ACCLAIM FOR A Question of Loyalty

This tale of the very human experiences of one Japanese-American family also shows author Malaghan's expertise in military hierarchy and the infrastructure of the armed forces. Many people are unaware of the struggles that Japanese faced as American citizens—scrutinized over their loyalty to the US while still connected to family roots in "enemy" territory—but Malaghan brings this psychological battle to the forefront and renders it understandable.

YAYOI WINFREY, DIRECTOR, *WAR BRIDES OF JAPAN, A DOCU*MEMORY*

A Question of Loyalty transports readers back to the Hawaii of World War II. Mike Malaghan has once again, as in *Picture Bride*, created a work so atmospheric the reader is immersed in history as if it were the here and now. We walk in the shoes of characters both exotic and familiar as we experience their sorrows and joy, defeats and victory, fears and heroism.

From page one, we share the shock of Pearl Harbor with picture bride Haru and her family. We share her fears for the safety of two children trapped in Japan. We are outraged at the humiliation of the Nisei summarily discharged from the Hawaii Territorial Guard simply for being Japanese, but we swell with pride watching those men form the Varsity Victory Volunteers to prove their loyalty. We are awed by the 100th Battalion's courage under fire in Italy as they prove their loyalty with blood. There is more, much more, but you get the idea. *A Question of Loyalty* is a page-turner.

KELI'I AKINA, PHD.
TRUSTEE-AT-LARGE, OFFICE OF HAWAIIAN AFFAIRS

On one level, *A Question of Loyalty* is a family story with memorable characters—sometimes flawed, sometimes a model of citizenship; love is given and affections are betrayed or poignantly unrequited. On another level, this is a stunningly detailed history of America's rejection of immigrant families who never give up on America. As the story unfolds, the price of blood is paid and shames America into acceptance and respect.

MARIKO MIHO, DAUGHTER OF 552ND ARTILLERY SPOTTER KATS MIHO
EXECUTIVE DIRECTOR OF FOUNDATION AND VICE PRESIDENT OF LANAKILA PACIFIC

This is a "must-read" book that provides an in-depth description of the thoughts and raw emotions of the Nisei civilians and Nisei soldiers before and during World War II. Historically accurate and fills many gaps in the knowledge base concerning the Nisei during that time!

L. STUART (STU) HIRAI
BOARD OF DIRECTORS, GO FOR BROKE NATIONAL EDUCATION CENTER

Michael Malaghan does an excellent job of detailing the struggle of our Nisei soldiers. You will cheer the Nisei fight for the right to defeat fascism while changing America's attitudes towards Japanese Americans.

BRIAN YAMAMOTO
LEADER OF 100TH/442ND TOURS OF FRANCE, 2014 AND 2019

Inalienable rights of American citizens were stripped from Japanese Americans in the aftermath of the Pearl Harbor attack of December 7, 1941. *A Question of Loyalty* brings to life the conflicts within a nation and the turmoil of families divided by war and geography. It chronicles, in graphic detail, how Nisei soldiers answered the call to duty. Michael Malaghan's exhaustive research into a very important time in American history provides lessons for future generations.

CYRUS TAMASHIRO
ADVISOR AND PAST PRESIDENT, UNITED JAPANESE SOCIETY OF HAWAII

An amazing work. A fascinating piece of both fact and fiction that brings the reader back in time. Michael Malaghan brings to life the Nisei who courageously fought to protect America while their families and loved ones endured prejudice, persecution and mass incarceration by that same country.

SHANE SATO, AUTHOR/PHOTOGRAPHER
THE GO FOR BROKE SPIRIT: PORTRAITS IN COURAGE, VOLUMES 1 AND 2

A Question of Loyalty

A NOVEL

BOOK TWO OF THE PICTURE BRIDE TRILOGY

In appreciation for all the good work of the Japan Society of Boston

Mike Malaghk
_5-21-20_

A Question of Loyalty

A NOVEL

BOOK TWO OF THE PICTURE BRIDE TRILOGY

MIKE MALAGHAN

LEGACY ISLE
PUBLISHING

Front cover photos:
442nd Regiment inset courtesy *The Honolulu Star-Advertiser*
Clockwise from upper left: Exclusion Order posted at First and Front Streets – Dorothea Lange, US National Archives and Records Administration; Young Oak Kim Silver Star presentation – University of Southern California, Korean American Digital Archive; Private First Class Genkichi Akamine of Honolulu, Hawaii, sniper, 100th Infantry Battalion – US Army Signal Corps, "Hawaii War Records Depository, HWRD 1434," UH Manoa Library Digital Image Collections; Pearl Harbor, Dec. 7, 1941 – Dept. of Defense / Dept. of the Navy, Naval Photographic Center, US National Archives and Records Administration; girl with luggage, spring 1942 – Dept. of the Interior / War Relocation Authority, US National Archives and Records Administration

Back cover photo:
Manzanar Relocation Center, 1943 – Ansel Adams, Library of Congress

ISBN 978-1-948011-21-1
Library of Congress Control Number: 2020901412

Legacy Isle Publishing
1000 Bishop St., Ste. 806
Honolulu, HI 96813
www.legacyislepublishing.net
info@legacyislepublishing.net

10 9 8 7 6 5 4 3 2 1

Printed in Korea

Dedicated to the twenty-one Japanese-American Medal of Honor recipients and the twenty thousand Nisei soldiers who served their country in World War II

∞ Acknowledgments ∞

So many supporters have helped bring *A Question of Loyalty* to term.

Bestselling historical novelist Bill Martin red-penciled my early writing with a savage pen, "Stop telling, show!" When it counted, Bill gave me the early encouragement to follow my post corporate "retirement" dream. "You can be a writer. Just keep at it."

Longtime editor, going back to my business writing days, Vicki McCown suffered through all my early drafts. "Didn't you cover this before?" "Who is _____ that just appeared?" "Cut the adjectives and find a strong verb." "What has the paragraph to do with the arc of the story?" And so it went. The faster pace of the novel has much to do with Vicki's relentless "Why?"s. And there is my dyslexia, which appears in an interesting fashion. Vicki's humor helped me avoid embarrassment and save you phrases like "Deer mom" and "Can you here me?"

Once Vicki and my collaboration was finished, I was fortunate to have the help of the editor of the *Hawaii Herald*, Karleen Chinen, who knows more about the Nisei heroics than I will ever hope to have. As a newspaper editor, she brought a new rigor to my writing, corrected factual errors and added critical clarifications.

Behind her, my publisher recommended I have one more person review to tighten the narrative. I am thankful we brought Christine Thomas to the project, who helped me cut at least two percent of my verbiage.

100th/442nd/MIS historian Isami Yoshihara often catches "minor" mistakes in my Facebook postings on Nisei heritage. When he volunteered to review the manuscript for possible errors, I jumped at the offer. And a good thing I did. He found some. He has served my future readers well.

Blog writer and wife Tomoko's patience was challenged by many "Can I ask you a question?" *A Question of Loyalty* has many scenes in Japan and getting the food, the mood, the use of the occasional Japanese word … all those little things that bring authenticity to the project—she was always there to help render an accurate perception of Japanese life.

Thanks to my Legacy Isle publisher liaison, Dawn Sakamoto, who gives a final reading to the project. Sure enough, she still finds needed changes.

Despite all this help, no doubt mistakes remain. The author takes full responsibility for such errors and welcomes reader corrections for future editions. You can email me at mgm@malaghan.net.

A special thanks to Karleen Chinen for serializing *Picture Bride* in the *Hawaii Herald* and beginning the serialization of *A Question of Loyalty* with the September 6, 2019, edition of the *Herald*.

❧ CONTENTS ❧

PART I

DAY OF INFAMY

∽ CHAPTER 1 ∾
December 7, 1941

THE EMPEROR'S CARRIER, THE *AKAGI*, powering its way across the Pacific, launched its adrenaline-fueled airmen towards their cataclysmic destiny. In minutes, the elite pilots would be eyeing the orange halo of sunrise while picking up the faint sounds of KGU Radio's ukulele serenade—radio signals that grew increasingly clearer as the airborne armada drew closer to its rendezvous with infamy.

One hundred miles away on Queen Emma Street in Honolulu, Haru stirred from a restless night. In just a few hours, she and Kenji would be homeward bound. Not homeward to Japan, but to Waimea, on the Big Island of Hawaii.

Thirty-two years earlier, Haru had arrived on the shores of Hawaii from Hiroshima, Japan, as the young "picture bride" of Kenji Takayama, a man she knew only through his photograph. He, likewise, knew Haru only through the photograph her adoptive parents had mailed to him in Hawaii.

Despite Haru's having lived a favored life as the wife of one of Oahu's leading Buddhist priests, and their six children having been raised in Honolulu for most of their young lives, she had never really felt at home in Honolulu. Not the way she had in Waimea. With each passing year, that first decade she and Kenji had spent in Waimea appeared sweeter and more precious in her rearview mirror.

Haru pictured the land as she had last seen it. Her land. Well, her family's land, which Haru had purchased as a result of Wellington Carter's stewardship of Parker Ranch. Such an arrangement would be impossible today, although it seemed so natural back when horses trotted along the town's crushed-lava roads.

The slow, rhythmic bells of the nearby Cathedral of Our Lady of Peace tolled seven times. The bells might be Catholic, thought Haru, but the gentle meeting of iron bronze on iron bronze reminded her of the ancient bells of her adoptive father's temple in Hiroshima. *What flutters our emotions when bells peal for God in his many ecumenical manifestations*, she thought. For a brief second, Haru could see a thirteen-year-old waif pulling hard on the temple bells, celebrating Admiral Togo's victory over the Russian fleet. *Regardless of our notion of God, why*, she wondered, *do we tether his bells to military triumphs and catastrophes?*

In five hours, Haru and Kenji would board a Matson interisland ship for their journey home. A real passenger ship this time—not like the cattle transport that brought her to the Big Island as an eighteen-year-old bride in the autumn of 1909. Haru craned her neck to watch her sleeping husband. Before his kidney cancer operation, Kenji would have already slipped out of bed and set the kettle on the stove. He would be sitting at the kitchen table, writing the day's lesson plans for his language school, lessons that taught more history and cultural principles than grammar and *kanji*. Nisei students attended the classes after finishing their public school day.

All of Kenji's pastoral responsibilities were now behind him. Months ago, he had turned over his Moiliili parish, bordering the University of Hawaii campus, to a younger pastor and moved into their home on Queen Emma Street to convalesce. Every morning, Kenji walked a slow thirty minutes to the Fort Street Hongwanji where he sat at the corner desk facing the lush ascent of the Pali while writing *The First Ninety Days at Your New Parish*, a manual for newly appointed parish priests. He finished his workday in time to be home for lunch. Dr. Tebbits had assured Haru that all of the cancer had been cut out, but something in Kenji's body and spirit had been exorcised along with the yellow mass of runaway malignancy. Knowing that any movement of the mattress would wake Kenji, Haru got up gently and tiptoed to the bathroom.

As eight bells pealed, Kenji's shoulders shifted ever so slightly.

A minute later, the upstairs flushing sounds announced that Tommy, the third of Haru's and Kenji's six children, would be the first downstairs. Tommy, whom they had named Tomio at birth, had recently been inducted into the 299th Infantry Regiment. He was home on a weekend pass after completing his basic training and had caught the university football game the night before.

Another son also wore army khaki, although a different uniform than Tommy. Yoshio, the Takayamas' second son, served in Japan's Manchurian army. He had been drafted out of Tokyo Daigaku university—Todai for short—because he could not be bothered to wait two hours in line to obtain his American passport before departing Hawaii for college.

Kenta, the youngest of their four boys, had joined the University of Hawaii's ROTC program to prove his loyalty to America. "Just marching fodder for upperclassmen chasing army careers," Kenta had glibly assured his mother. But Haru's fears had not been eased in the least. If war came, as the daily news reports shrilled, those ROTC boys would surely be activated.

Even their daughters were not out of harm's way. Sue, the baby in the family—the daughter they had named Sachiko—was now an au pair living with the local FBI director and his wife. Her older sister, the hardheaded Hiromi, had refused to leave Tokyo on the last ship carrying war-expectant expatriates back to Hawaii.

"Don't worry, Mom," she had written. "Japan might attack Malay or Indonesia to replace the raw materials that warmonger Roosevelt is embargoing, but their army is not so foolish to fight America."

Banging pans and the exuberant closing of kitchen cabinets reminded Haru that Tommy enjoyed preparing breakfast. If only his omelets were as good as his intentions.

Haru saw Kenji rousing. "Tommy burning us some eggs?" Kenji asked in his soft, morning voice.

"Let's hope it's just toast," Haru said, laughing.

Haru had come to like Western breakfasts. Her guilt over abandoning traditional rice-centered breakfasts were assuaged when she read that Emperor Hirohito had switched to a Western culinary start to his day after visiting the English royals as a twenty-one-year-old prince in 1921.

As she traipsed into the kitchen, skirting packing boxes that covered nearly every inch of the floor, she heard a bike crunch up the pathway to the back door. Taka, she guessed. Haru's heart swelled with pride as she thought about her number-one son's work with the Council on Interracial Unity, which was dedicated to keeping Hawaii's Japanese out of the rumored internment camps if war came.

Maybe Taka could rescue his brother's eggs without Tommy losing face. She wondered if Kenta would drop in for his parents' last breakfast in Honolulu.

∞ CHAPTER 2 ∞

THE AROMA OF PANCAKES, FRESH COFFEE AND SIZZLING BACON wafted through the room, waking Kenta. A cacophony of distant propellers buzzed his thumping head. He groaned and eased his legs over the couch in the Walters family's den and sat up ever so slowly. The engine of a recreation boat smothered the propeller chorus. Kenta got to his feet and peered out the picture window, waving at a girl water-skiing, her blonde hair flaring wildly. She skimmed past the Walters' dock facing Ford Island's precision-lined PPY bombers and the nine grey monsters of Battleship Row. The radiant-faced teenager did not see him. Kenta would later wonder what happened to her after it all began.

Kenta had spent the night on the couch at Bobby Walters' house instead of catching a cab back to campus after one too many beers at the O-Club after the University of Hawaii's football victory. He took a deep breath and squeezed his eyebrows together as if to expel the pain behind them, then stepped listlessly into the dining room.

"Who ordered planes to fly on a Sunday morning?" he asked Bobby's dad, who was carrying the coffee pot from the kitchen. He raised his voice, hoping to be heard over the propeller thrum approaching the house.

"It sure wasn't the navy," Captain Walters replied. "We're too civilized to screw up a Sunday morning. Sit down and eat. Your two hungover friends are taking a shower. You can make nine o'clock services if you want to join us."

"Sure," said Kenta. Though Buddhist, he didn't mind attending other people's church services. After all, two of his five siblings had converted to Methodism. As he filled his plate with pancakes and scrambled eggs, a squadron of planes buzzed the Walters' home.

Bobby bounded down the stairs. "Isn't that a little too close, Dad?"

"Damn right it is," said Captain Walters, his voice nearly drowned out by the din of churning propellers. "Who are those idiot cowboys trying to impress? I'm calling Hickam!"

As he rose from the table and walked over to the phone, Mrs. Walters and Eddie entered the dining room, both staring at the ceiling as if it were glass.

A burst of explosions froze everyone in place.

The captain sprinted through the open sliding glass door to the backyard with the boys at his heels. Roaring propellers reverberated through Kenta's groin as he gawked at the whirling armada, their fuselages emblazoned with the insignia of a bright red rising sun.

"No. No! NO!" he shouted.

"Jesus Christ!" bellowed Bobby.

"You boys get inside," barked Captain Walters. "I've got to get into uniform and report," he said, rushing back into the house.

The boys stayed put.

Kenta's line of sight riveted on the flitting faces of the enemy—faces that looked like his, framed with fur-lined caps and eyes masked by aviator goggles. For the past four years, dinner talk at his home often centered on the worrisome personal consequences of war between America and Japan.

We Japanese are in for it now, he thought.

Kenta shook his fist at a grinning pilot who waved at him from his open canopy as if promoting an upcoming air show rather than being seconds from releasing the finned torpedo clasped to his plane's undercarriage.

"You dirty rotten stinkin' Jap!" he called out.

As Kenta watched the torpedo separate from its fuselage, he thought of his father. The FBI had been to their home twice. Priests like his father were expected to be arrested when the war started. But a war in Asia, not here.

The image of his father's "just in case" suitcase, already packed and sitting at the foot of his parents' bed, flashed before him as he saw the torpedo enter the water and head toward the warships.

☙ CHAPTER 3 ❧

THE BREEZES OF PUOWAINA, THE "HILL OF SACRIFICE" that the locals referred to simply as Punchbowl, swept scents of plumeria blossoms through the open kitchen louvers of the FBI director's home. The sun sparkled off dew clinging to lime-hued banana tree leaves hanging over the back porch.

Inside, a young girl hovered over the kitchen stove, keeping one eye trained on the sparrows fluttering beneath the bird feeder's deep-slanted roof, designed to keep out curious pigeons. Her nearly dry hair shimmered all the way to her shoulders and her Jane Wyman bangs bounced against her forehead when she walked fast, as she often did. Her marigold-colored dress caressed her calves and the double-stitched hem of her sleeves reached halfway to her elbows.

Sue, Haru and Kenji Takayama's youngest child, hummed Glen Miller's latest hit, "Chattanooga Choo Choo," as she dropped another egg into the sizzling bacon drippings in the frying pan. She had already placed the pot of hot Kona coffee on the dining room table, which she had set for three the night before. Next on the table was a colorful bowl of mango slices and pineapple chunks.

The twenty-year-old university student had lived with Robert and Corrine Shivers as their au pair for two years, ever since Robert had arrived in Honolulu to head the newly opened FBI office in the fall of 1939. Sue was just about to start her freshman year at the University of Hawaii at the time. Although she was not privy to Shivers's FBI work, since the early days living with his family, she knew that the United States government planned to intern Japanese community leaders when the expected war with Japan began. Her eldest brother Takeshi—"Taka"—worked for the committee formed to prevent mass internment in the advent of war. Still, Sue was unaware of her role in the internment plans debate preceding Pearl Harbor. Her dinnertime conversations with the Shivers had never touched on Mr. Shivers's work or political topics.

"You being just an ordinary American teenager can make a huge impact," the politically astute Taka once told her. She had smiled, certain her brother's flattery lacked credibility and was based on fanciful notions. She was an au pair for a family that loved her—what did that have to do with world politics and war?

While Robert Shivers never talked about the possibility of internment with Sue, her presence in his home had impacted him so fundamentally that he had recast his mission. He had arrived in Honolulu to open the FBI office and prepare for mass internment of Hawaii's Japanese community if war broke out. Then he had met Sue, whom he had reluctantly taken on as a temporary au pair as a courtesy to Charles Hemenway, chairman of the University of Hawaii Board of Regents and Hawaii's former attorney general.

"Many of our community leaders find it convenient to have a live-in student, someone to help with light housework," Hemenway had explained. "In turn, it helps students afford college."

"Just until you find a permanent home for her, Charles." Shivers tactfully succumbed. With no children to attend to, what help did they need washing the dishes?

Within weeks of Sue's arrival, however, they realized that while they didn't need help with the housework, Sue was like the child they were never able to have. Shivers knew it bothered many in the white community when he introduced Sue as his daughter. But no daughter was ever more loved than Sue.

On Sue's first day at their home, Robert had wandered into the living room and found Sue absorbed in the *Pacific Liner*, his wife's favorite Hollywood magazine.

"I see that you and Corrine have the same interests," said Shivers, sitting down across from Sue. He had been waiting for an opportunity to question her. His plan was she would be gone in a week and Shivers could not pass up on this window of opportunity to learn about the loyalty and intentions of Japanese people.

"Who's your favorite movie star?" he asked, his FBI instincts kicking in.

Sue tensed at her first one-on-one conversation with the serious-faced Shivers. "Clark Gable. But I like Errol Flynn, too."

"So, you don't go to Japanese movies?"

A perplexed expression had washed over Sue's face. "I can't speak Japanese very well," she said, feeling a bit guilty. Trying to recover, she blurted out, "I went once with my mother, on my tenth birthday, but I fell asleep."

"So, your mother goes to Japanese movies?"

"Sometimes. But not so much anymore. Mother likes Ronald Reagan. She thinks he's handsome. But when he speaks, you can tell he's just memorized the lines. He's not very believable," Sue opined.

Remembering her mother's admonishment that a polite lady shows interest in others, Sue bravely asked, "Who is your favorite movie star?"

Shivers's G-man instincts urged him to snap back that *he* was the one who asked the questions, but he resisted. He could not help but smile as the names rolled out of his mouth. "James Cagney and Bette Davis."

As Sue caught a glimpse of Shivers's teeth, she was reminded of his wife's welcoming remarks: "Now you just ignore Mr. Shivers's severe face; it took me months before I ever saw his teeth."

Her voice still a little tight, Sue asked, "Have you seen *Dark Victory?* It's playing downtown right now."

"Actually, Mrs. Shivers and I saw *Dark Victory* in Washington just before we left."

Shivers abandoned his interrogation persona and went on at length about how he'd enjoyed Bette Davis's portrayal of a vacuous socialite suffering from a malignant brain tumor. He gazed at Sue's expectant eyes and reminded himself why he had asked Corrine to give him some time with the new houseguest before dinner.

"Did you go to a Japanese language school?"

Sue's lips turned down, telegraphing unhappy memories.

"Yes, my father runs one of those schools. We—that is, my brothers and sister and I—we hated it once we got to junior high school."

Trained to ignore such protests from hundreds of suspects he had interviewed, Shivers continued. "What did you learn at your father's school?"

"I can write my name in *kanji* and read simple signs over Japanese shops in our neighborhood. Father taught us Confucius's golden rule: 'Do not impose on others what you do not wish for yourself.' Respect the elders;

take good care of them. Honor our teachers. Bathe twice a day. Wash your hands after you ..." She blushed.

Shivers locked onto Sue's eyes. "What do you think of the Emperor ... Hirohito?"

"He likes horses."

Shivers's face betrayed his confusion.

Seeing his reaction, Sue hurried to explain. "I don't know much about him. But we have his picture in our home. He's sitting on a white horse." Sensing that did not sound quite right, she rushed on. "His picture is right next to President Roosevelt's, who is sitting in a car. I think this shows America is more modern." Her voice rose at the end of her sentence, making it sound more like a question.

"But Japan has modernized very quickly. You must be very proud to be Japanese."

Sue snapped her shoulders back. "I am *not* Japanese!" She placed her right hand over her upper chest. "I am an American!" Leaning forward, she pressed her fingers harder. "I'm proud to be an American, Mr. Shivers."

In the days immediately after that conversation, which had challenged his very purpose in Hawaii, Shivers studied the Asian faces he passed on his drive to the office each day and thought of Sue: the Hollywood movie star posters on her bedroom walls; her worries about applying just the right amount of Elizabeth Arden makeup; her fascination with the log cabin tale of Abe Lincoln, a favorite story of his during his own school days.

Shivers's futile efforts to find any spies over the past two years paralleled the growing affection he and his wife felt for Sue. All of his instincts, nurtured by decades of experience, were being challenged. Despite Washington's hysteria prophesying their disloyalty, any first-generation immigrant Issei, or second-generation Nisei in Hawaii would love nothing more than to be approached by a Jap agent so they could turn him in to the FBI. Sure, some of the Issei might support the Imperial forces if they attacked America, but sympathy for Imperial Japan is not the same as sabotage. Still, the havoc that one well-trained Japanese agent could cause worried Shivers. That "it only takes one" rejoinder frequented Washington's response to his reports that America had little to worry about its Japanese living in Hawaii.

So, Shivers stood ready. All of his agents had the list of leaders who were to be picked up the moment war began. Most on the list, if not all, were innocent of sabotage intentions. But that did not matter. Only a vigorous sweep of those influential Japanese men would reassure Washington. The roundup of the few would have to protect the majority.

Sue had overheard enough breakfast conversations between Shivers and Honolulu detective Jack Burns, the police liaison to the FBI, to know, more than any of her fellow university students, of the plans to keep Hawaii's internment numbers low if and when war broke out. She took quiet pride in Burns's reports from his task force looking for Japanese spies. "Not one," he often stated. Respectful of Shivers's trust in her, Sue never offered an opinion on the internment possibilities that often highlighted campus gossip, and the students, knowing her as the "FBI girl," respected her reticence.

On this morning, she reflected on the conversation that had taken place the previous Friday as she and Angelina ate their lunch with a group of Nisei students. As usual, she remained a diligent eavesdropper.

"You would think," said a boy with a crew cut whose father Sue knew because he supplied vegetables to Honolulu's grocery stores, "that when those California farmers envied the Japanese fields—their straight rows of celery and weedless strawberry patches earning top dollar from produce wholesalers—they would copy a winning hand that's in plain sight."

"It's not about farming techniques," said Angelina, one of the few Japanese females to be so bold as to articulate an opinion or dabble in sarcasm. Sue admired Angelina for what others called "unladylike manners." Rather than parting her hair down the middle as most Japanese ladies did, Angelina parted her hair on the side with hanging curls brushing her neck in the style of Bette Davis, her favorite actress. Angelina even dressed differently—no standard white blouse for her. She wore cheery blues and greens with skirts in similar hues below the knees, albeit barely beneath her knees. From early grammar school, she worked on speaking "American English" rather than Pidgin English.

"We 'alien' Japanese got the second-rate farmland," said Angelina. "How dare our slanted eyes and brown skin produce better crops than the supreme white race?"

An angry male voice punctuated with a shaking fist jarred Sue's calmer demeanor. "Those envious big noses *want* a war with Japan—an excuse to get rid of us. It wasn't enough that California passed laws forbidding us 'aliens' from buying land. A war would drive those earlier buyers off of their farms. This call for internment isn't about sabotage—it's about eliminating the competition. Al Capone would understand."

Sue noted that no one on that angry day admitted that the Japanese in Hawaii lived under no such threat. Certainly, those same Nisei student debaters understood that Hawaii's white community, referred to as "haoles," seldom regarded the agriculture and fishing success of "their" Japanese with envy; rather they viewed the Japanese commitment to food production as a needed service requiring work more arduous than most whites wanted to embrace. Sue, like all Japanese in Hawaii, acquiesced that haoles comprised the managerial class.

We Orientals are the working class. Like the Hindu caste system, Sue thought—a comparison she kept to herself.

But on the loyalty issue, Sue observed haoles were divided. Even those who claimed Japanese in Hawaii were loyal, hedged their bets. How often had student gossip sessions repeated the *Advertiser's* refrain cloaked in many nuances: "Better to be careful than sorry."

Despite her brother's assurances that mass internment wouldn't happen in Hawaii if war broke out, Sue often tried to imagine what life in an internment camp might be like.

"Ouch!" yelped Sue as a spurt of grease rocketed from the sizzling bacon to her face. She stepped back and rubbed her left cheek with the bottom of her apron while using the long fork to flip the offending bacon onto its paler side.

"Sue, are you all right?" "Mom" Shivers's slow Southern drawl drifted into the kitchen.

"Just a spot of grease, Mom Shivers," said Sue, who had come to feel she now had two mothers.

Despite Sue's assurance, Corrine Shivers, dressed in her Sunday church-going white *muumuu*, entered the kitchen.

"Let me see," said Corrine, putting her fingers under Sue's chin and gently tilting the girl's head. "Yes, it's OK."

Dropping her hand, Corrine wrinkled her brow. "I do wish our pilots wouldn't practice on Sunday mornings. It interrupts church services," she said, referring to their regular Sunday service at Kawaiahao Congregational Church on Punchbowl Street.

Focused on the lyrics of "Chattanooga Choo Choo," Sue had hardly noticed the drone of engines. But now that she thought about it, today's maneuvers did seem rather loud.

She picked up the spatula and slid two sunny-side up eggs on each of the three plates sitting on the scarred sideboard. Special Agent Robert Shivers, dressed in a white, long-sleeved shirt with a blue necktie, had already seated himself at the dining table across from Corrine. Sue set their plates down in front of them and then brought in her own plate and took the seat next to Mom Shivers, who then bowed her head and blessed their meal. Just as Shivers wedged a piece of bacon onto his fork, the phone rang.

Sue jumped up and scooted the few steps to the black phone attached to the dining room wall near the entrance to the kitchen.

"Good morning, the—" Before she could say "Shivers' home," she lifted the phone from her ear to escape the frantic screaming from the earpiece.

"I need to speak to Robert *NOW!*"

Alarmed, Sue held out the phone.

Shivers heard the shrill voice from across the room and had already risen from the table to take the phone.

"What?!" His voice trembled, betraying incredulity. "I'll be right down." He turned to Corrine, who was slathering a piece of toast with pineapple jelly she had bottled herself. "We have been attacked. Those planes we heard are Japanese." First glancing at Sue, he turned to his wife and paused until the lump in his throat cleared. "Corrine, take Sue wherever you go; don't let her out of your sight."

"My mother ..." Sue squeaked.

Shivers knew Haru was scheduled to sail to the Big Island that day. Sue had planned to walk to the harbor later to see her parents off.

"The switchboard ladies must have all the lines available for military and security." A stupendous noise like rolling thunder stopped Shivers's explanation. "I have to go ..."

∞ Chapter 4 ∞

"OUR BASIC TRAINING GRADUATION IS WEDNESDAY," said Tommy, greeting his brother.

"Wouldn't miss it for the world, little brother," answered Taka, a Harvard Law School graduate who addressed all five of his siblings as "little brother" or "little sister." Seeing his mother's concerned eyes as she focused on the bowl of cracked eggs, Taka—short for Takeshi—smothered a laugh. The boys greeted their mother and then Taka continued. "Tommy, why don't you chop some onions and tomatoes and I'll make us an omelet."

Delighting in a new audience, Tommy recited the fitness trials he had performed under overbearing sergeants and his rifle competition triumphs. He pointed to the marksmanship patch on his upper shirt sleeve. Neither brother noticed their mother's deepening worry lines.

Haru no longer heard the soft music wafting from the radio. Taka's and Tommy's war talk had reminded her of a time when her hawkish convictions surpassed even theirs. She remembered hearing Hiroshima's cannon booming, signaling a great victory, and running outside from her bedroom barefoot so their temple could be the first to ring the bell in celebration. She had exulted in Japan's naval thrashing of Russia in 1905. Seventy-eight-thousand mothers lost their sons fighting the Russians.

"You boys had an uncle who was killed in the Russo-Japanese War." *Oh, why did I blurt that out*, she thought immediately.

Tommy and Taka swiveled around toward their mother, their faces mirroring confusion.

"You never told us," said Tommy.

"No, and I never intended to."

At that very moment, Admiral Yamamoto was pacing the floor in the map room of his Yokosuka naval station headquarters, envisioning the bombers that had lifted off of his aircraft carrier and were approaching Battleship Row at Pearl Harbor.

Haru began to tell her sons her story, shuddering as she remembered.

"Your uncle left Amakusa for work. For a few months, he sent a little money home, as sons were expected to do. The money was desperately needed for food. You boys do not know what hunger is. I do."

Haru let that sink in for a few seconds, watching the astonishment grow on their faces as the mixture of eggs and vegetables congealed in the porcelain bowl.

"But then the money and letters stopped coming. After years of not knowing the whereabouts of my brother, I received notice that he had been killed fighting the Russians. A week later, a letter arrived from the Emperor, inviting me—I was only a thirteen-year-old student then—to witness his soul being added to the book of heroes at Yasukuni Shrine." Haru paused, her regret evident.

"Oh, the pride. My brother died for the Emperor! That day at Yasukuni, I felt the Tenno's godly presence as I watched him, so splendidly dressed in uniform, riding a magnificent white stallion into the shrine. I vowed to have many sons so they could serve and even die for the Emperor."

Haru hadn't heard Kenji enter the kitchen. His soft hands began massaging her shoulders. Her eyes glistened.

"I glorified war …"

She was about to say, "I don't want any of my sons to die for Roosevelt *or* Hirohito," when the drone of airplanes roared overhead.

The brothers ran outside.

Kenji shouted over the noise of the retreating planes. "All that noise over at Pearl Harbor sounds like Chinese New Year!"

Wide-eyed, the boys rushed back into the house.

"The planes," said Taka somberly, "are Japanese."

The music broadcasting from KGU stopped abruptly. Moments later, the radio crackled back to life.

"We are under attack! This is a not a maneuver! This is the real McCoy!"

Haru grabbed Kenji's hand, her frightened eyes searching his for an answer: *What will happen to our children?*

∽ CHAPTER 5 ∽

KENTA PUMPED HIS FIST LIKE A LINEMAN who had just sacked the quarterback on the opposing team as he watched the first ashen puffs of antiaircraft fire soar into the fleet of Zero fighters. The dancing ordnance burst into fireballs, then faded like Fourth of July pyrotechnics. Cheers erupted when an exploding disk ripped the wing off a "Kate" bomber, sending the Nakajima B5N torpedo bomber into a fiery downward spiral.

The percussion of exploding bombs pained Kenta's ears. Flaming pools of oil laced the water. Fire and smoke rose from the battleships. Two neat rows of Ford Island's patrol bombers burst into flames under the rat-a-tat-tat onslaught of the Zero machine guns. Beyond the devastation unfolding before his eyes, fear crept into Kenta's soul: *Dad will be arrested by nightfall. What will happen to Mom? Will we all be sent to internment camps on Molokai?*

The detonations billowed into gray towers, then morphed into a charcoal veil. Three successive booming blasts pivoted Kenta's attention to the bowline of a ship. Bobby yelled to Kenta over the tumult of whining propellers, explosions and antiaircraft fire.

"Shit! That's the *Oklahoma*. It must have been torpedoed, but how the—"

A bone-shattering boom assaulted Kenta's eardrums, followed a nanosecond later by a massive fireball that momentarily blinded him. Shock waves blew back his hair and singed his lungs. The Walters's sliding glass doors shattered behind him. Shrapnel rained down. Kenta jerked as a small steel chunk sliced his thigh, although he neither felt pain nor noticed the blood. Instead, he thought of his older brother's work as secretary to the governor's Council on Interracial Unity: All that planning to avoid internment camps for naught.

Kenta's sight returned in time to witness an exploding battleship shudder and rise from the water in its death dance. Suspended for a mere fraction of a second, the USS *Arizona* tilted and then sank before his unbelieving eyes.

What will the army do with Tommy, stationed at Schofield? Will they take away my brother's rifle? Cashier him out of the service? Put his entire Nisei battalion in the stockade?

On his far right, Kenta spied a lone P-40 Warhawk rise from adjacent Hickam Air Base and fly into a flotilla of Japanese bombers. In small backyards facing the smoking fleet, wives and children, half of them flanked by their Japanese maids, raised their fists, cheering on the lone pilot.

Do those cheering people see me as an American, or just another Jap?

Kenta swelled with pride as he watched sailors scramble to man more antiaircraft guns. Ack-ack booms soon became an orchestra almost drowning out the clacking of airborne machine gun fire. Kenta wondered how any plane could pass through the maze of exploding gray clouds of steel. But they did.

He thought of his sister Hiromi and brother Yoshio who had chosen to leave their country to live on foreign soil. Hiromi was an office worker in Tokyo, and Yoshio was serving in the Imperial army in Manchuria.

What does this declaration of war mean to their fate, he wondered.

∞ CHAPTER 6 ∞

"I HATE TOKYO DECEMBERS," MURMURED HIROMI, surprising even herself that she had spoken up. It was just an hour after lunch but already the amber sun had begun fading into broken patches of orange glow peeking between Marunouchi's skyscrapers. Her co-worker's furtive glance at her declaration lasted but a second. Hiromi's head slumped over a Remington typewriter in the middle table in a row of sixteen cramped, unvarnished wooden desks. Her Propaganda Section of the Ministry of Foreign Affairs, or *Gaimusho*, had donated their steel desks to the War Ministry to smelt into steel for tanks and shells for the never-ending China war—a war for which she wrote "news stories" of predictable victories for the English language press.

Six months ago, Hiromi had been an employee of Dentsu, Japan's most prestigious public relations firm, where she translated advertising copy for Procter & Gamble soaps and cosmetics. When she turned down the offer to leave Dentsu to work for the *Gaimusho*, she learned that the alternative to refusing was receiving a visit from the *Kempeitai,* the dreaded military police.

"Besides," reasoned her boss at Dentsu, "the drying up of American imports means your job is disappearing."

Hiromi's stomach churned and her neck ached, as if her body parts were determined to punish her for the latest drivel she had typed. She glanced at the wall clock. Time to submit. As habit prescribed, she read her copy with a whisper one more time to test its cadence and feel the flow of the words.

> *December 8, 1941. Once again, the devil without a tail, Cordell Hull, the nefarious Secretary of State for the world's most arrogant country, has issued his latest demeaning ultimatum under the guise of negotiations: "Get out of China, or else." Never mind about American colonies in Guam, the Philippines and Hawaii, or the British, Dutch and French occupiers …*

"Much better," intoned the flat voice of Takashiro Murakami, the *bucho* or section head. Hiromi hadn't noticed the soft-heeled approach of the stiff-backed veteran of the Russian war. His well-manicured fingers picked up the "news" release. Hiromi, seething inwardly, raised her head and smiled. Murakami enjoyed her expression all the more because of its insincerity.

Before lunch, Hiromi had written a much more balanced version of the current negotiations, although still very much slanted toward the Japanese position.

"No more *tofu* writing, Hiromi," Murakami had smirked through gapped teeth. She had controlled the urge to wrinkle her nose at his lack of dental hygiene, which spread invisible clouds of halitosis over her desk. "We need the hot pepper sauce perspective."

Now, as he read her "correct" interpretation of the exchange of diplomatic letters between Japan and America, Hiromi thought of her decision to flee Hawaii, where "I am treated as a second-class citizen," she had often said, and subsequent letters to her mother validating her decision. "Here, I am treated as an equal," she wrote home, but no matter how perfect her Japanese grammar was, or the depth of her vocabulary, her accent always revealed that she was *gaijin*, a foreigner.

Hiromi thought of Haru's latest letter with its usual plea to "come home—before war is declared." Yes, Hiromi thought, war might well come. America was squeezing Japan in a vain attempt to end her war with China. Anyone reading the newspapers knew of Tokyo's military plan to deploy rifles and ships to replace the lost oil and steel from America. Indonesia's oil wells or Malaya's rubber trees loomed as obvious targets for the Imperial Japanese Army. Rice rationing had started six months ago. What choice did Roosevelt's embargo leave Japan?

Hiromi had begun to admit to herself that the Imperial democracy she had migrated to three years ago had morphed into a military dictatorship.

The Kempeitai, sitting in newspaper offices, guaranteed that the "news" reflected the government line. She knew her neighbors had been interviewed about her, "the American." More than once, she had spotted a man in a black suit furtively following her after work.

Oh, how stubborn I have been, she thought. *I will get on the next ship to Hawaii. But now that the Kempeitai is watching me, I will have to leave home with nothing but my purse.*

"Good. Good," said Murakami, snapping Hiromi back to the here and now. "Send this as-is to the *Japan Times-Advertiser* with the usual suggestion that they might want to publish it in tomorrow's paper. Dispatch it to Reuters, as well."

The sounds of boots closing in broke her reverie. Her gaze snapped to the front door where the lead man in an ill-fitting Western suit, followed by two others outfitted in olive-green uniforms, were marching straight toward her. The silly train conductor caps worn by the soldiers didn't seem so silly now. As they approached her desk, Hiromi stood up.

The man in the suit addressed her. "Takayama Hiromi!"

"*Hai*," she said, almost at attention.

"You must come with us."

"I am a Japanese citizen," she blurted out. Under terms of a Japan-America treaty, any Nisei born before 1924 was automatically deemed a dual citizen of the two countries. Later, she wondered whether she should have said, "I am an American citizen. I want to talk to my embassy." But she knew it would not have made any difference.

"Do not worry. Come with me. We need to ask you some questions."

The two uniformed men took a step forward.

"*Hai*." Hiromi picked up her purse and followed the men.

In the hallway, she heard shouts of "*Banzai!*" By the time the elevator reached street level, a cacophony of discordant honking cars filled the street.

"Hiromi-*san!*"

Hiromi looked up. Murakami, leaning out the second floor window, leered triumphantly. He had addressed her honorifically. She had never seen him smile so widely.

"We just sank your Pacific Fleet."

The man in the black suit grabbed her upper arm from behind and led her toward a stout, four-door Mazda that matched the color of his jacket and trousers. One of the green-uniformed men at the side of the idling car opened the back door. Hiromi felt the hard press of a hand pushing her head down.

"Get in."

Ducking, Hiromi thought of her mother. War meant the cessation of postal services and letters from home. *It might be years before my mother hears from me again. If ever.* She stopped like her feet had been nailed to the ground.

Does this mean I have lost my American citizenship? And what about Yoshio? Would he lose his citizenship, too?

∽ CHAPTER 7 ∽

Y OSHIO SQUATTED OUTSIDE THE WOODEN GUARDHOUSE and scarfed down a lunch of rice and a stringy green Chinese vegetable in a *bento* tin that the patrol truck had delivered. He was enjoying the rare day outdoors, not confined inside the border hut as he stared across the Khalkhin-Gol River, dividing the Russian People's Republic of Mongolia and the Japanese puppet state of Manchukuo. It was blanketed with fresh snow and scarred by the imprint of reindeer hooves, the Siberian wind whipping across its span. By mid-day, the wind had slowed considerably and Yoshio felt the warm rays of the sun penetrate his padded woolen jacket. Later today, he would snowshoe over the mile-wide frozen expanse to the Russian side and barter *sake* and rice for beef, vodka and beets.

The Russians had crushed the Japanese army's 1939 attempt to settle a border dispute on their imperial terms. With neither nation wanting a war on two fronts, they found it in their interest to sign a nonaggression treaty in April 1941. The poor showing by Japanese troops changed the Imperial government's designs—from what had been planned as the "Northern Strategy" to conquer Siberia for its natural resources, to the "Southern Strategy," leading to the planned invasions of British and Dutch colonies in Southeast Asia. The Russian Siberian troops had left a month earlier to defend Moscow from Germany's *blitzkrieg*. *Maybe in a few months*, thought Yoshio, *I'll be facing Allied German troops across the border.*

Before this, he had thought that guarding Chinese mine workers, who were more like slaves, was the worst possible assignment. His sergeant had abused him miserably. When Yoshio had enough, lost his temper and hit back, his sergeant had laughed at him and in broken English snarled, "Good, Yank. Don't worry. No brig for you. You good guard. You get promotion."

Yoshio had arrived at the Siberian border station in August, at the height of the mosquito season. He had welcomed the crisp September freeze that sent the buzzing devils into hibernation. His fellow guards were all misfits: Koreans who had signed protest letters, petty thieves who joined the army in lieu of prison and old men unfit for combat. A certain camaraderie had developed among them. Even the sergeants and the lieutenant were almost civil in this remotest of remote outposts.

And then there was the cold. Those who had already been there a year laughed at his complaints.

"Cold, Yoshi? This is just an appetizer. In January, you will learn why the Mongols have a dozen words for cold."

Each miserable day reminded him of his discussion with Tommy about the Christian concept of hell. "The real pain of hell is not the fire, or even the hopelessness of eternal punishment, but rather being there by the choice you made."

Yes, thought Yoshio, who liked the Buddhist idea of reincarnation a lot better than eternal punishment for a single mistake. *I couldn't be bothered to stand in line at the Federal Building in Honolulu to obtain my American passport before leaving for Tokyo. I should be chatting up girls at Todai instead of eating stale rice in this polar hell.*

Yoshio picked up a fistful of snow to clean his chopsticks before sticking them back in his inner pocket. He decided to walk along the river before the sun escaped, and hadn't been gone even ten minutes when he heard a shout behind him.

"*Banzai! Banzai!*" Yoshi turned to see Fumio running toward him. "We bombed Pearl Harbor!"

Yoshio stared at the soldier, understanding the words but finding their meaning incomprehensible. War speculation centered on Asian oil and rubber countries. But Hawaii? Impossible. While denial froze his steps, Fumio, breathless, caught up with him.

"Well, Yank," Fumio sneered, "which side are you on?"

Yoshio ignored the often-used slur. He wondered when he would receive a letter from his mother. Considering how many years Japan had been at war in China, he thought it might be a year—if he stayed alive.

❧ CHAPTER 8 ❧

KENTA FAST-STEPPED TO THE RIFLE QUEUE, where a sergeant issued his Springfield. Strutting over to join his squad, he heard the raised voices of his men feeding each other "genuine" rumors.

"They spotted landing craft off Barbers Point," said square-faced Chad, the unit's harmonica player, his instrument, as ever, peeking from his shirt pocket.

"My brother got a report that we sank a Japanese carrier!" said lanky Henry, whose father regretted his son's choice of college over being groomed to take over the family's small fleet of three fishing boats.

Waving an *Advertiser* EXTRA! still damp with fresh newspaper ink, a cadet pointed to the front page. "The army says saboteurs landing on the North Shore of Oahu were wearing red circle patches on their shoulders."

"There were at least a thousand men aboard the USS *Arizona* when a bomb detonated the powder magazine."

That quieted the crowd until a low, deep voice broke the lull.

"I delivered the first blow from our ROTC unit," said Shigeto "Fats" Fukuda, whose love of rice and doughnuts earned him his nickname. "So, this morning, my father barges into my bedroom yelling 'Japan is bombing Pearl Harbor!' From the window, I see smoke rising over Pearl and hear shouts from the upstairs window. '*Banzai! Banzai! Banzai!*'" Fukuda threw his arms up to punctuate each "*Banzai!*"

"My idiot neighbor upstairs writes articles on Japan's right to acquire territory and how the Hearst newspaper 'invented' the Rape of Nanking. A real Mr. Right Wing, let's kiss the Emperor's ass kind of guy. He keeps shouting, 'Banzai!' like some zombie. I grab my mom's butcher knife, run upstairs and kick in his door." Fukuda kicked out his left leg. "I rush past him and tear down every picture of Hirohito in this guy's stinkin' apartment. Then I smash his Shinto shrine to pieces against the wall. Well, I can tell you, he's not shouting '*Banzai!*' anymore. The little shit is squatting in the corner, eyes bulging, his knees shaking like cane stalks in a storm. I go over, crouch down real close and swish the knife at his face."

"I hope you cut him up," said Kenta's dorm mate Short Pants, whose diminutive size had earned him his moniker.

"Not that I didn't think about it, but lucky for both of us my father came in. So, I left the bastard quivering like spilt Jell-O on the floor. When I got downstairs, my mom told me I had to report to the gym."

Kenta started to recount his boat rescue efforts when a burly sergeant who taught ROTC classes burst through a side door near the basketball hoop. He eyeballed Kenta.

"Follow me and bring your squad."

∽ ∾

Kenta and his men followed the sergeant to the back of the gym, where several closed doors lined the wall. He had never seen those doors open and assumed they led to a utility room housing pipes and wires. A brass ring holding a half-dozen, four-inch-long keys dangled from the sergeant's hand. He pulled off one key and handed it to Kenta.

"Open the doors." He turned back to the rest of the squad and ordered, "You men go get five tables and a dozen chairs."

"But there aren't any tables here," Kenta's rail-thin, tough-as-nails dorm buddy Stonehead protested, belatedly adding, "Sir."

The sergeant glared at Stonehead. "That's why, genius, I'm ordering you to go find some."

"To the cafeteria!" bellowed Fats.

Their nonchalant stroll toward the cafeteria door elicited a quick rebuke from the sergeant. "On the double, ladies. There's a war going on."

As the men broke into a run, Kenta forced his key into a matching slot. It took several grunted efforts of escalating pressure to force the key to turn the stubborn tumblers. He pried open the squeaking door, exposing greenish metal bins, rusted at the edges, jammed tightly on narrow wooden planks. Caked dust covered square tubs, stenciled letters spelling out "Ammunition," "Firing Pins" or "Firing Pin Springs." A single unlabeled box held grungy chamois cloths and odd-contoured screwdrivers. Kenta wondered whether the ancient bullets could even fire.

He turned back to face the sergeant just in time to see the only non-Nisei in his squad, Carlo "Azore" Carlesso, running toward him with two chairs in each hand. Behind Azore, whose nickname revealed his heritage—parents who had been recruited as sugarcane laborers from the Portuguese Azores at the turn of the century—came the rest of Kenta's squad, hustling as best they could while hauling tables and more chairs.

The sergeant took back the door key and then fired off an order to Kenta. "Pull out those metal boxes and set them on the tables. Then start inserting those firing pins into your Springfields."

Kenta's bewildered eyes told the sergeant that he might as well have asked him to explain Einstein's theory of relativity.

The sergeant shook his head in disgust. "Shit! If the Japs break into the gym are we supposed to hit them on the head with rifle butts? Set the bins on the tables!" Once the steel trays were lined up neatly by category, he pointed to a canister of firing pins caked in gooey packing grease and grunted, "Start cleaning." He then pointed to Kenta. "Hand me your rifle."

Kenta handed the rifle to the sergeant while thinking that in almost two years of ROTC training, he had never fired the rifle—or any rifle.

"Watch me," barked the sergeant, taking a seat at the table. "The rifles you have been drilling with can't fire a bullet. No firing pin. We're going to fix that." He pulled back the bolt on the rifle and unscrewed the

Springfield's trigger housing, placing it reverently on the table. Next, he picked up a wiped firing pin. The 2.286-inch pin ended with a rounded protrusion that provided maximum impact to ignite the deadly projectile's charge. The sergeant held the firing pin high for inspection. Satisfied, he reached into a metal box and extracted a steel coil spring. Pinching the spring, he slid it over the pin. Holding tight, he slotted the firing pin into the trigger housing, giving it a twist to hold it in place. Finally, he screwed the now-lethal trigger housing back into the rifle's firing chamber.

"Now you all do it." The sergeant walked around the tables supervising the squad's clumsy efforts. He glanced at the milling ROTC and shook his head once again. "I don't have enough time to train everyone. I'm going to order each squad in rotation to present their weapon to you, and you will insert the pins." He paused, eyeballing Kenta.

It took a few seconds for Kenta to finally understand the sergeant's meaning. "Yes, sir!"

Kenta wondered what quirk of fate had caused the sergeant to pick him out of the crowd to open the doors holding the firing pins. Cadets continued to straggle in and find their group. Territorial Guard officers and senior non-coms moved in and out of the gym engaged in agitated discussions, but no one seemed to be taking charge. Kenta hadn't seen Major Frazier for over an hour.

Kenta wanted to call home, but the military, needing all the lines, decreed "No calls for any reason."

∞ CHAPTER 9 ∞

"There's the major," said Short Pants.

The volume of murmurs dwindled as Kenta watched a clearly agitated Major Frazier rush over to ROTC Captain Nolle Smith, captain of the University of Hawaii football team, and the sergeant.

Major Charles "Rusty" Frazier, deputy commander of the Hawaii Territorial Guard, was a third-generation *kamaaina*—Hawaiian for a "child of the land," a native-born resident, Hawaiian by blood or not. Streaks of gray now dulled his once fiery-red hair. As with many of the white leaders, he stood a shade over six feet tall and exuded an easy air of authority.

The cadets coalesced into formation by squads. Frazier, Smith and the sergeant fast-stepped to the middle of one side of the gym and ascended to the third row of bleachers. Frazier said something Kenta could not hear, but he saw the sergeant draw himself up.

"Atten … shun!"

The men snapped their boots together and stood rigid. They stomped their rifles firmly on the ground at a forty-five-degree angle and focused straight ahead.

Major Frazier's eyes scanned the room as he moved his head in a slow arc. He cleared his throat.

"Today, your country needs you. Our battleships have been sunk. Our planes destroyed. While there has been no bombing since ten o'clock, there have been reports of invasions, including, moments ago, an unconfirmed sighting of Japanese paratroopers landing on St. Louis Heights, just beyond this campus."

Frazier waited for the stir to die down.

"This would *not* be the first time that Japan's soldiers followed a surprise naval attack. In 1905, without a declaration of war, Japanese warships entered the Tsar's Manchurian harbor of Port Arthur and opened fire on the unsuspecting Russian fleet. Nearby, Japan landed ten thousand marines, unchallenged." Frazier wiped a sweat bead from his eyebrow with the little finger of his right hand. "We're the only military unit in this area. The burden falls on you to face the enemy."

"Men," he said, his voice raised, strong and confident, "we are moving out. Captain Smith is taking charge of the operation."

Speaking with equal authority, Smith picked up where the major had left off. "The major has already requisitioned shovels from the groundskeepers' shed. They're being delivered outside as I speak. Three shovels per squad. We'll be digging some foxholes." Smith scanned the men. "Takayama, Okamoto, Ogura … take your squads out now. Spread out across the bottom of the hill. If anybody shoots at you, fall down, shoot back and start digging."

Dumbfounded, Kenta asked himself, shouldn't an experienced officer lead a patrol? Prior to today, Kenta's military "career" had consisted of marching to student officers' drill commands, and thoughts on Stephen Crane's *Red Badge of Courage*, required reading for freshman literature. *Will I run if rifle-firing soldiers shouting "Banzai!" charge down the hill to kill me? Japan has been fighting the Chinese for six years. Now these same combat soldiers might be less than a mile from here?*

Kenta hoped no one noticed his wobbly knees. He tightened his grip on his rifle barrel and addressed his squad. "Let's do our duty."

Seeing the sergeant stepping down from the bleachers directly in front of him, Kenta felt the impulse to shout, "I will fight the invader," but his voice came out squeaky, albeit with resolve. "We're ready."

"Good," said the sergeant. "If you see a Jap soldier, shoot him."

"Yes, sir," said Kenta, his vocal cords almost normal now. Seeing the uncertainty in the sergeant's eyes, he added with firm conviction, "I'll shoot to kill."

Buster Sugi, who had earned his nickname from mimicking the voice in the Buster Brown radio ad—"I'm Buster Brown and I live in a shoe"—held up his rifle. "What happens if I shoot all five bullets?"

"That's when you find out if you really believe in God," snapped the sergeant. "Now get going!"

∞ ∞

"They wouldn't put us up there if the army had any troops to spare," said Azore, sidling up to Kenta.

"Even if they did, the Schofield troops couldn't get here in time," said Kenta, dropping his voice to match Azore's.

"Do you really think there are Japanese soldiers on St. Louis Heights?" asked Fats.

Kenta noticed his men perking up upon overhearing the question. "Let's find out," said Kenta. "Let's prove we are just as American as any haole."

Kenta glanced at the men milling about the gym, their eyes filled with uncertainty. He caught Captain Smith's eyes on him. Kenta raised his hand, shaped it into a pistol and aimed at the double doors leading to the Heights. *Well, somebody has to go first.*

"Grab a helmet and a gas mask."

Kenta walked over to twin piles of World War I helmets and gas masks stacked like pyramids outside the adjoining supply doors. He picked up his set, adjusted them, and then checked on his men. Satisfied, he ordered, "Follow me." Without glancing back, emulating Errol Flynn in *Captain Blood*, Kenta marched out of the gym.

∞ CHAPTER 10 ∞

KENTA'S SQUAD MARCHED DOUBLE-TIME into the rice fields adjoining the campus. As they crossed the trickling Manoa Stream at the bottom of St. Louis Heights, he wondered whether the FBI had arrested his father.

Back to the mission at hand, he reminded himself. He surveyed the shrubbery, the wild grass and stubby trees covering the hill. No movement. Then again, seasoned troops would remain concealed until their officers ordered them to charge.

"Spread out," said Kenta, sweat dripping down his face from the sun—and fear. "But not too far. Stay within voice communication of your nearest neighbor."

"Do you think these old bullets still work?" asked Short Pants.

"Lean forward, everyone," Kenta ordered, ignoring the question that fueled his own doubts. "Let's not give them a big target." The cadets, eyes surveying places to dig if fired upon, hunched over like old men with bent spines and hugged their rifles snug to their chests.

A quarter of the way up the hill, Captain Smith caught up with them, three more squads in tow. He squatted and pulled out his field glasses.

"There's movement on the right side," said the captain, his binoculars still covering his eyes.

CRACK! Kenta and Short Pants fired simultaneously where Smith had pointed. Cordite perfumed the air.

"Hold your fire, goddamn it!" ordered Smith. "Who told you to start shooting?!"

"I thought … " Kenta started to say.

"Shut up!" hissed the captain.

Kenta had never seen this side of Smith before.

"Look!" screamed Short Pants, pointing to a scrub line that moved.

The sound of rifle bolts pulling back rang out. Smith turned around to face his men.

"Hold your fire! Dig in, boys! Share a shovel. Keep your eyes alert."

Most of the ROTC cadets had worked on sugar plantations or in pineapple fields. Digging holes was easy. In no time, shallow foxholes marred the landscape. The men lay prone, their untested antique rifles aimed at the top of the hill defining the eastern rim of their campus. Captain Smith moved around the defensive positions, redeploying the squads to form a double line.

"Azore, that's a cracking good foxhole," Smith encouraged. "Hideo, the reason you are digging is to keep your ass *out* of the firing line of sight, so how about lying down in that nice hole you dug?"

Kenta flipped up his shirt collar to give his neck relief from the blazing sun. He had inhaled some of the dirt kicked up by the trade winds. *All's quiet on the eastern front,* he thought.

Like his older brother Taka, Kenta devoured books, especially those that illuminated history. At age thirteen, he had read Churchill's *The Great War*. This year, he had argued that Hemingway's *For Whom the Bell Tolls* had proven once again that the "Great War" had not been the war to end all wars. He swatted away an ant crawling over his wrist and suddenly felt an urge to pee.

Until just a few hours ago, history had been something other people lived, not someone like himself. Now he realized that this day, this place and these actions would be forever fixed in the annals of history.

Kenta spoke in a low, hushed voice to his foxhole neighbor, Hideo Karamatsu, whose nickname "Hero" was the English translation of his first name. "How could they do this to us? Bomb us, kill us—the only place outside of Japan with nearly a majority of Japanese. It's such a … a betrayal. And so ruthless and cold, so sneaky."

"Hey, I live in a Korean neighborhood," Hero said. "They've been pissed since they lost their country to Japan thirty-five years ago. Lots of stories about atrocities, conscripted labor, shaming of their queen and so on. Are they going to see me as a Japanese or as an American?"

"I'm more worried about the haoles, Hero. They're going to look at our faces and think, 'You're the enemy.' Those embarrassed admirals have been telling Washington that Hawaii is safe and unapproachable. Whose fault then is this attack? Must be spies, a fifth column. Us! You've walked past Honolulu's train terminal. Machine guns mounted and pointed where? *Not* out to sea to shoot invaders, but up the street to shoot saboteurs." Kenta hammered his chest with his forefinger. "Except for a few people like Frazier, they'll never trust us."

Hero shook his head. "Most of the white power structure is OK with us, Kenta. Think about it. As soon as we got attacked, they gave us all guns. And who did they send up the hill to fight the Japanese? Us!"

"Maybe they just wanted us to get shot," said Kenta, his trigger finger firmly in place.

"Nah, they trust us. More than that, they *need* us."

Crack!

"Sorry," sputtered Kenta. "I was holding the trigger too tight."

Collective groans filled the hot, breezy air.

"How come we don't see any soldiers?" someone shouted.

"Maybe because there aren't any, jerk off," Smith replied. "Otherwise, they would have shot the first idiot that yelled." He spied Kenta three foxholes away and raised his voice. "OK hotshot, let's you and me sneak a peek up the hill."

As they rose to their hunchback crawl position, Kenta saw something white waving over a bush near the crest of the Heights. He and Smith both aimed their rifles.

"Raise your hands and come out slowly," shouted Smith. He turned to Kenta, "Can you say that in Japanese?" Before Kenta could answer, a silver-haired man waving a white handkerchief over his head came out slowly and cautiously from behind the bush. A little girl no taller than his thigh clung to his pant leg.

"My granddaughter and I were taking a hike ..." said the old man.

Smith and Kenta lowered their rifles. "You didn't see any Japanese soldiers?" asked Smith.

The man's knees wobbled. "No," he said, dropping his hands.

"Someone must have seen you on the hill and reported a Japanese landing," said Smith.

"Kenta, escort this family to the gym and report what we have seen to Major Frazier."

At 3:11 p.m., Smith received orders to stand down.

∞ CHAPTER 11 ∞

BY 3:25 P.M., ALL THE HILL DEFENDERS WERE BACK IN THE GYM. Late arrivals had swelled the ranks to almost four hundred young men, all untrained, but eager. They were forming up again at the sergeant's command. Frazier climbed the bleachers for the second time that day, and the student soldiers drew to attention. Beads of sweat dribbled down Frazier's forehead, his nearly drenched uniform stuck to his chest. After thanking the men for going out on patrol to defend St. Louis Heights, he got to the point.

"Governor Poindexter has issued a proclamation stating that all of you are eligible to be activated into the Hawaii Territorial Guard. Those who volunteer will remain at attention to take the oath; those who wish to remain a civilian, fall out."

Only the drone of American planes, taken too late to the sky, rent the silence. Smith's round eyes challenged his mostly almond-eyed assembly.

Kenta's voice rang out. "We know but one loyalty, and that is to the Stars and Stripes. We wish to do our part as loyal Americans."

As the gym broke into cheers, the sergeant handed Frazier a note. The major read it and then nodded. He had the sergeant give the attention order to bring the young men back to order. Satisfied, he addressed the assembly.

"I have just received word that Governor Poindexter has declared martial law." Question marks registered on the men's faces. "The governor has stepped down. General Short is now the military governor of Hawaii. All civilian courts and the Legislature have been disbanded, and the Hawaii

Constitution has been suspended. General Short will rule by decree. Whatever he orders or proclaims has the force of law. You must obey."

No question mark appeared on Kenta's face. He remembered the foretelling, that Sunday dinner three years ago when his brother Taka had announced, "Plans for martial law in Hawaii are in place in the advent of war with Japan."

Their mother had asked the questions that went to the heart of the matter: "Why Hawaii? What does it mean to our home?"

"The 40 percent," replied Taka. Everyone at the table knew what Taka meant. "Martial law means Japanese newspapers and radio stations will cease operations. Your shortwave wireless that brings Tokyo radio stations into your home will be confiscated. Japanese fishing boats will be grounded; they won't be allowed to leave shore."

Kenta glanced over at Akira Otani in the next squad. His father's fish market would disappear. Where would Hawaii get its fresh fish? Japanese made up 40 percent of the population, more than twice that percentage in the fishing fleet.

Major Frazier's "Raise your right hand" order brought Kenta back to the here and now. Frazier administered the oath to 363 young men and announced that they would enter the Hawaii Territorial Guard at the rank they held in their ROTC units. Kenta, who had been promoted to corporal only two weeks earlier as an incentive to sign up for next year's ROTC junior class, took back his defeatist thoughts. *Maybe this war will be an opportunity to move up the social ladder.*

Captain Smith's voice filled the room. "Listen up!" he said, holding a clipboard in his left hand. "Company A, find some shovels and get out to Kamehameha Highway and start digging trenches. Don't ask me where. Pick a high spot with a good view of anyone coming down. The buses that brought you here are on standby. Grab one. Try to be nice about it.

"Company B, you are being deployed to the power stations. See that big guy in the yellow hard hat? He's the chief engineer. He has a bus waiting for you."

Smith turned his booming voice toward Kenta. "Your squad has Washington Place."

The governor's office and residence, thought Kenta. He caught himself. The military governor's office and residence. Only a five-minute bike ride to his parents' Queen Emma Street home. Maybe he could stop by. A thought hit him and he rushed outside.

He hustled over to the bank of payphones, dropped in a nickel and dialed. He and many of his fellow cadets ignored the order forbidding civilian use of phones to keep the lines open for the military. *I'm not a civilian anymore*, Kenta thought. On his eleventh attempt, he finally got an operator. Kenta identified himself as Corporal Takayama and gave the operator his parents' phone number. He held his breath—and then breathed easier when he heard the familiar clicks of the operator connecting the number with her switchboard. The Takayama family had one of the few residential phones in Hawaii, a privilege of his father's religious position. That privilege, however, also earned Kenji Takayama continual FBI scrutiny.

"*Moshi moshi.*" It was his mother's voice on the other end.

Suddenly, a meaty hand reached across Kenta's face and slammed the receiver down, cutting the connection.

"Now unless I disconnected your call to General Short, get your sorry ass on a bus," the sergeant ordered, pointing to a row of school buses gathering in the parking lot next to the gym.

"Yes sir!" snapped Kenta. Given the sergeant's mood, Kenta didn't think it wise to explain that his company had been ordered to bike to their Washington Place assignment. Kenta hoped the phone-banging sergeant would not be assigned to his unit or notice his absence during his planned detour to his family's home.

As he walked to the bus line, Kenta's eyes lit up as he spotted a pretty Nisei girl in a sleeveless white dress peppered with blue polka dots, Angelina Muramoto. Then again, his girlfriend's beauty captured everyone's attention. She rushed up to Kenta and started speaking animatedly, her hands flitting about like an Italian, a fitting gesture given her name.

A bubbly cheerleader type of gal, despite having lived in Japan for four years from the sixth to ninth grade and being the daughter of conservative parents, Angelina had abandoned her Japanese reserve and adopted a carefree haole demeanor that was even more unconstrained than most haoles. Kenta, in an undeclared state of love and awe, found himself both drawn to and intimidated by her social prowess.

"They arrested my dad!" she cried. "He expected it, being a *kibei*, but still ..." "Kibei" were American-born but educated in Japan.

"Dad's the least political person. We just own a liquor store." In Japan, Angelina never thought of herself as kibei since she had attended the Heishikan, an all-Nisei school where English was spoken in many of the classes and on the playground.

One of the better kanji students at her neighborhood Hongwanji's Japanese language school, Angelina was placed in the advanced class at the Heishikan, where once again she excelled. Gifted in math, she loved the logic of kanji—how one symbol often served as the basis for another word or thought. The ideogram for tree was a stick with "branches," a copse was double the symbol and triple for a forest. She hated the symbol for noise, which was the kanji character for a woman written three times.

Thinking of his own father, Kenta said, "I'm sorry, Angie."

"Dad's sick, lying in bed in his pajamas, when some badge-waving haoles force their way into our house. Dad stumbles into the living room. One FBI guy pokes a gun in his stomach. A gun! He says, 'Out! Now!'

"My mom's yelling at them to wait; she'll pack him some clothes. The big guy points the gun at her and says they are leaving, right now. They push Dad out the door."

The same sergeant who had slammed down the receiver when Kenta was making his pay phone call eyed the crowd gathering around Angelina.

"We have to go, Angie," said Kenta, catching the sergeant's scowl. He gave the sergeant a quick nod and then addressed his squad. "Let's grab our bikes and get going."

Kenta turned to walk over to the Atherton Hall bike rack, and Angelina grabbed his left arm.

"What about your dad? He's more high-profile than mine. Did they get him, too?"

"I don't know, but he has a bag packed."

∞ ∞

Dusk was settling in as Kenta led his bike-riding squad down University Avenue and then right on Kapiolani Boulevard. As he approached Washington Place, it occurred to him that he had not waited for instructions. But he worried for nothing. On the mansion's front lawn another sergeant with a khaki sleeve full of chevrons stood astride a machine gun and three bulky canvas bags, each the size and color of a baby elephant.

Kenta's squad dropped their bikes on the lawn and formed up. "Corporal Takayama reporting as directed ... *sir!*"

Stubble covered the sergeant's square jaw, testimony that he had been awakened by the early morning bombing. A scar on his skull that ran behind his ear suggested a grazing bullet. Kenta guessed he had seen action in France during the Great War.

The sergeant studied the college kids. At Fort Benning he would have greeted them as "ladies" and ordered them to hit the ground and give him fifty pushups for their spotted shoes, less-than-crisp uniforms and sloppy formation. But not today. These kids were all he had—and all the governor would have for weeks, even months, until enough fresh army units could be moved here. That is, if the Japs didn't land in hours, or days.

"At ease, men." He kicked one of the bags. "These are tents. Each sleeps four. Five in a pinch. You men will sleep here." He zeroed in on Kenta. "Four armed men on duty at all times. Ten men must be on the grounds at all times. That allows two at a time to go into town."

"Understood, *sir!*" shouted Kenta.

"Fall out," said the sergeant. "I don't suppose any of you knows how to fire this," he said, pointing to the .30 caliber heavy machine gun. He let the no response stand. "We are placing this on the roof. I will show you how to use it. We can't practice firing it without making everyone think the Japs have landed."

Thirty minutes later, Kenta learned that every fifth bullet would be a tracer that lit up to show where they were shooting. Over the next week, his men would be rotated to a firing range to learn how to shoot.

∞ CHAPTER 12 ∞

NEWLY MINTED CORPORAL KENTA TAKAYAMA assigned himself the midnight to 4:00 a.m. guard assignment. This would give him time to help set up the tent, bike home, check on his family and then return for a catnap before his midnight shift.

As he tugged the strings on his tent bag, Azore, who shared Kenta's tent and shift, leaned over to him. "Get out of here. You're the only one with a family close by."

Kenta grabbed his Schwinn and sped off into the eerie darkness.

∞ ∞

The bright lights of the night before had disappeared completely. The island had been plunged into the total blackness of martial law. The streets seemed abandoned. Kenta thought of Edward R. Murrow's "This … is London" radio newscasts describing Hitler's nightly bombing.

He pedaled with his rifle slung over his back. The strap bit into his shoulder blades. He had tied a piece of white cloth to the tip of the Springfield in a makeshift attempt to be seen by trucks, army jeeps, the occasional bus and ambulances rumbling along the streets absent headlights. Two blocks up Punchbowl Street he ended up in a ditch when an oncoming firetruck hugged the shoulder.

His thoughts came fast and scrambled. Nobody had said anything about what would happen if Japanese troops landed in force and took over the island. Where would he find his place in the new topsy-turvy chaos? He drifted into the fantasy world of a resistance fighter: he and his Hawaiian buddies would hike into the mountains and set up camp in the North Shore's Kaneana Grotto and other ancient caves, where they would plan the retaking of Hawaii.

His reverie stopped the moment he saw the moonlit shadow of two V-8 Fords parked in front of his family's home. The distinctive oversized running boards told him his worst fears were being realized and he pedaled faster. The entire family had long prepared for this visit while also hoping it would never happen.

∞ ∞

The inviting aroma of fresh-cooked tempura wafted out the open door of the house. In the dim of flickering candles, Kenta quickly removed his army boots in the hallway and walked into the living room. Four men right out of a Bogart movie turned to face him: dark suits, white shirts, narrow ties, black shoes, fedora hats. The buttoned suit jackets did not hide the menacing bulge below each man's left armpit. One man held a flashlight.

Kenta saw the men focus on the rifle he held. He read uncertainty on their faces.

The hiss of Prankster, the family feline, from under the couch echoed Kenta's thoughts. He caught sight of his mother wearing a Western dress, something she never did at home. He had not seen her at first, but her muffled sobs diverted his attention from the men. She made a show of inspecting the curtains taped to the edge of the windows to comply with the blackout orders. Her trembling hands held the masking tape. All of the pictures of the emperor had disappeared. Kenta smelled the burning trash. Taka had warned their mother that in case of war she should destroy anything Japanese.

Haru's shoulders slumped. Kenta had never seen his mother appear so small. The confident mother and respected wife of an eminent priest had disappeared, replaced by a clone of a self-effacing woman selling trinkets at the Saturday flea market.

The man with the flashlight aimed it at Kenta, who answered the question before he even asked it.

"I live here. Now step outside and take your shoes off. And while you're at it, your hats, too."

"We're real Americans. We don't take our shoes off," said the lead agent who, on previous visits, had taken off his shoes. But he had been by himself, and there had been no war.

Kenta stacked his Springfield against the sofa and moved toward the nearest suit, his hands curled into fists.

"Kenta!"

At that moment Kenta's sixty-five-year-old father entered the living room wearing his black bishop's robe, ringed in a gold sash hanging from his waist.

Kenta stopped. "*Otosan*, these men …"

"Please forgive my son," Kenji said smoothly, bowing low to the suit who seemed in charge. "He has been called to active duty to defend our islands against invasion. He finds your presence troubling. However, I have prepared for this hour."

"I need to take any papers you have," the agent said, walking toward a small room off the living room.

A smile crept across Kenji's face.

"You might like what you find," he said, his tone cordial. "It is today's sermon, urging my congregation to be always loyal to the country that provides them their home."

Haru waved a candle and a match, her eyes asking the FBI agent the question.

He eye-checked the covered windows and nodded.

Haru lit two candles. "Ken-*chan*," her wavering voice called out. "You look good in your uniform."

Kenta knew his mother hated military uniforms. A bone for the FBI. He turned to his mother. "I've been sworn into the army, Okaasan. I can't stay long—our squad has guard duty at Washington Place."

Haru stepped toward her son. "You are an American soldier. Your country is America. Our country, Japan." A sob choked her words, but she mustered on. "Our country has attacked your country. That makes us … your enemy, Ken-*chan*. If it is your duty to shoot us, we will be proud of you."

The FBI agent studied his shoes.

Haru's fear-driven declaration shamed and angered Kenta.

"Don't talk foolishly, *Okaasan*. American soldiers are *protecting everyone*."

"Grab the Motorola," said the younger agent. "Shortwave."

Kenta stepped over to the radio. "Let me help you." He picked it up, strode out onto the porch, down the steps and heaved it over his head, smashing it on the stone walkway that led to the front door. He picked it up again and ran to the curb. In front of the FBI's black Ford, he lifted the radio again and heaved it against the curb. Calmly, he wiped his hands, executed a military about-face and marched back to the stunned FBI agents who had come out onto the narrow porch.

"Take it!"

The younger agent had drawn his gun and aimed it at Kenta. "I'm arresting you."

Kenta offered out his hands. "Cuff me."

The older agent placed a restraining hand on his over-eager colleague. "Put the gun away and just stick the radio in the trunk."

Kenji had picked up his suitcase and walked out the door. He stood beside the two agents as straight as his five-foot frame would allow. His Buddhist training told him his son had violated the serenity of his home: Kenta had resorted to violence. But in that moment, the father in him swelled with pride.

Kenta relaxed his threatening posture and casually walked up the steps to his father. As he started to bend over to pick up the suitcase, his stoic father did something he had not done since Kenta's infancy. He hugged his son, then stood back and grabbed Kenta's shoulders.

"I am Japanese. I honor the emperor. As an American soldier, you must defend your country. Do not bring shame on your country, yourself or your family. Do your best, even if you must give your life." The older man's eyes bored into his son. "Okaasan and I have already agreed on this." His voice softened. "All wars end, Ken-chan. I will be okay."

"I already took the oath to join the Guard, but seeing ..."

The father gripped his son harder. "No buts. You did right, Kenta."

The older agent clamped Kenji's elbow. "We have to go, Mr. Takayama."

Kenta grabbed the suitcase. With his back straight and head lifted high, Kenji strode to the curb as if he were walking down the aisle of his Moiliili Hongwanji Mission temple.

The son pushed his own shoulders back and walked beside the prisoner, doing his best to emulate the dignity of his father.

Watching the scene from the front door, Haru put her hand to mouth. "Otosan! Your shoulder bag." The bag held Kenji's toiletries. "Wait!"

Haru ran back to the bedroom, grabbed the small bag and returned to the front door. The doors of the Ford had already closed and the car was pulling away from the curb. Kenta banged on the rooftop.

"Stop!"

Haru hurriedly cut across the yard at an angle. Running at a speed that astonished Kenta, she reached the car as it started to pick up speed and threw the cloth bag for Kenji through the open window into the back seat.

∞ CHAPTER 13 ∞

THE FBI SEDAN TAKING KENTA'S FATHER AWAY TURNED THE CORNER and vanished from sight. On the island's inky western horizon, fires at Pearl Harbor still flickered. At ground level, only the glimmer of an occasional candle seeping out from a carelessly taped window broke the night. Above, a highway of stars glittered. Kenta lifted his arm at an angle so that the face of his watch reflected in the moon's light. He squinted, barely making out the location of the hands: 8:17 p.m. A little over twelve hours ago his thoughts had been of pancakes and exams. Now he had to comfort his mother and then return to his military unit and prepare to pull the trigger if invasion rumors proved true.

What would it feel like to kill a man? He envisioned a Japanese soldier charging, eyes bulging, teeth grinning. Kenta would shoot to kill. He was certain of it.

He turned and walked back to the front door. The soft rumble of a car stopped him. He pivoted. The starlit silhouette coming his way suggested the FBI had doubled back. Kenta clenched his fists. Now what do these bastards want?

The black car glided to the curb. A haole woman in a blue dress stepped out of the driver's side.

"Mom Shivers?" Kenta could hardly believe his eyes. Then a horrible thought sunk in the pit of his stomach: Something has happened to Sue. Before he could utter a word, he saw two more heads pop out from the other side of the car. Even in the dark he recognized them.

"Taka? Sue?"

His brother hurried up the walkway to join Corrine Shivers. Taka wore a dark suit with a white shirt open at the collar and a skinny yellow tie, its knot askew. In un-Japanese fashion, the two brothers embraced.

Kenta admired his big brother. The esteemed Hung Wai Ching had personally recruited the family's first university graduate to serve as secretary to the Committee for Interracial Unity. Kenta and Taka stood back from their embrace.

"Did you see Dad coming up the road?" asked Kenta.

"Well, I saw the government-issued cars. Mrs. Shivers and I suspected he might be in one of them," said Taka.

"And you couldn't do anything to stop these men from arresting your own father?!"

"Kenta ..." Taka placed his hand on his brother's shoulder. "Father knew and approved of the committee's preparations for a war with Japan, even if it meant interning a few to forestall the vultures who want to ship us all to Molokai." Taka glanced at Corrine. "Mom Shivers's husband is arresting Japanese leaders: Buddhist priests, school principals, union leaders and the like. It's a well-thought-out response designed to avoid the West Coast brand of racial hysteria that screams, 'Throw the Japs out.' We know there will be calls for mass internment. We're doing our best to see that it doesn't happen here."

Kenta brushed his brother's hand off his shoulder and moved closer. "And putting Dad in jail is part of some master plan to keep the rest of us out of prison?"

Taka stepped around his brother and answered Kenta's strident tone with a warm voice.

"Let's go inside. Mom doesn't need to see her two sons arguing just minutes after the FBI took her husband away." Sheepishly smiling at Corrine, he added, "I'm sorry, Mrs. Shivers."

"Nothing to apologize for. I can imagine my reaction if my father were arrested."

"When can we visit him?" asked Sue.

"Let's go inside," Taka repeated. As they approached the front door, Taka tapped Kenta's arm. "Is that a corporal's patch?"

Kenta nodded, but suppressed a proud grin.

They entered the candlelit gloom. Taka bowed to his mother.

Haru had long ago come to grips with the strange dichotomy that Sachiko—Sue—lived in a haole home where the Shivers family treated her as a daughter, not a servant. Her daughter had renounced her Japanese passport and legally changed her name from Sachiko to Sue to please her second "parents." Haru was awed by Corrine. Such important people who loved her daughter. She understood that they not only protected her daughter, but she felt in some way that the entire Takayama family would be under some kind of protection if war broke out. Now it had, but under conditions that no one had foreseen.

Haru bowed deeply to Corrine Shivers—so deeply that it embarrassed her three children. Corrine had grown accustomed to the fawning. She understood that her husband's position, more so than her own power, engendered exaggerated deference. Corinne used her Southern charm to put people at ease.

"I will do what I can to find out where Reverend Takayama will be sent," she said. Corrine had never figured out what to call a Buddhist priest. She had not heard her husband refer to them as "Father" or "Reverend," but she had been raised to refer to men of the cloth respectfully. She held law enforcement officials who referred to Japanese as "heathens" in low esteem. Sue and her Nisei friends, while not Christians, certainly were not heathens nor anything else that pejorative implied.

"I will prepare tea," said Haru.

"Okaasan, we can't stay," Taka explained. "I biked over to the Shivers' home to check on Sue and then planned to bike over to see you and Dad. Mrs. Shivers suggested we take her car."

"What's going to happen to us?" asked Kenta.

"Right, I wanted to tell you that the FBI included Dad on the 'first-day arrest' list. No one else in our family will be arrested. I just came from a committee meeting chaired by General Short. He vouched for the loyalty of our Japanese community. The military needs the Japanese—the welders, rivet men and machinists—to get those ships raised from the Pearl Harbor muck and sailing again. Short approved Ching's recommendation that we rename our Committee for Interracial Unity the Morale Committee, since the crucial mission has changed. We need to organize local Japanese support for the war effort."

Taka turned his attention to Sue. "You should be able to go back to classes by Thursday. And you might want to volunteer with the Red Cross."

Haru perked up, her confidence rebounding in the aftermath of her husband's arrest and the sudden appearance of Corrine Shivers.

"Your father and I agreed we will close the temple and our Japanese language school," said Haru. "It isn't as if we were not prepared. Like everyone else, we just didn't think it would start so suddenly."

"What about weddings and funerals?" asked Kenta.

"Wives can handle the ceremonies quietly," said Haru.

"Mom's right," said Taka. "Most of the temples, language schools, festivals—anything that people can point to as un-American needs to—" He stopped, searching for the right word.

"Rest," said Haru.

"Yes, that's a good way to put it," said Taka.

"What can I do?" asked Haru.

"Okaasan, it would help if you could organize the temple women to tear sheets into bandages and take in laundry from the hospitals. There's enough work for everyone. And you, Kenta," he said, his words encouraging, "you are doing exactly what you should—serving your country in an army uniform, letting everyone know that we Japanese are first to defend *our* country."

"Okaasan," said Sue, "What about your hotel in Waimea?"

"In good time, Sue. Right now, I'm needed here."

Taka had moved his gaze back to Sue. "We need haoles seeing you in a Red Cross uniform. We'll counter their prejudices and fears with what their eyes see."

"Somebody must have told the general that most of the Hawaii Territorial Guard members are Japanese."

"You're right. At the same meeting, a Colonel Schneider said something like, 'We can't be 100 percent sure where their loyalties lie'—'they' being Japanese Americans. But Short cut him off. 'Colonel,' he said, 'we need *all* Americans protecting our island.' He stared down the colonel until he got a 'Yes, sir.'"

Taka paused as four trucks loaded with soldiers roared past from the opposite direction.

"And then … something really amazing happened. Shivers said, 'General, now that you have issued that proclamation ordering Japanese to turn in their shortwave radios, guns and fireworks, it might be a good idea to have Nisei soldiers handle the confiscations.'

"Everybody saw Colonel Schneider roll his eyes, including General Short, who jumped right on him. 'Herr Colonel Schneider, there are ninety-eight Germans on the pickup list. How many are in custody?'"

Taka grinned at Kenta. "That Kraut bastard squirmed. And I swear he stuttered when he said, 'Almost half of them, sir.'" Taka laughed. "You just had to be there."

For the first time that day, Kenta smiled. "Funny, Taka." The smile curved back to a frown. "But not as funny as my going off to fight my own kind."

"You know what 'they' did in Nanking. They're anything *but* our own kind."

"You're right," said Kenta.

Taka walked over to give his mother a kiss. "I have to get back to the Morale Committee."

"And I have to get back to guarding the governor," said Kenta.

∞ CHAPTER 14 ∞

KENTA DID NOT BIKE DIRECTLY BACK TO WASHINGTON PLACE. He diverted to a wood-framed house further down Queen Emma Street and leaned his bike against a palm tree. As he walked to the familiar porch, a figure rose from a white wicker chair. He hadn't seen her sitting there.

"Kenta! I thought you were guarding Washington Place," whispered Angelina.

"I am. I have the midnight to four shift, so I need to get back before then."

"Have you been home?"

"Yeah, got there just in time to see Dad taken away. At least the G-men treated him better than they did your father."

Angelina rose. The clingy green silk robe she wore accentuated her curves. Her normally perfectly curled hair hung down, wild and unkempt.

"I guess they knew your brother's connections with the big *kahunas*." She sat down on a front porch step and patted the spot next to her. Kenta plunked himself down.

"Everybody's spooked, Kenta. Scared the midnight boots will march into their home. Scared a neighbor will twist some innocent remark and suddenly any one of us will be hauled off to jail."

A sharp breeze whipped across the porch. Angelina hugged her chest.

Kenta ached to put his arm around her. "Taka told me something else, Angie. Short will be issuing a decree forbidding any Japanese to own a liquor store."

"Kenta! That's the only income we have!"

"Tell your mom to sell her store tonight. She'll get less than what it's worth—but more than she will get after Short issues the decree."

A rifle shot startled them.

"Oh my God, is that gunfire?" asked Angelina. She grabbed Kenta's hand.

Four more shots rang out.

"Sounds like they came from the power station," said Kenta. "I think Ueda's squad is guarding it. Probably just someone shooting at shadows, but I'd better get over there."

He released Angelina's hand and then kissed her on the cheek. As he trotted down the sidewalk, Angelina called out, "Be careful, Ken-chan."

Kenta noted the use of "chan" after his name, conveying a warm tone of affection instead of her usual sarcasm. "I will, Angie-chan."

He pedaled toward the electric station. A smudge on the sky obscured the stars over Pearl Harbor. The trade winds blew in the smells of smoldering steel and rubber. Two more shots rang out. Revved engine sounds growled from the direction of the armory.

Kenta arrived at the power station and dropped his bike on the grass. He crouched low and duck-walked to the steel-mesh fence, sliding along it, searching for the entrance. He pulled back the bolt of his rifle.

The moon and stars illuminated Ueda's profile and another face Kenta didn't recognize. The two soldiers were squatting behind a coiled transformer with rifles aimed up the hill. Kenta puckered his lips and gave a "pssst" sound. Ueda swiveled around and aimed his rifle at the sound.

"It's Kenta! Don't shoot!"

Ueda lowered his gun.

"How do I get to you?" asked Kenta.

"Middle of the fence. Gate's open. Just keep coming," said Ueda.

Still hunched over, Kenta trotted to the gate and joined the nervous defenders. All three scouted the elevated area covered in shadowy grass and shrubbery.

"We saw something move. We shouted, 'Halt and stand up.' It moved. We shouted again, louder. It continued to move, so we shot it. Maybe something hit the ground, maybe not. But the movement stopped."

"Shouldn't we go out there and check?" asked the soldier Kenta didn't know.

"There could be fifty enemy soldiers out there for all we know," said Ueda.

The sound of a jeep braking on gravel saved Kenta from having to make a combat decision. He turned and shouted, "Up there!"

Three soldiers jumped out of the jeep before it rolled to a stop.

"I think we shot something," said Ueda.

"You all stay here and cover us," one soldier said.

A minute later, a soldier hollered from the hill. "Congratulations, you just killed an enemy cow."

PART II

DISCHARGE

❧ CHAPTER 15 ❧

Honolulu – December 17, 1941

A LONE.

A lonely ghost adrift in the sun-starved gloom, thought Haru, trying for the umpteenth time to express her feelings about her new normal—everyone's new normal—on an island paradise with golden beaches now lined with ever-increasing rows of barbed wire instead of tourists basking in its iconic sand and surf.

Haru's heavy eyes stared blankly at the amber glow bleeding through the mud-colored muslin taped snugly to the window frame. She had awakened as the stars began to lose their glimmer to the creeping dawn that the blackout "curtains" smothered.

Not ready to face the day, she thought instead of her close-knit yet scattered family. Her husband—still recovering from cancer, now incarcerated in a tent-style prison camp only a few miles from their home yet forbidden from receiving visitors. Three boys in uniform with another regretting he wasn't, portending his future in khaki. Two children in Japan: a son in Tojo's army, a daughter translating for the Ministry of Foreign Affairs. Haru feared it could be years before she heard from them now that postal service routes had been severed. Would the Red Cross deliver their letters? If so, when? And how often? If Yoshio were killed in Manchuria, how would she know?

The night before, she had draped an apron over a reading lamp to skirt the lights-out regulations. She distracted herself from the melancholy of the long night by reading Ernest Hemingway's *For Whom the Bell Tolls*. A war novel, the wrong type of book for her to read, and yet it was so compelling: a young man succumbing to the lure of war, a cause and love. Haru's mind seesawed between the novel's bitter reminder that combat awaited her sons and her enthrallment with Hemingway's portrayal of a love triangle in the midst of the Spanish Civil War.

Alone.

Still listless, Haru elbowed her way to a sitting position on her forlorn marriage bed. She rounded her hips and let her legs dangle. Inhaling the room's stale air, she longed for the sweet scents of pikake, ginger and plumeria blossoms from the nearby lei-makers' huts. The Hawaiian ladies were still there, but now instead of stringing flowers they wove camouflage nets.

Alone.

And quiet. Haru missed the happy chatter of children walking to school, which remained shuttered, and the murmurs of early-evening passersby strolling to restaurants or movie theaters. All nightlife shut down an hour before sunset so patrons and workers could rush home before the stillness of curfew.

The six o'clock rumble of cars and trams scurrying to their last destination of the day foretold the coming silence, broken only by stridulating crickets and the boot clicks of wardens scrutinizing windows for light leakage.

Alone.

Haru's thoughts wandered back to yesterday's boisterous activity on Hotel Street. The noise had penetrated her Queen Emma Street cottage. Bars were celebrating the end of the prohibition that had been imposed following the attack on Pearl Harbor. The raucous din of sailors and soldiers reminded Haru of a lurid life that could have been hers, as well. She refused to judge the girls working on Hotel Street. But for the grace of Buddha, that would have been her life, too.

As an Amakusa Island girl just reaching puberty, she had been willing to sacrifice herself to such a life for her parents' well-being. Though Haru's parents had already been paid for their daughter's bondage to a Sandakan brothel, at the last moment they suffered seller's remorse and arranged for her escape. Haru walked all night on mountain paths to the other side of Amakusa to surreptitiously board a coal collier to Hiroshima. Up until the moment the scow left the mist-enveloped harbor, she had feared that the procurement man would find her and drag her instead to the ship sailing for British-run northern Borneo. Would she still be alive today? A mistress to a businessman? A madam? Too much time alone conjured up so many "might have been" scenarios.

Alone.

On her rare shopping trips to sparsely stocked grocery stores, Haru felt the burn in the haoles' wary eyes. She knew they wondered about her loyalty, and yet she empathized with their prejudice. Their fear, however irrational, meant many haoles went to bed each night wondering if Tokyo would order people with eyes like hers to rise and knife them in their sleep.

Alone.

Haru padded over to the Motorola in the living room and fumbled with the knobs. At least radio stations—English-language radio stations only—were allowed to broadcast again. In the kitchen, she dropped a slice of bread into the toaster and set a pot of coffee on the stove to percolate. Until a week ago, Haru had never eaten breakfast alone. Not that a piece of unbuttered toast and cup of coffee could really be called breakfast. Her clothes had begun to sag on her. How often had she counseled parishioners in distress to keep up their strength?

"Don't give into the temptation of not taking care yourself," she had urged. Now *she* understood the demons they had felt.

Alone.

Haru scrutinized Ume's letter lying on the kitchen table. Ume had been a fellow picture bride and had become her close friend. She recalled the day Ume, then three months pregnant, had shown her the blotch on her neck that sentenced her to a long and slow death in the settlement of Kalaupapa on the island of Molokai. It had led to Haru's promise to her dear friend that she would pick up her baby shortly after birth. Now Ume was in her final days of life in the isolated Hansen's disease settlement. Haru knew that a *kokua* helper in the early stages of the dreaded disease had penned the letter for Ume, who had not been able to write for years. Her scribe had faithfully conveyed her tone.

Ume was writing to say good-bye. Haru had planned to visit her after she and Kenji moved back to the Big Island, but the bombing of Pearl Harbor had upended their scheduled sailing by four hours. Now with the shipping ban, her postponing of their final farewell for a convenient time had robbed her of a final, loving good-bye.

Haru had raised Ume's child, Kenta, faithfully. Kenji had urged her to forego the voyage, as if he had known what would happen. Her miscarriage on the Kalaupapa beach followed the ship's tempestuous passage, and Haru still carried the guilt to this day. Her real son would be alive today if not for her insistence that she keep her promise to Ume to pick up her baby in Kalaupapa.

Ume had seen an opportunity for both women, and insisted that Haru take her baby to Oahu but raise the child as her own, to replace the child Haru had lost.

"We have secrets here. We keep them here. You know how Irie is," said Ume, referring to her husband. "He will struggle to give this baby a good home." Haru knew too well Irie's struggle with *sake* since Ume had left for Kalaupapa.

The subterfuge. Especially to Kenji. A never-told secret, until four years ago when Kenta showed a romantic interest in Ume's oldest daughter—his biological sister. She recalled the trepidation as she told her son the truth, the tingling goosebumps as Kenta took her hand.

"You will always be my mother," he said. "Thank you for the life you have given me."

Afterwards, Kenta began sending chatty letters to his "Auntie Ume," giving her insight into the life of the son she would never know. Haru would send Ume a family picture, knowing the only face Ume would notice, if she could still see and were still alive, would be Kenta's.

Alone.

Had she bathed last night? Haru always bathed before bed. She just felt so tired. How could having nothing to do be so tiresome? Her rational mind kicked at her melancholy.

Thousands had died on December 7. Her family had survived. Takeshi served as the Morale Committee's secretary and had access to information not privy to the public. He assured his mother that the Sand Island internees, his father among them, had plenty of food and medical attention if needed.

Alone.

She heard a knock at the kitchen door followed by the twisting doorknob. Haru realized she had forgotten to lock her door the night before. But it must be someone she knew—a welcome relief from her boredom.

In strolled Takeshi. He glanced around and for a split second frowned at the half piece of toast on an otherwise empty kitchen table. Through the open bedroom door, he noticed her disheveled bed.

"Okaasan, the Morale Committee needs your help."

∞ CHAPTER 16 ∞

LESS THAN A MILE FROM HIS PARENTS' HOME, Kenta was waking up slowly, sluggishly. Unlike his mother, Kenta's lethargy was the result of overindulgence. Smuggled beer from a Fort Street bar had fueled a bullshit session that had lasted past midnight. As he pressed his fingers into the sides of his head in a fruitless effort to relieve the pain, the sounds of early-morning chattering and the clanging of tin coffee cups outside his tent suddenly stopped.

"Good morning, men," a voice of authority boomed through the canvas.

"Good morning, sir!" came the automatic response of Kenta's squad.

Kenta stuck his head outside the tent. It was Governor Poindexter.

Kenta jammed his legs into his trousers and slipped on his boots without lacing them. Still buttoning his shirt, he stepped out to greet the governor.

"Relax, Sergeant," said Poindexter, pausing and eyeing each man in turn. "We're mighty proud of how you all volunteered for the HTG," he said, referring to the Hawaii Territorial Guard. "You stepped up when your country needed you. You could have stayed in school."

"It's our duty, sir," said Kenta, suddenly realizing that the governor had just addressed him as "Sergeant."

Poindexter shook his head sadly. "My visitors are complaining that when they pass your tent, certain ripe smells are spoiling our aloha fragrances. What do you have to say for yourselves?"

The governor smiled as he saw discomfort registering on the young men's faces. "We've designated a bathroom with a shower for you. Two of you can follow me now. The next two can show up in rotation. After everyone is presentable, join the breakfast chow line in the ballroom."

At Kenta's nod, Short Pants and Buster followed Governor Poindexter inside.

"Yes!" Kenta whispered to the rest of his squad, giving them the thumbs-up sign. "My brother knew this would be our chance."

"What chance?" asked Azore.

Kenta's squad closed in around him. "Taka said the war would give us an opportunity to prove our loyalty. People will respect us and look at us differently."

"Maybe you ought to read today's *Advertiser* before you go too far with that," said Fats, holding out the newspaper. "Read the headlines."

JAP MAIDS FAILED TO REPORT TO WORK DECEMBER 7.
WHAT DID THEY KNOW?

WERE LANES CUT THROUGH CANE FIELDS TO GUIDE JAP PLANES?

REPORTS OF LOCAL JAPANESE STALLING THEIR CARS TO BLOCK ACCESS TO PEARL HARBOR AWAITING VERIFICATION.

SABOTEURS LAND HERE.

"Let me read the article that goes with this last one," said Fats.

NAVY WIVES TELL OF TREACHERY

Navy wives fleeing war-ravaged Pearl Harbor arrived at San Diego last night claiming fifth column betrayal. Nancy Pringle, wife of Navy Captain John Pringle said, "There is no way the Japanese could have pulled off this dastardly sneak attack without local accomplices."

"We know that's a crock," said Kenta. "None of it is true."

"Truth isn't the point," said Fats. "It's what people believe. For every person who tells us what a great job we're doing, there's a pair of suspicious eyes waiting for a reason to tell their neighbor 'I told you so.'"

Kenta picked up the dented aluminum coffee pot from the *hibachi* grill and poured a dark stream into a tin cup. "The governor has invited us to shower and eat. *In his home.* Let's cut the negative crap and see how fast we can get cleaned up."

An hour later, Kenta and his squad followed a governor's aide into the ballroom where the aroma of scrambled eggs, bacon, coffee and cigarette smoke filled the air. A smattering of applause greeted them as they walked in. Kenta poked Fats in the ribs as if to say, "I'm right again."

Moving down the buffet line, they loaded their plates with eggs, bacon and toast.

"Hey! Quiet!" All eyes turned to the booming voice of a soldier standing next to a large radio.

"... *confirmation a Japanese Zero pilot was killed December 13 in Hawaii's westernmost island of Niihau. The pilot crash-landed on December 7 and was taken prisoner. Yuya Harada, a Nisei born on Maui, was asked to guard the prisoner. During the evening, Harada freed the pilot and the two of them took prisoners at gunpoint and threatened to kill anyone who resisted them. A standoff followed. Four days ago, Ben Kanahele, a Hawaiian field hand, rushed the pilot. Despite being shot three times, Kanahele kept charging and broke the pilot's neck. Harada then turned a rifle on himself, ending the hostage crisis.*

"*The obvious question is—if one Japanese born in America has turned traitor, could there be others?*"

With a promise to give updates as they came in, the radio announcer moved on to the weather forecast. The soldier turned down the radio and took his seat. No one spoke. Kenta surveyed the room. All eyes in the ballroom were on his squad.

Later, as they were leaving, Fats murmured to Kenta, "I just overheard that Short got the boot. A new general, Emmons, arrived yesterday to replace him."

Kenta shook his head. "Who cares? This Harada sabotage story just screwed us."

Familiar with Hawaii from his 1934 to 1936 posting at Fort Shafter, General Delos Carleton Emmons had never attended a meeting of the Morale Committee, which before December 7 was known as the Committee for Interracial Unity. On his first-day inspection of Oahu, Emmons noticed the Asian faces guarding power plants and the telephone exchange. There were even armed and uniformed Asian faces at hospitals, on the beaches and in the governor's office.

The navy presented Emmons with its report on the Niihau incident: "The fact that a Japanese who had previously shown no anti-American tendencies went to the aid of the pilot indicates the likelihood that Japanese residents previously believed loyal to the United States may aid Japan if further Japanese attacks appear successful."

The navy report failed to mention the army officer, First Lieutenant Jack Mizuha, a Maui-born Nisei, who organized a landing of soldiers on Niihau to capture the freed Japanese pilot. By the time Mizuha landed, the pilot had already been killed.

In response, navy intelligence instead recommended the internment of all Japanese.

⌐ CHAPTER 17 ⌐

Tokyo – December 22, 1941

BANGING AWAY AT HER TYPEWRITER, Hiromi smelled the Brylcreem before she even saw him approaching. She tilted her head just in time for Murakami-*san*'s tobacco breath to overpower the reek of his hair tonic. *What is it with Japanese men over forty?* Yellow teeth. Slicked-back hair. Slithering eyes passing over her breast line.

Murakami set a folded page from a three-day-old *New York Times*—courtesy of the Japanese Embassy in Switzerland—on the edge of her desk.

"Translate this—" ordered Murakami, his raspy voice pausing for effect. "And properly ..." Another pause. "To encourage our home front." He fingered the headline: "HAWAII MILITARY ARRESTS MORE JAPS." His silence now signaled Hiromi to start reading.

The first paragraph summarized the continuing arrest of Japanese priests, teachers, journalists and business leaders in Hawaii. The *Gaimusho*—the Foreign Ministry—ordered Hiromi to "translate" the *Times* article into invective propaganda attacking America's claim of being a democracy, the hypocrisy of Roosevelt, and the low status of Japanese in America.

Hiromi's thoughts turned to her father, who likely was among those arrested and incarcerated. *A prisoner. Such injustice!* Hiromi had renounced her country. Or had she really? Surreptitiously, she had kept her American passport. The military now ruled the Japan Hiromi had embraced so eagerly just three years ago. Translating news articles sure beat joining interned Americans in Japan's hinterland. But twisting translations into daily vitriol that betrayed America was more than she could tolerate.

Why didn't I board that last ship before the attack? Why did I let my stubbornness blind me to Tojo's military intentions?

Today she would stand her ground. If not today, then when? This could be a long war. She had been so confident while rehearsing her "I am a translator, not a propagandist" declaration in front of her vanity mirror that morning in her rabbit warren of an apartment in Nihonbashi.

As Murakami leaned in, her resolve took a hit. Hiromi glanced at him to catch his attention and then dropped her eyelids in respect. In a voice just loud enough for Murakami to hear, she began, even as she felt her vocal cords tighten: "As a professional, I will translate. But if you want the news changed to propaganda, you must have someone else in the ministry make the changes."

Murakami glanced around the cavernous room of paper patriots trolling through data, magazines and newspapers, all searching for news articles they could rescript into press releases to stoke the public's support for attacking America. Noticing the feigned stares into periodicals of those nearby who pretended not to notice Hiromi's tone, Murakami teethed a false smile.

"Of course, truth is of the essence. Come. Let's discuss this important subject in my office."

Murakami turned and ambled toward the back of the room. Her confidence ebbing with each step, Hiromi lagged behind, enjoying the lingering fragrance of *hinoki,* a type of Japanese cedar, used to build their new desks.

Hiromi felt as if she shrank in size as she entered Murakami's office for the first time. Eight steps into the room she stopped behind two shoulder-high chairs facing an executive desk piled high with English and Chinese publications. On the credenza behind his desk sat an oversized, gilt-framed picture of Murakami stoically receiving an ornate medal from Emperor Hirohito.

Don't these people ever smile, thought Hiromi, realizing a split-second later that she was one of "these people." She certainly hadn't done much smiling lately.

Hiromi took a close look at Murakami sitting across his desk in an elevated chair. Her eyes darted to where his manicured hands rested on his polished mahogany desk, a curled forefinger caressing a single manila folder. On the tab was her name, handwritten in bold, black *katakana*. On top of the file lay an American passport. Hiromi felt her gut clench. She grabbed the back of the left chair. *I will not faint*, she resolved.

"Sit down," said Murakami in an unexpectedly warm, grandfatherly voice. "Your lack of dedication to your new task has been disappointing. And not just today. I had planned to meet with you after lunch. But your remarks suggest that now is better."

Hiromi walked around the chair slowly, holding on to its back until she eased herself into the cushioned seat.

Murakami let the silence linger. Then, pushing the passport aside like a fallen leaf, he opened the file. "You are a very interesting person, Hiromi."

Hiromi's folded hands tightened. Anger competed with fear. Murakami never addressed his female staff by their last names, as he did the men. And now he had even dropped the honorific san.

"You told your Dentsu interviewer that you chose to live in Japan." Murakami stopped talking and took his rimless glasses from the breast pocket of his suit jacket. Slowly, he put them on the bridge of his nose with his right hand while picking up a sheaf of paper with his left.

"This is your exact statement: 'I am tired of being treated like a second-class citizen in Hawaii and want to live in Japan for the rest of my life.'" Murakami raised his eyebrows. "Then you told Dentsu, and later my assistant, that you never applied for an American passport." He picked up the passport, opened it to the first page and laid it down facing Hiromi.

Her name. Her picture. Her passport.

"Hisayo! How could she!" blurted Hiromi.

Murakami's soft voice turned to steel. "How could you put your friend in such danger by asking her to hide your passport?"

Someone had clandestinely turned in Hiromi's passport. He, or she, had wrapped it in brown paper, dropped it off at the ministry's front desk and walked away. Murakami suspected it was most likely the Hisayo frequently mentioned in Hiromi's file. "If the Kempeitai knew of your friend's complicity, where would Hisayo be now? And if your friend had not turned your passport in to our ministry, instead of the military police, where would *you* be now? Perhaps Hisayo hoped the ministry wouldn't turn you in. Or perhaps she just didn't want the certainty of putting you into a Kempeitai interrogation room."

Hiromi still had a little fight left in her. "I was born in America. I have the right to be treated as an American. There is nothing wrong with my having that passport."

"Perhaps you would like to assert your rights to the Kempeitai? Murakami suggested. "Tell them why you were hiding that passport and passing yourself off as a disaffected American?"

"I am not a spy."

"Ah, but you made the connection," said Murakami, making a show of putting Hiromi's passport into his desk drawer and then closing her file. "Those Americans registered with your embassy are in camps for noncombatants. While they live in barracks without any contact with the outside world and are fed a—" Murakami wore a sardonic smile. "A nutritious, but less-than-appetizing meal, you live in an apartment near Ginza, surrounded by movie theaters and good Japanese food. And what does your job require? Translating hard news stories with an angle that provides comfort to a nation at war. Don't forget, *your* country really did arrest 'Japs.'" Murakami's face twisted in anger as he uttered the word. "And, yes, your fabled FBI holds your father prisoner."

Hiromi raised her eyebrows.

"I have news that might interest you." He sat back in his chair, stretching out the suspense in a show of petty bureaucratic power.

"Late in the evening of the attack, the police rounded up the last of our consular staff in Hawaii. A Swedish fishing trawler brought them back to Japan as part of the exchange of diplomats. They arrived two days ago and are providing us with last-minute intelligence."

Murakami paused again. Hiromi resolved to show no emotion.

"You have a brother in the University of Hawaii's student ROTC program. They were activated into the Hawaii Territorial Guard. So now you have three brothers in the military—two on the American side, and Yoshio on *our* side." He glowered at Hiromi, then reached into the inner pocket of his jacket and pulled out an envelope, its flap already slit open, and handed it to her. Her mouth fell open.

A letter from Yoshio.

"You can take a break and read it," said Murakami, his voice returning to its grandfatherly tone. "And then, please have that *New York Times* article translated … in the proper fashion." His burrowing gaze and unctuous voice demanded an answer.

"I will do my best."

"There is one more matter," said Murakami. The pause, the insincere smile. "You have missed your last two *Tonarigumi* meetings."

Hiromi hated the neighborhood association system that had been instituted a year earlier. Each Tonarigumi association consisted of about ten households. In reality, they were just a shade better than neighborhood spy systems monitored by the Kempeitai. The groups' chairmen organized send-off parades for new inductees; decided where to build trenches, as if America could bomb Tokyo; and distributed rice ration coupons that Hiromi had picked up from her chairman's home without hearing any complaints about her absences from events. Or so she had thought. The worm!

"I will not miss the next meeting," said Hiromi. Murakami held his stare. "And I will attend events."

Murakami picked up a copy of Hong Kong's two-day-old *Morning Post* and began reading.

Hiromi took the cue and rose. Weak-legged, she scurried off to the ladies' room and retched as quietly as she could so as not to attract attention or emit any sound that might hearten Murakami. Moments later, she squatted in the stall to read her brother's censored letter. Any reference to weather or food, their favorite subjects before the war, had been inked over. But Yoshio seemed in good spirits. Hiromi folded the letter and stared at the stall door. Murakami had not said, "If you don't translate news into propaganda, I will turn you over to the Kempeitai." Nor had he threatened to make Yoshio's miserable posting even more miserable. He didn't have to.

Hiromi plodded over to the dull porcelain sink and swirled some water around her mouth. She slapped her cheeks with the tips of her fingers and splashed some water on her face. After applying fresh lipstick, she forced herself to return to her desk with enthusiasm and rolled a clean sheet of paper into her Underwood carriage. She would first rewrite the *New York Times* article, which in her mind she had labeled "a propaganda script," and then translate. Her use of kanji characters lacked nuance, but she knew copy editors would polish her work.

⚭ CHAPTER 18 ⚭

Koko Head, Oahu – December 28, 1941

B*ANG! BANG! BANG!*
"Two bull's eyes!" Kenta exclaimed, louder than he realized. He had forgotten that he was wearing ear protectors. Kenta was only into the second hour of his first day on the Koko Head firing range, a few miles east of metropolitan Honolulu. He hadn't seen the firing instructor coming up behind him until he heard his booming, authoritative voice.

"You got a sniper's hands and eyes, kid. And you didn't let the Springfield's nasty shoulder-kick get the best of you. Take a break."

A short time later, Kenta joined the burger line inside the open-air mess hall. The salty breezes swept away the smells of cordite and cooking oil. As Kenta waited in line, a green army sedan screeched to a halt at the curb. He recognized the haole officer, Tony Jenkins, as he jumped out and fast-stepped it into the mess. He had graduated in Taka's McKinley High School class. As the young man walked up to the commanding officer, Lieutenant John Naumu, the server on the other side of the counter brought Kenta's attention back to lunch.

"You ordering food or just contemplating life?"

"Sorry," said Kenta. "Cheeseburger, fries and a Coke."

"Onions, lettuce, tomatoes?"

"Yeah, the works."

"You better get that to go, Kenta," said the lieutenant, who had approached unseen. He nodded toward Jenkins. "They want you downtown."

Kenta scarfed down his burger and fries in the backseat of the car while Jenkins sat silently in the front passenger seat, next to their Filipino driver. Kenta was wiping away ketchup from the corners of his mouth when the driver pulled up in front of the Dillingham Transportation Building. Jenkins jumped out and opened the rear door for Kenta. He then escorted him inside to a small, bare room with only a folding table flanked with two wooden hardback chairs. A naked low-watt bulb hung from the ceiling.

"Wait here," said Jenkins, not quite slamming the door behind him.

Kenta sat, fidgeting, wishing he had something to read to take his mind off what might be coming. Half an hour later, the door swung open. Kenta jumped to his feet and saluted.

"At ease," said the tall, silver-haired man dressed in starched khaki with knife-like creases. "Sit."

Kenta obeyed. The man took the other chair.

"I am Lieutenant Colonel Robert Lewis Stevenson."

"Like the author?" asked Kenta, wishing a second later that he'd kept his knee-jerk remark to himself.

"Have you met anyone that might raise some questions?" asked the colonel.

"I don't think so, sir. I'm staying with my squad, guarding Washington Place. We have tents there and I—"

"It is to *whom* you spoke while on guard duty," the colonel said, detailing a chance meeting Kenta had had with a childhood classmate from Waimea. He was walking by the governor's mansion when they spotted each other.

"Oh … yeah. I mean, yes, sir. Yasuda was a buddy of mine. I guess you've heard of his brother, nicknamed "The Emperor." He used to give speeches claiming Japan had a right to compete with France and England for Asian colonies." Kenta gave an indifferent shrug. "Yasuda and I were catching up with each other about our families. Shortly after their arrests, both Yasuda's brother and my dad were moved from the city jail to the internment camp at Sand Island."

The colonel asked a few more questions that covered the same ground. Then, without a word of explanation or a good-bye, he stood up and left. Kenta remained, wondering if he should get up and leave, too. The Filipino driver answered his question when he poked his head in the door.

"I'm to take you to Washington Place."

That evening, Kenta related the incident at chow.

"You're lucky you have a brother on the inside," snapped fellow squad member Tommy Ogi, who had been dubbed "No Ticket" for his habit of showing up to the movies without any money. Catching Kenta's confused expression, No Ticket elaborated.

"The FBI picked up your pal last night. Yasuda was sent to Sand Island."

"This might be my last breakfast with you guys," said Kenta.

"Maybe not," scoffed No Ticket.

He was right. The army never questioned Kenta again.

∞ CHAPTER 19 ∞

Washington Place, Honolulu – January 19, 1942

THE RAINDROPS TAP DANCING on their canvas ceilings had lulled Kenta's squad to sleep on the night of January 18. The rain and rustle of winter trade winds whipping their tented walls just after midnight drowned out the odd-hour comings and goings at the governor's mansion.

By mid-January, the fears of an invasion had subsided. The Niihau incident had proven to have been an anomaly. US Navy air reconnaissance had spotted the Japanese fleet near Midway on Christmas Day, heading home to Japan.

Kenta's guard duty became more relaxed. At night, only one soldier stood watch, and only for a two-hour shift. Food peddlers setting up their sidewalk canteens in the early morning hours continued to shout greetings when they arrived, thus ensuring that the sentry knew their footsteps and dark shadows were friendly ones.

The greatest danger turned out to be the coconuts dive-bombing from one of the palm trees where a badminton net had been strung up on the governor's lawn. Kenta's squad mingled easily with the governor's staff at breakfast. They had all attended the opening of *The Maltese Falcon* together. The girls, even the haole ones, had flirted with them.

Angelina dropped by often, sometimes with a batch of homemade cookies for the squad. She and Kenta sometimes walked over to Aloha Tower. When she spied Kenta chatting with a haole nurse's aide one day, she said, "You were much too friendly with that Goldilocks." Kenta laughed it off, but, inside, his confidence swelled. He had never thought of himself as an object of jealousy.

Just a day earlier, Taka had also visited Kenta. "Our Morale Committee is getting the job done. While the calls for internment are getting ugly in California, Hawaii's newspapers are printing most of my 'Hawaii's Japanese are supporting the war effort' articles. The editors have stopped publishing rehashed sabotage rumors. Maybe it's because not a single allegation has ever been substantiated."

That night, Kenta dreamed he was pushing a stroller along Waikiki Beach with Angelina at his side. The barbed wire was gone, and the swimmers and sun worshippers were back. "I think we're winning the war against prejudice," Kenta told Angelina as they walked along the waterfront.

"Wake up, Kenta," said Short Pants, shaking Kenta's shoulders. Raindrops fell from the bill of his cap onto Kenta's face.

"What the—!" cried Kenta, clearly irritated. "It's too early!"

Other men in the tent stirred, agreeing that Short Pants should "go fuck himself."

"It's Nolle," said Short Pants, loud enough so everyone could hear. "He said Frazier wants all of us at Lanakila HQ at six—with our rifles."

"That's an hour from now," said Kenta. "How long do you think it takes us to put on a pair of pants?"

"Nolle gave me the keys to two jeeps. You'll find them at the armory." Short Pants nodded toward the hidden, granite building.

"Maybe we're getting some type of recognition," said Fats.

"What's really strange is that Nolle said Carlos should stay behind," added Short Pants.

"Well, somebody has to stand guard," Kenta surmised.

The rain had stopped by the time Kenta's jeep, jammed with Hawaii Territorial guardsmen holding their Springfields close to their chests, pulled up at Lanakila School, a short ride from Washington Place. The moon danced in and out of clouds racing to the sea and the stars came out just in time to meet the glow of dawn. The air hung heavy, damp and sweet.

"Must be good news," said Ted Tsukiyama, entering the cafeteria. At age twenty-two he was an "elder statesman" in the ROTC–Territorial Guard, holding leadership positions in student government and the YMCA.

Kenta frowned. "I've never known a haole to call a meeting before the first rooster crowed just to deliver good news." He quickly surveyed the room. "Hey, why only Nisei?"

"I heard they're going to make us regular army, now that we've proven our loyalty," Ted retorted. "If that happens, I bet that any Sand Island internee who has a son in the army will be released. Your dad might be home in a week."

"I hope so," said Kenta as he looked at the sleepy-eyed assembly, many of whom were still tucking in their shirts and lacing up their boots. He meandered through the expectant gathering.

"They raised the *Nevada* this morning," one voice said.

"A buck says we get an award. Since we've been guarding the beaches, no Nippon soldiers have dared to land," laughed another.

"They released twenty-two men from Sand Island yesterday!" claimed an exuberant soldier.

No Ticket yelled, "We're going to the Philippines to kick some Hirohito ass!"

"Atten-shun!"

Three hundred and seventeen Nisei soldiers fell silent. Their clomping boots formed neat rows at attention. Kenta, standing in the front row directly across from Nolle Smith, noticed that the captain did not make eye contact with him. A hinge squeaked. Kenta's eyes refocused on the wall behind Smith. He studied Major Frazier as he strode in from the same kitchen doors, his gait as firm as usual but somehow not quite the same, either. It was more like he had sucked in his breath and forced himself to walk with a purpose that had come naturally as part of his leader persona, until today.

Frazier pulled up next to Smith. Kenta's radar ratcheted up as he noticed the wrinkles in Smith's normally crisp uniform and the chestnut half-moons outlining its armpits. Pinched furrows gullied his forehead. His teeth were clenched and jawline tight.

The gust of wind rattling the jalousie windows broke the silence.

"At ease," ordered Smith.

Together, the men swung their right legs eighteen inches to the right while simultaneously extending their left arms to hold their Springfields out straight. Each right hand snapped behind its owner's back. They kept their eyes straight and their heads rigid.

Kenta's gut fluttered as he watched Nolle hesitate, as though struggling to find the right words. *This isn't going to be good.*

"Men ..." Smith's voice faltered. Long, tense seconds passed. "Men, I have been proud to be your leader. You are good soldiers. There is no decent way to tell you what I must say." Smith's moistened eyes roved the uniformed contingent. "I have been ordered—*ordered*—to discharge all the men of Japanese ancestry from the Hawaii Territorial Guard, effective immediately."

Smith looked at Frazier, who moved one step forward. His voice wavered. "Your dedication. And your loyalty ... have been beyond reproach. You don't deserve this," Smith continued. He let a pause linger and then continued. Kenta heard genuine heartbreak in the captain's voice. "There is nothing, nothing more I can say. Stack your weapons and—and go home."

The men facing Smith froze—as stiff and numb as a contingent of terracotta warriors. Their eyes said they didn't believe it was really happening.

Stunned, his knees weakened, Kenta squeezed his rifle for support. *How will I tell my father?*

The thwack of a rifle hitting the hardwood floor shattered the silence. "Our country needs men!" shouted Short Pants. "But not us! We are less than men! We're useless and unwanted!"

Kenta felt the urge to follow suit, to have everyone throw their guns down on the floor. Pride trumped anger instead.

"No! We can't leave like this! We can't prove the naysayers right."

The rest of the stunned soldiers turned toward Kenta's booming voice. He picked up Short Pants's discarded rifle and held it out to his friend.

"America is the only country I know," spat Short Pants, keeping his arms at his side. "Now I'm told I can't be trusted. I won't touch that man's rifle again."

He spun away and headed for the nearest door, where he stopped and turned to face his friends. "All our lives, we've been Americans. Our friends are Hawaiian, Korean, Chinese, Filipino, Caucasian—didn't matter. We never thought of ourselves as better or worse than anyone else. Now, suddenly, we're different—outsiders. Rejected. The fucking enemy!" Shorts Pants pivoted and stormed out.

A few others dropped their weapons and started to leave.

Kenta turned to face his remaining squad members and bellowed, "Staaack arms!" He joined his rifle and Short Pants's rifle together and then stretched his vocal cords.

"We will leave in dignity. We will not bring shame on our families."

Fats placed his rifle in the correct position next to the two Kenta held to form a perfect pyramid stack. The remaining soldiers—ex-soldiers now—followed suit. Within minutes, all the arms were stacked in perfect alignment according to code.

Kenta commanded his men for the last time. "Forwarrrrd ... march!" He led them in a column of two toward the exit. Other forlorn patriots formed a human snake and followed. At the door, Kenta shoved the handlebar and marched out. He squinted in the early morning sun, its crimson halo morphing to amber as it rose over jade-tinted mountain ridges, a gilded sunrise of shame imprinting January 19 into his memory forever.

For seven steps, Kenta's military gait masked his humiliated spirit, and then he broke down. With his shoulders slumped and his teary eyes downcast, Kenta kicked a pebble. He clenched his fists while fantasizing that he had slugged the pale-skinned army brass who had stolen his pride. He envisioned himself bayoneting a cringing Japanese soldier in front of a row of those spineless generals to prove they were wrong.

Yesterday, the governor was falling all over himself, thanking my squad for guarding his mansion. And today us slant-eyes can't be trusted! Was all that democracy stuff just a crock of shit?

Short Pants strolled over, ripped off his shirt and rolled his trousers up over his knees. As steady as an acrobat, he balanced on his left leg while lifting his right foot and placing it against his standing leg to unlace his boot. He yanked off the boot and hurled it against the wall of the building.

Ted walked up behind Kenta. "Some award we got."

Kenta turned. Most of their squads—his and Ted's—hovered.

"When I worried about a dawn meeting, I never expected this, this shame," said Kenta. "The bigots have won."

"And the timing makes it twice as bad," said Stonehead. "Now it's too late for us to get back into school."

"I don't have a joke," said Buster. "But I know who's laughing his ass off. Tojo. He got Roosevelt to shit-can his most loyal soldiers."

For most Americans, December 7, 1941, was a day of infamy. For the Japanese-American soldiers discharged on January 19, 1942, infamy came in pairs.

☜ CHAPTER 20 ☞

Lanakila HQ – January 19, 1942

"LOOK OVER THERE," SAID FATS, pointing to the gnarled banyan tree whose leafy canopy had eavesdropped on lunches and impromptu meetings for generations. A middle-aged Chinese man sat cross-legged under the tree. He wore workman's clothes, not the tailored suit the public was used to seeing in his newspaper photos. Hung Wai Ching had buttoned up his plaid shirt to meet his long neck. His familiar rimless eyeglasses had slipped down his nose, and his narrow face and jutting jawline sagged. He had not slept the night before.

As the director of the YMCA's Atherton Hall, Ching knew many of these young men by name and had known their families for years. He trusted that these boys—he often referred to them as "my boys"—would behave themselves. If they'd been Chinese, they would have ripped off their uniforms and marched to Bishop Street waving homemade banners protesting the absurdity of American democracy. But these boys, no— they wouldn't do that. They would slink away, too ashamed to rage in public. He feared they would turn cynical, lose faith in the country they had served unquestionably and faithfully, and become a lost generation.

Ching's contact at army intelligence, Colonel Kendall Fielder, had called him at midnight the night before to warn him of the impending discharge of the Nisei from the Hawaii Territorial Guard—on the condition that Ching would not rush to Hickam in an attempt to overturn the decision.

Ching's attention turned to the issue before him. He knew Washington needed someone to blame for the sneak attack on Pearl Harbor. In two short hours, a few hundred Japanese pilots had humbled and humiliated America. A shocked public cried treachery and the media stoked the xenophobia. Calls for internment mounted. General Emmons, the military governor, couldn't resist the pressure to do something to appease Washington's howl for Japanese blood.

Ching believed the hysteria would eventually die down and American common decency would once again prevail. But it would be fruitless to toss such a bromide to his humiliated boys at this moment. Another tack would have to be used to save these boys from making decisions that would handicap their futures. They had to be protected, not only for themselves, but for the community as well.

What had his Cantonese father told him? "Don't fight a losing battle; find one you can win and focus on that." Three hundred young men needed help to cope with the injustice heaped upon them. That would be his mission.

Kenta strode over to the familiar face and squatted across from him. "I guess you know what happened."

Misty-eyed, Ted dropped down next to Kenta. "Mr. Ching, if they had dropped a bomb in our midst, we could not be more devastated."

Kenta let his eyes drift across the school lawn, his gaze hollow. "Being rejected by our country is like taking a rifle butt in the gut."

Ching put his hand on Kenta's shoulder. Noticing the gathering crowed squeezing forward, his voice rose. "Yes, you boys have been treated unfairly." He fixed his eyes on Kenta's. "What do you plan to do?"

What does he mean? wondered Kenta. He had no answer for the YMCA leader. Although he had been taught to conceal his emotions, shock, hurt and disappointment were written all over his face and he could not stop his silent tears.

"Sit down," said Ching softly.

Kenta switched from a squat to a *seiza* position, his rump resting on his calves and feet. The stunned former soldiers, now numbering close to fifty, dropped to the ground in a half-circle, some sitting seiza like Kenta and others sitting cross-legged. The trade winds mixed the scents of trampled grass and a nearby aromatic jacaranda tree.

If anyone understood tough times, it was Ching. His father had fled China with fellow revolutionary Sun Yat-sen to settle in the Kingdom of Hawaii. Sun Yat-sen later returned to his homeland to become the father of the Republic of China. Ching's father remained in Hawaii, sired six children and then died, leaving his family to fend for themselves in the mixed-race slums abutting the Nuuanu YMCA. Ching sold newspapers to pay for his grammar school fees, and as a teenager ran the YMCA programs in Chinatown's tough streets. He graduated from McKinley High School in the famous leadership class of '24 and then earned a degree in civil engineering from the University of Hawaii. Instead of building roads and bridges, however, he followed his heart back to the YMCA and became a director. In the depths of the Depression, he took a sabbatical to earn a master's degree in divinity from Yale.

Ching's commitment to a society of meritocracy and equality earned him the respect of people of all races and the recognition of community leaders who had called on him to help develop a contingency plan to avoid a racial cauldron when the expected war with Japan broke out.

Angry voices charged the air.

"We did everything they asked. And this is how we're repaid? It ain't fair!"

"We're sacrificial lambs for a bunch of admirals playing golf while Jap airplanes came in undetected."

"They're not doing this to Germans and Italians."

Ching opened his thermos and poured tea into its cup. He passed both around for the boys to take a sip. He opened a bag of rice crackers and shared them, too. As they vented anger and frustration, Ching nodded his head in understanding and made little guttural sounds that confirmed his interest.

Short Pants shouted his complaints, but he did so using the Chinese honorific. "Ching-*Xiansheng*, three days after Pearl Harbor a Japanese sub popped up and fired a series of flares and artillery shells. Most were duds. The next day, a Seabee came and asked for volunteers to help dig up unexploded shells." He pointed a thumb toward his chest. "We stepped up. *We* put our shovels into ground that might explode and maim or kill us. Sure, we were scared, but we did it anyway. For our country!"

Hero, also known as "Little Caesar" for his zeal in translating Caesar's *Gallic Wars*, said, "We were born here, went to school here just like every other kid. For the past five weeks, I have been willing to die for my country. But our eyes are slanted so we're the enemy. Everything I believe …" He closed his eyes for a moment and shook his head. "Everything changed fifteen minutes ago."

Ching nodded silently, raised his eyebrows and leaned forward, scanning the group as if to say, "What else?"

"Most of us have never been to Japan," said Stonehead.

"We don't speak the language," chimed in Buster.

"This is so, so … discouraging," said Harry "Einstein" Nakata, the squad's math whiz. "And there's nothing we can do about it."

Ching pounced. "Nothing?" He stood up. "Did you say there is nothing you can do?"

The group piped down and trained their attention on Ching.

Ching's eyes challenged the men. He waited. He recalled the words he had rehearsed just hours ago. He understood that he had a two-minute window of opportunity to salvage this disaster. From behind the school, the bark of a dog could be heard. The breeze rustled the palm trees, and someone suppressed a cough.

"Why are you just howling at the wind?" asked Ching. He paused, waiting for the labored transmission sounds of a truck to pass. "Why don't you men show what you're made of?"

His eyes roved, boring in on each young man. If the men had expected handholding and sympathy, they were in for another shock. Ching pumped his fists. "Why don't you *do* something?"

Kenta jumped to his feet. "Like what?" He faced the assembly. "The army's in charge of our island. They've made their decision." The group murmured their assent.

"We're fucked!" shouted someone in the back.

The men applauded.

Kenta dropped his hands, palms out. He stood abreast to Ching, a man he knew well from his Atherton dorm but also whose home he had often visited with his oldest brother Taka.

"Mr. Ching, we all know you and your committee worked hard to prevent this sort of thing from happening. You tried. We tried. We failed."

"The brass says you cannot be trusted as soldiers," said Ching.

"No shit!" yelled Stonehead to a smattering of cynical laughter.

Ching ignored the interruption. He stepped into the first row of sitting men. His voice rose. "What happened to you was so wrong. So unjust. You can't do anything about their decision. It's an outrageous test of your character." He softened his voice. "Yes, an outrageous test of your character, but a test, nevertheless."

Ching walked through the assembly until he reached the rear. The men twisted their bodies to follow him. Kenta sat down again. "You, and you alone, can decide how you respond to this outrage." He summoned his orator's voice. "Do you rage about this injustice and prove the doubters right? Do you go back to your homes and accept this defeat?" he asked, peering into the eyes of each man. "Or, do you show them who you really are, and where you stand? Surely, there must be something you can do to demonstrate how much you love and support your country."

A long minute passed, but in that minute, Ching knew history could be rewritten. He saw a glimmer of determination replace despair, anger soften into contemplation. Not all of them had made the journey from hopelessness to possibility. But some would be good enough. *I can't build the fire, but I can provide the spark.*

"Gentlemen, I leave you to determine your own fate. If you are willing to answer the question 'What can we do?' please come to my office this afternoon at three o'clock. With a slight nod of his head, Ching left the group and strode to his car.

Kenta watched Ching's retreat. He respected the man and for a moment tried to accept what he had said, to pick up the challenge and keep fighting this injustice somehow. Then the memory of his visit with his father the previous Sunday at the Sand Island internment camp flashed in his mind. As men in US Army uniforms, he and brother Tommy had been among the first to be granted visitation rights. Otosan had lost weight and was sharing a tent with six other men. He had to use an open latrine. His father, a respected Buddhist priest, had raised his sons to be loyal to the Stars and Stripes—and how did the army acknowledge his father's admonition to serve in the military and be willing to die defending America?

Fuck it! I don't need this, thought Kenta. *The army has spoken. They don't want us. Fine.* He walked over to his former squad in time to hear No Ticket say, "Let's join the others downtown at the Y. We can talk about what Hung Wai said."

The men turned to Kenta, the question burning in their eyes. He squatted next to No Ticket but avoided eye contact. His evasive tone betrayed the certainty of his words. "Go ahead. I'll catch up with you later. I promised Angelina I would go see her."

No Ticket frowned, rolled his eyes and shook his head. "Yeah, right."

Kenta started to walk away.

"*Kenta!*"

"Don't try it, No Ticket." He reached into his pocket, pulled out the keys to his jeep and tossed them to No Ticket. "I'll walk back. I've got some things I need to think about. I'll catch up with you later. The guys are waiting for you."

∞ CHAPTER 21 ∞

FIVE MINUTES INTO WALKING ALONG KUAKINI STREET, Kenta heard a car horn behind him. Caught up in his own world of despair and anger, it never occurred to him that the toot might be for him until it sounded again, this time louder and longer, followed by a woman's voice.

"Kenta!"

Kenta stopped and turned around as an avocado-green Studebaker sedan pulled up alongside him and stopped. It was Angelina! He had lied to No Ticket about going to see her, but suddenly his lie had turned into truth. Kenta stuck his head into the passenger window.

"Taka called me," said Angelina.

"So, you know."

"Yes, I know."

Kenta opened the passenger door and slid into the car.

"A terrible day," said Angelina.

"More than terrible." Kenta slammed the dashboard in frustration. "We tried so hard, Angelina! We gave everything we could give!"

She wrinkled her nose. "I'd say you need a shower and some breakfast." Struggling with the gearshift knob, Angelina wiggled it until she engaged first gear. The car bucked forward.

After giving her a summary of what had transpired in the gym, Kenta asked, "Did Taka tell you they're sending Dad from Sand Island to a stateside prisoner of war camp?"

"Oh no!" she exclaimed, turning to Kenta. The car nearly veered off the road. "If your father is leaving, my dad will be sent, too."

"Maybe so. They do what they want with us. And our parents keep telling us to not bring shame or dishonor on our family and heritage."

"What did Hung Wai say?"

"He wants us to swallow our pride and fight back by doing something for the country, but he didn't say what." Kenta shook his head dismissively. "Some of the guys are going downtown to the Y. They think they can dream up ideas for how to help the country that just rejected them and arrested our dads."

"So what are you going to do?" Angelina asked, turning onto her street.

"Our country has made its decision, and I'm making mine." The anger in his voice left little doubt of his choice.

Angelina eased to a stop in the oil-stained driveway of her home. "You're not even going to the meeting to talk about what you all can do?"

Kenta put his hand on the door handle. "Mom's talking about going back to the Big Island to run our hotel. She'll need help."

"Well, sure. I guess she will," said Angelina, resisting the urge to argue, opting instead to wait for a better time to challenge his decision. Instead, she stayed upbeat. "Come on, let's go inside."

They walked up the stone path to the front door of the Muramotos' white, wood-sided home. Kenta held the screen door open as Angelina unlocked the interior door.

"Where's your mom?"

"Visiting friends." Angelina pushed the door open. "Yesterday morning, Mrs. Hirakawa picked her up and they drove to Kaneohe. They're having a picnic there today with other wives whose husbands are incarcerated."

Kenta followed Angelina into the kitchen. "What's for breakfast?"

Angelina turned and pinched her nose. "You stink. Take a shower first. You can wear my dad's clothes. I'll throw yours in the Maytag."

Kenta's jaw slackened. He couldn't maintain eye contact with Angelina. An inner light snapped on, almost erasing the last hour's humiliation. It suddenly occurred to Kenta that he had never been alone with Angelina—not in either of their homes. In a few minutes, he would be naked—if only in the shower.

Angelina grabbed his shoulders and swung him 180 degrees like a mother would a wayward child. "No shower, no food," she ordered, marching him toward the bathroom.

She disappeared into her parents' bedroom and came back with fresh clothes from her father's closet. Kenta grabbed them and turned abruptly, crimson that Angelina might notice the telltale effect her presence had on him. In the bathroom, he shucked his clothes and began emptying his bladder.

"Throw your clothes out the door," Angelina yelled from the hallway.

He stopped urinating midstream, wondering whether she had heard. "OK," he replied. Kenta stood at an angle behind the door, opening it just enough to toss his khaki uniform into the hallway.

"You're not wearing any underwear?"

"Yeah, just a minute." He flung his skivvies through the crack in the door.

Kenta stepped over the lip of the bathtub and turned on the shower. When the water warmed, he moved under the showerhead and began lathering his body, stroking the source of his throbbing. He certainly did not want to walk around the house with a hard-on. Eyes closed, luxuriating in the pulsing stream of water, he neither heard the bathroom door open nor saw the figure moving toward the shower curtain.

Suddenly, the curtain slid open.

"Angelina!"

There she stood, wrapped in a white towel.

While Kenta's hands rushed to cover his groin, Angelina let her towel drop to the floor.

Before today, the only naked women Kenta had ever seen were in the pages of *National Geographic*. His eyes riveted on Angelina's breasts and then descended to the silky threads of her body's triangle, then back up to her pink pointed nipples, just inches away.

"What are you doing?" Kenta asked, his voice thick.

"The shower is running, and I don't have any clothes on. You get one guess," said Angelina.

Like a man in a china shop full of expensive antiques, Kenta eased aside, careful not to touch the fragile object of his daydreams. He had been attracted to Angelina's nontraditional ways since they were in junior high school. Her easy flirting. Her shorter skirts. Her chatting with haole boys. It seemed everyone on campus knew her—the Japanese girl with a bounce in her step. He took delight in calling her his girlfriend, often wondering why she had chosen him.

In the face of temptation from the nearby Hotel Street brothels, Kenta had clung to his virginity. He skipped standing in queues for a seven-minute "quickie." The idea of a furtive release in his first experience with a woman didn't appeal to him. Instead, he daydreamed of a meaningful event. But even in his wildest daydreams he never imagined Angelina naked, let alone showering with him.

Inside the steamy enclosure, Angelina took the bar of soap from Kenta's hand. Smiling impishly, she lathered a washcloth, gently turned Kenta around and slathered his back down to his buttocks. Privately, she had concocted scenarios of her first magic moment with Kenta.

Angelina loved Kenta. More than once, she had argued with herself about bringing up marriage. About being "a good Japanese girl" and waiting for marriage to lose her virginity. But the shock and injustice of this day had cast aside ingrained taboos. Besides, she rationalized, the few girls who had crossed the line didn't seem to be any worse for it.

"Relax," she said. "You've had a bad day. Let's make it better."

Yes, she was making it better. When Angelina drove to the school looking for Kenta to invite him to her home, she told herself it was only to make breakfast for a friend who needed comforting on the worst day of his life. It was a chance to show Kenta that she cared for him no matter the circumstances. Deep down, though, she knew that being alone with Kenta would be a temptation. The wetness she had felt as she drove to the school, looking for him, had told her that she could change his memory of this day to a better one.

Angelina brushed his shoulders. "Now the front." She washed his face as a mother might for her newborn. She was rougher on his chest but moved softly over his stomach. Kenta's mesmerized eyes closed in antici-pation. Angelina dropped her soapy hands to wash the inside of his thighs.

Kenta groaned and let go, shooting Angelina on her belly.

"Oh, God … I'm sorry."

Angelina giggled. "Better the quick trigger now. You'll control yourself better in a few minutes."

"But …"

"I know, Kenta. Your mother told you to never take advantage of a girl. But what about the girl? This is not Hiroshima in 1910, and I am not a picture bride who has to arrive intact."

Kenta opened his mouth to reply. Before he could utter a word, Angelina placed her forefinger over his lips, leaned forward and kissed him, drawing his hand to her breast. Releasing the kiss, she whispered, "I love you."

Kenta held her tightly, wanting to say, "I love you." He didn't under-stand why his words would not come. He held her closer, hoping she could read his mind. The feeling of warmth and well-being that came with just holding Angelina naked in his arms overwhelmed him. He had no idea he could feel this protective, this loving, of another human being. He clasped her tighter and took pleasure in the hot shower cascading over their en-twined bodies. He had been right to skip his initiation into the pillow world on Hotel Street. One moment would always have been hidden in shame—today could be openly shared forever.

Angelina tapped him on the shoulder. "I have to breathe, Kenta."

He unwrapped his octopus embrace, gently held her head in his hands and kissed her on the nose.

She turned off the shower, toweled him dry and then, holding his hand, led him to her bedroom.

∞ CHAPTER 22 ∞

"I WORRIED THAT YOU'D BE CLUMSY," said Angelina.

"You thought about this?"

"Of course. You think only boys fantasize?"

"But that's so … so …"

She brushed his lips with hers. "So what? Un-Japanese?"

"You sure you won't get …"

"I told you my period is due to start in a day or two."

"If we hadn't been kicked out of the army …" Kenta didn't know how to complete his sentence.

"Maybe you should call General Emmons and thank him," Angelina said as she wiggled out from underneath Kenta. She kissed him on the forehead and sat on the edge of the bed.

"I will always love you, Ken-chan."

Angelina tossed a four-egg omelet with sautéed onions into the air. It landed perfectly back in her frying pan. This omelet didn't have its usual Wisconsin cheddar cheese, a staple she had taken for granted before the start of war rationing. On the stove's other burner, a small pot of miso soup simmered.

Angelina popped two slices of bread into the GE toaster as Kenta sauntered into the kitchen. She gave him a peck on the cheek. "Have a seat," she said, setting a plate of eggs and a bowl of steaming soup on the Formica tabletop in front of him. She sat next to him.

"I thought a couple was managing your parents' hotel for them, Kenta. Is your mom going to fire them?"

Kenta studied the soup as if some inspiration would flash a poetic line sanctifying this morning's experience. He almost didn't hear Angelina. His thoughts were still on what had just happened between the two of them. It felt more than incredibly good, more than exciting, more than sensational. It had been almost spiritual.

Angelina picked up her fork. "I mean, if your mom is going back and she keeps the couple on, what will you be doing?"

Kenta cradled the hand-sized bowl. "You have given me such a precious gift, Angie. I could never have asked you to do this."

Angelina took a bite of her omelet and made a face. "Oh, rats, I forgot to add salt and pepper," she said, picking up the two bottles and shaking them over both of their plates.

"I mean, it's nice to help your mother, but the hotel seems to be doing well even with your mom in Honolulu. What would you do that isn't being done now?"

"Angie, don't you feel special?"

She laid her hand atop Kenta's and squeezed gently. "Kenta, your words are so sweet. But now you're saying that you are going to leave me."

"Parker Ranch is being converted into a Marine training base, which means even more construction jobs. Our hotel is on the edge of the ranch. We should be pretty busy."

"So—you would manage the hotel?"

"No, Mom is really good at that. I'd just help out."

Angelina looked deeply at Kenta. "What about us, Kenta? If you are on the Big Island, how can we see each other?"

Kenta stared blankly at Angelina. In his euphoria, he hadn't even considered the consequences and responsibilities of the last hour. Not knowing how to answer, he changed the subject.

"You know that Hawaiian guy who got shot three times rushing the pilot on Niihau? Taka told me he's getting a special award from Governor Poindexter." He stabbed at an errant slice of onion. "I wonder if I would have had the courage to do that."

Angelina held his eyes with hers.

"We never know what we will do until the moment comes, Angelina."

"So, what are you going to do with your moment?"

"My moment?"

Angelina let her silence do the talking.

Kenta wiped his mouth with a napkin. He thought of his father's stoic acceptance of arrest in order to dampen calls for mass internment. And he thought of his mother, turning their home into a clubhouse where her temple ladies wrapped bandages and sewed uniforms for Red Cross nurses. And then he thought of Angelina's morning gift and of the possibility of that gift continuing. He thought of her breakfast goading, suggesting her admiration if he took up Hung Wai Ching's challenge. He thought of Ching's words and his men at the Y, and he, the leader, shirking his responsibility by not leading.

Angelina maintained her silence. She firmed her grip on Kenta's wrist, slowly sliding her fingers into the palm of his hand.

Kenta grasped both her hands. "Can you give me a ride to the Y?"

"As soon as we celebrate your decision to do the right thing," she replied.

Angelina stood up and walked around the table. She took hold of Kenta's hand and led him back to the bedroom.

"Fumiko tells me it's better the second time," said Angelina, referring to her best friend who had married a week after graduating from high school. "Slow is good, Kenta."

He couldn't believe that anything could be better than what had happened before breakfast. But twenty-two minutes later, he was a believer. This time his entire body tingled at the moment of ecstasy.

⚭ ⚭

An hour later, Kenta walked into the YMCA to a smattering of cynical applause and rude remarks. He took a seat in the back. A group of discordant voices filled the room, but no one had stepped forward to take charge and run the meeting. After thirty minutes, he could no longer take the drivel that was getting them nowhere. He was so tempted to get up and scream, "Hey! Quit complaining and let's *do* something." Instead, he stood up, clapped his hands and walked over to the blackboard at the front of the room. He picked up a piece of chalk.

Kenta waited for the voices to quiet down. "OK, let's show those haoles how they just made the biggest mistake of this war since Pearl Harbor." He wrote the numeral "1" on the blackboard. "What suggestions are we kicking around? Stonehead, you go first."

For the next hour, Kenta jotted down ideas on the chalkboard, asked questions and ran the meeting of almost two hundred men as they discussed a variety of practical and not so practical approaches.

Ted, who was normally quiet, stood up, and the room quieted down. "Y'know, we've been at this for several hours now. It comes down to do nothing or do something. I move that we do something, and that is offer ourselves to the military and let them decide—if they accept our offer."

Before Kenta could ask for a second to Ted's motion, the room resounded "second." "All those in favor, say 'aye.'" The room thundered with "ayes." There was no need to ask for a vote by those opposed, although Kenta spotted a few men sulking silently.

"Ted," said Kenta, "You're the writer here. Maybe you can be our Jefferson and draft the resolution."

Ted retreated to the YMCA office and sat down at a typewriter.

Word of the meeting had reached Shigeo Yoshida of the Morale Committee. Shigeo had been a leading proponent of statehood during the 1937 hearings. He had quietly slipped into the room halfway through Kenta's chalkboard exercise. He waited ten minutes and then followed Ted into the YMCA office.

"When you finish, do you mind if I take a look?" Shigeo asked. A short time later, he was reading the draft. "I know how the brass likes to have memos presented. Do you mind if I edit a bit?"

With the afternoon sun slipping through the shutters, the discharged men soon queued to sign the petition:

> Sir,
>
> We, the undersigned, were members of the Hawaii Territorial Guard until its recent deactivation. We joined the Guard voluntarily

with the hope that this was one way to serve our country in her time of need. Needless to say, we were deeply disappointed when we were told that our services in the Guard were no longer needed.

Hawaii is our home; the United States our country. We know but one loyalty, and that is to the Stars and Stripes. We wish to do our part as loyal Americans in every way possible and we hereby offer ourselves for whatever service you may see fit to use us.

Respectfully yours,
University Students

That evening, Kenta, Ted and four other squad leaders stood at the door of Ching's home with the petition addressed to General Emmons and signed by one hundred sixty-nine dismissed men of the Hawaii Territorial Guard.

"Ching-xiansheng, we decided that nothing can beat us down," said Kenta. Then, borrowing words from the petition to volunteer for non-combat duties, he continued. "Nor will we do anything to dishonor our Japanese heritage. We are Americans. We are determined to serve our country. By our actions and dignity, we will shame those who doubt us. Our goal is to wipe out the stigma of our hyphenated designation and simply be called 'Americans.'"

⧈ CHAPTER 23 ⧈

Sand Island – January 19, 1942

UNAWARE OF KENTA'S HUMILIATING DISCHARGE early that morning, Haru quickened her pace as she approached the metal gate of the Sand Island encampment, the bleak tent city that imprisoned her husband. At last, the authorities had allowed a family visit. Matson piers flanked the five-acre coral peninsula that jutted out into the harbor, crowded with longshoremen unloading netted crates. She studied the tall barbed-wire fence, the rifles on the right shoulders of guards patrolling the fence, and the stunted canvas pyramids staked a foot off the ground to allow breezes to fan the prisoners' cots. She tried to block out the image of the tent's dirt floor turning to sludge when it rained, as it often did during winter.

Haru threw back her shoulders and parodied a smile. Although still a good fifty paces from the gate and not yet able to see Kenji, she wondered if he might spot her approaching. She knew that slumping shoulders and a labored shuffle would only add to her husband's worries. In truth, Haru was getting better at coping. Taka's pre-Christmas visit had lifted her out of depression.

"Okaasan, we need your help," Taka had said as if all were well with her. "Our Japanese are answering the call to volunteer—wrapping bandages at the hospital, digging ditches and laying barbed wire on the beaches—but not in sufficient numbers and not in an organized way. We need more visibility to show the local haoles and military whose side we are on." She knew that the Morale Committee, led by Hung Wai Ching, was well organized and Haru gratefully accepted the call to action.

To comply with the martial law decree, Haru invited former parishioner wives to her home in groups of fewer than ten. Within days, the Issei women and their children were furrowing their grassy yards into neat rows laced with vegetable seeds. They lined up at blood banks. And wearing their newly acquired Western dresses that had replaced familiar and comfortable kimono, they marched into Red Cross offices where they packed donation kits destined for American soldiers under siege in the Philippines. Although Admiral Nimitz had suspended sailing of relief ships to the Philippines—and history would show he never lifted that suspension—the presence of so many Japanese women at Red Cross offices had sent the right message.

Haru's hands tightened around the corded handle of the flowered *kinchaku* cloth bag, which was wrapped around a *bento* box filled with rice, boiled carrots and tuna bits, remnants of the previous day's visit to the Otani Fish Market. Akira, the teenaged son of owner Matsujiro Otani, another Sand Island prisoner, had apologized for the scarcity.

"Since we lost 80 percent of the fleet," he said, referring to the directive forbidding Japanese fishing boats from leaving the harbor, "we must restrict what each customer can buy."

Amidst the Japanese prisoners in black pants and white T-shirts and the Caucasian soldiers standing guard in their khaki uniforms stood a tall man dressed in hospital whites. Haru knew this haole man very well.

It was Dr. Bernard Tebbits, the Takayamas' family doctor since their days in Waimea on the Big Island. He had assisted the internist who operated on Kenji's cancerous kidney. What was he doing here?

The doctor spotted Haru near the gate. He waved and smiled and then rushed toward the entrance. As Dr. Tebbits talked to the guard, Haru lifted her right hand waist-high and wiggled it, palm outward, signaling for him not to intervene on her behalf.

A few minutes later, Tebbits greeted Haru as she entered the prison compound. Reading the surprise on her face, he answered her question before she could ask it.

"Gertrude …"

Haru nodded. "I know her father supported Hitler's National Socialism. But it's been twenty years since Gertrude immigrated to America. She's an American citizen now."

"And it's been thirty years since you left Japan, Haru." He paused. "However, as you probably recall, we visited Germany last year."

Haru remembered well the dinner discussion she and Kenji had had with Bernard and Gertrude in happier times. They had struggled with the question of whether to visit Germany, which was now at war. But given her father's failing health, Gertrude had argued, "Who knows how long the war will last?"

"There is a women's section next to the Japanese men's encampment, which holds forty Issei," said Tebbits. He pointed to another cluster of tents. "The adjacent fenced-off area houses about twenty-five Germans and Italians.

"The FBI did not include my name on the 'to be arrested' list. I reminded them that I had traveled to Germany with my wife. I said, 'Arrest me, too.' But 'Not on the list, can't be arrested,' the FBI told me. Then I asked if the camp had a doctor and offered my services." A self-deprecating smile played on his lips. "I have no status, really. I'm not even sure if I can leave the camp or not, but with Gertrude here and the need for a doctor, I will stay for the duration."

Haru gazed beyond the doctor's shoulder and caught sight of Kenji in a grassy area near the fence. Her heart quickened as she watched him move in their direction, his gait forced and unsteady. Tebbits spoke softly into Haru's ear, gently restraining her elbow as she started to move toward Kenji.

"He's weak, Haru, but he's getting a decent diet and walking every day. The twice-daily roll calls have ended. Since Emmons' decree that we are to be treated as detainees rather than POWs, we now have access to toothpaste, razors, soap …" As Kenji drew closer, Tebbits rushed to finish his assessment. "He needs his wife to cheer him up."

Kenji carried a tuft of grass with full roots to be planted as the beginning of a water barrier around his tent. He smiled as he recognized the shape of the bento box at the bottom of Haru's tote bag. Like most Japanese couples, Haru and Kenji did not kiss or hug, although in the privacy of their home Kenji had come to appreciate the intimacy of Haru's warm embrace. But never in public.

Taka had urged his mother to bring Kenji English-language books that wouldn't raise eyebrows. Haru twisted open her bag and took out three volumes that had been sitting atop the bento box: for escapism, Agatha Christie's *Evil Under the Sun*; for literature, Pearl S. Buck's *Dragon Seed* and for nonfiction, William Shirer's *Berlin Diary: The Journal of a Foreign Correspondent, 1934-1941*.

Suddenly a familiar male voice sounded behind them. "*Berlin Diary* would be my first choice."

Haru and Kenji didn't have to turn around to see who had spoken. "Taka!" they exclaimed in a quiet Japanese tone so as not to attract attention. With a quick excuse about needing to see patients, Tebbits left the family to their reunion.

"Let's sit in the dining room," said Kenji.

"Dining room?" Haru looked around for what could be a dining room.

Kenji laughed. "It's that big tent over there. We call it the dining room."

Taka fidgeted while Haru and Kenji caught up on daily life. What he was about to tell them would make these tidbit exchanges inconsequential. He also shouldered the burden of telling them about the dismissal of soldiers like Kenta. Finally, at a pause, Taka broke in.

"I have good news."

His parents faced him expectantly. Noting Taka's eager smile, Haru jumped to her long-held hope. "You have a girlfriend you want us to meet?"

"Better than that, Okaasan. Mr. Hemenway saw General Emmons and vouched for Otosan's loyalty. Emmons agreed and ordered Otosan's release. It will take a few days, but by the end of the week, he can go home!"

Kenji's face showed no joy. "But … what about the other priests, Takeshi?"

"Otosan," said Taka, his deflated face noting his father's rare use of his full name. "The army and the FBI cannot let everyone out. You know why. But it's not just you. Several other people were released this week."

"Mostly small business owners or name mix-ups. No priests, language school teachers or journalists, Takeshi."

"Yes, but exceptions are being made every day," Taka argued. "Hemenway made a big withdrawal from his goodwill account with Emmons to get your release, Otosan."

Noting the angry frustration creeping into his son's voice, Kenji managed a small smile. "You acted with good intentions, Taka. It would have been better if you had asked me first. You assumed something … that I cannot do."

Taka let out a long, loud exasperated sigh. "Otosan, think of Okaasan. She needs you." Taka turned to his mother, expecting her support.

"I would be ashamed if my Otosan took the offer, Taka."

"But just look at Otosan! His health is deteriorating. He could die here, or possibly in some camp far away where we would never see him again. There will be no Dr. Tebbits or bento wherever they send him."

"A short life with dignity is better than a long life without honor," said Kenji.

Taka was overloaded with adrenaline. But before things could escalate further, a pimply-faced teenager in uniform walked over and pointed his bayonet at Haru.

"Visiting hours are over."

"And not a moment too soon," said Taka, rising and stomping out without as much as a good-bye, and without telling his parents of Kenta's dismissal from the Hawaii Territorial Guard. He was already outside the gate when he was overwhelmed with shameful regret.

"I am so sorry, Otosan," said Haru, watching their son's retreat. "This is a horrible way to end a visit."

"It will pass, Okaasan. Takeshi is more upset about his loss of face with Hemenway than my health or your loneliness at this moment. In time, he will regret making this goodwill withdrawal from his relationship account with Hemenway."

The guard moved closer, his bayonet held high. "You must obey the regulations, or you cannot come back."

Haru rose.

"It has been a good day, Okaasan," said Kenji, getting to his feet as well and escorting Haru outside the tent. "I have seen my wife. Now, a good meal and good reading await me." He held up the books and the bento. "You have brightened not only this day but many days yet to come."

Followed by the overzealous soldier, they walked together to the waiting gate as if they were strolling along Waikiki Beach. At the gate, they bowed to each other, both straining unsuccessfully not to part with moistened eyes. Haru walked past the guard post on the freedom side of the fence. She took a dozen steps and then turned and waved at Kenji, wondering if and when permission to return would be granted.

Kenji turned to the young guard. "You are a good soldier. I hope my sons in the Hawaii Territorial Guard and the 298th Infantry Regiment follow orders as well as you do."

PART III

REPRIEVE

❧ CHAPTER 24 ❧

Washington Place, Honolulu – January 20, 1942

Lieutenant General Emmons's stubby fingers snapped the eleven-by-fourteen legal sheaf of white paper. He had reread the last paragraph twice. A collection of signatures, all Japanese surnames, skirted the sides and bottom of the text. Behind him, an open jalousie window revealed a full moon evaporating into the dawn. His snow-white hair, combed straight back, framed his pie-shaped face and bald head, and his easy, grandfatherly smile belied no-nonsense decisiveness.

He had arrived at Washington Place at his customary 5:30 a.m. starting time. In his first hour of work he handled overnight communications from Washington, where they were already halfway through their working day. He had agreed to meet the Morale Committee's key members—Hung Wai Ching, Charles Hemenway and FBI director Robert Shivers—at 6:30. The early morning guests sat in three ornate armchairs in front of a sandalwood desk. Six overhead steel pendants hung in a row from the ceiling, each encasing a 150-watt bulb that gave the men's skin tone a convalescent's pallor. The lack of an ashtray explained the sweet, clean air.

"What kind of men do you raise here, Charles?"

"None like I've ever heard of before, General," replied Hemenway.

Emmons read the last paragraph out loud: "'Hawaii is our home, the United States our country. We know but one loyalty, and that is to the Stars and Stripes. We wish to do our part as loyal Americans in every way possible, and hereby offer ourselves for whatever service you may see fit to use us.'"

Emmons set the paper down on his desk as gently as one would handle a sacred parchment. "I can't tell you how much my first inspection tour of civilian installations shocked me. At every hospital, power station and government office I saw armed Japanese standing guard.

"'We got here too late,' one of my aides said to me."

Hemenway, Shivers and Ching gave a tired laugh to what had become an oft-repeated line, allowing Emmons the satisfaction of delivering the Jack Benny one-liner.

"A day later, I visited Admiral Nimitz at Pearl and told him what I saw. He stood up and strolled over to the window facing the harbor. 'Come here,' he said, then raised a hand and waved me over. He pointed out the window and said, 'Look at my sunken ships.'

"And what do I see? More Oriental faces. Driving forklifts, lugging cables over their shoulders, welding iron plates, hammering rivets. 'Chester,' I said to him, 'I always wanted to visit Yokosuka, and you've brought their navy base here.'"

"So, what are you going to do?" asked Ching.

"Damn it, let me finish," Emmons growled.

Ching flushed and bowed his head slightly.

"The following week," Emmons continued, "I had the police and FBI work with military intelligence to do a little background checking on the Japanese dock workers."

"And what did you find?" asked Hemenway.

"It seems like they are evenly split over whether Williams, batting over four hundred, or DiMaggio, with his fifty-six-game hitting streak, deserved the Most Valuable Player award."

Picking up a cable without reading it, Emmons said, "The debate over the evacuation of Japs from the West Coast is over. It's just a matter of timing the announcement and building the camps." Emmons pushed two forefingers across his brow. "You know, Charles, I harbor no personal animosity toward your Japanese community. I understand the argument that if the local Japs were going to sabotage anything, they would have done it by now."

Hemenway gave a resigned shake of his head. "They're all busy trying to prove they are more loyal than the rest of us."

With a sudden burst of energy, Emmons thrust his right finger in the air. "But! But you say *because it has never happened* guarantees it *won't* happen. That's like leaving your car unlocked because no one has ever stolen it." Emmons sank into his leather chair, clearly unhappy. "Not my words, gentlemen, but I cannot dismiss them either. Pearl Harbor is the prime example of that kind of 'It can't happen' thinking. Charles, I know this issue is somewhat personal for you from the last war."

Hemenway shifted in his seat. "When we declared war on Germany in 1917, I sat on the Board of Regents at UH. We had a German woman, a professor, who refused on principle to renounce her German citizenship. She claimed she had not done anything disloyal. Despite my argument that taking away a citizen's rights for no reason other than ancestry undermines what we stand for, the university dismissed her."

"Point taken, Charles, but we've been attacked on our own soil. Most of Europe and Asia are in the hands of modern Attilas and Genghis Khans. The survival of our nation is at risk. We are fighting so that when this war ends, we will still have all those rights."

Hemenway moved his hand toward the pack of Chesterfields lodged inside his jacket pocket, then caught himself and instead dusted off an imaginary piece of lint. "We understand the political pressures you're facing regarding our so-called disloyal element."

Emmons's mouth tightened and he picked up a newspaper. "Charles, can you straighten these guys out?" He fingered a front-page editorial headlined "THE MOLOKAI SOLUTION." "The goddamn *Advertiser* is demanding that I pack off 40 percent of the population to your leper colony."

"I'll take the editor, Farrington, out to lunch for a 'harmony' meeting at the Pacific Club, Del. It's time for me to cash in a few chits."

Ching cleared his throat. "We understand that if you don't do something to address the hysteria, you will be forced to follow the West Coast model and intern Nimitz's work force."

"No shit! It's more than the local rabble-rousers stirring up xenophobia." Emmons paused and ran his fingers across his brow again. "What the hell! If I can't trust you, who can I trust?" He reached into his briefcase and took out a manila folder, untied a blue ribbon around it and pulled out several sheets of embossed stationery. "This is from General Marshall: 'Round up twenty thousand of your most dangerous Japanese.'" Emmons skipped down the page. "'Immediate removal of the most dangerous twenty thousand people to either the island of Molokai or to a concentration camp located on the US mainland.'"

He then switched to a page of handwritten notes. "Here is a quote I wrote down when I talked to Knox. Only yesterday, our Secretary of the Navy told me, 'Personally, I shall always feel dissatisfied with the situation until we get the Japanese out of Oahu.'" Emmons then plucked the letter with the presidential seal. "This is a copy of FDR's letter to Knox." He scanned it until he found the sentence to make his point. "'I have long felt that most of the Japanese should be removed from Oahu to one of the other islands.'"

Emmons placed the three documents across his desk for his guests to read. "See for yourselves."

Shivers, Ching and Hemenway leaned forward and read the letters and notes in their entirety.

Ching spoke first. "It's curious. The president feels the Secretary of the Navy is 'dissatisfied,' and yet there is no direct order from the Secretary of the Army. Unless you have another letter?"

Emmons shook his head. "Not yet."

"It would seem there just might be the tiniest bit of wiggle room, Del," said Hemenway.

"Agreed. There's no Sherman-like order to these 'cover their asses' letters," said Emmons. "I couldn't act immediately even with a direct order. I don't have the transport. I'm using anything that floats to move the remaining fifteen thousand military dependents to the Mainland." Rubbing his forehead, Emmons continued, "So, you all are *sure* that removing the Japanese community would cause far more problems than it would solve?"

"Absolutely!" said Hemenway.

After remaining quiet for the entire conversation, FBI director Shivers spoke his mind. "There is no sabotage threat, General," said Shivers. "As you know, Hoover fought internment. He's insulted that the military doesn't think the Bureau can ferret out any fifth column operators on its own. We're confident that we've already picked up anyone who might cause trouble."

Ching turned to Shivers. "You've got almost two thousand internees living in appalling conditions at the Sand Island camp, Bob. What's going to happen to them?"

"We're running background checks, but most will stay put," said Shivers.

Ching smiled. "Frankly, General, the only reason Sand Island is secure is that the prisoners have accepted their confinement. If you really thought they were dangerous, the fences would be higher, you would not let them roam around within the camp and you would be assigning a lot more guards."

"Perhaps you can respond to these letters in the same manner the president does at press conferences," said Hemenway. Seeing the general's raised eyebrows, Hemenway explained. "When he's asked a question he doesn't want to answer, he simply answers the question he wishes had been asked."

A smile filled Emmons' face, and he smacked his hand on his desk. "Exactly. I'll start by wiring the president that all Japanese in the Hawaii Territorial Guard have been mustered out."

Ching put both his hands on Emmons's desk. "And tell him also that as soon as the War Department gives you a place to send them, you have two thousand POWs ready to go."

Shivers rapped his left knuckles on the arm of Ching's chair. "You're one sly old Chinaman."

Ching broke into his "Confucius say …" Chinese accent, camouflaging his distress over the racial pejorative. "I have known many gifts and insults." His frown morphed into a smile.

"Today I am giving you a gift—a workforce for Nimitz." Shivers picked up his briefcase and placed it on Emmons' desk. He snapped open the latches, took out a bound report and handed it to the general. "This is my FBI report on the Sand Island internees. I played up the cooperation the FBI has had with Fielder and his military intelligence team."

"Good. Our Washington desk jockeys love reports, the longer the better. But Bob, could you just summarize it for me so I can include it in my reply to the president?"

"Every week that we drag our feet on this internment directive gives us a chance to find another excuse the following week," said Hemenway.

"Right. I'll muddle along unless I get a 'remove, or else' from FDR. I don't want my command distracted by having to round up tens of thousands of families and constructing a city to house them. That's a fucking waste of time and resources." He locked eyes briefly with each of the men across his desk. "None of you ever heard this from me. Got it?"

Ching leaned forward and pointed at the petition.

"Yes, the petition," said Emmons, picking it up again. "This Kenta Takayama has a sense of history, given the size of his John Hancock at the bottom. You would almost expect the first words to read, 'We hold these truths to be self-evident.'"

"It's not just that, Del," added Hemenway. "I know these boys. They are as loyal as Americans you find anywhere." He sat up straighter. "After the war, General, you will move on to your next assignment. We will still be here. Hawaii is our home—for life. Think of the resentment that will fester if you deny these boys their plea to serve. In a decade, these Nisei will make up the majority of Hawaii's voters. What kind of citizens they will become may rest on how you respond to this petition."

After a heavy pause, Emmons spoke. "Hung Wai, I suppose you have a recommendation. Let's hear it."

"If I understand your Washington orders, General, you are to reconstitute the Hawaii Territorial Guard after removing the Japanese, correct? There's nothing that says you cannot squelch the Nisei students' anger—and their loyalty to our country—by putting them to work as civilians. You could give these plantation boys picks and shovels to build roads, put up fences and buildings and dig trenches."

Emmons picked up the petition again and studied it in his mind.

"Another point to consider," said Hemenway. "These boys have already sacrificed their lives for their country. They served on December 7 and they also gave up enrolling in school to join the Guard."

Emmons glanced at Shivers. "I assume the FBI has no objection?"

"None whatsoever, General," said Shivers. "Giving these boys jobs to support the war effort means they will not be wandering the streets with time on their hands and huge chips on their shoulders."

Emmons rubbed his brow. "God knows we need all the construction workers we can find. None of our bases or beaches are fortified properly, and the Jap fleet has thousands of landing craft."

"Sounds like you're in deeper shit than even Washington knows," said Hemenway.

"Let me put it this way," said Emmons, leaning across his desk. "If I were Yamamoto, I'd invade."

Emmons's words hung in the air.

Ching gave one of his discreet little coughs. "Excuse me, gentlemen, the question to ponder is *how* can these Nisei help?"

Emmons appraised Ching, then the petition. "How about we attach them to the 34th Engineers at Schofield? They'll be civil servants, wear some sort of uniform and live on base. I have already asked the 34th's CO, Colonel Kauai Lyman, to be here this morning for another matter."

"Very good, General." Ching said, smiling. "The Varsity Victory Volunteers."

Emmons raised his eyebrows. "What?"

"That's what they call themselves, the Varsity Victory Volunteers."

"Hmm, clever. Has a nice ring to it. Maybe we can get the fellow who came up with that to work on some new Burma Shave signs."

The men facing Emmons understood they were being dismissed and rose to their feet.

Emmons rose, too. "One more thing, gentlemen. While I am inclined to act favorably on this petition, the timing is important. Washington has been told I cleansed the army of 'Japs.' I can't come back a day later and report 'Well, not really.' So, let's get moving!"

As the three men headed for the door, Emmons barked into his phone, "Get the admiral on the line …"

"Chester, those Nisei I discharged yesterday won't go away." Emmons's words were tough, but his tone demonstrated admiration. Given the petition on his desk, the building pressure from Knox, FDR and Marshall, and the frank comments in this morning's meeting, Emmons explained, "I'm getting it on all sides."

"Del, whatever you do, don't get rid of the Japanese working on my ships," the admiral warned. "I need those welders, tool machinists and all those tradesmen. I'm getting shipwrights from California, but not fast enough."

"I'm an army officer, Chester—not a politician."

"Wrong, Del. Once we got our second star, we became political warriors. That's why we command at our level."

"Sacrifice some to save the others."

Silently, Emmons mulled his dilemma. The visibility of Nisei in uniform disconcerted the Washington brass and stoked local xenophobes. The next group of "visibles" were the Japanese civilians working in army offices. They'd have to go eventually, but not now. *The brass has been notified that the Nisei are out of the Guard.* For now, that was enough chum in the water for the sharks. *I'll wait a few weeks and then dismiss all Japanese civilians from the army. That will protect Chester's tradesmen.*

"All right, Chester, I'll see what I can do," said Emmons, ending the call.

He stabbed the petition with his finger. One hundred sixty-nine signatures of men who wanted to prove their loyalty to America stared back, challenging him. He was a goddamn three-star general. He would find a way to put those men to good use.

On February 19, the men of the Varsity Victory Volunteers were sworn in as a labor battalion and assigned to Schofield Barracks. They were attached to the 34th Combat Engineer Regiment. They weren't regular army, but not exactly civilians, either.

Just a week earlier, Emmons had dismissed all Japanese civilians from the army.

∞ Chapter 25 ∞
Schofield Barracks Army Base – Early March, 1942

KENTA AND SHORT PANTS AMBLED FROM THEIR TENT to the mess hall for their morning fare of greasy ham, burnt toast, runny eggs and room-temperature oatmeal. Their army-issued T-shirts hung outside their trousers and their work boots showed off weeks of scars and not a single coat of shoe polish.

The misty central Oahu rains dampened their ill-fitting denim uniforms. Daily rain clouds drifted in from the North Shore and collided with the eastern slope of the Waianae Range, bringing downpours that fed the reservoirs. The sun's rays slanted in at sharp, early-morning angles. A double rainbow curved into the mountain forest, once abundant with sandalwood trees that had been Hawaii's treasure. A crisp outer ring of yellow, blue and red arcs rimmed a faded replica shimmering underneath.

Short Pants hummed "Chattanooga Choo Choo" while Kenta pounded a scruffy baseball into his fielder's mitt, hoping to pick up a game of catch after breakfast.

Soon Kenta and Short Pants left the fresh air smells of dawn and entered the steamy breakfast odors of Building 442, the mess hall. A year later, Short Pants would claim the number had been a secret prophecy, the kind of the thing Nostradamus would have understood. At the moment, the only number holding Short Pants's attention was forty-five—the amount on the pay stub in his pocket from his first two weeks of wages. He had to speak loudly to be heard over the din of clanging dishes, banging pots and hundreds of chattering men.

"Until I stood in line yesterday and actually got the cash, I didn't really believe this shit." His eyes lit up as all the ways to spend the money ran through his head. "Forty-five bucks every two weeks!"

Spud, who favored potatoes over rice, had caught up with them as they joined the tail end of the chow line. "It's real, all right. The first day we had PX privileges I bought a box of Tampax for my sister at half the price of Wong's Pharmacy in Chinatown."

"Jesus," said Kenta, "do you have to talk about shit like that? I'm getting ready to eat."

Spud ignored the rebuke. "Things are good, Kenta. We get to sleep in tents big enough to stand up in. We're next to the showers, get steak every night, all the butter we want and free movies!"

"But we wear the ugliest shirts and baggiest dungarees in the weirdest blue colors ever imagined," grumbled Short Pants. "God forbid anyone think us funny-eyed workers are in the *real* army."

"At least no one seems to mind that we don't wear those goddamn green-felt armbands with VVV sewn on them," said Spud.

Kenta broke into his good-news smile. "Hung Wai is working with UH to have professors come out here and offer a few courses for credit. He's going to teach a business class."

"Sign me up, Kenta," said Spud.

"Right now, I'm concentrating on getting all the gym time I can get," said Short Pants, who had won his first boxing match the previous weekend.

The conversation lapsed while they loaded their trays. They found a table that had just been vacated except for their squad mate, Seiji Fukayama—"Chuckles" to them because he laughed at his own lame jokes.

Spud poured sugar into his coffee as though he were making molasses and noisily clinked the inside of the cup as he stirred the sludge. "Let's see if I understand the army. They didn't trust us guarding civilian installations, but it's okay for us to be inside an army base?"

Spud enjoyed the status of a *Sansei*, a third-generation American of Japanese ancestry, or AJA. His father was born three days after annexation, thus becoming Hawaii's first person of Japanese heritage to hold US citizenship. The local press had not reported the event, but his plantation village on the island of Kauai had celebrated for three days. Two decades later, Spud's father became a union activist in the failed sugar strike of 1923 but fared better when he and Kenta's father led the successful strikes in 1939.

Chuckles drowned his scrambled eggs with ketchup. "How's this for crazy? My brother didn't join the VVV, but he got a communications job at the Maui naval station."

Spud stopped stirring. "Communications? *Honto ni!*"

"Yeah, really!" said Chuckles. "He reads all the messages between Nimitz and his ship captains. And you don't think they keep an eye on him? Just in case he wants to send smoke signals to a Japanese submarine."

Four regular army enlisted men joined their table, which seated eight. "Good morning," they mumbled. Kenta and his group answered with their standard "Aloha."

Kenta poked Spud's arm. "Don't turn your head now, but have you noticed that sergeant two tables behind you staring at us?"

"You mean the one whose face broadcasts that his parents lost a bet with God?" asked Spud. "Reminds me of Willie Whacker. Remember him? We used to call him Whack-off Willie. He squeezed his zits until his face mirrored Capone on a bad day."

Chuckles wiped his mouth with his sleeve. "That's the same guy who cut in front of me in the chow line. He kind of bumped me when he did it, but instead of apologizing he just sneered at me. 'Japs at the end of the line.' What an asshole."

The soldier sitting next to Kenta pointed his fork at Chuckles. "Stay away from that fucker. That's Sergeant Davy Crockett." When the other three army guys laughed, he explained. "His real first name is Randall, but he makes sure everyone knows he's a real hard-ass Texan who is some twice-removed cousin of Davy Crockett."

"Yeah," said another private. "Claims letting you people on an army base is the worst thing that's happened since Lincoln freed the slaves."

∽ ∾

By the time Kenta and his buddies left the mess hall, the sun had burned off the morning mist. The rainbows had disappeared, but clouds still hugged the mountains, waiting for their stormy afternoon companions to join them.

The back area of Schofield had previously been an open range. Scavenging cows would occasionally meander through the scrub, scouring for rare sweet grass working its way up through the rocky volcanic earth. Kenta's squad had been assigned to fence it in. Since most of the VVV boys had been raised on sugar plantations, it didn't take much training to show them the army's method of perimeter security. If they kept up their current pace and the afternoon rains remained light, they could finish their assigned section today.

As Kenta jammed a fence post into a freshly dug hole, a jeep rumbled to a stop behind him. He welcomed the interruption. Wiping his brow, he took off his heavy gloves and walked over to greet Major Walsh.

Walsh had been an eight-year lieutenant in the peacetime army when war broke out. At five and a half feet, his height corresponded to the Nisei men he commanded, but his broad shoulders and barrel legs gave him an imposing twenty-pound advantage. Walsh's freckles and fair skin betrayed a Celtic heritage, as did the beginnings of a red drinker's nose. A two-inch scar over his right eye and a missing chunk of ear on the same side suggested his usual genial demeanor could change when challenged, especially when under the influence.

"Hey, Kenta, we're supposed to lay down four miles of road parallel to the north perimeter. Gotta crush some rocks for the bedding."

"That sounds like about twelve tons of gravel," said Kenta. "When do you need it?"

The major checked his Timex. "It's almost eleven. How about by three this afternoon?"

"Hell, Major, why wait till three? We'll just deliver all twelve tons to your office by two and take the rest of the day off. That is, unless you want us to build a new barracks hall before we go home."

"Tell you what. Since I'm in such a good mood, how about a ton every three days? I wouldn't want to cut into your surfing time."

"Man, you are *too* good to us." Kenta nodded back at the direction of the compound. "This Sunday, we're roasting a couple pigs behind our barracks. If you and your officers want to take a break from the mess hall food, you can get a taste of real Hawaiian chow. You know, to show our appreciation."

"That purple poi shit you guys eat is so tempting, I don't see how I can pass it up."

Chuckles had meandered over. "Hey, Major, if that doesn't sound good, we can always whip up an Irish gourmet dinner instead." Chuckles's giggles swelled to guffaws, making it difficult for him to deliver his punch line: "A six pack and a baked potato."

Kenta cringed, wondering if Chuckles had gone too far.

Walsh just laughed and pointed to the water barrel on the back of his eight-seater jeep. "You fellows might want to refill your canteens."

Kenta lifted his canteen from his belt and walked behind the jeep. The rest of the squad dropped their shovels and picks to form a queue, glad for the break. Kenta took a swig and twisted the cap back on. "Actually, I'm glad you showed up. I forgot our plumb line. We're used to building roads and fences without one, but you army types are a little picky when it comes to straight lines."

"You need a lift back to the barracks? Hop in."

Four minutes later, Walsh skidded to a stop in front of Kenta's tent. "I'll stay put," he said, lighting a cigarette. "Make it snappy."

"You can time me," grinned Kenta.

He sprinted to the canvas barracks, shoved the flap back and bounded in.

He stopped short.

At the far end of the row of cots, a man in uniform with his back to Kenta was stooped over Buster's locker, rifling through its contents.

⌘ CHAPTER 26 ⌘

"HEY! WHAT THE FUCK ARE YOU DOING?" Kenta demanded. The uniformed man bolted upright and turned.

"It's you!" shouted Kenta.

Sergeant Crockett, holding some of Buster's civilian clothes in his hands, wore a sneer of superiority. "Yeah, Jap-man. Me! What I am doing? I'm doing what somebody should be doing every day, slant-eyes. There's a codebook or a radio transmitter somewhere, and I'm gonna find it. Why they let you little bastards on an army base in the first place, I don't know."

"Get outta here!" ordered Kenta in a voice loud enough to be heard through the canvas walls. "You don't belong here. You got a problem, take it to your CO."

"Like I take orders from some enemy pipsqueak who can't even speak proper English."

A figure loomed in the doorway. "What's going on in here?" demanded Major Walsh as he tossed his half-smoked cigarette behind him. It bounced off the inside of the flap and rolled on the canvas floor, where it began smoldering.

"A thief," said Kenta, pointing to Buster's open locker.

Crockett stood, facing his challengers. His crew cut brushed the slanted tent top as he stepped away from the locker into the middle aisle, a cot flanking each leg. "I'm checking for sabotage," he said, his voice insolent.

Walsh stepped forward. "Save the bullshit for your CO, Sergeant. You know everybody's out on the site, so you sneak in here to do some pilfering. And when you're caught, you *claim* you're on a spy-catching mission." The major stared down Crockett, letting the silence stretch before finally speaking again. "Apologize and I'll forget this happened."

The Texan spat. "I'll be court martialed before I apologize to a Jap."

"Fair enough," said Walsh. "Now, Sergeant, you are ordered out." He noted the soldier's nametag and unit badges. "I'll be reporting this to Major Wilkes."

Crockett sulked out, followed by Walsh. Kenta grabbed his plumb line and returned to the jeep. Walsh hit the gas pedal and pulled a swift U-turn.

"I'm sorry, Kenta. That guy is just some redneck jerk who doesn't know any better." When Kenta said nothing, Walsh added, "Look, this isn't going to end here. I'll talk to Wilkes and we'll find some way to ship that guy out of here."

Walsh had taken his eyes off the road, so he didn't see a pothole. The jeep hit it hard.

Kenta bumped sideways off his seat. "Christ, this is not my day," he said, trying to adjust the loose seat cushion.

"By the way," said Walsh. "I haven't seen Stonehead today. Anything I need to know?"

Kenta put a steadying hand on the jeep's frame. "Stonehead got a call after breakfast. Said he had a family emergency and had to go."

"You need to report those kinds of things, Kenta, so the upper brass doesn't think I don't know what's going on with my own unit." Walsh softened his voice. "Hey, I owe you for what just happened, so I'll just let it pass this time and won't dock Stonehead a day's pay."

෴ ෴

Late that afternoon, Stonehead pushed open the flap to the barracks just before the returning work detail. Clutching a pair of scissors, he stomped over to his bunk at the far end and yanked open the lid to his locker. He pulled out his two sets of uniforms and began hacking away at them.

"What the fuck are you doing?!" cried Buster, just minutes before the crew returned to the barracks. The rest of the squad had opted to first hit the head.

"They arrested my dad this morning," said Stonehead, anger written all over his face. "I'm outta here." He spoke in a methodical cadence, his violent slashing punctuating each word.

"Haven't I been a good American?"

Snip! A shirtsleeve fell to the floor, joining other bits of his sheared blue uniform.

"When they asked me to join the Guard, I didn't hesitate."

Snip! A pant leg gaped on its way to being severed at the knee.

"When they kicked us slant-eyes out, I signed the petition saying I would do anything for my country, no matter how low and disgusting the job might be."

Snip! Stonehead gripped harder to slice the seams crowding the trouser crotch. By now, his audience had grown as the squad trickled in from the head.

"When they changed our draft status from '1-A' to 'Enemy Alien,' telling us we're 'not acceptable because of our ancestry,' I didn't complain."

Snip! Snip! Stonehead had moved on to a shirt. The scissors slashed easily through the back.

"When the Businessmen's Military Corps restricted its membership to Caucasians only, and they put in their goddamn charter, 'Our main job is to watch the local Japanese,' I let that pass, too."

He stopped his angry cutting. "So why did they have to take my dad?"

"Hell, Stonehead," said Fats, "you thought they were going to pick him up in the first round of sweeps. Besides, you told me you hardly ever talked to your dad."

"That's not the fucking point! He taught at a Japanese language school. Yeah, the students learned some Japanese history, but the history books stopped at World War I, so what's the big fucking deal? We hate the Nazis, but our own SS goons are just as bad—they just couldn't leave him alone. The son is good enough to dig ditches on an army base, but the father belongs in jail? Fuck the FBI! Fuck the army! Fuck the good ol' US of A-holes!"

Kenta came over and put his arm around Stonehead's shoulders. When his friend shook him off, Kenta sat down on a bunk.

"Hey, you're not the only one whose dad got thrown in a prison camp because of this war."

"Maybe not, Kenta. But you and your dad knew Buddhist ministers would be arrested if war broke out. Hell, you weren't even surprised when your dad got picked up on the first day. But the FBI has had three months to see that my dad's been working as a longshoreman, unloading goods for the island since the attack. They know that his son quit school to serve his country." Stonehead dramatically waved his hands in the air, scissors in one hand and shredded shirt in the other. "There hasn't been one incident—not *one!*—of us Japanese doing anything that could be called suspicious. Other than looking Japanese."

Kenta sat mute. All he could do was confirm the truth in Stonehead's words. No one in the unit noticed that someone had entered their tent and remained quiet.

"Attention!" ordered Sergeant Crockett.

The VVV boys, dismissed from the Guard only a few weeks ago, assumed the position. When Kenta recognized Crockett, he used his strongest command voice.

"Sit down, guys. We're civilians and this guy has nothing to do with our squad." He refused to make eye contact with the sergeant.

Crockett walked down the aisle flanked by the foot-ends of wooden cots. "You think I didn't see what this traitor just did? He destroyed government property and desecrated the American flag."

Hero stood up. "What you talking about? It's just a civilian work uniform."

Crockett picked up a sleeve that Stonehead had cut off. "You runts fake patriotism and sew American flags on your yellow arms." He shoved the sheared sleeve under Hero's nose. "This flag is cut in half." He turned to Stonehead. "You're under arrest."

"Don't mind him, Stonehead," said Kenta, who turned on Crockett. "You have no right. You don't …"

Crockett had pulled out his pistol, pointed it at the canvas ceiling and fired. Then he aimed the gun at Stonehead.

"Anybody else want to talk about rights?" No one spoke. "Yeah, I didn't think so. That's because you don't have any *right* to be here, Jap-boys." He jerked the gun at Stonehead like a teacher with a pointer. "March! We're going to the brig."

Stonehead stared at the gun inches from his eyes. "Fuck you! Go ahead and shoot me, pock-face."

Several Nisei from nearby barracks, their numbers sprinkled with haole soldiers, slid through the flapped entrance of the tent, forming a crowd that kept pushing forward like a wave.

Crocket jammed his gun into Stonehead's forehead.

Stonehead glared at the Texan and pressed his head into the barrel.

The swelling crowd was now just an arm's length away from the two men.

Uncertainty flashed across Crockett's face. "Clear the way!" he shouted. "This is an arrest."

A sea of smoldering almond eyes challenged the sergeant. Not one Nisei moved. Two MPs worked their way through the impassioned huddle.

"I'm glad to see you guys," said Crockett. "I've discovered a traitor. I'm ordering you to take this man to the brig."

Before the MPs could respond, a familiar voice boomed, "What the fuck is going on?!"

Buster pressed a fish knife into Kenta's hands.

The crowd cleared a path for Major Walsh.

Stonehead moved aside. Crockett kept his gun hand steady, which left the major now staring down its barrel.

"Sergeant, that weapon you are holding is aimed at a major in the US Army. Drop it."

"I just caught this man …"

"I said to drop it, soldier, or I will order the MPs to shoot."

∞ Chapter 27 ∞

THE MPs DREW THEIR SIDEARMS.

Crockett's face twisted like an enraged grizzly. He tightened the grip on his revolver. Not a murmur, a movement—not even a breath of wind could be heard. The click of the hammers from the MPs' weapons broke the silence. Crocker let his hand fall to his side. "Fucking Japs," he muttered as he shoved the gun into his holster. Only then did the MPs lower their weapons.

Crockett softened his glare at Walsh. "No disrespect intended, sir."

"Show's over," said Walsh. "Everybody back to your barracks." He turned to the MPs. "Escort Sergeant Crockett outside and take his weapon. Make sure he gets to his quarters."

Crockett walked to the front of the tent. Kenta surged forward, his own anger contorting his face. He pointed his finger at the taller man and raged.

"You're from the same family that couldn't hold a fort from a ragtag outfit of Mexicans! You Texas losers shout 'Remember the Alamo!' like you're proud of the massacre of your family. Let's see how you cowards fight without a gun aimed at an unarmed man."

"Step aside, Kenta," ordered Walsh. Crockett passed. Walsh turned and blocked Kenta, grabbing his arm with the hidden knife. His anger came through the whisper. "If I don't see it, this stops right now. Understand?" He held Kenta's forearm until he got a nod and felt the muscles relax.

"Kenta, I want all the Nisei to stay in their barracks while I sort this out. Don't let this cretin win by creating a shitstorm. Got it?"

"Yes, sir."

An hour later, as the sun was setting, Colonel Lyman gathered all the VVV boys between the Nisei barracks.

"Gentlemen. A month ago, I stood up for you when General Emmons asked if I could use some good men. Now I am asking you to stand up for me and call this incident closed. Let the army take care of this. We don't take kindly to men drawing weapons on patriots."

⌒ ⌒

The next day, Kenta's morale-wounded squad started busting rocks for the foundation of a dirt path they were turning into a tar-covered road. In a year, a new army division would be living and training on the now-barren parcel. As far as the eye could see, both sides of the road were lined with rough pyramids of rocks that had been dynamited from the granite hills.

The dust had painted their torsos a slick, reddish brown. By noon, a fine filter of sand had dried on the road, and the occasional vehicle driving by swirled powdery grime that lingered in the air. Kenta took a swig of water, now warmed by the heat, from his canteen. *Where are those trade winds when you need them?*

After lunch, the sun burned even more fiercely without any usual clouds drifting in. Beads of sweat fell from every brow as the men brought their sledgehammers down in harsh harmony. The squad did not complain—rather, they kept swinging their sledgehammers, albeit with less vigor and decreasing intervals between checking the time. There would be no time for a quick baseball game before curfew tonight. Stonehead's departure and yesterday's run-in with Crockett had sucked the joy out of the day more than the sun drained their energy. But they kept swinging away.

Major Walsh showed up driving a flatbed, which he parked in the middle of the seldom-used road. That meant it was time for a water break. Walsh scrutinized his weary crew and declared, "My watch says it's 4:00 p.m. Grab some water and hop in. You Charles Atlas boys knocked out two days of rock breaking."

The honking of a horn directed everyone's attention to a dust cloud barreling down the road. The driver kept pressing the horn as if to say, "Get that goddamn truck out of my way!"

Walsh checked the flatbed. "They can get around, but they'll have to slow down."

The driver of the oncoming jeep slammed on his brakes ten yards from the flatbed, bringing the jeep to a showy skid. Just as he was about to give the men a piece of his mind, he spotted Walsh's oak leaves and snapped his mouth shut.

Kenta's eyes popped.

Seated next to the driver was mean-faced Sergeant Crockett. An over-stuffed duffel bag filled the back seat. Crockett glowered as his jeep crawled around the flatbed, directly in front of the VVV boys. Kenta locked eyes with Crockett, knowing he had achieved some sort of victory. Then he saw something that lifted his spirits more than any forced apology ever could. The sergeant chevrons that were on Crockett's shirt yesterday were gone. The only evidence of Crockett's tenure as a sergeant were the wisps of red threads that now lay limp.

Walsh laughed and turned his back. "Well, well, if it isn't *Private* Crockett slinking away via the back gate, gentlemen. While I have my back turned, you might want to give him a proper send-off salute."

With parade-ground precision, Kenta's squad flipped the bird at Crockett, whose crimson face and taut neck veins betrayed his shame.

Walsh turned around again and watched the jeep gather speed into a new cloud of dust.

"Crockett has been banished to some godforsaken place in Mississippi to count T-shirts in a supply room. He *volunteered* to take a cut in rank rather than face a court martial. You won't see him again."

The men climbed onto the flatbed, and Walsh cranked the engine. He spoke to Kenta, riding shotgun, but in a voice loud enough for all the men in the back to hear.

"I hear there's a group of rowdy new Texan recruits itching for a ball-game. Do you think you could use me at third base and show those boys how Hawaiians play the game?"

"Let's do it," yelled Buster, thrusting a fist in the air.

Short Pants took out an *ukulele* from his bag and strummed a familiar chord. The men broke into a raucous army ditty they would not be sharing with their mothers.

☙ CHAPTER 28 ❧

Washington Place – April 6, 1942

Emmons wearily strolled around the brightly lit map room, which had been renovated into a room-within-a-room to comply with blackout requirements. The room stank of stale tobacco, hours-old bologna sandwiches and rank body odor. Emmons pulled out a stick of Wrigley's peppermint gum from its packet as he glanced up at the bank of international clocks on the wall. It was 11:00 p.m. today in Honolulu, 5:00 a.m. tomorrow in DC and 5:00 p.m. tomorrow in Tokyo.

Five minutes ago, Emmons had dismissed everyone and ordered them to go home. The wall maps were hardly reassuring. On one wall, red pins marked the depleted but still formidable German armies clawing at the gates of Moscow, Leningrad and Stalingrad. The Asian map showed the fallen Dutch East Indies, Singapore and Hong Kong, now part of the Japanese Empire. He knew the last blue pin, Corregidor, an island in Manila Bay, would soon be replaced with a red pin. Wainwright's troops on the island were hunkered down, trapped and starving in an under-ground fortress.

He stared at the Pacific map as he unwrapped the piece of gum. Midway lay to the northwest, Johnston Atoll to the west, and Christmas Island to the south. Yamamoto's carriers were back in the Pacific. Slipping the gum into his mouth, Emmons reflected on his preparations for a possible in-vasion of Hawaii or Midway. His Mainland counterpart, General John DeWitt, commander of the Western Defense Command, was squandering precious manpower rounding up West Coast Japanese. That, in turn, was putting pressure on Emmons to follow Knox's internment orders.

This idea of putting a third of Hawaii's population into camps gnawed at his sense of mission. He rose and headed for his office, fighting the urge to detour to the side room where he kept a bunk for late nights like tonight. An idea had been percolating for several days now. He had seen the VVV boys building fences and roads at Schofield, and the Japanese nurses at Tripler caring for wounded sailors. He knew the wives of incarcerated priests were making bandages with donated sheets from their temple parishioners.

Rather than just carp about the absurdity of using the Marines and soldiers to round up a hundred thousand Japanese, why not take the initiative? He had been on the verge of discussing his idea with Hemenway and Hung Wai Ching but had decided to wait. He could predict their level of enthusiasm for the idea. Why set up a false set of expectations? Everything he had learned at West Point validated the idea; yet, darker political considerations were ascendant in Washington. No, he would have to do this himself. Not even his staff could know about it. He knew that his proposal would enhance military capabilities and that a positive response from the Department of War would inadvertently boost the civilian morale of Hawaii.

He sent the terse memo in code.

To Secretary Knox: There are now two thousand Nisei serving in various military units in Hawaii, having been drafted prior to December 7. They want to keep serving. Request permission to organize an all-Nisei unit to fight in either North Africa or Europe. The unit would give a good account of itself.

More than a month passed before Emmons received a response from the Department of War.

Regarding memo of April 6, 1942, requesting formation of all-Nisei unit. Not favorably considered.

Six weeks later, Emmons shook his head in disbelief as he read orders to send his Nisei 298th and 299th Hawaii National Guard units to Wisconsin for combat training.

∽ Chapter 29 ∽

Honolulu – May 28, 1942

DEEP WRINKLES ETCHED HARU'S BROW as she surveyed her silent living room. The mid-morning sunbeams accented the reflective sheen of the freshly polished cherry wood dining table. Six lacquered chopstick sets rested in porcelain holders parallel to pleasingly shaped hand-decorated plates lying on woven bamboo placemats. For the first time since that dreadful day when Haru watched the FBI agents take her husband away, all her children living in Hawaii would be together.

Angelina, who was almost another daughter to her, bounced in through the front door. "Auntie Haru, look what I have!" She raised a Coca-Cola bottle half-filled with rationed cooking oil in one hand and a bottle of *daiginjo sake* from her family's private stock in the other. Haru turned to look, and Angelina immediately lost her peppy demeanor. Shocked by Haru's pallor, Angelina blurted out, "Are you OK, Auntie Haru?"

"Just a cold coming on. Didn't sleep well last night."

Considering the news Tommy had delivered that morning that his unit would soon be shipping out of Hawaii for combat training in Wisconsin, Angelina accepted Haru's reply with skepticism. She rushed ahead to cover the awkward moment. "Where is everyone?"

"Kenta called from Schofield. He's buying all the vegetables he can. Some of his squad members are helping out," said Haru. The VVV boys were using their PX ration privileges to compensate for the civilian food shortage in Hawaii. Many Japanese truck farmers, who produced half the island's fruit and vegetables, had stopped planting after FDR issued Executive Order 9066, rounding up all West Coast Japanese and herding them into camps. "And Sachiko's out back cleaning fish. She was lucky—she reached the Aala fish market just as a three-man boat docked and unloaded four ice chests filled with mahimahi."

Haru began to explain that Tommy had phoned to tell her he'd catch the next bus from Kaneohe but stopped. "I will be right back down," she said, and hurried up the steps with a forced smile and gritted teeth. She made it to the toilet bowl just in time to kneel and heave, Tommy's words still echoing in her head. "Okaasan, the army is making us a combat unit."

As Tommy had rattled on about earning a day pass and calling for a celebration, Haru's memory sped back twenty-six years to the Yasukuni Shrine. Once again, she saw the emperor riding tall on his white steed, honoring the latest soldiers—including her brother—who had given their lives in the Russian war. She could not expel her thoughts of that day. Bowing deeply to the man-god, pledging to give birth to sons who would die for him. Had she really done that?

Haru's hands gripped the bowl's edges for support as she rose, then wobbled over to the sink to rinse her mouth. *Combat means my sons might die. I despise the prejudice that kept my boys out of combat because of their Japanese ancestry. Yet, that prejudice kept three of my boys safe. I should be ashamed of feeling this way, but I cannot bear the loss of even one son.* Haru reached for her toothbrush. *So many sons. What are the odds all will survive?* She squeezed the Colgate onto the bristles and began brushing her teeth. Hard.

Foolish Yoshi. Now stationed on the Siberian border, she hoped he would not see combat since the imperial army did not trust posting Japanese Americans on the front lines.

Haru rinsed her mouth again. *Today, it is Tommy. Can Kenta be far behind? Unless my boys fight, they will never be trusted, never be treated as real Americans.* She peered into the mirror and rubbed her cheeks. *Tommy must not sense my conflicted thoughts. This is his day.* A day he had hoped for. A day Kenta and Taka hoped for. A day their father understood. Haru wiped away a tear. *They are standing up for America. I am proud of them.*

Jaw set firmly, she stepped out of the bathroom and returned downstairs.

By noon, everyone had arrived. Angelina placed lacquered bowls of miso soup at each setting. In the kitchen, Haru dipped the last wedges of sliced pumpkin and eggplant into the tempura batter and dropped them into the bubbling cooking oil, creating soft sizzles and inviting fragrances. At just the right moment, she worked her chopsticks and hoisted the crispy pieces of tempura from the wok, placing each piece on yesterday's newspaper to catch the oil before deftly transferring them to a wooden platter shaped like a banana leaf. She turned off the gas grill. *Done.* Pleased with her efforts, she turned to Sue.

"Call everyone to the table."

The familiar sound of chairs scraping across the wooden floor mixed with the melody of treasured voices was music to Haru's ears. Her hand brushed her left breast, feeling the precious airmail parchment tucked under her *fudangi,* her casual house kimono. Until Kenji's first letter arrived from the Santa Fe POW camp, she had not realized she had married a chef and a romantic poet. His latest correspondence shared recipes he had cooked for his fellow priests in the barracks and the nascent vegetable garden he tended. She suspected that he overstated the positive and passed over the negative. He closed each letter with a *haiku* poem he had written, including his most recent:

My grumbling wife —
if only she were here!
This moon tonight …

She picked up the tempura platter and carried it into the room as if carrying a priceless crown on a red velvet pillow. She gave a slight bow to acknowledge the applause of her children and placed the platter in the middle of the table. She then took her seat at the head of the table, which, in normal times, would have been reserved for Kenji. But of course, normal no longer existed.

To her left sat Sue and Angelina, still dressed in their nurse's aide uniforms having started the day at Queen's Hospital. Taka had tracked them down as soon as he heard that Tommy had a gotten a day pass.

Tommy took the seat to his mother's right. He looked handsome in his army uniform, still displaying the soon to be replaced 298th Infantry patch. Next to him sat Taka. Always dressed for a seemingly important meeting, he had arrived in a brown suit and white short-sleeve shirt. At least he had taken off his tie and stuffed it into the pocket of his jacket, which he had draped over the couch when he entered the house. Haru hung it in the closet where it belonged. She had also picked up the gas masks her children had tossed on the couch and taken them to Sachiko's seldom-used bedroom.

Kenta had commandeered the chair next to Angelina. They touched hands as they put their napkins on their laps, as if they were invisible. He felt her bare foot touch his leg. So concentrated on their subterfuge, they missed the knowing smiles around them.

"I wish our dads could see us in our nurse's aide uniform," said Angelina. "By the time I graduate next year, there will be a cadet nurses' corps. I'm joining." A frown quickly punctuated her pause. "If they let us …"

"Mrs. Shivers says in a year people's attitudes will change," said Sue a bit smugly, knowing her residence in the Shivers's home gave her access to information others might not have.

"What do you mean?" Angelina asked, her eyes narrow and suspicious. "Don't tease me."

Taka shook his head. "This is no teasing matter, Sue. You have played an important role in this whole drama, although you don't know it."

"Me? How?"

"Do you remember when you first went to live with the Shiverses?"

"Almost three years ago," she said, wondering where this was leading.

"Do you remember when Mrs. Shivers took you to see *The Wizard of Oz*?"

Sue relaxed, her smile warm at the memory.

"Oh, right. Mr. Shivers had taken a Pam Am flight to Washington earlier that week. Mom Shivers and I walked into town every couple of days. We saw that movie the opening week. We tried singing 'Over the Rainbow' while walking back home, but we were pretty awful." She laughed. "I especially remember that trip because when Mr. Shivers got back, he started to introduce me as their daughter."

"Well," said Taka, "I have a bit of an inside track on what happened that week."

Sue's eyes widened as she leaned forward, and everyone at the table grew quiet. The only sounds came from the curtains slapping against the open windows.

Taka smiled at his sister. "When Mr. Shivers returned, loaded down with more pressure from Washington's 'ship 'em all out' crowd, he told his wife, 'I can't send Sue to the camps. It would ruin her life. And there are thousands of Sues.'"

Sue sat still, staring at her brother, her dark eyes growing darker.

Haru's eyes moistened and her voice had a sting to it. "You never told us about this before, Taka."

"Okaasan, I didn't know until last week. Hemenway told me the story. Mrs. Shivers told him one evening when they had the Hemenways over for dinner." Taka turned back to his sister. "Shortly after sharing his conflicted thoughts with his wife, Shivers, along with Hemenway, established the Committee for Interracial Unity, which set the stage for Hawaii to avoid mass internment."

"My sister, part of history," said Kenta.

"And so we all are," said Taka.

"Taka, what is it like working with someone famous like Hemenway?" asked Angelina.

"Yeah, that guy's a legend," said Kenta. "He's been in Hawaii since 1899. Came over to teach math at Punahou. A Yale grad."

Angelina gently elbowed Kenta's ribs while keeping her gaze on Taka.

"Did I ask the barefoot boy in shorts? I know *who* he is, that he started out as a teacher, but quit to become our attorney general. Now he is Mr. Everything." Angelina ticked off each accomplishment on her fingers. "President of the Hawaiian Trust Company, president of Queen's Hospital, president of the Chamber of Commerce. He even founded the College of Agriculture and Mechanical Arts, which became our University of Hawaii. But *what* is it that makes him so special?"

Taka studied his siblings as if searching for the right words to explain a mystery he had pondered many times. "Hemenway lost his only child in his early years. So, in a way, students became his children. He always treated everyone the same. Race or color or religion never mattered to him. He always had time to do what he liked best: talk to us kids."

Around the table, chopsticks stopped clicking. Expectant eyes fixed on Taka's earnest face.

"He is a man of deeply held convictions, passionate about fairness and opportunity. But that wouldn't matter if not for one quality Hemenway possesses in abundance."

"Courage," said Haru. All eyes turned to her. "He is not afraid to stick his neck out. Otosan said he protected us Japanese from people who say we don't belong here."

"That's right, Okaasan," said Taka. "He saw the real danger."

"The real danger?" asked Angelina.

"Yes. The real danger to us doesn't come from the super-patriots screaming, 'You can't trust them.' The greater threat comes from the larger group of whites, many of whom work with us and do not personally doubt our loyalty. But they are afraid to face up to the noisemakers. Hemenway stands up for us. He believes in our loyalty *and* does not hesitate to say so. He has used his reputation and stature in the territory to hold back the dam of suspicion and hatred."

"So, they'll close the camps and Otosan can come home?" Sue asked.

A surge of electricity shot up through Haru's throat, and a fresh layer of perspiration appeared on her forehead. She looked at the stern photo of Kenji on a nearby table.

"Possibly, Sa-chan, but I doubt it," said Taka. "I asked Hemenway the same question. He just sighed and said, 'We are not there yet.' The committee is still getting hysteria calls. Every time the Japanese win a victory in Singapore, Hong Kong or Manila, the telephone rings demanding that the committee 'quit coddling the Japs and send them off before they kill us in our sleep.' There's one bit of irony. Remember the outcry from navy wives claiming their Japanese maids didn't show up for work on December 7 because they knew of the attack? Their latest complaint is that their maids are quitting."

"Good for them!" cried Sue. "Some of them are working with me at the hospital for better wages."

Taka shrugged his shoulders, resigned to such absurdities. "Yeah, typical haoles, want to have it both ways. We have to explain, politely, that with labor shortages the maids are switching to better paying jobs."

"God forbid a haole wife should have to iron her own dresses," groused Angelina. "But if Tojo can't invade California, then what's the reason for the camps?"

"If only the threat of invasion were the reason for internment," said Tommy. "We're the scapegoat, the people who look like the enemy, the people who had Hirohito pictures hanging over the Shinto shrines in our homes. I'm lucky to still be in the army. Until two weeks ago, the 298th drilled without weapons. They keep paying us, but they don't know what to do with us."

"At least you didn't get tossed out like a dead rat," said Kenta.

"No, but not because a lot of folks didn't want to. The brass had a helluva dilemma because we had already taken the oath and had been inducted. They started teaching us how to use dynamite to blow up bridges only two weeks ago."

"For months, your CO, Colonel Turner, has been asking General Emmons to send the 299th stateside for combat training. Emmons supports sending your 298th off to fight, too," said Taka.

"That's what we want to do," insisted Tommy. "Before they gave us the dynamite lessons, we were painting trash cans. There have been fistfights, talk of going AWOL and—"

"Please let me finish," said Taka, raising a placating palm. "HQ has been complaining about how your endless marching is affecting the morale of all of the military units. Until last week, Washington kept turning down Emmons." Taka flashed a politician's grin. "That's why you guys are going to the States for training and then being deployed to fight as an all-Nisei battalion."

"What about Turner? He's pushing fifty," said Tommy. "We know how the army feels about 'old men' leading combat units."

"You're right. When Turner heard that he might be relieved, he made a fuss. I guess his fire and energy—and the good will contacts he has here in Hawaii—served him well."

"And Tommy's unit is going where exactly?" asked Sue.

"That's still a secret," said Taka. "But you will be fighting," he said, turning to his brother.

"What about us?" asked Kenta.

Angelina poured some tea into Haru's cup, gently massaging the older woman's shoulder with her other hand.

"Don't know," said Taka. "It stands to reason that if Tommy's unit does well, then it will pave the way for the formation and deployment of other Nisei units." Not wanting to add to his mother's worry, he stopped there. He would tell her later of his plans to volunteer as a civilian for army intelligence, which was desperately in need of Japanese linguists.

"Philippines?" asked Tommy.

"What!" exclaimed Sue.

"I'm guessing they will land us in the Philippines." Tommy cleared his throat and glanced at the kitchen clock. "Oh wow! Okaasan, I have to go."

"Me too," said Kenta.

"Let me drive you back," offered Angelina. "Tommy, I can drop you off at the bus station on the way." She smiled at Tommy's raised eyebrows. "Since the war, more women are learning to drive, and they're doing jobs that used to be reserved for you guys."

"Like what?" asked Tommy.

"Well, like working on cars. Two girls I went to high school with are helping out at the American Motors dealership, changing oil, checking tire pressure—maintenance things."

Haru held her tongue, straining to control her emotions. A husband in the camps, one son heading off to war and another eager to join him. She wondered if her entire family would ever sit together again.

They would not.

On June 5, Tommy's unit shipped out on the SS *Maui* as the Battle of Midway raged. Despite orders to keep the departure secret, several hundred families gathered at the pier before dawn. The entire Takayama family lined up as close to the guarded entrance as was allowed. Angelina called out Tommy's name when she spotted him.

He turned just in time to see his brothers salute him and his sister wave good-bye. And his mother wipe away her tears.

❦ CHAPTER 30 ❦

August 12

Angelina and Kenta strolled into Kapiolani Park. They paused for a few seconds to watch a handful of surfers riding the waves under the August sun. Angelina held a picnic basket in one hand; her other was hooked around Kenta's arm. A pair of Coca-Cola bottles and a steel bottle opener clinked in the burlap bag Kenta carried, a rolled-up straw mat tucked securely under his arm.

"Over there," said Angelina, pointing to three palm trees that formed a triangular canopy. They had learned to avoid picnicking under leafy banyan trees, where hordes of pigeons cooed and roosted. Diamond Head rose behind them while the hustle and bustle of Waikiki was just down the street. A half-dozen families had staked out shaded oases hosting corroded barbecue pits and chipped concrete tables.

Obon season without the bon dance and food kiosks just didn't feel like obon, mused Angelina forlornly, recalling the thousands who had gathered in the park just a year ago—and every year before that—to welcome home the spirits of their departed loved ones on their annual pilgrimage to the land of the living. The trade winds had swirled the aromas of simmering noodle pots and vats of bubbling oil cooking varieties of tempura. She loved *tonkatsu*, the Japanese version of deep-fried pork cutlets, and mahimahi filets.

She could still see it in her mind: the skewers of tightly packed chicken breast pieces, ginkgo nuts, eggplant slices and chunks of sweet pineapple roasting atop a glowing charcoal grill. Perspiring women heaping scoops of rice onto paper plates while men served sake in small paper cups. Muscular *taiko* drummers clad in red *hapi* coats, secured at the waist with a simple *obi* sash, beating a steady rhythm. Nisei girls dancing in colorful *yukata*, often joined in costume and exuberance by Caucasian, Filipino, Korean and Chinese friends and schoolmates. The colorful *chochin* lanterns strung up throughout the park drew Honolulu's diverse community into the welcoming spirit of the annual festival.

But not this year. Not after Pearl Harbor.

"Not one person wearing traditional dress, Ken-chan."

Kenta squeezed Angelina's hand, an endearment gesture reserved for when they were alone. "This year it's lipstick, Barbara Stanwyck hairdos and polka dot dresses. Nobody wants to be the nail sticking out of the board."

"Kenta, when the war ends, will they still hate us?"

Kenta shook his head. "Is it hate or is it fear?"

"Fear leads to hate," said Angelina. "But when it's all over, we will still look like the enemy."

Kenta spread the straw mat under the palm trees.

"We're going to be facing the sun, Kenta," she scolded.

"At noon? You move it."

Angelina put her hands behind her back like an innocent young girl and kissed him on the forehead.

"You're so cute when you get mad. The sun *sets* in the *west*. And it moves every minute. In an hour, the sun will be at an angle blasting our eyes. I suppose the army only teaches such details to its officers, not to mere ditch diggers."

With a roll of his eyes, Kenta repositioned the mat. "In a city of ten thousand sweet and polite Japanese girls, how did I find the only one who doesn't know how to bow?"

"Would you feel better if I walked three paces behind you?" she teased.

Angelina sat down and leaned against the tree. Then she reached into her handbag and pulled out a letter. "It's from Tommy. Your mom gave it to me yesterday when I dropped by the temple to pick up the laundered nurses' uniforms for Queen's."

Kenta reached for the letter, eager to hear the latest from his brother. Although Haru received weekly notes, the last *real* news from Tommy had been a phone call to dispel rumors that Nisei units were being sent to internment camps.

Angelina held the letter playfully, just out of Kenta's grasp. "Make yourself useful and take out the Cokes, then give me the bag." Kenta handed it over and Angelina folded it several times then laid it on her lap as a pillow. "Put your head down."

After Kenta had stretched out and made himself comfortable, Angelina handed him the letter. Instead of taking it, however, he folded his hands on his chest.

"No, you read it, Angie, since the sun is at such a good angle," he said pointing skyward. "If you run across any three-syllable words, I'll help you out."

"Since the letter is from a member of *your* family, I can't image that will be a problem," she said, running her fingers through his hair to soften the words. With that, she began reading.

Dear Kenta,

What a hectic six weeks. Other than the weekly aerogram to Mom, I haven't had time to send a REAL *letter to anybody.*

First, the good news! We got a huge morale boost upon our arrival in Oakland. We are no longer the Hawaiian Provisional Infantry Battalion, the name they gave us before we left Hawaii. We are now the One Puka Puka—the 100th Infantry Battalion. INFANTRY!

Old Man Turner says that means we will be trained to fight. He told us to talk like Americans. We got the hint. Except for when the poker stakes are high, we talk only in English, even if it is our favorite Hawaiian English—Pidgin English, of course!

The people of Wisconsin treat us well. We wondered how folks would take to hundreds of us short, brown-faced GIs with strange-looking eyes living in their little town of Sparta, the place closest to Camp McCoy. At first they stared at us like we were animals in a zoo. We heard a few mumblings like "What is Roosevelt thinking?" We wondered if they were going to throw peanuts—or rocks.

But then, as we'd go in to buy sodas at Walgreens or buy stuff at Woolworth's, people got to know us. Many townspeople had relatives in Germany, so they made the connection. They knew parts of America where anti-German immigrant feelings ran pretty high. Many of them lived through the anti-German hysteria in the Great War.

Angelina let her hand holding the letter rest on Kenta's shoulder.

Anyway, back to the beginning. Thanks for seeing us off at the pier. Most of the guys couldn't contact their folks. The army tried to keep our departure secret. After all, there were Japanese submarines between Hawaii and the West Coast, so you could see their point. You can imagine the cheers on our third day at sea when the captain announced that our navy had sunk most of the Japanese fleet trying to capture Midway.

Angelina paused to take a long sip of Coke and then resumed reading.

Our seven-day journey across the Pacific started with most of us puking our guts out. This is nothing like sailing from Hilo to Oahu, although if you remember I threw up on that trip, too. By the third day, most of us had gotten over it. We were eating well and keeping our food down and settling into hour after hour of boredom—broken only by rolling the dice in craps games.

Larry Sakoda of D Company designed our battalion's colors with an eagle's beak holding a banner with our motto: Remember Pearl Harbor.

You won't believe what I saw the first day we landed in Oakland. Haole people doing dirty work! All the longshoremen are haole. We passed a waterfront canteen—all the waitresses were haole. The truck drivers are haole. White people even collect the garbage!

Kenta sat up.

"It's hard to imagine haoles doing that stuff."

"Maybe 'haole' doesn't always mean 'boss.'"

Kenta sat cross-legged, motioning Angelina to continue reading.

The army couldn't get us out of Oakland fast enough. They bussed us from the pier to the train station at night—"for our safety." We gave two bits to grinning colored porters to send our telegrams letting everyone know we arrived safely.

We boarded this really dirty, smelly train. It burned charcoal, so we were covered with so much soot we could have been mistaken for Amos and Andy. The food tasted like it had been dropped on the coals and left there. The officers ordered the shades pulled down. I guess they didn't want the locals thinking Tojo had invaded. It took us four days to reach Wisconsin.

The first day of man-to-man combat training provided a few laughs. After a demonstration of a bayonet charge by a group of big haole trainers, they asked for volunteers. Six of us with kendo training jumped up. You should have seen the shock on those haole faces when they all hit the dirt. They took it pretty well and seemed impressed that we had come to fight. They told us we were the first group that never had anyone drop out on the morning runs. We might have thrown up, but we didn't fall out. We know we're guinea pigs. If we do better than anyone else, maybe the army will let more of us enlist.

We share training with the Texas 2nd Division. They're loaded with Mexicans. Big guys. We found that sort of strange, given all the Remember the Alamo history. But the Mexicans found us strange, too. At first, a lot of them called us Japs. I guess they thought they could get away with that—they must have thought our small size made us pushovers. We cleared out the cafeteria twice with fights, giving better than we got. A couple of our boys spent a night in the brig, but they never again called us Japs. Earlier, the Mexicans were fighting the Texan white boys after being called greasers and wetbacks. Sometimes it's hard to remember that the enemy are the Germans and Japanese, not us fellow Americans.

Last weekend, our squad had a three-day furlough. We went to Chicago. Nobody seemed to mind that we were Japanese. Of course, we were wearing army uniforms. The first two drinks in some bars were free. On short trips, most of the taxis refused to take our money. We popped for Glenn Miller tickets. It seemed half the audience were wahines who wanted to be showgirls. Wahines outnumbered the guys, 2-1. Some of us got lucky.

Kenta checked Angelina's eyes, wondering how much she read between the lines.

She reached over, swatted his head and rolled her eyes. "Men!"

Kenta closed his eyes as Angelina resumed reading.

Wisconsin is hot in the summer. We were told to enjoy it, because we're going to freeze in the winter. Our barracks don't have any stoves. Not that it would matter much when we're freezing. The gaps between the boards are big enough for a small dog to squeeze through. If we had built the barracks, it would have been done right.

There are two families here that treat our squad like ohana. They invite us to Sunday dinner. Both families have sons in the army. I've attended the Lutheran church and USO socials a couple times. A few gals flirt with us but we are still too shy to ask any of them to a movie. Our eyes are at bust level. We don't want to start something with the locals.

The Schneider family—they own a dairy farm—invited our squad for dinner. Their son is serving in Guadalcanal. You'd think they would hate anyone Japanese. But they said we are just as American as their son. Before eating dinner, we all held hands and told each other what it meant to be an American. We all cried more than once.

Angelina read on about their daily activities, their food and requests from Tommy's friends to call their parents and let them know their sons are doing fine. Then she suddenly stopped.

Kenta opened his eyes and saw embarrassment written all over Angelina's face.

"It's … about me." She thrust the letter at him. "You read it."

Kenta hesitated, then took the letter and read silently.

Little brother, keep a close eye on Angelina. She's a heartbreaker. Take good care of her. I doubt you'll ever get tired of her, but if you do, tell me first.

Just got the two-minute warning for lights out. Keep building those roads.

Tommy

Kenta folded the letter and sat up, resting on his haunches. "You're pretty popular, Angelina."

"I never said anything to him, Kenta." She dropped her chin.

Kenta grabbed her hands. "He's lonely. He's telling me to take care of you. He just wishes he had someone like you, Angie-chan. He knows we care about each other and he wants that, too."

"Just 'care,' Kenta?"

"More than care, Angelina. You're special. When this war is over, we can talk about the future."

"But you can't … say the words, Kenta?" Angelina stared off into the roiling surf. "What is it about Japanese families? We were all brought up here but emotionally you men are back in Hiroshima and Kyushu."

Kenta wanted to say the words. He had never said them to anyone. Never heard anyone in his family say them. Such sentiment was understood. He wondered if Tommy would have said them.

Seeing Kenta's inner turmoil, Angelina relented.

"Come on, let's eat."

Her smile made everything right again.

⚭ CHAPTER 31 ⚭

Waimea, Hawaii Island – August 14, 1942

THE POSTMAN ROLLED HIS BIKE to a stop in front of the Takayama Hotel. Standing up and balancing the bike between his thighs, he tugged his cap down over his forehead. He searched his leather bag for the hotel's mail bundle and didn't notice the hotel's front door opening, nor the middle-aged woman in a checkered housedress coming down the steps, holding something wrapped in wax paper.

"Good morning, Mr. Fehner," Haru called out, holding up her hand and a package as she descended the weathered wooden steps. "Fresh out of the oven."

Haru accepted the letters with one hand while offering warm, aromatic baked bean cakes to the postman with the other. She noticed the edge of a blue aerogram sticking out from the bundle. From Kenji she hoped. In May, a few days before the FBI had sent him and other prisoners to a camp in Santa Fe, he had urged her to return to Waimea "at least for a few months. The hotel needs you."

"But the Fort Street Hongwanji …"

"Can get along without you," interrupted Kenji gently. He knew this was the last time he could offer advice, help his wife adjust to the new reality. "You have been telling me how you have recruited ladies to take turns running water, pulling weeds, even some painting at the temple." He paused for effect as much as for his weakened body, that didn't have the energy to debate it once had, to speak with some authority. "Go to Waimea. You've said Sam and Kame need help." Left unsaid was Kenji's worry that Haru had overextended herself with all the volunteer work organizing bandage wrapping, bond drives and food packages for his fellow prisoners. He didn't like the weary eyes that faced him.

Haru made a point of deferring to Kenji. She recognized her own declining energy, but didn't know how to back away from the whirlwind of war support activity she had created. Granting Kenji's pleas was a going-away boon to him while his "demand" offered a graceful excuse to return home. At least for a few months. Taka had moved into her Queen Emma Street home. She could return.

Haru broke her reverie to study Fehner, who had been one of the first haoles she met after arriving in Waimea as a young picture bride. He chewed and swallowed the bean cake and with an air of satisfaction said, "We're all proud of your boys over in Schofield and Wisconsin." Then with a wave, he mounted his bicycle and moved on to the next house.

Haru watched Fehner pedal away. For the first time in all her years in Hawaii, she asked herself why Japanese never applied to work at the post office. Those types of federal jobs were for whites—less educated whites than the haole bosses, but still white. It had been that way forever and no one had ever questioned why it was so. *We work in the fields, and they have the clean jobs.*

Haru walked back up the cobblestone path to the hotel. Still two years away from her fiftieth birthday, Haru's complexion remained smooth, her gait strong and her mind sharper than ever. Many of her friends had aged more quickly. Decades of fieldwork on sugar plantations had etched deep lines on their sunburnt faces and bleached their original midnight-black hair to the color of thunderclouds. As the wife of a Buddhist priest, Haru had always been active in helping relieve the sufferings of others, but such work did not come with the same physical demands of watching the sun rise with a hoe in your hand day after day.

Haru smiled at the freshly painted dark red window frames and white porch railing. Despite rationing, some of the contractors staying there had "found" a little extra paint and picked up a paintbrush to show their appreciation for her well-run hotel.

Haru dropped all the mail except for Tommy's letter into a Chinese porcelain pot resting on the third step of the four-step *kaidan tansu* staircase-style chest next to the front door. She walked to the kitchen through the family room, still trying to get used to the extra chairs and card tables that had been put up to accommodate the surge in guests. Although she had always set aside two rooms for hotel guests, Haru had never envisioned a commercial enterprise on this scale.

She strolled over to the four-burner Tappan gas stove Kenji had presented her on their thirtieth wedding anniversary, the first such appliance in the Japanese community. Haru took a long match from the small lacquer box she had found at the Yamanashi Dry Goods Store. The purchase was a rare splurge, bought with the understanding that she could return it if the matchsticks did not fit. She struck the match against the top of the stove, turned the knob on the right front grill already holding a pan, and with no need to bend and aim, stuck the match up to the pinprick holes on the grill. At the sound of the "whoosh," she jerked her hand back and reduced the flame before placing the rice pot atop the rear grate.

Next, she turned her attention to the coffee urn, swirling its burnt-brown contents. After four hours, it was a bit sludgy. But she wanted to read Tommy's letter now rather than take the time to make a fresh pot. Haru poured the dregs into her stained coffee cup and sat down at the kitchen table.

Happy Thanksgiving, Okaasan!

Remember Yoshihara-san, the basketball player whose dad had a heart attack last year? He met a girl at church the first week at McCoy and is now engaged! The first marriage in our unit to a gaijin. Two wives from Kauai arrived in early November with only Hawaii clothes. It didn't take them long to understand the real meaning of the word cold. Their husbands worried whether they could find families willing to rent to us Japanese. After a somewhat rough start, enough of the townspeople adopted us.

I visited Otosan at the Camp McCoy Detention Center on Sunday. Color is returning to his cheeks and he's gaining weight again. It still seems strange that I am training to fight Germans in North Africa while my father is a POW a short jeep ride away in this same camp. He is always upbeat and encourages me to never let down the Takayama family name. I will try my best. Please take care of yourself, Okaasan.

Aloha,
Tommy

Haru put down the letter. From Taka's phone call yesterday, she had learned that the army had transferred Kenji to a POW camp in Louisiana— one expected to house Germans captured in the upcoming North African campaign that was no longer a secret. Haru hung her head as she thought of her husband being treated as a prisoner of war.

☙ CHAPTER 32 ❧

Schofield Barracks Army Base, Oahu – December 14, 1942

ASSISTANT SECRETARY OF WAR JOHN J. MCCLOY arrived to inspect Hawaii's military facilities. At the end of one of his briefings with

General Emmons, he asked about the Oriental workers he had seen, some repairing a bridge and another group laying gravel on a new road. He didn't stumble upon the VVV work brigades by accident. Hung Wai Ching, who had been asked to escort McCloy for part of his inspection, had carefully orchestrated it.

"Splendid chaps, John. They call themselves the Triple V—the Varsity Victory Volunteers. They really are remarkable. Do you remember the orders to get rid of the Japanese from the Territorial Guard?"

"Sure, I remember. What a dichotomy. While the army prepared to intern the Japanese on the West Coast as potential saboteurs, the same army deployed armed Japanese American soldiers to guard the port and other facilities in the territory under the threat of an invasion."

"Quite right. After we stripped the men of their uniforms and weapons, I expected them to go back home and lick their wounds. I just hoped they wouldn't cause any trouble, not that their kind is inclined to. Well lo and behold, that evening, I get a petition from them saying they would dig ditches to help the war effort and prove their loyalty to America."

"Rather unexpected, given the circumstances."

"The best part is how we move the VVV brigades around the base to work next to our lads, some of whom need a burr on their ass to work at full speed. These VVV boys report to work every day as if the invasion were tomorrow." Emmons rapped his knuckles on his desk and leaned forward, his body language demanding a response.

"A lot's happened in a year, Del. The Japanese-American unit training in Wisconsin has impressed the officers. They're tough, eager to fight. Maybe it's time to put weapons back in the hands of the VVV boys."

Emmons opened his desk drawer and pulled out a file. "John, I'd like you to read these."

McCloy perused the documents chronicling Emmons's proposals to recruit and train a Japanese American unit to fight in Europe, along with the Department of War memos rejecting the idea. He laid the file back on the desk and sat back, one hand massaging his tired eyes.

"Things have changed, General, I'll grant you that. Frankly, we need all the good men we can get our hands on."

"I suspect our Japanese would relish the chance to show us what asses we have been for not letting them join the army in the first place," said Emmons.

McCloy nodded slowly. He stared at the framed photographs of President Franklin D. Roosevelt and General George Marshall mounted on the wall behind Emmons as if he were asking them for help framing his answer. He put his hands together and cracked the knuckles of each forefinger. His eyes came back to Emmons, and he dropped his voice a half octave.

"I think FDR has had second thoughts about these mass internments. But, politically, he doesn't dare make any public admissions. Perhaps putting these boys in uniform could be a way of making amends—and give us the kind of motivated men we need to win this war."

∞ CHAPTER 33 ∞

Schofield Barracks Army Base, Oahu – January 28, 1943

MAJOR WALSH GRABBED AN EMPTY TIN COFFEE POT from beside the electrical heating unit and clanged it against the nearest metal-framed bed. In his free hand, Walsh fingered a yellow square of paper with a telex message pasted on it.

The VVV boys froze in various stages of dress. Engine noises from passing jeeps and water running in the showers competed with a radio blaring an ad for Honest John's Used Cars. Kenta stood next to his bed—the one the major had just assaulted with the pot—in nothing more than his skivvies.

"Get the men from the shower," Walsh ordered.

Kenta dashed for the showers. "Short Pants, all you guys, get your ugly asses in here. Something important may be happening."

"The radio," said Walsh as Kenta rushed back into the barracks.

"You, too, can own a Chevy convertible for just $290! Come on down to—

Kenta twisted the radio's volume knob to zero. The interrupted commercial would forever be seared into his brain. At radio silence, the sound of shower taps shutting off heralded the arrival of three dripping-wet men, towels wrapped around their hips, who joined the huddle forming around Walsh.

"Gentlemen, listen up. General Emmons just sent me this from Secretary of War Harry L. Stimson himself."

Kenta could guess the contents. Taka had given him a heads-up three weeks ago but swore Kenta to secrecy.

"It is the inherent right of every loyal citizen, regardless of ancestry, to bear arms in the national defense. Loyalty to country is a voice that must be heard."

The men stepped closer to Walsh. He dropped his arm holding the telex.

"This morning, Stimson announced President Roosevelt's decision to reverse the draft status of American citizens of Japanese ancestry. You men are no longer enemy aliens classified 4-C. Effective immediately, you all are 1-A."

The stunned men stared at their major and then each other. Then Kenta jumped in the air, one fist raised. "We did it! We won!" shouted Kenta. "They couldn't hold us back!"

The VVV boys tossed towels and work caps into the air. They yelled and stomped their feet. Chuckles attempted a back flip and landed on his back. Buster strummed his ukulele. The men slapped each other on the back and exchanged hugs.

Walsh pumped his open hand into the air to quiet the exuberance.

"There's more. Since you are no longer classified as aliens unfit for military service, the army is …" Walsh's eyes dropped down to the telex message. "The army is 'accepting Japanese American volunteers for the purpose of creating an all-Nisei combat regiment.'"

A second round of pandemonium broke out.

"I'm coming back a hero in a pine box," shouted Short Pants.

Spud looked at Kenta and in a fierce tone just loud enough for those around him to hear, he said, "If we die—and some of us will—they can't treat us as second-class citizens anymore."

The barracks payphone rang. It took a half-dozen rings before anyone noticed.

"It's for you, Kenta," called Fats, waving the phone.

Kenta raised his voice. "Hey, you guys, quiet down! The major's not finished. Fats, tell whoever's on the phone I'll be there in a minute."

"Men, meet me here after breakfast. We need to—what's the expression you fellows use? 'Tidy up the nest.' This is your last day here."

Whoops and horseplay punctuated the major's parting words. Kenta evaded a towel snap from Short Pants on his way to the phone.

"It's your brother," said Fats.

"Kenta!" Taka's raised voice came across the line. "Judging by all the noise, I guess you heard."

Kenta plugged his left ear with a forefinger. "You had it right, Taka, but it sure was hard keeping it a secret."

"You did good. Listen, word is you'll be dismissed by lunchtime. We're trying to arrange a proper mustering-out ceremony in a day or two. Let's meet at the Red Rooster on Hotel Street around two."

⸂ CHAPTER 34 ⸃

Six hours later, Kenta stepped off a bus crowded with ripe-smelling GIs. As a first timer to Hotel Street, he was awed by the wild sanctuary catering to the libertine needs of sailors and soldiers. Shoeshine boys tugged at standing trouser legs. Photographers stood in front of cardboard cutouts. Fifty cents bought a snapshot of Hawaiian paradise—grass huts, white-sand beaches, towering palm trees and native beauties baring tanned midriffs dancing the hula in grass skirts.

Teenaged Hawaiian girls hawked leis. Filipino and Chinese kids waved arms laden with watches, chanting "Cheap! Cheap!" Lights blinked outside Portuguese tattoo parlors. Live Dixie quartets and 78 rpm records blasted from bars, almost drowning out the corner hula bands. Tatty kiosks peddled penny postcards, gaudy jewelry and native carvings. Eager sailors and soldiers, weighed down with passports of cash, waited in long queues at the bottom of stairwells leading to pleasure cubicles upstairs over the roaring salons. Kenta knew from the risqué chatter in the Schofield mess that three bucks got you three minutes with a whore in an assembly line operation Henry Ford would have envied. *Welcome to wartime Chinatown*, he thought.

Kenta brushed by a popcorn vendor, which reminded him that he had skipped lunch. He reversed course and exchanged a nickel for a hot, butter-stained bag. He walked briskly, keeping his eyes peeled for the Red Rooster's sign.

The flushed Caucasian faces—ignoring, jostling and stink-eyeing— told Kenta he didn't belong. In a few weeks, however, he would be wearing their same uniform. Maybe this was why his brother had invited him here. The raucous mood of Hotel Street, coming on top of the army accepting him into its ranks, flooded his body with adrenaline. He could leap tall buildings and run faster than a speeding bullet.

Kenta slowed as he came to the end of the cacophony of crowds. Had he missed the bar? Loud, tinny hula music resounded from the doors he passed, competing with a Tommy Dorsey recording trumpeting from a loudspeaker in a bar across the street. A huge red rooster blinking through the window stopped him in his tracks. A sign under the rooster put out a challenge: "Bar reserved for the biggest cocks in town."

Kenta jaywalked across the street, dodging taxis to reach the flashing lure. With both hands extended, he pushed through the swinging saloon-style doors. Breathing in the stale beer and swirling sawdust, Kenta couldn't stifle a trio of sneezes. He felt like a tuna wrong-turning into a frenzy of sharks. He smiled at the sea of white-faced stares. *Fuck it*, he belonged here as much as anyone else. Maybe even more so. He had *earned* his way into the club. He strutted into the bar, scanning.

Taka rose from a table in the back highlighted by a gaudy chandelier. Kenta took Taka's right hand and then the beer his brother extended to him.

"If you're going to join the army, it's time to take a peek at the new life that awaits you," said Taka.

"I have to confess. I'm not sure if I'm joining to prove my loyalty or to find some excitement. You know. War. Adventure."

"It's both, and it doesn't matter. What matters is you're in."

"When can we sign up?"

"Whoa, Kenta! Relax and drink your beer. Today's announcement is just the beginning. It primes the pump. This is the government we're talking about. They don't move so fast."

Kenta took a long, foamy drag of his beer. "OK, so what's the first step?"

"They've got to set up the process to recruit volunteers and then settle on a place to train."

"How many people?"

"They're talking about a full regiment."

"That means four to five thousand men, depending on the mission," replied Kenta. "Is this going to be an all-Hawaii regiment?"

"Hell, no. You'll only be about a third of the group. There are twice as many draft-eligible Nisei in the relocation camps as there are in Hawaii."

Just then a six-foot, two-hundred-plus-pound sailor in drill uniform bumped their table, followed by a slurred challenge.

"Hey, you! Your kind—you don't belong here."

Kenta and Taka ignored the interruption and kept talking.

The boisterous camaraderie near their table quieted. Eyes bleary from beer focused on the big sailor. The bartender retreated to the cash register and dropped his hands. The white sailor kicked the table leg and showed a malevolent grin, exposing two missing front teeth.

"You got a fucking hearing problem to go along with those slant-eyes? I'm gonna say this just once. Get out!"

Kenta ignored the warning signal on Taka's face and stood up. His eyes came level with the top button of his antagonist's shirt.

"I am an American about to be inducted into the US Army to fight Germans. I have as much of a right to be here as you."

"You want a right? Well here's a right." The uniform pulled back his right arm.

Kenta shot out his left leg, smashing the sailor's right shin with his steel-toed work shoe. As the man collapsed, Kenta spun around and drove his right heel into the sailor's left kidney. As the bully pitched forward, Kenta's fist hammered the back of the man's neck. If he had delivered a karate chop with the edge of his hand, the blow could have been fatal.

The sailor's buddy charged forward. Kenta hit the bridge of his nose with the heel of his hand, then followed through with a full-force kick to the man's groin. Kenta spun around once more, slamming the man's upper leg with his heel as he toppled to the floor.

The scuffle was over so fast that drinkers in the front section of the bar had no idea that a confrontation had taken place. The men in back watching the fight reacted according to the color of their uniform. The white uniforms stared belligerently. The khaki uniforms gawked, amused. A voice emerged from the khaki crowd.

"Hey!" called out a tall, big-nosed man wearing sergeant chevrons.

Kenta peered into the gloom to see who had spoken, wondering just how many more he would have to take on.

"You're one of those VVV boys, ain't ya?"

Kenta nodded to the sergeant.

"We heard you guys got the green light to join the army. We've seen you out on the road, diggin' those ditches and doin' other dirty work. You're a gung-ho bunch."

The sergeant raised his mug in a salute to Kenta, then stared at the white uniforms, daring them. "He's one of us."

Taka waved a five-dollar bill at the bartender, who had hurried down to the end of the bar wielding a well-used Louisville slugger.

"How about a round of drinks for everyone?"

The bartender didn't move, indecision on his face.

"These two Dempseys started something they couldn't finish," said the sergeant. "No one else is involved. A free beer sounds like a good idea."

The men on the floor groaned. Their mates ignored Kenta and tried to help the fallen heroes get back on their feet. Kenta took the hint when Taka laid his five-dollar bill on the table, and the two brothers walked out the back door.

"Jesus, little brother, where did you learn that?"

"I decided not to take any more shit from anyone. We've been accepted in 'The Man's' Army. They will treat us with respect or pay the price."

"No, I meant ..."

"I know what you meant. We've been practicing karate and kendo for a year. We learned to hit fast, hit hard and hit in threes."

Wonder spread over Taka's face. "What happened to my happy-go-lucky little brother?"

"He died the day they stripped him of his uniform. A year building roads, learning self-defense and finally being accepted into the army means I don't have to sit back and take it like a good, quiet Japanese kid."

Taka gave Kenta's shoulders a quick squeeze. "I like my new brother."

∽ ∾

Two days later, the army formally disbanded the Varsity Victory Volunteers in Schofield's auditorium. Charles Hemenway delivered the keynote address, closing with:

> You have carried on through your first year with the same spirit of loyalty that was the basis for your offer to serve in whatever way the commanding general could use your help. You have held fast to your ideals. You have made an outstanding record and have won the respect and admiration of many who were doubtful of the stand which you citizens of Japanese ancestry would take. You have fully justified the confidence of those of us who knew that you are as loyal as any other citizen of other racial descents. I am proud of what you have done.

On March 30, fifteen thousand cheering people jammed the grounds of Iolani Palace for an induction ceremony with fresh flower leis for all the proud recruits.

PART IV

SOUTHERN HOSPITALITY

∞ CHAPTER 35 ∞

Camp Shelby – February 1943

LIEUTENANT COLONEL FARRANT TURNER reached for a short stack of folders on the left corner of his recently constructed pinewood desk and scooped up the top file, labeled "Lieutenant Young-Oak Kim." It had been just seventeen days since he left the snows of Camp McCoy, Wisconsin, and Turner didn't need another experiment on top of what was already an experiment. He was certain Kim had no desire to be the sole Korean in a group of Japanese whose forefathers had brutally occupied Korea since 1905. Kim's time at Camp Shelby would likely be short.

With no deployment mission assigned even after six months of training in Wisconsin, he had finally received a wire from General Mark Clark: "Your Nisei battalion is welcome to my command." The men would be moving to the swamps of Louisiana for combat training—they would fight. Letting the Korean lieutenant go would clear one more distraction from the mission.

Turner gazed out the window at the piles of lumber and building materials stacked in quadrants being leveled by Caterpillar loaders. His fourteen-hundred-strong 100th Infantry Battalion, mostly away on field training, would soon be joined by four thousand Nisei recruits who formed the 442nd Regimental Combat Team. The first foundations for hundreds of new sixteen-man hutments would be laid by week's end.

Turner pressed the buzzer connecting him to his aide.

"Send in Lieutenant Kim," he commanded his orderly.

In minutes, the lanky Korean strode into Turner's office, snapped to attention and offered a smart salute.

"Lieutenant Kim reporting, *sir.*"

His voice was strong and confident, and his demeanor suggested he was not concerned about being summoned to the battalion commander's office the morning after his arrival.

"At ease, Lieutenant." Unless the meeting promised to be lengthy, men visiting Turner's office stood. Turner had learned that the level of kibitzing dropped when visitors remained on their feet.

"Congratulations on graduating at the head of your class at Officer Candidate School."

"Thank you, sir."

Turner let out a small sigh. "I don't think you realized that this is a Japanese unit. And you're Korean. Historically, the Japanese and Koreans don't get along, so don't worry, I'll have you transferred."

Kim did not hesitate, his voice remaining steady. "With all due respect, sir, they are Americans and I am an American. We are all going to fight for America. So, I want to stay."

Turner tilted his head and pursed his lips. His fingers tapped the file while he thought through a response. "All the other officers who preceded you who were not Japanese wanted out. The process has been set up. I can have you transferred in the morning."

Turner stared at the new officer, then let his eyes fall back to the file. Kim took this as permission to continue speaking.

"After being drafted two years ago, the army sent me to Fort Benning for basic. At the end of training, the army awarded me this badge," said Kim, pointing to a rifle patch on his left sleeve. "Number one marksman in my class of four hundred men. The next day, my sergeant gave me a choice of either being assigned as a cook or a clerk. When I asked why not infantry, he said, 'Wake up! You got the wrong-shaped eyes and the wrong color skin. People like you can't be soldiers.'

"Then the war gave me another chance. But even finishing first in my OTC class—well, I expected to be shoved in some out-of-the-way admin post. Here, with you—I will have a chance for combat. If you transfer me out, I'll be hidden away. No one is going to give me command of white troops. I volunteered to fight, sir—not push paper."

Kim's last words could have been Turner's own just six months earlier. As executive officer of the 298th Infantry of the Hawaii National Guard, he had initially been passed over to command the 100th Infantry Battalion, which combined the Oahu-based 298th and the 299th, made up of neighbor island prewar draftees.

While Turner studied the file searching for a rebuttal, Kim broke the pause.

"One other thing, if I may?"

Turner nodded.

"My parents owned a grocery store in the Bunker Hill area of Los Angeles, surrounded by Mexican, Chinese, Jewish and Japanese communities. We all went to school together. Some of the Japanese became my friends. They were sent to the Rohwer internment camp in Arkansas.

"When I graduated from OCS, I took a bus to Arkansas to visit them. I arrived at Rohwer late at night in my new second lieutenant's uniform. The guards gave me an icy stare and ordered me back to town until they could sort things out. But I had taken the last bus, so they were stuck with me. Those privates, who should have been saluting me instead of holding me at gunpoint, kept me waiting at the gate in the falling snow for two hours until they found someone who had the authority to let me in.

"So, you see, your Nisei boys and I—we're both fighting for our dignity, for the right to be accepted as Americans."

Turner put up his hand. "I get the point, Lieutenant. Well, you can stay, but you'll be on probation to see how well you get along with the men."

Turner rose from his chair and held out his hand, but Kim ignored the dismissal handshake.

"There's something else I'd like to discuss, Colonel."

Irritated but intrigued by the young man's brashness, Turner nodded. "Go ahead."

"Sergeant Kitaoka briefed me upon arrival yesterday. During our exchange, I learned that your men are receiving the same basic training they received in Hawaii and then again in Wisconsin."

Turner frowned but did not interrupt. Kim continued, "They march in the morning. Get a lecture. Have lunch and return to camp. Not only is their morale a problem, sir, but no one in the unit has combat training."

"And you do," challenged Turner. Behind his words, however, he recognized the deficiency. Kim had brought Turner's nagging guilt to the surface—that he spent too much time organizing lodging, arranging food supplies and sorting out personnel assignments at the expense of training. He knew all too well that much of the army brass thought this Nisei unit was a dangerous waste of time. He had been proud of their training record in Wisconsin, where the 100th acquitted themselves above average. At Shelby, they were repeating the grade.

"Yes, sir. My OCS training emphasized the new combat doctrine of working as a unit, not as individuals. Give me a typewriter and twenty-four hours, and I can deliver a training program proposal."

Cheeky, thought Turner. Still, what had he to lose? "Take it up with your commanding officer, Major Jack Johnson."

∞ ∞

The fifty-year-old National Guard officer, whose career could be summed up as an ROTC drill instructor, knew his limitations all too well. He listened to Kim's proposal.

"You got it right. I don't know anything infantry. I'm worried the men will be sent into battle with inadequate preparation. We need to change the training method, but I don't know how."

"The plan starts," said Kim, "by changing the emphasis on individual training to team training."

"OK. You've got the twenty-four hours you asked for," said Johnson. "Write it up. But let me run interference for you with the other captains. Doing this only with my squad doesn't make sense."

∞ CHAPTER 36 ∞

S.S. *Lurline* – March 28, 1943

BUGLE REVEILLE PIERCED THE SILENCE in the VVV barracks at Schofield at 3:30 a.m. Sunday morning. For some, it would be their last day on Hawaiian soil. Ever. Kenta wondered if he would be one of them. Putting the thought aside, he yelled, "*Gambarimasu!*"—Let's do our best!—to his drowsy but anxious bunkmates, then shed the underwear he wore as pajamas. Grabbing a towel, he bolted down the dimly lit corridor to be among the first to shower.

He fingered the locket—Angelina's—hanging from a silver chain around his neck. The glass side displayed her picture winking at the camera. Between the picture and the locket's silver backing, Kenta had wedged strands of her silky ebony hair. He smiled remembering the moment she had gifted it to him. His lips touched hers and she whispered, "Just something for you to anticipate—when you come back." The erotic replay hardened him, so he switched his thoughts to yesterday's grand money exchange to keep from becoming the butt of everyone's jokes.

Kenta had watched the paymasters unwrap boxes of crisp US bills. As a precaution against providing Japanese with a bonanza of US dollars if they occupied Hawaii, the US mint had begun superimposing the word "HAWAII" on the island's currency, making the stamped bills as worthless as Monopoly money in the hands of the Japanese. The disbursement officer announced he had $300,000 available so the recruits could exchange their "Hawaiian dollars" for regular greenbacks now that they were departing Hawaii. His condescending tone suggested that he thought this was way too much for this sorry-assed group of misfits the army had misguidedly selected for combat training.

After just a dozen swaps with more than fifteen hundred to go, the paymasters exchanged whispers. One then hurried out the door. When the money quickly ran out, the senior officer—resisting an urge to shake his head in disbelief—announced, "The paymaster is bringing back another $400,000." Kenta laughed as he recalled telling Major Walsh how family and friends had loaded them up with *senbetsu*, or "send-off best wishes money."

By dawn, the recruits had departed Schofield for the Iwilei train station. At 8:00 a.m., the boys began the mile-long march from the railroad station to the pier, each carrying a duffel bag that weighed nearly a hundred pounds. As he hoisted his bag over his shoulder, Kenta felt confident that the past year with the VVV had prepared him well. He swelled with pride as he walked, seeing the thousands of family members and friends that lined the road to cheer them on. *So much for military secrecy*, he thought.

The men slogged onward, wilting under the tropical sun that burned above in a cloudless sky. No one had thought to fill a canteen with water. Some tossed items on the roadside to lighten their bag—personal treasures that had seemed indispensable the night before. Any semblance of military order disappeared as every man fixated on placing one overburdened foot in front of the other, conscious of the sorry sight they were displaying to the community. Soldier after soldier stopped to rest, only to hear the bark, "Get a move on, soldier!" from the nearest non-com.

As Spud trudged along next to Kenta, his mother spotted him and ran out to give him one last hug. A burly MP stopped her.

"This is a military march, not a picnic," he snapped, shooing her back into the crowd. For years, Kenta would remember her tears and humiliation, and regret that he had not challenged the MP.

As more men faltered, Kenta's anger rose. "This is all wrong," he said to Spud. "Some of us are not coming back. A mother's last image of her child should not be of him dragging a duffel bag like some ox."

Spud wiped his grimy brow with his sleeve. "Yeah, this stinks. The army could have loaded our bags onto trucks and let us march past our families. They could have had a military band play marching music. It would have been a proud memory our parents could cherish. Even now, we're still treated like runaway plantation workers."

∞ ∞

The three-foot-tall hands of the Aloha Tower clock pointed straight up as the pre-war luxury liner S.S. *Lurline* pulled away from the pier to shouts and tears from ten thousand people. A wind gust swept away the white "Dixie Cup" cap of the sailor casting off the last mooring into outstretched hands on the pier. Pressed together like sushi, the soldiers waved to family and friends, wondering if they would ever see them again.

Kenta nudged his way to the mahogany railing of the bow. He checked his pockets again for the envelopes stuffed with cash. As the ship eased away from the pier, he spotted his mother and Taka standing outside the barrier. When Kenta could no longer make out their faces, he focused on Hung Wai Ching, who had permission to be inside Pier 11 to see his boys off at the gangplank, until Ching, too, faded into a stick figure.

∽ ∾

As the *Lurline* shrank toward the horizon, Haru, who had returned to her Queen Emma Street house the previous month, remained rigid at the rope restraint. Thirty-eight years ago, she had watched excited men board ships in Hiroshima on their way to Manchuria to fight Russians. She had yelled "*Banzai!*" and waved a little white flag with a blood-red circle in the middle. She thought of her brother, forever a teenager, buried somewhere in Manchuria, and prayed for her sons.

She prayed for *every* son.

∽ CHAPTER 37 ∾

THE *LURLINE* ROLLED GENTLY in ten-foot swells as it turned east for the long journey to San Francisco. A sense of finality had gripped Kenta when the tip of Aloha Tower disappeared from view. He wondered how many of his three thousand fellow Nisei shared his thoughts: *Will I ever see that tower again? Will I be shipped back home in a pine box?*

Kenta was soon distracted by laughter and the loud voices of his fellow recruits. Few had ever left Hawaii before, and now they were sailing aboard a luxury liner—albeit repurposed as a military transport—on their way to prove themselves in a faraway place.

The *Lurline* shined as the proud symbol of the renowned Matson fleet. Founder William Matson had fallen in love with the "*Lurline*" moniker when he skippered a yacht of the same name honoring the Rhine River nymph made famous in an 1860s opera. The luxury liner was halfway to San Francisco the morning Japanese pilots bombed Pearl Harbor. The ship had continued on to California at maximum speed. It then returned to Honolulu, refitted with supplies and loaded with Marines.

The ship's captain, rather than joining a navy-escorted convoy zigzagging at varying intervals to avoid incoming torpedoes, pushed the throttle to full power in a straight line to reduce time at sea and hoped to hell that no one spotted them. Despite the breakdown in security, the *Lurline's* captain assumed no one who had come to the pier that day had called the Emperor. The captain chose the straight line dash option to reach San Francisco in the near-record time of just over four days, trusting that the Eastern Pacific's run of no loss of ships since January would hold.

On this crossing, thirty-five hundred military personnel had to be accommodated on a ship advertised to hold seven hundred fifteen passengers. Upon boarding, Kenta and his squad had dragged their duffels down two flights of stairs to Deck Four, Room 201—a nice two-person stateroom that prior to the war had been appointed with cushioned armchairs, a writing desk, closet, storage chest and vanity table, and now had been gutted and refitted with four triple-tier bunk beds. No allowance had been made for personal items or duffel bags. The smarter men dropped their bags on their preferred mattress, like a dog marking its territory. Others gave into fatigue and dumped theirs on the floor.

∞ ∞

Hung Wai Ching rushed off from the pier to catch a military transport flight to Oakland. He had convinced General Emmons that he needed to be in California ahead of the Nisei's arrival so he could lobby General DeWitt to treat his boys with respect. He landed in Oakland ten hours later, unprepared for the chilly wind of San Francisco in April. His reception was about to get colder.

Based on his experience with General Emmons, Ching was confident his appeal to General DeWitt, head of the Western Defense Command, would be favorably considered. He remembered Emmons's arrival in Honolulu, intending to ship all one hundred forty thousand Japanese to the island of Molokai. Although he had ordered the disbandment of the Hawaii Territorial Guard to rid the unit of all Americans of Japanese ancestry, Emmons had not been driven by hate. Rather he followed orders, which were soon tempered by his own good common sense. When he learned how loyal the local Japanese were, he became their booster and protector. Agent Shivers had gone through a similar metamorphosis a few years earlier.

Ching assumed that anyone promoted to Emmons's or Shivers's level of responsibility shared their professionalism and leadership characteristics. Thus, he entered DeWitt's office like a soldier who stands up in his foxhole thinking the battle is over, only to be hit by a bullet.

As DeWitt's orderly began to introduce Ching, DeWitt cut him off.

"Who in the hell do you think you are, barging in on a secure military installation?" DeWitt leaned over his desk like an enraged hawk poised to swoop down on an unworthy prey. His horned-rimmed glasses were pinched tight to the ridge of his beak, emphasizing the hard eyes of a man who squashes problems "once and for all."

When pressed by Roosevelt for evidence of Japanese sabotage two months after Pearl Harbor, DeWitt wrote the president, "No subversion discovered to date." In the next paragraph, however, he insisted, "This only proves a disturbing and confirming indication that such action *will* be taken." The president agreed, overrode the objections of FBI director Hoover and issued Executive Order 9066, giving DeWitt authority to declare parts of the United States "military areas from which any or all persons may be excluded." The order did not name any particular group; it did not have to. The exclusion order enjoyed widespread support up and down the West Coast. When asked about the racial selection of the internees, then-attorney general of California Earl Warren declared, "When we are dealing with the Caucasian race, we have the methods that will test the loyalty of them. But when we deal with the Japanese, we are on an entirely different field." DeWitt had argued vigorously against formation of the Nisei regiment and wanted the new American soldiers just off the *Lurline* to know it.

Ching resisted his instinct to step back. Holding his ground, he reached into his coat pocket and pulled out a piece of paper, which he unfolded and placed on the edge of DeWitt's desk. He scanned the general's taut neck muscles and sixty-two-year-old cobalt eyes. Unlike Shivers or Emmons, who were inclined to listen and consider before acting, this self-righteous bigot forged ahead based on an unwavering prejudice—facts be damned.

DeWitt dropped his eyes to the letter of authorization signed by Emmons.

"You used this letter—from *another* general in *another* command—to compromise security on *my* base? You belong in the brig, not in my office."

Ching stood straighter and inched forward. "I am on a mission authorized by the general of the Pacific Command. Listen to why I have come all this way before you throw me out of your office."

The white-haired DeWitt glowered at the clearly uncomfortable orderly who still stood by Ching. "Call the MPs."

DeWitt leaned forward, his fingers like an eagle's talons clutching the edge of his desk. "I know why you are here. You want me to coddle those Japs from Hawaii. Treat them with 'due respect.' They shouldn't be here; they shouldn't be in the army. Emmons will rue the day he didn't throw out the lot of them. If one Jap wanders off that ship he will be arrested. If one soldier lifts a curtain on the train to Camp Shelby, I will stop the train and court martial everyone on that carriage."

Two large MPs strode into the office.

"Take him to—" DeWitt blinked. The veins in his neck recessed back into his throat. "Escort this Chinese 'gentleman' off the base."

⊙ CHAPTER 38 ⊙

WHILE CHING LOCKED HORNS with the great protector of the West Coast, Kenta and the boys were busy throwing up in the toilets, in the showers and over the deck's railings. On the fifth day, just as most of them began finding their sea legs and holding down solid food again, a cry went up: "Land ahoy!"

The jubilant men rushed deck side to stare at the San Francisco skyline. Unaccustomed to the cold and gusty winds of the North Pacific and temperatures below sixty degrees, the men donned their newly issued woolen winter coats, which spilled over their shoulders and draped down to their shoelaces.

As the late afternoon sun set behind them, the *Lurline* passed under the Golden Gate Bridge in all its reflected brilliance and then passed the infamous Alcatraz Island. Alcatraz had many lives: lighthouse, fortified defense post, military prison and the address of recently released mobster Al Capone and current residents, gangster Machine Gun Kelly and murderer Robert Stroud, known as the Birdman of Alcatraz.

"Look at that!" shouted Short Pants as the *Lurline* slowed to berth. "Haole stevedores!" The muscled Caucasians went about hoisting bundles, carrying picks, pulling carts and lifting bags, oblivious that they so enthralled the young men gawking at them as though they had spotted tigers mating in a zoo. Thinking back to Tommy's letter noting the same phenomenon, Kenta turned his attention to a waiting gangplank where a company of uniformed men stood at parade rest—rifle butts on the ground, each right hand gripping the end of the barrel at a thirty-degree angle.

Kenta's eyes widened. At the bottom of the gangway stood Ching in a black suit, tie and fedora. Unbeknownst to Kenta, inside his white, long-sleeved Hathaway shirt, Ching wore all four T-shirts his wife had packed for him to cushion him from the cold. A Kodak Brownie camera hung from his neck. The first lieutenant at the guard gate, more impressed with Emmons's introductory letter than DeWitt, had given Ching pier access while dutifully admonishing him not to take pictures of the port. He could and did take publicity photos of the boys walking down the gangway, not only for posterity but to improve the odds that the guards would be on their best behavior.

DeWitt had ordered that the Nisei be escorted from their ship to buses taking them directly to the train terminal. Each bus would transport forty men to the station and return six or seven times until the entire regiment had been moved.

Ninety minutes after docking, the ship's intercom bellowed, "Group twelve, go to the gangplank on mid-ship deck four and proceed to shore."

"That's us," said Short Pants.

Minutes later Kenta watched the last school bus leave with only the second wave of disembarking recruits. The need for Matson to disembark the soldiers quickly so the ship could turn around with men and supplies needed for Hawaii, coupled with a shortage of buses, allowed the recruits to mill about in the confines of the port facilities. MPs at each exit ensured none of the "suspicious characters" wearing the same uniform they wore tried to break out and occupy the city in the name of the emperor.

Once on the ground, Kenta marched over to Ching. "Are we soldiers or prisoners of war?" he asked, pointing to a guard who must have overheard.

Ching put a calming hand on Kenta's shoulder.

"These white boys with guns are just doing what the overzealous brass tells them to do. Remember, your mission is to prove those old farts wrong." He turned to the other squad members gathering around, listening to the exchange. "We Orientals have never had a chance to prove ourselves. Now FDR has given you that chance." Ching returned his gaze to Kenta and gave his shoulder a supportive squeeze. "Seize the opportunity."

While Ching calmed Kenta, Chuckles strolled by the row of shops in the civilian port complex and drifted into a cafeteria. Twenty minutes later, he skipped back to his squad, who were entertaining themselves by rolling dice on the tarmac across from the *Lurline*. No Ticket had borrowed Spud's ukulele and was turning a ribald ditty he had picked up at Schofield into a Hawaiian tune.

"Hey—look at me! I'm an emperor!" roared Chuckles. "I just ordered a white woman to bring me a Coke and a hamburger—and she did!" His buddies turned and stared at him in disbelief.

"You gotta see this. Go to the cafeteria," Chuckles said, pointing to the shops. "Don't worry, I'll watch the bags."

Kenta's squad rushed to the cafeteria and ordered the daily special—a hot turkey sandwich—just so they could write home that a white woman old enough to be their mother had wiped their table, taken their order and served their food. The boys relished leaving her a big tip and were surprised by the sincere thanks from the woman.

Kenta's squad enjoyed the Bay Area sunset until it was their turn to board the buses to the railroad yard.

Later, as Kenta's train chugged into night, an officer addressed the men: "Keep those curtains down. We don't need the locals calling in reports of Japanese landings."

Kenta stood up. "Sir, where are we going?"

The officer gave a wry smile. "You will know when you get there."

⊙ CHAPTER 39 ⊙

AT DAWN, THE TRAIN SLOWED for a brief stopover at the former gold rush city of Marysville, California. The previous summer, the city's racetrack had been a holding area for twenty-five hundred internees, including Marysville's own sizable Japanese population, until they could be shipped off to a permanent camp. Building internee housing for one hundred ten thousand displaced American citizens and their parents had taken months to construct.

As the train pulled in, an announcement told the recruits they had thirty minutes to stretch their legs.

"May be trouble ahead, Kenta," said Short Pants who was peering down the track. Kenta poked his head out the window. "There must be hundreds of people, like a mob."

Earlier, DeWitt had issued an advisory to the citizens of Marysville that a trainload of Japanese soldiers in uniform would stop there to replenish water stores. The warning, intended to allay the townspeople's fears and keep residents from the station, instead set hospitality wheels in motion. More than five hundred citizens—all of them white—showed up with homemade banners reading "Welcome to Marysville" and "Cheers to the fighting Japanese Americans." Chocolate cakes, apple pies, baked hams, cribbage boards and Monopoly sets sat atop colorful homemade quilts covering portable card tables.

Kenta stared out at the crowd with a surprised smile.

"Can you believe this?" asked Chuckles.

"I wouldn't if I hadn't seen it with my own eyes." Kenta reached up to the rack and pulled down his duffel bag. "I've got a lei made of *puka* shells in here," he said, finally holding up the strand.

"Right," said Chuckles, pulling a harmonica out of his pocket. Others followed their lead, searching to find Hawaiian treasures to share.

A man with a bullhorn, who turned out to be the town's mayor, stood in front of the enthusiastic crowd.

"The city of Marysville is proud to have you stop here." The mayor's voice wavered as his misted eyes surveyed the young men on the platform. "Marysville has many Japanese Americans among her citizens—our neighbors and our friends. We miss them."

Kenta walked over to the mayor and placed the puka shell lei over his head. Chuckles played a few bars of "Little Grass Shack." Half a dozen soldiers started strumming their ukuleles, serenading the cheering well-wishers with a medley of Hawaiian songs. After the impromptu concert, Chuckles presented his ukulele to a blonde, pig-tailed girl who, according to her little brother, had turned ten that very day. Two train cars down, another squad broke into a hula. Townsmen shook the soldiers' hands and wished them good luck. The women passed out hot coffee and homemade baked goods. Thirty minutes had stretched to sixty by the time the train left the station.

∽ ∾

By midmorning, the early spring marigolds and petunias of Marysville had been replaced by snow-covered granite of the Sierra Nevadas. At noon, the train stopped for another water refill at the Donner Pass Township and with whoops of delight, the Hawaii boys engaged in their first snowball fight. The first winter after California became part of the United States following the War of 1845 with Mexico, eighty-one pioneers attempted to cross this pass. Just forty-five of what became known as the Donner Party survived—and then, only because some survivors ate those who did not.

Once the 442nd recruits passed the California border, beyond DeWitt's command, the officers ignored the curtain rule. The new soldiers did what soldiers have done since the time of the Hittites. They gambled, carped about the food and bitched about not knowing where they were going. Kenta had read about the vastness of America, could name the forty-eight states, and knew the prominent geographic features of most of them. Still, nothing had prepared him for the rich agricultural lands of the rain-favored western side of the mountains, the first majestic crossing of the High Sierras and the water-starved eastern side of the range where nature had carved sculptures from mesas and granite outcrops.

At the Salt Lake City water and refueling stop, a few long-time Japanese families residing there, along with a small group of Hawaiian Nisei Mormons—students attending Brigham Young University—greeted the train. From there, the train moved through the Rockies in Utah and Colorado and then into the flatlands of Kansas. Kenta found it hard to believe that a hundred years before, when Honolulu hosted a bustling whale port, Indians and buffalo had populated this part of America.

He watched the evolution of American agriculture roll past the train's windows. Farmers drove John Deeres to grind soil for spring planting while their poorer counterparts, often on small plots tucked between big farms, walked behind mules pulling tillers cutting furrows for seeds they would plant by hand. Half the men on the train knew from experience exactly how grueling that process could be—experience that would prove invaluable during the Italian campaign.

As the train left the wheat fields of the Midwest for the cotton fields of Missouri, Kenta watched farming practices regress. No coloreds and few whites had mechanized equipment. Dark-skinned men strapped to a tiller or grader grunted and pulled as men had for ten thousand years. The lucky ones had a mule.

Hero nudged Kenta, pointing to shacks the colored families called home and the shabby unpainted frame wooden houses reserved for the slightly better-off whites.

"It doesn't pay to lose a war, Kenta. You would have thought Sherman had marched through here last year."

Kenta didn't bother to correct Hero by telling him Sherman never got close to Missouri.

∞ Chapter 40 ∞

Hung Wai Ching watched the last 442nd train leave Oakland, then took a taxi to the airport to catch a Pan Am Clipper to Washington, DC. General "Tight Lips" DeWitt had inadvertently given him the information no one else would—the destination for the 442nd: Camp Shelby, Mississippi. It was the worst possible choice—the Jim Crow South, where social order divided everything from toilets to bus seating between two—and only two—races. The Japanese would have to be assigned one of them. He expected and feared his brown-faced recruits, owning the eyes of the enemy, would be treated as colored. This would destroy the morale of the Nisei brought up in a multicultural community. Whites might top the social and power hierarchy in Hawaii, but everyone shared the same public bathrooms. No cultural or racial group suffered any impediments when registering to vote or entering the university. Nisei boys were not lynched for talking to white girls.

Ching arrived in Washington just after the city's three thousand cherry trees, given to President Taft by the people of Japan in happier times, had shed their last blossoms. The Japanese Cherry Blossom Festival had been renamed the Oriental Cherry Tree Festival as an alternative to chopping down all the trees. He had slept little since his disastrous meeting with DeWitt. While in flight to Washington, DC, he rummaged around in his imagination for a strategy to keep the 442nd boys from going to Mississippi. He could come up with no approach other than begging the army for reconsideration. The furrows in his forehead deepened as he foresaw a looming catastrophe.

Upon arrival, Ching taxied directly to the Hawaii congressional delegate's capital office. A young greeter immediately ushered him into Joseph Farrington's inner sanctum, Ching's new Samsonite still in tow.

"Aloha, Hung Wai." Farrington came around his desk to exchange a Hawaiian hug. He stepped back. "I have never seen you so frazzled." He eyed Ching's suitcase. "I insist you stay with us. Elizabeth won't forgive me if you don't."

"Mahalo. We need as much time together as possible to avoid a calamity in the making." He recounted his disastrous meeting with DeWitt and his discovery of Camp Shelby as the eventual destination for the 442nd. "We are talking about a helluva morale crisis, Joseph. You know our boys. Give them a taste of the Jim Crow life and they'll riot. The sugarcane strike will seem like a Kapiolani Park picnic compared with what will happen in Hattiesburg."

Farrington lit a cigarette and then offered his guest a Camel. Ching accepted and lit it with the tip of Farrington's cigarette before resuming.

"We need to make some calls. Our boys come from the fields, the farms and tough city ghettos. You piss off one of them and the whole gang 'makes beef,' as they would call fisticuffs defending their honor. They don't think.

One insult and the fists fly." Ching's forehead creased deeply. "Can you imagine the reaction the first time someone says, 'You can't drink from that fountain'?" He let his shoulders slump. "This entire enterprise could be abrogated in a series of racial incidents."

Farrington took a long drag of his Camel. "You have a couple of unlikely allies in keeping the Nisei out of the South, Hung Wai. Let me read excerpts from a recent speech by John Rankin, a Mississippi House Representative. We serve on the same subcommittee on territorial issues. He's the one who tried to pass a bill requiring that only nonresident whites be appointed to high-level federal government positions in Hawaii. A few years later, he led the charge to frustrate Hawaii's ambition to statehood on the basis of our mixed-race population."

"Excuse me, Joe, I was there at that time."

"Right." Farrington picked up what resembled a newspaper, but not quite.

"This is an edition of last year's Congressional Record." Farrington began reading, mimicking an exaggerated Southern drawl. "'You cannot regenerate a Jap, convert him, change him and make him the same as a white man any more than you can reverse the laws of nature. Damn them! Let us get rid of them now.'"

Farrington swapped it for a *Washington Post*, turned to an inside page, and resumed his slow, Dixie impersonation. "'I am shocked beyond expression to learn that several thousand Nisei troops are training in Mississippi. More trainloads of Japs are coming to my home state.'" He took a pull on his Camel. "He delivered that little gem yesterday on the House floor."

After he and Ching discussed strategy, Farrington called Assistant Secretary of War John McCloy. He and Ching took turns explaining the problem. When McCloy complained, "It's late in the day" to bring this to his attention, Farrington reminded McCloy the army revealed the destination only yesterday.

McCloy replied, "You know the boys from the 100th are already there, don't you?"

"Yes," said Ching. "But that group is smaller in number and has been subject to army discipline for almost two years, including a year of combat training in Wisconsin. The 442nd is just off the plantations. They'll be tough soldiers—as you will see the first time they are insulted for not having eyes shaped like the grandsons of Jefferson Davis." As he said the words, Ching felt as though he were talking to the wind.

But not one to give up, he placed a call to Eleanor Roosevelt, whom he had met the previous year on her trip to Hawaii. During a photo shoot, she had shaken his hand and maintained a steady gaze. "Let me know if you need help."

Evidently, she had meant it. To his surprise, Ching got through to her.

After listening to Ching's concerns, Mrs. Roosevelt said she would call McCloy and see what she could do. Then after a pause, she added, "Mr. Ching, since you are so close to the White House, I will send a limo over to pick you up. I think the president might like to see you. That is, if you have the time."

∽ CHAPTER 41 ∽

THE FIRST LADY GREETED CHING at the White House entrance. As she escorted him to the empty cabinet room two doors from the president's office, Mrs. Roosevelt shared some mixed news.

"I talked to Mr. McCloy. Your Nisei will be going to Hattiesburg." Ching struggled to hide his disappointment but did not restart his argument. He had been heard.

"But, Mr. Ching … I do believe Mr. McCloy knows that I have a personal interest in how those young men are treated." She smiled as she opened the door. "I will leave you here to ponder all the decisions our republic has made in this room."

Surveying the many portraits covering the century-old walls, Ching's eyes came to rest on an unexpected portrait of Woodrow Wilson, the twenty-eighth president, which was so large it dominated the room. He would have guessed that Washington, Lincoln or Jefferson would hold that commanding spot, yet on reflection, it made sense. The current president had served as navy secretary in Wilson's war cabinet.

Ching had just moved to a window facing the Rose Garden when he heard a knock on the door. He turned to find an attractive young woman entering the room.

"Mr. Ching? Good morning," she said, her voice low and pleasant.

"You must be Grace Tully," said Ching. "Your newspaper photos do not do you justice."

The woman blushed and let the compliment pass. "The president is ready to see you. Please follow me."

As Ching walked down the corridor, his sense of intimidation eased. His mission dominated his thoughts, strengthening his wobbly knees. Yet, as Grace Tully held open the door to the Oval Office, Ching admitted a sense of awe to himself. *If only my immigrant father were alive to know that his son sat in the White House foyer, about to not only meet the President of the United States but to express his views on national policy.*

As Ching entered the world's most famous office, the stench of cigarette smoke filled his nostrils. It had the odd effect of steadying his nerves by taking his mind away from meeting the president, even if only for a few fleeting seconds.

"Mr. President, this is Mr. Hung Wai Ching," said Harry Hopkins, the president's diminutive personal advisor who sat across from Roosevelt. Hopkins stood up and shook hands with Ching before guiding him around the *Resolute* desk to FDR, who also stood and offered a handshake. Like most visitors before him, Ching did not know that the president was crippled by polio and normally confined to a wheelchair. However, when sitting in a normal chair behind the presidential desk, President Roosevelt could use his upper body strength to lift himself up to standing, seemingly without effort, and shake hands with visitors.

The man who greeted Ching radiated vigor. Roosevelt grasped Ching's hand firmly and locked onto his eyes, then motioned his guest to take a seat. As he sat down across from the president, Ching noticed a lit cigarette, snug in its signature holder, resting in an ashtray shaped like the continental United States. The president eased back into his chair, opened a teak wood box and offered a Lucky Strike to Ching, who accepted. When Roosevelt flicked his silver lighter, a flattered Ching leaned over the desk for the President of the United States to light his cigarette.

"So, you are the man who keeps the lid on the Jap community in Hawaii— the same man who thwarts my orders to remove them to a safe place."

President Roosevelt's oft-photographed smile took the edge off his words. But they reminded Ching that even one incident of sabotage in Hawaii would send all the Japanese to Molokai.

"Quite the contrary, Mr. President. On the small islands of Hawaii, it's easy to keep tabs on everyone. The quick action by the police and the FBI removed anyone with even the slightest potential to do damage. I believe on the day of the Pearl Harbor infamy, we arrested more Japanese in Hawaii than were picked up on the entire West Coast. We were prepared."

The White House photographer stepped into the room. Rather than respond to Ching, the president said, "Mr. Ching, why don't you come over here to my side of the desk and we'll get a picture together." While FDR said something to Hopkins, Ching snuffed out his cigarette and cupped it in his hand before dropping the memento into his pocket and moving beside the president. The photographer snapped away with Ching standing next to Roosevelt, the president's head tilted up with his cigarette extending from its holder, wearing an election-winning smile.

As soon as the photographer left the room, Harry Hopkins coughed and stubbed out his cigarette. "The president is under enormous pressure, Mr. Ching. We are both aware that so far not a single rumor of sabotage has been verified. But you can imagine the uproar if even one such event occurred. It would open up the president to charges that he failed in his duty to protect the country. Civil rights simply have to take a back seat when the very existence of our nation is under attack in both Europe and the Pacific."

Ching remained impassive, fighting the urge to offer a counter argument on civil rights. He simply held Hopkins's gaze, noting how the other man's pale, narrow face made him appear ill, despite his strong voice.

Hopkins lit another cigarette with a gold-plated lighter. "Mr. Ching, are you aware of the Japanese spy ring on the West Coast?" His cold eyes challenged Ching.

The expression on Ching's face said he did not.

"In 1940, the Japanese consul in San Francisco began recruiting local Japanese as spies. The consul gathered intelligence from Japanese agents standing on hills commanding a bird's-eye view of the San Diego Naval Station. Other spies sent reports regarding factories, port facilities, military installations and utility locations from Seattle to the Mexican border. We found no evidence of planned sabotage, but that doesn't mean there were no plans. And in war, behind-the-lines information is often as important as an aircraft carrier."

"I had no idea," said Ching.

"No reason you should have. In Hawaii, only Shivers and Emmons had the need to know. The spies were picked up and interrogated. No doubt the Japanese guessed they had a leak that led to the arrests," said Hopkins, even though he knew Japanese message codes had been broken months before war broke out.

"You haven't mentioned Hawaii," said Ching.

"If we had found a single spy in Hawaii, all the Japanese would have been evacuated," said the president. "I still think they should have been, but I've let Emmons drag his feet."

Hopkins sat back. "In Hawaii, the Japanese consul apparently felt no need to recruit spies. With all of our ships berthed in one harbor, he could drive up just about any hill that affords a view of Pearl and count the ships."

"And maybe he feared approaching any local Japanese, knowing he would learn that their loyalty lay with America," said Ching. Behind him, the sound of a female voice startled him. He had not heard the door open.

"Mr. President, Milton has arrived for your meeting," said Grace Tully.

Ching recognized the dismissal and rose to leave.

"You are doing good work, Mr. Ching," said the president. "I am not unaware of the contributions your Morale Committee has made to the war effort. I am sure the Nisei will acquit themselves well in Europe."

"Thank you, Mr. President."

Ching followed Grace Tully out the door. As she escorted him, he nodded to the man who passed him. Ching recognized him as Milton Eisenhower, the director of the War Relocation Authority. Eisenhower was in charge of the ten internment camps holding the uprooted West Coast Japanese. Ching wondered if the chance passing had been inadvertent or a contrived warning of the yet-undetermined fate of Japanese residents in Hawaii. He decided to report to Emmons and Hemenway that his meeting with the president and Hopkins had been de facto recognition of the status quo. He knew about FDR's penchant for sloughing off the delivery of bad news to his staff, saving the good news to announce himself.

That evening, the phone rang as Joseph Farrington twisted a corkscrew into the cork of a bottle of wine. Farrington picked it up on the third ring while pointing to the corkscrew stuck in the bottle of merlot. Ching took over as sommelier.

"No interruption at all, Mr. McCloy." While Farrington listened, his faced rounded into a wide smile. Ching suspended his screw twisting. "Why, yes, that is very good news, welcome and unexpected."

Seconds later, following a warm "Good night," Farrington dropped his hands, palms out. "You never know the consequences of not giving up. McCloy is sending his personal aide to Hattiesburg tomorrow to let the brass know Mrs. Roosevelt expects 'her Nisei' to be treated like any other American soldiers. And," Farrington's smile broadened, "McCloy has arranged for a special rail pass for you from here to Hattiesburg."

Merlot had never tasted so smooth.

With the expedited rail pass, Ching left the next morning so he would arrive in Hattiesburg a couple of days before the 442nd. He knew that the 100th Battalion had been in Camp Shelby since February, but discovered that another cadre of Mainland Nisei soldiers had preceded them. These soldiers, drafted before Pearl Harbor, were culled from their scattered units and drawn to Camp Shelby to be trained as noncom officers for the 442nd. By day, they carried out their military drills. By night, they worked as plumbers, electricians, carpenters and latrine diggers to prepare the barracks for their incoming charges.

A fourth group of Nisei had also begun straggling into Hattiesburg. These eight hundred volunteers from the ten internment camps would be melded into the 442nd. There were no rousing bands or patriotic parades to send them off. Most had slunk away in predawn hours to avoid confrontations with those who called them traitors for fighting for a country that had imprisoned them and their parents.

∞ CHAPTER 42 ∞

CHING'S TRAIN SLOWED AS IT PASSED THE SIGN that read "Hattiesburg. Pop. 21,026." *Probably double that by now*, he thought. The April rains increased, and the wind blew harder, as if to say, "Don't overstay your welcome." The only pedestrian Ching saw through the rain-splattered window was a bent-over colored man walking into the wind.

Once part of the Choctaw Indian Nation, Hattiesburg typified the post-bellum South. Four hundred men and women of Irish, Scottish and English heritage—most of them from Georgia and the Carolinas who sought refuge from the lingering ravages of the war—founded the town and its pine lumber-based industry in 1882. Of course, the coloreds followed, but no one counted them as early settlers. Two years later, the railroad built a new line between Meridian, Mississippi, and New Orleans, Louisiana, and chose Hattiesburg as a way station. Timber mills and the turpentine industry flourished. The town received another boost in World War I when the army chose the area just south of Hattiesburg as a recruit training center. Then, depleted forests and the end of "the war to end all wars" fueled a two-decade depression until the army reopened Camp Shelby in the wake of Pearl Harbor. The town bitched and boomed as residents pined for more tranquil times while building new homes.

Ching balanced on the oscillating connecting plates between two carriages. The wind buffeted his face, marked by two days of stubble. As the train screeched to a halt, Ching spotted the first batch of "Japs, Go Home" posters plastered on the coal dust–coated red-brick columns that supported the station roof. He felt his heart beat insistently inside his chest. Judging from the partial scraping of rectangular shapes on the walls, a few of the signs had been torn down, although many were freshly posted. Not a good omen, especially since Ching had telegraphed ahead his arrival time to the chief of police, the mayor and the editor of the *Hattiesburg America*. He had emphasized his desire to help the community adjust to the influx of the Japanese. The newspaper's editor telegraphed an invite to visit his office, just across from the railroad station.

Ching stepped down onto the platform into typhoon-like gusts of frigid air. Early April in Mississippi felt more like February. He set down his Samsonite to button his coat, regretting he had buried his woolen scarf in his suitcase.

A colored porter wearing a billed cap with the name of the hotel embroidered on it met Ching. "You must be Mr. Ching, suh. I'm to walk you to the newspaper office. I'll take your luggage directly to the hotel a couple doors down."

Ching smiled with wry amusement. "Who *doesn't* know that I am arriving?"

The white-haired porter stared at him, uncertainty in his big brown eyes. "Suh?"

"Never mind," said Ching. He palmed the man a quarter and followed.

All eyes turned on Ching when he entered the newspaper building. Conversations ended mid-sentence. He responded with a wide grin and a tip of his fedora, dripping with rain, to show his appreciation to all who interrupted their work in his honor. The smell of fresh ink, smelted lead and stale cigarette smoke hung in the air. The curious stares followed as Ching strolled confidently ahead to the glass-enclosed room at the back, assuming it must be the editor's office. Passing an untended reception desk, he walked right up to the closed door.

Inside, two men sat on opposite sides of an oversized desk cluttered with papers. The thin, doughy man who faced his direction locked curious eyes on Ching. The sleeves of his white shirt were rolled halfway up his forearm and a narrow black tie hung askew. A ribbon of a black mustache divided his face in half. The other man wore a tight-fitting police uniform, his bulging back indicating a portly figure. Ching knocked on the door just as the receptionist came hurrying up behind him, a woman whose deeply wrinkled face suggested she had held her job since the days of Woodrow Wilson.

"Sir, sir!" she huffed. "I'm sorry, but you can't just go in there." Ching smiled, but did not move. The woman grasped his elbow. "Please come over to my desk and I'll check my appointment book and see if Mr. Logan is available."

The door swung open before she could steer Ching away from it.

"I'm so sorry, Mr. Logan," the woman said to the thin, mustached man. "I just stepped away from my desk for a moment to powder my nose," she said, slightly flushed. She glanced at Ching with disapproval and embarrassment.

"It's OK, Mrs. Harwood," said the man, who then greeted Ching in a deep Southern twang. "Welcome to the pride of Mississippi." He turned to the woman. "Could you please bring us all some fresh coffee?" Turning to Ching, he added, "Sorry, we don't have any tea."

Ching ignored the presumption. He wondered if his subtle Hawaiian Pidgin accent might be just as difficult for them to decipher as their Dixie drawl mystified him. But he had adjusted to various accents in Hawaii and felt assured he would quickly adjust to Mississippian pronunciation.

"I'm Johnny Logan, the editor," said the man, ushering Ching into the office, heavily laden with cigar smoke. "This is Chief Jack Ditmar." Ditmar made a half-attempt to squeeze out of his chair, but its rosewood arms seemed to pin him to the seat. The white crew cut he sported gave him the air of a longtime master sergeant.

"Pleased to meet you," the chief grunted. "We are all admirers of Madame Chiang Kai-shek."

Ching, who considered General Chiang Kai-shek and his politically astute wife a corrupt anachronism spawned by the worst of Chinese war-lordism, smiled graciously.

"Thank you." He refrained from adding, "And I am a longtime admirer of Huey Long."

The receptionist brought in a Dixie flag–emblazoned tin tray on which sat three cups of coffee. She served the men in frosty silence and quickly left, shutting the door behind her a little more forcefully than necessary.

The chief swiveled his chair to face Ching. "Your Jap boys are causin' quite a stir, Mr. Ching."

"That's why Assistant Secretary McCloy thought it might be a good idea for me to help smooth the way. Our boys will be just as nervous as you are about coming here. I understand a few have already arrived. Have you had any trouble?"

Ditmar lifted a hand to his ample chin as if to give his answer greater weight. "No, most of 'em have been right polite. There've been a few scrapes over the use of the word 'Jap,' but that's about it."

Ching smiled at both men. "Well then, that is easy to fix." He let that observation linger a moment. "Yours is a peaceful town, well-steeped in Southern hospitality, according to the military brass I've talked to in

Washington. The signs at the train station … I would think they don't fit well with the genteel reputation cultivated by three generations of Hattiesburg citizens."

The chief made an attempt to sit up a bit straighter. "We keep takin' 'em down and them agitators keep puttin' 'em back up."

"I suspect …" Ching paused for emphasis, "your word is the law when you want it to be." Not waiting for a reply, he opened his briefcase and took out two editorials echoing Representative Rankin's alarm over the "stationing of Japs at Shelby." He placed them on Logan's desk. "You and I have been working hard to have those boys trained in the North. We both lost. Now thirty-five hundred of them will be here in a few days. Your editorial stance recommending how Hattiesburg should receive these young men who volunteered to fight for their country will be extremely important, Mr. Logan."

He changed his attention to the chief and got to the nub of the matter. "Where will these boys ride on your buses?"

The chief smiled, a bit condescendingly. "Why, we consider those Ja—those Nisei boys—honorary whites. They will ride at the front of the bus, be allowed to enter the white theater entrance to see a movie and drink out of the white drinking fountain. And use the white toilets."

The news, like a shot of Jack Daniel's, eased the tightness in Ching's neck and shoulders.

"Mr. Logan, some of the national media have picked up on the story of Americans of Japanese descent volunteering to fight for their country—even in the face of discrimination and being sent to internment camps. I think you will agree that this is a great human-interest story. I have taken the liberty of notifying the *New York Times*, *Chicago Tribune* and other newspapers of the Nisei's arrival. This will be a grand opportunity for you to correct some misconceptions about your town."

Ching left unspoken that after a year and a half of blindly supporting the government's internment policy, a few publications were re-evaluating the proposition. In February, *Newsweek* and the *New York Times* had responded to the announcement of the formation of the 442nd in a neutral manner—a small start to the pendulum swinging back to America's founding values. *Time* had picked up coverage from the *Honolulu Advertiser* and run a story with the headline, "THERE ARE GOOD JAPS," accompanied by a photograph of the Nisei signing up to join the army. Ching read Logan as a fair man—as fair as a white man raised in the Deep South could be. His editorials had argued against the Nisei training in Shelby, but his writing lacked the rancor of a DeWitt or Rankin. Ching sensed that neither Logan nor Ditmar wanted a series of unpleasant incidents focusing unwelcome scrutiny on their town. An eternal optimist, Ching thought that just maybe his Nisei soldiers were close to their first victory without firing a shot.

∞ ∞

The chief watched Ching's back as he made his way out of the newsroom.

"Cheeky little bastard, ain't he?" he said, swiveling around to face Logan. "This is one fucked up world if I have to listen to a Chink tellin' me how to handle Japs."

Logan opened the bottom drawer of his desk and pulled out a thermos and two glasses. He poured a measure of golden liquid into each and shoved one over to Ditmar. "For sure we don't want this Jap group stirring up our colored folks, Jack."

Ditmar raised his glass and tilted it in a salute before taking a generous swig. "That's why the City Council agreed to treat 'em as honorary whites."

"Well then, maybe you want to make sure the Klan stops putting up any more signs."

The chief raised an eyebrow. "I have nothin' to do …"

"Cut the crap, Jack. You're not talking to the FBI." Logan fished a stogie out of the ashtray and relit it. "The only reason we don't wear the sheets is our position in the community. Not only do the signs gotta go, but I think it's time to welcome the boys with an editorial thanking them for volunteering."

The chief emptied his glass and then pried himself out of the chair. "We can keep 'em on our side until this damn war is over."

Logan drew on his cigar and admired the uniformity of the tip's red glow. "The Nisei will come; they will go. The colored are ours forever."

∞ CHAPTER 43 ∞

PLEASED WITH THE SEEDS HE HAD PLANTED, Hung Wai Ching surveyed the street for a luncheonette. He could have eaten at his hotel, but he knew that a local diner would give him better insight into the community. He almost thought he was in Honolulu as he caught sight of three Asian ladies walking down the street, umbrellas shielding them even though the rain was now just a drizzle. He recognized one of them—Judy Oda, wife of Mathew Oda of the 100th Battalion. The other two women looked vaguely familiar, but he could not attach names to their faces. He cupped one hand around his mouth.

"Judy! Judy Oda!"

All three women raised their umbrellas and turned their heads, shouting in a chorus.

"Mr. Ching!"

They started heading toward his curb, but Ching raised his hand like a school crossing guard.

"Wait right there, I'll come over!" he shouted.

Much against his law-abiding nature, he glanced left and then right and then quickly jaywalked across the street. He barely heard the honking of an annoyed driver as he calibrated this unexpected intelligence opportunity.

Ching skipped to the curb and bowed low.

"Judy, so nice—*so* nice to see you. I heard that some of the wives had followed their husbands here." He smiled at the other two happy ladies expectantly.

"Mr. Ching, this is Mary Sato from Maui and June Okamura from Kaneohe."

Ching's smile held a question.

"You most likely met them when they were Hitomi and Megumi," explained Judy. "But even those who are not Christian like me take on Christian names so Mainlanders can pronounce and remember them."

Ching nodded. "*Ah soo desu ka.*" He patted his flat stomach and asked, "Where can I take you ladies to lunch?"

"We've already eaten, but we would love to have some coffee and cake while you have lunch. We can go to the Dixie Grill, just around the corner."

The dwindling all-white lunch crowd turned to the high-pitched jangle of the bell above the grill's front door. One diner frowned as the four Asians entered; the others, many in uniform, gave them a curious glance and then continued eating. The waitress, just a year or two out of high school, flashed a smile of recognition. She wore a pink blouse, its top two buttons opened to reveal a glimpse of generous curves, and a short skirt with a white ruffle trim hugging its hem. A matching bow adorned her blonde bangs. Ching wondered how she could stand all day in high heels more suited for a night on the town.

"*Ohayo gozaimasu,* Judy. We didn't fill you up the first time around?"

"We have a new customer for you, Mabel-san." Judy did not correct Mabel's misuse of the greeting, which meant "good morning." "This is Mr. Hung Wai Ching, from Hawaii. He would like to order lunch. And we will have some of that German chocolate cake we passed up earlier."

Once he had ordered, Ching lowered his voice and asked, "Is everyone as friendly as Mabel?"

"We wish," said Mary softly. "But almost everyone treats us at least civilly. Sometimes we have to pretend we don't hear someone mutter the word 'Jap.'"

Ching pulled out a pack of Luckys from his coat pocket and offered them to the ladies, who demurred. He lit up. "What about housing?"

Mabel arrived with four cups of coffee. Only Judy added cream, although she didn't bother stirring it in.

"It's sure not Wisconsin, where so many people remember the anti-German discrimination they faced in World War I. In Hattiesburg, it took a lot of 'I just rented my last room' rejections before we finally found a widow who had sent her three sons to join Eisenhower in North Africa. She said she heard how neat the Japanese were and rented us her boys' rooms. The first weekend that our husbands joined us, she insisted on cooking us a real Southern dinner."

"To be fair," said June, "housing for army wives is tight. If any wives of the 442nd boys follow their husbands here, they'll have a tough time finding rooms."

"But getting a job is easy," said Judy. "We all work at Best Clean Laundry as seamstresses. They like hiring us Japanese because they rarely hear complaints about our work."

Mary cleared her throat. "Most of the boys here in the 100th Battalion are single. The one time they went to a USO dance, they were allowed in with the white boys, but most of the girls refused to dance with them and after a while, they gave up. It's not a big problem since the 100th is on maneuvers in Louisiana and will be shipped overseas soon after they get back. But the 442nd boys might have a problem with it."

A look of concern suddenly filled Ching's face. As he gathered his thoughts to respond, Judy leaned over and gripped his arm. "We all know you are trying to help us. We're not worried about the insults. But, Mr. Ching … I'm pregnant. You know my father. He ran a Japanese language school and is now in a POW camp in New Mexico. I don't want my baby to be treated like him or me." She tightened her grip. "Our husbands are fighting so our children can live with honor as loyal Americans. Please see that my husband is sent to fight. We …" She paused as her eyes moistened. "We know that some of our husbands and brothers must die. Guarding prisoners of war or moving supplies won't bring us the respect that only … only death can bring."

"*Wakarimashita*," said Ching, assuring her he understood.

The conversation moved to updates on the 100th boys. As he took the last bites of his meal, Ching motioned Mabel over, marveling at her thick makeup. "Could you please put an extra piece of cake in a paper bag for Judy's landlady, Mrs …." He turned to Judy.

"White. Mrs. Betty Lou White," Judy responded. Her eyes crinkled in pleasure.

∞ ∞

The ladies walked Ching to the nearest bus stop and waited with him until the Camp Shelby bus arrived. He joined the queue with the whites and dropped his nickel into the cash box attached to a metal pole next to the driver. He then took a seat in the third row. After all the whites had boarded, Ching saw the coloreds, mostly in uniform, follow. There weren't enough seats in the colored section to accommodate all the Negro passengers. Although seats were still available in the white section, the last two colored soldiers stood in the back of the bus, behind an empty "whites only" seat. Ching fought his urge to object to this absurd injustice, reminding himself that he had come to Hattiesburg to protect his boys, not to challenge Jim Crow.

Along the nine-mile ride south to Camp Shelby, the only thing Ching observed was pine trees and more pine trees, with an occasional break of shacks huddled together or clusters of nightclubs. Once inside the Shelby gate, the standing colored soldiers moved forward and sat in the vacant seats reserved for whites. The driver frowned, but his authority to enforce the laws of Hattiesburg stopped at the camp's entrance.

Camp Shelby bristled with activity consistent with a training facility hosting a transient population of up to a hundred thousand men living in fourteen thousand tents and hundreds of wood-framed barracks. A civilian army of hardhats drove tracked Caterpillars and operated Deere backhoes. They shoveled dirt, hammered boards, ran electric wiring and installed plumbing. Khaki-clad soldiers marched on the grounds not reserved for construction. Including leased land, Camp Shelby consisted of almost eight hundred thousand acres, with ample room for battalion-sized training exercises, tank maneuvers and firing ranges for every type of weapon. Ching heard what he guessed were tank or artillery barrages in the distance. No one else on the bus seemed to notice.

The driver dropped him off at the 442nd headquarters, which was still a work in progress. Uniformed men with Asian faces moved in and out of the building. As the bus steamed away, a sergeant rushed out the door, bounded down the steps and came to a stop in front of Ching.

"You must be Mr. Ching. We have been awaiting your arrival." The soldier took Ching's briefcase and introduced himself as being from Berkeley, but more recently from the Manzanar Relocation Center in California. Inside the building, the strident scent of freshly cut pinewood planks fought against the ever-present cigarette stink. Men at desks, mostly Caucasians, shoved papers, signed requisitions and gave orders. An orderly moved toward a door and placed his hand on the knob.

"Colonel Pence is expecting you."

Ching's peripheral vision had spotted a sign over an open door just to his right. He put a gently restraining hand on the orderly's arm to read it: "Reverend Joseph Adcock."

"One moment, please." Ching moved to the open door and peered into the office, where he found a big man sitting behind a desk, his short, blond hair in the early stages of going gray.

The man took in Ching in his black suit and ventured a guess. "You must be that wonderful Chinaman everyone talks about," he said, rising from his chair and offering his hand. "I'm very pleased to meet you. I want to hear all about the good work you are doing with the YMCA."

Ching smiled and reached over to shake Adcock's firm hand. "I see you have done your homework, Reverend Adcock. A lieutenant colonel," he added, his voice reflecting his admiration.

Adcock beamed. "I guess they want a career fellow working with … ah … this special unit."

Ching surveyed all the plaques hanging on the wall. Most of them had the words "Southern Baptist" prominent in their lettering. "Quite impressive."

Adcock came around his desk and put his arm on Ching's shoulders. He then lowered his voice to a conspiratorial tone.

"As a fellow Christian, you can see the opportunity to bring the Bible to these Buddhist heathens now that they are out of the influence of the plantation."

Ching felt his adrenaline rush demand a sharp retort. He smiled instead, as if Adcock had complimented him on his tie.

"Colonel Pence is waiting for me, but I did want to introduce myself. If you will excuse me …" Ching backed out of the office. "I'm sure we will meet again."

Ignoring his neck's suddenly knotted muscles, Ching froze his composed face and followed the orderly into Pence's office.

Colonel C.W. Pence, not a man given to smiling often, made no exception when Ching entered. From the time he dropped out of college in his senior year to enlist in the army during WWI, Pence had built a reputation as a man of serious intentions that were seriously undertaken. He comported himself more like a professional athlete in the twilight of his career than a twenty-six-year Army veteran, thanks to his time spent at DePauw University playing football, basketball and baseball. In college, he bussed tables to pay for his incidentals, yet somehow managed to maintain close to a 4.0 average. He still ran hard with his troops to maintain his thirty-inch waist and tough demeanor. Someone like Pence might have intimidated a lesser man than Ching. But Ching had worked with driven men like Emmons and Shivers who concentrated on getting the job done and were not sidetracked by ideology, prejudice or bureaucracy.

He respected Pence's spartan office. The unfinished pine walls displayed no adornment other than a world map on the left wall dotted with blue and red pins. A single peg snagged an Army-issue rain jacket on the back wall. A file basket on the right side of Pence's desk contained a few papers. Next to it sat a short pile of folders. A squat inkwell rested next to a day calendar and a bare, leather-edged ink blotter in the center awaited paperwork. A white, wooden plaque rested at a forty-five-degree angle on the front edge of the desk, its boldly etched letters heralding "Col. C. W. Pence." The black phone at his right elbow suggested that Pence preached "minimum motion serves best." It reminded Ching of his own habit of keeping his toothbrush, toothpaste, straight razor, badger hair shaving brush and lather bowl perfectly aligned in order of use on a side table next to the sink. The only personal item in the entire room sat on Pence's desk: a glass globe containing a miniature forest engulfed in water that looked like a snowstorm when tipped upside down. Ching guessed it must have been a gift from a grandchild.

The colonel stood and offered his hand. Ching had learned to provide a firm handshake and eye contact with military officers, quite different from the gentle clasp of hands exchanged in his Hawaii business dealings. He knew this first exchange must be one of equals. The crisp creases of Pence's khaki shirt and trousers validated Ching's decision to change into a freshly starched shirt as the train had approached Hattiesburg.

"*Ni hau,* Mr. Ching?" said Pence, greeting him in Mandarin, asking him how he was.

"*Hen hau* … Very good," replied Ching, adding, "Colonel Pence, your years in China have given you a better command of Mandarin than I have."

Remaining standing, as he usually did to keep such meetings short and to the point, Pence said, "I developed a certain affection for China during my deployment. I suspect the army has given me this posting because of my experience in the Far East." He gave a rueful shake of his head. "Of course, you and I know the Chinese and Japanese cultures are quite different. I'm now in the process of learning how Nisei culture differs from what we would find in Japan." He changed his expression to a near-smile. "Some things still translate, though. I am reminded that Asians love their rice, so I have asked the quartermaster to do what he can to get some."

"Anyone who spends time in Asia learns how to adapt and appreciate cultures different from his own," said Ching, pleased with the direction of his first conversation with the man who would have control over his boys.

Pence waved off another orderly who stood at the door with files in hand.

"Just this morning, Lieutenant Colonel Turner, the CO of the 100th, bragged that his young men have acquitted themselves very well. Last week, they captured the entire enemy headquarters unit in war games. Caused quite a stir."

Ching saw the opportunity he had hoped for. "Will they see combat?"

"That I cannot tell you. Eisenhower is not on board with this 'Nisei experiment.' But second-in-command General Mark Clark has told Colonel Turner that he will take anybody who will fight." Pence paused as if he might add something more, but apparently had a second thought and let the statement hang.

"Colonel, those boys want to fight. It is a matter of pride for themselves—and honor for their families."

"I accepted this command because the army designated the regiment a combat unit, but it's out of our hands, Mr. Ching. Not everyone in Washington and North Africa is convinced that these boys have what it takes to be a fighting unit, even putting aside loyalty issues." Pence cleared his throat. "I know you're concerned about the morale of the 442nd. We share that concern."

"I'm encouraged to hear you say that, Colonel. Perhaps we could address a few of those issues today." At Pence's nod, he continued. "First, I am worried how the young men will be treated in Hattiesburg."

"Well, this is the South. The locals don't want the Nisei here, but have agreed to treat them as honorary whites."

"So I've heard, but it is a little more complicated than that." He told Pence of the conversation with the Nisei wives about the USO and then offered a solution.

"Go ahead and make some calls, Mr. Ching. You have my backing," said Pence in a voice suggesting an end to the meeting.

"One more thing," said Ching in a soft, urgent voice. "I'm sure you are aware that most of the men are Buddhists."

Pence sat quietly for a moment. "I'll admit I hadn't given it all that much thought."

"I just met Reverend Adcock. A fine man." Ching began to relay his conversation with the reverend.

"I see where you are going with this." Pence motioned to a chair. "We'd better sit down. What do you have in mind?"

Ten minutes later, Ching left with an agreement that two chaplains from Hawaii would be sent for, both Christians since all of the Buddhist priests, save one, had been incarcerated. Chaplains from Hawaii had grown up with the spirit of aloha and an understanding of both Buddhist and Christian traditions.

Ching's focus on the religious and racial issues obscured two other simmering volcanoes. He hadn't failed to notice that the Mainland Nisei spoke "white" English instead of the Pidgin English favored by the Hawaii boys, yet had given little thought to the language disparity and its consequences. Further, he raised no alarm when Pence commented, "We scoured the military for Mainland Nisei who were drafted before Pearl Harbor and promoted most of them to sergeant. We have been training them since February to be the noncoms for the 442nd."

For years, Ching would wonder how he had completely missed what should have been so obvious, ignoring the fact that no one else had foreseen the circumstances that would almost destroy the entire Nisei experiment.

∽ CHAPTER 44 ∽

Saint Louis, Missouri – April 12, 1943

WHEN THE TRAIN PULLED INTO SAINT LOUIS, the curtains were drawn and the Nisei were forbidden from disembarking, even to stretch their legs. The men peeked out through the edges of the curtains and saw for the first time a large population of Negroes.

An officer wearing a major's stripes swung up the steps and into the coach.

"Listen up, recruits," he said. All of the men fell instantly silent. "While we have a few minutes of relative quiet, let me explain the ways of the South. You boys are from Hawaii. Lots of races mix, but you don't have many coloreds. You will find the South different. Jim Crow means whites and coloreds each have their own role in society. You might think it strange or even repugnant. Our job is to get ready to fight Germans, not get involved in Southern social issues." He gazed around at the somber faces. "Do I make myself clear?"

Kenta broke the silence. "And what exactly are we?"

"I'm just getting to that. You are 'honorary whites.' You are to use white-designated drinking fountains and toilets, and you sit in the front of the bus. You are *not* to use the colored facilities."

Most of the men stared blankly, hearing but not registering.

The officer moved on to the next train cab and Harry Nakata took out a map. "We're running out of geography. My guess is we're heading for Camp Shelby."

Hero studied the map. "A buck says it's Fort Benning, Georgia."

Chuckles opened his wallet and pulled out a crisp bill, which he waved at the two of them. "The 100th is in Camp Livingston, Louisiana. I bet we join them there." He laid his money on the side table that folded out just below the train's window.

Nakata held his ground. He and Hero each threw a dollar into the pot. Spud and Fats, who had watched the exchange without comment, figured there must be more than two Army camps in the South. With the odds in their favor, they joined the pool.

The next day when the train slowed coming into Hattiesburg, they accused Harry of not playing fair.

"You must have overheard the officers talking," grumbled Chuckles.

"Hey, I don't need any 'inside information' to beat you knuckleheads," grinned Harry as he scooped up his winnings.

∞ ∞

The Nisei arrived in Hattiesburg in mid-afternoon but were ordered to remain on the train until nightfall. Kenta peeked out from the edge of the curtain. The only posters he saw on the freshly scrubbed brick station walls and pillars promoted war bonds. Leaking clouds and angry winds exaggerated the chilly temperature Kenta felt in his bones when he cracked the window to freshen the sour air inside the overheated carriage. His eyes widened. There, standing under his fedora, was the unmistakable Hung Wai Ching. "Mr. Ching! Mr. Ching!" Heads craned out the windows.

Ching broke into a wide smile, tipped his hat and boarded the train. He visited each carriage. "The military has decided it best not to parade a thousand Japanese through downtown Hattiesburg in broad daylight." The men had heard it all before. As nightfall conquered dusk, Kenta's squad hoisted their duffel bags and descended the train's grated steel steps into the damp, cold wind. They meandered over to the station entrance where a fleet of two-and-half-ton transport trucks was just pulling up. While searching for his assigned truck, number 61, Kenta spotted a newspaper boy. The skinny ten-year-old white kid had waited all afternoon, shrewdly guessing that with so many soldiers on the train a few of them might want to buy a paper. Kenta whistled him over and handed the boy a nickel. In seconds, a sea of khaki-attired arms surrounded the boy. In minutes he had sold out.

"You guys are weird," he said. "Most of the regular army guys don't buy newspapers. Just a few officers." As he cycled off to get more papers, he suddenly stopped, turned and with a grinning face shouted, "I'm Bobby! I'll be right back, so don't buy from anyone else!"

Kenta stared after the kid, grinning at Bobby's compliment. One glance at the newspaper headline, and his smile turned to a scowl. "A JAP'S A JAP." The Nisei had arrived in Hattiesburg the same day that General DeWitt presented testimony to Congress.

"Listen to this," shouted Short Pants. "Here's what DeWitt said: 'They are a dangerous element. There is no way to determine his loyalty. It makes no difference whether he is an American citizen. Once a Jap, always a Jap.'"

"He's not the only one against us," said Chad, holding up the paper. "There's some guy named Rankin that the paper claims is the 'distinguished' representative from our new home state of Mississippi. Here's his welcome: 'Hawaiian-born Japanese are being sent into the South where we don't want them and where an invasion would surely occur if the Axis ever attempts it. Instead of sending those Jap troops into Mississippi, as the army is now doing, they should be put into labor battalions and be made to do manual labor.'"

"Good," said Kenta.

"Good?" Short Pants waved the paper in the air. "Are you fucking crazy?"

"Listen, we know DeWitt and what's-his-name speak for a lot of people. Now it's out in the open. What's he going to do when we kill a ton of Germans? The more assholes like him talk stupid, the more dramatic our sacrifice."

Short Pants threw his paper on the cement floor. "I guess you failed the course on logic."

Occupied with ranting over DeWitt's front-page remarks while bundling up in their overcoats to cope with the near-freezing temperatures, hauling their duffel bags with guitar and ukulele necks protruding and hunting for their assigned trucks, the Nisei took little note of a photographer snapping pictures of their arrival. Nor did they bother to read the editorial Johnny Logan had published that day, asking the citizens of

Hattiesburg to keep an open mind on the arrival of this volunteer group. Logan had closed his editorial with a quotation from another politician: "The principle on which this country was founded and by which it has always been governed is that Americanism is a matter of the mind and heart; Americanism is not, and never was, a matter of race or ancestry." The words of the president, uttered a mere two months earlier.

∞ CHAPTER 45 ∞

"I FOUND IT!" YELLED BUSTER, pointing at their truck.

Kenta's squad rushed over to truck number 61 and tossed their duffels into the back. They scampered up the steel-strutted ladder bolted to the rear of the truck and shivered together on the two cold, steel benches running parallel to the truck's chassis. Kenta was the first on; he sat with his back pressed against the cabin. He turned to peer through the cab's smudged rear window and exchanged smiles with the driver.

The two-and-a-half-ton transport with a canvas cover pulled onto Main Street. The driver stepped on the gas after passing the city's last streetlamp. Icy wind and drizzle cut through the flapping tarpaulin. Their fingers numb from the cold, the men struggled to pull their oversized pea jackets tighter around their bodies.

"Hey, Buster," said Chuckles, "where's that guitar of yours?"

Buster reached down and freed his guitar from his duffel bag.

"Man, this might hurt," he said, staring down at his cold, stiff fingers. For nearly a minute, he alternated between rubbing his hands together and blowing on his digits before he started strumming "Boogie Woogie Bugle Boy." Chad pulled out his harmonica from the pocket of his trousers and blew a chord. The squad broke into song. Chuckles screeched out new ribald verses that somehow had escaped the Tommy Dorsey Band.

As the truck slowed, the men stopped singing to focus on their surroundings, squinting through the cab's window. Bright lights outlined a white archway flanked by twin guard stations.

"We're here!" shouted Short Pants as the truck passed the guard gate.

To Kenta, "here" meant a whole lot more than simply a place. "Here" proved that they had never given up—even after the betrayal of their parents' homeland and their humiliating dismissal from the Hawaii Territorial Guard. "Here" gave them the chance they hungered for—the right to fight for their country like any other American.

The truck rumbled along freshly rolled asphalt, then cornered into a poorly lit gravel track. The driver downshifted to a halt. The men piled out of the truck in front of a cluster of less-than-welcoming oblong huts. Low-wattage door lights haloed a washed-out yellow glow, revealing pine plank construction.

A shadow stepped from the door and into the gloom.

"Welcome to Hutment 714," said a radio-perfect haole voice spoken by a Japanese face. He saluted. "I am Sergeant Johnny Doi, your squad leader."

Squad leader? Kenta felt as if someone had punched him in the gut. He wanted to yank the chevrons off of Doi's arm and shout, "What gives you the right to take my job?" True, he had been sworn in as a buck private upon induction, but he assumed that he and the other VVV boys would be promoted to the ranks they had held in the Guard.

Kenta swallowed his rage and masked the disappointment on his face. He saluted Doi. *If I am the leader I claim to be, I will not appoint myself chairman of the bitch committee.* Kenta was so preoccupied with controlling his thoughts that he missed Sergeant Doi's "Follow me" order, but he fell in with his squad as they hoisted their duffel bags on their shoulders and marched toward the squat building's front steps.

Doi faced his new unit. "Us noncoms have been working nights and weekends to try to make these hutments livable. It's not much, but it's home."

He hopped up the four steps, his men close behind.

Chuckles stepped inside and quickly scanned the interior. "What a shit shack."

Doi pivoted, his face twisted. He had been hoping for a chance to demonstrate his authority. What had he learned in noncom leadership training? *Establish control early. Beat down any attempt to usurp your authority.*

His gaze zeroed in on Chuckles. "You, what's your name?"

"They call me 'Chuckles.'"

The men behind Chuckles laughed.

Doi's voice rose. "I don't want some chicken-shit nickname." His voice increased another decibel. "State your full name. And you will address me as Sir."

"Seiji Fukayama … sir."

"Congratulations, Private Fukayama. Your cute remarks just earned you the first latrine duty. Grab a shovel after dinner." Doi stared at Chuckles, who took a long moment to understand the strained silence.

"Yes, sir."

"Dump your duffel bags on a bunk, then follow me. The made-up bunk near the stove is mine."

Chuckles is right, thought Kenta. *These barracks are a shit shack.* As he took in the flimsy pinewood walls, he thought of his mother's descriptions of early housing for sugarcane workers. He brushed off a drop of water that had splashed on his neck. The floors squeaked as the men moved about, staking out their bunks with their duffel bags. No windowpanes, just a wooden hatch window cover lashed shut with string wrapped around a nail. The front door didn't close tight; it didn't fit the frame and had been cut a half-inch short. *Tents would have been better*, thought Kenta. *They sure couldn't be any worse.* Months later, he would reappraise his first impression.

The squad crowded into the room. No chairs, just bunks. Doi pointed to the squat black iron stove.

"We used this in winter. They decreed winter ended April 1 and base housing HQ no longer delivers coal."

"Where's the john?" asked Kenta.

Doi's eyes flared, fixated on Kenta.

"I mean … where is the toilet, sir?"

"You boys don't hear so well. A latrine means there is no toilet. There is a trench behind each row of hutments. That's why the latrine must be cleaned daily. Let's go to the mess hall."

∞ ∞

Doi's tough-guy attitude could be seen as ironic, given his own military experience. He had been drafted before Pearl Harbor. Despite his college background and excellent Army test results, he, like all the Nisei, never saw the inside of an Army specialty school. After December 7, 1941, the army confiscated his rifle and instead handed him a shovel and a potato peeler. Serving on active duty was of no help to his parents, who were sent away to an internment camp. Doi considered going AWOL, but accepted his humiliated status, too shocked to protest.

That all changed in December 1942. The Army assigned Doi and a chorus of Nisei soldiers collected from scattered units to Camp Shelby. No one told him why, but he got his rifle back. He took part in drills during the day, and at night, he hammered, caulked and painted the prefab hutments. Without any plumbers, he dug narrow-slit trenches that the men could squat over. When Doi asked why the Nisei had to do these jobs, he discovered the joys of latrine duty. He seethed as he shoveled shit into wheelbarrows, then pushed the wheelbarrow outside the housing area where he dug a deep pit and emptied the shit into the hole. Then he shoveled the dirt he had just dug up back over the hole. He pushed the fetid wheelbarrow to the tool shed and hosed it down.

The speculation over why they had been sent to Camp Shelby ended on January 28, 1943. At noon, the frustrated drill-and-paint Nisei were assembled to meet their permanent commanding officer, the newly arrived Colonel Pence. Blank faces greeted his introduction.

"The War Department has decided to create an all-Nisei combat regiment." Pence paused to let his words sink in. He watched the puzzled look on the men's faces. "You men have been chosen to be trained to provide the noncommissioned leadership for this volunteer unit. You are all being promoted, effective immediately, to sergeant." A lone soldier clapped in the stunned silence, followed by a spontaneous crescendo of applause. Pence waited for the commotion to die down and then continued to address the men. "Many of you will be promoted again to staff sergeant or even sergeant first class by the time the volunteers arrive in early April."

The cadre of drafted Nisei spent three months learning to be sergeants. Doi got the point about giving orders, expecting them to be obeyed without question and punishing any infraction. Upon graduation, two-thirds of the group received promotions to staff sergeant or sergeant first class. But not Sergeant Doi. He convinced himself that his performance had been just as good, but since he wasn't an ass-kisser he hadn't received a fair assessment. He'd show the brass that they had made a mistake. He couldn't wait for the new recruits to arrive; twelve of them would be his to whip into shape. Someone else could shovel the shit.

One might expect the new sergeants—who had been subject to prejudice in the army and whose family members were incarcerated because of their ethnicity—would be empathetic to their own kind. And some were. Others, like Sergeant Doi, could not make the connection. In his mind, underlings needed to be put in their place. Unpleasant duties could be fobbed off. Discovering rule infractions gave Doi bolts of euphoria and inflicting punishment for those infractions, particularly for lack of respect, afforded long moments of righteous satisfaction and assuaged fears of inadequacy.

The two approaches to leadership could be seen in Doi's response to a directive put out the day after the Nisei arrived. The quartermaster, who slept in warm quarters, ordered that all comforters be returned to the supply room since, according to the army manual, cold weather had ceased. Some sergeants found a way to keep the comforters a little longer, reasoning that it would take a few days for the supply personnel to track down four thousand comforters.

Not Sergeant Doi. He marched his men, comforter in hand, to the supply unit within hours of receiving the directive. That night, he alternated between being pissed off at other sergeants who had ignored the order, and berating himself as he shivered in bed, for being a damn fool and complying so promptly.

∞ ∞

Sergeant Doi's alarm clock clanged fifteen minutes before the bugle played reveille. The first-up tactic buttressed Doi's strategy to land those unjustly denied staff sergeant's stripes.

"What the fuck?" complained usually quiet Harry Nakata. "Who's the asshole who set off the alarm?"

"That remark will cost you an extra day of latrine duty, soldier," said Doi, proud of his swift response to the day's first challenge to his authority.

"Aw shit, man, that ain't fair," said Harry.

"You want fair, you should have stayed in Hawaii planting pineapples. Your bitching just earned you another day of shoveling shit." Doi grabbed his clipboard hanging on a nail over his bed and made two ticks with the pencil attached to the board with a string.

Kenta threw aside his light blankets and stuffed duffel bag he had used as a comforter and arose to meet the coldest morning of his life. He surveyed his new home, which was definitely not up to VVV standards. The glow of hanging light bulbs revealed haphazard carpentry. Cold air seeped through air slits between the uneven pine boards—the window latches did not fit tight and nails were not pounded flush against the wood.

Doi stomped his feet on the floor. "All right ladies, time to boogie. We start with a ten-mile run and then breakfast." Wearing a Cheshire Cat smile, he mulled over a suitable punishment for slackers. He bristled that the entire squad had helped Chuckles clean out the latrine after dinner the night before. While he admitted that the trench now had deeper-cut walls and a more firmly tamped rim, he dreamed up scenarios in which he demanded two hundred push-ups from his too-clever pineapple squad for challenging his authority. He opened the door and started jogging.

Kenta knew they couldn't all leave in their current state of dress and was certain that Doi had planned it that way so he could dole out a fresh punishment to the stragglers.

"Short Pants, you're ready. Get going. We will leave one at a time, as we each get dressed. Just make sure one of us always leaves in time to see the person in front. When the last guy leaves, we will all catch up to our *luna*," using the Hawaiian term for hated Portuguese plantation overseers.

If Sergeant Doi thought he could run his charges into the ground, he was sadly mistaken. His squad had toughened up during their year of construction work as the VVV. No matter how fast Doi ran the Hawaii boys kept up with him, sensing his run-them-into-the-ground objective. The men had a more difficult time keeping up than their outwardly effortless pace revealed. They each worried that they would be the one who breathed loud or developed a cramp. A few paces behind Doi, Kenta smiled through the pain as he noticed the sergeant's back expanding and contracting rapidly, making room for larger gasps of air.

∞ CHAPTER 46 ∞

April 26, 1943

"I'M HUNGRY," SAID FATS. "Let's get some chow."

The men changed into aloha shirts and shorts and ambled over to the mess hall where an angry and out of breath Short Pants and Buster ambushed them.

"We were just told that they don't sell toothpaste to Japs at the PX," snapped Short Pants.

"Tell the clerk to go fuck himself and check out with another cashier," said Fats.

"The cashier practically kowtowed to the haole bullies," said Buster.

"A wimp," said Short Pants, his breathing almost back to normal. "A bunch of shit-ass Sixty-Ninth New Yorkers just coming off maneuvers started in with the 'You Japs don't belong here' crap. A few more guys came over. Five or six of them against the two of us."

"That's it!" hammered Fats. "I'm finished pretending I don't hear those racial slurs."

Kenta's face tightened as his mind flashed back to the two haole soldiers hitting the floor at the Hotel Street bar, which replayed like a movie trailer. "Right Fats, I'm tired of hearing 'you Japs' every time we go to the PX. It's time we stood up for ourselves. Let's go over there and settle this."

"We ain't gonna take this shit anymore," said Short Pants, leading the charge.

Kenta fast-marched the seething soldiers to the PX. On their way over, they tore down army propaganda posters showing slit-eyed soldiers grinning sinisterly as they bayoneted children. What a motley bunch the Nisei looked as they entered the PX adorned in their mishmash attire of aloha shirts, T-shirts or unbuttoned uniform shirts, straw *zori* or half-laced army boots, and shorts or floral-themed drawstring trousers.

"There they are," said Short Pants, pointing at a table of beer drinkers in the canteen section of the PX.

"Let's all get a tube of toothpaste and get in line," said Kenta.

The half-dozen juiced-up drinkers quickly noticed the strutting Nisei as they entered the PX. A beefy soldier with a skull and crossbones tattooed on the back of his neck jumped up and roared, "I had a brother die in Guadalcanal. Let's teach those Japs a lesson!"

His tablemates jumped up and hollered, "America for Americans!" They scoured the eyes of their beer-guzzling buddies at the other tables as if expecting support.

Nobody else stirred.

A master sergeant, drinking alone at a table in the corner, opened his mouth and was just about to say something but held back as he watched the Hawaii boys queue at the checkout, their jaws set and eyes steely. *More interesting to see how this plays out*, he thought.

Short Pants led the toothpaste brigade to the same clerk who had earlier denied him service. He thrust the tube of toothpaste and a dollar at the clerk, a bald, fortyish, squinty civilian sporting a wrestler's physique. The man pivoted from the cash register and leaned over the counter.

"I guess you Japs don't hear so well. I don't have to sell to your kind."

Short Pants reached across the barrier, grabbed the clerk's shirt with both hands and jumped like a kangaroo. He headbutted the man's shiny dome twice. The double *kotonk bong*, immediately followed by the clerk's bellow, brought the PX patrons to a shocked standstill.

But only for a second.

Blood sprang from the clerk's right eye and streamed down his face. He stumbled backwards, knees buckling and crashed into the iron railing separating the cash register lines. His dazed expression morphed into fiery rage. Like a boxer hit hard—but not hard enough to send him to the canvas—the clerk launched himself off the rail and swung a muscular arm, his whirling fist smashing Short Pants's left cheekbone. Short Pants's admiration of his handiwork caused him to duck a fraction of a second too late.

Short Pants fell backwards like a fifty-pound sack of rice falling off the back of a pickup truck. In his fuddled state, Short Pants didn't hear the stomping, beer-drinking Yankee yell, "Remember Pearl Harbor!"

The rabble charged the checkout counter. Their flushed faces, clenched jaws and eager strut said they expected their short, skinny, brown opponents to fold in fear.

That was their first mistake.

Behind them, the enraged clerk stepped around the cash register and picked up Short Pants. He hoisted the now-limp figure over his head, roaring like Tarzan, "Get out and stay out!" and then tossed him toward the front door.

Short Pants hit the pinewood floor and rolled over until a pair of gleaming boots stopped him.

In that instant, the tallest Yank charged Stonehead like a raging bull. A Golden Gloves boxer, Stonehead ducked while his practiced hammer to his attacker's gut doubled him over and a fist to the back of his ear put him on the floor and out of the fight.

Kenta, Spud, Fats, No Ticket and Chuckles formed a circle, their backs to each other like the gang in the Charlie Chan movies. All except for Spud and Fats had earned black or brown belts in karate. The last three white boys came flying in for the kill, not a bit worried about being outnumbered by little runts with slanted eyes who were only as tall as their Adam's apple.

Kenta delivered a kick to the shin of the short, would-be thug, swiveled three hundred and sixty degrees and landed a second kick to his jaw. The man stumbled backwards into a table, flipping it over and landing hard on his butt. No Ticket used the momentum of the skinny one to spin him into a metal pole, his slide to the floor punctuated by a savage kick to his gut. The third attacker, the one with the crew cut, swung at Chuckles who easily stepped aside and delivered a devastating chop to the back of the man's neck, sending him to his knees. Behind them, the clerk closed in on Short Pants, flailing like an upended cockroach at the base of a man's shiny boots.

A voice at the top of the boots boomed. "Who wants a court martial?"

A John-Wayne-built master sergeant loaded with chevrons stood over Short Pants, still dazed, and eyeballed the crowd.

"These Japs attacked me!" said the lone standing assailant, somewhat shakily.

Kenta wheeled around and kicked the man in the groin with his heel. The six-foot-four-inch-tall soldier crumpled back to the floor.

The master sergeant stepped over Short Pants and stopped abreast of Kenta. "Do you want to try that on me?"

"Only if you call me a 'Jap' and refuse to sell me—an American soldier—a tube of toothpaste … *sir*."

The sergeant gave Kenta a long, cold stare. "Get your toothpaste and go back to your unit."

"You're not going to call the MPs?" challenged the clerk.

"I could call them and you could file charges. I watched you refuse to sell toothpaste to that soldier. How far do you want to go with this?" He surveyed the battered Yanks. "I saw you guys charge these men."

"And you didn't stop it?" asked the clerk.

The master sergeant answered the question while staring at the triumphant Nisei. "Well, I'd heard stories that these Nisei wouldn't stand up in a fight. I thought I'd see what would happen."

A tall, gangling staff sergeant walked into the PX and surveyed the damage. He spotted Kenta and broke into a malevolent smile.

"Crockett!" shouted Kenta.

"No, asshole! *Sergeant* Crockett," Kenta's Schofield nemesis smirked. "You dumb shit, you believed that charade about me being busted to private? When I knock out one of your teeth, I bet you'll put it under your pillow expecting the tooth fairy to leave you a quarter."

Crockett surveyed the shambles before bringing his eyes back to Kenta.

"I'll see you later when your gang isn't here to back you up."

PART V

Jim Crow, Kotonks and Buddhaheads

⚮ CHAPTER 47 ⚮
May 2, 1943

PENCE HELD A TIN MUG OF COFFEE in his left hand. The worried cleavage between his eyebrows pinched together as he studied the four-foot-high map on the wall to the right of his desk. The sea of red push pins identifying Hitler's and Tojo's armies and the blue pins representing the defending Allies reminded him of the military rationale for the December 1942 decision to create an all-Nisei combat regiment. Men were needed to fight.

The year 1942 had been horrible. The Axis powers were winning, although the final outcome was still in doubt. Except for Midway, the Allies had lost territory and ships on all fronts. In February, the Japanese navy had smashed an Allied fleet at the Battle of Java. The fight for Guadalcanal hung in the balance. The Philippines had fallen to the Rising Sun. Singapore and Hong Kong had surrendered. Japan had occupied Burma and its amassed troops near India stood ready, waiting for an expected uprising against British rule. And that was just in Asia and the Pacific.

On the European front, German troops seemed ready to enter Stalingrad, Moscow and Volgograd. The Wehrmacht had taken Sevastopol, giving them control of the Crimea and the Black Sea. Paris, Copenhagen, Athens, Oslo, Amsterdam, Sophia, Belgrade and more—all had fallen under German rule. The British had surrendered twenty-five thousand troops after losing the first Battle of Tobruk. Montgomery's counterattack in Tobruk had, by the slimmest of margins, kept the Germans from occupying Cairo, but Rommel still controlled most of North Africa. Anglo-American troops had landed in French Morocco and French Algeria. Eisenhower's armies suffered inglorious defeats in their first confrontation with Rommel's Afrika Corps. As Churchill said of the Axis 1941–1942 European/North African onslaught: "This was their finest hour."

Pence felt confident that the worst was behind them. As awful as 1942 had been for the Allies on the ground, the factories of America had produced forty-eight thousand planes and fifty-six thousand tanks, and the army had mobilized a fighting force that had grown to seven million men.

Pence almost allowed himself a smile, remembering a recent letter to his mother in which he had taken credit for the Allied turnaround since his January 1943 appointment as commander of the 442nd. RAF bombers dropped their payload on Berlin during January 30 speeches by Goebbels and Goring celebrating the Nazis' tenth year in power. On February 2, the Russians broke the siege at Stalingrad and captured ninety thousand German troops. A week later, American Marines broke the aura of Japanese invincibility by winning a vicious victory at Guadalcanal. Pence moved the pins in North Africa. Eisenhower and Montgomery had Rommel's Afrika Korps squeezed in a giant pincer. Pence wondered if the Allies would invade France or Italy this summer.

Eisenhower. If only he would let Pence's men fight. But the colonel had no control over that decision. He could only concentrate on training his men for combat and dare the brass to pass over men willing to die for America. *Willing? More like eager.*

"Sir?" The orderly at the door had repeated the word three times before the colonel snapped out of his reverie.

Pence turned from the map. "What is it, Corporal?"

"You said you wanted to know when Master Sergeant Forte arrived."

"Send him in."

Forte entered, shaking his head. Despite the chill, his shirt showed half-moon sweat marks outlining his armpits.

"How bad was the boys' first run, Sergeant?" asked Pence, interpreting Forte's head shaking as bad news.

"You won't believe it, sir," Forte said in a Louisiana drawl softened by his French accent, courtesy of his parents speaking the language at home while he was growing up in rural Lake Pontchartrain. "Not one of those Hawaii recruits dropped out of the ten-mile run. We had the usual number stop to throw up, but they puked and then ran to catch up to their squad."

"That might be a first, Sergeant. Tomorrow I'll join the men on the morning run. Let's bump it up to twelve miles and have them carry an empty pack. You said the Hawaii boys?"

"Yes, sir. They seem different than the Mainland boys."

"How so?"

"More gung-ho, more likely to help each other out."

Forte, used to Pence's no-nonsense meeting style—"Just get to the nub of the topic at hand"—stopped there.

But Pence wanted more. "You've been going to their mess and walking around their hutments since they arrived. I want to know your impressions."

"The mess is a good place to start, sir. The Hawaii boys form instant groups at the tables. They're boisterous. Very social. Lots of talking and laughing. Everyone seems to know everyone else. The Hawaii boys were proud to show me pictures of their big Honolulu send-off ceremony. They had those flower garlands—leis, they call them—draped around their necks, thousands of well-wishers all around—white, Asian, Hawaiian.

"The Mainlanders, on the other hand, walk through the chow line silently. They eat alone, even at the long tables." Forte's voice dropped to a more somber tone. "Can't say I spent any time with the Mainlanders. They eat, maybe have a Coke and then shuffle out … like, like they're going to a funeral. All that Hawaii exuberance must get under their skin, considering the send-off they had, if you can even call it a 'send-off.'"

Pence stabbed his forefinger on the map of North Africa, next to the blue pins representing American forces under the command of General Mark Clark. "General Clark opposed putting all those families into camps, and I agreed with him. It's not only morally questionable, but Tojo uses the internment as propaganda proving America demeans and brutalizes the Japanese. Given the Mainland boys' treatment by our government, I'm surprised we got even nine hundred to volunteer."

Pence raised his coffee mug toward Forte, an invitation to tell him more.

"When I talked with the Hawaii boys, I asked them why they volunteered. They got pretty fired up and shouted out the usual responses: loyalty to country, sense of duty, seeking adventure. Some said they didn't want to have to explain after the war why they hadn't fought. But the answer that really got me came from the young man they call Short Pants: 'Respect, sir. To be regarded as an American, not a hyphenated American.' I could see that sentiment on all those young Japanese faces. And their eyes bored into me with an intensity you rarely see in recruits."

Pence put his coffee cup down and folded his arms. A second later, he raised his right arm and rested his chin on his fist like Rodin's statue, *The Thinker*, a habit Forte recognized as the colonel telegraphing, "You have my attention."

"Contrast that with what happened just before I got here," said Forte. "I found two Mainland volunteers waiting outside my office. 'We've had it. We're resigning,' they told me." Forte allowed himself a wry smile. "After I explained the court martial process, they went back to their units."

Pence took out a cigarette. "Three of a kind beats a pair."

Forte lifted his eyebrows and moved his neck forward, looking like a human question mark.

Pence lit his Lucky and took a deep draw. "I've had three junior officers request transfers. They say they don't want to command Japs. They left my office with a clear understanding that we don't use the word 'Jap' and that their present assignment is their chance to demonstrate leadership. I didn't paint the alternative, but they got the idea that it would be a lot worse than staying put."

Forte touched his shirt pocket. "May I, sir?" Pence nodded. Forte pulled out a pack of Chesterfields, flipped out a cigarette and then stuffed the pack back into his shirt pocket.

"You know how the Mainland cadre resented the hutment repair detail." Forte, wiggling his Chesterfield and looking at the tip of Pence's Lucky, said, "May I?" Pence handed Forte his cigarette. "And the results show it."

Forte used the tip of Pence's cigarette to light his own before continuing. "The Hawaii boys have been fixing leaks, resetting doors, painting—basically fixing everything that's not right. Lots of them were raised on plantations, where they learned to be handy with tools." He handed Pence back his Lucky, then put his own cigarette to his lips, drawing it in thoughtfully, then slowly exhaling. "But you can see the downside to all this repair frenzy."

Pence lifted his coffee cup to take another gulp. Empty. He instinctively glanced at the coffee urn, then thought better of it and put the cup back down. Instead, he took a drag of his cigarette before settling into his chair.

"We invested three months into developing confident officers … and then their men show them up on their first day."

"Yes, sir. The Hawaii boys have no idea that the Mainlanders left families living in conditions worse than the hutments."

"Good job, Sergeant," said Pence in a send-off voice. Then he quickly raised a hand, waggling his index finger. "Oh! Did you find your medics?"

"Too many. There are twenty-seven pre-med students among the Hawaii recruits and double that number with hospital experience. I turned the files over to the doctors. Let them pick and choose. I also found out that the Records Department finished tabulating the intelligence and aptitude tests the Hawaii boys took at Schofield just before they shipped out. The average IQ is 121. Almost all are high school graduates, and more than half have at least some college education. I bet we have more college graduates among our regiment's enlisted men than all of Mark Clark's Fifth Army."

Pence had been reviewing the 442nd personnel files since the regiment arrived a week earlier and knew his command was comprised of the most intelligent and best-educated regiment in the history of the US Army.

Forte drifted over to the side table where the coffee urn sat. He filled a mug about one-fourth full. "Half come from plantations. They speak a Pidgin English that is less understandable than Cajun. Yet their written tests are the King's English. How can that be?"

"Education mamas."

"Excuse me, sir?"

"I saw some of that when I was stationed in China and visited the Japanese concession in Port Arthur. The Chinaman, Hung Wai Ching, confirmed my reasoning when he visited here. The Japanese mothers are fanatical about their kids' education, especially their sons. Those boys are raised believing they will go to the university."

Forte tipped his cup to finish the small jolt he had poured himself. "Will that be all, sir?"

"Yes."

∞ CHAPTER 48 ∞

June 4, 1943

IN THE SIX WEEKS SINCE the 442nd arrived, migrating Canadian geese had begun clouding the skies. As the weather warmed, a more menacing airborne traveler rose from Camp Shelby's marshes. Regular DDT spraying kept the mosquitoes down to a mere nuisance level within the camp, but morning marches seemed timed to match the breakfast habits of the ravenous droves of bloodsuckers lurking outside the spray zone.

Yesterday, the ever-vigilant Sergeant Doi had led the squad on its first twenty-five-mile hike with a full backpack. This morning, they had slithered hundreds of yards under live ammunition, navigated an obstacle course and stabbed stationary sacks with their bayonets. After lunch, they were trucked to the rifle range. Doi's disappointment with the Hawaii boys' expert marksmanship—due to their pig-hunting forays back home in the Islands—showed through his grim composure.

As soon as Kenta returned to his hutment, he high-tailed it to the communal shower. The Hawaii boys, used to swimming in the buff at isolated beaches and river spots and even in plantation irrigation ditches, walked naked to the showers with their towels slung over their shoulders. The more reserved mainlanders draped their towels over an arm strategically pressed against their stomach.

∞ ∞

Oh, for those wonderful, brisk days of early April when freezing their asses off seemed the worst weather the recruits could endure. Short Pants sat on a log adjacent to a creek during a break on another Doi-led hike. He pushed and pressed the skin around his ankle.

"Another fucking chigger!" He interrupted his squeezing to move his arms like fans about to bust loose from the ceiling. "I swear to shit the chiggers got a deal going with these swamp mosquitoes. They wait till you're getting rid of the chigger and zoom in like a bunch of Zeros." He kicked the ground. "You'd think with all the snakes around here they'd eat the insects. Isn't that how it's supposed to work? And the fucking humidity ..."

"We got it," said Doi, who had acted almost human during the march, maybe because he fretted that his tough Islanders would handle the endurance challenge better than he would. He let a weary smile creep into his voice. "Let's saddle up, Buddhaheads." No one, not even Short Pants, had complained about the hike. After all, that's what the army did. Hike.

"But why," asked Short Pants, "are the Washington numbnuts training us in a swamp if we're going to Europe?"

Doi poked Short Pants's shoulder. "Good news, we're going to outrun the mosquitoes." He regarded the rest of the squad as he put on his light backpack. "It's only six miles to home, men. Let's do it in double time."

Chuckles capped his canteen, forcing a laugh before he offered an exaggerated, "Thank *you*, Sergeant Kotonk."

The good-natured exchange of slurs, much like friendly Italian and Irish brothers-in-law might greet each other as "Mick" and "Wop," camouflaged the tenuous camaraderie of Doi and his men. The relationship between the Hawaii soldiers and the Mainlanders had deteriorated with each passing day. A week after arriving, a Manzanar recruit, listening to a Hawaii recruit's Pidgin English snickered "Buddhahead," a clever amalgam of *buta,* meaning pig in Japanese, and Buddha, whose religion most Mainland Nisei had dropped, unlike their counterparts from Hawaii. In the melee that followed, the rough-and-tumble Hawaii Nisei beat up the less pugnacious Mainlanders. When one of the Mainlanders hit the ground hard, a Maui boy had shouted, "Kotonk!" Hawaiian slang for the sound a falling coconut makes when it hits the ground. By the end of mess that evening, the 442nd's vocabulary had been universally enriched by the two newly minted pejoratives.

Doi's squad—or Kenta's squad as the men under Doi still thought of themselves—broke into a trot of a hundred and eighty paces a minute rather than the normal hiking pace of around one hundred and twenty beats, a spacing and pace designed for men with an average height of five feet eight inches. Most of the Hawaii boys were shorter, many hardly breaking five feet. They had to stretch further and move their legs faster to make up the difference. But they did so without complaint; to do otherwise would suggest that they were not as tough as the white soldiers.

Kenta broke out of the pack to take his customary position behind Doi.

Doi seethed at this constant reminder of Kenta's confidence. He vowed to assign Kenta another round of latrine duty. What would it take for that Buddhahead to make the connection between his assumption of leadership and shoveling shit? His anger rose another notch as he thought about the previous night.

"Men, we need to gather some wood for a fire and organize the food," Doi ordered upon arriving at the campsite.

"Yes, sir," Kenta replied and immediately began assigning individual tasks to the men. It was so effortless for Kenta. Doi watched, barely able to control his rage, knowing he couldn't complain.

Within minutes, the wood had been gathered and a fire had been lit. Chuckles started dancing like an Indian medicine man, flapping his elbows and moving his neck back and forth like an ancient Egyptian chorus girl, yelling, "Pluck, pluck!" Even Doi had to laugh. Chuckles picked up his knapsack and raised it up to the sky. He let out an alley-oop whoop, reached inside and pulled out a live chicken.

Doi opened his mouth to object. Before he could spit out his words, however, applause and catcalls rose not only from his squad but from other nearby squads. Doi had no idea how to kill a chicken or pluck its feathers. He watched in amazement as Chad and Henry did what they had done since they were kids back in Hawaii.

With little need for communication, the Hawaii boys moved swiftly into action. Chad opened his Swiss Army knife and slit the chicken's neck in one smooth stroke. He held the chicken out over the ground and let its blood drain. Short Pants cut two limbs from a nearby sapling—each one forming a "Y" shape—and stuck the pointed ends in the ground on either side of the fire. Fats foraged through the brush to find a slender, fairly straight branch and set it horizontally in the crook of each Y. Henry then filled his helmet with water from his canteen and Chad's and hung it by the chinstrap on the branch. When the water came to a boil, Chad dipped the chicken into the helmet in sections and easily plucked off its feathers. Henry chopped the defeathered body into eatable chunks and tossed them directly into the fire. Minutes later, a flurry of fast-as-a-magician hands snatched up the sizzling pieces and tossed them into waiting upturned helmets.

Doi thought they were nuts, but had no problem eating his share or accepting the approbation of a captain who strolled over to congratulate Doi's team on their ingenuity. Fuming inside, he vowed to find a way to impose his will on his squad.

∞ CHAPTER 49 ∞

THE WARMING SUN HADN'T YET REACHED its noon zenith when the men left the pine woods and quick-marched down the hutment subdivision's dirt path toward their barracks. "Charge!" they shouted. Kenta stepped up the pace. "Remember Pearl Harbor!" he rang out. Sergeant Doi knew his lieutenant might congratulate him for bringing in his men with such a gung-ho spirit. But, once again, Kenta had taken over his squad, and with only three words: "Remember Pearl Harbor."

Doi might have excused his men's excitement as a natural consequence of their hope for weekend passes. Not all at once, mind you. *Wouldn't want to overwhelm the sensitive citizens of Hattiesburg with an invasion of four thousand young, horny Japanese men.* The commotion, or lack thereof, in front of the hutments told the story of the winners and the losers. Short Pants sprinted ahead upon spotting an envelope nailed to the door of their hutment and took it down.

"It's for you, Sergeant."

Doi approached Short Pants at a measured pace, took the envelope and opened it so carefully that one might think he hoped to reuse it. His face turned into a question mark as he read it to himself. At that point he became aware of his expectant squad.

"We've been ordered to report to the mess hall at 4:00 p.m. in fresh uniforms. Everyone, except for Private Karatsu."

"What about our passes?" asked Spud.

Doi waved the paper. "Nothing."

∞ ∞

When the squad arrived at the mess hall, they found that they weren't the only ones who had been summoned. A couple hundred men were taking seats facing the front.

"Atten … shun!" A haole sergeant, his short hair the color of nickel and his face lined with history, stood rigid on the one-foot-high wooden platform. Everyone rose, assuming the position. Colonel Pence sauntered across the stage, his body language telling the men to relax. His first words into the stand-up microphone soothed the khaki-clad audience.

"At ease, men, and—" A high-pitched screech tore out of the sound system, cutting off Pence's next few words. The soundman fiddled with the dials and then gave a hand signal to try again. The colonel tapped his fingers against the microphone. At the sound of the muffled pop, Pence resumed speaking.

"At ease, soldiers. Be seated." His eyes roamed the room, making fleeting contact with everyone. When the only sounds came from the soft whirling of the overhead fans, he began.

"You men have made me proud to be your commander. When you run, you don't drop out. When you tackle an obstacle course, you climb, you crawl, you slither … you do whatever it takes to get through in record time. The medics report the fewest visits from a unit this size in their memory. You came to prove your fitness to serve—and you have. Keep up the good work."

His face then grew stern and he added bite to his voice.

"However … my desk is littered with reports of fighting between Mainland soldiers and the soldiers from Hawaii. We are here to fight Germans, not each other." He paused and let his eyes scan the room again, slower this time, but with a more intense gaze. "Do you understand?"

The men responded with a resounding, "Yes, sir!"

Pence paused to let the men think about what he had just said. The rumble of a slow-moving truck could be heard outside the closed doors. When it stopped, Pence continued speaking, dialing his face to his good-news mode.

"You men have been selected for the regiment's 522nd Field Artillery Battalion." The noise blast of a cannon firing a blank shell shook the wooden building. Many of the men jumped. Shock morphed into a sheepish "you got me" expression as soon as the men could make the facial switch. A bugler blew the cavalry charge. Soldiers opened the doors where a smoking 105 mm howitzer greeted them.

"Go outside. Take a look," Pence ordered.

Kenta, sitting in the back, rushed out to reach the khaki-green-colored cannon first. He caressed the base of the barrel. The new wide-eyed 522nd soldiers circled the weapon, almost like one would do viewing a relic of an ancient saint's skull. Kenta walked under the tip of the barrel so he could see the three metal plates, all bolted together, shielding the lower front of the howitzer to provide bullet and shrapnel protection to the men behind the barrier. He knew enough about machinery to understand that the cast-iron metal trough under the barrel had plenty of extra length to handle recoil. He surmised that the three ten-inch steering wheels attached at different positions along the barrel handled the sighting. He dropped back and bumped into Short Pants.

"All those days at Schofield where we saw these things ..." said Kenta. "When we signed up for the infantry, it never occurred to me that I would be working with one of them."

"Back to your seats," barked the sergeant into the microphone. The sound of his command voice left little doubt that he meant right now.

On the platform, an officer stood beside Pence at the microphone. He equaled the colonel in height, but that's where the similarity ended. No one would call his back ramrod straight. His full face and not-quite-trim waist provided another hint that he, like most officers at the lieutenant colonel rank and below, had been a civilian on December 7, 1941. But it would be nondescript men like him who would win the war.

Pence introduced Lieutenant Colonel Baya Harrison, who, until recently, practiced law in Tampa, Florida. Harrison stepped up to the mic to make a speech in front of the largest audience he had ever faced.

"I'm a Florida cracker," he said in a drawl to the men of the 522nd who were puzzled by this term they had never heard before. "I can tell you a lot more about good Tampa cigars and refried beans than artillery shells. We have ourselves a mighty fine weapon here; in fact, we will soon have a dozen of those little monsters, making us the only regiment in the whole US army with our own artillery battalion.

"A 105 mm howitzer is so named because the diameter of the shell is a hundred and five millimeters, or just over four fat inches. In a pinch, you can send off ten rounds in a minute, and, with a range of up to seven miles, it can bust up a Panzer attack.

"This is a breech-loading weapon ... better than a muzzle-loading cannon where you just drop the ammo in the mouth of the tube and stand back. The 105 resembles a naval gun. You lift the shell knee-high and load it at the rear of the barrel, or the breech. Got it? Breech-loading.

"When muzzle-loading, you stand in front of the cannon where the enemy can shoot you. In breach-loading, you stand behind your weapon's metal plate. Breech-loading is quick. With a muzzleloader, you have to load the projectile and its separate charge into the top of the tube. With our 105, you just shove the projectile into the breech. As you step back, the gunner yanks a short cord called a 'lanyard,' which ignites the primer.

The primer then ignites the charge at the end of the rocket, sending it on its flight.

"This is an air-cooled cannon, but in rapid fire, I'd keep a bucket of water handy. The recoil is slowed down by a constant hydropneumatic shock absorber.

"Each of you has been assigned to either a gun battery consisting of four howitzers and one hundred and thirty men, a headquarters battery of a hundred and seventy men that chooses targets or a service battalion of eighty to keep the cannon stocked with ammo. We'll have a medical detachment of three doctors and thirteen medics. A ten-man officer corps will make up my leadership unit."

Harrison checked the three-by-five card in his hand. "Together we will learn to support our infantry. We are a motorized unit. A truck tows the howitzer. You will ride in flatbeds. On Monday, you will be taken to the firing range and see these babies in action. In the meantime, I am happy to issue my first order as your commander. Your sergeant is authorized to give everyone a weekend pass."

Garrison caps shot into the air like graduation at West Point. Doi collected the pass forms from the master sergeant. He then called out his men by name, signed their pass and handed it to them. When everyone but Kenta had his pass, Doi turned to the men.

"I need to talk to Private Takayama."

☞ Chapter 50 ☜

Kenta felt a snake crawling in his stomach but managed to show a row of perfect teeth. That pissed off Doi, whose own mangled teeth had been ignored by his penny-pinching parents.

"You joining us for a beer, Sarge?"

"Any beer that you will be drinking tonight will be right here, Private."

"What?! Nah, you can't do that! The colonel just ..."

"I can't do this?!" Doi straightened up. "*I can't* do this?!" His hands had bunched into fists.

Kenta stepped back and immediately regretted the retreat.

Doi gloated. He had just learned something about Kenta from the outburst: When challenged, the big-mouth Buddhahead backed away.

"Oh, I *can* do this. You should try listening as well as you speak. If you cleaned the shit from your ears, you would have heard Colonel Harrison say, 'Your sergeant is *authorized* to issue a pass.'"

Kenta inched forward and regained the space he had conceded. He assumed the at-ease posture with his hands behind his back and legs spread apart.

"Come on, that isn't fair. I've worked hard, performed well. You know what Harrison meant. Everyone from our new unit is going into town."

Doi wanted to end the confrontation, as nearly everyone in the room had cleared out. Pence and Harrison were on the stage talking with a tech sergeant who eyed Doi and Kenta. Doi smiled at Kenta—the type of smile that suggests there is a way out, but at a price.

"The wooden window shutters over my bed don't fit right. But I tell you what. You fix it and I'll leave a pass for you at HQ. You can pick it up when the window is fixed. But I'm warning you: If the shutters don't fit snug, you'll be cleaning latrines for so long you'll miss the smell when we ship out."

Doi made a flourish of printing "Kenta Takayama" in bold letters on a blank pass, then folded it and stuffed it in his shirt pocket. He snuck a peek at the tech sergeant, but he had turned away. Doi figured he'd covered his ass.

Short Pants had hung back at the mess hall entrance. "So, what did Doi want?"

Kenta raised his eyebrows and shrugged his shoulders, obviously perplexed. "He's up to his usual nasty self." Kenta explained the window assignment. "No big deal," he concluded. "You go ahead. I'll meet you later at the USO. It shouldn't take long."

Kenta knew exactly what was wrong with Doi's window shutter. The kotonk sergeants fucked up the hutment construction. Kenta and his squad had repaired their shoddy work.

They had inserted slivers of wood into the pine board gaps and caulked smaller apertures and rehinged the front door.

Doi hadn't helped with repairing the hutment, so the refurbishment gang passed over his window. They had only reset the latch so it would stop banging. The shutter should have fit snug into the windowsill, but the frame needed to be trimmed a quarter inch. Kenta would need a planer, a screwdriver and, to be on the safe side, a new set of hinges.

But it was already five o'clock and the maintenance and supply rooms were closed.

Had Doi known this? Had he set up Kenta to fail? Regardless, Kenta was determined to find a way to fix the window. He walked over to the nearest construction site, hoping his faith in the local crews' sloppy work habits would be rewarded. The foreman must have been one of the fussy ones—everything had been put away. Twenty minutes later, he hit pay dirt at the second site he visited. He found a toolbox snug against a lumber pile.

Within forty-five minutes, Kenta had removed the shutters from their hinges, measured, planed the edges and put them back up, perfectly snug. He adjusted the inside latch and cleaned up any mess.

Another shower, even a cold one, beckoned. Who knows? One of the USO girls just might take a liking to him. After slipping on an aloha shirt—word had gotten around that the boys in aloha shirts were generous tippers—he raced over to the 442nd headquarters, happily kicking a few pebbles along the way and humming "Boogie Woogie Bugle Boy."

By then, night had fallen. But at seven o'clock, even allowing for the bus ride to town, a full evening of revelry beckoned. He skipped up the stairs to the 442nd HQ and saluted the Nisei duty sergeant—he recognized him from the UH ROTC program. The sergeant had been a captain back then—he used Kenta and other freshman as marching fodder to practice giving drill orders. Kenta glanced at his badge to recall the name.

"Sergeant Kago, I'm Private Takayama, sir. I'm here to pick up my pass."

The sergeant's face registered a question mark. "Pass?"

"Yes sir, Sergeant Doi signed a pass and said he would leave it here for me to pick up after I completed an assignment." The snake slithered loose in Kenta's stomach.

"I haven't seen Sergeant Doi or anyone drop off a pass," said Kago. Seeing the anxiety on Kenta's face, Kago checked his desk and then asked two privates typing up reports if they knew anything. Lastly, he checked the tops of all the unoccupied desks. He turned to Kenta and shook his head. "Sorry, Private, nothing here."

Kenta's fists clenched.

"But he promised." He relaxed his hands and placed them on the edge of the sergeant's desk and leaned over. "Can you help me out here, sir, and give me the pass?" Kenta replayed the meeting with Doi.

As duty officer on a Friday evening, Kago listened patiently. After all, Kenta was a fellow soldier from Hawaii. Inevitably, though, he shook his head again, slower and sadder.

Kenta wanted to keep talking until the sergeant could see the injustice of the situation. He finally realized, however, that Kago could not, or would not, issue the pass. Doi had screwed him over. He thanked the sergeant and trudged over to the mess hall, just in case his worst fears had been misplaced. Maybe Doi was still eating dinner and just hadn't had time to drop by the HQ.

His spirits rose when he saw a sergeant from one of the nearby hutments in the cafeteria. He rushed over to the young man's table. "Sir, have you seen Sergeant Doi?" asked Kenta as the sergeant wiped his mouth with a paper napkin.

The sergeant dropped his napkin on his plate, which was covered with the scraps of a hamburger bun and a few skinny french fries lying in a smudge of catsup.

"Sure, he left here a half-hour ago to catch the bus to Hattiesburg. I'm meeting him at the Rainbow Club—some of the noncoms hang out there. Did you want me to tell him something?"

Kenta got the sergeant's message. The club did not welcome the lower ranks. He also got the stronger message: He had been fucked. A lightning kaleidoscope ripped across Kenta's brain. He saw himself in action, flipping the table, saying, "Yeah, I have a message. Tell Doi he's a fucking coward, a misfit, a ..."

The electric arc passed. He gritted his teeth.

"Nah, nothing. It can wait until Monday."

He turned around, wanting to board the bus and find the Rainbow Club. He wanted to call out Doi in front of his peers and thrash him. He could see it all: Doi would take a few swings. Kenta would play with him, deliver a few body shots with his fists and kick him in the thighs—enough to hurt him, but not enough to put him down. Doi would be in pain and want to quit, but with everyone watching, he would have to let the *kabuki* drama play itself out, one in which the audience knew the final act. When Doi could hardly stand and could not protect himself, Kenta would walk away, leaving Doi's lack of leadership exposed to all of the other sergeants.

The fantasy passed.

Kenta slumped out of the mess defeated. Without a pass, he could not leave the base. The security detail at the gates checked everyone.

What had he done wrong? He obeyed orders and never slacked. He accepted latrine duty and did the push-ups when Doi had a spur up his ass. Kenta started walking to the PX to buy a case of beer and take it back to the hutment to drink while reading John Kennedy's book, *Why England Slept*.

The combination would put him to sleep. Then, he saw his salvation. This time, the flash of fantasy could be acted upon.

"Bobby! Hey Bobby!" Kenta called out to the newspaper boy hawking papers from his bike inside the camp.

Bobby rode over and pulled out a *Hattiesburg American.*

"You want a paper? Friday's edition lists all the clubs." Then he lowered his voice. "I'll give you the names of a couple clubs that don't advertise," he said with a wink.

For a boy of fourteen, this kid has a lot of street smarts, thought Kenta— and that worked well for the plan that had just popped into his head.

"What I want, Bobby, is your bike."

He pulled out a George Washington and explained. Bobby nodded, and then gave him an even better idea.

∞ CHAPTER 51 ∞

Camp Shelby's immense size—nearly 135,000 acres—and its lack of a security threat made it a virtual undefended border. Perfect for his plan, strategized Kenta.

With Bobby perched on the handlebars, Kenta pumped away on the teen's bicycle. When they reached the nearest bus stop inside the gate, Bobby jumped off and Kenta continued on, turning right into an access road parallel to the fence. After pedaling for what he guessed was about two miles, he glanced back to see the lights of the last tent city fade into a yellow glow. He had bought six copies of the *Hattiesburg American* from Bobby to lay over the barbed wire and either crawl over or between the strands.

To add a bit of combat fantasy to the scheme, Kenta imagined himself on a mission to infiltrate German lines, knowing he had to rely only on guts and ingenuity to complete the operation. As it turned out, all that separated him from freedom—other than his naïve underplaying of the consequences of getting caught—was a four-foot-high chain-link fence. *What can they do—give me lifetime latrine duty?* he laughed to himself.

Kenta had planned to ride the bike into town and then leave it for Bobby at the newspaper office. But Bobby, ever the entrepreneur, suggested that for another dollar he would flag an incoming taxi and hold it outside the gate at the Camp Shelby pick-up zone.

∞ ∞

Forty-five minutes later, the taxi dropped Kenta at the Front Street USO. He swaggered into the building like Gary Cooper playing Sergeant York, the famed hard-drinking World War I hero and Medal of Honor awardee. Friday-night "just got paid" GIs jammed the converted warehouse. The colored band was slamming "That Old Black Magic" to a jitterbug beat. Smells of beer, sweat and the USO gals' generous applications of perfume drifted like waves, ebbing and flowing with the movement of overhead fans and countless bodies in motion. Nearly all of the fifty or so USO hostesses were dancing. Kenta knew they tried to dance and chat with ten times that number of lonely GIs, so he knew he would get his shot.

He wandered around the haoles for a while. It didn't take long for his confidence to melt away as he pretended to not notice the stares, not all of them friendly. There were a few Asian faces in the place, but none that he knew. Had his guys given up on him joining them? As he started to walk out, he spotted a Hawaiian-print shirt—and then a half-dozen Hawaiian-print shirts—behind the bandstand. He slung his shoulders back and reset his swagger.

"Hey, you pineapple bumpkins," he said. Kenta nodded at the beer in Chuckles's hand. "You guys drinking by yourself? I made the mistake of thinking you losers would be on the dance floor."

"OK smart-ass, now that you've sucked up to Doi by fixing his window, why don't *you* ask one of those haole girls to dance?"

Kenta swiveled his hips twice, hula style. "Watch me, Short Pants. Take notes."

He strutted toward one of the few haole girls without a dance partner. He had taken only a few steps when a panic attack mugged his bluster. If not for his boasting, he would have walked right past the girl and gone to the bar for a slug of courage. He didn't need eyes in the back of his head to know that his squad was watching his every move. He approached the plain-Jane dishwater blonde girl, careful not to get too close. She gave no indication that she had even noticed his presence. Aware of his skeptical beer-guzzling audience, Kenta radiated his cocky smile.

"Hi, my name is Kenta. I'm from Hawaii." He nodded toward the gy-rating dancers. "We have an Island version of the jitterbug. Want to try it?" He offered his hand to take her to the crowded dance floor.

She considered him coldly, as if he were a menu and she wasn't impressed with the dishes being offered. "I'm resting at the moment," she replied in a clearly bothered voice and turned her back on him.

Kenta tried his luck with another girl. Netting the same result, he slinked back to his buddies.

Less than a minute later, both girls were on the dance floor. A group of GIs standing at the bar gave Kenta's group the stink-eye.

"Let's get outta this place and catch some action at the railroad bars," Buster suggested.

At that moment, Kenta spotted a girl standing alone, leaning against a pillar. Her long dark hair fell over her shoulders almost in a Japanese way. Her slim figure resembled that of a silhouette. When she caught his stare, she dropped her eyes demurely, again, more like a shy Japanese girl than an American one.

Men see what they want to see. Kenta approached fantasia. She stiffened but managed a faint smile. He heard sincerity in her words.

"I'm sorry. I really ... I just can't." She felt the eyes of the haole group at the bar openly staring at her and Kenta. Rather than be put off by the rejection, a rejection not of the girl's own making, Kenta concluded that this gentle girl *really* wanted to dance, but the stares of those goons were intimidating her. Well, fuck that.

He reached out his hand. "Let's just finish the dance," he said.

Bad timing.

Just then, the band switched to the Rodgers and Hammerstein cheek-to-cheek dance from *Oklahoma*, "People Will Say We're in Love." It didn't matter that the guys and gals rarely touched cheeks at these well-chaperoned USO dances. Slow dances gave the couple a chance to actually talk to each other, which was impossible to do during the upbeat numbers. The girls focused on giving as many young men as possible a chance to chat with them. When the young USO girls ran into a soldier with more problems than they could handle, they passed him off to the older matrons. These kind women listened to and often counseled the young GIs who needed to cry their heart out over a "Dear John" letter, or just to talk about their deep loneliness at being away from home, often for the first time.

The girl talking to Kenta held up her hand and softly placed it on his chest, almost like a caress, but definitely to put the brakes on Kenta's advance. She murmured a plaintive, "I'm sorry." The girl's innocent gesture gave the pretext that the beer-guzzling white boys at the bar had been waiting for—a chance to defend a white woman's inviolate Southern decency from a stinking Jap.

Chests out, the defenders of white women's honor marched into what promised to be a wonderful donnybrook.

Patrons cleared a pathway.

At that moment, Kenta, totally smitten, would not have noticed the *Titanic* sinking. He peered into the girl's pleading green eyes and uttered a strained, "I understand."

With fists clenched and eyes radiating "let's beef," Kenta's squad strode toward the haole "saviors."

The USO was no stranger to fights. Seeing the converging combatants, two burly MPs blew their whistles and shoved their way through the crowd. Gawking drinkers, talkers and dancers parted like the Red Sea, giving the charging warriors an arena to settle their differences.

The commotion jerked away Kenta's attention in time to see the haoles closing in from just ten feet away. Kenta prepared himself, knowing he would get in the first blow with his legs. Then, as suddenly as he prepared to fight, he bowed to the girl.

"I'm sorry to have bothered you." He turned to face the angry men, arms bent at the elbow, palms facing outward, giving the universal "take it easy" gesture. "My mistake, guys. Don't worry, we're leaving."

Confused and disappointed, the approaching men stopped, just in time for the MPs to step between the antagonists.

Kenta backed over to his squad. "Let's go."

Short Pants tugged on Kenta's arm.

"Why'd you back down? We were right behind you." A look of disgust and confusion filled his face. "I thought you were the 'I ain't taking no more shit' guy."

Kenta bent over and whispered in Short Pants's ear. "I'm AWOL. Let's get outta here."

Back on Front Street, lined with ivory magnolia blossoms radiating a spicy-sweet bouquet, Kenta explained the consequences of being caught and reported AWOL by the MPs.

When Kenta started to repeat himself, Chuckles cut him off with a wave of his arms.

"OK, OK, we get it. But I came to party. If the haoles don't want us here, let's walk across the railroad tracks to the colored USO. It's on Sixth Street."

"How do you know?" asked Little Caesar.

"Remember that colored pilot visiting from Tuskegee that I told you about? The one who asked me to buy him a six-pack because he couldn't go into the Sixty-Ninth PX? He told me they have great parties at their USO."

Fats tilted his head right and raised his eyebrows. Pursing his lips, he queried, "So, he invited us?"

"Well, not like that. Not straight out. More in like a Japanese way. I mean, why would he tell me what a great party they have if he didn't want us to come?"

No Ticket twisted his face. "You know what they've been telling us. We are 'honorary whites.' Don't drink out of the colored water fountain; don't sit in the colored theater section, don't …"

"Oh, is that right?!" challenged Little Caesar, anger sweeping over his face. "How come one of the kotonks got yanked out of the line at the movie theater last week by a cop yelling, 'You're colored! Go where you belong!'?"

"That's a mistake," said Kenta. "I heard later that the movie theater manager explained to the cop …"

"*Fuck!*" shouted Chuckles.

Everyone froze and gawked open-mouthed at Chuckles.

"Fuck! Are you guys going to debate all night or party?" Chuckles paused three seconds for effect. "If we're honorary whites, those girls would have danced with us. I'm going over to the colored USO."

All eyes turned to Kenta, who let out a sigh of resignation.

"OK, let's go."

With that, Chuckles led the charge down Front Street, which was crowded with boisterous soldiers that had changed the town.

Staid storefronts were dressed up with patriotic red, white and blue bunting. Retail shops offered payday loans, and dress shops had been converted into hamburger and beer joints. Beauty parlors promoted perms *and* tattoo artists.

Everything changed at the railroad tracks—it was like a border where a man's color was his passport. The coloreds who crossed from their own side approached the border sauntering and laughing. But as soon as they crossed the tracks, they switched their gait to a shuffle and kept their heads down, their appearance and mood transforming as seamlessly as a chameleon changing colors.

The noise from the brothels wafted as the Hawaii boys ambled across the railroad tracks.

"*That's* where we should be going," said Short Pants, pointing to a row of houses parallel with the tracks a quarter mile down the road.

"Maybe later," said Chuckles. "Right now, I'm a-keepin' to the mission."

No one else responded to Short Pants's effort to move the excursion to the whorehouses. None of them had ever visited one. Embarrassment overrode desire, albeit by the slimmest of margins. Six weeks ago, these young men steeped in the tradition of respecting women were eating their *sayonara* meals with their mothers and sisters and promising to stay out of trouble.

The boys in aloha shirts heard the jazz music before they even saw the USO building.

Chuckles felt his gut churn with apprehension, like a gerbil spinning in a cage. But he forced himself to keep walking at a sauntering pace. *What am I doing here? Am I breaking some rule with a bad outcome in the making? Like, what's the fuss about us Japanese staying away from the coloreds? We both know something about being at the bottom of the social pile.*

The gerbil-spinning turned erratic when Chuckles spotted a group of colored GIs standing outside their USO. Their easy chatter ceased as they stared at him and his mates.

Chuckles slowed and then hesitated.

Kenta walked up beside him and gave him a reassuring grin.

"I wouldn't worry, Chuckles. They probably think we're from the Ku Klux Klan, hunting for someone to hang."

Behind them, Little Caesar added, "Sure, other than getting kicked out of the MIS while the print on the transfer papers is still wet, what's to worry?"

"What's this about the MIS?" asked Chuckles.

"This is my last night with you guys. Pence told me I'm being transferred to military intelligence since I speak fluent Japanese."

"Hell, for sure we gotta get you laid," said Chuckles.

"More like you're gonna get us killed," said Little Caesar, nodding ahead to the colored group standing in front of the USO.

"Let's just keep smiling," said Kenta.

Suddenly, Chuckles threw a fist in the air.

"Jonesy!"

The tallest of the Negro GIs peered down the street.

"Hey, Six-Pack! You've come to the right place!"

The stares along the USO's sidewalk turned from suspicious to curious. Broad, white teeth gleamed in the flare of light shafting from the building's entrance. Copper, brown and black hands exchanged handshakes. Lieutenant Roscoe Jones gripped longer and squeezed a welcome on the men's shoulders with his other hand. As if on cue, the band played Billie Holiday's "God Bless the Child."

As Jones grabbed Chuckles's shoulder, his eyes surveyed the group like a preacher on Sunday.

"You Jap boys are welcome here. We all need to stick together."

"Japanese, not Japs," challenged Kenta, his fists clenched and stomach muscles taut.

The band's vocalist tormented the night with her sweetly melancholic notes. Jones turned to Kenta and let out a lamentable laugh. He brought his head low to peer at Kenta, eyeball-to-eyeball.

"Us niggers welcome you Japanese boys. Whatever we call ourselves, whatever they call us, we sure know the white man don't want to share what they got with no one else."

Two colored USO hostesses pranced outside.

"Hey, fellas, whatcha doin' out …"

Mouths fell open as they spotted the Hawaii boys. Then the one with the caramel complexion put her hands on her hips.

"Lordy, lordy. Where you boys get them colorful shirts?"

Chuckles took in the friendly faces. This is the way it's supposed to work. The gals come to us.

"If you all allow us to buy a round of beers …" Chuckles glanced at the men outside to make sure they knew he meant *everyone*. "… I'll tell you where."

Halfway through their beers and well into the Chuckles-Kenta tag-team stories about aloha shirts, endless summers of surfing and fish that practically jump into boats, the band broke into Duke Ellington's "It Don't Mean a Thing (If It Ain't Got That Swing)."

The stouter girl with midnight black skin and wearing the dress of a temptress, broke into the boys' story. "Do they do the jitterbug where y'all come from?"

"Do they ever!" shouted Spud, grabbing her hand. He let her lead him to the dance floor.

Chuckles bowed low and twirled an extended hand at the tall girl, just like an English knight. He followed her to the dance floor.

The beer and the joy of being accepted did their magic: The boys put on a show. Other girls came over. Soon, all the Hawaii boys were dancing. They stayed on the floor for "Pistol Packin' Mama" and thanked the girls, knowing it was bad manners to monopolize them. The band slowed the pace to Ellington's "In a Sentimental Mood."

The sound of approaching sirens was largely ignored by the Hawaii boys. In the few hours they had spent in Hattiesburg, sirens, raucous GIs, music, taunts, crowds egging on fights were but background hubbub exalting the good times of a weekend pass. They noticed the sudden change in facial expressions and the jerk of fearful heads toward the entrance, as if a thirsty vampire had winged in to choose a neck. Dracula would have been more welcome.

∽ CHAPTER 52 ∾

FOUR POLICEMEN DRESSED IN KHAKI UNIFORMS pushed through the swinging double doors; two held snarling dogs on short leashes.

The band stopped playing. The colored MPs retreated to the back of the room.

The heftiest cop, his intimidating gut straining his shirt's buttonholes, stepped ahead of his companions. He eyed the room like a viper sensing prey and then settled on the confused eyes of the Nisei. He pointed his nightstick at them.

Chief Jack Ditmar spoke slowly and conversationally, confident that no sound would compete with his voice.

"You Jap boys know you don't belong here. Come along now and don't make a fuss. We'll escort you to the white side of town."

Fresh sirens wailed. At least one, maybe two cars, screeched to a halt. Car doors slammed and four more sets of boots came stomping in.

No one spoke or moved.

Kenta's short temper pushed aside his AWOL status and common sense. He stepped forward, addressing the burly uniform in a fractious tone. "Did you forget something, sir?"

The chief relished smart-ass challenges to his authority. It was a chance for a little "entertainment." He smiled like a hangman who enjoyed pulling the rope. All eyes focused on the developing drama. Raucous sounds wafted from the other side of the tracks. Smells of perfume, sweat and fear hovered.

"And just what might that be, son?" asked the chief.

Kenta regretted his rush to dangerous humor. He could've ended it right then by saying, "I'm sorry. Nothing, sir." But compulsion overcame prudence. "Your swastika. You forgot your swastika."

Ditmar let his face slide into an indulgent smile that did not match his cold, malevolent gray eyes and ambled over to Kenta. The chief's neck and shoulders showed no tension. One hand rested easy on his nightstick, the other hung loose on his side.

"That's just the kind of thinkin' we expect from a Jap. I could arrest you for disturbin' the peace, insultin' a police officer and violatin' city ordinances on racial mixin'. But I'm not gonna do that, 'cause I am a man who likes to give a troublemaker a second chance." He stopped talking and turned around. Seemingly pleased with the positioning of the dogs and his officers, he addressed the tall, lanky one. "Ain't that right, Earl?"

The only skinny cop in the group broke into a nasty smile, matching his boss.

"Captain Jack, sometimes I think you show too much compassion to the riffraff. But I admit you do one thang right."

Police Chief Jack Ditmar raised his eyes and stood a little taller. "Remind me, Earl."

Earl scratched his groin. "You always be sparin' the judge of the nuisance of gettin' out of bed for night court. You always say, 'Instant justice is the best justice.'"

Ditmar nodded, as if reminded of a truth of biblical proportions. "Why yes, Earl, I do believe I have been known to say that." He turned to Kenta and smiled as broadly as he could without showing his teeth.

The dogs growled low and strained their leashes.

The night truncheon came out so fast that Kenta had no time to respond. The cop jabbed it deep into Kenta's gut. He fell forward, giving the police chief a chance to whack his back twice before he hit the floor.

A cultured voice rang out.

"You can't strike an American soldier." Lieutenant Jones stepped forward. "I am a lieutenant in the Air Force, and I will be reporting this."

Ditmar lived for confrontations like this—just him and a small group of police officers staring down a crowd of niggers. He could hardly wait to regale one of the town whores with the story. His one-eyed snake hardened in anticipation.

"My, my. A smooooooth-talkin' coon. I bet you even graduated from a u-ni-ver-sit-ee, you be readin' and writin' so good. You must be one of them Tuskegee flyboys. I just imagine Hitler's about ready to surrender now that he knows we be lettin' niggers fly airplanes."

Jones stepped closer, his long jaw jutting out. "I don't have to …"

"Boy … if you want trouble, you've come to the right place. Earl, give them dogs a little more leash."

Both German Shepherds were brought to their hind legs as officers twirled their wrists to let out the leash a dramatic yard. The dogs lurched forward, testing the arm strength of their handlers, one almost breaking loose.

Women shrieked. The room scattered.

Jones jerked back, his fifteen seconds of defiance over.

Pleased with the show of mass cowardice, Ditmar slithered his eyes to the reception booth where an older Negro woman sat with her hair wrapped in a yellow bandana. Her ample body was draped in an oft-washed purple dress with a white gardenia print. The woman's violet-painted lips quivered under the scrutiny.

"Miss Beatrice," addressed Ditmar, "I'm a mite disappointed. We let you open this place to cater to the colored boys in uniform. Yes, I'm disappointed you be a-breakin' the law, lettin' these Jap boys in here, especially with me hirin' your daughter to cater food to the city prison."

The woman rose—she was even bigger than the captain. "Yessuh, Captain Jack. I make a plenty-big mistake. No more Jap boys in here."

The captain ambled over to the woman and leaned forward, his mouth almost kissing her ear. He grunted softly.

"How about you tell your daughter to be bringin' a sandwich by my office around midnight?" He pulled back, giving her a knowing grin. "We understand each other?"

The woman's loud, trembling voice filled the room. "Yessuh, Captain. I sure don't want to break any laws."

Ditmar pointed his nightstick at Jones.

"Make sure you don't go over the speed limit, y'hear?" He didn't wait for an answer, turning his gaze instead to the Nisei. "You boys follow me." He slow-pivoted and sauntered out like he owned the joint, which, in a way, he did.

Short Pants extended an arm to Kenta and helped him up from the floor. He whispered hoarsely, "You forget you're AWOL?!"

Kenta did not acknowledge the rebuke. He kept his head up and his back stiff. His shuffle behind the strutting cops reminded the crowed of who had won.

Outside, Ditmar reached into his shirt pocket and pulled out a hand-sized notebook, the kind housewives take to the supermarket with their grocery list. He thumbed the worn edges of the blue cover until he found an empty page.

Kenta stifled his urge to comment, "Since your little book is almost full, ever think of thumbing from the back?"

Ditmar took out a nub of a pencil and licked the lead tip. "Now what I need is your names and units. Here's what I'm gonna to do, me bein' a compassionate man and all. I'm gonna report you to your Colonel Pence."

Kenta's eyes widened.

Ditmar picked up on it. "Of course, we know who you boys belong to. Why do you think we have half the police department workin' tonight? First night they let you Jap boys out in the town is sure to cause trouble."

Ditmar enjoyed watching the strain on the boys' faces and knowing his police force saw how he could control a situation.

"I'm goin' to report that a bunch of his … *nee-says* … crashed the colored USO." He smiled, mimicking a grandfatherly countenance, and then twisted his face in triumph. "Against his orders!" He let that sink in, watching them squirm. "But," he said, waving his little book, "I am not goin' to give him any *names*. No sireee. This here is my first offender's book. No one in this book wants to be stopped a second time. Do we understand each other?"

The Nisei heads moved up and down. Faces relaxed, none more so than Kenta's.

Ditmar focused on Kenta. "OK, big shot, you first."

Once he completed the name-taking, Ditmar ordered the boys into three of the patrol cars and instructed his deputies to follow him in his lead vehicle. He ordered the dog handlers back to the station. Ditmar then draped a fleshy arm around Kenta's shoulders.

"You're ridin' with me." The chief got into the backseat with Kenta and nodded his head from the back window at Chuckles, hovering nearby. "You … ride in front with Earl." He tapped Earl on the shoulder. "I think we need to show these boys where they can have a good time without causin' a disturbance."

"You mean …"

"Don't go dense on me, Earl. Of course, that's what I mean."

In the back seat, Ditmar's arm once again found Kenta's right shoulder, his meaty fingers pinching the muscle tissue. He noted that the kid didn't wince. A good sign, he thought.

"You're Ken."

"Almost, sir. Kenta."

"You boys are all Americans, right?"

"Yes, sir."

The chief relaxed the pressure. "Then you are right familiar with nick-names. So, it's Ken. Now, Ken, I am appointin' you one of my ambassadors. You know what an ambassador is, doncha?"

Kenta twitched the aggravated muscle. "Yes, sir. Like a representative from one country to another, but I think you want someone to represent you."

"I knew that under that smart-ass temper, there just might lie a brain. You see, Ken, we got colored folks and white folks. Everybody knows their place; everybody gets along. Once in a while, an agitator comes a-callin', tryin' to stir thangs up. We deal with that. But you Hawaii boys … you don't quite fit, do you?"

"We are Americans, sir."

The chief dug his fingers deep and squeezed the muscle near Kenta's neck.

The suddenness of it caused Kenta to flinch.

Ditmar's tone turned rough. "I said you were smart. Now don't go and disappoint me. You get to talkin' to these colored folks and get them all riled up. Then you know what happens?"

Ditmar did not wait for an answer. His voice rose. "We have to come down hard." He twisted Kenta's neck even harder, ignored Kenta's yelp and twisted it again.

"Maybe next year, you'll be in North Africa shootin' Krauts. But we still got some of our colored folks all hot and bothered and we have to take …"—another twist—"… strong measures to put thangs right. You hear what I am sayin'?"

"Yes, sir."

Ditmar loosened his grip on Kenta's shoulder. "It's good that you do. Now you tell the other boys. You don't want to be responsible for people like that nice lady Miss Beatrice fallin' onto bad times now, do you?"

Kenta remained silent until the chief slowly raised his arm.

"No, sir."

By then, Earl had crossed the rail tracks. Instead of turning left toward the railroad station and downtown, he swung right.

The chief pulled out a cigar from his shirt pocket. His words turned friendly. "Well, now that that's settled, you keep an eye on those houses ahead."

∞ Chapter 53 ∞

Kenta spotted the blinking lights maybe a quarter mile down the road. The parade of cop cars passed warehouses and the railyard. The acrid smell of coal filled the air, prompting a sneeze from Kenta. The car slowed as it neared a patch of two-story houses framed with Christmas tree lights.

The chief took the wrapping off of his cigar. "We've got some fine girls here, most from Jackson or Mobile, but a few from as far away as Atlanta. I passed the word. You will be welcome."

Earl stopped the car at the third house. The chief reached back into his shirt pocket, wiggled his fingers and pulled out a matchbox. "Earl, wait a spell while I introduce Ken and his boys to Miss Lillian Delight."

The chief, Kenta and Chuckles got out of the car. Behind them, the opening and closing of the deputies' patrol cars disrupted the Dixieland jazz sounds coming from the antebellum home. Ditmar lit his cigar and then noticed the hesitation on Kenta's face. His voice hardened.

"You're not a puff, are you?"

"No, sir, it's just that …"

The chief laughed, grinned at his deputies and boomed, "We got ourselves a cherry!" He took a deep draw on his cigar and then pointed it at his deputies. "You boys run along and patrol downtown."

Like a pudgy pied piper, the chief led his army of aloha shirts up the wooden stairs to the veranda, forlornly populated with a mismatched assortment of empty wicker love seats. Kenta paused on the top step to read a hanging sign illuminated by the red ceiling light: "The one-eyed snake never sleeps here."

A pianist had started banging out "Deep in the Heart of Texas" to the accompaniment of an off-key inebriated chorus.

Several soldiers brushed past the Hawaii boys on their way out after the girls clad in pink had given each of them a peck on the cheek. "Y'all hurry back now," they called out.

Kenta, whose hesitation with the chief had been induced by thoughts of Angelina, grew hard.

Chuckles put the excursion into perspective. "All those as hard as a *daikon*, forward march."

Cheap perfume permeated the air. Ditmar tipped his hat at the stout, middle-aged woman dominating the center of the room. She could have been five years on either side of forty.

"Good lord, Chief, did we lose the war?"

The chief roared laughing. The Nisei squad behind him had to smile. They'd heard the slur before, but never so good-naturedly from a woman with such voluptuous breasts that were so generously displayed.

Kenta's eyes scanned the room, like Alice coming out of the chute into Wonderland. The ample woman wore a hot pink, sequined dress that kissed her hot pink heels. Pink was everywhere—a pink Kama Sutra tapestry hung on the chartreuse-and-pink walls, and a fresco of naked mermaids swam on the salmon-hued ceiling. Blush-colored upholstery covered the sofas and chairs and a pink veneer covered whatever color the furniture might originally have been. Even the piano and its colored pianist with white hair were dressed in the shade of a rosé wine. He wore a pink tuxedo. Although the working girls' dresses varied in erotic design, all had been cut from the same bolt of hot-pink fabric.

The chief's ever-changing demeanor had moved into the realm of geniality. "Boys, this here is Miss Lillian Delight."

The woman's lips, caked with hot-pink lipstick, opened wide. "Oh, you fine-lookin' boys. Welcome to the Pink Palace."

One of the girls handed the chief a tumbler of whiskey.

"Thank you, sweetheart." He swallowed the double shot in one gulp and then sent a knowing glance Lillian's way.

"Well, I best be about the people's business. Maybe I'll come by for lunch tomorrow," he said with a wink and then turned to Kenta. "You boys'll be right fine. See you don't cause no trouble, y'hear?"

He left to a chorus of "Yes, sirs."

Lillian placed her hands on her hips and pushed out her chest. "You hula dancers ever drink pink champagne?"

The expression on the boys' faces suggested that she might as well have asked if any of them had been to the moon recently.

Lillian sighed in feigned exasperation. "So many firsts for you boys. Come on, then. Pony up to the bar." She signaled at the curvaceous redhead behind the bar adorned in a pink frock with a plunging neckline, so plunging that her nipples peeked over the edge of her dress like a second set of eyes. "Sadie, pour these boys a flute of bubbly." Pink, of course.

While Lillian had been performing, her stable of young hopefuls were sidling up to the boys. Each grabbed a hand and led her guy to the bar.

"That drink will cost each of you boys a buck," said Lillian. She waited for the astonished faces. *Got 'em*, she thought, smirking. "And along with that first drink at the Pink Palace, the young lady will take you upstairs for ten minutes of her time."

"Let's not waste any time at the bar," said Chuckles, guzzling his champagne. He banged his glass on the wooden bar—pink, of course—and squeezed his girl's hand. "Lead on, angel!"

Except for Short Pants and Kenta, the boys pranced upstairs. Kenta nursed his drink while his dick debated with his feelings of guilt.

Short Pants grinned. "Kenta, it's going to be a long war. She doesn't really expect you to be a choir boy."

The girl holding Kenta's hand let her fingers glide over the urgent part of the debate. Kenta finished his drink and half-turned to her. "Let's go," he said weakly, surrendering to his dick in the argument. Having assuaged his pal's weakening guilt, Short Pants, with his "date" in tow, followed a few steps behind, making sure Kenta did not have any second thoughts and turn around.

If Kenta's girl had given him her name, he had already forgotten it. He really didn't want to know it. He wished he could tell her that he had a girlfriend, a wonderful girl, that he loved. He started mumbling something about a girl in Hawaii as they entered a room, which was more like a cubicle, and pink, of course. The working girl murmured "Mmmmm" and "Nnn hah," all the while undressing him, methodically using one hand when possible and stroking him with the other. When she put the condom on him with her mouth, Kenta almost exploded. She led him over to her bed, covered with a pink sheet, laid him prone, and mounted him while placing his hands on her apple-sized breasts. It was all over in a few jerky thrusts of their hips.

"Relax, sweetheart. Stay put," said the girl, giving him a wicked smile. "We still have nine and a half of our ten minutes."

Kenta's dick, still hard, but not so needy now, returned to the debate. This time, though, his guilt-sodden brain took charge. He rolled over, almost throwing the girl off of the bed.

"I'm sorry. I can't ..."

His eyes glanced around the room and saw what he needed. He tiptoed over to the pink floral waste can and threw up in it. He gave the girl a one-dollar tip, hastily put on his clothes and rushed downstairs to the bar. He bought his first whiskey to wash away the bitter aftertaste. He owed Angelina a letter, but how could he write her after what he had just done? He finished his shot of whiskey and ordered a second.

He didn't notice the slim girl slide onto the bar stool next to him until he felt her hand. He turned to brush it aside and send her away—until he found himself staring at the most beautiful girl he had ever seen. She had lustrous black hair, straight bangs to her eyebrows and silky tresses covering her ears and innocent face. Her satiny hair draped low on her back—a style out of fashion and all the more dramatic for it.

"Tell me about Hawaii," she said with a throaty voice.

Kenta muttered something about surfing and palm trees while the girl's fingers brushed ever so gently over his thighs. It was more casual stroking than a rough sex grab. Her other hand massaged the back of his neck. She leaned into him. "I'm Natasha," she whispered. "And you are very cute." She moved both hands, one closer to his groin without touching and the other combing the back of his head with her fingers.

"The second time is so much better. I like it slow, very slow." She grabbed his hand and rose to walk upstairs.

Kenta's brain maintained control. "I can't," his puppy-dog eyes begged.

Most working girls would have accepted the rebuff and butterflied to the next john. Natasha turned the fewest tricks yet earned the most money in Miss Lillian's stable. The other girls could not figure out how she did it, even as she told them her secret.

"Fuck with their minds, become the fantasy girl next door and don't peek at the clock."

Natasha let Kenta's hand drop and sat back down. "Tell me about her."

Kenta spilled his heart out, surprising himself as he described the first time he and Angelina had made love. All the time, Natasha caressed the back of his neck, tussled his hair and rested a chaste hand on his knee.

Lillian had learned to give Natasha up to ten minutes chat time, understanding the dividend that would be earned later. But now she walked over. "You have a visitor."

Natasha whispered in Kenta's ear. "Write your letter. Trust me, women in war know their men give in to loneliness. They don't want you to tell them who and where, but they understand. Don't waste guilt on what doesn't harm anyone." She touched the side of his face. "Remember me, I'm Natasha," she said, a hint of forlorn in her throaty voice and then floated away.

Kenta's eyes followed her as she crossed the room to greet her visitor, regretting that he hadn't seen her earlier when it mattered. He suddenly realized that his entire squad had returned to the room.

Chuckles pointed to the door. Kenta nodded and jumped up from the stool.

Miss Lillian saw them out. "You big-spendin' stallions welcome to come back anytime."

A jeep rolled to a stop in front of the Pink Palace. Four sergeants, all white, jumped out. Kenta's group stopped and stared, their mouths wide open.

"Oh shit," said Chuckles. "It's him."

The tall sergeant with pock marks on his face hitched his pants and sneered at the Nisei group. He turned to his mates. "It's our lucky night, boys. These girls hardly had to work with these short-dick Jap boys."

Far fewer insults had ignited many a fight. Kenta's squad, knowing his AWOL status, kept walking down the road. The other sergeants, more interested in screwing than brawling, walked up the steps. One called out, "Hey, Crockett, let it go."

"Private Takayama!" shouted Sergeant Crockett.

Kenta slowed, but resisted the urge to turn around. With Short Pants tugging on his flapping shirt, he resumed their normal pace.

"This is not the end," shouted Crockett. "There will be a time when it's just you and me." Crockett showed Kenta's back the finger and walked into the Pink Palace.

∞ ∞

The small group of alcohol-buzzed soldiers, newly pussy-whipped and deprived of sleep, nodded at a honking vehicle and jammed into that single taxi.

"To the USO," ordered Kenta.

"You gotta be kidding me," said Chuckles. "I don't remember the warm welcome."

"We're not going to dance," fired back Kenta. "Where else can we crash for the night?"

The new initiates in the art of late-night carousing straggled into the USO. Nearly a hundred other GIs lay sprawled on mattresses scattered on the pinewood floor. An enterprising group of young women offered laundry service—two bits would get a GI a pair of pajamas for the night and their freshly cleaned clothes delivered in the morning.

After handing over their clothes, the boys collapsed onto the closest vacant mattress. Tonight, they had conquered the railroad houses. Tomorrow: Hattiesburg.

∞ CHAPTER 54 ∞

June 6, 1943

KENTA'S BLADDER WOKE HIM BEFORE DAWN. Lights—harsh lights—hung from the ceiling. Outside the windows, city street lanterns radiated amber halos. Silverware and cups and saucers clinked, foretelling coffee and doughnuts. The room stank of stale beer and jockstrap sweat. Kenta credited Lillian's generous snack trays for the taiko drummers in his head pounding at half-strength.

He picked up his freshly laundered clothes sitting on two, long folding tables next to the coffee and doughnut counter, then followed the arrows on the floor down a hall to the shower. Fear outweighed his fleeting thoughts of guilt over his thirty-second liaison the night before. First anger, and then alcohol, had numbed his brain to the consequences of being AWOL. Standing under his first hot shower since arriving in Mississippi, he realized how lucky he had been. No way would he press his luck with a day in town. He would be on the first bus back to Camp Shelby: You needed a pass to get out, not to get in.

Kenta returned from the shower to find Short Pants munching on a jelly-filled doughnut. Specks of powdered sugar dotted his chin. Short Pants growled, "My headache is growing, and after the Pink Palace raid on my wallet, my funds are shrinking."

Kenta grabbed a glazed doughnut, took a big bite, and began speaking with his mouth half-full. "Get your sorry ass in gear. We're lucky. The first bus of the day, mostly for locals working on-base, will be here in less than five minutes."

Once on the bus, Kenta and Short Pants found empty seats up front, but standing room only in the back, suggesting the bus must have started its route on the colored side of town. They took seats in the front row, near the driver, who did not seem pleased to see brown faces with funny eyes sitting so close to the front. At each subsequent stop, they watched the Mississippi version of a kabuki play, as mostly white riders boarded the bus. Three stops later, there were no more empty seats.

On the outskirts of town, neighborhoods once again reflected a change from white to colored residents living in hamlets on the road to Camp Shelby. When the bus stopped, all the whites standing got off and stepped aside. They waited for the few colored riders to disembark. Then the Negroes waiting at the bus stop got on, followed by the whites who had disembarked earlier. No one spoke, not even among themselves, and neither group ever acknowledged the other with eye contact.

Kenta's neck muscles tightened. His headache worsened as the dance of injustice played out in front of him. At least the Jim Crow antics diverted his attention from worrying about his own precarious position.

Until he saw a sign: "Rainbow Club."

Three white soldiers were waving down the bus under the blinking neon sign. *Shit, isn't that where the sergeant said Doi would be hanging out?* The snake in Kenta's stomach thumped. He instinctively reached for his missing cap left at the USO—to pull down to his eyes. The bus stopped. Kenta bent down to pick up an imaginary gum wrapper when the soldiers stepped onto the bus. The snake quieted as the soldiers walked down the aisle, ignoring Kenta and Short Pants.

With ninety-thousand soldiers on base, what are the odds of one of those haoles recognizing me? wondered Kenta. He began to breathe normally.

Short Pants gave him an elbow and a smile that said, "You're one lucky son of a bitch."

As the morning sun slanted through the bus's scarred windows, a shack-lined crossroads came into view straight ahead. Two colored men in uniform stood at the bus stop pole. The bus slowed and the driver peered through the windshield.

"Ain't got no more room for niggers," he mumbled.

"Ain't that the truth," said a gap-toothed bubba sitting behind the driver wearing workpants smeared with gray paint.

The driver hit the gas pedal.

As the bus shot forward, Kenta and Short Pants yelled out, "Hey!"

"We've got room for those guys," protested Kenta. "They're soldiers."

The driver spat tobacco juice on the floor. "You're lucky I let *you* on. Only did it 'cause I have to."

Kenta jumped up and cuffed the bus driver on the shoulder. "Stop the bus!"

"Sit down, you fuckin' Jap!" shouted the bus driver.

Short Pants, right behind Kenta, knuckled the man on the head.

The bus swerved. The driver took his foot off of the gas pedal to regain control. Again, the bus slowed.

Everyone on the bus went silent. All eyes focused on the battle upfront. Then, from the back came, "Stop the bus. That's the rule."

The driver jammed the gas pedal, jerking the bus forward. The passengers who had been standing quickly grabbed on to a pole strap or a seat back to keep from falling.

Kenta wrapped his right arm around the pole to which the coin box was attached and grabbed the driver's ear with his left hand.

"You pick up those soldiers or I'll rip off your fucking ear," Kenta demanded. He planted his feet on the floor of the bus and pinched the driver's earlobe like a pair of pliers, pulling as hard as a knight trying to extract a sword from stone.

The driver wrenched his head right. The coin box pole blocked his attempt to slug Kenta, who increased the pressure, twisting the earlobe violently.

The driver jammed hard on the bus's brakes. Kenta lost his grip and banged his head on the front window. The bus stopped. The driver opened the door, then got up from his seat. Using his truck-tire belly, he bumped Kenta toward the door while swinging his right arm into Short Pants's gut.

"Get off—now!" He took another step forward, again bumping Kenta backward. His arrogant smile told his audience that he was enjoying this drama. "So long, Jap-boy." He took a bigger step and gyrated his gut forward for the coup de grace. Short Pants slipped behind the driver.

As Kenta fell back, he grabbed the driver's shirt pockets with both hands, karate-style, and steadied himself at the edge of the step, bending his knees. Before he could pull forward, Short Pants guessed the maneuver and kicked the driver in the ass. Gripping the driver's shirt tighter, Kenta launched himself backward. The driver lost his balance, flailed his arms and shot forward. Kenta hit the ground rolling, just in time to avoid being crushed. The driver's face slammed into the gravel. His left arm draped across Kenta's chest like a lover's would. Kenta twisted and got to his feet. He jumped over the driver and ran up the steps of the bus. Short Pants sat grinning in the driver's seat, his hand on the clutch.

The bubba in the paint-smeared pants started to rise. "What the hell?! You boys can't …"

A white soldier put a restraining hand on his shoulder. "This isn't your fight," he said in an accent that pegged him as a Red Sox fan. The rest of the passengers remained silent.

Short Pants shoved the gear stick into first. With some difficulty, the driver rolled over onto his knees and lifted himself up from the ground. Short Pants stepped on the gas while easing his right foot from the clutch. The driver, his dirt-smeared face bleeding, swiped at the closing door a second too late. As the bus pulled away, he pummeled its side with three futile thumps.

Short Pants U-turned the bus to pick up the colored soldiers. The laughter on their ebony faces suggested they were Northerners with no memories of men wearing coned hoods and white sheets with eyeholes to intimidate them. Short Pants pulled up to the colored soldiers who wasted no time scrambling up the steps.

Kenta rushed off of the bus to pick up a wallet that had fallen out of the back pocket of one of the soldiers. He hopped back on, watching the driver, his chest heaving, hopelessly lumbering toward the bus, shaking his fist. "You fuckin' Japs!"

Kenta took little note of the few passing taxis, including one with three gawking soldiers. He slumped back into his seat, his knees shaking. A middle-aged white man sitting behind him leaned over and whispered in his ear.

"They may be only niggers, but it ain't right to not pick 'em up. We always treat our colored folks right. I hope you boys don't get in no trouble."

Kenta managed a "Thank you, sir," and fantasized a good outcome. *Really, how much trouble did the driver want to get into? Why would he*

want to tell the bus company that he lost control of his bus because he had vi-
olated regulations about picking up all passengers? Kenta was sure he would
flag a taxi and come to Shelby to retrieve his bus. He wouldn't want to
advertise his screw-up.

Short Pants slowed down at the main gate expecting to be challenged,
but the MPs just waved him through. He braked at the first bus stop, opened
the door and stood up to get off. Agitated murmurs ran though the bus.

"Hey, you can't just leave us at the gate," called out one of the passengers.
"We gotta get to work."

Short Pants ignored the plea and continued getting up from the
driver's seat. Kenta stood at the door, preparing to disembark. He
stopped before taking a step. The blood drained from his face. The
snake twirled, slithered up his gullet and then retreated to whirl out of
control in Kenta's innards.

A smirking Sergeant Doi stood at the door.

∞ CHAPTER 55 ∞

"WELCOME HOME, PRIVATE TAKAYAMA. Perhaps you would like to
step down from the bus? You too, Private Moto."

Two MPs stood next to a paddy wagon, the military police vehicle for
prisoners. As Kenta and Short Pants climbed down from the bus, one of
the MPs asked, "Do we need to cuff you?"

"No, sir," said Kenta.

"Where are you taking him?" asked Short Pants, wondering why no
one asked him why he had been driving the bus.

"The brig, of course. Whaddya think, this is a tour bus?" snorted Doi.
He turned to Kenta. "You're not the sharpest knife in the drawer, Takayama.
You must think you're invisible. Sergeant Butler told me that he saw you
guys leaving the USO." He affected an incredulous tone. "Including 'that
private that asked for his pass.'"

"The sergeant at the mess hall?" asked Kenta. "But he said he'd see you
at the Rainbow Club."

"He did. But first he checked out a new bar across from the USO and
saw you guys coming out." Doi let out a harsh laugh, more like a grunt. "I
guess you neophytes learned fast that the USO is not the friendliest place
for Japanese."

"You promised me a pass."

Doi cast an eye at the MP. "I did." He pulled out the pass from his shirt pocket. "I planned to let you stew in your juices for a night and give you a chance to think about respect and *then* see to it that you got your pass today."

The MP raised an impatient hand. "Enough. Let's go."

A taxi pulled up beside them. The right rear door flew open and the bus driver pried himself out.

The snake quivered.

Seeing Kenta about to enter the police van, he flashed a smile of triumph, but said nothing. He climbed on to his bus as if he had just taken a toilet break and drove off.

The snake snuggled down. Kenta figured he had been right about the driver's wish to hide his humiliation. He stepped inside the paddy wagon.

Minutes later, the van pulled up to the Camp Shelby prison.

"Follow me," ordered the MP. Handcuffed soldiers, bandaged soldiers and MPs were all crowded into the reception area. Typists clacked away. A desk sergeant handed Doi a clipboard with a form attached to it.

"Grab a pencil and fill this out."

After a thirty-minute wait, a captain approached. "What's the charge?"

Doi stood up. "AWOL, sir." He handed the sheet to the officer.

The captain glanced down at the paper. "Where did you find him?"

"Getting off from the bus at the gate, sir."

The man's head snapped up at hearing Doi's response. "You're not saying inside the camp, are you, Sergeant?"

"Uh … yes. Sir," Doi replied fumble-mouthed.

The officer exaggerated a shoulder droop. "Sergeant, I got brawlers here tearing up bars, shoplifters insisting they're innocent, whores claiming a soldier didn't pay and then beat them up, men picked up in Mobile who really *were* AWOL. And you bring in someone who you claim is AWOL … on base?" He stared at Doi, exasperation in his eyes. "What are they teaching you people?"

Doi blushed. "But he left …"

"Get out of here. You filed a report. It's been noted. Your CO will get a copy."

Doi's flush deepened. He mumbled a "Yes, sir," performed a crisp about-face and quick-stepped out the door.

Kenta followed him, suppressing a smile.

Doi's face had turned an unattractive shade of burgundy. His neck muscles coiled as taut as Apache bow strings and his lips were pulled back from his teeth like a bulldog ready to bite. He whirled around to confront Kenta.

As Doi snarled his threat, Kenta smelled the vile stench of his breath.

"Before you go bragging to your Buddhahead buddies about how you beat being tossed in the brig, you'd better think about what your life will be like shoveling shit and doing push-ups, because I will press forward with charges at regimental HQ."

He spat out the entire sentence without taking a breath, the last words barely more than angry gasps. He balled his fists and then turned and stormed away.

Kenta had no intention of bragging. He'd been caught. The snake in his belly rumbled. His heart thumped. *Why couldn't I have just stayed back and read my Kennedy book instead of sneaking off base? I wouldn't be on report for being AWOL. I wouldn't have betrayed Angelina. I wouldn't have been on the bus. I wouldn't have that little kotonk turd dedicating his worthless life to thinking up ways to get back at me … not just because he couldn't throw my ass in the brig, but for being shown up by a haole officer with me watching.*

ᇮ ᇮ

It was a long walk to his hutment, but Kenta knew he needed to cool off, to think. Revenge dominated his thoughts. He envisioned himself pounding Doi into a bloody pulp. Visualized Doi begging for mercy as Kenta landed another blow to his face. Satisfying, but the consequence of a few years in the brig wasn't appealing. After his third imaginary thrashing of his tormenter, Kenta's face brightened. The answer! *Yes!* He shouted, at the top of his lungs, ignoring the amused passersby. He broke into a trot, then a run. It was important to get back to the guys—his guys—before Doi.

Back at the hutment, an out of breath Kenta could hardly contain himself while revealing his plan. The perfect plan. Chuckles tossed a playful punch at Kenta's shoulder. "Now that is a stealth plan that is fun *and* gives us military practice. The only question is: Will the message get through?"

ᇮ ᇮ

While Doi's squad feigned deep sleep that night, marauders raided Hutment 714. They taped Doi's mouth, tied up his legs and jammed a pillowcase over his head. They hoisted him out of his bed and carried him outside, where they pummeled him with fists and soccer kicks for a long minute before fleeing. Hearing the ruckus outside, Doi's sleepy-eyed squad crowded the doorway yelling, "What's happening?" "Who's out there?" They struggled to restrain their urge to laugh as Doi moaned and tried to right himself. Then they ran to his rescue.

Once untied, Doi ripped the tape from his mouth. "Ouch!" he screamed, then glared at his men accusingly. "Where were you guys?"

"Right here … sir," said Short Pants. "We were awakened by a whole lotta commotion just outside our door. Thank God we woke up in time to save you … sir." A chorus of men added their own "me, too." But nothing could placate the sergeant.

Kenta noticed blood dripping from Doi's forehead.

"Somebody get a clean T-shirt," he called out. Kenta got down on one knee to examine the cut. "You might need some stitches, Sergeant. And the way you're holding your side … you'd better get checked for a broken rib."

Doi later learned that he was one of five sergeants who had been taken to the hospital that night with a similar story. Old-time sergeants knew there would be at least another five in the days to come. The men whose sergeants were beaten up owed a favor to the messengers. Three nights later, Little Caesar, Kenta, Chad and No Ticket got up after midnight to visit the latrine. Forty-five minutes later, they returned after completing their side of the bargain.

"My last risky adventure," Kenta swore to himself. He felt like he had slid under a tag at home plate twice. He had snuck out of his hutment at midnight without waking Doi, and he had commandeered a bus without being arrested or charged. From here on out, he vowed to avoid being the nail that stuck out.

⊚ CHAPTER 56 ⊚

TWO DAYS LATER, MASTER SERGEANT FORTE briefed Colonel Pence on the latest sergeant attacks and on the scraps between the Hawaii Buddhaheads and the Mainland kotonks. Then, Pence turned his attention to his huge wall map.

Forte picked up the cue. "The Allies are starting to win."

Keeping his eyes focused on the map, Pence answered, "We are losing our internal war, Sergeant. I don't want to have to close down this Nisei experiment."

Before Forte could respond, an orderly stuck his head through the door. "Sir, that Korean lieutenant is here."

"Good, send him in." "Stay," he said to Forte in a lower voice. "Turner agreed to transfer Kim to us until the 100th deploys to Africa in late summer."

Forte trained his eyes on the map with blue and red pins. "Africa? Is that official?"

"Grapevine official," said Pence. "When Ike turned us down, Clark told Marshall he could use all the men he could get."

The orderly returned with the Korean lieutenant who brandished a smart salute.

"At ease, Lieutenant," said Pence. "Colonel Turner thinks our 522nd Field Artillery Battalion can use some of your team-building magic."

Kim fought to keep his pleasure from showing. "Perhaps the colonel is aware of the artillery training I received shortly after finishing basic OCS," said Kim, referring to his Officer Candidate School experience. "As the only regiment to have its own artillery, we have a tremendous advantage. We never have to ask for a share of the division's artillery."

"The advantage only works if we meld infantry and artillery seamlessly," added Pence.

"We can do that, sir," said Kim in a quiet voice that radiated confidence. "The 522nd drew together exceptional men—the makings of an elite unit."

∽ ∾

The early sun busied itself turning the dew on the trees and shrubs surrounding Camp Shelby's barracks into haze, and then humidity. Chad and No Ticket argued whether the snake they found under the doorstep presented a threat as a deadly coral or was a harmless grass snake. They followed the well-worn dictum: When in doubt, stick it with a bayonet. Ignoring the snake murder, Short Pants slathered indalone all over, on his neck, face, arms, trying out the newest Army concoction to repel mosquitoes.

At 8:00 a.m. sharp, the first of a fleet of trucks arrived at the hutments to transport six hundred fifty soon-to-be cannoneers to the firing range. The lead truck held Lieutenant Kim, who made sure he got on last.

"This sure beats the shit out of walking," said Chuckles, climbing in.

Short Pants shared his wisdom. "Who would have thought that fixing tractors, building culverts at Schofield and doing our trig homework would mean we'd get a pass on digging foxholes?"

∽ ∾

First stop, the target zone, was eight miles behind the howitzers. Squads tramped and milled around the site like packs of eager tourists at the Gettysburg battle site during the first week in July. Kenta turned to Kim as the truck rolled to a stop. He swatted at a fly dive-bombing his ear.

"I guess we lucked out. Firing guns behind the lines is a better deal than being at the front."

Kim opened his canteen and surveyed the eyes of the squad in the back of the flatbed. He took a swallow before twisting the cap back on and then began speaking at a deliberate cadence. "If we learn to do our jobs right, we save the lives of our men on the front line. That's the mission." He waited for his words to sink in.

"Follow me," Kim ordered, jumping down from the back of the truck. He walked the squad through the target zone of dilapidated cars, foxholes and cardboard men. After the impact zone inspection, the truck ferried the squad to the observation post at the end of a line of twelve alligator-green 105 mm howitzers stationed atop a rise, each twenty yards apart.

How can twelve guns protect a regiment of four thousand men? Kenta wondered, although he kept his skepticism to himself.

Five-man artillery gun crews from General Bolte's Sixty-Ninth Division stood next to each howitzer. Behind them, another five men fronted ammunition racks. A voice roared, "Commence firing!" The gunners' synchronized movements reminded Kenta of a war dance. Twelve gunners simultaneously rammed thirty-three-pound projectiles into the backs of their cannon barrels, and another soldier stationed at each howitzer pulled the detonating lanyards.

Charges at the base of each cannon cylinder exploded, thrusting the missiles at a banged-up Chevy that served as a simulated tank target. The earth shook and the noise deafened. A short, eerie silence followed, settling over the observers, broken only by the quacking ducks flying toward the target zone. Quick-moving gunners shoved another shell into each smoking howitzer.

The second launch fired. Two seconds of silence. Then, the sounds of the first volley's distant rumble bounced off the low hills, followed by a smoke cloud emanating from the target zone. A third firing before the second volley landed. The frenzied action lasted three minutes. The impact sector's sky changed from Monet blue to storm cloud gray. Wisps of smoke swirled from the smoldering jaws of the cannon. The gunners stood at attention.

The newly formed 522nd applauded and were then trucked to reinspect the target zone.

"All of the cardboard soldiers are torn apart," said Kenta in a subdued voice.

"Once a car, now just twisted steel," added Short Pants in the same tone.

"Notice the foxholes," emphasized Kim. "Except for one direct hit, they're all good and safe. Take a lesson: When under fire, either charge or stay in your hole."

"The trick," explained the Brooklyn gunner who had accompanied the men, "is setting the fuses on the antipersonnel shells." He pointed toward the trees. "Those shells were set to let loose at fifty feet to convert the trees into whirling daggers. If you set the fuses to blow at twenty feet, the shrapnel will kill anything moving within a hundred yards."

Kim held up his hand to stop his men boarding the truck. "Gentlemen, let me assure you that when we finish our training, we will put on a demonstration that will leave nothing standing or intact." He pulled out a pack of Luckys from his shirt pocket, took one for himself and then held out the pack to Kenta. "Take one and pass it on."

∞ CHAPTER 57 ∞

THE NEXT MORNING, Kenta was just sitting down to a plate of french toast in the cafeteria. Before he could even put a bite in his mouth, he heard a shout, "Private Takayama?"

Kenta shifted his body to face the entrance, where a young soldier stood looking among the crowd uncertainly. "Yo! Over here!"

The corporal made his way over to Kenta's table. "Private Takayama, Colonel Pence wants to see you."

The old snake woke up with a jolt in Kenta's stomach. His voice faltered. "What's this about?"

"No idea, Private. Let's go."

Kim was reading the day's *Stars and Stripes* on the HQ steps when the corporal dropped off Kenta. He delivered a smart salute to Kim, who stood up and returned the salute. Kim folded the paper and stuck it in his back pocket.

"What's this all about?" Kenta asked again.

Kim's words came out quick and harsh. "Are *you* dumb, or do you just think *I'm* dumb?"

"I know ... last weekend," replied Kenta, weak and nervous.

∞ ∞

Twenty minutes later, an orderly came out and asked Kim and Kenta to step into Colonel Pence's office. Kenta spied four file folders spread out across Pence's desk.

As Pence rose to his feet, Kenta snapped to attention and saluted. "Private Takayama reporting, *sir.*"

Kim saluted without coming to attention. "Good morning, Colonel."

Pence, stone-faced, returned the salutes and sat down. The spring scents of fresh pine needles wafted through the open windows, tamping down the aromatic mix of brewing coffee and fresh cigarettes.

Pence opened the file to his far left and picked up a sheet of paper. He began reading.

"Mrs. Haru Takayama." Pence raised his eyes and locked onto Kenta's before resuming. "You have given a soldier to the army of the United States. He has arrived here safely, and I am happy to have him in my command. By your sacrifice, you have enabled him to enlist voluntarily and become a symbol of the loyalty and patriotism of our Japanese American population. Without compulsion or perusals, he made the brave and manly choice to exercise the responsibility of his citizenship. With the soldier you have given to us, and others like him, we shall make a glorious record for Japanese Americans in our country."

Pence returned the letter to the file and closed it. His steel-marble eyes focused on Kenta. "I obviously wrote this prior to this past weekend." He fingered another file.

Kenta's mind swirled. He saw himself on a train back to San Francisco.

"Here is a report from the chief of police. You are accused of throwing a bus driver out on the street and commandeering the bus."

Pence picked up a lettergram. "Do you recognize this?"

"Yes, sir." Kenta had wondered what had happened to that letter. He had forgotten to mail it to Angelina. He stared at the letter in the colonel's hand and envisioned a judge pounding his gavel, intoning his verdict. "Court-martial." The grill of a prison door slamming shut flashed before Kenta's eyes.

"You apparently dropped it during your scuffle with the bus driver. But prior to that, you had already gotten acquainted with Chief Ditmar. He claims you crashed the colored USO."

"Yes, sir." He had been wrong in thinking that the bus driver wouldn't want anyone to know that he had lost control of his bus. Kenta saw Doi behind this.

Pence picked up another file. "Your name came across as the first member of the 442nd to have an AWOL violation, although Sergeant Doi went back to retrieve the complaint, saying it had all been a mistake. He had a bandage on his head, according to a note here."

Pence finally flipped open the fourth and last file.

"You may stand at ease, Private," he said, keeping his eyes on the pulled papers pinned with yellow tags. He held them up and then flipped through them like dealing a deck of cards. His voice rose in pitch and speed with each document he slapped on his desk: "President of your high school class for three years; quarterback of your football team; captain and pitcher for the freshman college baseball team; 3.8 GPA; sergeant in the ROTC; service in the Hawaii Territorial Guard and a similar rank for your civilian service working in the Army Corps of Engineers … the Varsity Victory Volunteers. Letters of commendation. Higher than average IQ."

Pence closed all the files with exaggerated care. He raised his right fist and parked it under his chin in his great thinker mode. "Who *are* you?"

I'm beginning to wonder myself, thought Kenta. Buoyed by Pence's tone suggesting his punishment would be less than a court-martial, he declared with more confidence than he felt, "I want to prove to you that I am the person you described in the letter you wrote to my mother."

"Lieutenant Kim will decide your punishment." Pence leaned back in his chair. "I did hear from the CO of the colored unit, who reported the bus incident from his men's perspective."

Did I just detect a hint of admiration in the colonel's tone? Kenta wondered.

"I don't approve of the way the South handles its colored people. But we are in Mississippi for one purpose. Do you know what that is, Private?"

"Yes, sir. To train to fight Germans."

"Almost, Private. We are here to train to stay *alive* to fight Germans. Dismissed."

"Thank you, sir." Kenta was about to add, "I deserve a more severe punishment," but thought the better of it and made a smart pivot while thinking he had just dodged a bullet, a huge change of life bullet, foretelling a life of failure that began with being drummed out of the army.

Lost in the fog of relief, he didn't hear the boots behind him.

Kim penetrated the fog as he stepped aside Kenta walking down the steps of the 442nd building. "I believe you know where the camp's brig is located. You are in charge of the prison latrines for the next two weeks—and I expect you to have a good attitude about it."

Kenta said nothing, merely nodding. Kim's next words were a bit lighter. "I know that it's a shitty detail—forgive the pun—but you could have been court-martialed and thrown in the brig for sixty days. However, the colonel and I have a hunch …"—Kim threw a glance at Kenta—"… that beneath that anger and stupidity lies a leader-in-waiting. You've been given a second chance. Don't make me look like an idiot when it comes to judging character. Save your cravings for a just America for when you return to Hawaii."

"Yes, sir."

Kim walked over to a jeep parked nearby and opened the driver's door.

"Jump in." He started the engine and turned to Kenta. "This is all behind us now. You take the punishment, no bitching. Do the job right. You are one of the squad, equal to all others in my estimation."

With that, Kim shoved the gearshift into first and held it there without releasing the clutch.

"By the way, Sergeant Doi has been promoted. He is now Staff Sergeant Doi, assigned to the rifle range. That means you guys will be getting a new sergeant."

⊚ CHAPTER 58 ⊚

June 19, 1943

COLONEL PENCE JUMPED OUT OF HIS JEEP, paying little heed to the nighttime jazz and swing bands of Hattiesburg's bar scene. He noted the huge banner draped over the entrance of a converted Catholic Church: "HAWAII USO." He stomped his feet to shake the Camp Shelby grit from his boots and inhaled the scent of the magnolia trees, oblivious to their heavy perfume. The cool breezes relieved the early June humidity, although the troubled Pence did not notice that, either.

MPs from the 442nd stood in front of cardboard cutouts of palm trees, hula dancers and King Kamehameha, Hawaii's first king. It was an idyllic evening … except for the ring of MPs guarding the entrances and the hushed, worried tones coming from the building—signs of an experiment going horribly wrong.

The phone call to Pence's living quarters had come at 22:50. He had been reading Thucydides's *The History of the Peloponnesian War*, which his father had given him in his freshman year of college. Within the first one hundred pages he had recognized his calling. He re-read the classic every ten years as a reminder of its military lessons and as a check on how he had changed from the last time he had read it.

The phone interruption had startled him. Minutes earlier, he had swirled his cognac, breathed deeply over the lip and sipped slowly from a carefully measured two-jigger glass. He had picked up the custom in China while working alongside French officers in the foreign concessions.

Pence's stomach tightened upon hearing Master Sergeant Forte's voice at the other end of the line. Unless shit happens, master sergeants do not interrupt their commanding officers late on a Saturday night.

After a dozen "uh huhs," Pence ordered. "Just make sure no one leaves the building until I get there."

He was angry. No, boiling mad—not just because he would have to change from his soft, comfortable robe into a uniform and drive into Hattiesburg, and not just because of the embarrassment this donnybrook would cause him. No, he was pissed because these young Japanese American zealots, so eager to prove their patriotism, had allowed their infantile, barbaric nature to jeopardize everything they claimed to hold dear. *How could men who were breaking training performance records be so blind? These men who displayed such impressive unit cohesiveness on maneuvers ... How could they be so stupid?!*

Pence's infuriation turned into hopelessness as his driver sped along the ill-lit highway from the base to town. Every bone in his body told him that he could lead these men successfully into battle against Italians and Germans. These Nisei would fight if they made it to Europe. But they might never get the chance. Pence envisioned these boys being shipped back home for these ongoing Buddhahead-Kotonk donnybrooks. And without a regiment to command, he would be relegated to teaching military courses at OCS—or maybe ordered to write a two-volume report on "The Perils of Ethnic Units in the Army."

Pence returned the MPs' salute. He pushed his shoulders back, lifted his chin and tightened his jaw. He didn't want to enter the USO as a defeated commander. Rage twisted his gut as he surveyed the carnage: overturned tables, busted chairs and bottles strewn about, many broken.

The Hawaii USO had opened only yesterday with so much hope and exuberance. Hung Wai Ching had performed a minor miracle. When told there were no Army funds for a Japanese American USO, he had raised the money in Hawaii and come back with a Hawaiian band. Ching had found this little-used church, and had it fixed up, Hawaiian-style. He had visited the Arkansas Japanese relocation camps and had arranged for a busload of Japanese girls from the two camps to attend the opening dance. Pence had used the occasion to plead for peace and harmony between the Buddhaheads and the kotonks, emphasizing the risk if they continued fighting. They listened and they applauded, but they hadn't heard a fucking thing.

The girls from the camp, many of them quietly sobbing, huddled together near the bandstand. Pence knew they were inadvertently contributing to the problem. They tended to socialize with the more sophisticated

Mainland boys with whom they shared a common experience. It did not help that the Hawaii boys insisted on sticking to their Pidgin English, which the girls barely understood.

The two divergent Nisei contingents claimed opposite sides of the main hall. One group had dressed in natty clothes suitable for Saturday night at a Los Angeles jazz club; the other side sported casual aloha shirts and trousers that were more appropriate for a *luau* pig roast. A half-dozen MPs stood in the middle. Master Sergeant Forte; the new chaplain, Hiro Hamada; and two sergeants—one white, one Nisei—wearing MP bands, walked over. Pence addressed the white NCO.

"If you can have your MPs keep folks from entering, that would be helpful, Sergeant. Our MPs will handle the inside."

As the sergeant led his men out, Pence flipped his right hand, palm out, pointing to Forte. "What happened?"

"Well, we talked to the bartender who heard the whole thing," said Forte. "I guess one of the Hawaii boys complained about the kitchen running out of rice. He told a Mainlander that if everyone chipped in a quarter, the kitchen could buy more. The Mainlander said something to the effect of, 'You Buddhahead bumpkins need to start eating American food.' A Hawaii boy got right up in his face and shouted, 'You cheap kotonks are tighter than a cockroach's asshole.' A few shoves quickly escalated into a no-holds-barred brawl."

Pence held his silence and shifted his gaze to Hamada. "Where were you when all this happened?"

"Sergeant Forte and I were finishing up dinner at the King's Lair, a couple doors down. We heard some yelling and saw MPs running down the street toward our USO, so we followed them." Hamada stopped and flashed Forte a guilty grimace. "I just remembered—we didn't pay for our meal."

Forte ignored the remark and returned to the conversation. "By the time we got here, the MPs had started to gain control. I shouted the loudest 'Attention!' of my life. That ended it. Then I called you."

Pence walked along the two sides of the room, eying each man. At least the Takayama kid and three others he had reprimanded were not here. The men stood subdued, dropping their eyes when Pence surveyed them. He had seen the same ashamed faces after other incidents. The boys had good intentions, but the gulf between these two groups stretched as wide as Mississippi's whites and colored.

"Sergeant, tell the boys to return to the base. Flip a coin to see which group leaves first. Then join the chaplain and me at that restaurant you left."

Pence surveyed the worried faces of the girls standing across the room. "Give me a minute," he called out to Hamada and Forte.

Pence walked up to the ladies from the Rohwer and Jerome camps. They had bussed all the way from Arkansas for this weekend of social events with Japanese American soldiers. The ladies had gotten all gussied up in party dresses and jewelry, their well-coifed, hot-ironed hair set in the style of Rita Hayworth's famous do. The smells changed from beer and sweat to powder and perfume.

"Ladies, you are the angels of Hattiesburg, doing remarkable work. My deepest apologies. We will see to it that you get back to your camp tomorrow. We're closing the USO for the weekend."

The tallest girl stepped forward. Colonel Pence recognized her as Mary Nakahara. Everyone recognized Mary, already a legend at nineteen.

"Colonel Pence," she said in debutante English, "we are here for the weekend. Please do not close the USO. I cannot predict the future, but I believe the shock of tonight will guarantee good behavior for at least one night."

Colonel Pence studied the faces of the other girls. Saw the disappointment in their eyes. Turning his attention back to Mary, he showed her something no one at Camp Shelby had ever seen. A warm and genuine smile. "You would charm Joe DiMaggio out of his favorite bat, Mary."

After making sure the girls had a bus to take them to their tent barracks at Camp Shelby, Pence strutted over to the restaurant.

∽ ∾

Chaplain Hamada had gone ahead to the King's Lair, which was modeled after a typical British pub, complete with dartboard and King Henry VIII posters. He apologized to the manager, explained what had happened, and then paid the dinner bill. Given the late hour, he had his pick of the empty tables. Hamada chose one at the rear of the restaurant. Forte joined him a few minutes later. He knew Pence well enough to confidently order three Millers.

Hung Wai Ching had recruited Hamada upon his return from Camp Shelby in late April. Hamada had the broad shoulders of a middleweight boxer. At five-foot-two, he had fought as a Golden Gloves welterweight until his ordination. He believed that an omnipotent and loving God had sent the Great Buddha to Asia as one of his messengers and, five centuries later, sent his only son with the final message. Not given to proselytizing, the chaplain extolled good character from whatever source it sprang forth. Rather than preaching, he found listening a more effective tool for healing. Known for his soft-spoken voice, Hamada always needed the microphone at full volume to be heard at assembly.

Pence entered the pub and paused for a second to allow his eyes to adjust to the dim lights. "Over here, sir." Spotting Forte and Hamada, the colonel ambled over to their table. Taking his seat, he thanked them for ordering him a beer.

The colonel wasted no words on small talk. "Chaplain, we need a miracle. We can't take this group to Europe as they are."

"The 'I told you so' ghouls like DeWitt might be right after all, Colonel," said Forte.

"I'm not ready to pack it in yet, Sergeant, although I realize that disbanding the unit is an option."

"Colonel, I have an idea that might result in a small miracle," said the chaplain.

Pence listened closely as Hamada laid out his suggestion. Pence then shifted his gaze to Forte.

"What have we got to lose?"

For the first time in two hours, Pence's face looked drained of its tension. The colonel relaxed into his great thinker's pose. Forte and Hamada lifted their beer mugs, eyes down, sipping slowly to fill the prolonged silence they had learned to expect from their leader as he mulled over a problem. They knew that the longer the pause, the more likely an affirmative response—maybe not for the idea exactly as presented, but at least for the nugget of the idea. The awkward dead space meant that bursting arcs of mental electricity were at work inside the colonel's calculating brain.

Pence placed his hands on the table. The furrows lining his forehead deepened and his steel-gray eyes were full of purpose.

Pence lifted his mug, inviting Hamada and Forte to clink their glasses with his. "Gentlemen, let's make it happen." The three men took a deep gulp.

"All right, one week from today," said Pence wiping the foam off his upper lip with a napkin.

⸙ CHAPTER 59 ⸙

June 26, 1943

FORTY-EIGHT HAWAII BOYS, INCLUDING KENTA and his Young Street neighbor Danny Inouye, Short Pants, Chuckles and Chad assembled at the main road leading into the hutment community. Each wore starched khakis with sharp creases and just-shined boots that were so shiny the morning sun bounced off of them. The men had stuffed their bulging backpacks with a change of clothes, a towel, mosquito coils, grass skirts and *omiyage* purchased at the PX to gift to their camp hosts.

Kenta slapped another mosquito biting his cheek. He examined the bloody corpse and then flicked it away. Sweat beads trickled down his face and his khaki shirt clung to the middle of his back like sticky rice, although he didn't notice.

The chosen were waiting to leave for a party weekend at Camp Rohwer in the southeastern corner of Arkansas.

"Hey, you gonna play that thing or just take us on another snipe hunt?" asked Kenta, pointing to the ukulele in Short Pants's hands. The allusion to Short Pants leading a group of four kotonks on a snipe hunt never failed to rouse a chorus of chuckles. Short Pants started strumming. The men took a collective breath and launched into "My Little Grass Shack."

Colonel Pence, Chaplain Hamada and Master Sergeant Forte strolled over to the truck. The men started to form up.

"At ease, men," ordered Pence. "The orders of the day are simple: Enjoy your leave, but remember, you are the 442nd's ambassadors to Rohwer's eight thousand residents." The colonel's eyes twinkled. His voice then broke into mock seriousness. "Can I count on you to tell the Nisei gals that you appreciate their coming to our USO dances?"

"Yes, *sir!*" roared the soldiers.

"Well, what are you men waiting for?"

The men piled into the back of three open-air troop-transport trucks. *Oh, to be the guy who sold green paint to the army*, thought Kenta.

Chad pounded the top of his driver's cabin. "*Ikimasho!*—Let's go!" he shouted.

The engines sprang to life.

Danny raised his hand, revealing two dice between his thumb and forefinger. "Wimps to the front, men to the back."

The first of the trucks moved forward. Short Pants hit a chord on his ukulele, and the party boys resumed singing "My Little Grass Shack."

⚭ ⚭

They sang until they began to worry that they would be too hoarse to perform at the camp talent show. They switched to swapping recycled jokes. Their warm mid-morning beer washed down ham and cheese sandwiches, inducing fitful naps under the brutal sun. At noon, they crossed the Mississippi River into the Arkansas Delta and stopped at a Howard Johnson's for ice cream cones. They had to settle for Popsicles due to a rationing of dairy products. They licked quickly to keep the sugary dribble from running down their hands.

Danny's pockets bulged with his winnings. With only a sliver of frozen juice left on his Popsicle stick, he announced, "I'm renting a bus to New Orleans for the July 4 weekend. And don't worry about a place to stay; I already cut a deal with Tulane. It's summer break. We can sleep in their dorms."

The trucks rumbled along State Road 65 toward the rural township of McGehee.

"High cotton," said Kenta, standing and holding on to the side rail. "I never understood those words before. They're more like snowball trees."

"Sure," muttered Short Pants, pointing at a group of stooped Negroes. "Except for their color, that could be me pulling weeds in cane fields."

"Man, this is just hell with humidity," said Kenta, wiping his brow with his shirtsleeve.

Chad stood up and faced his mates, bracing against the truck's cab. He began crooning an unhurried rendition of "Summertime." Chuckles pulled out his harmonica and placed it between his lips, charging the air with plaintive notes. Everyone else hummed along.

The truck stopped at the McGehee Township for gas and directions. Within minutes a black, bubble-topped Hudson marked "Chief of Police" rolled up. A uniformed man, just under six feet tall, emerged from the driver's side. He appeared to be in his mid-thirties and was blessed with the waist of his high school days. Kenta and Danny, who could switch from Pidgin to perfect English when the occasion warranted it, jumped down and walked over to the car. They offered a smart salute.

"Good afternoon, officer," said Kenta.

Sunglasses masked the officer's eyes. He swiveled his head silently.

Kenta bluffed an air of confidence. "Sir, could you point us in the direction of the Rohwer Camp?"

Still nothing.

"Maybe you heard about the Japanese American soldiers training at Camp Shelby?" He punctuated his question with his most engaging smile. "That's us. We're going out to Rohwer to meet some of the folks."

The chief scrutinized the truck filled with young men with funny eyes in wilting khaki. On the door, stenciled in white were the words "US ARMY." He watched as several jumped off the truck and plugged nickels into the Coke machine. He spat a stream of tobacco juice on the road, but away from Kenta and Danny's polished boots.

"Yeah, we heard about you boys. A good thing y'all are doing."

The tension quickly drained from the two soldiers' faces.

"Watchu wanna do is mosey up the road about three miles. You pass a big sign, 'Bright's Fish Farm,' then watch for the next road. That'll be Highway 1. It'll pass through the town of Rohwer. To git to the camp, you take a left on State Road 138, only it's not marked. If you come to the railroad line spur that goes to Rohwer, you've gone too far."

Danny and Kenta smiled in tandem.

"Thank you … sir!" With a salute, they trotted back to the trucks.

A few minutes later, Chad called out, pointing ahead, "Look over there!"

A rectangular sign with large white lettering that read "Rohwer Relocation Center" hung from a five-foot-high knobby wooden pole. The trucks slowed, bounced over railroad ties and came to a stop. The men jumped down from the trucks, stretched and walked to the side of the sprouting dandelion-flanked road, peed, targeting grasshoppers resting on the froth-covered drainage ditches. Bees droned; butterflies danced.

The drivers U-turned into what they hoped was State Road 138, a gravel lane hardly wide enough to let another vehicle pass without violating the rough shoulder. Recent rains had worsened the ruts in the road and the sun had baked them tough. As they passed meandering bayous, Chad lifted his warm Coke and nudged Kenta. Both kept one hand on a support bar that butted up against the driver's cabin.

"I still can't figure out why only us Hawaii guys were invited."

"It's easy," said Kenta, although not as sure of himself as his words conveyed. "It's recognition of our gung-ho attitude—we're tough, we're determined and we're full of enthusiasm. We *want* to be here. Those kotonks have an attitude problem. Last week, two of them claimed allegiance to the emperor. They got the general discharge they wanted and were sent to Tule Lake."

Short Pants stood behind them, balancing like a sailor riding rough seas. He flipped a pair of dice in the air, caught both in one hand and eyed the outcome with a grin.

"Gentlemen, the odds favor us. There'll be no smooth-talking mainlander gigolos schmoozing the gals this weekend."

"And we'll have some delicious *udon,* tempura and *teriyaki,*" said Chad, licking his lips. He raised his voice, pointing. "Something's up ahead."

The men stirred and stood up. They peered through the shimmering heat. An amorphous outline emerged like a giant chess set, its castle pieces set at fifty-foot intervals. They cheered, stomped their feet and slapped each other on the back. Short Pants strummed another encore of

"My Little Grass Shack" before switching to "Tiptoe Through the Tulips." Exuberant voices belted out the lyrics.

As the trucks slowed, the medieval silhouettes suddenly turned sinister, morphing into wooden guard towers. The shouting stopped and the singing faded into silence. Mouths fell open. Only the squawks of a crow flying overhead broke the stunned quiet.

∽ CHAPTER 60 ∾

KENTA'S EYES RIVETED TO THE TOP of the nearest tower where three soldiers manned a machine gun with a ribbon of bullets feeding it … aimed downward, targeting inside the camp. Kenta gripped the truck's railing tighter. White boys his own age wearing the same khaki uniform he wore, stood ready to fire on people who looked like him, *because* they looked like him … because they looked like the enemy.

The three trucks crossed a small bridge spanning a lazy bayou inlet. A twelve-foot-high barbed wire fence snaked beyond eyesight on either side of the fort-like entrance.

The transports slowed to a halt at the gate. No one spoke. Movement inside the camp caught Kenta's eye. Men, women and children were spilling out from rows of wooden barracks, like prisoners answering a roll call.

Several white soldiers swung open the gates, outward. A pimple-faced corporal, holding his hand up more like a Nazi salute than a command to halt, stood under the gateway's arch. Two rifle-toting squads marched out of the gates behind a sergeant with a taut jaw. Holding their Springfields snugly against their chests, they flanked the trucks.

"Welcome to Rohwer Camp," the sergeant called out. "Get down and form up in lines of six."

The confused Hawaii boys fell in as ordered.

"Everyone must be frisked before you can enter," said the sergeant.

One squad of mean-eyed soldiers stood sentinel while the others patted down their fellow soldiers. The only difference was the shape of their eyes. The soldier running his fingers over Kenta hit his groin with the edge of his hand. Kenta saw it coming and held back a grimace. *What a fat fuck. One kick and the bastard would be out like a deer shot between the eyes. What kind of soldier is given guard duty in a place like this?* he wondered.

"Back on board," ordered the sergeant.

Swirling dust rose as the trucks crunched over the gravel road through the gate. The camp detainees, dressed in their Sunday finery, stood waving small American flags in front of their row-house barracks wrapped in tarpaper. A ghetto in the middle of nowhere. Mothers carried their babies. Toddlers waved as they do at all parades, even a parade of three Army trucks.

Kenta turned an ashen face to Short Pants, his voice hollow, but his smile firmly in place. "These families are welcoming us to their prison as if we were arriving for a Waikiki Beach Sunday barbecue," said Kenta, gesturing a thumbs-up at a child holding a flag.

Short Pants's eyes glistened. "See all those kids?" He flicked away a teardrop with his pinkie, as if the casual motion could hide his feelings. "They're all American-born."

"Who can't even speak Japanese," added Chad.

The trucks rolled into what Kenta guessed was the "town square." Girls adorned in party dresses and high-heeled black pumps jumped up and down, waving at the boys as if they were the latest heartthrobs in Tommy Dorsey's band. The trucks pulled to a stop and Kenta dropped to the ground.

Young ladies holding homemade leis gathered around the arrivals. A girl with a red paper bow in her shoulder-length hair skipped up and placed her lei of dandelions over Kenta's neck. She wore a lime-green sundress that accented her lithe figure. He thought he recognized her from the USO, but knew he hadn't talked or danced with her.

"Welcome!" She paused for a glance at Kenta's nametag. "Welcome, Private Takayama."

Kenta bowed. "*Domo arigato.* It's the most beautiful lei I have ever received. Please, call me Kenta."

She blushed. "I ... I'm Jane Doi. My parents would like to invite you to join us for dinner tonight."

Kenta's face went blank. *Dear God, let this be a coincidence,* an inner voice pleaded.

"You might know my brother. He's a sergeant."

Kenta's knees turned wobbly. His face flushed, as though stricken with malaria.

Jane's eyes widened and her hand flew to her mouth. "Are you OK?" she asked with deep concern.

"Yes, I'm fine. I got a little motion-sick riding in the truck." He paused and took a few deep breaths as the flush in his face dissipated. "I do know your brother—actually, our squad had him as our sergeant for a few weeks. But he ... he received a promotion a few days ago." Kenta's stomach knotted as he imagined the horrible stories her brother must have told her about his "misfits" from Hawaii. He relaxed as he saw Jane's smile widen.

"When he received his draft notice, you would have thought he won the Irish Sweepstakes. We had a big party. Of course, we never dreamed that six months later, we would be at war." She brushed her dress as though whisking away errant ants. "Let's go. We're having an early dinner so we can all enjoy your show."

Kenta started to stroll ahead up the main thoroughfare. "Going somewhere?" Jane teased, standing in place and pointing to a side lane. Kenta stopped and pivoted back to his host.

"Let's go this way," said Jane. "It's more interesting." As they walked, Jane pointed to the corner building ahead and to the right. "This is my high school. I should have graduated last year, but ..."

"Yeah, all the traveling."

Jane rolled her eyes. "The traveling was the least of it. We only had three days to sell our produce market and house." Her voice trailed away. "We were each allowed to bring only one suitcase. Then we were herded onto a cattle train and transported to a racetrack, where we were assigned a horse stall as our temporary home. They slapped a coat of lye on the wooden slats. Can you imagine the horrid smells?" She shuddered. "Lye, moldy hay and horse poop."

Kenta nodded, thinking of the Parker Ranch stables near his family's hotel.

"We were supposed to stay at the stables for just a couple of weeks. But the army engineers took a month just to drain the Rohwer swamp." Jane stopped walking and turned to Kenta. "Get this ... when the government hired local tradesmen to construct this camp, the workers were harassed by KKK types. The governor had to send the highway patrol to keep the troublemakers at bay. Only after President Roosevelt personally asked the governor to give a speech about Arkansas's patriotic duty to take in Japanese internees did the tire punctures and demonstrations stop."

Jane glanced at the bulge in Kenta's shirt pocket. "Is that a pack of cigarettes?"

Kenta raised his eyebrows.

"Don't be silly," said Jane. "The rules for 'proper ladies' died the day we boarded the trains."

Kenta shook out two Luckys and put both sticks in his mouth. He lit them both and then handed one to Jane. Her lingering brush of fingers at the hand-off hinted that the game was on. A slight stirring in Kenta's trousers confessed his hope for intimacy.

Jane inhaled a ladylike puff.

"When we arrived at what the army told us would be 'a model American city,' the buildings were only half-completed. The high school turned out to be a few stakes in the ground." Her voice turned hard. "But it really didn't matter because we didn't have any teachers. The feds offered to hire teachers at high salaries because it would be a twelve-month assignment and the living conditions …" A sweep of her hands made any more words unnecessary. "But the Arkansas State Teachers Association threatened to blackball any camp teachers from ever teaching in Arkansas again."

Jane resumed walking. Kenta followed her, comparing Jane's family's loss with that of his own. Although Kenta's own father was being held in a similar camp, his sister lived in the home of the FBI director, his mother owned a hotel and his older brother held an important community position.

They rounded to the path that ran along the back of the barracks. Muted sounds of children playing hide and seek lightened the mood, giving the camp a sense of normalcy. Drying laundry fluttered on ropes strung between pine trees. The smells of rotting vegetation drifted in from the bayous.

At the elevated wooden walkway, Kenta nodded and asked, "A bridge?"

Jane laughed, her voice girlish once again. "Hardly a bridge, but Rohwer is crisscrossed with streams and drainage ditches."

"Nothing is growing on either side," noted Kenta as they crossed the wooden walkway.

"We keep it that way to keep the mosquitoes away."

"Doesn't the army spray DDT?"

Jane shook her head and exhaled a long, slow stream of smoke. "You have a lot to learn, Kenta."

Changing the subject, Kenta pointed to his right. "Is that cotton?"

"Well, we're not growing scoops of ice cream. Ask my dad about cotton."

A hodgepodge of improvements graced the barracks. A few enterprising families had built their own porches. Tree trunks sawed in fat, two-foot lengths had been transformed into chairs and tables that dotted most backyards. Everyone tended to a vegetable plot. Kenta inhaled the pleasing scent of fresh mint.

"This is amazing … how all of you have turned a swamp into a truck farm."

"It's all out of necessity," Jane said. "The army's food budget is forty-five cents per person per day. Part of the money I make waitressing at the army cafeteria helps to pay for vegetable seeds."

"Forty-five cents a day?" Kenta's voice challenged the figure.

"Mom works in procurement for the camp mess. She gets a cut of the camp's forty-five cents a day food budget to buy meat from local farmers." Jane paused. "That's not all," she said with a testiness in her voice. "The Army built a hospital—but didn't recruit any doctors. They built a power plant—but didn't hire any engineers. They built a kitchen—but didn't hire any cooks. Thank goodness we're resourceful," said Jane with a defiant pride in her eyes. "We created a city with all the services we need. When we're short of technical people, we train them. As Mary Nakahara likes to say, 'Let's get better, not bitter.'"

Kenta's eyes turned to the stacked chunks of timber.

"If you had been here last winter, you would have started a log pyramid early, too. There's no heating in our barracks. That's how Dad contracted tuberculosis."

Kenta stooped down to stop a bouncing ball and rolled it back to a bunch of kids playing dodgeball. "Instead of moping, you are coping."

Jane laughed. "You're funny, Kenta, but you have a ways to go before you can enter a poetry contest." Then her face turned serious. "Our improvised 'city building' impressed the WRA," she said, referring to the War Relocation Authority, the camps' civilian administrators. "The bureaucrats there urged the federal government to recruit our camp's engineers to work on the Hoover Dam to alleviate the labor shortage on a dam project in northern Arkansas. But our 'Nazi' governor, 'Adolf' Adkins, refused to accept Japanese workers. In Arkansas, colored people are suitable for picking cotton and digging ditches, but skilled construction jobs are reserved exclusively for whites."

Kenta stubbed out his cigarette on a tree and started to flick it away but caught himself. Embarrassed not wanting to tarnish the camp's pristine appearance, he walked over to a recycled flour barrel and lifted the lid. Then he stopped himself again. Amused, Jane pointed to a cracker barrel where he disposed of his cigarette.

"It's crazy," said Kenta. "Putting bigotry ahead of national security. In Hawaii, we helped restore sunken battleships. In Arkansas …" He shook his head, left his thought unfinished, and gave a thumb-sized rock an angry kick.

"It's the reason you won't be seeing my younger brother, Patrick," said Jane. "He accuses you, Johnny— any Nisei in the army—of being traitors. He says the army trusts wops more than us. After all, furloughed Italian POWs earn two bucks a day weeding for the same peanut farmers who wouldn't hire our boys. Patrick didn't join any protests, though; he fears being sent to Tule Lake. He knows we need the $16 a month he earns at the sewage plant."

Kenta pointed at a row of narrow wooden cubicles sitting on a patch of land between two drainage ditches. They were separated by a five-foot-high corrugated iron fence. "Is that what I think it is?"

Jane frowned. "The army only knows one way to provide toilets and showers. The left side is for women, the right for the men. All the stalls are open. There's no privacy when you sit down to do your business. Open showers, too. It took my grandmother weeks before she overcame her shame and took a shower—but only late at night with me standing guard."

Kenta turned to Jane. "Grandmother?"

"Yes, my mother is Nisei. Grandmother arrived in Hawaii in the closing days of Hawaii's monarchy. She moved to California the year Hawaii became a territory. My father arrived toward the end of World War I. He met my mother, an English teacher, when he attended a school for new immigrants. When you hear him speak English, you will know why we still tease him that he must not have been a very good student.

"This is our castle." Jane pointed to one of six barrack entrances. "The one with a porch." Wooden shingles, curled by the baking Mississippi sun, garnished the oddly slanted roof. Raised shutters revealed screened windows with no glass. Pinewood benches flanked a well-joined picnic table, crowding the yard. Someone had given the garden loving attention. Tomato plants hugged the building. Neat rows of carrots, lettuce, radishes and daikon ran parallel to the tomatoes. The scent of fresh herbs—basil, rosemary, thyme and chives—wafted from a stubby wooden planter atop the porch.

As Kenta and Jane climbed the steps pulled together with scrap lumber, her parents appeared at the back door. Jane introduced everyone. Kenta bowed to the waist. Shigeru Doi, his eyes sunken and sallow, returned a dilatory quarter bow. Jane's mother, Fumiko, younger looking and more vibrant than her husband, bowed deeply and motioned Kenta and Jane inside.

On a narrow bed pressed against the far corner of the small room sat a stooped-back elderly woman, hunched over. Jane greeted her grandmother, who responded by gazing at an imagined spot on the wall.

Fumiko welcomed Kenta in hushed tones. "We speak softly. We can even hear the broom strokes of our neighbors though the walls." Kenta stared at the sheet rock partition separating the family next door. It rose seven feet high and left a four-foot gap at the peak of the A-frame.

"I've grown used to the loud snoring of the man at the end," said Fumiko.

Jane could not resist adding, "And our nighttime entertainment comes from the rhythmical thumping of ..."

"Jane!"

Fumiko shot her daughter the stink eye, followed by a quick nod toward her two youngest children, a boy and a girl, who stood next to a makeshift kitchen counter covered with pans and vegetables, but no faucet. The boy—Kenta figured him to be eleven or twelve—stood almost at attention in a sharply creased, wrinkle-free Boy Scout uniform. He saluted Kenta, who returned the greeting. The little girl flashed an impish smile at Kenta, revealing toothless gaps. The wild violets pinned behind her ear set off her immaculate, navy-blue party dress. Kenta felt guilty about the languorous walk he and Jane had taken. The little girl, around six or seven years old, must have been penned up inside until the visitor arrived. He squatted down and dug into his rucksack, pulling out a Walt Disney wind-up cat from the movie *Pinocchio*. She reached for it at the end of Kenta's outstretched hand. After a quick inspection, she widened her engaging smile.

"My name is Ruth," she said, her eyes shining. "I'm in first grade."

"I'm pleased to meet you, Ruth. My name is Kenta."

As he stood up, Jane introduced the boy as her youngest brother, Gabriel. Once again, Kenta dug into his rucksack.

"I think I have a genuine army knife in here I bet you could …"

"That's very generous of you, Kenta," interrupted Jane, tussling her brother's hair, "but we are not allowed to have weapons."

Kenta surveyed the twenty-by-twenty-foot room. Surrounding a table were four unfinished, straight-back chairs and three handcrafted stools, stacked one on top of the other. A thin mattress covered the small, steel-framed bed where Jane's grandmother huddled with rolled bedding. Kenta guessed that a *futon* comforter was squeezed underneath.

Shigeru coughed into a handkerchief and pointed to the ceiling. A naked light bulb was screwed into a ceramic socket. It was tethered to an outside power line by an electric cord hanging from the ceiling beam.

"Patrick and I built an attic," said Shigeru, catching his breath. Wooden planks had been laid across the struts, leaving two rows of space to shove boxes through.

Jane tapped Kenta on the shoulder and pointed to a couple of folded army cots leaning against a wall. "We fold them up during the day. Mom and Dad sleep on those. The rest of us sleep on the futon." She pointed to a guide wire dividing their cubicle. "We hang a sheet over the wire at night to get a little privacy."

Kenta's eyes circled the room again and then broke the awkward silence.

"How can they do this to you?"

Fumiko's eyes kept Jane silent. She spoke to Kenta in a weary voice. "Japan attacked Pearl Harbor. And because we are Japanese, we must accept this … this exile. *Shikata ga nai*—it can't be helped; that's the way it is." With a wan smile, Fumiko excused herself and went outside.

Kenta walked over to a picture of a young man in uniform that hung next to the front door. "That's a good picture of Staff Sergeant Doi."

Jane joined him. "We were living the American dream when Johnny received his draft notice. We had a profitable grocery store, big house, good neighborhood, a Packard in the driveway." She bit her lower lip. "When Johnny visited us at the racetrack, he cried." Jane's eyes grew hard. "He told Father he would rather go to prison than return to his unit." She cast a glance at her father, who sat misty-eyed. "Father told him that he had to prove America made a mistake. So, Johnny went back. On his next visit, he told me, 'Dad was right. Military service is proving we are Americans in our hearts.'"

Kenta spied a newspaper page pinned on the wall next to the bed. The yellowing sheet displayed pictures of six young men, dressed in jacket and tie. Someone had scribbled "Heroes" over the page in red crayon. More than twenty signatures crowded the bottom and edges.

"Who's that?" asked Kenta.

Suddenly, the door behind him banged open. Everyone turned. A young man wearing a baseball uniform and a smirk barged into the room.

"Patrick," said Jane, her wide eyes and taut neck muscles registering alarm.

"This is our guest," implored Shigeru quickly.

"Of course, Father. Don't worry," said the young man.

Kenta offered his hand. "You must be Patrick. I'm Kenta."

Patrick ignored the proffered hand and walked over to the newspaper clipping. "You want to know who these guys are? They are the true heroes of our prison, the no-no boys." The tone of Patrick's voice accused Kenta of ignorance of the rejectionists.

"The men who stood up for what they believed in, right?" asked Kenta.

Contempt clouded Patrick's eyes. "So, you've heard of them. But, tell me, have you read exactly what they refused to sign?"

Kenta paused. He knew the gist of the controversy. When the army decided to accept Nisei into the armed forces, all draft-age males in the internment camps were required to fill out a loyalty questionnaire. The WRA jumped on the idea and decided to use the survey to expedite clearance for students hoping to attend college and workers wishing to accept jobs outside the camps. All internees were compelled to fill out the questionnaire. The attempt to justify a horrible policy would have been a harmless bureaucratic exercise, if not for the two odious questions that had created a moral dilemma for many internees.

Patrick stabbed his finger on the newspaper page.

"Read it."

∞ CHAPTER 61 ∞

"PATRICK, YOU PROMISED ..." said Jane.

"No, it's OK," assured Kenta. "Your brother is right. I *should* read it."

Patrick dropped his hand. His expression still defiant, but now tinged with uncertainty as Kenta focused on the offending questions, reading it silently. Feeling the stares of the others in the room, he decided that reading the questions out loud would defuse the tension.

"'Number twenty-seven: Are you willing to serve in the armed forces of the United States on combat duty, wherever ordered?'" Kenta turned to Jane. "Women, too? Did they have to sign this?"

"Everybody, even *Obaachan*," said Jane, glancing over at her grandmother. "Even those who can't read a word of English or speak English."

Kenta continued, his voice more subdued. "'Number twenty-eight: Will you swear unqualified allegiance to the United States of America and faithfully defend the United States from any or all attacks by foreign or domestic forces, and forswear any form of allegiance or obedience to the Japanese Emperor, or to any other foreign government, power or organization?'"

Kenta rolled his eyes. "This is so stupid. If a survey could determine loyalty, why didn't they do this a year ago and avoid all this misery?" He shifted his gaze to Patrick and asked, hesitantly, "So you signed it?"

Patrick took a deep breath and exhaled slowly. "I wrote, 'I'll sign if all other Americans have to declare the same loyalty. I recited the Pledge of Allegiance at school for twelve years. Does that count? Has anyone considered that a real spy might answer both questions with a "yes"?'"

"But you're not in Tule Lake," said Kenta, referring to the camp where all the no-no boys—the young men who had answered "no" and "no"—were sent.

Patrick's shoulders slumped, the challenge in his voice having lost its power. "The next morning, I tore up the page with my first responses, what I really felt in my heart. Then I swallowed my pride ... again ... and answered 'yes' to both questions. I didn't want to cause trouble for my parents."

Jane walked the few steps to her father. "My father faced a special dilemma: If he forswears allegiance to Japan, he forfeits his Japanese passport and citizenship. But the law in America does not allow him to become an American citizen. Not ever. So, by answering 'yes' to question twenty-eight, he becomes stateless, a man without a country.'"

Shigeru cleared his throat. He waited until he had everyone's attention. "The government did, finally, change the wording for us Issei. The statement read, 'We would not do anything to harm America.'"

"Unfortunately, by that time, the camp protests were in full swing," said Jane.

Kenta saw Patrick's jaw tighten. "You see, by saying *I forswear allegiance to the emperor* suggests that before … I *did* have such an allegiance. But that's not true!" Patrick's words came out in a heated blast that seemed to surprise even himself. "You can't imagine the anger I felt when Japan attacked *my* country. I am as American as any white person."

Kenta could imagine, but he allowed a painful silence to settle over the room. Then he asked, "Is there … do you have a pen?"

Gabriel reached into his pocket and pulled out a fountain pen. He handed it to Kenta with an infectious grin. "A Boy Scout is always prepared."

Kenta smiled back and took the pen. Under the word "Heroes," he signed his full name under Patrick's signature and then turned to Patrick.

"For me, joining the army was the right decision, but I understand and respect the no-no boys. They acted in good conscience. I'll be fighting for them, too."

Jane moved toward Patrick to give his arm a reassuring squeeze, but her brother shook her off. Instead, he grabbed a towel and a change of clothes and stomped out.

Their father dropped his head. Jane turned to Kenta, fighting back angry tears. "I'm sorry."

Kenta smiled. "Don't be. I get it."

"Can we go out and play?" asked Gabriel.

Fumiko nodded to her two younger children. "Be back before dinnertime." She turned to Kenta and forced a smile. "Usually, we walk to the big mess hall, where you will be performing tonight. Tomorrow morning, you can stand in line with us for two hours with our begging pails." Fumiko's last words could have been bitter, but her laugh softened them.

Her husband lifted his head and gave Kenta a wide smile that revealed misshapen teeth. "Come. Let me show you something."

"OK," said Kenta. He bowed to Jane's grandmother, reclining on the bed. He wondered if she had any idea of the drama taking place. Kenta followed Shigeru outside, where the sounds of wood-chopping drowned out the call of the birds.

"We will eat on this picnic table that I made," said Shigeru. "But that's not what I want to show you." He shuffled on the balls of his feet to a pair of sheds—one wood, the other corrugated metal—at the edge of the drainage ditch.

The smell of baking bread danced in the moist air. Shigeru pointed to the source of the delicious aroma. "Later. Come … come." He reached into his trouser pocket and took out a small wooden spoon with a brass key dangling from a piece of red ribbon. At the ill-fitting door of the wooden shed, he attempted to insert the key quickly to hide the slight tremble in his hand. He succeeded on the third try.

By now Kenta had learned to ignore the older man's soft but constant cough.

Shigeru opened the door and walked in. He reached up and pulled on a dangling string. The bare light bulb sprang to life, revealing a spinning wheel. He smiled like a boy who has just caught his first fish.

"Before California, our family leased farmland outside of Hiroshima. We grew hemp, which my mother spun into a *kaya,* a mosquito netting that she sold at the Friday market. She also spun cotton and made our clothes. I helped her, and being someone who likes to tinker, I built a lighter, smaller spinning wheel, more suitable for her small size."

Kenta clapped in appreciation, running his hand over the spinning wheel, which he then plunged into the attached wooden box holding raw cotton. He fingered the spindle, fat with cotton thread, blinking at such an unexpected discovery.

"This is amazing," Kenta said, giving the wheel a gentle spin. "All those years you kept the skill. I remember my okaasan telling me about this." Kenta fabricated this last bit of ingratiation since he could not remember Haru ever mentioning a spinning wheel. He wiped his eyes with his shirt-sleeve as casually as he could.

"Next door smells good," said Kenta.

Shigeru took the hint and reversed the locking process. He then labored the dozen or so steps to the corrugated metal shed, picking up a handful of splintered wood from a short stack of logs by the doorless opening.

"Go inside," he commanded with pride in his voice. "Our barracks group built a kitchen from discarded building materials."

Fumiko stood in front of a pot on a circular grill supported by metal struts over flaming logs. Beads of sweat trickled down from her hairline to her chin as she stirred its steaming contents. Next to her, a middle-aged woman lifted the lid of another pot over the same flames. The woman stabbed at the rice inside and sampled a bit. Her face broke into a smile, showing twin dimples and a row of yellow teeth.

"*This* is real rice," the woman said, nodding her approval. "From California, just for this special occasion. Not that Louisiana rice that falls off your chopsticks."

Shigeru squatted, his knees perilously close to the bread oven. "A pottery crafts teacher made this kiln from bayou mud and straw," he said, feeding firewood into the flames.

Kenta, searching for something to say, volunteered, "Now I understand why you have all those logs."

The sweat-drenched women left the hotbox to catch a breath of fresh air, although no amount of breeze could alleviate the stifling heat. Kenta followed the women outside.

"This is our neighbor, Yoshie Nakahara," said Fumiko.

"Are you Mary's mother?" asked Kenta.

Yoshie gave a self-deprecating laugh. "Yes, I am. Ever since Mary organized the letter-writing campaign to all the boys in the military, I'm simply known as 'Mary's mother.'" With more pride than most Japanese mothers allow themselves, she added, "I think she has a chapter of letter writers in every camp now—except Tule Lake."

Kenta bowed slightly. "She's a teenage legend."

Fumiko brushed the sweat from her face with her sleeve.

"What Mary does is even more remarkable when you realize what happened to her family after Pearl Harbor. Her father died shortly after leaving the hospital and being arrested by the FBI," said Fumiko. "She has good reason to be bitter about all that has happened, but ..." Fumiko's eyes clouded, her distress evident. "She believes in the American ideal that I have trouble accepting. I can only hope she is right."

"I'm sorry," said Kenta turning to Yoshie. "The FBI took your husband out of the hospital?"

A hint of breeze finally passed through the trees. Yoshie wiped her hands on her apron and gave Kenta a sad smile. "Not quite. The story is a long one." At Kenta's nod of encouragement, she sighed and continued.

"My husband descended from a *samurai* family. He left Japan in 1921. We had a good business selling provisions to Japanese naval ships visiting Long Beach and San Francisco. One of our hometown friends, an admiral in the Japanese navy, gave us his ship's supply business. He often stopped by our home on the way to Washington, where he served as a military attaché.

"Just before his last visit, he sent a telegram saying he had to fly directly to Washington and would not be visiting us. The FBI intercepted the telegram. That same day—December 6—my husband came home from the hospital after treatment for diabetes …"

"… And Japan attacked Pearl Harbor the next day," said Kenta.

"Before nightfall that Sunday, the FBI barged into our home. They woke up my husband—he was so weak he could barely stand—they accused him of being a spy and took him away. They would not even allow him to change out of his pajamas."

Yoshie twisted the edges of her apron. "They interrogated him for two weeks. I guess they found nothing because they released him. But by then, he was just a ghost of the man I knew." Her eyes misted. "He couldn't talk; his mind, which was so sharp before, had deteriorated terribly. All his pride and dignity were gone. He died three days later. Later, we found out that the FBI had rented a house across the street a year earlier to keep tabs on us because of our connection with the admiral."

Yoshie sat, hands relaxed and composed. "A month on, when we were all living in the horse stables, Mary organized her first letter-writing campaign to divert our attention away from our plight. At first, we wrote to orphans and people in old folks' homes and then later to the boys in the service. Mary works at the camp mess hall to help pay for postage." Yoshie shook her head. "Some people make fun of my daughter, accusing her of being a naïve idealist who doesn't understand anything. But those same people always show up for the social activities she organizes."

As if on cue, Mary stepped out of her family's barracks. She wore a white, short-sleeved dress with a modest V-neck. A magenta-colored paper bow crowned her upswept hair. Her creamy skin attested to an avoidance of the sun's rays. Chad trailed behind her. In an instant, Kenta knew that Chad having been assigned to Mary's family had not been left to chance. While Mary treated every GI as her best friend, she had spent more time with Chad, who was one of the few boys who had not come on to her.

Mary gestured for Kenta to come over, comfortably taking charge as if she were the camp's master sergeant. "Let's put our two picnic tables and benches together," she said. Kenta was learning that when Mary said, "Let's," she really meant, "You do it."

"I'll bring out some lemonade," she said.

Chad brushed Mary's hand as she got up from the table, as if they were both invisible to watchful eyes. Kenta and Jane played along, refusing to smirk or raise an eyebrow. They carried their table over to Mary's backyard while Chad retrieved the benches.

Mary returned, carrying a tray with a pitcher of lemonade and four Kraft Swanky Swig jelly jars. Kenta thought about how he had always drunk lemonade with ice, as though the frosty ice cubes were an ingredient in lemonade. Now he gratefully settled for anything wet to quench his thirst. His saliva glands puckered his mouth. Kenta downed the entire glass of lemonade in one, continuous gulp.

Mary refilled his glass.

Kenta let out a sigh of satisfaction.

"How do you manage to stay happy? You, Jane … the busloads of girls who come to the USO dances in Hattiesburg like you had just left a New York penthouse."

Ignoring Japanese cultural restraints, Mary placed her hands on Kenta's arm.

"What would you have us do? Mope around, complaining about how our lives have been torn apart?"

"Besides, we love to see you guys!" said Jane. "For us, it's a weekend escape—a chance to be happy, a chance to make others happy!" Jane paused. It was the kind of pause that commanded everyone but the most impatient to wait. "True, we haven't spent much time with you guys from Hawaii."

After asking her mother if she needed help, Mary said, "The morning after the big brawl between our kotonk guys and you Hawaii boys, Chaplain Hamada came over and talked to me. I agreed with him that you folks needed to see how we live our lives. More than that, we want you here! I'm setting up a USO inside the camp."

Fumiko came over and handed Jane a bed sheet. The four young folks each grabbed a corner and spread it over the picnic tables.

Mary poured the rest of the lemonade. "I bet you guys don't know that some people live here voluntarily."

Kenta and Chad raised their eyebrows.

"Including Jane." Mary tilted her head toward Jane. "You tell them."

Jane paused, her eyes drifting to where her father struggled to uproot weeds under the tomato vines.

"Father was not the man you see now. His vigor and enthusiasm infected our family and our employees. In the early days after Pearl Harbor, the government warned us Japanese that it would be better to apply for permission to move inland. So, we did, and were accepted as volunteer evacuees. Most Japanese thought the hysteria would blow over soon. We sold our store at a huge discount, but it was nothing like the giveaway prices other Japanese had to settle for a few months later.

"We moved far inland—to Glendale, Arizona. My parents rented a two-story, Spanish-style stucco building a block west of Main Street. Our street ran parallel to the railroad tracks that divided the town in half. We lived upstairs while Dad prepared the downstairs to become our new vegetable store. My older sister and her husband found a place on the opposite side of the tracks, just a ten-minute walk from our home. Since the better high school was east of the tracks, on my sister's side, I registered as living with my sister.

"Two months later, President Roosevelt signed Executive Order 9066, calling for the evacuation of all Japanese from the West Coast. General DeWitt included the western half of Arizona to his designation of the West Coast, using the railroad tracks that cut through Glendale and the rest of Arizona as the dividing line. You know that expression—'the wrong side of the tracks'? That's where we lived. So, for the second time in just eight weeks, my parents had to leave their home and business, but this time in just forty-eight hours, and this time, by force into a camp surrounded by barbed wire fences. Since I officially lived east of the tracks, I could have escaped detainment."

Kenta and Chad listened in disbelief, nodding their heads attentively.

"Every family here has a story," said Mary, softly. "Should Jane have stayed with her sister, graduated from high school and gone on to college? Does her family need her here? What right does the government—of the people, by the people, for the people—have to force us to make those kinds of decisions?"

"I need help in the shed," called out Fumiko.

"Be there in a minute, Mom," said Jane.

Mary shifted her attention to Chad. "You guys in the army are proving every day that America made a mistake. This is still the greatest country in the world. Someday, America will recognize its mistake."

Mary rose to her feet. "Let's put the food on the table."

"Sergeant Mary" had issued her order. The privates replied: "What can we do?"

After a dinner of delicious, home-cooked food and colorful stories about California and Hawaii, Jane turned to Kenta.

"Your education is almost complete. Let's take the scenic route to the recreation hall."

∞ CHAPTER 62 ∞

AT SEVEN O'CLOCK IN THE EVENING, the sun was still high in the sky. "That was a delicious meal, Jane," said Kenta. "On forty-five cents a day, you can't do this very often."

"Oh, you innocent boy. The families pooled this week's ration coupons and donated them to the host families. Those with jobs kicked in coins so Mom could buy extra vegetables in town."

A wave of shame filled Kenta's face. "They shouldn't have …"

"No, Kenta, we should have. Other than visits from our soldiers to see their families, we rarely see other people. This is the biggest event in the history of our camp."

Kenta tried to think of an appropriate response but avoided uttering a bland bromide by pointing at a two-story-tall obelisk ahead of him. A sharper focus revealed white stones on the ground, laid out symmetrically.

"That's our cemetery, Kenta. Mostly older people are buried here— people who built lives in America, owned homes, sent their children to universities. They came to America chasing a dream and made it come true for the most part. And then they ended up dying in this prison."

Jane walked over to a whitewashed cement headstone. "But not only old people." She pointed to the headstone. "Kato Asao Miriam, 1922–1943. Just 21 years old."

Kenta kept his eyes on the other headstones. *How did she die?* "*Seppuku?*"

"Hanging from an American flag tied to the archway fronting the camp commander's house isn't exactly ritual seppuku, but she died with honor. We've had two girls hang themselves from a rafter in their barracks."

In the Shinto tradition, Kenta bowed his head at the tombstone and lightly clapped his hands three times in reverence.

Without thinking, he took Jane's hand in his as they continued. She didn't pull away until they neared the recreation hall.

"It wouldn't do to start gossip," she laughed. "But … after the show to-night, I might come back to the cemetery." She gave Kenta an encouraging poke in his back.

One by one, the Hawaii boys gathered at the rec hall. They seemed more like zombies than entertainers. Danny rose gloomy-faced and turned to his buddies. "I know none of us feels like dancing and singing."

"You got that right," said Short Pants.

"It might be days—maybe longer, maybe never—before we can adequately express the shock we're feeling," Danny said. "But as we can see, these folks haven't given up. They have welcomed us with warmth and generosity. We have an *on* to repay, a true debt of gratitude."

When it was time for the Hawaii boys to perform, their song and dance routine brought the audience to their feet so often that soon, no one was sitting.

And then it was time for the finale. "Short Pants, hit it," Kenta called out.

Short Pants started strumming. The men, who were really still boys, reverted to their happier, carefree days of singing and dancing after a day of pulling weeds in the pineapple fields, cutting cane, planting seeds or doing other plantation work. The dancing Hawaii boys created a sensual mood—for which they might have to answer to the parents after the show.

⚭ ⚭

Kenta slipped out the back door after the show. A guard tower spotlight caught him square in the face, blinding him. He jerked his head away and swung his right hand over his eyes. The guard light passed and continued its lazy arc. Kenta raised his contorted face. Each of the six guard towers panned a light beam over the barracks, the cafeteria and the fences. Kenta froze and waited for the arc to double back, certain that a guard would spoil his coming liaison. But the arc maintained its leisurely swivel.

Kenta sprinted forward, dodging the light beams, toward the unlit area of the cemetery. He appreciated Jane's chosen venue. None of the guards bothered to turn the searchlights on the dead.

He reached the obelisk. Waited. Waited more. Maybe Jane had had second thoughts. Not that he assumed anything to come from their rendezvous, but his expectations had risen each time he spotted her smiling face in the audience. The feelings of guilt that had plagued him when visiting Miss Lillian's Pink Palace had dulled. He thought of Natasha, with whom he had not slept, rather than the Pink Palace tart who had given him thirty seconds of passion and whose name he had already forgotten.

Then he heard something. He stopped; listened intently. A soft note floated his way. It was a very poor excuse for a whistle, but enough to establish direction. The snake in his stomach stirred. His eyes roved. A lone silhouette of a small building, maybe the distance from home plate to second base, broke the moonlit row of headstones in the right corner of the graveyard. The whistle, louder this time, beckoned, triggering a stiffening below his belt. Anticipation sucked the saliva from his mouth as Kenta aimed for the stone shed, the only hiding place within distance of a whistle. As he got closer, he heard a soft whisper. "Inside …"

A ring of sweat beads on Kenta's forehead bubbled. His heart pulsed. The insistent snake roamed his gut like a cobra eyeing a mouse. Kenta pushed the door, which resisted. Determined, he pushed harder.

"Wait!" demanded an urgent whisper.

Kenta dropped his arm. The cobra thumped the insides of his stomach.

A soft voice laughed. "Don't Hawaii doors ever open outwards?"

The door squeaked open a scant foot toward him.

As Kenta grabbed it, a slender hand reached out. It pulled him inside and spun him around. Jane brushed his lips with hers as she hooked the bottom of the door with her raised toes and tugged the door close.

Kenta stood still. He barely noticed the wheelbarrow tilted upright against the back of the shed, or the shovels, hoes and pitchforks hanging on hooks. His eyes riveted on Jane.

She posed flirtatiously. Beams of moonlight slipping through the slats revealed a coquettish smile. The bodice of her dress framed her hard nipples. Jane leaned forward and kissed him again. She closed the narrow gap between their bodies and put her hand behind his neck. Then he felt her tongue slip into his mouth.

Taken aback by Jane's urgency, Kenta pulled away. "Are you … you sure this is okay?"

"Kenta, we live in strange times. Normal rules don't apply." Jane's fingers were undoing the top button of his khaki shirt. "I don't want to hear about any girl you left behind in Hawaii," she said, her voice husky. "And I'm not going to tell you about my high school sweetheart who is being held just like all of us, but in a camp in Manzanar, California."

Two more buttons found freedom. Kenta inhaled her sweet ginger-and-*sake* breath, which was more arousing than any exotic perfume. His knees were like putty. Jane placed one hand on Kenta's bare chest and freed the button just above his belt. "Do you think you can unzip the back of my dress?" She pirouetted daintily.

Kenta's shaking fingers fumbled with the tongue of her zipper.

Jane giggled. "How do you ever manage to clean your rifle, soldier?" She reached behind her back and in one fluid, practiced motion caught the zipper pull and slid it down.

Kenta let out a short breath at the sight of her copper-hued back, shimmering in the moonlight and promising a bit of heaven. He did not ask her how she had smuggled a sheet and a towel into the shed, nor where she had hidden her bra. Instead, he bent down to untie his army boots, muttering a soft curse as he inadvertently knotted the laces in his haste.

"Kenta, I promise not to run away before you figure out how to take off your boots," said Jane, turning around, her hands hiding her womanhood.

Kenta tossed his boots, stood up and kicked his trousers to the side.

Jane cupped her breasts. "Our time is short, but that doesn't mean we skip foreplay."

Kenta wondered what experience had brought forth such a knowing comment. He had learned one thing early on with Angelina—the rewards for a few strategic kisses and patience were enormous.

When they finished, Jane lifted up Kleenex tissues and a Campbell's soup tin of water.

"What did my little brother say about being prepared?" she said, smiling. "I will leave first. Wait two minutes and then join your group in the rec hall," said Jane, knowing that was where the Hawaii boys were sleeping.

∞ ∞

At the first sliver of dawn's light, the doors of the cafeteria/recreation hall banged open.

"You're lucky we open early," said a woman, her voice sandpapery from years of smoking. The sounds of door latches being unfastened and window shutters being pried open awoke the men. Pleasant breezes from the bayou swept out the unpleasant odors of body sweat and burnt mosquito coils.

"How are we so lucky, *Obasan*?" asked Chuckles.

"Because if you move quickly, you won't have to stand in line for a shower."

The men stirred. They rolled up the futons families had provided and grabbed their towels from their backpacks. Marching around to the back of the barracks, they kept an eye out for an open shower stall as the obasan had advised. The soldiers found the showers empty. *By design?* wondered Kenta. They also found that the word "shower" was a misnomer. A trickle was more like it. They kept their voices low.

"How can our government do this to its own people?" asked Chad.

"My dad's in a camp like this one," said Kenta, "but we still have our home and our business. It reminds me of that saying, 'I complained because I had no shoes … until I met a man who had no feet.'"

"I'm ready to head back to Shelby. This place is depressing," said Short Pants.

"Not yet!" stressed Chad. "Mary has a full day planned for us," he added, concern and challenge evident in his voice.

"No need for the sales talk, Chad," Kenta assured him. "We're not going anywhere."

∞ ∞

The group applauded the morning skills demonstration by the Boy Scouts and Girl Scouts.

That afternoon, Kenta pitched for the 442nd baseball team. He threw fat pitches down the middle. The infielders missed easy grounders, and the outfielders were slow to chase well-hit drives. At the end of the first inning, the Rohwer Rangers led, 4–0.

Mary charged into the Hawaii boys' dugout. "Don't you dare insult us!" She tore into the boys for a full two minutes. The 442nd boys from Hawaii played their best for the rest of the game and won, 10–6.

At dinner, the Hawaii boys declined the courtesy of being at the head of the line. They spent the next two hours talking with the camp residents waiting for their turn to eat.

There were enough musicians gathered on the cafeteria's makeshift bandstand to form an eleven-piece band, so they played all the latest Miller, Dorsey and Sinatra songs. The music brought couples who had not danced at all since being incarcerated to the dance floor.

Kenta and Jane danced the first cheek-to-cheek number. Jane whispered, "Last night, Patrick noticed that I got home late, so he told me that he's going to walk me home tonight."

∞ ∞

Before departing for Camp Shelby the next morning, the Hawaii boys attended an ecumenical church service in the cafeteria after breakfast. Buddhist priests and a Protestant minister offered prayers of gratitude for the wonderful weekend and prayed that the boys would come back home safely.

Outside the church, the soldiers bowed, shook hands, and in a few cases hugged women their mothers' age who acted as their surrogate okaasan that weekend. Kenta's eyes roamed over the group several times feigning nonchalance. She wasn't there. Would he see her at the USO, or would she feel she couldn't attend because of what happened? What would he do if she showed at the USO? What seemed so natural, so urgent, now seemed a bit tawdry given the consequences in their culture.

He almost bumped into Mary. Stopped. Shook her hand softly with both of his. "Arigato, Mary. You have given us a memory." Men were loading into the trucks. He heard his name called. All of a sudden, he had much to say, but said nothing as Mary filled the gap.

"You have given us memories to fill our days for a long time, Kenta."

Speechless, Kenta ran to the truck, jumped and turned in a single leap and landed on the back edge.

∞ ∞

When the trucks finally drove back down through the main thorough-fare to the gates, the residents once again waved their American flags and shouted, "Domo arigato!" The Hawaii boys in the 442nd forced smiles and waved back. The sun was cooking the bayou once again, pro-ducing the sour, rank smell the boys had come to hate. Once outside the gates, their mood turned sober—no singing, no gambling, not a word, just haunting silence.

The youngest of the soldiers, the normally exuberant Danny Inouye, spoke what was on everyone's mind. "I wonder what I would have done if it had been me and my parents inside that camp. Would I have volun-teered for a country that betrayed me? Remember, we volunteered from a close-knit community that is generous and supportive of what we're doing. Our families haven't been forced out of their homes and herded into back-woods prisons—never knowing when it will end or what kind of life is possible when this camp nightmare ends. But those mainland boys vol-unteered while in these camps, willing to die for a country that locked up their parents and siblings."

"One thing is for certain," added Kenta. "Our war with the kotonks is over. We are one; the only enemy is in Europe."

PART VI

FAMILY REUNION

THE SETTING SUN GAVE ENOUGH LIGHT for Kenta to finish his weekly letter to Angelina. He regaled her with his 522nd forward observer exploits calling in coordinates that caused a shelling of a jeep holding a case of a colonel's whiskey. "Since no alcohol is allowed in live training sites," he wrote Angelina, "I got off with a scowl." He sat outside his hutment on a makeshift bench, arms resting on the picnic-style table the squad had fashioned from planks they had "found" at a construction site. He caught a sudden movement from the corner of one eye, causing both to widen in surprise.

"Tommy!"

"Hey, little brother. What's with your uniform? They don't issue belt buckles and shoes to you sorry-ass pineapple grunts?"

Kenta stood up to give his older brother a hug, then stepped back for an appraisal. "I thought you were on maneuvers in Louisiana."

"Just got back a few hours ago," said Tommy. "We'll be in Shelby for a month before shipping out to join Ike in North Africa.

"For a guy who trained in the Wisconsin winter, you sure have a helluva suntan. What gives?"

By now, Spud, Fats, No Ticket, Stonehead and Chuckles had come outside the hut to greet Tommy.

"Hey, are all you guys still together as a squad? Whose ass did you kiss for that?"

"We're not the only ones," said Kenta. "Some of the other VVV squads have been kept together, too." He jerked his head westward. "Most of them bunk in those hutments."

Tommy sat down on the bench. "I just spent three months as dog bait off the coast of Mississippi, a nowhere place called Cat Island. And I'll punch out the first wise ass who asks, 'Does it rain cats and dogs there?'"

Tommy lowered his voice. "I participated in a secret mission to prove that Japanese smell different than other races."

"We know *you* do," said Chuckles, wrinkling his nose.

Tommy quickly flipped him the finger. "You guys gotta listen to this. Cat Island is a marshland with mosquitoes as big as sparrows. The brass picked this armpit for a hush-hush experiment because it's supposed to resemble a tropical South Pacific island. Some Swiss know-it-all convinced the White House you could train dogs to enter caves and hiding places in the Pacific to find and attack Japanese soldiers because of our 'unique smell.' Supposedly the dogs take one sniff and know the difference between white and Japanese soldiers."

"You're shitting me, right?" said Fats.

With a six-pack of Budweiser swinging at the end of each arm, Hero joined the group to a round of applause. He put the beer on the table, pulled a church key from his Bermuda shorts, and grabbed a Bud. After punching two triangular holes in the top, he took a long, thirst-quenching gulp. Kenta grabbed the opener and poked two more Buds, handing one to Tommy, and then passed the opener to Chuckles.

"The idea isn't as farfetched as it sounds. It's based on diet."

"What do you mean, 'diet'?" asked Fats.

"As in what you eat. Haoles eat meat and potatoes, Asians eat fish and rice." Tommy waited until everyone had a beer in hand. "The animals were pets, donated by people responding to the army's plea for dogs to be used for guard duty or search missions. Little did they know what horrors awaited their pooches.

"At first, the dog handlers tied raw meat around our necks so the dogs would get used to chasing us—like a game. These were big dogs: German shepherds, Saint Bernards, giant schnauzers, and even one Great Dane. The dogs were also being taught basic obedience commands."

"So, you proved dogs like meat. That's a good way to spend a month," said Spud.

"Almost like that," said Tommy. "We'd run. The dogs would catch us. We'd fall down. They'd gnaw at the meat, maybe lick our faces." He took a long draw on his Bud. "But once the dogs got used to playing chase, the rules changed. We were given knobby sticks and ordered to beat the dogs until they attacked us."

All attention riveted on Tommy. The only sounds were the murmurs in nearby hutments and the cackling crows that came each evening scrounging for scraps.

"The theory was that the dogs would learn to associate our smell with the abuse and attack anyone that smelled like us."

"Jesus, Tommy," said Kenta.

"So now the dogs hated us. I don't know if smelling us made them want to attack, but for sure when they saw us, they got riled up. The army started sending us into the woods and then let the dogs loose with orders to kill. One of the dog trainers lost a brother at Pearl, and I think he held us personally responsible for it. You had the feeling when he shouted 'Kill!' he really meant it."

"I'd be scared shitless," said No Ticket. "Didn't you get bit?"

"We were wrapped up in protective padding and wore metal mesh masks to protect our faces—you know, like the kind fencers wear. But I still got bit through the clothing." Tommy held out his arm and rolled up the sleeve. "And I got plenty bruises from dogs that didn't let go with the first whack. We wore extra padding over our nuts and pecker. After a while, we got used to the dogs but not the heat. And toward the end, we were more worried about snakes and alligators."

Tommy tipped his empty beer can upside down and then slammed it on the table. Fats took the hint, opened another and handed the can to Tommy.

"Every day, same routine—two hours of running for our lives, sweating like sons-of-bitches, getting chewed to bits by crazed animals—followed by twenty-two hours of boredom. We fished and hunted wild pigs—and gambled."

"How did it end? I mean, can dogs really tell the difference between us and haoles?" asked Kenta.

Tommy took a long swallow then set down his beer can, staring at it for a moment.

"How did it end?"

He gave a little shrug, as if to shake off the memory. "Not well. A bad ending to a stupid idea."

He stopped again, and Kenta saw pain behind his brother's eyes.

"What happened?"

Tommy took a big breath. "A week ago, five of us Nisei were stationed about fifty yards from the kennel, ready to run as soon as they let out the dogs. There were five of them, barking and snarling, trying to jump through the fence. Eyeing those dogs, all wound up and itching to get at us, I worried we didn't have enough padding. Then the handler who hates us came out, opened the pen and yelled, 'Kill! Kill! *Kill!*'"

Tommy took another swig and wiped his mouth with the back of his hand.

"But instead of coming after us, the schnauzer, first out of the cage, leapt on the handler and went right for the throat. The other four dogs followed in a frenzy—biting the guy's arms and legs, whatever they could reach. The handler started screaming and tried to roll into a ball. But the dogs were wild, out of control, like monsters in some horror movie."

"Did you try to help?" asked Spud.

"Yeah," said Tommy, but his voice sounded leaden. "As soon as we saw the attack, we ran back, yelling at the dogs and waving the sticks over our heads, but that didn't stop them. We started beating the dogs with the sticks. They turned and attacked us—except for the one sinking his teeth into the handler. By then the guy lay motionless. Blood geysered out of his leg. I threw my stick at a dog to back it off then dropped down next to the handler and pressed my padded hand on the hole in his leg. The other guys kept fighting off the dogs, which finally backed away. About then some other handlers arrived carrying shovels and hoes to drive off the dogs. And then they … they … started shooting and … they killed them all. They killed all those dogs we turned into beasts. And just a month ago, they'd been pets … beloved family pets."

No one spoke for a long while. Then Chuckles broke the spell.

"What happened to the guy, the handler?"

"Oh, he survived. But the scent experiment died."

Another solemn silence settled over the group until Fats let out a juicy belch. Everyone burst into laughter, thankful for the change of mood.

"Hey," said Tommy "What's this I hear you have a kim chee-breath *yobo* for an officer."

"Them's fighting words big brother. You're talking about Samurai Kim," said Kenta. "Truth is, I used those same words when I found out our lieutenant was Korean. And a ninety-day wonder out of OCS at that. It didn't take long for our attitudes to change.

"With our CO's backing, Kim trashed our previous training and jammed in a whole new regimen. We were in the field from dawn until sunset. Charging pillboxes spewing live bullets—two guys from Maui got bloody butts. When Kim shouted: 'The squad leader is killed. Private Takayama, you're in charge,' I had to take command on the spot. No waiting for the squad lieutenant to give an order.

"It took us a while, but we got the point. In war, we need to step up when a man goes down. When moving, one squad shoots while the other two move and then rotate seamlessly. Other companies are laughing at us because of our hours and constant drills, but I think when the shooting starts, we'll have a better chance of winning and surviving. GI Kim is no longer referred to as our yobo."

Tommy raised his eyebrows. "GI Kim? Samurai Kim?"

"It's about respect," snapped Kenta. "Earned respect. If you 100th don't fuck up over there, we'll see Europe, too. I like our chances of standing up to the Germans a whole lot better with the training Kim and Major Johnson have given us."

"What are we doing here drinking beer, when Hattiesburg beckons?" said Short Pants, breaking the tension.

∞ Chapter 64 ∞

KENTA SPLURGED FOR A TAXI. After all, his brother was joining him, and it was time to flee Camp Shelby for the promise of Hattiesburg. He and Tommy squeezed into the front seat, while Short Pants, Buster and Chad piled into the back.

Kenta absent-mindedly cracked his knuckles, half listening to the yammering between Short Pants and Buster. Chad said nothing, focused on the pages of last year's bestseller, *The Robe*, an odd complement to the ribald backseat argument.

"If we hit the USO first, the Rohwer girls will get us revved up without knowing it. We'll behave like gentlemen because we know an hour later, we can walk our daikons over to Lillian's," said Buster.

"That won't work," argued Short Pants. "Your pecker'll be a-twangin' and all you'll be able to think about is Pink Palace pussy. You won't hear a word the girls are saying and they'll get pissed. Let's go now, get our wickets waxed and we won't have to act like gentlemen."

Kenta wondered if Webster and Clay had been as passionate arguing the Missouri Compromise. He let the debate prattle on. It didn't matter. He had already made the decision where they would go first. He wanted to see Natasha early, before her card filled. Thoughts of Natasha had never been far from his mind. Kenta could not explain the fascination he had for this woman whom he had not slept with, had spoken to for fewer than fifteen minutes and whose time had to be paid for at a premium.

He thought of her most when he wrote letters to Angelina. The more he envisioned Natasha disrobing, the greater the intensity of his prose. Angelina welcomed his affection and wrote back, "Loneliness and distance have taught you how to express your feelings." He agreed with her, acknowledging a disquieting awareness his writing had changed more than he realized. He worried whether his sudden ability to write with greater passion would eventually sound alarm bells. Would Angelina suspect another root of his new introspective writing skills?

Time to end the backseat drivel. Kenta poked Tommy in the ribs and wiggled his forefinger as he faced the back seat, signaling: "Watch this."

"This endless bullshit shows why I played quarterback and you lug heads got stomped on at the line. Boys, it's double-header time. We'll drop by Lillian's now and get a smile on our faces. Then we'll trot over to the USO, chat up the girls, eat and drink beer." He broke into a salacious grin. "Then we go back to Lillian's for dessert."

He glanced at Chad, who was not smiling.

"Of course," said Kenta, "before our first stop, we'll drop off Chad a block from the USO so he can help Mary with the dance preparations. And being the good friend he is, Chad will lie and tell Mary ..." Kenta did his best to mimic Chad's higher-pitched voice. "I couldn't wait to see you, so I left those slow-pokes behind at the base."

∞ ∞

Kenta grew hard walking up the Pink Palace steps. He and the gang strutted into Lillian's. His eyes rummaged the room for Natasha. Instead, he spotted Sergeant Doi chatting to Lillian at the grand piano. They hadn't seen each other since Doi had been transferred out of the 522nd. Kenta had played out the inevitable meeting in his mind dozens of times.

Since the Rohwer visit, the mood between kotonks and Buddhaheads had changed. Hamada's ploy had worked beyond his and Pence's expectations. Hawaiians greeted Mainlanders with a new respect, made an effort to join them for meals and bought them beers when the chance appeared. They might even offer a "You guys really got the short end of the stick" or "We were lucky to avoid the mass internment." When a Mainlander, slow to catch on to the new spirit, shot a verbal zinger about the Hawaiian dress habits or pidgin talk, the Hawaiians laughed it off with a zinger of their own, but in jest rather than a challenge to "beef."

Doi's laughter stopped when he saw Kenta come straight for him, with Short Pants, Buster and Tommy right behind. His jaw tightened. His fists closed.

Lillian picked up on his alarm and casually stood in front of Doi as if to greet the Hawaiians, but Kenta's warm smile broke the unnecessary tension.

"Congratulations on your promotion, Sergeant." He turned to Lillian. "Please put the staff sergeant's drink tab on mine. His parents hosted us at Rohwer. Great folks." Before Doi could respond, he lowered his voice and asked Lillian, "Where's Natasha?"

Doi and Lillian started to talk at the same time.

Kenta smiled at Doi and then nodded to Lillian. She glanced at the naked mermaid clock over the bar. "You're lucky. You have time for a drink before she comes down."

"How's a Pabst Blue Ribbon sound, Sergeant?" Tommy asked Doi.

Doi waited a beat before answering, struggling to navigate the new landscape. "Uh ... good ..." His eyes fell to the floor then rose again. "I think at Lillian's we can drop ranks."

Tommy and Short Pants gathered up five foam-topped beers from the bar and brought them over to the piano. Short Pants grabbed one, took a long drink, and then turned to Doi.

"Man, I have to say ... we visited Rohwer. I mean, we had no idea ... what you, your families went through. We had to ask ourselves what we would have done in your shoes."

"Like I said, I stayed with your family," said Kenta. "Your sister told me how you wrestled with the decision." He took a good gulp from his beer. "If you feel like talking about it ... well, we'd like to hear."

Doi lifted his glass as two girls drifted over after waving goodbye to their customers. They smiled coyly at Doi, whom they seemed to know. When Doi cast a sidelong glance at Kenta, the girls switched their gaze to him. Kenta stared back at Doi, ignorant of the handoff.

Tommy laughed. "You will have to excuse my baby brother. He's barely out of the crib." He waved to the bartender, held up two fingers and then pointed the same fingers at the girls.

Kenta spotted Natasha coming down the stairs behind her client. He threw her a smile and turned to the piano player. "Can you play 'Summertime'?"

Natasha winked at Kenta and sashayed her hips suggestively in sync to the piano. Her black hair hung to her shoulders, a few seductive strands drifting over her eye. Her ruby—"deep pink," she'd argued to Lillian, who gave her number one mare a pass on the house dress code—velvet dress hugged her knees, ruffled sleeves stopped just past the elbow and the narrow V-neck swooped to her navel, revealing the flanks of pear-sized breasts. She sauntered over to the piano.

Kenta handed her a box of chocolates from the PX, which she set on the piano.

Eyeing the firm nipples outlined by the dress's fabric, Kenta said, "You might want to open it now."

Natasha turned to the bar, giving Kenta a sidelong glance.

He nodded to the redhead behind the bar.

She began pouring vodka into a cocktail glass.

Natasha ran her fingers along Kenta's arm. "I've been hoping you'd return." She opened the box of chocolates, ignored the five-dollar bill lying across the top and selected a piece. She bit half of it, smiled wickedly and placed the other half in Kenta's mouth.

He caught a wide-toothed grin from the piano player as the baritone voice finished the last "Hush, little child" refrain.

The redhead delivered the vodka concoction to Natasha and shamed the rest of the Hawaiian boys into ordering another round for their girls. Natasha lifted her glass languidly to her lips and sipped, a sensuous move reminiscent of Greta Garbo in *Mata Hari*, but held the glass there until the liquid disappeared. She placed the glass on the bar.

"A little buzz improves performance." She grabbed Kenta's hand and led her willing prey upstairs. She whispered into his ear, "Tonight is lesson one."

Kenta embraced lesson one. "Go slow" had its rewards. Each time he started to buck like a wrangler breaking a mustang, Natasha would grab his shoulders. "Slow down, cowboy, slow down." By the third time he had it right, maybe because by then, he needed the time.

Natasha accepted the generous two-dollar tip and promised, "Next time, if you prove you've mastered lesson one on the first go-round, you will be rewarded with lesson two."

Kenta opened his mouth to say, "I'll be back at midnight for the second lesson," but dampening his eagerness, Natasha placed a silencing finger on his lips. "One lesson at a time." She gave him a quick hug and his testicles a gentle squeeze. "Come tomorrow with the vigor you displayed tonight."

How Japanese, thought Kenta. *Rather than say "I am too busy," she washes her rejection in compliments.* He winked and displayed a knowing smile to indicate he understood the scene well.

Kenta, the last of his group to complete his mission, joined his mates at the bar where Doi was butchering his attempt to speak Pidgin with Short Pants but providing delicious entertainment for Lillian's girls.

Kenta paid the bar bill. He checked his wallet. "Men, it's time we found a place where two bits fills a mug."

Doi and Kenta let the group stroll ahead of them as they walked together toward town. They discovered both were Red Sox fans and agreed Joe DiMaggio couldn't hold Ted Williams's bat.

Doi said, "Joe's the better fielder."

"True but, like, how many great catches win a game?" asked Kenta.

"Is baseball big in Hawaii?" asked Doi.

"Bigger than big," said Kenta. "We play baseball better than we box, and you have seen some of our matches." Kenta regretted the statement as soon as he made it. He had been referring to the Camp Shelby boxing events but figured Doi would take it as a dig over the Mainlanders' poor fighting performance against the Hawaiians.

"We could organize an all-star Nisei team," said Doi. "There's a loud-mouthed, nasty-faced Texan I have to put up with at the firing range. He and I have the same job, me with the 442nd and him with the Sixty-Ninth. He was with a Texas outfit. Transferred to the Sixty-Ninth under a cloud according to a sergeant I talked to. Wasn't for the war, he said he'd have been cashiered out."

Kenta stopped. "Tall, lanky guy with a history of smallpox tattooed on his face? Claims he's the reincarnation of *the* Davy Crockett?"

"That's the one. Doesn't really think we belong. When he's not telling us about his family history, he explains he's the Dixie version of Bobby Feller."

Kenta grinned. "Interesting. I'm a pitcher too."

Doi's eyes lit up. "I'm a catcher."

"Us Japanese are as good at preparation as the Texans are at arrogance. I just bet they would put some money on beating us little brown runts."

∽ CHAPTER 65 ∽

July 20, 1943

BEHIND HOME PLATE, COLONEL PENCE SAT next to General Charles L. Bolte, commander of the Sixty-Ninth Division, both men perspiring under the Mississippi sun. The two senior officers had a bet. If the Sixty-Ninth New Yorkers prevailed, Bolte received a dozen cartons of sweet, ripe pineapples airlifted from Hawaii. If the 442nd won, Colonel Pence would get twelve bushels of McIntosh apples from upstate New York, courtesy of General Bolte.

The two men maintained a testy professional relationship. Fights be-tween the two contiguous units broke out frequently. Invariably some Yankee uttered "Jap." The 442nd men never asked, "What did you say?" or demand an apology like in the movies. He who struck first owned the advan-tage, and the Nisei swung fists and kicked groins in a Pavlovian whirl. The

Sixty-Ninth learned, and Jap-baiting largely ceased except for Neanderthal Klan types who needed only a few beers to forget their last beating.

The fact that the much smaller men of the 442nd won more skirmishes rankled Bolte as much as the fighting undercut his reputation. He had been heard to complain, "My men shouldn't bait the 442nd. But if they start something, they should finish it." Bolte expected his "real" Americans to win the battle of America's pastime against the undersized Japanese who, truth be told, had no business being in the military regardless of all the training records they were setting. He took grim satisfaction in knowing "those little men" would soon find out soldiering was altogether different when the other side uses real bullets.

Pence felt just as confident about his team, and for better reasons. He recalled the meeting two weeks earlier with Kim, Doi, and that private … *What was his name? Takayama.* They had come to him with a proposal— put together a baseball team made up of Nisei Mainlanders and Hawaii boys as a way to continue the bonding process begun with the trips to Rohwer and Jerome.

"We got a guy in the 100th. An outfielder from Waialua, on the North Shore of Oahu who has been scouted by the San Francisco Seals. Joe Takata," said Takayama. "If he hadn't been drafted, he might have been a major leaguer."

Pence dismissed this as hyperbole but accepted that this Joe fellow could be a hidden weapon best not bragged about.

"My guess," said Kim, "is that the Sixty-Ninth boys will stumble through a few intramural games with teams that won't challenge them. They'll likely spend more time bragging than working hard at being good." He waited a moment for emphasis. "I propose that our squad plays some real games with a few Hattiesburg teams."

Doi broke in. "If your office contacted the city league, we could schedule four or five games before we play the Sixty-Ninth."

Kenta turned to Kim. "The lieutenant here is our first baseman and cleanup hitter. The Yanks don't know he made the all-star team in college."

Pence couldn't keep the small smile from his face. "And what about you? What position do you play?"

Kenta flushed at this attention. "I'm a pitcher. My fastball is faster than my size suggests, and I can throw a curve."

Pence nodded his approval. "It seems you have come a long way since our last meeting, Sergeant." He relished the prospect of putting the Yankee Doodle Dandy boys in their place.

"Private … sir," said Kenta, wishing he could learn to keep his mouth shut.

"The first thing a newly promoted sergeant should learn is to think before correcting officers," said Pence. "Lieutenant Kim recommended you for sergeant and I have signed the papers." Pence turned his attention to Kim. "Work with the morale department and schedule those games. You are authorized to approve leave for anyone practicing. Gentlemen …" Pence stopped to give his words import, his eyes resting on each man in turn. "I don't take well to losing."

The Nisei had lost their first exhibition game against a Hattiesburg team 4–12, but then won four games straight. Kenta averaged more than a strikeout per inning in his three outings.

Now, boisterous crowds crammed backless benches, jammed aisles, stood in back of the rafters and squeezed the life out of scrabble grass on the open fields along the edge of the foul lines. Hot dog vendors sounded off. Infield dirt swirled as the ground crew swept the base paths.

Kenta warmed up alongside Crockett, who had been chosen to pitch for the Sixty-Ninth and bat fourth. He had little control over his fastball or his mouth.

"Before we ship out, I'll find you when you're not surrounded by your pineapple protectors." Ball, high. "Tell your slant-eyed friends not to stand too close to the plate." Ball, wide. "Your big brother playing second better be wearing shin guards. We slide hard." Right down the middle, a hitter's dream.

Kenta feigned to ignore the prattle even as he wondered if bragging to his teammates about Tommy's fielding skills had brought his brother into danger not of his making. The more Crockett goaded him, the more the Texan's pitches missed the plate. Kenta warmed up at quarter speed until the last three pitches, all nipping the edges of the strike zone. The Mississippi sun burns hard in August, and Kenta vowed to guard his strength. He hoped Crockett would pour it on from the first inning.

Pence and Bolte recognized the danger of what was intended as a friendly match turning into a donnybrook. The two senior officers counted on their presence to mitigate the men's brawling instincts. Pence agreed with Bolte and shut down beer sales after the fifth inning. Beefy MPs from a Wisconsin unit filled the front row of both sides as guests and added incentive to keep the game clean.

Recently promoted Master Sergeant "Sunny" Carter shook hands with the hardened Master Sergeant Brixton from the New York Division. Private Danny Inouye and a private from the Sixty-Ninth mimicked the hand shaking of their senior non-coms. They all sat on the bottom row of the spectator seating. A burlap bag of cash sat at their feet.

A week before the game, Inouye had watched Kenta help mow down a Hattiesburg team 7–0. After the game, Danny joined the team for hamburgers at the Dixie Grill and bought the first round of beers. "Let's really challenge the Yanks!" he had shouted. "$1,000!" He delighted in the shock value of his challenge. "I'll off-load bets at two bucks a shot." Inouye, who had built a good stake with his poker skills, lifted his beer glass high. "I'm in for ten bucks."

Mary had bused in two hundred USO girls from Jerome and Rohwer as a cheering section for the game. Tonight, they were hosting a USO send-off party for the men of the 100th, who were shipping out to North Africa in a few weeks. A dozen wives and their husbands of the 100th sat together with more on their mind than a baseball game.

The crowd buzzed when the 442nd's favorite Hattiesburg waitress, Mabel, strode in holding hands with Chuckles. They sat with the Nisei wives. In a feeble attempt at modesty, Mabel buttoned her snug-fitting blouse to the top, but her short skirt rode high enough that by the end of the first inning, everyone opposite her seating section knew she wore red panties. When they arrived, astonishment more than anger registered on the Sixty-Ninth side. Mabel had become a minor celebrity among the recruits, with her flirty banter, short skirts and revealing blouses. They mumbled the usual rant: "Why would an eye-popping girl like that go for a slant-eyed guy like him?"

Her parents shared their view. When Mabel talked of marriage, her mother, eager to discover proof of Chuckles's character flaws, wrote to his school. Letters came back from the principal and teachers praising his schoolwork and character. "Lucky is the woman who finds a man who will listen," wrote his senior English teacher.

∞ ∞

The Nisei won the coin flip deciding who would be the home team and bat last. Their first base dugout consisted of a string of benches and a corrugated roof to keep the sun at bay, but only when it shone directly overhead. By three o'clock, the sun would bend behind home plate and blaze directly into the pitcher's eyes.

The Sixty-Ninth Divisional Band and the 442nd Regimental Band played the "Star-Spangled Banner," the last four bars obliterated by the roar of the crowd.

The home plate umpire, one of three hired from Hattiesburg, bellowed, "Play ball!"

Kenta threw the first pitch too close to the middle of the plate. The batter swung from his heels, made good contact and took off for first base. The speedy centerfielder ran down the ball on the first bounce and kept the runner to a single. The second batter hit a 2–1 pitch that skated past Kim's outstretched glove to right field for a single. The next batter hit it up the middle toward center field. The second baseman dove, made a spectacular grab on the edge of the grass, threw to Kim from his knees, but without enough zip to double the runner at first.

Men on first and second, one out and Crockett batting cleanup at the plate. Kenta threw the first ball inside. Crockett laughed and pointed his bat at Kenta, a challenge to "bring it on." Kenta looked the runners back to their base, took the sign and placed his fingers against the seam to throw a curve.

The hit and run was on. The runners took off as soon as Kenta committed himself. The pitch broke over the middle of the plate, but low. Crockett hit a squibbler to the first baseman. Kenta raced over to cover the bag, catching Kim's toss just as Crockett's left shoulder sent him sprawling. The ball stayed in his glove.

The crowd behind first base rose and yelled. Kenta shouted "Interference!" at the umpire. By the time he remembered there had been runners at first and second, one had crossed the plate and the other stood on third, a mocking smirk on his face. The umpires, ignoring a chorus of boos, ruled the bump an accident.

The next hitter had a Babe Ruth physique—a barrel chest set on spindly legs. Kenta stared down Doi for the sign and wondered if he had the guts to throw a brush-back pitch. He answered his own question when the batter hit the deck on a high, inside fastball. The Nisei crowd whooped their approval; the New Yorkers let out a slew of obscene catcalls.

The next pitch buzzed even closer to the batter's head, who once again ate dirt.

The benches cleared. The MPs jumped to their feet. Pence and Bolte stood up. Both teams rushed to the foul line. Base umpires faced each team. "Back to your benches," they ordered.

The plate umpire strode to the mound, his gait urgent and angry. "You've made your point. Now pitch."

Kenta threw the next pitch an inch inside at the knees. The batter flinched. The next three pitches were inside but over the plate. The batter kept his bat on his shoulder for the first two, called strikes and weakly whiffed at the third. The Nisei roared.

The game settled down until the seventh inning with the Nisei leading 5–4, thanks in great part to Joe Takata's three doubles. The taunts had tapered off. Crockett, who had struck out twice since the first inning grounder, led off the seventh inning with a routine fly to short left field. He ambled down the line, in no hurry to be out, only to have the outfielder lose the ball in the sun. Although safe at first, Crockett had to listen to heckling from both sides of the field for not hustling. Sixteen thousand people knew he should be standing on second base.

The next batter hit a double-play ball to the second baseman, who bobbled it. He recovered in time to toss the ball to Tommy, covering second. As Tommy pivoted to throw to first, a sliding Crockett came in, spikes high. Tommy went down with a thud. Bloodstains blossomed on his pant legs.

Kenta rushed off the mound. His first and third basemen rushed faster to intercept him. "Start a fight Kenta, and Crockett wins," said Kim. Feeling his third baseman's arms pinning his waist, Kenta stopped pushing. He glanced at both teams standing at the ready to charge the field. "Right, next at bat, I'll find out how fast he can duck."

Tommy, standing now, brushed his trousers. "It's all right Kenta. Nothing a Band-Aid won't take care of."

Kenta walked back to the mound thinking of Crockett's next at bat with a vengeful relish.

Back in the stands, Bolte turned to Pence. "He's out of there. New Yorkers play tough, not dirty." The outcries from the Nisei were not countered by a rebuttal from the Sixty-Ninth, their honor tarnished by Crockett's Ty Cobb imitation. The Yanks hated losing, but honor stood above all else in the Empire State.

At a nod from Bolte, the umpire sent Crockett to the showers.

Kenta mumbled a "damn," his chance at instant payback robbed.

The incident sucked the fighting spirit out of the New Yorkers, but not Kenta's fast ball. The Empire Staters never threatened again, losing 6–4.

∽ ∾

Bolte and Pence issued weekend passes generously. The streets of Hattiesburg swarmed with khaki. Except for one fight over a hooker well beyond her bewitching days, the New Yorkers accepted the hospitality of the Hawaii boys who ordered beers for any Yank they encountered.

Not so Sergeant Crockett. He drank by himself. "Vengeance is mine, sayeth the Lord" kept popping into his head. "I ain't waiting that long," he muttered to himself.

⌒ CHAPTER 66 ⌒

August 4, 1943

CROCKETT HAD A WEEK BEFORE SHIPPING OUT—a week to exact revenge. He grinned, admiring his flash of brilliance on how to overcome the sneaky judo tactics and clannish nature of the Nips. They always walked, ate and drank in groups. *Christ, they probably screwed in groups.* The brown-faced cowards wouldn't accept a one-on-one fair fight. They would jump to their mate's defense.

Tuesday morning at Hutment 714, Buster scooted out the door, first to enjoy the relief of an early morning pee. When he saw the envelope on the door, he brought it inside.

"For you," he said, handing it to Kenta.

Kenta tore the end of the envelope, pulled the folded sheet from inside and read the note typed on military stationery.

"Meet me at 6AM at HQ. Kim."

Kenta peeked at his watch—5:45. "Shit, I wonder what this is about." He showed the note to Buster who read it out loud.

"No shower for me, guys. See you at mess," said Kenta, buttoning his shirt.

A fifteen-minute sprint separated HQ from the hutment. He would be late. He could knock the time in half if he cut through the sewage processing plant. He started running. What could be so important that necessitated a 6:00 a.m. meeting? Why hadn't Kim just knocked on the door and talked to him last night instead of leaving a note? By the time he thought of a third question—Why had Kim bothered to find a typewriter instead of just handwriting the note?—a knot of suspicion had formed in his gut. Just as the words "snipe hunt" crossed his consciousness, he spotted Crockett emerging from behind one of the sand-colored buildings.

Kenta had never seen such malice in a man's eyes. His scarred face, narrow eyes and toothy sneer like the Joker in *Batman* comics all radiated evil. He wore his baseball uniform, but it didn't seem to fit him. It was too bulky. He moved steadily forward, lips moving but the words drowned by the rumble of the plant's machinery and the hiss of the outdoor aeration sprinklers.

They were alone. Crockett had picked a killing zone.

Kenta faced Crockett—anxious but confident the odds favored him. A man driven by hate would make mistakes because he assumed his hate would be enough to carry the day. Once again, arrogance would be Crockett's downfall. Kenta stood his ground, feet planted to give him maximum balance for a deadly judo kick. Or if Crockett lunged for him, Kenta could grab his shirt and use the momentum to throw Crockett down.

Crockett held his hands loose at his side like a gorilla.

Kenta caught a glint off the inside of Crockett's hands. Brass knuckles. He watched as Crocket strode toward him like Gary Cooper striding down a deserted Main Street. Kenta kicked his leg straight ahead as soon as Crockett's belly came within range. His army boot saved him from a broken foot. While the kick pushed Crockett back, a metal plate covered with a piece of rug, primitive but effective protection, absorbed the impact. A second kick, this time to the leg, hit football pads.

Confusion flooded Kenta's brain and Crockett moved in. His brass fist hit Kenta's unprotected face hard. Skin split, bone crunched and Kenta's body crumbled. Crockett's boot found Kenta's ribs. A loud snap told Kenta at least one rib had broken. He rolled over and almost made it up when the brass knuckles hit him on top of the head like a sledgehammer pounding nails into a railroad tie. Kenta sprawled flat again. Blood poured from his cheeks and head. He curled into a ball and closed his eyes. The rain of kicks continued. He felt the metal fist explode into his kidney.

I'm going to die. Kenta could make out this thought in his foggy brain. He thought of his mother and Angelina. There was so much he wanted to say and now he would never have the chance.

The beating stopped. He cautiously opened an eye and saw a knee on the ground. He breathed heavily. The taste of blood made him nauseous.

"We're even, Jap-boy. You thought you were going to die, didn't you? But if they found you dead, who are they going think done it?" Crockett gave a nasty chuckle. "On the battlefield, that's a different story. You ever see me out there, don't turn your back."

Kenta lay still for a full minute after the footsteps faded. His thoughts returned to Angelina. He swore he would not betray her again.

∞ ∞

Tommy was standing outside the hutment when a bloody Kenta limped back.

"Jesus H. Christ, what happened to you?"

"I fell down. I'll tell you later."

Tommy stepped closer. "You need to be cleaned up." He examined Kenta's face. "And you need some stitches."

Kenta winced. "I think I broke a rib or two."

"Let's get you fixed up fast. We need to get to Camp Livingston."

Kenta turned up his face. "I need a doctor and you're talking about going to Louisiana?"

"To see Dad," said Tommy. "He's been moved from Santa Fe to Camp Livingston's POW camp." Tommy waved a telegram. "I got this an hour ago. The guy at communications knew the 100th was shipping out in a week and sent it over. There's a 2:00 p.m. bus from Hattiesburg that gets into Alexandria around midnight."

Short Pants flagged down a jeep and got Kenta a ride to the clinic. Tommy, still in pain from the cut shins, tracked down Kim, who wrote out a three-day leave for Kenta. By noon, the two brothers had packed knapsacks and caught the bus from the base to Hattiesburg. Kenta shrugged off the stares at his bandaged face and head with the usual "You should see the other guy."

Once he told Tommy the tale of his mismatched fight with Crockett, Kenta felt a release. With the help of a Miller washing down four aspirins, he drifted into a fitful slumber for most of the bus ride. He woke at each station stop. His stiffening muscles sent sharper waves of pain. He forced himself to get off at stops to walk it out.

When they arrived in Alexandria, Tommy called Camp Livingston from the station.

"This is Sergeant Takayama. My brother and I would like to visit our father, who is stationed at your camp."

"Did you say sergeant?" asked an uncertain voice. "As in, an American army sergeant?"

"Yes, sir."

"You are ... American GIs ... with a dad in this POW camp?"

"Yes, sir. My dad is a Buddhist priest. Kenji Takayama."

"Oh ..." Tommy heard a softening in the man's voice. "That would be the group that came in two weeks ago. Let me check the list." Tommy pressed the phone piece to his ear, tapping his toe on the dirty floor of the bus station. Two minutes later, the voice returned. "He's here. Who's your commanding officer?"

Tommy gave the names of both his and Kenta's COs.

"It's going to take you a while to get here. You'll need to take a taxi at this hour. I'll wait until five to wake your dad. You probably won't be here before then."

∞ ∞

The officer of the day surprised Kenta and Tommy at the gate. He gave them a sincere smile, greeted them by rank, offered a cup of coffee and didn't bother to pat them down. He cast an appraising eye at Kenta's bandages. "You've got some strange headgear," he said, then escorted them to a Quonset hut, an oblong building with a curved roof design lifted from Iroquois longhouses.

"We've got some of your 442nd boys guarding German prisoners. One of them had his dad arrive with yours. The two men visit every day. Your dad's group is easy—very well behaved." He pursed his lips, as if he had something more to say on the subject but didn't want to let it out. They continued the walk in silence. At the Quonset hut's door, he dismissed the two guards assigned to the visiting quarters. When he noticed Kenta gazing at the "Speak English Only" signs, he said, "You can ignore those." He jerked his head toward the door. "Go on in. Your father's waiting for you." With a smart salute, he moved on.

Kenta pulled out a small bottle, extracted two aspirin tablets, and chucked them into his mouth.

"I'm more nervous now than when I had to enter Pence's office." He turned the door handle, drew back the door and gestured to Tommy to enter first.

Dozens of gray wooden tables and hundreds of dreary matching chairs populated the room. War bond posters hung haphazardly on the walls. The arched roof and dim lighting reminded Kenta of the Makua cave on the Waianae Coast of Oahu. A man sitting at a table in the middle of the room rose.

Kenta and Tommy took but a few steps before bowing and saying simultaneously, as if rehearsed, "*Ohisashiburi desu*," the traditional salutation used when greeting a person after a long absence.

Their father returned the bow. "Welcome, samurai."

The two brothers weaved among the empty tables. Kenta controlled his urge to rush to the other side of his father's table and do something he had done only once before, when the FBI arrested Kenji—hug him. He pushed the thought aside, knowing it would embarrass Kenji. At the same time, he resolved that when he had children, he would hug them like the Hawaiians did at home.

As he approached the table, Kenta studied his father's face. He had expected a sickly pallor and defeatist eyes like the faces of older men at Rohwer. Instead, he found a robust complexion, eyes firmer in purpose than ever, a face radiating pride. Kenji had lost none of his dignity since the night Kenta had carried his father's suitcase to the waiting FBI black Ford. He did catch worried eyes taking in his bandaged face.

Kenta forced a laugh. "I fell down a gorge on maneuvers."

As agreed beforehand by the two brothers, Tommy changed the direction of the conversation. "Otosan, you look terrific."

"Sit, sit. You can't imagine how surprised and happy I felt when they woke me saying you boys were coming."

The brothers sat down on the gray-metal folding chairs and Tommy began with an apology.

"*Gomennasai*, Otosan. We only have two hours. We have to catch the noon bus back to Camp Shelby."

Kenji's eyes glistened. He waited until he could control his voice. "That's a shame because we're putting on a *sumo* exhibition for the German POWs tonight. Immediately following the bouts, their symphony orchestra is conducting a welcome concert for us."

Missing the main point of his father's remark, Kenta reached across the table and grabbed his father's arm.

"That's not right. You shouldn't be in the same camp with Nazi war prisoners."

Kenji put his other hand over his son's. "Not Nazis, Kenta. The SS prisoners go to Kansas. Most of these German Afrika Korps soldiers grew up on farms. They're boys like you and Tommy. Some are working in the nearby peanut fields as farm laborers. Italian POWs, too."

Kenji lifted his hand off Kenta's, reached inside his denim shirt's wide pocket and pulled out a letter. "Angelina writes your unit is winning training awards." He glanced at Tommy. "And you are going to Italy soon?"

The two boys exchanged sheepish looks. "I should have told you myself," said Tommy. "I ... I promise to write more often."

"We think about you every day, Otosan," said Kenta. "I'm not the greatest letter writer. I figured Mom would pass on anything important. I do manage a short note to her weekly." Then he added feebly, "And to Angelina."

Kenji waved away their apologies. "Don't worry about that. I am proud of both of you. What you are doing is already helping us inside. The guards in Santa Fe treated us better after they heard about the 100th and 442nd.

You saw how the officer here acted. Your visit reminds everyone we are loyal to America."

Tommy pointed to the patch covering his father's shirt pocket. "Otosan, what's this 'Mayor, 4th Regiment'?"

Kenji extended his hands palms up and pulled his shoulders back slightly. "I've been voted mayor of our barracks group. It's how the army organizes the Japanese camp. With Germans and Italians, it's by their senior officer."

Tommy rose from the table. "Excuse me, I have to answer the call of nature."

Kenta thought it odd that Tommy exited the building instead of heading toward the "TOILET" sign. "Is everyone here from Hawaii?"

"No. We're barely a majority. Most in my regiment are priests. We have different Buddhist sects, Christian priests, Protestants and Catholics, including some Issei from Panama, Peru and Brazil. Among all these men of God, eight Japanese submarine sailors, rescued after the Battle of Midway, have been assigned to one of my regiment's barracks."

Kenta leaned forward. "How does everyone get along?"

Kenji shrugged. "On our religious differences, quite well. We plan to put on lectures for the camp, giving our different perspectives. We had our first one last night on miracles. A quite revealing debate. While each religion believes in its own miracles, the claims of 'miracles' in other religions are considered to be a sham or simple idol worship. We had quite a lively debate but civilized and even entertaining. The real problem is politics. I hope we do better here than in Santa Fe."

Kenta raised his eyebrows. "Mainlanders and Hawaii folks?"

"I wish," said Kenji. "Japanese sympathizers, a troublesome minority of mostly Mainlanders, start each day by bowing to the east and hanging homemade Japanese flags in front of their barracks. Fights break out between prisoners rooting for America to win the war and those yelling 'Banzai!'—especially early in the war, when Japan captured Hong Kong, Singapore and the Philippines. The arguments between priests who cut off allegiance to their main temple in Japan and those who insist on keeping the affiliation are the ugliest."

"And the camp commander doesn't intervene?" asked Kenta. He fought the urge to pull out his pack of cigarettes and light up, not sure how Kenji would react to his new habit.

"The authorities try to avoid confrontations. Some of the Italian and German internees display pictures of Mussolini and Hitler. As long as no one causes a disturbance, prisoners are left alone to express themselves. Camp harmony improved in Santa Fe when the more rabid protesters were shipped to Japan as part of the exchange program. The Spanish ambassador, representing Japan's interest in America, visited Santa Fe several times to handle these cases.

"Most of the time I deal with less weighty matters, like settling disputes on whether to keep the door open to let in a breeze or keep it closed to keep out sand and bugs." He stopped and fixed a familiar piercing gaze on his son. "But tell me about your training."

Ten minutes into the telling, Tommy and the officer of the day strode in with broad smiles.

"Good news, Otosan," said Tommy, beaming at Kenji. "We're spending all day and tonight with you."

Kenji's eyebrows lifted, his eyes moving from his son to the officer. "How—?"

"Your son volunteered to give a talk about Nisei soldiers," said the officer, cutting off Kenji's question. "Since the entire camp will be turning out for the sumo tournament and concert, I called the camp commander. He agreed this would be a big morale booster to the Japanese internees and an education for the German and Italian POWs."

Kenta noted how the officer differentiated between calling the Issei internees and captured soldiers POWs, even though in reality the Japanese in camp were also POWs, arrested rather than interned. As prisoners, this mostly professional class was incarcerated without their families.

"And so, my CO called Pence. He OK'd the invitation for you boys to address our camp tonight."

Kenji stood up and saluted. "Thank you."

"Hey, it's a great opportunity," said the officer. "I'll see you tonight." With a wave, he turned and pushed his way through the door and out into the humidity.

"So much depends on who is in charge," said Kenji. "The first commander at Santa Fe took rice off the menu for two days when a group of diners banged forks on their table to protest small portions. Later, we got a new commander. When he found out the camp struggled to raise $10 to buy special rice for the New Year's *Oshogatsu* celebration, he bought it himself with personal funds." He stood. "All this talk about food makes me hungry. Time for some breakfast. Come, I will show you around and take you to our mess."

◈ CHAPTER 67 ◈

ON THE WAY, THEY STOPPED AT KENJI'S BARRACKS for a quick tour. Tommy surveyed the room full of bunks and footlockers.

"I feel right at home, Otosan."

Kenta stared, incredulous, at the golf clubs leaning against the wall next to Kenji's bed.

Kenji caught his look. "In Santa Fe, the military allowed golfers a day of recreation at the nearest golf course every week. Since most of us sought any excuse to leave the confines of the gates, we took up the game. It was the same with eye exams. Only once a year, but we welcomed a day in town. We were all bused in and allowed to shop and walk the streets between our appointments. Most of the townspeople there are Indian or Mexican. They had the same color skin we have. They didn't look at us suspiciously. They smiled at us and we smiled back."

Tommy peered at his watch. "What time do they stop serving breakfast?"

"You're right, we should go," said Kenji, who couldn't keep the corners of his mouth from curling up. "I am so excited to see you boys I forget that time does not stand still."

◈ ◈

Most men had finished breakfast and were leaving by the time Kenji and his sons sat down at an empty table to eat.

"Sorry for the bland fare," apologized Kenji. "In a few months it will change. I've already been allocated a half-acre for a vegetable farm."

"It's fine," said Tommy, smiling.

A few internees meandered over to be introduced to Kenji's sons, and when the last of the well-wishers left, Tommy watched two short and stocky men walk vigorously through the chow line, then clank their food trays on an empty table at the far corner of the room. The remaining diners avoided eye contact.

"Those two men don't look like priests or doctors," said Tommy.

Kenji exchanged head bows with the two men. "That's Kin-san and Gin-san, the event organizers from our Santa Fe days. They are in charge of tonight's activities."

"How did they pick up nicknames that mean 'gold' and 'silver'?" asked Kenta.

"They're the top two event facilitators for the Tokyo Club," said Kenji.

"*Yakuza?*" Tommy whispered.

"Where did my innocent boys hear of this California gang?"

"Dad, everybody knows the Tokyo Club controls prostitution and gambling in the Japanese community on the West Coast," said Kenta. "What are those guys doing here?"

Kenji allowed himself an indulgent smile. "Like me, they are leaders of their community. But here in camp, they are very humble. In the pre-war days they took a percentage of almost every type of Japanese event. At camp, they've put their experience to good use. It's a rare night when we don't have a lecture, a ball game, a Noh play or some other activity. They are the ones who convinced the authorities to let us out for our weekly golf game."

"How come we don't have a Tokyo Club in Hawaii?" asked Tommy.

"We did, fifty years ago. But for some reason, all the early members were killed in the plague of 1900—maybe because they all lived together. After that, we were vigilant preventing them from starting up again. We had our homegrown hooligans but nothing like the yakuza. It's a lot easier to keep them out than to kick them out. Yet, they also do some good things. They give to charity. In times of flood or earthquake, they are the first to organize relief. There is good and bad in yakuza—as is true with most of us. Kin-san and I often share *shochu* together."

"When did you switch to shochu, Otosan?" asked Tommy.

"The Japanese Red Cross sends it, since we are listed as POWs."

"Wait," said Kenta, "are you saying you're actually friends with this guy?"

Kenji smiled wanly. "The limited size of our incarcerated world makes for unlikely relationships. Kin-san is an intriguing character." He hesitated. "I probably shouldn't repeat this …" Kenji stopped again and examined his fingernails.

"What?" asked Tommy. "Tell us. Are you in any kind of danger because of these guys?"

Kenji smiled and shook his head. "No, no, nothing like that. They are likable, friendly—cause no problems. But … they come from a very different world. The story goes like this. When I first met Kin-san in Santa Fe, he didn't say much about his life in California—only hinted that he was part of gang discipline. But later, as we got to know each other during meals and on the golf course, he talked more about his job back home. He bragged about his role as the boss's main enforcer. If a gang member skimmed money, Kin-san made them disappear. But 'disposal' posed problems. At first, they hid the bodies in the mountains. Later they took them out in a fishing boat, cut them into parts, stuffed the parts into fishing nets with cement blocks and dropped them overboard."

"That's murder!" said Kenta.

"Yes," said Kenji, "but Kin-san defended the action. He explained it this way: 'We're like soldiers. When you join our family, you know the life or death rules. But we don't kill civilians.'"

Just then a young, freckled-faced private approached the table. "Are you the boys from Shelby?"

Tommy's expression hardened. "I'm Sergeant Tommy Takayama. This is my brother, Sergeant Kenta Takayama. At our base, privates salute sergeants and they don't call non-coms 'boys.'"

The freckled face flushed, anger dancing in his watery-blue eyes.

Tommy and Kenta kept their eyes on the private, and the stare-down went on long enough for other diners to stop and watch the drama unfold.

The private finally gave a sloppy salute. "The commander needs to see you." He stood spine stiff, chest out. "*Now … sir.*"

Moments later, the brothers entered the commander's sparsely furnished office, saluted and sat down as ordered. The commander's face was pinched with deep worry lines. From the first word, his tone of voice portended bad news.

"The *New York Times* has broken a story on the Bataan and Corregidor march."

"March?" asked Kenta.

The CO picked up a copy of the local newspaper that lay on his desktop and lifted it so Kenta and Tommy could see the entire front page. Their eyes widened at the quarter-page headline: "death march."

Kenta and Tommy stared blankly.

"Well, I can't say I'm surprised at your reaction," said the commander. "Let me fill you in. Two years ago, seventy-two thousand soldiers surrendered after the three-month siege of Bataan. At the end of the following week, only fifty-four thousand had survived the sixty-mile gruesome march to their jungle prison camp. Each prisoner subsisted on a daily bowl of gruel. Those who dropped out due to exhaustion were left to die where they fell. Stragglers were beaten or stabbed, complainers beheaded. Thousands more died in the prison camp."

He paused for a few moments, closed his eyes and pinched the bridge of his nose as if this would help rub out the pain of human suffering.

"The army received reports but kept it quiet, not wanting to upset wives and parents. So … you can imagine how today's shocking revelation has put my camp guards on edge. A few people here had brothers on that march.

"I just had a meeting with my officers. We will do everything we can to keep the guards under control. We do not want an incident, so I'm canceling your appearance tonight."

Tommy sighed and ran a hand through his crew cut. "I understand," he said, dispiritedly.

"If I may, sir?" said Kenta.

The commander nodded.

"Our talk tonight is about loyalty and our faith in America. Ten thousand men tried to enlist in Hawaii. I have always felt lucky to be part of the just one in three men who were selected. I think what I have to say will help you with both the internees and the men assigned to guard them."

⊙ CHAPTER 68 ⊙

THE SUMO WRESTLERS FORMED A CIRCLE around the *dohyo*—the elevated sand ring where the bouts would soon take place. Kenta sat in the first row next to three actors dressed as early eighteenth-century warriors to promote the camp rendition of the *47 Ronin* the following week. Given the Bataan news, Kenta wondered why someone had not thought to tell the performers that today of all days was not a great day to dress as samurai.

Following the camp CO's introduction, Tommy stood barefoot, but otherwise in full uniform, on the dohyo, holding a microphone. His previous singing experience consisted of one year in the school choir as a way to meet girls. Tonight, he was making his solo debut. Issei prisoners provided a six-piece orchestra, which swelled to support Tommy after he sang the first five words, "O, say can you see …"

Kenta stood, raised his right hand to his forehead in salute to the American flag and sang softly. So did the samurai.

Tommy's voice filled the auditorium.

Kenta would never have guessed he had a brother who could sing so well. He listened to "the bombs bursting in air" while his mind raced with images of the afternoon in the wake of the Bataan Death March news. The camp smelled of fear and danger. The friendly banter between the guards and the guarded ceased. The few Japanese flags flown by angry men demanding to be included in the next exchange were taken down. Prisoners took great care in avoiding any rule violation. When an errant baseball rolled near the fence during a game of catch, it stayed there, no one wanting to defy the rule that marked six feet from the barbed wire as forbidden territory.

Eight Japanese sailors rescued in the Battle of Midway and assigned to the Livingston POW camp were trucked from their barracks in the general population to the camp prison guarded by senior non-coms and officers. The camp's Sumo Association dropped two wrestlers with known pro-Japanese sympathies.

Kenta wondered if he would have been better off agreeing with Tommy and the commander and returning to Shelby, but it was too late. Besides, he would face worse dangers in the coming months.

"… and the hoooome of the brave!"

The crowd of Issei broke into sustained thunderous applause. The Germans and Italians maintained glum silence.

The sumo matches went forward without incident, aided by beer rationing which limited each person to one coupon. In the wake of the news, Kin-san shelved plans to serve sake. In between each bout, Gin-san explained the winning strategy. By the fourth bout, the Germans and Italians were beginning to understand and cheered the winners.

After the last contest, Tommy once again stood on the dohyo. Determination blazed from his eyes. "I hate Japs," he said, and took a deep breath. "I am not a Jap. I am an American. Japs bombed my home island. They killed two of my friends. They are my country's enemy and my enemy." He paused, seemingly unsure how to continue. "But there is someone here tonight who can better express what I am trying to say—my brother, Kenta."

When Kenta reached the dohyo, Tommy handed him the microphone and took his chair.

Kenta focused on his father and remembered how he would always wait patiently for his congregation to settle down before speaking. He gripped the microphone tighter and brought it to his lips.

"My father came to America forty years ago. That's him in the second row." Kenta pointed to Kenji, who stood up amidst polite applause. "He is a Buddhist priest. My mother landed in Hawaii as a picture bride a few years after my father. They raised four sons and two daughters. Three of their children serve in the US Army. We are American citizens.

"By law, my parents cannot become American citizens. If they had been allowed to apply for citizenship, as Germans and Italian immigrants were, they would have done so. They love America. They taught us to love America.

"Tommy and I are willing to die for America. Not because we think America is perfect." Kenta paused and eyed his father. "We are fighting for America because of America's journey to fulfill its promise 'that all men are created equal' and each of us has a right to 'the pursuit of happiness.' No other nation makes this pledge. We want to be part of that journey. We cannot lose this war, for to do so would mean the light of freedom would be extinguished for all of mankind.

"Tommy and I were lucky to have been born in America. When I left Hawaii on a boat bound for the US, my father admonished, 'Do not dishonor our family.' In our culture, that means it is better to die than to retreat. Tommy is going to Italy next week. I will join him early next year."

Kenta's eyes found Kenji's. "We will not dishonor our father."

Silence enveloped the room.

And then the camp commander stood and began to clap. All but a few of the Japanese followed suit, and the applause became almost deafening.

Kenta surveyed the crowd and saw with surprise that upon hearing the translation the Italian and German prisoners also stood and applauded.

While the crowd clapped, Tommy asked Kenji to come to the dohyo. Kenji refused until the crowd, seeing Tommy's entreaty, cheered louder. The two brothers and father bowed to the crowd, then exited off the dohyo stage toward the commander, who had waved them over.

"Absolutely inspiring," said the commander pumping Kenta's hand. "I'll admit, I am envious of Colonel Pence. I wish I could lead young men like you into battle."

∽ ∾

The next day, on the ride back from Camp Livingston to the Alexandria bus station, the boys watched Caucasian men in POW uniforms weeding peanut fields.

"It's still hard to see that they still don't trust our kind to work outside the base," said Tommy. "The 442nd pulls guard duty on German POWs, the Krauts are granted furloughs to harvest peanuts for wages, but not our dads, whose sons are about to be sent into combat. Different up North. Japanese internees plant and harvest potatoes in Idaho, harvest beets in Eastern Oregon and weed wheat fields in Kansas. Some camps are making it easy for students to get furloughs to attend universities."

"Let it go, Tommy. We joined the army to prove America made a mistake. Let's concentrate on that."

"You better hope we kick some German ass or you'll never leave the swamps of Mississippi."

"I'm counting on it," said Kenta, dropping his arm over his brother's shoulder.

∽ PART VII ∽

THE WOMEN

∽ CHAPTER 69 ∽

Honolulu – April 1943

WHEN FDR SIGNED PUBLIC LAW 77-554 on May 15, 1942, establishing a Women's Army Auxiliary Corps, Angelina took little notice. Not that she hadn't seen the page-one story in the *Advertiser*, giving it a cursory glance before moving on to more interesting stories. The idea of a woman of Japanese descent volunteering for the army did not register for her any more than if she had heard volunteers were being accepted for a polar expedition.

Her attitude began evolving after January 28, 1943, when FDR decreed Nisei eligible to enlist in the army. The same month, Angelina began working at Tripler Army Hospital. If Japanese American men could join the army, why couldn't Japanese American women join the WAAC? Two weeks after Kenta sailed from Honolulu, the sight of the first WAACs in Hawaii walking through Tripler's trauma recovery unit kindled her awareness. A chance lunch with two WAAC nurses in the hospital's cafeteria stoked her interest, and over the next weeks the flames grew brighter. Finally, the dawdling ended. The Angelina who awed Kenta with her determination swung into action—to her mother's chagrin.

∽ ∽

Angelina dropped her bike on the crushed seashell pathway leading to Haru's back door and then barged into Kenta's mother's kitchen. Haru was wiping the insides of kitchen cabinets with a soapy rag, and was surprised to see Angelina burst in, but not offended.

"Mother's thinking is still on the farm in Okayama, Auntie Haru," Angelina exclaimed. "If my brother and your sons can join the army now, why can't I join the Women's Army Auxiliary Corps? Right?"

Haru gave Angelina a wordless smile. *Kenta has got a handful*, she thought, and not for the first time.

"Sorry, Auntie," said Angelina. Eyeing glasses and dishware stacked on the counter, she remembered her manners. "Can I help put those back in the cabinets?"

"Maybe later. I am about finished scrubbing. Time for a break." She motioned Angelina to take a seat at the kitchen table. "I have enough coffee left for two cups. Let's hear about this WAAC thing," she said, letting Angelina know she was well aware of the Women's Army Auxiliary Corps.

"The haole WAACs told me the army is accepting five hundred Japanese-Americans in the Women's Army Auxiliary Corps. I am a qualified lab technician working at Fort Shafter's Tripler Army Hospital *and* taking courses in nursing." She paused for Haru's objections. Receiving a nod of the head instead, she went on. "It's not like we don't need the money since the government made us sell our liquor store for peanuts. WAACs get paid twice what I'm getting from Tripler. My brother, my ... and Kenta are serving. Proving their loyalty. Mom doesn't want me to leave home. This is war. People leave home. Traveling to new places is exciting. It's not like Mom has no friends. She must be in every volunteer group ever imagined. It's not enough to *say* I am patriotic—I want to *show* I am patriotic. And when the war is over, I will be at the head of the line for a civilian job. I will be a veteran with new job skills."

Haru never failed to be astonished by Angelina's breathless promulgations but knew her mother's objections well. The army was almost all male. Stories floated that WAACs were loose women despite there being no evidence to support such gossip.

"It's almost like Mom is accusing me of being a ..." Angelina held back. "A woman who easily swoons in the presence of any man in uniform."

A much better way to say it, thought Haru. Relieved, she said, "Takeshi has told me that some haoles have invited WAACs to share a home-cooked meal. Maybe we could show a few Mainland army ladies some aloha."

Angelina leaned in as Haru detailed what she had in mind.

⁂

The following week, half a dozen WAACs from Illinois and Minnesota savored their first taste of Japanese food alongside family-sized bowls of spaghetti and meatballs. The Midwestern girls gushed over the tempura prepared by Angelina's mother, and by the time the WAACs and Japanese came to the end of an evening of exchanging family stories, Angelina's mother announced, "My daughter is sending in an application to join soon." There was a spontaneous outbreak of applause, and Angelina lifted a hand to cover her face. She didn't know whether to cry or laugh, so she did both.

The following morning, Angelina registered at the WAAC recruiting office and received two pairs of silk stockings. But the following Sunday she was back at Queen Emma Street, this time tapping out three polite knocks before entering. Angelina managed to hold back until she and Haru sat at the kitchen table, each holding a steaming cup of coffee laced with sugar and a drop of precious war-rationed cream.

"They say they want us, Auntie, but, but, but … look at all this paperwork!" Angelina opened her bag and dumped the forms on the checkered linoleum floor. "This isn't all. They want records. High school. College. Referrals from Tripler. On it goes. They invite us to go swimming but tell us to stay out of the water."

Lucky for Angelina, Taka had dropped by that Sunday, too. He laughed as he came downstairs.

"What's so funny?" snapped Angelina, tears of frustration leaving a trail of mascara down her cheeks.

"Not you, Angie," said Taka, using the nickname Angelina hated, though she had never told Taka. His accomplishments—Harvard, the Morale Committee—intimidated her. "I'm laughing because, where I work, we just *love* forms. We love covering our … backsides. No one wants to be the bureaucrat who leaves the door open for a traitor. Then there are those who just plain don't think you belong. Surprise, surprise."

Angelina stomped her foot. "Well, it's working! This traitor won't be in the WAAC."

Grinning, a hint of laughter still in his voice, Taka said, "Since I am the family member sentenced to lawyerly ways and a member of an almost-government agency, I understand how these folks work. Why don't you leave that pile of papers with me?" He paused. "After you pick them up and organize them."

Haru plucked a tissue from a box on the counter and handed it to Angelina.

"Really?"

"Yes, really, Angie. We are like family. Just give me a few days."

Taka held a sisterly affection for Angelina. He suspected that Angelina regarded Haru as a surrogate for her own beloved—but correct to the point of being cold—mother. He speculated just how Angelina had sealed her ties to the Takayama family but kept his thoughts to himself. Like Scarlett O'Hara, Angelina knew what she wanted out of life and set about using charm and ambition to reach it.

It took him forty-eight hours to complete the forms. He used his admin and schmoozing skills to gather the docs and jump-schedule Angelina's physical. Taka reveled in the approbation that came his way when busting bureaucratic barricades.

Angelina couldn't claim to be the first Nisei WAAC. That honor went to Frances Iritani in Denver. Angelina joined the contingent of Hawaiian inductees. Days after the welcome ceremony, she returned to Haru's home for a final goodbye.

"Fort Oglethorpe, Auntie. They are sending us to Georgia for training. How far can that be from Uncle Kenji's camp in Louisiana?"

"First Sherman, now you," said Haru.

"Who's Sherman?"

Haru kept laughter from conjoining her smile. "You will find out soon enough."

⨯ CHAPTER 70 ⨯

Late June, 1943

FOLLOWING A DOZEN DAYS OF DRILLS, with enough time for two softball competitions, Angelina and sixty-one other young ladies sailed to the West Coast. They represented the Islands' ethnic salad bowl—German, Chinese, Irish, Korean and Filipino—but the majority Nisei. While the Hawaii WAAC didn't get quite the dramatic sendoff of the 442nd recruits months earlier, they were feted and celebrated.

From Oakland, their train chugged leisurely and made many stops, allowing the ladies to dance hula and sing Hawaiian songs at various USOs, including Amarillo, Texas, and Memphis, Tennessee. Whatever anti-Japanese sentiment existed when the war started or was still held by a few, the ladies never experienced it. Local media gushed over the "patriotic Hawaii ladies volunteering for the war effort." Train-stop cities' newspapers featured stories of Nisei ladies whose husbands were soon to be fighting the Huns in Italy.

On arrival in Oglethorpe, a letter from Kenta waited atop her assigned bunk. "The 100th guys are leaving Shelby at the end of August for Hampton Roads and then it's on to Africa before joining Clark in Italy. Us 442nd fellows hope to join them next year." She ignored his stupidly insensitive close: "We hope the Germans haven't surrendered by then." Her daydream was to bus to Shelby the first weekend, but Angelina soon realized that six weeks of required basic training meant none of the WAACs would be leaving the Fort Oglethorpe base overnight.

∽ ∾

Midway through basic, the WAAC trainees were asked to list their service preferences. Given her Tripler Hospital experience, Angelina checked off the nursing corps as her first choice. As an afterthought she ticked clerical, because she could type, and air force technical, which just sounded interesting.

Angelina sat down on her bunk to write to her mother, Kenta and Haru: "I expect to be assigned to an army hospital. Best guess, Camp Polk, Pennsylvania. US Nisei WAACs will not be in segregated units like our men. We are treated the same as haole WAACs. Training is a little boring. Saturday day trips to Chattanooga are a nice diversion, even if we have to return for 9:00 p.m. curfew. No visits to Shelby. Too far for a day trip."

Given that Angelina spoke Japanese at home and had an IQ of 127, the testing officer had instead forwarded her application to the Military Intelligence Service. Unbeknownst to both MIS and Angelina, other forces thousands of miles and many time zones away would soon influence her assignment.

∽ **CHAPTER 71** ∾

August 20, 1943

MABEL'S MOTHER FACED A DILEMMA. Her prejudice had convinced her that Chuckles's school would send back letters exposing him as unsavory. Because Mabel had such confidence in Chuckles, she had agreed that if the school reports validated her mother's concerns, she would dump Chuckles straight away. Mabel also trusted her mother that if the letters supported Mabel's instincts, her mother would keep her promise and step aside.

The glowing letters flowed in. Sitting with her daughter while reading yet another sterling letter, Mabel's deflated mother gritted her teeth. "Well, I hope you know what you are doing," she muttered.

Mabel checked her enthusiasm and said softly, "Thank you, Mother." She knew she needed to accept her reluctant acquiescence without pushing for more.

Mabel's father, a career postal sorter, came home every day at 6:00 p.m. as if punching a timecard—after stopping at the neighborhood bar for three pints of Schlitz on tap. Quiet and almost—but not quite—drunk, her father never asked Mabel about her schoolwork or, until Chuckles appeared, cared about who she was dating. Mabel had once asked her mother, only half-joking, "If Dad died, how would we know?"

At dinner the evening after Chuckles's school reports arrived, her father finally weighed in. "You're going to do what you are going to do, even though the Bible forbids mixing. So get this straight—I don't want no Jap boy in my house. I don't never want to see any half-breed Jap kids in my home."

Mabel packed her bags that night and moved in with one of the Nisei wives whose husband had gone on maneuvers.

The US Army frowned on sudden marriages to local girls who were suspected of coveting spousal benefits more than their spouse. But Colonel Pence approved Chuckles's marriage without hesitation. As a patron of the Dixie Grill, he recognized the genuine affection between them.

And while Mississippi refused to marry mixed-race couples, Louisiana stood almost alone among the former Confederacy in allowing folks to marry whomever they pleased. "New Orleans is a better place than Hattiesburg for a honeymoon anyway," said Chuckles as they boarded the Greyhound bus to their future.

∞ CHAPTER 72 ∞

August 27, 1943

KENTA PLANNED TO VISIT FORT OGLETHORPE in a few weeks when Angelina's basic training finished and she received her weekend pass. It was good timing, since the now mostly faded bruises he got from his encounter with Crockett meant he wouldn't have to invent a story. Kenta did not want Angelina to visit Hattiesburg, in case the local Nisei wives knew about houses of pleasure, the 442nd visits to them, or his relationship with Natasha. If they did, most likely they wouldn't act as informants. *Most likely. Why take the chance?*

But Kenta had not counted on the combined ingenuity of Angelina and Mary Nakahara. Kenta had written to Angelina that when they wanted to get something done everyone went to Mary Nakahara. So, when Angelina wrote Mary to ask her to help arrange a surprise trip to Hattiesburg for her and her fellow Nisei military ladies—now WACs instead of WAACs, since the unit had converted to active status and dropped the Auxilary designation in July—on their first weekend pass, Mary lived up to her reputation. She arranged for them to stay in the same barracks tents the USO girls from Rohwer used during their Hattiesburg visits.

"I'll be on base to welcome you to your canvas home along with a few of our Rohwer gals who always enjoy time away from our camp," Mary wrote.

Soon Angelina and all her sister Nisei WACs were exchanging hopes and dreams, picturing the shocked and happy smiles they'd see after surprising brothers, fiancés, husbands and friends. They bought crates of Georgia peaches and bags of the state's famed peanuts. The giddy excitement masked the realization that soon, some of their loved ones would never return home. Alive.

∞ ∞

The Nisei WACs arrived at their tented barracks Friday afternoon to shouts of jubilation. Happy chaos reigned as family stories were brought up to date and gifts were opened. Angelina asked for Kenta, and his 522nd field artillery buddies had a pretty good idea where to find him—the same place he went every time he got a pass.

"Kenta said he wanted a change from cafeteria food," said No Ticket. "He might have gone into Hattiesburg for a meal." A moment later, he left on a mission.

Sergeant Doi was clearing up a baggage allowance misunderstanding with No Ticket at Hutment 714 when news of the girls' arrival swept the barracks. He trotted along with the artillery lads to greet them. Thanks to Kenta showing off his picture of Angelina, Doi quickly spotted her. He wormed his way unnoticed to within eavesdropping distance, and overheard Angelina's inquiries. His face froze, imagining Kenta straddling Natasha—Natasha, whom Doi fancied but was never able to reserve time with.

Despite the good feelings he and Kenta had shared after the accidental meeting at the Pink Palace, Doi felt his dark side wiggling its way back. He had begun to see his promotion to the supply unit as a sidestep to deny him command of an elite unit. Worse, Kenta had also been promoted. Never short a weekend pass, Kenta had visited Rohwer again, while he hadn't been once. Reading his sister Jane's gushing words about Kenta, Doi suspected Kenta had been intimate with her, but had avoided a family confrontation due to his father's declining health.

All these thoughts swirled for attention as Doi listened to the happy chatter between Angelina, her WAC friends and the guys of Hutment 714. No one had even bothered to introduce him. Feeling left out as usual, Doi moved to the ice-filled cooler, helping himself to one Bud and then another in the span of just a few minutes. As he finished his second, he saw No Ticket hurry off and guessed his intention.

Doi ambled back to Angelina, trying to act casual and indifferent. "Did I hear you ask for Sergeant Takayama?"

Angelina flashed a Pepsodent-perfect smile. "Yes! Do you know where he is?"

"As a matter of fact, I do. He and I are friends. I served with the 442nd until being promoted to managing the 442nd warehouse about the time Kenta and my squad were transferred to the 522nd artillery section. One of the perks is that I have access to a jeep." He gave Angelina a stiff smile. "I was just about to drive into town. If you like, I can give you a lift, check out a few of the usual places he and his squad hang out. We might run into him."

Doi figured he had at least an hour head start on No Ticket, who would rather wait for the bus than pay for a taxi.

∞ ∞

"That's the spot, Kenta. Gentle, gentle. Yes! Yes! That's it. Don't stop." Natasha moaned as Kenta's newly trained fingers brought her to climax. "Now it's your turn to enjoy—what do you call it? The thunder and clouds?" An hour later, luxuriously exhausted and sponge-bathed by the attentive Natasha, Kenta dressed. He put ten dollars on the table, double the usual amount.

The night before, he had cleaned up at poker, bought drinks for everyone, and still had enough left over for a special meeting. *The absolute last*, he vowed. He loved Angelina. Yet he hadn't been able resist satisfying his urges—not only with Natasha, but also with Jane at Rohwer. The urge. The prospect of intimacy. He liked Natasha and felt genuine fondness for her. But love? No. Still, the hour with her transcended magic. He couldn't imagine doing the same things with Angelina, if for no other reason than she would ask where he had learned such techniques. But he would be more patient, more sensitive to her needs. Natasha would make him a better husband. But enough was enough. In a week or so, he would be visiting Angelina.

I will savor today as a last memory, but there is no reason to tell Natasha. No point in creating drama. And he suspected that, down deep, Natasha viewed him as just another customer. Nicer than some, but nonetheless simply a client—not a lover.

"Oh, this is too much, Kenta," said Natasha, who promptly wedged the tenner into her purse even as she wondered if the big tip signaled something. Why probe? Kenta wouldn't be the first customer who swore off commercial sex only to return a few weeks later when the memories begged to be renewed. Her motto had always been *be the best at what you do and let nature take care of the rest.*

They sauntered to the head of the stairs, Kenta cradling Natasha's waist nonchalantly.

⚭ ⚭

Doi gripped the steering wheel harder with both hands as second thoughts crept into his head. He shook them off. After all, how could Kenta betray such an innocent girl? *His despicable behavior should be exposed, and he should be punished for the cad he is.* A chastised Kenta would be pissed but, in a month, no doubt, return to the Pink Palace, while Angelina would be crushed, her life devastated. *But she'd be better off for knowing the truth.*

What will Jane say when she hears what I am about to do? An unwelcome prick of conscience invaded Doi's thoughts and his better nature almost prevailed. He would stop at a few bars and restaurants and make perfunctory inquiries. Who knows, he might even find him. But he recalled Kenta boasting, "I always come to the Pink Palace before dinner when the girls are fresh, and my pecker isn't drowning in beer." *A few stops,* thought Doi, *and then back to the base empty handed.*

That's the way it would have played out. If only.

At the edge of town, Angelina started in on how wonderful Kenta was. The quarterback of his football team. The captain of his baseball team. The president of his senior high school class. He almost singlehandedly organized the Varsity Victory Volunteers brigade.

Doi wanted to shout, "Enough already! Your two-timing boyfriend is the snake of all snakes." So he drove faster, and straight to the Pink Palace. This bragging dolt would shut up the moment she stepped into the doors and recognized what kind of club Kenta frequented. As soon as he asked for Kenta, one of the working girls would say, "He's upstairs" or "He hasn't come in yet." Either way, this talking machine would soon know Mr. Perfect pays for pussy at a whorehouse.

Suddenly, Angelina stopped talking. She sensed she had gone on too long, had exposed what a small-town girl she was. She chastised herself for being an impolite bore and changed the subject. "So … why did you join the army, Sergeant?"

Doi missed the question. He ripped around the corner onto the street that fronted the railroad tracks. At the Pink Palace, he braked the jeep hard. The noise from inside blared, accompanied by raised voices and raucous laughter. Doi jumped out, ran to the passenger's side and pulled open the door. A real gentleman.

"Get out, come with me." He instantly regretted the harsh tone that provoked wariness to cross Angelina's face. "I'm sorry. I'm mad at myself for the quick stop. My daydreaming almost caused me to drive past," Doi improvised, adding a toothy smile. "I bet Kenta will be so happy to see you. He talks about you all the time."

Doi hopscotched up the steps. The music grew louder. The smell of beer wafted. Two laughing soldiers walked out the swinging door and passed Doi and Angelina, both giving the young woman a long appreciative glance. From inside, female voices sang, "Hurry back."

Doi pushed through the doors, Angelina following in his wake. She blinked under the assault of pink. The piano player missed a beat, caught off guard at Doi bringing in a girl.

Lillian stood next to the piano. Her eyes widened. Only girls in the trade came in to visit, and one glance at Angelina's Asian eyes and conservative dress said she did not belong. Lillian had no idea why Doi was bringing in a civilian, but she knew trouble when she saw it. She learned long ago, one does not wait to see how trouble develops. She ambled over to the girl.

Angelina stared open-mouthed at the full-size Kama Sutra artwork behind the bar and the young ladies dressed in provocatively cut pink dresses. She turned to Doi. "Is this some kind of joke?"

By now, Lillian was close enough to hear Angelina's question. She reached out to take Angelina's elbow with the intent to gently walk her outside to the porch where they could sort this matter out.

The intrusion might have passed as a rude stunt, with Doi being the dunce, when movement at the top of the stairs caught Angelina's attention. She froze in place, oblivious to Lillian's effort to maneuver her out the front door. The blood drained from her face.

Above, Kenta laughed intimately with the woman beside him. Heads bent together, Kenta's arm wrapped around Natasha's waist, they descended the winding staircase like Rhett and Scarlet. Kenta enjoyed a surge of pride each time he glided down the stairs with her, and scanned the room seeking the usual looks of envy and admiration.

Angelina! It couldn't be.

Kenta's face blanched. His arm dropped off Natasha's waist and he grabbed the handrail to keep his knees from buckling. The piano player stopped playing, the bar chatter stumbled and then halted altogether.

"Angelina!" Kenta gasped.

In an instant, Lillian, Natasha and the pink-clad whores understood.

The chalk-faced Angelina stared at the top of the railing as if seeing a ghost. "Kenta?" The words from her suddenly constricted throat floated like a prayer of denial.

"Child," said Lillian, settling a gentle hand onto Angelina's arm. "Listen to me. That man of yours loves you like the dickens. We just give him solace in his lonely moments. What happens here is not about you."

Angelina looked at Lillian as if facing a rabid Doberman. Then she snapped her head back to Kenta. "I loved you."

Kenta started running down the steps with Natasha on his heels.

Angelina grabbed Doi's hand and pulled. "Get me out of here."

While Angelina ran, spurred by disgust, Doi ran hastened by fear. He jumped into the jeep. It started at the turn of the key as Angelina flung herself into the passenger side.

Doi jammed the accelerator. Kenta grabbed the side roll bar but couldn't hold on. He shouted, "Angelina! Angelina!" until he dropped to his knees and pounded his fist into the ground.

He barely heard the crunch of tires as a car came to a stop next to him. "Kenta!" cried No Ticket.

Doi had been wrong about No Ticket's priorities. Cheap though he might be, when faced with the choice of saving a few bucks or saving a buddy, No Ticket had made the decision without hesitation. Seeing the long line at the taxi queue, No Ticket offered two dollars to the soldiers standing first in line. An easy sale. A moment later, No Ticket's taxi blitzed down the highway and turned down the road to Lillian's in time to see Kenta on his knees.

No Ticket opened the rear door. "Kenta! Come on! Jump in the cab, we'll catch up to them."

"No! No! No!" Kenta cried, his fists still abusing the battered street. "It's too late!"

A small crowd gathered, mostly patrons of the Pink Palace, including many of the 442nd boys who had been downstairs drinking. They told No Ticket what they had seen. Lillian, who had followed them out, filled in the details.

No Ticket's face reddened, and he glowered into the eyes of the Hawaii 442nd boys. "It was Doi," he said, resolve mirrored on his face. "Doi ... dirty, shifty, downright biggest asshole I've ever seen. He's gonna pay."

⌒ CHAPTER 73 ⌒

Tokyo – August 1943

Hiromi sat in front of the NHK microphone. Across from her sat the stern-faced Kempeitai man wearing a brown business suit that had seen better times. His right hand relaxed inches from the red button that would cut her broadcast if she diverted from the "Zero Hour" script. He would then escort her out of a life of wartime privilege and into a cell. Or worse.

"Greetings to America's sailors and soldiers. This is the voice of truth, your friend—oh excuse me, the enemy, your number-one enemy—Little Orphan Annie, bringing the latest American pop hits and the news your government hides from you. As always, our peaceful people reach out with love and sorrow. Sorrow because of what your superiors are making you do while young men who avoided the draft are making whoopee with your wives and girlfriends.

"A special welcome to the Boys of Rhode Island and Connecticut of the 43rd Infantry Division ready to land in New Georgia as part of Operation Toenails. So sad so many of you will be killed fighting brave Japanese soldiers who have liberated these people from the yoke of British colonialism in the Solomon Islands. There must be better causes to die for.

"Now, let's start our music with Peggy Lee and 'Somebody is Taking My Place.'"

Hiromi switched off her mic and pushed her chair back. Her minder's hand casually left his switch for a pack of cigarettes.

"Very good," said Goto, his English almost devoid of an accent, a result of spending his early school years in America where his father represented Mitsubishi Heavy Industries.

On her first day in front of the mic, Hiromi had patiently listened to him explain his function. Hiromi's fight-back impulses urged her to show a sullen face and closed mouth, but she answered "Wakarimashita" to keep him from repeating his threatening spiel as if she were deaf. A short man who no doubt would righteously send her to an executioner if she spit out, "I am an American held against my will" on the live broadcast, Hiromi oddly thought of him as a decent man. He was always polite, which was out of character for most Kempeitai. He talked about his wife and children as if to demonstrate she had nothing to fear sexually from the power he held over her—a relief from Murakami. Although she reported daily to the NHK studios, she continued to receive her salary and ration coupons from the Foreign Affairs office.

She still translated Allied newspapers and BBC broadcasts. She knew Japan was losing the war and wondered who else in the government knew. The general populace certainly didn't. The disasters at Midway and Guadalcanal were portrayed as victories. What did the leaders of the Japanese government think when they read her *New York Times* summaries of the build-up of the American armed forces and the flood of airplanes, ships and tanks from America's factories? Who read her translations? Was her own life threatened simply because she knew?

It had already been six months since Murakami told her to go to the NHK studios after one of the Tokyo Roses had suddenly fallen ill. Her instinct was to refuse, but of course she couldn't. She felt like the frog in the pan of water, only she knew what the frog didn't. But like the first and most popular Tokyo Rose, Ikuko Toguri, a Nisei from Los Angeles, Hiromi was a natural at the microphone. She kept her voice conversational as if she were chatting with friends, and she sounded good—too good. NHK wanted her on-air permanently. The offer came with perks: she would receive extra ration coupons and a National Rail Pass, which was extraordinary. Ministries issued local rail passes to ride back and forth to work as standard practice, but Hiromi didn't need one. Where would she go?

⌒⌒

After lighting his cigarette, the Kempeitai man began talking again, penetrating Hiromi's reminiscences.

"Your brother has malaria. Hiroshima has an excellent tropical disease hospital. I will see what I can do," he said, smiling without warmth. "I understand your grandmother lives in the Fudoin Temple."

Hiromi struggled to return to the present. *Yoshio, sick?* Hiromi had guessed as much when his last Manchurian border letter arrived. "I am in good spirits," Yoshio wrote. "Reminds me of the summer obon festival of 1939." Hiromi remembered that August—it was when their father underwent his kidney cancer operation. The joyful remark had gotten past the censors, but not Hiromi.

"Yes," said Hiromi, recognizing his sinister use of the carrot and stick. "My grandfather served as head temple priest for decades." Which, of course, he already knew. This was a hint that her brother's health depended on her delivering these Zero Hour broadcasts whenever NHK asked. The Kempeitai were not against using brute force, but this man had accorded her the opportunity to accept the pretense of him as a man interested in the welfare of her family.

Yoshio. How long had it been since they had seen each other? Both of them so naïve about the world and paying the price of being caught in a war zone that Hiromi now knew would get worse. She had translated the Allied bombing of Berlin. *How long would it take the Americans to capture an island close enough to Japan to begin bombing Tokyo?*

Her neighbors complained that the frequent bomb shelter drills served no useful purpose, and the idea of American airplanes flying close enough to Japan to actually bomb Tokyo was absurd. NHK and the *Yomiuri Shimbun* reported great victories, assuring them America would soon tire of their fruitless war. When neighbors asked "their" American about the likelihood of the US bombing Tokyo, Hiromi could only reply, "America does not have airplanes that can fly that far."

Hiromi eyeballed the man in the control booth. He held up two palms, all fingers extended. Ten seconds. She sat down in front of the mic with the news of the day scripted in front of her.

❧ CHAPTER 74 ❧

NATASHA DAMNED HERSELF FOR HAVING BEEN in such a hurry after her session with Kenta. Normally, she dawdled a bit to give her customers the feeling of not being rushed. It's part of what separated her from the other girls. Maybe the ten-dollar tip irritated her more than she knew at the time—a goodbye tip. She wished he had said something. But men like Kenta who suffer pangs of guilt don't like to talk about it. Instead, she had hurried once she saw the tip. If she hadn't, Kenta would still have been upstairs when the girl arrived, and Lillian would have put her back in the jeep. Natasha locked herself in her room. For the first few hours, Lillian indulged Natasha's self-pity, but business was business and her best mare needed to get back downstairs with the studs.

❧ ❧

Back in the jeep, Angelina leaned against the door, her face turned away from Doi who was now driving carefully. He could almost feel the sobs that wracked her body, deep and despairing, and had quickly given up his refrain of "I'm sorry. I'm sorry," since these pathetic mumblings only induced louder weeping. He drove into summer's purple sunset and considered what would happen next.

This is how it must feel when a parent or wife receives a death notice, Angelina thought, wondering if her loss might be greater. When a man dies in battle, a hero fighting the noble cause, his life is honored, and his family is proud. Kenta had betrayed her. She tried to erase the scene from her brain as she remembered all the letters she had written, showering him with intimate feelings. The close relationship with his family. The assumption that at the right time they would marry. *All gone.*

By the time Doi dropped her at the WAC barracks a little after 9:00 p.m., Angelina's shock had morphed to anger. *Doi.* She stood on the gravel road in front of her lodging, reluctant to enter the joy and laughter of the barracks and watched him drive off. *Why had he done such a despicable thing?* Was not his treachery the greater crime? If Doi had not taken her to that awful place, if she had met Kenta later at any other place, all would have gone forward as planned. She would not have known. Ever.

And even if she had known, if she had discovered the act but no one knew except she and Kenta, they would have had a row, yes, but he would have begged forgiveness and she would have eventually granted it. It's not like he was having an affair with her best friend. Angelina had driven past Honolulu's Hotel Street and seen the lines of white-capped men. It was nothing well-brought-up girls approved of, but they understood. In war, men who found themselves far away from home, obsessed with their odds of living or dying, had been patronizing prostitutes since time immemorial.

"Angelina!" One of the WACs wandering outside noticed her standing on the road outside the tents. "Did you find Kenta?"

Angelina remained mute.

"We're leaving soon to join the party at the USO."

Angelina shook her head slowly, and the girl walked over. "What happened?"

Angelina fixed her bleary eyes on her friend. "I can't talk about it."

The girl took Angelina by the hand. "You can't stand out here all night."

She led Angelina toward the tents. A small crowd of WACs who had been watching from the open tarpaulin door stepped aside. The girl nudged Angelina to her cot. Angelina sat down, the center of attention.

"Angelina! What happened?" another girl asked.

The WAC girls examined Angelina as best they could in low-wattage hanging bulbs.

"Are you okay? Has anyone hurt you?" came another voice.

"No … at least … not that way … but …" Sobs choked off her words. And then, when Angelina could breathe again, the words flew out of her mouth. She immediately felt horrified at her confession and regretted it. Now Kenta's sin became public. If she had just said she and Kenta had a fight … Letting her head drop, she said softly, "I should never have come here."

"Listen," said one of the girls, primping in front of a mirror. "Another bus with more of the 442nd boys is coming by to pick up us stragglers. You wash your face, put on some new makeup, and come with us."

"I … I can't," said Angelina.

"We can't leave you alone," said the girl. "And don't go telling us, 'Go on without me.' You know we couldn't do that. We wouldn't be partying tonight if it weren't for your letter-writing campaign." Her smile softened her words. "Angelina, we owe you."

Angelina went to the basin and splashed water on her face. One of the girls opened Angelina's locker, chose a fitted black dress with lace trim and took it to the ironing board.

∞ Chapter 75 ∞

THE WARM AIR BUZZED WITH MOSQUITOES and the smell of oily smoke coils to fend them off. Kenta, Short Pants and No Ticket sat at their hutment's picnic table, which had doubled in size, courtesy of the squad next door who had pulled theirs over to join the wake. They listened in outrage as No Ticket related the story.

A half-moon and low-watt streetlamps provided enough light to distinguish a Bud from a Schlitz. Plenty of both flowed, but not enough to drown the forlorn sergeant's sorrows. Kenta held his drooping head with both sweaty palms between long swigs of whatever beer had been placed in front of him.

Short Pants pushed a plate of SPAM toward the morose sergeant.

Kenta brushed it aside.

No Ticket finished his telling with the order, "Find Doi."

Kenta emerged from his drunken stupor. "Stop. I don't want you all out on some kind of witch hunt. It's not Doi's fault. I am guilty. I betrayed the woman I love, an angel I don't deserve."

Short Pants leaped up. He shook his fist like a one-armed man pounding rail ties. "Are you fucking nuts? Don't get started on a guilt trip. Why do you think the army makes us watch those films with swollen peckers dripping green pus? Why do they pass out free condoms? Why do the docs keep buckets of sulfur in the infirmary? We're soldiers going off to war. We get laid."

Short Pants bent over, so he came nose to nose with Kenta. "Doi is the only one that's guilty. Got that? Angelina, bless her soul, made a mistake with this surprise visit. And that evil prick fucked her up, fucked you up. He's going to pay."

∞ ∞

By the time No Ticket had issued his orders, more than twenty-five Nisei from surrounding barracks were milling around the picnic table, eager to avenge the betrayal. In less than a quarter hour, Doi was spotted entering the supply warehouse. No Ticket sent men to keep an eye on all exits.

"This is our hutment's responsibility. We clean our own nest." He hit his fist into his open hand. "What we need right now is a key to the warehouse."

"I know who has a key—and no love for Doi," volunteered one of the men.

"Send Doi a message, No Ticket, but no head wounds or broken bones," Kenta said. "Doi wins if one of you ends up in the brig."

"Yes, sir," said No Ticket, giving an exaggerated salute. "We'll get a second shot at that little shit in Italy."

The thought that Kenta's team shared his anger comforted him. His thoughts boomeranged back to Angelina. The next time he saw Angelina in Hawaii, would she be married? Pushing a stroller? Arm in arm with a handsome haole? He would never find a woman like her again. No matter whom he married, he knew in his soul that Angelina would be the only one for him—forever.

∽ ∾

A desperate Doi had ducked into the back door of the camp's football-field-sized warehouse unseen. Or so he thought.

As he huddled in the dark of midnight and fretted over how he would handle the inevitable confrontation with Kenta and his buddies the next morning, he heard a sound just outside the door. A few pidgin words filtered through. Doi stood, careful to make no noise, and retreated to the far side of the building. The dim light seeping through the metal security mesh over the windows cast faint shadows over rows of metal racks stacked with boxes of clothing, blankets, duffel bags and other supplies.

He heard the distinct metallic sound of a key twisting the door's lock. How was that possible? Only he and four other sergeants held keys. His heart rate stampeded. Electric arcs of fear constricted his chest. His eyes roamed for a place to hide. *There.* In the murky shadows, further along the wall. He tiptoed toward stacks of recently arrived uniform cartons jammed against the wall and wormed his way into the boxes. He could hear the squeaking steel hinges as he maneuvered one, two, then three boxes ever so slowly, willing them to close the gap without tumbling. He sat on his haunches, wondering how long they would search before giving up.

He heard them taking boxes off the racks and piling them in different parts of the building. He guessed they were blocking all three doors to cut off the exits. Doi was glad he was far from the doors. When an overhead box started to slide down, he caught it softly and then let it rest on his forehead. His bladder pushed down. Would his underwear and trousers absorb enough of the smell if he pissed in his pants?

Singsong voices began taunting him, reminding Doi of the high school bullies who used to steal his lunch. The men were spread out, as if they were on patrol, hunting for the enemy.

"Here, kitty, kitty," said a voice that sounded just like Chuckles.

Why had he let his anger get the better of him? He remembered his father throwing water on him to halt his temper tantrums as a child. Something as small as being denied dessert would send him out of control.

"We know you're here, Sergeant Doi," teased another voice—No Ticket. Then after a pause, "Sir."

"The longer it takes us to root you out, the tougher the punishment," said another—Henry—his tone like a teacher keeping a class after school.

Why hadn't he just slipped a note on top of Angelina's suitcase telling her the truth about her sainted boyfriend's whore?

"Remember your Shakespeare, Doi?" asked yet another, unmistakably Buster. "How many deaths have you suffered in the last five minutes?"

Why had he even gone over to his old squad to personally handle shipping arrangements? What was he trying to prove by making nice to those pricks? *I'm the black sheep, never got a break in life. My father always favored my brothers and sisters, barely tolerated me. The army fucked me over, undermined my authority with these assholes from Hawaii, and then humiliated me with a paper promotion to supply. They might as well have posted a scarlet "U" on my shirt for "unfit to lead a combat unit."*

Doi's descent into self-pity had so distracted him, he failed to notice the sound of scuffling footsteps drawing closer, and then the silence. He did now. His legs cramped. Then he heard breathing. He pissed in his pants.

"Oh, Sergeant Doi ... we're here," Chuckles whispered in soprano.

Doi cringed as the warm liquid trickled down his thighs and the acrid smell filled the small space. He squeezed his eyes shut. *Please, God, send them away*. He replayed the rumors of men killing hated officers in the midst of a firefight. Would Kenta's mates consider the forthcoming beating full punishment or just a down payment on a death sentence in Italy?

The cramps in Doi's calves twisted and he shifted involuntarily. A box fell. His heart thumped. He curled into a fetal ball, waiting for the beating he knew he deserved.

∞ CHAPTER 76 ∞

LILLIAN HAD NOT BEEN ABLE TO COAX NATASHA out of her room. Her eyes flicked up to the mermaid clock behind the bar—midnight. Too long. She surveyed the standing-room-only crowd and then slapped the piano. It was time to put on her madam's "heart of gold" persona. A catalogue of personas, on call to protect her business, lay behind the no-nonsense exterior of a brothel madam. If fixing a love relationship between her client and his fiancée would return her best whore to her back, then that's what she would do. She smiled inwardly as she prepared to go about doing Cupid's work.

She drained her martini and lumbered upstairs. She knocked on Natasha's door.

"Go away!"

"Honey, you gotta stop punishing yourself. Instead of wallowing in remorse, you should be ashamed of yourself for not doing something to put that boy's life back together."

"There's nothing I can do. I'm a fucking whore."

"Damn right you are. And not a very good one, either," said Lillian. With any of the other girls, Lillian would have threatened to throw her out if she didn't get back to work and that would be the end of it. But Natasha's ability to produce a high income and a loyal clientele was rooted in a human sensitivity—unique in her trade—that required another approach. "If you could stop feeling guilty for a minute because some asshole fucked up your best client's love life, I can tell you how to put that favorite of yours back together with his girl."

Natasha pried the door open halfway. Lillian almost gasped—Natasha's tousled hair hung dull and unkempt as Lillian had never seen it. Crying had tattooed dark rings around Natasha's eyes. But, more than that, the spark that always simmered beneath her beauty, that luminous, seductive light that every customer coveted, had burned out.

God, I hope this works, Lillian thought.

"Girl, let's talk." She put her hand on the door, opened it all the way and stepped inside.

∞ ∞

Forty-five minutes later, a refreshed Natasha strolled into the Hawaii USO as uncertain as a virgin GI entering the Pink Palace. The colored band, decked out in wide-lapelled tuxedos, scorched the latest Dorsey hit, "Besame Mucho." The dance floor sweated and rocked, more men than women. The WAC girls jitterbugged along with some of the gals from Rohwer. Raucous men jammed the bar five and six deep.

Natasha promenaded three strides inside the door, a question mark on her face. All eyes turned her way. She exuded poise, beauty, and, most of all, an irresistible sexuality exaggerated by her vulnerable, searching eyes. In deference to her mission, she had skipped her usual ruby-red lipstick and dark eye shadow, but it hardly mattered. All the WACs and Rohwer girls stared. Even the local Hattiesburg matrons, who kept a motherly interest in maintaining the highest USO standards, gawked. The men who recognized Natasha avoided eye contact, except for one drunk soldier who started forward as if to say hello before a pair of strong khaki-sleeved arms jerked him back.

Natasha spotted the information booth and walked over. The effervescent young woman manning the booth turned an expectant face her way.

"Where can I find Mary Nakahara?" Like anyone with any knowledge of the 442nd, Natasha knew about Mary. Natasha also assumed that if one lady would know what had happened a few hours ago, it would be her.

"I'm Mary," said the woman at the booth. Then in an incredulous voice she asked, "Are you here to volunteer?"

"I'm Natasha."

Mary's eyes widened. "Oh ..." she faltered. "From the ... uh ..."

"Yes, *that* Natasha."

Mary cast a quick glance over her shoulder. All eyes were ready to be entertained. The USO had been abuzz with the narrative of Doi's cruelty. Too many 442nd boys had been at the Pink Palace when Angelina walked in to keep such a juicy story from spreading like a plague of locusts.

"You know what I do, but that doesn't mean I don't want to help put this right."

Mary had not become everyone's confidante by casting judgments. She grabbed her purse. "Let's go to the King's Lair for a cup of coffee."

⸱⸱⸱

Natasha told her story at a back table, assuming that Mary already had been at least partially informed.

Mary leaned close, eyes on Natasha's, and offered an affirmative "uh-huh" every few sentences.

Although hesitant at first, Natasha soon found herself speaking freely. She wondered how her life would have turned out if she had directed her skills to helping people like Mary did. For this one day she would try.

"All evening, I've been replaying the anguish in that girl's eyes and Kenta pounding his fists on the ground in despair. I will never love—or be loved—like those two love each other." Natasha's eyes fell to her clenched hands. "I … I'm just a diversion for the men who visit me, comfort for hire, someone that women like Angelina are never supposed to know about."

Mary covered Natasha's hands with her own. "Natasha … you are also a person who cares." A mischievous smile lit her face. "And you're a much better person than some of the Bible thumpers I've met in Hattiesburg."

Natasha's eyes grew shiny. She took a few seconds to compose herself. "By the way, Chad has never been to Lillian's." She took a sip of the tepid coffee. "In fact, he's famous for being the straight and narrow guy in Kenta's squad."

Mary laughed. "I don't know if it's because he is faithful or too shy. We've never—"

"Enough!" Natasha put her fingers on Mary's hand. "You are a good person … someone I would like to have as a friend." A tear leaked from her right eye. "I have an idea how I might help, but I need you."

Natasha quickly explained her plan.

"Angelina was standing with the crowd in the back of the USO when you arrived. You can understand why I didn't tell you." Mary paused and got a nod from Natasha. "Wait here. Let me see what I can do."

∞ CHAPTER 77 ∞

AFTER FORTY-FIVE MINUTES PASSED, Natasha began to worry that Mary had failed to convince Angelina to show. She was picking up the matchbook on the table to light the Chesterfield dangling from her mouth when Mary finally returned with Kenta's wary-faced girl.

Introductions were not necessary.

The three ladies took their seats in awkward silence. Mary asked the waiter for two more coffees and checked her watch. If her timing was right, the 442nd soldier was now delivering her message to Kenta back at Shelby.

Angelina sat rigid and red-eyed, feeling conflicted, confused and angry. She did not want to be here with Natasha, but she did not want to be among all the happy people at the USO. She didn't want to be anywhere.

"If you have come to apologize, it's not necessary," said Angelina, looking Natasha in the eye.

"I have something important to tell you. Something you need to know."

"You're not—"

"Angelina, she is not pregnant with Kenta's child," Mary blurted. Street-smart Mary knew working ladies and maternity wards didn't mix.

"That's right," said Natasha, glad she hadn't had to answer the question.

Silence descended again as the waiter placed the coffees on the table and refilled Natasha's. There was more silence as the ladies poured, spooned and stirred their coffees.

"I understand … it's difficult to know your man visits someone like me. But you must also understand the role we play. We … relieve tension, we listen, we give comfort. We are just stand-ins for the women they left behind." Natasha folded her hands and glanced at the bar in the corner of the diner. "Can I have something stronger? This … is difficult to talk about."

"Of course. I'll be back in a moment," answered Mary, who wondered if Natasha wanted a one-on-one with Angelina as much as a shot of whiskey.

"Kenta …" said Natasha, her voice thick, locking eyes with Angelina. "Kenta always wanted to talk about Angelina. Angelina, who reminds him to write home. Angelina, his first and only love. Angelina, the most beautiful girl, so warm, so loving—"

"Angelina, so far away. Angelina, what she doesn't know won't hurt her," spat Angelina.

"That's the whole point, isn't it," Natasha said kindly. "If Japan had not attacked. If Kenta had not volunteered. If war did not create armies of men a long way from home."

Angelina's eyes dropped. "But I do know. All my friends know." She shook her head, long black hair dusting her shoulders. "I should never have come here."

Natasha placed her hands over Angelina's. "And yet, you have not said you no longer love Kenta."

Angelina remained silent.

Mary returned with three shots of whiskey, and Natasha downed hers in one gulp.

Angelina took a timid swallow, coughed, then said, "You don't understand the meaning of 'face' in our culture." She pushed her whiskey over to Natasha, who raised it and took a ladylike sip this time.

"Like Germans or the Irish or Jews don't feel the pain of betrayal, the loss of face and embarrassment? Come on—you are a special person to earn Kenta's love, but don't waste words on how your loss of face is unique." Natasha wanted to add, "Loss of face is something I gave up long ago," but suppressed the urge. Natasha poured half a shot back into Angelina's coffee. "The Irish understand how to flavor their coffee."

Angelina took a timid taste. Enjoying the warm feeling of the coffee sliding down her throat, she tipped the cup to allow a generous measure. Holding the cup with both hands, she said "Every …" Her voice caught. "Everybody knows."

Mary placed a gentle hand on Angelina's arm. "Everybody knows that when our boys go to Italy, a few cigarettes will provide comfort. We all live with that. The question now is, will you allow the treachery of one person, that lowlife Sergeant Doi who tricked you, to rob you of a lifetime of happiness?"

Natasha's eyes steadied on Angelina, at the girl she could have been, and said softly, "Years from now, when you see Kenta on the streets of Honolulu, will you regret that you gave up everything you love because of ten seconds of shock and shame?"

∞ CHAPTER 78 ∞

N ATASHA SAW HIM FIRST.
The door to the King's Lair opened slowly before a soldier and then Kenta entered the diner. Kenta's eyes searched the room, finally resting on the women's table, but he did not move. He gave nodded thanks to the soldier who had escorted him off base and watched him swiftly make his exit, glad to have no further part in the evolving drama. With their backs to the door, Angelina and Mary remained unaware of Kenta's presence until Natasha rose.

"You must choose between surrendering to love or letting the mindless gossip of a few people determine your life." She leaned over and kissed Angelina on the cheek. "If Kenta were mine—which he is not—I know which choice I would make." She gave a last squeeze to Angelina's hand. "Good luck. I wish only the best for you both."

As Natasha walked away, Angelina and Mary turned around to watch her and saw Kenta standing just inside the door. As Natasha walked passed Kenta, she stumbled. "She loves you. I hope that is enough."

The tears in Angelina's eyes told Mary she had done all she could. When Kenta approached their table, Mary stood, smiled and left.

∞ ∞

When Kenta and Angelina walked into the USO later that night they were holding hands. Kenta kissed Angelina on her forehead, let go of her hand and made straight for the bandstand. A woman in a slinky, sequined dress stood offstage, waiting for her cue to come out singing "In the Blue of the Evening." Kenta whispered urgently into her ear.

The vocalist walked over to the drummer who doubled as band leader. He stopped playing the song and banged the bass drum twice. The band stopped playing.

The vocalist took the mic. "We are happy to interrupt with an important announcement."

A drum roll rat-a-tat-tatted, building to a crescendo and then stopped. The drummer struck the symbols smartly. The vocalist motioned Kenta to take the microphone. He grabbed Angelina's hand and walked to the center of the platform. The vocalist lowered the microphone's pole to Kenta's height as the crowd quieted to a murmur.

"I'm happy … no, ecstatic," said Kenta, lovingly gazing at Angelina, "to announce Angelina has accepted my proposal of marriage."

The crowd erupted into applause along with a chorus of whoops from the servicemen. Kenta turned Angelina toward him and gave her a passionate kiss followed by a long, loving hug. As he led her down to the dance floor, the singer reclaimed the mic.

"This song is for Kenta and Angelina. May they enjoy a long and happy life together."

The band launched into Kenta's requested song, last year's Benny Goodman hit, "Taking a Chance on Love."

The crowd opened the floor for a proud-eyed Kenta and a teary-eyed but smiling Angelina to dance solo.

"Are you sure you don't want to marry now?" asked Kenta.

"No, I am not sure of anything Kenta except I love you and love is forgiveness," said Angelina. "To get married and then maybe see each other a few weekends before you go to Italy, and I possibly end up in some faraway hospital—no, that's not the way to start our marriage." She wanted to say they needed a period of time to prove Kenta could be trusted; however, some words were better unspoken.

⮽ CHAPTER 79 ⮾

WHEN ANGELINA RETURNED EUPHORIC to Fort Oglethorpe, she spied an official envelope on her bed, her name written boldly in capital letters on its face. It was not her own name that caught her eye, but the name of the sender: "From the Commandant." What had she done? Her fingers fumbled at the edges, careful to open the envelope without tearing.

"You are ordered to report to Military Intelligence, Camp Ritchie, Maryland, no later than 16:00, Wednesday, September 1."

Three days. She knew she had done well on her verbal and written Japanese tests but had not realized what now seemed so obvious. Several classmates had already been taken out of training and assigned to translate Japanese documents confiscated by American soldiers in the Pacific and forwarded to the Camp Ritchie army base. Her dreams of nursing were over.

When she checked into Camp Ritchie three days later, her first thought was "Little Tokyo." The WACs in her barracks were all Nisei, some from the camps and some recruited from parts of America not subject to internment. She recognized a few from Hawaii.

Angelina had the gift. She not only translated but often typed a second interpretation of what the words really meant. Letters stating Japanese fuselages were now made of wood revealed the obvious—a shortage of metal. But when one letter mentioned the type of wood, Angelina knew the species—a rare variety found mostly in Matsumoto in the foothills of the so-called Japan Alps. She thought this could be an ideal bombing site, as the American forces moved closer to Japan, so she reported *and* recommended.

When translating food references, she noted the deteriorating protein value of the food consumed. People must be starving, children's growth stunted. She wondered how Hiromi managed. Hiromi's few Red Cross letters, which Haru shared with her, mentioned little of living conditions. Angelina assumed it was to avoid confiscation by Kempeitai censors.

Despite the frequent praise for her interpretive translations, Angelina's quick promotion to sergeant bewildered her almost as much as how her life had turned onto a path she had never imagined walking.

⤜ Chapter 80 ⤛
Honolulu – August 1943

W HEN TAKA CALLED HIS MOTHER to invite her to lunch at the Natsunoya Tea House, Haru felt more than a flicker of anxiety. Not just because Taka had used his position to talk the Red Cross into allowing them to join staff and patients at her favorite lunch spot, now closed to the public.

She tried to convince herself he had settled on someone special, most likely Candi Ida, the sister of Horace Ida, one of the five accused defendants in the famous Massie trial. Taka had covered the "trial of the century" for the *Hawaii Hochi*. Candi had been his primary source on the background article he had written on the infamous Mosquito Flats, a mixed-race slum adjoining Chinatown in downtown Honolulu. News of an engagement to Candi would have been welcomed.

No, it must be something else. She knew Taka chafed at his civilian job, even as he recognized its importance. Her only son not in uniform, Haru fretted he would volunteer for active service. Adding to her anxiety, Taka had sent a car and driver to pick her up and deliver her to the tea house. Whatever Taka wanted to talk about, he didn't want to start the conversation in the car. She knew he liked to be prepared, whether writing articles for the *Hochi* or making a presentation to the Morale Committee. But all of this for his mother?

As much as she loved the restaurant's ambience and the commanding view of Ford Island, it was common knowledge that the restaurant's favorite and most famous pre-war customer, Japanese consul official Yoshikawa, had been a spy. He was a legal spy in the sense that he didn't pay money for information or break into government offices. He bought beers for the navy boys and listened to the stories, assembling pieces of information into a more cohesive mosaic.

Viewing anchorage in Pearl Harbor required only walking upstairs to the roof and peering over the naval station. He could scan the harbor using the telescopes in place for patrons to take in the view, but Yoshikawa instead counted big items like airplanes and ships and then wired the data to Yokosuka, headquarters for Japan's Pacific fleet. Haru imagined Admiral Yamamoto scrutinizing Yoshikawa's coded wireless reports. She did not know the American navy had already broken the code. The last report before Yamamoto sent the fleet toward Pearl verified all four aircraft carriers sat moored in port. Lucky for America, those carriers were out on maneuvers by the time the Japanese bombers arrived. By no means a military strategist, Haru still knew Yamamoto had not had a backup plan if the carriers were not in port. If he had, a section of his bombing fleet would have torched the oil depot, effectively grounding ships for months. The Battle of Midway would not have happened, and Japan would now occupy the Marshall Islands.

As Taka waited to see Haru exit the car in front of the covered entrance, his own anxiety grew. He began to regret his choice of venue. He should have handled the dilemma he faced at home over coffee. Yesterday, a two-minute meeting in General Emmons's office had overwhelmed him.

"Good morning, Takeshi," the general greeted him affably from behind his desk. Although a civilian, Taka stood at attention. "Relax," commanded the general, but he did not ask Taka to sit down. Instead,

Emmons reached across the desk and offered his hand to Taka, whom he had met while attending a few of the Morale Committee sessions. "I understand you are hoping to join the army and leave your critical role as secretary to the committee."

Taka understood an admonishment when he heard one, and although Emmons hadn't quite phrased his remarks as a question, they came close enough to demand an answer.

"Yes, sir." While other men would elaborate on their reasoning, Taka had learned generals were not interested in explanations unless they asked.

"As you know, a contingent of Nisei linguists is being sent to Australia. Some will stay and translate documents and wireless communications; others will join combat units as interrogators. General MacArthur has asked me to recommend a Nisei to his senior staff to help coordinate all the incoming data and provide a Japanese perspective."

Taka rejected the implication. He was not a Kibei with years of experience living in Japan. He wasn't in the army. He wanted to volunteer for the 442nd Combat Regiment. But he kept his mouth shut.

"If you accept, given your age and role working with senior leaders, you will be commissioned as a captain. No need to drill, so no basic training. You will be sent to MIS training at Camp Savage, Minnesota."

Haru's entrance into the dining room interrupted Taka's reverie. She spotted her son sitting at her once-favorite table on the lanai, with a favored view of the lush green hillside ablaze with jacaranda flowers.

Haru's irritation with this staged performance had grown with each mile the car ascended Makanani Drive leading to the tea house. She had hardly taken her seat when she asked, "Well, Taka, are you getting married or joining the army?"

Haru's uncharacteristic bluntness validated Taka's second thoughts over his plan. This was his mother. He had offended her.

"Gomennasai, Okaasan. I do have something important to tell you. I know you love this place. I wanted to share an important decision with my mom, and I thought this would be the perfect setting."

Haru's voice mellowed. "So, which is it?" Then seeing the consternation on her son's face, she smiled and added, "I am sure it is good news for you to bring me here. Let's order first."

Once the waiter had placed tea on the table and taken their order, Taka said, "Well, it's the army, but not like you think. No combat." Those were the words he knew his mother wanted to hear given her other three sons were carrying rifles. Yet Taka knew that no combat now did not mean no combat ever. He explained the meeting with Emmons.

"So, what did you tell the general?" Haru asked. Given Taka's harping on his civilian status, how could he not have given an immediate "Yes." But Taka surprised her.

"I told the general I would give him an answer by this afternoon." Taka left out the unhappiness that transformed Emmons's face. "Then I asked him if I could choose a Nisei secretary already translating documents at Fort Ritchie."

"Angelina?" Haru's stomach tightened. Taka had not thought this through. Helping Angelina negotiate her WAC application had been a thoughtful gesture, but bringing her to Australia was the height of imprudence. She smothered her instinct to protest. An admonishment would fall on deaf ears and doubting Taka's good intentions would only ruin the lunch. He didn't understand the danger of proximity, the urgency that war creates. Yet Haru did feel pride in the honor Emmons had offered her son—a captain assigned to MacArthur's Brisbane headquarters.

"Taka, ask to use the tea house phone and call General Emmons now and accept the offer unconditionally before he withdraws it. Don't say a word about the Angelina request. It will sound like a condition and only make the general doubt his choice. He has your request and will act accordingly."

Taka stared, bewildered. His mother was ordering him to accept? Was she dismayed he hadn't accepted on the spot? Then he thought of many big decisions in the life of the Takayama family. Haru was always the rock, the decision maker, the one who saw the tree in the forest. He rose.

"Then call Hung Wai Ching, who no doubt had much to do with the offer and most likely is aware of your dilly-dallying."

Taka headed for the phone—without delay.

Haru gripped her purse handle tightly as if squeezing the pain away. Despite assurances that Taka would be at headquarters, she knew from Guadalcanal stories that MIS soldiers went into combat zones to interrogate prisoners or serve near the front line to listen in on Japanese chatter on captured walkie talkies. *How long would it be before Taka tired of a desk job and asked for a "real" job?*

She had lost a brother in the Russian War. Now, she had four sons in this war. *Who would come back?* She couldn't see a future where all returned.

FIRST BLOOD

∽ CHAPTER 81 ∾

Oran, Algeria – September 19, 1943

*D*EAR *KENTA*,

Welcome to Goat Hill, a pile of rocks better called Sand Flea Biting Hill. On arrival in Oran, Algeria, September 2, we found no immediate assignment but rumored to remain in Algeria on guard duty.

We met a couple Algerian girls who wore white dresses and veils. They invited us to their home with a few words of English and sign language. Their family might be Moslem, but they served wine, much better than the suspicious water the locals tote home from the nearest municipal well. More adventurous girls work at the Villa de la Ross night club. The military allows it to open only on weekends.

My typist "skills" earned me punishment duty as an orderly. (Which explains why my letter is typed instead of my poor handwriting.) You might think one would embrace a cushy HQ job miles behind the front line, out of harm's way, but how am I going to answer my kids when they ask me, "What did you do in the war, Daddy?" Carped to Kim. He put his hand on my shoulder. "Button up, Tommy. Embrace the job as the best thing that ever happened to you. Trust me to get you transferred to the line when we see combat."

We learned to respect his leadership during our long month fighting mock battles during our Louisiana maneuvers. He stood out among the junior officers. Intellectual in his approach to tactics like a staff officer when explaining what we need to do, but as a line officer, eager to get his hands dirty. In Louisiana, he was a "leadership by example" commander. Comfortable making decisions. Took charge. We're glad Turner was able to pry him away from Pence permanently and have him assigned to the 100th.

As it turned out, the HQ task is an interesting window into what's going on behind the scenes. Keep the following to yourself until the war is over. Almost didn't get to Italy. When we landed in Algeria, two of General Eisenhower's senior officers made a courtesy call on old man Turner that wasn't all courtesy. Voices raised inside a tent drifted over to our adjacent canvas "office." Us lowly grunts couldn't hear the senior officers' first words, but assume it went something like "How are things going?" We certainly heard the rest.

Turner's irked voice came across loud and clear. "Not well. Not so well at all, gentlemen."

"If there is a problem, maybe I can fix it," said one of the officers in a tone I rated condescending.

"Since you are the cause of the problem, I would hope so. How can you assign our combat *battalion to remain in Oran? Guarding supplies!"*

All typing and paper shuffling stopped.

"An important assignment, Lieutenant Colonel Turner," said the second voice, slightly defensive. "These Arabs will steal the shirt off your back while you are napping." They're right on that point. The Arabs take anything not tied down. It's funny watching them walking around in trousers made from duffel bags, GENERAL ISSUE *stamped on their butts.*

Turner's voice turned steely in a way I had never heard before. "The 100th did not come all the way from Hawaii, spend a year in combat training in Wisconsin and Mississippi, just to do guard duty."

One of the voices grunted just loud enough for us to hear. "But can you trust your troops to fight?"

Our eyes were riveted on the canvas wall. We fist pumped when we heard Turner roar, "Absolutely!"

We went back to work. Didn't want to get caught eavesdropping.

Orders sending us to Italy arrived two days later. We were assigned to Major General Ryder's Thirty-Fourth "Red Bull" Division's 133rd Regiment ... well bloodied from fighting the Krauts in North Africa for a year. The Thirty-Fourth is mostly Midwest farm boys from the Dakotas, Nebraska, etc.

The first time we formed up with the rest of Ryder's division, the band played "My Little Grass Shack." Ryder delivered a welcome speech. His last words sent chicken skin down my arms. "You want to fight? Follow me!"

I guess Ryder figured that men eager to forsake behind-the-lines guard duty in exchange for a chance to die in combat are his sort of soldiers. I doubt Ryder truly understands the depth of our commitment. Only by blood can we prove our loyalty and show America they made a mistake doubting us. Right now, it's enough that Ryder accepted Turner standing up for us and gave us a chance to fight. We won't let Turner down!

Ryder's adjutant, Colonel Fountain, spoke too. He talked about his work with Nisei linguists in Guadalcanal and how we weren't Japanese but Americans. Then he looked over at us and said, "And don't call them 'Japs' or there'll be trouble." You can bet he saw a whole lot of smiles from our guys.

Our 100th baseball team beat another Thirty-Fourth battalion for the North Africa championship. No shithead Crockett in this game. A clean game. I got two hits but not surprisingly Joe Takata was the hero. Three hits including a homer. And here's the surprise. Ryder's men cheered us! The only argument was over who bought the first round of beers.

It gets better. Ryder passed out baseball caps with the Thirty-Fourth motto, "Attack, Attack, Attack." Our officers received new epaulettes with the same battle message. We are more determined than ever to validate his confidence in us. We will attack!

– Tommy

Tommy held the letter in his hand. The euphoria of writing—writing *secrets*—wore off. His eyes turned to worry. His hands, not shaking, not so steady either. How would he get this letter past censors? Suppose there was a search? Hadn't he been told, "What you hear, stays here"? All those posters like "Loose Lips Sink Ships" came to mind. Revealing a dialogue between Turner and Ryder wasn't a national security issue. Or was it?

What settled the internal debate were two simple truths Tommy admitted to himself. *If I am worried how to conceal what I wrote, I shouldn't be writing it. If I am worried about getting caught, it must be wrong.* Tommy rewrote the letter, keeping the meet-up with the Moslem girls and the baseball game. What to do with the offending pages? Just thinking of how to destroy them made him realize the consequences to him and the honor of the 100th. He tore them into tiny bits and over the next three days sprinkled them into the field toilets.

⋆ CHAPTER 82 ⋆

Salerno, Italy – September 25, 1943

A RUTTED THREE-STORY STONE BUILDING with five rooms, roof and walls still intact, served as HQ for the incoming 100th commingling with part of Clark's departing staff. In a room for staff support, Tommy was assigned a "desk" of a couple planks balanced over rescued bricks and a typewriter that must have come from a magician's hat normally reserved for rabbits. He was back from the chow line. Hot food on the second day after landing! He stepped into the commander's room, the war room, the map room. The colored pins of war. Blue for Monty's battle-tested Eighth Army. Red for Clark's Fifth Army. And black—perfect color—for German commander, Field Marshal Alfred Kesselring's 135,000 soldiers. Three hundred thousand men bent on a joint mission ... to kill as many of the other's soldiers as possible in the shortest possible time.

⋆ ⋆

Tommy stood over the makeshift latrine dug along a wall of what once was a building. Unbuttoning his fly, he came face to face with a photo of Kesselring, taped to the wall. A bullet hole punctuated the middle of his forehead. His eyes ... deep, piercing, commanding. A definite contrast to his fleshy face and hairless forehead. A man to be reckoned with.

Relieving himself, he thought of America's answer to Kesselring. He had seen Clark at HQ twice in the three days since landing. Determination written all over his eyes and demeanor. A study, Tommy thought, of a Caesar who expects to win. A skinny John Wayne. Roman nose, just like all the statues around here. Thick lips and a prominent Adam's apple. Three polished gold stars on his shoulders. Preaches harmony, but short-tempered. Given to sucking up to the press. Big PR staff churns out reports with his name mentioned three times on every first page. Tommy rebuttoned his fly thinking of the copies he banged out earlier today when a Clark PR blitz called for more typists. Tommy had wanted to shout, "You got the job!"

He walked back into HQ. Relatively quiet. A chance to write a letter before the next shit storm. Tommy sat down, shoved a piece of paper into the carriage, and hit the first key.

Welcome to Italy, Kenta. At 800 miles long, it's the world's largest boot.

We're bivouacking beneath the ruins of a Greek temple at the pre-Christ city of Paestum. Looks like those pictures of the Parthenon near Athens. Supposedly, we are sleeping on the same spot Ulysses did.

I am still assigned to HQ support. Typing forms might be frustrating, but I eat well and see the so-called big picture.

Tommy's hands dropped from the keyboard. Oh, how he wanted to write about that "big picture" his humble fly-on-the-wall typist's assignment had given him. How the HQ was pissed at Monty going over Clark's head to petition Ike for an extended campaign to drain German divisions from the Atlantic. "Land on Italy's toe. Fight and hold!" Clark was having none of it. He cited Napoleon: "Italy, like a boot, should be entered only from the top." *Salerno for sure isn't the top,* thought Tommy, *but we skipped the foot and a couple hundred miles of calf by landing a third of the way up the boot.*

Tommy's "Wish I could" moment passed, and his fingers went back to the keys.

When we boarded our troop carriers in North Africa, we were at war with Italy. By the time we landed a few days later in Salerno, a ninety-minute train ride away from Rome, Italy was our ally. A strange world, Kenta. The Germans are another matter. They anticipated the Italian collapse and are now running Italy as an occupied country.

So far, the most dangerous incident was the landing in Salerno. Landing craft are designed to land on the beach. As is often the case, our landing craft hit a reef outcrop. The fourteen-foot-wide steel bow door splashed down into surf. We jumped, shoulder-strapped to a fifty-pound backpack. Water neck-high, kicking my legs with everything I had. Bouncing off the bottom like a drunken kangaroo. There was a moment when I thought the Mediterranean was going to save the Germans wasting a bullet on me. Tell Short Pants to put balloons in his pockets.

The media met us dripping-wet Nisei on the beaches. The idea of an all-Japanese unit intrigues them. Maybe Dad and the families behind barbed wire will receive better treatment ... if we fight well.

– Tommy

Tommy wondered if the last sentence would get by the censors. A hope is not a military secret, but he knew the army was more than just a little sensitive about the internment situation.

He knew that the 100th were fortunate to land when they did. By the last week in September, Salerno's beaches had been cleared of Germans.

Tommy knew the numbers—190,000 troops had preceded him along with 30,000 vehicles. Kesselring had lost his gamble that he could let the Allies land then concentrate his forces to push the Allies back into the sea. But he made them pay. Dearly. In the ten-day battle securing a beach hold, the Brits and Americans took almost 10,000 casualties, including 1,500 killed.

Tommy licked the envelope, but his eyes looked at the row of mountain peaks in the eastern horizon … as he often did … thinking, worrying that those mountains and rivers of Italy give all advantage to the defenders. The Germans lost Italy as an ally but kept the mud and mountains on their side.

Tommy walked outside. A sunset marred by smoke rising from broken buildings where embers lingered. He heard the constant low rumble and roar of vehicles heading out. To war. A war he was about to taste.

Every breath Tommy took inhaled the stench of death. The dead and wounded had been cleared, but not the farm animals. Cows and pigs don't do well panicking among the shells and bullets of battlefields. Not a good environment to gather and butcher the slaughtered animal into steaks and chops. And so they lay in the fields, rotting. Stinking.

Hungry kids. Emaciated urchins followed him. Hoping, waiting for morsels of food he could not give them. He'd seen when a GI's broken heart prevailed over army rules and gave a child a C-ration only to be inundated by a mob of scrappy children who in a month had been transformed from polite students in schoolrooms into cunning hooligans roaming the debris of war and forgotten dreams. They hovered at garbage dumps like jackals. Never bathed.

He heard soft footsteps behind. Fast. Certainly shoeless. He turned to the expected ragamuffin. This one a little older. High school? "You like fucky fucky?" Looking at Tommy's shirt pocket holding a pack of cigarettes and without stopping he hustled on. "One cigarette. My sister like fucky fucky." Tommy threw his hand back over his shoulder to give the intended blow maximum impact. He stopped. Looked at the cringing kid. He reached into his pocket. Took out a cigarette. Gave it to the kid. "Go, go. Go away." Whether the kid understood the words, he understood the shooing hand motion. The kid scared Tommy. Not fear in the moment. But it scared him, wondering what he would do in such circumstances and tried to fight off horrible images of his sisters. *Facing starvation, what is the limit I would go to eat?*

He needed a beer. Companionship. He turned and walked back to the canteen, surprised he had walked so far. He stepped up the pace as if something evil was following him. Human and dog shit everywhere. Bombed-out houses everywhere. Packs of dogs everywhere. Tommy's heart sank as he watched old men with weathered lost faces and scarf-swathed grannies pushing wheelbarrows with all their possessions, looking for a place to sleep. All this misery under a temple reminiscent of the gods of Greece and Rome. Tommy wondered, *two thousand years from now, will people look at Jesus or Buddha like we do Zeus or Mercury?*

∽ CHAPTER 83 ∽

Salerno – September 28, 1943

KIM KEPT HIS WORD. Tommy was back to being a grunt. K-rations instead of hot meals. Goodbye canvas cot at HQ. He missed that luxury within hours settling on his "army futon," a sleeping bag in a pup tent on rough ground. In a few days, he'd look back on the comforts of *that* luxury. Tommy's smile was broad. He was back where he belonged. With his platoon. Proving as men of the 100th often repeated, "We are as patriotic Americans as any haole."

Tommy woke thinking, *Today is the day.* Standing at ease between two ancient Roman columns nicked by shells and bullets but still standing in defiance of yet another war challenging their endurance, Tommy watched Kim come to the center and face his men. "Eat a hearty breakfast, it might be the last warm meal for weeks. We got motor transport heading east twenty miles or so, and then turn north for eighty-some miles to the front line." Kim let his words linger. Tommy felt his testicles tighten. *My* Red Badge of Courage *moment is hours away. Enemy soldiers will be shooting at me.* Before Tommy could take his thoughts further, Kim looked at his watch, resumed talking. "Oh-seven-hundred. Be back here. Trucks will be waiting, engines running."

∽ ∽

At 7:00 a.m., the men boarded their green army trucks. At 7:10 a.m., they disembarked. Rookie driver had them stuck in the mud. Back wheels spinning, whining and not moving an inch. Kim didn't issue an order. A test on his training methods. Would his men just get the job done or wait until someone told them what to do? He held back a satisfied smile as he watched Tommy scrounge branches and others picked up rocks to jam behind the back wheels. Without orders, the platoon PUSHED. Pushed harder. The truck engine strained, the wheels spun, found the slimmest traction and budged. Encouraged by the slight progress, the grunting men pushed all the harder. In seconds the truck was back on firm ground.

Breathing heavily, Tommy climbed back on the truck. His spirits rose when Joe Takata squeezed in behind him. Everyone admired Joe. Mr. Baseball.

Takata rested his Thompson submachine gun on its stock butt between his legs. The magazine shaft held thirty .45-inch bullets sticking out of the barrel chamber.

As Takata lit up a Lucky, Tommy studied his face. *So calm.* He had to ask. "Aren't you shitting in your pants?"

"Took a dump after breakfast to avoid that." He laughed, but not a real laugh. *Maybe he's scared too.* "The best way to face a fastball pitcher is to crowd the plate. I hate a good fastball pitcher. He has an edge. I have to show him I ain't intimidated. So, I take a quarter step closer. Maybe lean over the plate, daring him to aim at my head. Same with the Krauts. That's why I asked Kim to designate me to the lead squad. I'll be first up the hill. It's how I conquer fear."

Takata inhaled his Lucky. Deeply. Handed Tommy the cig. He inhaled the one good draw left. "Mahalo." Tommy held his breath, then slowly exhaled. Feeling a slight euphoria, he asked, "How'd you get the Tommy?"

"Sergeants of rifle squads are supposed to get one. I'm one of the first in the 100th." Joe shrugged his shoulders. "I guess hitting that homer against the Thirty-Fourth didn't hurt me on Turner's priority list."

Tommy snapped his smoking butt into the mud. He picked up Joe's gun. At eleven pounds, heavy but not too heavy. "I like the feel. I'm qualified on the weapon."

"A stick of destruction," said Takata. "On fully automatic, the clip empties in three seconds if you keep your finger pressed on the trigger."

Tommy handed the Thompson to Joe. "Keep your batting eye on me. When I see a Jerry, I'll point." At that moment, Tommy knew he could do this recon thing. *Something about Joe makes you certain.*

Everybody on the truck went silent as they drove by a jeep on its side, the engine blown half out of its nose. Minesweepers don't get them all.

Takata broke the silence. "German brutality." He looked at Tommy. "Villagers facing starvation as Jerry seizes livestock. Able-bodied men are Shanghaied to the front to dig ditches. Bad for the Italians, but good for us."

"We'll be welcomed as liberators," said Tommy.

Kim, sitting across, used his presenter's voice that carried to all on the truck. "At last night's briefing we were told that as soon as retreating

Germans leave, villagers come out of hiding in shell-hollowed stone dwellings to mark the mines. When our mine sweepers arrive, skinny kids, scarf-covered women, bent old men point at buried mines not marked."

"How stupid can the Krauts be," said Tommy. "Turning yesterday's ally into today's hateful enemy eager for revenge."

The convoy slowed, stopped, slowed, stopped. Kim barked. "Out of the trucks. Form up!" As much as Tommy hated pushing and shoving trucks, he felt queasy watching the green transport leave. In the distance, he heard the intermittent rumble of artillery. *My baptism of combat only hours away.*

Kim's platoon marched through trampled vineyards on the outskirts of Montemarano. Taking a pee on top of the vineyard hill, Tommy stared down at a once-upon-a-time stone church, its walls blasted into granite remnants sticking up like a dinosaur's mangled teeth. The altar—unharmed—faced the open rubble as if waiting for a priest to begin outdoor services. Shrapnel-twisted trees in the plaza and a splotchy white gazebo with only a few bullet tattoos. Rows of stone houses abutting each other, each with its own shell or bomb history. Walls sheaved off. Roofs—now timber chunks—strewn over what might have been an attic. Gaping, football-sized shell holes punching still upright walls.

Tommy's eyes lingered over the rubble. *Looks like a Spanish Civil War newsreel. If Picasso wants to paint a sequel to* Guernica, *he should come to the war-ripped Italian mountain villages.*

The platoon bivouacked along the side of the road outside Montemarano. Out came the trench tool, a stubby shovel. The bed maker.

"Men!" shouted Kim. "We're in artillery range. Dig slit trenches—not foxholes. Shallow, but coffin deep, so you can lie prone below ground level. You can't avoid a direct hit, but you will be protected from swirling debris."

No shelling on their position that night. Instead, intermittent thunder and lightning burst like the devil's alarm clock. Rain. Lots of it turned the men's trench beds into mud reservoirs. As the mud soup reached crotch level, Tommy restored his dirt bunk by scooping out the slurry. Four times. Doze and dig. Doze and dig. Doze and ....

Montemarano – September 29, 1943

Up before dawn. Way before dawn. Tommy rubbed a little soap on his stubble, slid his Gillette over his face. He rinsed his blade in his helmet half full of rain. He finished his cling to civilized niceties by splashing the remains of his helmet water over his sudsy face.

The platoon squatted around Kim, who had converted his helmet into a coffee pot. In a low voice causing the men to lean in, Kim delivered his version of the Knute Rockne pep talk. "Today is the day. Our orders—throw Jerry off the ridge west of Montemiletto." Kim pointed to the northwest mountains. "All your demands to let you fight, all the training, all the yammering, all the fear-masking braggadocio are behind you. Behind us." Kim thumped his chest, punctuating the word "us." "Now the reality of this first battle test: How well will we fight? Will the Germans know they are facing greenies and overwhelm us?"

"We're ready," said Takata in his soft, steel-laden voice.

The growl of a jeep interrupted the fist-pumping reaction to Takata's declaration. Eyes widened. Turner roared up to the men. As soon as the jeep stopped, Turner stood up in the back, uniform limp from rain. A scrap of bloodied toilet paper stuck to his chin. His eyes were bloodshot, but his voice firm. "Our job over the next few months is climbing hills and taking out well-protected German positions at the top of those hills." Turner coughed. Cleared his throat. "The Allies have been pushing Germans back one hill at a time for six weeks. A hard-won ninety miles of blood, mud and stone. The Krauts don't retreat easy, but they retreat. Our turn to take a hill."

A chorus of "yes, sirs" resounded. Turner saluted and sat down. Immediately, his driver ground into first gear and the jeep bounced slowly over the rough terrain due west where Company C waited for the order to attack.

The platoon rushed to the field kitchen chow line. Men wolfed down the unexpected hot meal and were told again, "This is your last hot meal for a while." Slurried eggs, syrup-laden pancakes and greasy donuts washed down with rich Moroccan coffee never tasted so good. Tommy told Kim, "I need to take another dump." Tommy ran into the bushes and upchucked his breakfast. *Does this foretell that I'll run when bullets start flying?*

Into the misty gloom of pre-dawn, the men formed into a single line and marched smartly through Montemarano. A ghost town. The rain had washed away the stink of death. A single candle glimmered through a boarded, first-floor window in a house whose second floor lay collapsed.

Tommy was not aware of his knuckles going white from squeezing the stock of his rifle. Fear pumped a steady stream of adrenalin heightening alertness. *I won't run when fired on. But do I REALLY know? Until I march into people shooting at me, I won't KNOW.*

The platoon slogged through the mud along the twisting roads, passing farmhouses without a hint of human habitation. All uphill. Tommy's legs were seasoned, but he was breathing a little heavy by the time the platoon was ordered to stop in Chiusano. The rumble of German artillery in the direction of Montemiletto silenced the banter.

Chiusano was not abandoned. People emerged into the roadside mist like Frankenstein ghouls. No men. Old women and kids stared dull-eyed. Shell-shocked? Starving? Numbed for sure. The soldiers didn't offer food. By orders and by common sense. Who knew when rations would be resupplied? One gray-haired lady's leathery face nodded at the men, made eye contact with each as if praying the Americans would make the Germans pay for taking their men.

A gray dawn oozed over the mountains. A crack of lightning flashed a fleeting northeast view of Montefalcione, the German-held redoubt on the road to Montemiletto. Kim led his men off the road into an olive orchard to avoid detection.

A sunrise without the sun. Light rain danced on the mud. Eight sloshy miles left to march up the Avellino Road through the now quiet village of Castelvetere. A road is a road, by any other name it is a road. No! Not so in Italy's mountain villages. Deep ruts, muddy and slick. "Donkey season," according to the *paisanos*, what the men called the locals. Even in the dry season, a truck would be challenged by the skinny roads built in medieval times that barely allow two carts to pass.

Ahead, the nearby hills of Chiusano and the further dull outline of Montefalcione. A couple miles more north, Montemiletto. The objective.

Mud marching equaled soaked boots. Seemed important until the men heard the thunder of fresh artillery firing. A different sound than the division's 105s.

"Jerry letting us know they know we're coming," said Tommy.

"Yeah," replied Takata. "But their random shelling broadcasts, 'We don't know your exact location.'"

Yet, added Tommy ... but only to himself.

Amid the rubble and destroyed dreams of the sorry villagers, Tommy noticed patches of picturesque vineyards, unblemished postcard-worthy stone homes on cobblestone roads. *Will they last the day? Will I last the day?*

At 10:00 a.m., incoming mortar fire from the Chiusano hills welcomed the men to the front lines. Two shells exploded to Tommy's right. He hit the ground. Dust and pebbles rained down. Luck counts. Not a nick. Tommy's worried eyes glanced at Kim.

Kim raised his hand, turned and pointed. "Halt! Don't bunch up. Krauts on that ridge." Tommy looked far up the hill as if he were going to see a German tour guide wave a swastika. Almost virgin hill. Trees still standing. Fuzzy scrub huddled around granite outcrops.

Despite Kim's photographic memory, he still checked the map. Punched it with his finger. "Everyone, dress up!" Tommy stuck bush branches behind the back of his collar, down the insides of his trousers. He rubbed fresh mud on his exposed skin. *This is the moment we all feared, anticipated, demanded, hungered for. The moment where death is certain for someone, but hopefully the bullet or grenade fragment doesn't have your name on it.*

Kim looked to his right. "Takata!" Joe turned to Kim. "You wanted the lead. Take your squad to the far left and advance slowly, about twenty yards. Don't shoot unless I give the order, or someone shoots at you."

"Yes, sir!" Tommy saw the anticipation in Joe's eyes. Daring the pitcher to throw one anywhere near his head.

Kim, his radioman and Tommy hunched down behind a scrubby stone wall long in need of repair. "OK, Tommy, pay attention." Kim's voice sounded no different than if he had asked Tommy to grab a couple hot dogs at a ballgame. While Tommy's eyes focused on the map, Kim said, "We're here. Start crawling up and drift left. Signal when you spot a German."

"Yes, sir." *No "if," only "when." Jerry's gotta be looking for someone crawling around.*

Tommy angled his right hand in his jacket pouch for his field binoculars. Took them out. Scanned in a slow, 270-degree arc. Nothing. He stuffed the field glasses back in his jacket pocket. No hanging around the neck like in the movies. Sunlight reflection gave you away. He checked his M1. Again.

Time to go.

Tommy squeezed through a breach in the stone fence. Duck-walked up the hill. *Who sees who first?* His fist tightened around the barrel of his M1. *If I have to use it before Kim orders an attack, I've failed. It means THEY saw me first. Their recon spotter won!* Tommy bent into an elbow and knee crawl.

Somewhere ahead, Germans lay in wait. But where? So many hills, gullies, farms, orchards and roads for Krauts to watch and protect. Lots of angles on every hill for them to hide. But that same topographic confusion along with drizzle and sun-hiding clouds offered stealth protection to the platoon edging up the hill. *Until it doesn't*, Tommy thought.

Tommy's eyes searched for bushes, earthen outcrops, stone walls, anything that concealed. Then his testicles bunched up. *A German!* A quarter of the way up. Mean-looking fucker behind a rocky outcrop mid-hill. Holding the stock of his machine gun. Tommy flattened down slowly. The German didn't move. *He hasn't seen me. At least I don't think he has.*

Tommy slow-twisted his neck to eyeball Kim. Muddy hand ready to give the signal. Halfway through his neck twist, it wasn't Kim whom Tommy saw, but Takata. He was acting as his own spotter. AHEAD *of me. Why?!* Takata's squad crawled behind him.

Takata's roving eyes picked Tommy up. Tommy pointed to the German. Takata followed Tommy's line of sight. Tommy aimed his rifle at the German, his finger light on the trigger. The German dipped into his nest nonchalantly. Tommy let out a deep breath.

Takata moved further right. He and Tommy slithered, snake-like, undetected. Takata crawled toward a depression, not quite a gully. The plan was to maneuver around the hill and surprise. Just like playing capture the flag. Each team hides the flag. The first team who finds the flag wins. Same here, but instead of flags, it was soldiers. The first team that found people shot them.

Takata's knees and elbows were churning fast. Kim frantically hand-gestured him to slow down. Takata did. Barely. Aggressive on the bases, aggressive on the attack.

A sudden crescendo of machine gun fire opened on the right. Joe's squad spotted. Mortar shells slammed into his position. Heads in dirt. The thump and terror of artillery shells shook the earth.

Tommy poked his head up inches, peeked. No direct hits on Joe's men. *But with that much fire power, only a matter of time. A* Jerry machine gun fired from another angle. *Where are those fuckers?! Have I been spotted?* Turtle-necked, Tommy scanned the hill. Rotated his eyes thirty degrees. Nothing. Granite outcrops surrounded by foliage. *So much cover. The Jerry emplacements, how far up?*

Takata's squad fired scattered volleys. Tommy looked over the short distance. Heard Joe's voice command, "Stop firing. We can't shoot what we don't see. Need to draw fire. I'm going up. Keep your eyes open! Don't fire until you have a target!"

Joe didn't wait for the "yes, sirs." He popped up like one of those spring-loaded toys. Standing, he saw a machine gun poking out of sandbags. Joe blasted away. His Thompson was on auto in a tight, three-second arc. While Joe ripped out the empty cartridge and jammed in a replacement taken off his belt, Kraut machine guns burst.

Tommy barely made out sandbags covered in foliage. No mistaking the blink of machine guns. He opened fire to draw fire.

Mortar fire. Exploding earth. Shrapnel spinning.

A brief lull and then words rang out that Tommy never would forget. "They got Joe!"

Tommy spotted Takata, his head dripping blood. A steel fragment stuck out of his skull. Tommy pulled his M1 trigger eight times, as fast as his finger could move, to cover Joe. The empty cartridge clip automatically popped out. Tommy jammed in a fresh clip. Fired. Joe kept crawling forward. Tommy screamed, "Medic!" Joe's corporal crawled up to him.

Tommy jammed in a third cartridge. Firing in slow cadence, he crawled toward Takata. Joe jerked his hand in a forward command gesture, all the time yelling "Carry on! Carry on! Carry on!"

Takata's head thumped on the ground.

Joe's squad rushed the German nest. Krauts fled.

Tommy ran hunched over to Joe. Dropped to his knees. Put two fingers on Joe's neck artery. Barely a pulse. Medics arrived, carried Joe's prone body downhill.

Twenty minutes later, same medics back. Shaking their heads. The head corpsman looked Tommy in the eyes. "Joe didn't make it."

The guns went silent. The platoon gathered on the captured hill. Tommy's shoulders drooped. Trudging up the hill, he composed the letter he would write his brother. *Joe Takata will go down in history as the first Nisei to give his life for America, to give lie to the charge we are not loyal, that we won't fight. Joe was our best baseball player. Some of us thought he might make it to the Bigs. I'm proud of what he did even as it reminds me I could be next.*

∞ CHAPTER 84 ∞

Chiusano – Noon

TOMMY JOINED THE SAD CONCLAVE at the top of the German abandoned hill. A victory in their first hours of combat, but no joy. *Why Joe? The best of us. A* SOMEBODY. *Who would be a somebody. A Big League player. A coach for St. Louis or McKinley high school.* SOMEBODY! Tommy struggled with the inner conflict of being relieved to be alive. Unwounded. Yet wondering if it would have been better if he'd gone down instead of Joe.

"Men listen up and listen fast," commanded Kim. "The Germans still control the ridge. We're out of machine gun range. Until we advance. And we are going to advance. That's why we are here."

Tommy noticed movement down the hill. "Lieutenant, looks like the company CO." Kim followed Tommy's line of sight.

Sure enough, Captain Taro Suzuki was trotting up the narrow stone road. Eyes out of focus. Reached the top. Didn't talk. Head jerked down at the cry of "medic." Stared down at a bleeding man carried on a stretcher, tourniquets twisted around both thighs, a medic holding up a blood sack, tube stuck into the soldier's arm. A mortar shell exploded in range of the men on the hill … but off by twenty yards. A dazed Suzuki gawked at the hole in ground the mortar shell "dug."

Kim turned from his disoriented commander, looked at his staring men and barked, "Scatter. Stay off the road. Don't make it easy for them to zero in on us." Kim looked at Tommy. "You and the radioman stay here."

Kim's order jolted Suzuki out his stupor. "No! No! Stay on the road. That's the HQ command. Charge the road and take out Jerry's machine gun nests."

Kim stood his ground. "That's dumb. We'd be open targets. Once the enemy has us in range, we need to leave the road. Look at where the firing is coming from. We move up that road, we're in 'fish in the barrel' range. Leaving the roads gives us trees, brush, rocky outcrops for cover. We can zigzag up to the Krauts in minutes. We move fast, that hill is ours."

Suzuki dug in, eyes wide. "No!!! Up the road. Those are our orders!"

"Those orders were given before we knew where the Germans planted their guns. Now we know. Instead of being targets, we should get off the road and attack through that gully."

Suzuki raged, "Stay here! I'll be back."

Minutes later, Suzuki returned with a flush-faced Turner. "Lieutenant Kim! Follow the order of your commanding officer."

"No, sir. I will not lead my men into a free-fire zone when I can move left under concealment and go straight up the hill and take out that German nest."

"If you leave this road, I'll court martial you," Suzuki snapped.

Tommy, standing like a statue and ignored by the officers, knew he shouldn't be hearing this exchange. But he was spellbound. No one was looking at him. Like he was not there. He stayed.

An angry challenge in Kim's rising voice. "Go ahead, sir. If I get up the road in full sight of German gunners, some of my men will die, others will be wounded. Unnecessarily. Look!" He aimed his finger at the ridge. "You can see a Jerry tank waiting for us to get in range. Our bullets won't carry that far. Our rifles on the open road can't fire back until we've advanced a hundred yards. For the Germans, it will be like target practice." Pointing to his left, Kim's voice returned to normal Kim calm. "We can veer off to that gully safely. We still might lose some men, but we will be fighting the Germans on our terms."

"This is a command," said Turner. "We can't have every lieutenant disobeying orders. Headquarters has ordered us up this road. You will march your men accordingly."

"This isn't World War I, sir. My first duty is to protect my men."

Turner gave Kim "the stare." Then he and Suzuki stalked off.

Doc Kometani, seeing the growing confrontation, had moved close to Tommy. As Turner and Suzuki exited, Kometani ambled the few feet to Kim. His voice, low, urgent. "You don't want our first day in battle to end in a court martial. Think what it will do to the Puka Puka reputation. What will your refusal to follow a direct order do to the Nisei experiment?"

Kim respected Kometani, a dentist who at age thirty-five gave up his practice to become the 100th's morale officer. Kim was aware he had convinced the men to donate two dollars a month for the establishment of a post-war club.

Kim's voice dropped, but Tommy was close enough to hear his steely words. "I hear you, Captain. But you can see the tank. This isn't speculation. Doc, you took the Hippocratic Oath to do no intentional harm. Would you lead men into deadly fire when a safer way lies a few yards off the road?"

Doc cocked his head toward the ridge. "Yes. I can see the tank. But it is better to have some casualties than a court martial."

Kim's shoulders slumped. Resignation clouded his eyes. "For you, Doc, and the reputation of the 100th, I will lead my men up death's road. But you and the brass better take responsibility for the men who will die in the open. For surely they will. Better get your medics and stretchers ready."

Tommy still stood transfixed. More scared than he had ever been. *Why did Kim give up? Even I, a lowly grunt, know we are sitting ducks. I'm going to die in the next five minutes.*

∞ ∞

Tommy underestimated Kim.

Kim led his platoon of thirty-nine men up the road. Right on schedule around the first curve, the German tank fired. A mortar shell exploded off the road where Tommy had been marching seconds ago. A cloud of gray debris fell harmlessly.

As soon as the curve took Kim's men out of sight, he broke into a hunched jog and pivoted left into a copse of chestnut trees. Jerked his right fist in the air signaling, "Get your asses moving." His stride burst into a sprint. Up the hill. Straight to the Jerry tank firing at the road.

"*Yes!*" shouted Tommy as if his school just scored a touchdown.

Tommy peeked back. The third squad wasn't following! He spotted Keichi Tanaka looking his way. Tommy was frantically jerking his hand in the "Come here now!" motion, when Tanaka's head exploded like he had a stick of dynamite stuck between his ears. Tommy stopped. Froze. Watched Tanaka's headless body remain standing. Blood spurted like a fountain. In seconds, he collapsed like a rag doll.

Machine gun fire resounded. The Jerry tank fired at will. Kraut mortars found range on the men on the road. Soldiers flung themselves into water-filled culverts lining the sides of the road. Bodies jerked as the hail of bullets and shells ripped flesh and bone.

The ammo carrier poked Tommy in the ribs. Tommy's mouth was still gaping. *A grisly lesson on two alternative fighting tactics.*

"Tommy!" the ammo man shouted, fear in his voice, looking into Tommy's zombie eyes.

Tommy snapped back. He dashed to catch up with Kim. *I wonder if anyone will remember Keichi. Not famous like Joe. Besides, who ever remembers the second of anything? I won't forget. I wish I could.*

Tommy, refocusing on his "be ready to scout" mission, ran to catch up with Kim racing into an olive grove gully. Machine gun fire split tree bark. Mortar shells, bursting a foot or two off the ground, sliced and spliced tree limbs into swirling scythes. *I know there is more land surface than German bullets can cover. But it doesn't seem that way. I'm fighting every instinct telling me to stand down, dig a trench, hide behind something.* Tommy ignored the whiz of bullets, the ground exploding. Hunched down to make the smallest target. Swerved every few steps. *Don't make it easy for snipers.*

The German tank turret sluggishly spun toward the olive grove. Kim motioned Jimmy Okada, the bazooka man, to join him and Tommy. Kim draped his arm on Jimmy's shoulder. "Time to see if this thing works." Dropped his arm. Zeroed in on Tommy. "Tommy, you're going to be the eyes." Kim pointed to a rock outcrop twenty yards left.

Tommy and Jimmy hightailed it to the granite knob. Knees on dirt, they peered over the smooth protective stone. The tank. Tommy half yelled, "We got a shot."

Tommy moved back. Jimmy rested the fifty-four-inch bazooka tube on the granite.

Tank turret stopped. Its deadly nose tilted down.

"Look!" shouted Tommy. "We're spotted!" On cue, Tommy put the end of the bazooka on his shoulder to help balance. Jimmy adjusted the angle of his tube. Excitement in Jimmy's voice. "We got him, hold steady."

Tommy willed himself to not shake. *Why hasn't that tank fired?*

Jimmy pulled the trigger. *Whoosh!* The shell hit the turf like a stone skipping on water and bounced into the back tread of the tank. *Wham!* Exploded. Lucky break.

Tank tilted maybe thirty degrees. Not much damage to the body of the tank, but without that piece of blown tread, it couldn't move. Turret pointed to the ground. Men jumped out. The first German hit the ground. Tommy saw his face. A baby face. Fear in the boy's eyes while loading his gun. *Why isn't he running? Why wasn't his gun already loaded? Dumb.* Tommy dropped to his right knee like in a practice drill, gun stock firm against his shoulder, aimed, fired. All in seconds. Microseconds. The German staggered back, face showing surprise, wonderment. Slumped against the side of the tank.

Kim's platoon climbed fast, shooting from the hip. Tossed grenades like Santa throwing sweets off the back of a fire engine in a Christmas parade. With no tank support and outnumbered, the Germans fled. Another hill belonged to the 100th. Six dead Germans. Two captured.

Tommy looked at the destruction behind him as he reached the hilltop. *What happens to the family who owns the ravaged stumps of olive trees that was, until minutes ago, their livelihood?*

Tommy found the body of the Jerry he killed. Eyes closed. Face serene, like he was dreaming of a good time. Tommy checked his pockets. A few lira and German-occupation marks. A picture of an older woman in drab clothes and two small girls snug against her skirts. Something scribbled in German. "We love you"? Then what looked like an address. Tommy put the picture in his shirt pocket. *Maybe I'll contact his mother after the war. What would I say? I am the American that killed your son. Absurd idea.* But Tommy kept the picture. *If a Kraut kills me and searches my uniform, he will find a picture of my okaasan. A note on the back. "Stay safe." Not Japanese to write "I love you."* Tommy's thoughts drifted back to Salerno where he had added Okaasan's address on the back of the picture. *Why? Not necessary for identification. Dog tags around our necks take care of that. Still, I wrote the address. Just in case.*

The third squad corporal—the one who'd failed to follow Kim off the road—joined him on the captured ridge. His eyes focused on the carnage below. His men. His dead men. "If I had followed you, Lieutenant, my men would be alive. I saw the culvert lining the road. Safety. I yelled, 'Jump!' I'm the leader. They obeyed, trusted me. Some dead; others bleeding out calling for the medics." Pain and humiliation in his voice. His fingers clutched the frayed corners of his corporal's stripe. Ripped it off in one angry pull. Tossed it into the mud. Rubbed his heel into the muck until the stripe disappeared. "I'm not fit to lead men in battle." He slouched off.

Including Keichi, three dead, seven wounded from the squad that stayed on the road. Without the medics, two of those seven wouldn't have made it. The rest of the platoon's three squads had five casualties, no KIAs.

A first lieutenant on Turner's staff caught up with Kim who was reviewing a map with Tommy. "You were right."

"You didn't have to expose yourself to incoming fire to tell me," said Kim, no "I told you so" in his voice. "You could have waited."

"No, I needed to let you know now. We blindly demanded you follow an order given early in the day. We're leaders on the spot. The real order … the mission was 'push the Krauts off the ridge.' We fixated on 'march up the road.' We should change tactics as circumstances demand. Your 'scatter and charge' got it right."

The lieutenant paused. Kim took half a step back and relaxed his shoulders. Kept silent. The lieutenant raised his head, looked Kim straight in the eyes.

"A little after noon, the Third Battalion's second platoon bunched up under an awning to keep out of a downpour. Two Kraut shells smacked in the middle and wiped out eleven in an instant." He stopped talking as if deciding whether he had said enough or more details needed to be added.

Kim made it easy for him. "Thank you, Lieutenant. Thank you for making this right." Kim reached out his hand. A goodbye shake.

Then as a second thought he extended his hand to Tommy. Tommy accepted, hid his surprise at the officer-to-sergeant exchange. Then watched the lieutenant retreat down the hill. *Why did Turner back Suzuki's misguided command? What would have happened to us if Kim simply complied? Would I have ended up like Keichi?*

The Germans retreated north. The 100th occupied the hills of Montefalcione. Hours later they were ordered to march two miles through veggie gardens and vineyards to bivouac in a town of the same name. The men had tasted victory. Men went down. The untested 100th proved they would fight. The took casualties and kept charging.

Tommy looked back where they had started in the pre-dawn. *Where is that* New York Times *reporter?!*

⚭ Chapter 85 ⚭

Montefalcione – 10:00 p.m.

Looking for a spot to set up his pup tent in the outskirts of the village abandoned by the Germans, Tommy bumped into the medic who was tending Joe when he died. "Turner's a mess," he said. "He's almost fifty, but it's his first time in combat. Not sure he was mentally prepared. After we brought in Joe and the other wounded, he didn't talk. Just sat and stared at the cots."

"Nobody was prepared," Tommy said. "We expect blood and death. Ol' Man Turner has been a paper pusher—a good one. But a few times on the firing range over a couple decades isn't exactly field experience."

The medic took out a Mars bar, tore it in half, and handed a piece to Tommy, who lifted the welcome treat over his mouth to catch the oozing caramel strands.

"I guess Turner didn't know what to expect," said the medic. "The burden of command—that must have hit him in ways he hadn't anticipated. Even though we all knew some of us weren't coming back." The medic paused to take another bite. "Turner's recommending Takata for the Distinguished Service Cross. Not because he was our first, but for the way he sacrificed his life."

"You know that Joe wasn't the first Nisei solider to die in this war," said Tommy. "Two months after Pearl Harbor, a Japanese sub sunk the *Royal T. Frank* carrying twenty-nine Japanese American soldiers from their Schofield training exercise to the Big Island."

"But Joe was the first to die in combat," said the medic.

"He showed us the way," replied Tommy.

⚭ ⚭

After the medic left, Kim wandered over to Tommy. "Despite Joe's loss and the disaster on the road, we prevailed, won our first battle." Kim stopped. Thinking there was more, Tommy remained silent. His decision was rewarded. "Here's a lesson in leadership. Did you notice that not only our platoon, but the entire company vastly outnumbered the Germans?"

"Actually, I didn't," said Tommy.

"At the prep meeting yesterday, Ryder's briefing officer told Turner, all of us officers, 'Your first action is against this set of hills. Lightly defended. The Krauts are not expecting a force of your size to attack.' Then Ryder interjected, 'No matter how easy the first battle is, the morale of the troops will never fail afterwards if you win it. I wouldn't take special care of you otherwise, but I will let you win the first battle."

Tommy pounded his right fist into his left hand. "Shit, you mean it was a set up?"

"No," snapped Kim. "If we hadn't charged that hill in the face of withering fire, kept charging despite casualties—" Kim paused for effect. "All the numerical advantage Ryder gave us on our first assault would have been for naught. We threw those Krauts off the hill fair and square. We proved to ourselves we could fight and win. Joe Louis's first fight was not against Max Schmeling."

∞ CHAPTER 86 ∞

Camp Shelby – October 1, 1943

COLONEL PENCE SIPPED HIS SECOND CUP of coffee as he read Mark Clark's telegram a second time.

> *This army rang with praises today for the "guinea pigs from Pearl Harbor," a unit of American infantry composed almost entirely of men of Japanese descent. Officers who witnessed the action were un-restrained in their admiration. They declared they never saw any troops handle themselves better in their trial under fire.*

Clark added a personal note to Pence. "I gave this statement above to the *Stars and Stripes* today: 'I never had such magnificent soldiers.' Send me all you got."

Pence put his cup back on his desk. Yes, the 100th had come under fire and taken casualties but kept pressing the enemy. If they had flinched, the whole Nisei experiment would have come under a cloud. They likely would have been relegated to the rear, carrying supplies.

Pence wanted to call out a doubting Washington that had ordered Clark to submit a daily performance report on the 100th. The skeptics had expected, even hoped for, failure. Nisei fighting success would give lie to their prejudice and throw doubt on the rationale for internment. He felt his shoulders relax and realized he had been holding his breath. He lifted his eyes and whispered forcefully to the map of Italy pinned to the wall opposite the world map.

"Thank you, boys. I knew I made the right decision to accept this command." The valor of the 100th assured the 442nd their own fighting time.

Despite the 442nd winning every performance award, the holdout doubt-ers still questioned: "But will they wilt under fire?"

Pence clutched the telegram. They would not.

Eisenhower's staff had outright rejected Nisei units. What would have happened if Clark had felt the same? Clark must be taking pride in the Nisei's vindication of his confidence in their fighting ability. Ike's misgiv-ings were misplaced while Clark's instincts were proven right.

The colonel studied the map. Italy's geography favored defense. Ranging from the Alps to the boot, the Apennines formed a granite spine creating a ribcage of mountains that cradled fast-running rivers feeding fertile valleys. The Germans retreated grudgingly. Their new mission: give their engineers time to lay mines, position booby traps and blow up bridges.

∞ CHAPTER 87 ∞

Approaching Benevento – October 2, 1943, mid-morning

INSIDE A FORMER GERMAN MACHINE GUN NEST, Kim and Tommy were matching map positions with the ground the platoon occupied and the likely next objective when a Turner messenger delivered orders. "Avoid infiltration. Spread out." His eyes radiating vexation, Kim's head swiveled, surveying his men's dug-in positions. He silently started counting to ten. At six, he told the sergeant, who was following Kim's line of sight, "If I had waited for HQ orders to form a line with foxholes ten yards apart, German scouts would be reporting on how Turner likes his eggs prepared. Walk the line if it pleases you, Sergeant, and report to Turner we have followed SOP when facing the enemy."

Now it was the sergeant's turn to pause. Anger in his eyes drained as he seemed to be making an effort to count to ten. "Yes, sir."

Tommy didn't hide a smirk watching the sergeant march down the hill. He turned to Kim. "I wonder if the sergeant had approached a white unit, would he have looked at the men's deployments before delivering orders and issued a 'Well done'?"

"Ah, the blindness of arrogance," said Kim shaking his head. "Ask all the officers and non-coms to join us."

Once the men reported, Kim held up the map. He stabbed at the rail-road junction in the center of the only decent-sized town. "Benevento. That's Ryder's next objective. Ultimate objective Rome, via Cassino." Showing a rare smile Kim added, "All roads lead to Rome, but all roads are mined." Serious again. "Clean your weapons, drink plenty of water and get what sleep you can. I expect orders to march tonight."

∞ ∞

A downpour thickened as Kim led his platoon off their hard-won hill on the stroke of midnight. Ahead, sixteen relentless hours of slogging through mud until they reached their objective: to secure a junction in close support of the Third Battalion's left flank, south of Benevento. Kim kept off the main roads to avoid German mines. Waded across the Calore River. Not a big river as rivers go, but the water rippled fast, footing was uneven. Carrying fifty pound backpacks, the soldiers climbed a series of 200-foot, 300-foot, ever higher, uneven rock-strewn hills.

Afternoon light was on the back stretch when Kim halted on the crest of the last hill for the day. In the distance, Tommy sighted buildings. Benevento. The first big town in days. Directly below, Tommy recognized the target, the road junction. He was checking his map to make sure when Kim sidled up. "No Germans," Tommy said with conviction.

"None we can see anyway," cautioned Kim. "If nobody starts shooting at us, here's tonight's home."

Like horses sensing their stable, the men trotted to the road crossing. Unlike horses, their wary eyes searched for an enemy lying in ambush.

Digging a foxhole in the fading sun, Tommy recognized the 45th Division's recon officer jogging up the hill. The officer waved. In seconds, he was scanning the nametag sewn on Tommy's shirt pocket. "Sergeant Takayama, Benevento is ours." Kim walked over and the officer shifted his attention. "The Germans have quit Benevento. You don't have to sleep on the road tonight."

"The Germans left?" Kim sounded incredulous.

"It's not like we haven't been bombing the city into rubble. The cathedral the Krauts used for HQ is a pile of medieval stones. The ancient Roman Theatre and the Arch of Trajan are still standing. If you step on it, you can find some standing buildings to bivouac."

Kim turned to Tommy as the sergeant took off. "Regardless of the sunny report, I want you to verify. Take that bike the paisano kid sold us and grab a flare gun. Most likely, the town is as vacant as reported. Find a set of houses where we can bivouac indoors. If all is OK, shoot the flare gun. I'll answer with a flare of my own." Another rare smile. Two in one day! "Hold for our arrival. If you see trouble, hightail it out of there."

Despite Tommy tightening the lug nut in the center of the bike's front tire, the wheel wobbled. Not a lot, but enough to warn that it wouldn't take much to flip. He strapped a six-pouch ammo bandolier belt around his waist, filled up his canteen, stuffed a couple Mars bars into his rucksack and slung the M1 over his shoulder. He cinched the strap so it wouldn't bounce as he pedaled up the hill to what he hoped would be indoor lodging. The incline punished his sleep-deprived muscles.

What was left of the town was eerily quiet. Not so the bike. The front wheel whined at half-second intervals.

No lights, not even a candle twinkle. Regiment recon had it right—no Germans, no anyone. *Now to find a standing house where forty men can sleep dry*, Tommy thought. Weaving around rubble, he spotted what must be the town square. Yes. The cathedral. Rather, an outline of partial walls of what had been a church. Kitty-corner and up fifty yards, a two-story building still standing. Tommy hit the pedals.

In his excitement, he bumped a stone and took a nasty spill. Bruised, but nothing broken. But now the front wheel wobbled beyond use. Tommy galloped up the street and entered the building carefully, checking for booby traps. Room by room, so far safe. He climbed atop the second-story roof. Tommy fired his flare gun. He munched a Mars while walking downstairs. Back at the entrance, he stood like a wary gold miner, staking his platoon's claim to quarters, appraising the destruction.

Suddenly—marching sounds, just like approaching Roman soldiers in a movie's opening credits. Stomping boots! Tommy's heartbeat raced. *No American patrol marches in jackboot cadence. German boots?* Tommy's stomach tightened. Denial. *Can't be Krauts. The town's empty!* Boots closer. At the head of the broken cobblestone road, a patrol entered from a side street. *Germans!* Holding rifles in both hands across their chests. Marching as precisely as if they were passing Hitler's reviewing stand. They didn't see Tommy. Yet.

Instinct kicked in. One quick step back into the building. Stop. Freeze. The flare. *Did they see it? If so, this is the first place the Krauts will check.* Tommy eased back into the street, two steps sideways. Pressed against the stone building, taking refuge in the shadows. Rain stopped. Clouds began breaking up. *Why now?!* The full moon bobbed in and out of parting clouds. *Why didn't I put on blackface to take away the shine?* Tommy's back was firm against the wall. More sidesteps. Then nothing against his back. A bomb-opened gap. He backstepped inside and turned. Half wall, half rubble. Scooted five steps, crawled over the rubble into a back alley. Safe for the moment.

Boots drew closer. Eight pair? Ten? His heart pounded. Cold sweat. Tommy's fist tightened on his M1. *If I'm spotted, fire a clip, then run.* He sprinted down an alley to a side street. Turned left. Standing buildings. He resumed sidestepping, back pressing against stone walls. His head clipped an angled edge of a metal grill guarding a window. He bit his lip to restrain a shout of pain. Boots stopped. Loud German voices. Boots again. Fewer. *Some soldiers must have entered the building where I launched the flare, others looking for me on the run.* Blood trickled down the back of his neck. *I need to go around the grilled window.*

The boots clacked louder. Tommy's bronze cheeks shone in the moonlight. He squatted and duck-walked under the window. Slow, careful not to make any sudden movement. Snarling winds swirled, returning rain blotted out the moon, cutting visibility. Stomping boots closed in, seconds from the side street hiding Tommy. *I'm going to be caught. Killed or sit out the war in a German POW camp.* He pushed hard against the wall as if he could shove it back. Sidled faster. Stumbled back into a recess to sharp pain. Again, suppressed the instinct to cry out. Something stabbed him just above the belt. Tommy reached behind and felt wood before his hand struck a metal door latch. His hopes rose. *Bear down … jiggle … press again.* Locked. Two German soldiers at the intersection. Two more. Fifty yards. His heart thundered. *In seconds I will be spotted.* Tommy brought his rifle to his shoulder. *My war coming to an end. How many can I take out before I am killed?* He lifted the rifle to aiming position, leaned against the door for support.

The door suddenly gaped open and Tommy toppled backward into blackness.

∞ CHAPTER 88 ∞

A CALLUSED HAND SMOTHERED TOMMY'S MOUTH. Bearded stubble sandpapered his left ear. A raspy voice hissed, "*Silenzio!*" Tommy inhaled a fog of rancid breath thick with tobacco and alcohol. Bile surged up his throat. The man's hand dropped from Tommy's mouth. A soft click. *He's closed the door.* In the dim, a narrow-faced old man turned around, grey hair frizzed over his ears, forefinger pressing his lips.

Tommy's heart thumped as the sounds of smacking boots pounding cobblestone drew closer. Jerries testing latches. Shouting. Rifle butts hammering doors. Stop and go. *Oh God, don't let there be enough manpower to smash open solid doors.* Boots stopped at the savior's door. A hard rap. Tommy's sphincter could crush an ant. A guttural, accented "*buona sera*" outside. Anger, deadly purpose in the grating voice. A firm hand on the handle, pushing down. The latch jiggled. A shoulder slam rocked the door. Another shoulder slam. Harder. *One more and that door flies open.* Tommy aimed his gun at the expected entry. A barked command and the latch stopped moving. A rifle butt hit the door as a soldier said something, frustrated, before moving on.

Or has he? Boots stopped. *Did they spot me in the shadows before I fell? Know I'm hiding here?* Through the slit in the curtain, a burst of light flashed and disappeared just as fast. Then another. *Let it be a cigarette break.*

Tommy's savior waved his arm, motioned him to follow. Tommy stumbled over a footrest, landed on all fours like a baboon, dropped his rifle. A dull clang on wood. Tommy froze for two deep breaths and then righted himself.

Boots resumed their drumbeat, fading as the Wehrmacht continued their patrol.

Tommy's savior parted a heavy dark curtain at the corner of a living room. Tommy followed him into a kitchen. Garlic permeated the air. On the left, a stubby candle, like a votive offering in a church, flickered dimly on a table covered with a red-and-white-checked tablecloth. Behind, a flower-embossed plate and mug rested on a sideboard attached to a small sink. A glass-fronted cabinet displayed bowls, dishes, cups and glasses.

The Italian stepped in close and examined Tommy's eyes like an optometrist. A grin revealed gaps between teeth. "One Puka Puka?"

"Yes, One Puka Puka." Tommy tapped his own chest. "Toe-mee."

The Italian extended a hand, firm and rough. "Bernardo." He pulled out a chair. "Wait." Opened a side door and a musty smell spilled out. Pointed his forefinger in the air. "Wait." He turned and descended. Careful, labored steps, then silence.

After several long moments, the soft clang of bottles. Bernardo ascended, steps more confident. At the top of the stairs, he smiled triumphantly. Wiped dust off a wine bottle revealing "Aglianico 1933."

Tommy hadn't a clue about wine, but the pride in the man's face promised a vintage fit for the wedding of a first son. He beamed in appreciation. *Am I sharing the man's excitement or am I just thankful I'm not marching as a POW?* "Bene," Tommy whispered. His heartbeat wasn't back to normal yet but slowing.

The old man set the wine bottle on the table like a priest settling a chalice on the altar. "Americans bene. Germans … shit." He shuffled over to the cabinet. He opened a drawer, groped through jangling utensils and extracted a corkscrew. He firmly pulled the cork in a single smooth motion punctuated with a soft whoosh. "Wait."

Wait for what?

Bernardo took a deep breath and exhaled while extending his hands. *It's like some type of unfathomable tea ceremony.* Tommy nodded his head and breathed, managed a *"Grazie."*

Bernardo took two glasses from the cabinet and put them on the table. Again: "Wait." He shuffled over to a side door, opened it and disappeared. *This place has more doors than a haunted house.*

Bernardo returned carrying a rifle marked "Carcano." Tommy studied the clunky bolt-action weapon, its stock weathered and scuffed. *A World War I weapon? Or older?*

"Partisan," said the old man, referring to his warrior status in the Italian resistance, tapping the rifle butt against his chest. "I kill two Germans." He placed the rifle on the table, careful not to point it at either of them. Bernardo lifted his leg, rested his foot on the edge of the wooden chair and rolled up his loose trouser. A red scar the size of a quarter, maybe two to three months old. The man's face drooped. "SS kill twenty boys."

Tommy nodded as the man eased his leg back on the floor. *Need to show I understand.* Tommy held up his fists, showed his index finger. "One German killed." Then he extended all ten fingers. "Hitler kills ten Italians." *Retribution works. Few partisans run independent operations now.*

The old man picked up the wine bottle and poured. Slowly.

Tommy reached for his glass.

"Wait."

Tommy snapped his hand back, aware he had violated some cultural taboo.

Bernardo hoisted his glass and swirled the wine gently, drawing it to his nose. Inhaled.

He's teaching the barbarian how to properly drink wine. Am I only fifteen minutes from being shot or captured by the real barbarians?

Bernardo sipped. Paused to allow his taste buds to savor the moment. He swallowed. Lips curved upwards, eyes sparkled. "Perfecto." He pushed Tommy's glass toward him. "Now."

Tommy mimicked the old man as he watched with approval. His taste buds exploded. *So this is what the rich haoles experience.* The thought evaporated as quickly as it formed. *I need to get back to my unit. Warn Kim.*

"One glass," said Bernardo. "German patrol leave. I take you to regiment. I know back streets."

"Bene. One glass." *Is he reading my thoughts? How does he know where the American army is advancing?*

"I have brother. Rhode Island," Bernardo said. He and Tommy

exchanged family history while savoring the Aglianico in small mouthfuls. All the while Tommy listened for the dreaded sounds of jackboots.

As dawn approached, Tommy took a long look at his watch, then gazed at Bernardo.

The old man took the cue, stood and snapped his shoulders back. Made a show of loading a six-bullet clip into his rifle's magazine. *Gun might be a relic, but it's rust-free and well oiled*, Tommy observed. "We go," Bernardo proclaimed, like Caesar commanding his legions.

Tommy followed out the back door into a narrow walkway. He welcomed the drizzle turning to chilled sheets of rain. *The same rain is falling on Jerry, sucking their enthusiasm to march, sapping their alertness and blurring their vision. Makes it tricky to distinguish between real movement and the nocturnal fuzz of shadows and rain.*

They cut between bombed stone houses, slunk down pedestrian cobblestone lanes. Then at a corner—with surprising strength—the old man grabbed Tommy's arm. "Germans," he murmured, then snorted. "Germans stop at Lucinda's whorehouse."

Tommy surprised eyes stared into Bernardo's. "Whorehouse?"

Bernardo ignored the question, stepped back, motioned Tommy to switch places and pointed upward. "Look." Three cigarette-smoking Germans loitered on a covered patio. They tossed butts over the rail and walked inside. At street level a Swiss-type Red Cross sign signaled an apothecary. *Buy your rubbers first downstairs or get a sulfur packet on the way out. The girls must be well known to the chemist.*

The old man tugged Tommy's arm. "Go back."

Tommy took one step back. "Wait!" he whispered, almost too loud. An idea was forming.

The old man raised his rifle. "Shoot Germans?"

"No!" said Tommy, his eyes alive. "POW. We capture." He raised his hands in the surrender gesture.

In the drizzle, Tommy sensed the old man ruminating. *He's fought and killed as a partisan.* Tommy lifted his hands again. "Intelligencia," Tommy said, trying to Italianize the word.

"Ah, intelligencia!" A sparkle in the crow's feet-bordered eyes. "The madam. She own apothecary." He grinned. "Stairs." His fingers mimicked walking. "Secret." Out came a set of picks like in some Bogart spy movie. Bernardo dangled them, simulated inserting into door lock. "Partisan tools. Germans chase us. We must hide." He grinned mischievously. "Hurry!"

The reborn soldier moved with a step that surprised Tommy. His confidence was catching. They scurried across the street, slunk into an alley behind the whorehouse. Stopped at a door adorned with a faded red heart pierced by an arrow, Cupid riding it like a cowboy. Bernardo tested the latch. It opened. Steep wooden stairs and another door to the immediate right. Chemical smells. German words filtered down. Tommy's heart leapt back into overdrive.

The old man unlaced his shoes, gesturing Tommy to follow. Tommy hesitated, "heard" the oft-given command: "Never take off your shoes." Tommy bent down. *No matter how softly I tiptoe in boots, barefoot's quieter.* Excruciatingly slowly, the laces loosened, and the boots eased off.

Bernardo crept up the stairs, Tommy at his heels. He stopped at the top, gripping his gun with both hands. The door just ahead was ajar. Tommy fingered his trigger. Guttural male voices mingled with that of an older woman. Soft laughter, the clink of glasses. *How many soldiers? At least two, more likely three or four. Probably not holding their weapons.* Old man whispered, "Four beds." *Must mean bedrooms.*

Tommy gestured to change places. *If I enter first with my M1 aimed at the surprised soldiers, I will be taken more seriously than the old man.* Bernardo nodded, stepped aside. Holding his rifle tight in both hands, Tommy lifted his right leg, put the toe of his boot against the barely open door, and pushed.

∞ Chapter 89 ∞

Tommy stepped inside as casually as if he was the next customer. No John Wayne–style busting the door open, guns blazing. Talking stopped. Tommy raised his gun waist high as his eyes surveyed the room. A kitchen. Four Germans sitting around a table with a big-busted woman in a frilly dress. Three wine bottles on the table. Men bleary-eyed. *Same soldiers from night patrol? Up all night? Advantage to me and Bernardo.*

Six German rifles were stacked against the wall adjacent to the kitchen sink. Tommy pointed his rifle at a soldier sporting a lieutenant's epaulets. He spotted the Kraut's pistol butt protruding from a leather holster on the right hip.

Bernardo, at a ninety-degree angle from Tommy, held his rifle menacingly. His wrathful eyes made clear his eagerness to pull the trigger. *Hope he doesn't, but also hope the Germans are thinking the same thing even as I see them all glance at their rifles. How lucky do they feel?*

Bernardo growled something. Tommy picked up the phrase "hands up" in German, not the rest.

Moment of truth. Surrender or shoot out.

The old warrior stepped closer to the table, rifle firm against his shoulder in firing squad stance. The hate in his face radiated the urge to kill. Fear shined in the eyes of the Germans. The lieutenant's hands rose. Others followed.

The madam looked at Tommy. "Don't shoot," she said in English. Turning to Bernardo, she let out a stream of Italian as she pushed her chair back, careful to keep her hands visible. She rose and retreated to a side table. Stopped talking. Opened a drawer under the tabletop while Bernardo clipped a few words. She pulled out a lady's pistol.

"Lucinda—she is one of us," said Bernardo. Lucinda's armed hand fell to folds in her skirt. She shuffled back to the table behind her former customers.

One German dropped his hand. Tommy barked, "Stoppen."

Focused on the one soldier, Tommy didn't catch the lieutenant dropping his hand until Lucinda placed her tiny pistol behind the soldier's ear. The shock of what might have been heightened Tommy's alertness. *There are six rifles, but only four Germans at the table.*

Bernardo hissed in German. Hands reached higher. Lucinda clicked the dainty pistol. *Maybe not so dainty on your skull.* After saying something in Italian, which resulted in Bernardo moving closer with his gun still in bull's eye aiming position, Lucinda addressed Tommy. "Better you take the guns from holsters." Tommy placed his rifle on the kitchen counter, walked behind the lieutenant and slowly withdrew his Luger. Tommy put his finger on the trigger. Having armed himself, Tommy rounded the table, stopping at each sitting German, jammed his newly acquired Luger into his back, withdrew each soldier's pistol, and stuffed them in his pockets until all the sweating Krauts were disarmed. Tommy walked to the drawer where Lucinda had removed her pistol and put the Lugers inside, save one for himself.

The men in the bedrooms. Do they have their pistols? Surely, they must. They'll soon notice the silence if they haven't already. "Bernardo," Tommy snapped quietly. As Bernardo turned, Tommy pointed his Lugar towards the corridor leading to what had to be the bedrooms. Following a head shake, Bernardo barked in German. The officer hesitated. Bernardo aimed his rifle at the lieutenant's forehead and tightened his finger on the trigger, as if willing the officer to go for his gun. *My God, don't pull the trigger.* The lieutenant spoke softly to Bernardo and then shouted in German. Bernardo eased the pressure on his trigger.

To keep out of sight, Tommy stepped sideways. A door squeaked. Footsteps. A soldier in trousers and half-buttoned shirt stepped into the kitchen. Saw Tommy. Looked right. A chair in the corner with two holsters, a Luger in each. *How did I miss that?!* The old man switched his rifle to the new arrival. The lieutenant spoke. The madam took the holsters and added them to the gun drawer. The spoils of war. Tommy eased over to the side table. *Sloppy. I am now visible to anyone in the hallway.*

A man's voice shouted from a bedroom.

Lucinda barked, "*Beeile dich.*" Tommy recognized the command to "hurry up." *Maybe this is going to work.* A door opened. A man, shirtless, buttoning his trousers. Didn't see Tommy immediately. Looked up. Lunged straight for Tommy who couldn't lift his Lugar in time. They crashed to the floor. Gunfire. The soldier jerked, tumbled off Tommy. He stared at blood leaking from a hole in Kraut's skull. He looked up. Lucinda. Wisps of smoke rose from her gun barrel.

Tommy let out a deep breath. *I almost get killed in a whorehouse.* "Grazie. Grazie."

Bernardo shouted in German, rifle trained on the men at the table. Lucinda turned her gun to the table. The soldiers raised their hands higher.

A whore from the bedroom shouted something in Italian. Lucinda translated. "Soldier jump." *Shit! Can't chase him. Will he bring back others? How quick?* Tommy looked again at the six stacked rifles. *Stupid! I assumed only six soldiers.*

Four girls appeared. Two in skimpy pajamas, one in a bra and panties, the fourth only panties. Tommy felt an instant stir in his groin. *How long has it been?* Lucinda addressed them and they clapped their hands. She opened another drawer and pulled out a roll of kitchen twine. The girls went to work binding the Germans' hands to chair backs. Tommy checked the knots. *Where did they learn that?!* The girl with bouncing breasts extracted wallets, took money, tossed empties. She screeched happily, waved a US five-dollar bill and stuffed it into her lacy red panties. Lucinda snapped something. Frowning, the girl handed the money to her madam.

Tommy eyed Bernardo. "POWs. How take to my regiment?" *Use his word for whatever he thinks my unit is. No time to teach "squad" or "platoon."*

"You don't," said Lucinda. "The Germans, they are leaving. The Americans, you are coming. The lieutenant," she said, pointing to the grim-faced officer bound to his chair, "he tell me, 'Big mistake. When commander say leave, we near here. Maybe last chance for girl for long time.'"

"Sophia." Lucinda's eyes shifted to the topless gal, whom she addressed in English. "Put clothes on. Take bicycle to main road. You come back with American jeep."

Lucinda eyed Tommy's bulging trouser fly. She smiled knowingly. "Sophia and I speak a little English. The other girls—they soon learn," she laughed. Tommy's eyes followed Sophia's sashaying hips down the hallway as Lucinda's voice turned angry. "Why you soldiers take so long? We must fuck these pigs for months. Some hurt the girls." Lucinda looked over at her oldest whore, maybe twenty-five, who was twisting a carving knife and staring at the Germans. "That Theresa. Germans take father and brother. Work brigade. She give her money to mother. Food for her three younger sisters and German baby." She spits. "Some of these pigs no wear blanket. Theresa won't drop baby. She worry about the Pope. The Pope! He sit in the Vatican. What's he do—" She stopped, once again turning on her madam smile. "But you are here now." She looked at one of the other girls and spoke in rapid-fire Italian.

Two girls started taking off the soldiers' trousers and underwear. Lucinda showed a hardened smile. "No clothes; no run away." She paused, her voice warming. "You One Puka Puka boy?"

"Yes." Adrenaline was wearing off, Tommy's hard-on easing.

The sun broke through the night sky. Sophia returned, dressed in church-going black. She carried two chairs and placed one next to Bernardo. He seemed relieved to be able to sit down. She brought the other chair to Tommy. He shook his head and pointed to Lucinda.

∞ CHAPTER 90 ∞

A GIRL TOMMY HADN'T NOTICED BEFORE sashayed out of the pantry, dressed in crotch-high baby doll pajamas. She carried a wine bottle snug in burlap. Lucinda produced a corkscrew. "We saved this for the day the pigs leave." She held out the corkscrew. "Bernardo, you do honors." Tommy heard the soft pop of a cork for the second time that night. *Am I fighting a war or on an Italian wine sampling junket?*

The jaunty temptress set four crystal glasses on the side table holding the Lugers. She threw Tommy an inviting smile. He held the look. She closed in on Tommy and rested her hand on his chest. "Gloria." Tommy broke eye contact as another part of his body went rigid. *No sleep for almost two days. It's not a good time for more alcohol or to jump in the sack. But not a good time to offend, either.* Tommy ignored the pleas from his groin. He looked at Lucinda. "I need to find my platoon."

She seemed to understand. "Yes, yes, but a taste now." Handed Tommy a glass.

Tommy sipped. His arousal retreated.

"Is good, no?"

"Si, bene." Tommy nodded his head with a vigor he did not feel. *My fatigue is at a dangerous level.*

Lucinda held the bottle high, catching the morning sun streaking through the window. Almost half full. She stuffed the cork back in. "We keep for you." A big madam smile. "Your unit, it is marching through?"

"Yes." Even in his addled state, Tommy caught the meaning.

"My sister has small stable in Salerno. She say Puka Puka boys very polite. Maybe we can do business."

"How much do the girls charge?"

Tommy caught the gleam in Lucinda's eyes. *I bet a month's salary that a "rich American soldier" price hike is about to be announced.* "We charge … fifty cents …" She eyed Tommy. *Waiting for a challenge? Am I supposed to negotiate?* "Or a pack of cigarettes," she concluded.

Tommy surveyed the room with a new perspective. Kitchen scrubbed clean. Colorful wide-blooming roses printed on white plastic tablecloths. Small wooden chairs occupied by silent Germans, accepting their POW fate. The smell of garlic gave the kitchen a homey feel. He strolled down the corridor, peeked inside rooms. *What used to be two bedrooms converted into four tiny cubicles like Honolulu's Hotel Street brothels. Lucinda's place is a cut above the instant cat houses we've passed since Salerno.* Tommy strolled back to the kitchen, eyeing Bernardo as if asking his advice. *A man I have known for only a few hours, but a fellow warrior who saved my life.*

"Lucinda's girls clean. No steal money."

Lucinda laughed. "A free sample for you. Which girl you like?"

Tommy shook his head. "Not me. When our soldiers arrive to collect the Germans, ask one of your girls to take Bernardo back home and stay long enough to give him a memory."

"I'll send two girls with him."

"Only Sophia," said Bernardo, not embarrassed.

The roar of a jeep invaded the kitchen. An American jeep. The screech of brakes riveted Tommy's attention to the window. *How did Sophia get back so quickly?* He strutted to the balcony. Looked below.

No Sophia.

Three haole officers and a raggedy-looking Italian kid. The 133rd's Captain Reich and two lieutenants. *Not good news. Don't know most of the 133rd's officers, but we all know Reich.* Despite Ryder's admonition to not use the word "Japs" and the respect the 100th had earned in the field, Reich was well known for calling the unit "dirty Japs." *The coward. He uses his officer's epaulettes to denigrate, knowing that retaliating with a punch would mean a court martial.*

The kid pointed upstairs. Lucinda, the tops of her hefty breasts on generous display, peered over the balcony.

Tommy watched Reich's upturned stern face shift to lascivious expectance in an instant. He handed the kid a pack of cigarettes. *No doubt what Reich has in mind.* The kid sped off into the rubble. *Tonight, his family eats. Better step inside.*

The sound of boots pounding up the stairs turned Tommy's eyes to the door. *I've had a shitty night and am not about to give in to this poster boy for racism.*

Captain Reich stepped in. Surprise in his eyes at the sight of trouserless Germans tied to chairs and a dead Kraut on the floor. The officer lifted an eyebrow, maybe a hint of approval. He took in the three young girls in revealing pajamas. Then his attention turned to Tommy struggling to control his rage as he watched Reich's calculating pose. *Rules be damned, I'm not saluting this shithead in a whorehouse.*

"Caught some Krauts with their pants down?" Reich nodded appreciatively at Bernardo. "Little help from a partisan. Well done. Once they put some pants on, you and my lieutenant can find your way to HQ for interrogation. Might even be a medal in it for you," he said dismissively.

Fuck him! I'm outranked. Outnumbered. Need to stall for time. Where are my guys? Tommy glanced over at the Germans. "If it weren't for the Italian holding the rifle, it would be me who's the POW."

"Right," says Reich. "Not a lot of rice and raw fish in a Kraut *stalag.*"

Tommy's eyes turned steely, but he kept his mouth shut. Didn't take the bait.

"You are ordered," Reich paused for emphasis, "to take the prisoners to HQ. Get them dressed." Before Tommy could blurt out a response destined to earn him a court martial, fresh noisy boots stomped up the stairs along with the ping of high heels. Reich eyed the door, a hint of uncertainty on his face. The door flew open. *My guys! Seven of them.*

No kitchen had ever been so crowded. Six pantless Germans, another dead, six hookers and eleven American soldiers.

Reich seized the moment. "Good. Now you have enough men to take the prisoners to HQ, Sergeant."

My moment of truth. "Yes, sir. Four of my men will take the prisoners. That leaves four of us from the 100th to take over the cathouse."

"Don't be impertinent, Sergeant. I have given you an order!" He stared hard. "You and your men will leave immediately with the prisoners."

"Captain, I captured these Germans. This is my unit's R&R facility."

Kats Hata, one of the recently arrived soldiers, known for his stoic silence, riveted his eyes on the captain. "The 100th has occupied the town for more than an hour. It's our bivouac town." Kats shifted his gaze to Tommy. "Lieutenant Kim sent us to find you. Except for these sorry asses," he said, noting the pasty-skinned Germans, "the town is Kraut-free." Nodding his head toward Sophia he added, "We saw this gal waving us down. We stopped and she told us about a Japanese soldier holding some Germans. Knew it had to be you." *Eat those apples, Captain Reich.*

"Evidently, some kid told the captain here about the whorehouse," said Tommy.

"No," said a smirking Reich, "the kid told me about the prisoners. I was shocked to find Jap enlisted men consorting with prostitutes."

Tommy couldn't hold back. "Do you always have a hard-on when picking up naked German men?"

Reich's neck veins popped. His face bloomed red.

"That boy is Pepito, butcher's son," Bernardo interjected. "He not know Germans here. You lie."

"Fuck off, old man, this is an American military situation," Reich said, clenching his fists. His face was cruel. He snapped at one of his lieutenants. "Get this old codger out of here."

A trigger snapped. All eyes turned on Bernardo. His eyes were defiant. "This my village. You liberator or Nazi?"

Short Fuse Arai picked up a wine bottle, hoisted it high in the air and slammed the bottle on the edge of the kitchen counter, leaving a jagged shank. Shaking his weapon savagely he snarled, "This is the same officer who refers to us as 'dirty Japs.'"

One of the lieutenants put his hand on his holster gun.

"OK," Tommy said, extending his palm to tell Short Fuse to ratchet down the volume. "We all know Reich is a West Coast racist. But he's an exception. Ryder and his officers treat us well." *I don't want Short Fuse to start a brawl that leads to the brig. On the other hand, the tension must have the captain wondering how far he wants to go with this. No matter the outcome, he'll have a tough time explaining why he was fighting for control of a whorehouse in a bivouac not his own. What do they call it, a Mexican standoff? Feels more like a movie where everyone stands still. Waiting for the first person to move.*

Tommy looked over to Lucinda's horrified face. "Maybe your ladies might want to give these officers a freebie." *Maybe a taste of free nookie will give the peckerhead some face-saving cover that just might make him back down.*

"Yes," Lucinda said, clearly relieved. "My ladies are a randy lot. Waiting for Americans." She said something in Italian and two girls sidled up to the lieutenants. "I no longer serve clients … except for senior officers." She twirled her pinkie in her mouth. "Like this handsome captain." The captain's eyes dropped to Lucinda's cleavage—not for long, but long enough.

The tension eased. Tommy eyed Short Fuse and signaled him to back down. He breathed easier watching Short Fuse set the serrated bottle-neck atop the sink board. A soft clink, a gentle roll and then it stopped. Tommy breathed even easier when he heard the disengaging trigger click of Bernardo's rifle and observed the lieutenant's hand move away from his gun to scratch his nose.

"Captain," Tommy said, "while your men are engaged, my men will see that the Germans get dressed. They'll be ready downstairs for your men to escort them to your HQ unit." *Hopefully Reich is smart enough to realize that bringing back prized POWs for interrogation is a better career move than busting up a whorehouse.*

"See that it gets done." Reich's voice was back to command level.

Having won, Tommy fought back a smirk. He snapped a respectful, "Yes, sir."

∽ ∾

While the captain and his men cleaned their ashes, Tommy lit a Lucky on the balcony and watched the Germans standing in front of the pharmacy, now fully clothed, hands tied behind their backs. *How Reich gets his prisoners back to HQ is his problem. March? Commandeer a truck? He's got a jeep. Let him figure it out.*

Tommy walked back inside in time to hear the defeated Reich strut smartly down the stairs like he had won. Wearing a triumphant smirk Tommy said, "Kats, why don't you hustle off and inform Kim you found me. But first, let me tell you the business arrangement I've negotiated with Lucinda. Perhaps you and Short Fuse can help me manage our new business." Smiles all around.

"What about Kim?" asked Kats.

Tommy didn't hesitate. "We'll cut Kim in for a share of the profits."

"OK," said Kats. "I'm off. Will find Kim."

Bernardo, who had never let the gun out of his hands until the Germans descended the stairs, said "I'm hungry."

Relieved laughter filled the room.

Lucinda, back again as if nothing had happened, said, "I cook you breakfast. Eggs. Sausage. Bread." *A whorehouse madam eats well, even in wartime.*

Halfway through their eggs over easy, a jeep roared up. Tommy's stomach knotted until Kim walked in the door.

Tommy stood and saluted. "I have a story."

Spotting the corpse on the floor, Kim said, "It better be good."

"It's better with eggs and sausages, sir."

A pause. Kim gave the order to clear the kitchen except for him and Tommy. Lucinda and her girls retired to the bedrooms, the soldiers took their plates and forks to the balcony. With Sophia clutching his arm, Bernardo, smiling like a child with its hand in the cookie jar, swaggered to the door.

Tommy told his story aided by strong Italian coffee. Kim listened. "Incredible. I spotted Reich transferring the German POWs to a truck. He was eager to give me directions here along with a story of how my depraved men were holding whores hostage. I'm not worried about Reich nor am I worried about the Kraut that escaped. He's long gone. Benevento is ours. Ryder has ordered the division to stop and hold. R&R for … maybe thirty-six hours." Kim paused, studied Tommy. "As your commanding officer, I don't approve or take part in running a comfort station." He allowed a savvy smile. "However, you'd better sleep here. A miner sleeps in his claim, lest a claim jumper move in." *I don't need convincing.*

Kim passed on Tommy's offer of a quickie. "Maybe later," Kim said. "Right now, I'll settle for eggs and sausage." Eyeing the dead German, Kim added, "Have your guys wrap him in a sheet and take him downstairs to the sidewalk. I'll order a body wagon to pick him up. Check his pockets first."

My cue to call Lucinda back in the room.

∞ CHAPTER 91 ∞

October 3, 1943

SOFT HANDS RUBBED A SLEEPING TOMMY'S SHOULDERS, then drifted lower, activating his libido. Breasts pressed against his back. Hands prodded Tommy to turn on his back. *Gloria! Naked. Thank you, Bernardo for bringing me here.* She lifted her hips. Tommy felt the warmth, the moisture.

The door burst open.

"The Germans are back!" Lucinda gasped.

"What?!" Tommy's erection shriveled.

Ignoring Gloria, Lucinda leaned over Tommy's face. "The fucking Krauts are back!"

⚭ ⚭

Tommy jerked up to the roar of artillery, the pop of rifles and the rat-a-tat-tat of machine guns. The burst of a shell slamming into an adjacent building jacked Tommy to full alert.

Lucinda, her eyes radiating terror, tossed Tommy his trousers. As he shoved his legs into his khakis, a familiar voice carried from the street below. "Tommy! Tommy! Where the fuck are you! Kim needs you *now*!" *Ohashi. What's he doing here?* Tommy streaked out of the bedroom toward the open veranda door. Buttoning his shirt, he spotted Ohashi who rapid fired, "Kraut tanks, rumbling into the city, shooting. Maybe a dozen of them. You got the maps?"

Tommy rubbed his hand over his chest. *Safe in a wax wrapper that only seconds ago I layered between my T-shirt and khaki tunic.* "Yes! I'm coming down."

Lucinda and her girls crowded around Tommy, who was lacing his shoes, on bended knee. Worried faces stared down. *Time for contrived reassurance.* "Don't worry, ladies. We will beat them back. You won't have to fuck Germans again."

Tommy stood, brushed imaginary dust off the upper legs of his trousers, took his rifle from a moist-eyed Gloria, hurried to the door and hopped down the steps.

Waiting at the exit, Ohashi was jogging in place. "Let's run." *I don't need any encouragement.* Incoming artillery and tank shells exploded against nearby buildings and roads. Descending debris bounced off them as the two sprinted toward the bivouac building. Ohashi panted, "Kim's up top."

Tommy dashed two steps at a time to the roof. The percussion boom of an artillery shell smashing the pavement he just left pounded his ears. He ducked instinctively, squinted behind, relieved Ohashi still followed. *If he'd stayed on the street, he'd be a KIA.* Sounds of rifle fire inside the building resonated. *Half our platoon must be shooting from the building. Are German infantry this close?*

On the building top, Kim wasted no time. He pointed. "What's the number of the hill at one o'clock?" Tommy's eyes followed. Three Tiger tanks. Smoke cascaded from their turrets. Kim had the telephone receiver in his hand. Wires dangled, leading to the stairs.

Tommy pulled out his map. Took only seconds. "Hill 553." *I'm getting good at matching what I see with hill numbers.*

Tiger tanks fired. Kim called in the hill number to the artillery unit. Shells from the Tigers exploded on unseen targets half a kilometer to the right. In ninety seconds, the first register shell slammed into Hill 553. Missed the tanks. Hard to impossible to score a direct hit on a target the size of a tank from two to four miles away. Kim shouted adjustments into the field phone. A rain of artillery shells pounded the crest.

With his binoculars, Tommy spied men moving back. *Not a good place for a human body without infantry support. Will the tanks stay? Can our bazooka boys get close enough to take out the tank? A direct frontal hit not effective, but a side shot might penetrate and certainly fuck up the treads. A tank that can't move is a tank with a short life expectancy.*

Standing next to Tommy, Kim, hands on his hips, surveyed the carnage. "Germans have a quarter of the town. But the advantage of surprise is gone."

At the sound of the dreaded "whoosh," Tommy screamed, "Down!" as if he were the only one that could hear the incoming mortar. As the men dropped to prone positions, a shell hit the corner of their building. Shrapnel whirled outwards. The angle of hit, the absorption of the blast by the stones, added to the mayhem even as the radius was lessened. Kim was still, even, calm. Before the dust settled, he stood.

What can I do but follow? Tommy stood, his knees shaking.

"We got a great view," Kim observed, as if admiring a Waikiki sunset.

"Right," said Tommy. *Yeah, a great view for every hilltop Jerry gazing down at two GIs on top of a building.*

Kim pointed up and left. Curling smoke from a copse of olive trees.

Tommy didn't wait for orders. Instantly scanned the map. Poking the corner, he shouted into Kim's phone, "Hill 668!" In minutes, whatever was under those smoke curls was disabled or in retreat.

After an adrenaline-filled seventy minutes running back and forth on the roof, there were no more targets to call in. The Germans had withdrawn.

Tommy bounded down the steps to join his unit forming to move out in pursuit. As he exited the building, a truck with a lone German driver turned his way. *Troop truck searching for stragglers?* The driver's face was shocked as a dozen GIs trained their M1s on his truck. *Is he going to plow into us for the Fuhrer?* The driver stopped the truck. Tommy breathed easier. The driver raised his hands. *Lucky German—his war is over.* The squad rushed forward. Ohashi opened the door.

"I surrender; don't shoot," the driver said in perfect American English. He studied their faces. "Japanese?"

"Yes," Ohashi deadpanned. "You didn't hear? Our emperor switched sides. Like the Italians. We're American allies now."

"Sometimes I listen to BBC but haven't for at least a week. My mother's American. Married a German visiting Milwaukee. We moved to Munich after Hitler seized power in '33. She left my father when we invaded Poland. The Reich wouldn't let me leave." Then it dawned on him. "Hey, how come you speak English?"

"Just keep your hands high," commanded Tommy, jerking his rifle up. "If you cooperate you just might get back to Milwaukee." *We have ourselves a POW eager to be interrogated.*

The rumble of demolition charges cast a pall over the brief joy of capturing the POW.

"German sappers blowing bridges and toppling buildings onto roads," said the prisoner, as if he were a scout for the 100th rather than a POW.

Ohashi turned to Tommy. "Give the Krauts credit. They know how to retreat."

∞ ∞

The pause in the fighting allowed the "post office" to catch up with the platoon. Tommy scribbled a quick letter.

> *Little Brother,*
>
> *All those Shelby drills paid off. Conditioning ensures endurance on the battlefield and adds the extra speed to dash to the next building or boulder before Jerry can mow us down. In training, we won awards for setting up a machine gun on average in five seconds—a third of the time, according to the manual, and half the time at OCS school. In Italy, that set-up speed translates into dead Germans instead of dead Americans. We hated Kim's gung-ho drills, driving us harder than necessary. We love him now.*
>
> *Looking forward to you joining us.*
>
> *– Tommy*

∞ CHAPTER 92 ∞

October 3, 1943 – Afternoon

AFTER SLOGGING FOUR MILES, Kim barked, "Fall out. Set up your pup tents. Dig your foxholes. Dig deep, we'll be on the outskirts of Montesarchio for a few days"

Tommy dropped his backpack on the ground. Shovel out, started digging next to Short Fuse who mused, "Four miles from Lucinda. Might as well be four thousand."

"What lucky stiffs are enjoying golden moments with Lucinda's gals?" said Tommy, pitching dirt behind him. Standing up to stretch to ease the back discomfort from digging, Tommy's face lit up. "Look!"

Everyone turned. Then, a roar of cheers as the men watched Italians cajoling their supply-laden mules across tobacco fields, churning them into muddy ruins. *Who knew the Italians grew the stuff?*

"Are those bags of rice on the next to last mule?" asked Short Fuse.

"George Grandstaff," said Tommy, referring to the battalion's supply officer, "has done it again."

"Right," said Short Fuse. "He's getting good at trading our division's standard kitchen rations to augment the rice allotment."

"For a haole, he sure picked up we were getting tired of potatoes pretty fast," added Tommy.

☙ ❧

Roadside kids ran up shouting, "Chinese! Chinese!"

"I don't care what they call us," said Short Fuse, "as long as they keep tossing apples our way."

One of the gangly kids, well into his teens, approached Tommy. *Lucky boy to have escaped being sent to a German labor battalion.* "You like rabbit?" the boy said in decent English.

"Rabbit?" said Tommy, who had learned early on that most gangs of kids had a least one English speaker to handle negotiations. Usually vegetables and maybe a chicken, in exchange for cigs.

"I show you. Many rabbits." He grinned. "Many cigarettes." He pointed at a white concrete building.

After telling Kim he had a line on rabbits, Tommy followed the boy. Sure enough, a whole hutch of maybe a dozen rabbits! He studied the building. "*Mediche*" something or other. *Nobody here. Fled when the Krauts passed through.*

Tommy couldn't believe his good luck. *A culinary goldmine! Good eats. Some rabbits for George to trade for more rice.*

After making the boy rich by agreeing to four packs of cigs, Tommy raced back to the top to round up the cigarettes and bags to carry the rabbits back.

☙ ❧

October 9, 1943

"Read this," ordered Kim, walking up to Tommy's pup tent where he was about to roll the dice in a fresh game of craps to ward off boredom after six days of rest and resupply.

"BEWARE: STOLEN MEDICAL EXPERIMENT RABBITS CARRY RARE DISEASE."

Tommy looked up without reading the full text. "This is HQ scare tactics, right? Some Italian complained and this is Turner's response. Right?"

"Maybe," said Kim holding Tommy's gaze. "But I'd check your stool the next couple days."

Before Tommy, less sure of himself now, could reply, the mountains convulsed.

"My God, an earthquake," shouted Tommy looking around, expecting houses to collapse, the earth maybe to open up.

Short Fuse from Hilo laughed hysterically, barely managing to speak. "You Oahu boys don't know what a real earthquake is." The earth was quiet. No houses had crumbled. No rifts in the earth. Short Fuse's voice had almost returned to normal, "This was just a mountain shrug. Come over to the Big Island where Pele knows how to set off a real earthquake."

Unrattled, Kim's somber voice cut off the squabbling. "Brutal news from Naples. The local folks rose up against the Germans, expecting the attacking Americans to enter quickly. Took us a week. The number killed in the uprising was in the thousands."

Shaking his head, Tommy said, "Well, if the Krauts wanted to make sure the Italians will help us going forward, they did it in spades."

"Before you get back to your game," said Kim in a lighter voice. "Let me read Clark's report to Ike. It was printed in the divisional newsletter.

The 100th showed quick reaction to hostile opposition and employed all weapons unhesitatingly. Hospitalization from sickness practically nil as men prefer to remain with command. Morale high. The 100th demonstrates a strong desire to be with their unit. Their combat reduced absences due to sickness and hospitalization almost to zero.

While the Japanese American battalion was acting as the advance guard for a regimental combat team, the battalion advanced approximately fifteen miles in twenty-four hours, operating day and night in the face of strong enemy resistance and over difficult terrain. Although suffering casualties, their advance continued on schedule. All of its weapons were used with complete assurance. A

Japanese American sergeant who lost his life in this action has been recommended for the Distinguished Service Cross.

As Kim strolled off, Short Fuse picked up the dice, "If you candy-assed Oahu boys have recovered from the deadly earthquake, the game is still on."

"If you have enough cash to cover your losses, roll'm," said Tommy.

∞ CHAPTER 93 ∞

October 15, 1943

RIVERS ARE LOVED BY DEFENSE, hated by offense. The Volturno is a cruel river to cross and a dream to defend from the concealing orchards, vineyards and reeds. Its military importance goes back to the Etruscan kingdom. Only 109 miles long, the Volturno River sources 1,600 feet high in the Apennines. From those heights, the river drops south, then halfway through its journey, meanders east. Finally empties into the Tyrrhenian Sea just a little north of Naples, a two-hour drive south of Rome. The muddy Volturno's oxbow loops and curves twist in devilish configurations. When you think you have crossed it, you find the snaky fiend has doubled back on itself and must be crossed again. And again.

The 100th's mission: Secure a bridge before the Germans could dynamite it. Kim led the march at double time, 180 steps a minute rather than the normal quick-time of 120 steps a minute, through back roads, orchards and creeks under the cover of artificial fog—a nasty smelling smoke screen. The platoon was a quarter mile from the bridge when they heard and felt a mammoth explosion. Minutes later, running ahead as the platoon scout, Tommy verified what they feared. He stared through fading fog and night drizzle at what was once a bridge, now a pile of cement and twisted steel. He couldn't stop sneezing from the concrete dust.

Tommy scurried back and reported to Kim. "The Krauts were a step ahead of us." Tommy's mouth was agape as a new sound, a terrifying sound, assaulted his ears. The sound that had been spine-chillingly described but not yet heard. An ear-splitting whistle, a rising crescendo heralding the Grim Reaper's imminent arrival. The Screaming Mimis. The six-barreled electronic Nebelwerfer rocket launcher fired in ten-second intervals. The three-finned rocket wasn't accurate but targeting massed troops didn't have to be.

Tommy's eyes locked on Kim's. "Incoming!" someone screamed as if no else could hear the dreadful foretelling. Tommy body-slammed the turf. Waited a split second, an eternity, as death selected its victims. Then the explosion. Like in training. Only not. This was for real. The second explosion closer. Mud splattered Tommy's face. Kim shouted, "Dig!" No shovels on this maneuver. The brass ordered the men to carry more ammo instead. Tommy's hands dug frantically in the soft mud. No foxhole, but deep and long enough so only a direct hit could take him out. He listened for the next one. Intently, expectantly. Seconds passed. His heart pounded. Nothing. He breathed easier. Only the rumble of distant artillery and intermittent pops of rifle fire. *Are the German rocketeers finished with our quadrant? Merely reloading? Retreating under our fire?*

"Party's over!" Kim shouted. He stood up. "No direct fire from the opposite riverbank. Let's tiptoe across." Tiptoe gingerly is precisely what they did, over fallen concrete chunks sticking out from the river bottom. In that fashion, the platoon used the dynamited bridge to reach the opposite bank. As scout, Tommy reached the German side first. He crawled slowly up the riverbank while sticking his bayonet in the ground ahead, checking for mines. When steel bumped steel Tommy froze. Felt cold sweat. Hyperventilated. Breathed deeply. Tommy tapped carefully in a circle to discover the edges of the mine. He stuck a branch on top to warn others. Then wiggled around the mine, probed for the next one.

In thirty harrowing moments, the platoon crawled to the crest. No one lost. Silence. Then, as if the men were on a Boy Scout badge-qualifying hike, they marched unopposed to the assigned road junction and took over abandoned houses to bivouac. Then waited.

The snowcapped Alps sent windy warnings of coming icy nights.

⊂ѻ CHAPTER 94 ѻ⊃

October 18, 1943

THE SECOND CROSSING OF THE SIDEWINDER RIVER. A night crossing. The mission: Protect the rear in case the Krauts tried a flanking maneuver. Kim halted near their assigned crossing at the edge of an olive orchard. He and Tommy pulled out identical maps. Kim ran his finger from the current spot to the river, separated by an open field a quarter mile away.

"Germans know we're coming. But they can't man the entire riverbank. Find a crossing." Kim pointed to an odd depression a half mile to the right. A feeding creek. *Maybe some cover.*

Kim motioned the platoon's Kraut-hating mule driver, Roberto, to join them. Like a genie, he always seemed to know when to appear. "Roberto, you will be taking our supply mules here. Once Tommy indicates his crossing point, you follow."

Kim turned to Tommy. "If you lose contact with Roberto, leave a stone, marking the direction you are taking."

Tommy and Roberto rolled and crawled to the river's edge where weeds and scrub offered camouflage. No talking. Sound carried better at night. They paused, lying on their backs. Caught their breath. Adrenaline pumped at turbo speed. *Recon is hair-raising, but you know you are alive like never before. The German patrols hunt for me, and me for them.*

Random shots punched the Nisei side of the river. Germans couldn't see them but shot randomly to let the 100th know they were planning a welcome party. Hunched over, Tommy waddled down the riverbank, scouting for that golden crossing point. *Don't like what I see. Too much exposure. Water moving too fast at narrow points. Might have to pick a least-worst option.* Then Tommy spotted a crossing that at first glance appeared daunting. High banks but undamaged scrub. *Good for crawling. Something for our hands to grab onto and our boots to push off from.* His binoculars searched the opposite side. An open field, but an orchard, apple this time, not all that far to the right. *Concealment!*

Tommy huddled with Roberto. "Stay here," he said, his voice a shade over a whisper. "I'll wade across."

Roberto anticipated Tommy's next instructions. "If nobody shoots, I go back, get mules. Tell Lieutenant Kim where you cross."

Tommy entered the water. Deeper than he had thought. At the center, chilly water up to his nipples. Ammo draped over his neck. M1 held high. *Being short is not an advantage walking across rivers. If I'm spotted, I'm KIA or POW.* Tommy crossed unseen—or at least, unfired upon. He alligator-crawled to the top, wet uniform slick with mud. No Germans. *Maybe they dismissed this crossing because of the high bank. Maybe. Doesn't mean they won't be here later.* Tommy looked back across the river. Roberto was still there, eyeing him. Tommy jerked his right arm in the "go, go" motion.

An hour later, the platoon crossed. A field greeted them over the cusp of the riverbank. The type of farmland where you expected to see cattle or horses grazing. Too open. Kim had to decide: Go slow and check for mines or sprint for the apple orchard before Jerry spotted them. "Double-time to orchard!" Kim half-shouted.

The men spread out, hunched low. Like shadows in the mist, they streaked to the apple orchard.

Rifle shots. *The Germans have spotted us. Us, valley; them, hill.*

Scattered rifle fire. No machine guns. Yet.

The platoon hit the orchard, maneuvered left, and kept running until trees met the mountain bottom. Men stopped to reform and catch their breath.

The radioman was already cranking in anticipation. Kim shouted into the phone, "We need smokescreen coverage!" He gave coordinates. Handed the phone back. Raised his rifle in the air. "Charge!" The men bent over and ran up the hill. German fire poured down. Squads took turns dropping to one knee to fire a cover volley as other squads climbed. Smokescreen shells that Kim ordered exploded ahead and to the left.

Rumors about Jerry running low on ammunition were overblown. Sharp winds broke up smokescreen cover. Deadly rifle fire. Climbing, Tommy tried to tune out the screams of "Medic!" *Snipers? Are we running the wrong way? Feeding a trap?* Machine gun fire. From the ridge. *No rookies. Seasoned troops.* The platoon advanced within thirty yards of camouflaged German machine gun nests. The Krauts blasted away.

"Retreat!" Kim commanded. Those who heard the order passed it on. Suppression firing from hips, they walked backward. An orderly, practiced retreat.

Except Thomas Yamanaga. He was on his elbows and knees slithering up. All German eyes followed the retreat, but they didn't peer directly down. A blind spot. Tommy quickly let his eyes rove, not wanting some Kraut to follow his line of sight. He aimed his suppressing fire at the machine gun nest near Yamanaga's turtle-paced crawl.

Then, like in the movies, the hero half stood, held a grenade in his hand, pulled the pin. Tommy saw him counting. *Throw the fucking thing!* As if reading Tommy's mind, Yamanaga did. The face of one German turned to horror. The grenade exploded in the nest, killing three Krauts instantly. Secondary explosions. Yamanaga ran down the hill at Jesse Owens speed. At the edge of the orchard, the retreated platoon blasted away to cover his escape.

In the gloom and drizzle, shadowy stretcher-bearers cleared the battlefield of bodies.

∞ CHAPTER 95 ∞

Leonardo Village, Volturno River – October 20, 1943

"**G**ET OVER HERE SERGEANT," Kim snapped.

Tommy turned to Kim. The harsh looks knotted Tommy's gut. *We won't be talking about coordinates.*

Before Tommy reached Kim, the pleading screech of "Medic!" pierced the night. Tommy scanned the hill. *How did I miss him coming down? Tommy puts the binoculars to his eyes.* The usual assortment of trees, shrubs, and granite…but no human outline. Jerry heard the agonizing plea as clear as the Nisei did. Random rifle fire. Scattered mortar shells. Rain stopped just when its sound suppression and visual camouflage were needed most.

"Medic!"

"That's Tochikawa!" yelled Tad Shikiya, rolling out of his foxhole. He sank into the field leading to the hill. "I'm coming, Tochi!"

"Shikiya, is that you?"

"I'll bring you in."

Kim ordered, "No firing. It will just pinpoint our position."

Tommy pressed his binoculars against his eye sockets. *This is going to work.*

Then light. Luminous German artillery shells turned night into day as Shikiya lifted Tochikawa over his shoulders at the hill's midpoint. *To have any chance, Tad must drop Tochi and run and weave with all that he has. But I know he won't. This is going to have a bad ending.*

Shikiya lumbered forward. Bullets streamed. So many weapons firing at a single target. Bullets ripped into them. Their bodies bounced in the air like rag dolls. Fell to the ground. Jerked and twitched as the monsters kept firing.

Kim shouted into the phone. Gestured for Tommy to join him. "Give me some coordinates on the fire source, including those shells." Kim hollered the numbers into his handset. The artillery opened up. Tommy kept converting what he saw in the hills into map coordinates, feeding adjustments and new targets. Ryder's cannoneers were deadly accurate and overwhelming. The ridge lit up. At least a half-dozen of the division's 105s blasted shells in five- to seven-second intervals.

Kim dropped the phone. His officers grouped around him. "Our artillery will keep this up another two minutes. It takes three minutes to run up that hill. Let's take out those arrogant motherfuckers before they realize what hit 'em."

Kim leaned toward Tommy. "I'm guessing the Krauts interpreted our artillery barrage as revenge and not the usual prelude to attack." He stepped out of the orchard and shouted, "Let's go!" Tommy struggled to keep up with Kim's lithe, long-legged speed.

A rout. The Germans were surprised, got off a few shots, but mostly ran. Kim ordered, "Stop! The hill is ours, let's not tempt fate and run into an ambush."

Two Germans in a blown nest stood up slowly, hands up. Guns swiveled in their direction. "No!!" commanded Kim. "Battle's over."

Kim turned to Tommy. "You take care of them."

"I believe we are low on ammunition," said Tommy.

"Yes, we are. Because a certain scout in charge of making sure Roberto knows where we are fucked up. Royally."

Shit. I was so scared, I forgot to mark my changed crossing point. Rookie mistake in a game of life and death.

"I don't want to hear it," Kim shouted, cutting Tommy off before he can respond. "Escort the prisoners down the hill. A HQ interrogation unit is either there or will be shortly." Kim's eyes stared, harsh. "Don't return until you find the mules."

Tommy pointed his rifle at the prisoners, wide eyed with fright. Tommy glowered at them. He hardly saw them as their Kraut uniforms triggered memories of Tochi and Shikiya being ripped to pieces. Tommy saw again the hail of bullets bouncing them in the air. *These bastards don't deserve to live!* The prisoners cringed under Tommy's malice-charged eyes. They lifted their hands higher.

"Beweg dich!" Tommy commanded to get them get moving. *Have they shot American prisoners?* Tommy's forefinger wrapped around the trigger. They began walking down the hill in the drizzle and dark. Shadows. Tommy's gun pointed at their backs. A random mortar shell exploded close enough that they all ducked. Tommy rose from his crouch, aimed his rifle with intent. *I want to fight Germans, not protect them.* The prisoners begin to move. Tommy held in place, his trigger finger expectant.

"I can take them," A calm voice ahead of Tommy intoned.

Tommy froze, finger tight on the trigger. He felt his body in suspension. *Where did he come from?*

The same soothing voice gently commanded, "I'm Lieutenant Wilson, HQ. I'll take the prisoners from here. Interrogation saves lives."

He knows. "Right," said Tommy. He lowered his rifle. "Did you see a mule supply train?"

Before Wilson could answer, like some kind of miracle, Tommy spotted Roberto leading a herd of mules out of the apple orchard. Tommy galloped down the hill past the prisoners, where Roberto greeted him with a smile that would light up Broadway.

"I go to meeting spot. You not there. Then I hear gunfire from my uncle's apple orchard. It must be you. I didn't see the marker. So sorry. But I think I take chance and hope I am not bringing supplies to the Germans." He laughed, but the humor was grim.

"I am just happy to see you, Roberto."

Above them on the hill, Kim looked happy to have his supplies

"There was no marker, Roberto," Tommy whispered.

"No, no. I should find. You no need to ... cover my ass by telling lieutenant it was your fault."

"Roberto, I never laid the stones. Kim knows."

Roberto put his hand on Tommy's shoulder. "It's a small thing. The *big* thing, no more Germans on hill."

But Tommy was not thinking about Germans no longer on the hill. He walked up the hill in silence, oblivious to Roberto's chattering about looking for him. *I was going to shoot those men. Wilson saved their lives. Saved me from a lifetime of guilt? What about next time? More of us killed. More stories of Nazi brutality and murder. Next time we are under fire and really can't spare manpower to take them to HQ—no Lieutenant Wilson to come to the rescue.*

Am I—are we—losing that thing called humanity? Is acting uncivilized the only way we beat the Germans and save civilization? The way of the warrior. The ugly side of bushido.

∞ Chapter 96 ∞

October 21, 1943

The following foggy morning, Tommy approached Kim as he sat on a granite slab, scooping the last of his slurried reconstituted eggs into his mouth. Tommy punched a finger into his map. "We're here." Tommy slid his finger to one of several swirls topped with three digits. "Here's Hill 529. If not for the mist, we could see it. Less than a mile. I can recon and be back in ninety minutes." *I am about to find out if I'm still a scout.*

Kim paused. Slowly finger-wiped some egg dribble off his chin. "Good idea."

Tommy let out his breath. "The hill's on the outskirts of a village. A tongue twister: Sant'Angelo d'Alife."

☙ ❧

After eleven wary minutes of running hunched over, ducking here, spinning there, Tommy reached the bottom of Hill 529. He stopped and dropped prone to the ground.

He peeked, listened. Nothing. He crawled forward, stopped, peeked, and repeated the process, again and again. Empty foxholes. An abandoned machine gun nest. *Where are the Krauts?* Then a mortar shell exploded in the distance. A month of combat had educated Tommy's ears. *Our artillery has cleared the Germans from the side facing us. Jerry doesn't know exactly where we are. They don't know I'm prowling at the bottom of their redoubt.*

The mist broke and Tommy spotted a medieval castle commanding the hill. Vines hugged its crumbling walls. Tree branches shadowed the long-abandoned dilapidated fortress. *Triumph and ignominy over so many generations.* Voices brought Tommy back to reality, too far away to distinguish words. He lifted his head. Krauts smoking, rifles slung over their shoulders. Four. They showed no worry about an imminent incursion. *Un-Krautlike lapse. A point for our team.* A flare brightened the mist. *Shit. Maybe not so sloppy.* Tommy slid and slunk back into the old machine gun nest he spotted earlier. No gunshots, but he felt their hunting eyes. Tommy stayed put until the parachuting flare died. No voices. No sounds of boots clumping down the hill. *Luck or German sloppiness?*

Tommy wiggled slowly back to level ground and started trotting. Then a silhouette of a man ten yards ahead. A uniform. Tommy hit the turf. Put his rifle to his shoulder. The man was moving slowly. More like a shuffle. No one else. Tommy rose, rushed forward, gun at hip. The uniform was American. *Infiltrator?* Rumors of Jerries in American uniforms have been reported.

"Halt or I'll shoot!"

The man halted. Raised his hands without turning to face Tommy. "I'm a Yank."

"Who's Johnny Vander Meer?"

"Pitcher who threw two no hitters. Back to back."

The man turned around slowly. A haole corporal with a parachute patch on his upper arm. He answered Tommy's question before he asked.

"Shacked up with a whore in Naples. Drank a lot. Fucked more. By the time I sobered up and got back to my unit, it was gone. Suppose I'm AWOL."

Nothing supposed about it! Tommy let him continue. *This might be good.*

The corporal threw out a hand. "Thompson. Just Thompson. I got lost and ended up behind German lines. Been living off the land for a week, dodging the occasional Jerry. During the confusion, I slipped through undetected. I watched them lay three strings of mines on that hill from top to bottom. Hey, where are we?"

"A long way from Naples. Take a look at the map." Tommy pointed to the current location.

"I could use a decent meal."

"You're in luck. We just got a new supply of SPAM. Ten minutes if we jog."

Kim was beside himself. "You're better than a POW," he said, almost laughing. "You know what's happening and you speak decent English. Turner sent the word. Our company is to take that hill. Our platoon will take the center."

Thompson caught on quick. "I can lead and avoid the mines. We can move faster without the mine-clearing boys ahead of us. Let me warn you. The Germans mean to hold that hill. Artillery in place. Mortar units setting up. Didn't see any tanks, but I bet a few Tigers are nearby."

A tin of SPAM and a warm can of Campbell's tomato soup—along with being the center of attention—did wonders for Thompson's demeanor. He morphed into self-assurance consistent with the cachet surrounding paratroopers, remarkable considering his recent checkered history.

"Might put me in good graces with my lieuy. You know, the whole AWOL misunderstanding."

Kim raised his eyebrows. "Lead the way safely and I'll put in a good word."

Forty-five minutes later, Thompson charged up the hill like a Boy Scout leader sprinting ahead of the pack. Five steps behind, Tommy yelled, "Slow down!" The last words Thompson heard. He stepped on a mine. A big one. Blasted straight up. Body parts flung in an ice cream cone arc. Stunned, Tommy was unscathed other than falling debris including bits of bloody flesh. *His recklessness saved my life.*

No time to dwell on the caprice of survival. The explosion alerted the Germans and all hell broke loose. German mortar shells pounded the hillside. Their artillery and tanks joined the mortar bombardment. Two German Stukas strafed. American tanks and support vehicles scattered, some pinned down by fire, others stuck in the mud. Nisei fell like ten pins. German flares. Never enough to illuminate the entire hill at one time, but always lighting up some of the hill. A hill that in peaceful days, Sunday picnickers would climb in a few hours.

Kim kept the platoon maneuvering, digging, plodding, crawling. All initial advantage to the hilltop Germans. Day turned to dusk to night to dawn to another day. *What must the Germans be thinking? They are throwing everything they have, and we are still here. A little closer.*

Kim and the other company's officers never stopped struggling up the hill despite prudent military doctrine that a tactical retreat would bring no dishonor. Medics, stretcher bearers and ammo resupply soldiers. The 100th refused to buckle. Relentless.

As another evening approached, the tide changed. The division's artillery concentrated its fire power on the hilltop. Ryder's tanks regrouped, fired in tandem. The platoon's mortar shells found targets.

The Germans made their point and retreated to their next defended hill.

It was a victory without celebration. In thirty-six sleepless hours, the 100th took the hill. At a cost. The worst yet. Another twenty-one KIAs and sixty-seven wounded.

Exhausted, Tommy sidled up to Kim who was spooning a mouthful of K-rations. Tommy pointed down to the opposite side of the hill just conquered. "I suspect the Germans are retreating to their next defense line … not the next village. Any troops lying in ambush anticipating our hot pursuit most likely have withdrawn by now."

"OK," said Kim, his weary eyes drooping. "Check it out."

Tommy's thoughts wandered as he wove, crouched, and loped toward the village. *I still think it would have been better if we had been sent to Guadalcanal or somewhere in the Pacific to fight Japs. There is a rumor that we are here because we don't mind killing whites but maybe not our own kind. Tojo's soldiers are* not *our kind.*

No ambush. Even in the starless night, Tommy could see that the houses were chiseled out of the mountain. The villagers lived in granite houses, the same granite that when cut and polished became the floors of kings. The village appeared empty. *But is it?* Tommy moved stealthily. He entered battered doors in gun jerking moves. Nothing. Not even a dog barked.

I have taken my first town! With his last ounce of adrenaline, Tommy scampered back and delivered an out-of-breath report to Kim.

"No Krauts, but lots of indoor sleeping."

∞ CHAPTER 97 ∞

October 24, 1943

IN RESERVE. THE SOLDIERS RESTED AND WERE RESUPPLIED. They shared housing in Sant'Angelo d'Alife with Italians who drifted back to their homes only to find them occupied by Japanese Americans. They welcomed their liberators. Food was shared. Nothing like a SPAM pizza!

∞ ∞

Tommy was catching some rare sunshine while oiling his rifle on the doorsteps of "his" stone sculptured home when a ragamuffin wearing a long black dress much in need of washing approached him. "Give me SPAM. I am hungry. My mother, sister hungry. I fuck you. You give me can of SPAM."

A pained Tommy observed the war on her face and her bony body. Childhood lost. *We're not supposed to share food. Hard enough to keep us supplied. And if we share with one, all expect a handout.* But Tommy reached into his shirt pocket and pulled out a Hershey bar. She lifted her dress halfway. "Inside." She turned and took a step inside the doorway.

Shocked, Tommy stammered, "No fuck, no fuck." He handed her the Hershey. Told her, "Go," flicked a backhand to shoo her away.

She stared at her chocolate bar. A tear formed. "Grazie." She backed away three uncertain steps, turned and ran. *I wonder how many people will share her treasure.*

Tommy watched her run and then stop. She bent down, looked at something sticking out from under a jagged piece of concrete. A doll's head. Tommy sprang up, screeched, "*Nooo!*" Her hand was on the doll. "*Nooo! Nooooo!*" The last "No" was obliterated by a detonation. Tommy ran as fast as he had ever run. The platoon filled the street, guns at the ready. Tommy reached the girl. What was left of her. *The bomb must have gone off belly high.* Her pitiful little body was split in two. A couple of "What the fuck" shouts. Then silence. The men have seen mutilated bodies. But a girl. *A girl who should be in grammar school learning her times tables.* On his knees, Tommy pounded the ground. A piece of flesh dangled from the edge of his palm. Tears. He couldn't stop them. *I don't give a shit who sees them.*

Tommy was well aware that the Krauts were really good at booby traps. A child's doll, mess kits, bottles of wine, GI-issued canteen, chunk of coal, shaving brush, even a chocolate candy bar. Snap off a piece, ba-boom! *Any Nazi prisoner of mine will never make it to HQ.*

By night, Tommy was drinking wine he found in a cellar. The whole bottle. Still not enough to bring sleep. *If I had accepted her crude offer ... would she still be alive?*

⚏ CHAPTER 98 ⚏
October 26, 1943

TOMMY WAS SCARFING DOWN A SECOND PLATE of pancakes when Kim strolled over with a tin plate of scrambled eggs in one hand and a puny sausage at the end of a folding fork in the other.

"How would you like to fly instead of crawl?" A smirk. A second later, he added, "Ryder wants our recon guys to have a wider perspective of front lines."

"You don't mean going up in one of those Piper Cubs," Tommy said with less enthusiasm and more anxiety than he wanted to show. *We all appreciate the gutsy pilots flying their drab olive-green Cubs slowly over Kraut lines. Just the presence of those Grasshoppers suppresses German artillery and for good reason. When German troops or artillery are spotted, the pilot radios coordinates and in minutes, thirty-two-pound exploding artillery shells arrive in twelve-second intervals. And that's if only one of the four cannons in a unit is firing.*

"Exactly." Kim smiled, enjoying Tommy's discomfort.

"When?" Tommy replied with feigned readiness.

"Well, if you have to take a pee, I would do it now."

"You're kidding. There's no plane, no runway." Even as he spoke, he heard the faint sound of a propeller. *Or do I imagine it?*

"Any flat surface half the length of a football field will do."

Definitely propeller sounds. Tommy's head tilted to the sky. Single engine plane, canopy back. The pilot, in goggles and leather cap like a football helmet, waved. He aimed at a level patch of what before the war might have been a cow pasture. Tommy jammed a pig's portion of pancakes into his mouth, scurried behind a jeep and, still chewing, emptied his bladder on the front tire. He heard the plane bounce as he buttoned up his trousers.

Goggles lifted, the pilot was all grins. "Which one of you daredevils is my copilot?"

The entire platoon rushed forward to examine the canvas-covered toy. Tommy raised his hand.

"You flown before?" It was more of a challenge than a question.

Wordlessly, Tommy stared.

"A virgin." The pilot laughed. "You want to stick your finger down your throat now or throw up later into the barf bag?"

The idea of getting into that dinky single-prop plane almost induced Tommy to throw up right then and there. He'd seen the planes maneuver sharply, avoiding ground fire. "Be right back," he said, choking out the words. Tommy scurried back to the jeep and chucked up breakfast before his fingers were halfway down his throat. Then he trotted over to the plane and started to climb in.

"Not so fast, soldier. First put this on," the pilot ordered, handing Tommy a stinky leather helmet. "You have to help me start the engine. Stand behind the propeller. Grab the prop with both hands. When I say 'Spin,' you pull down and step back."

You got to be kidding. Tommy fastened the helmet strap. *But the guy's face tells me otherwise.* He saluted. "Yes, sir…" Glanced at his name tag. "Captain Bogan."

"This isn't a Pam-Am Clipper with an audio system for passengers. Engine's too loud for talking. If I see something, I'll point. If you see something, tap my shoulder and point. Maybe scream something in my ear. We'll be flying around three hundred feet off the ground at about fifty-five miles an hour … unless someone shoots at us. Then I rev the engines. You'll get the thrill of your life as we shoot straight for the sun. Our sixty-five horses can gallop ninety miles an hour in a pinch."

Tommy walked under the wing, his helmet not quite touching, and stood behind the prop as directed.

Bogan climbed in. "OK, pull down smartly and step back."

Tommy yanked, the engine coughed and the propeller struggled to make a revolution. Tommy stepped back. The propeller spun faster, like an electric fan warming up.

"Hop in," Bogan barked over the engine noise.

Tommy hoisted himself up in the back and twisted onto the thinnest cushion over the hardest seat. Steel. He grabbed the edge. Thick. Maybe three inches. Then it hit him why.

Bogan flipped some switches and studied the instrument panel. He pulled back a stick and the plane jumped forward. Bouncing. *The cow field wasn't designed for this!* Tommy stared at the back of Bogan's head, trying to decipher some body language that might reassure him. Before Tommy could worry more, they were airborne. The earth receded and his fear evaporated. *There's so much to see!* The plane tilted left and then quickly righted itself, heading straight toward German lines.

The plane flew low. Very low. *Bogan's "three hundred feet" looks a lot closer.* Treetops. An unblemished olive orchard. Scraggly vineyards. Men! German troops. *Shit.* Rifles rose. Popping sounds. Puffs of smoke. Bogan banked sharp right and up. He was talking into his radio. He circled. He returned farther up from the German troops. *A tank! Another one. Turrets can't shoot in the air.* But the rifle-armed soldier exiting the tank could. Tommy heard a ping. *Did a bullet hit something or is it my imagination?* A wave of nausea enveloped him. Tommy pulled back the seat pocket. *Where is that barf bag?* He pulled it out just in time. Nothing but a little gastric acid.

Bogan leveled out and Tommy's stomach settled. His eyes hunted for tanks and artillery. *I am a recon man, after all.* Nothing. But then Bogan lifted his arm and pointed. Tommy's eyes followed. Still nothing, then … *those branches don't look right. Camouflage. Underneath, steel tubes on wheels. German 88s.* Bogan was already on the radio, shouting coordinates.

Below, rifle fire again. Then the muffled rat-a-tat-tat of a machine gun. Another sharp zigzag. Bogan pulled back on the stick and the plane shot up like a carnival ride. Tommy's stomach was a hundred feet behind.

Bogan aimed the Cub back to friendly territory. *Boom!* More booms. Tommy twisted to look back. Ryder's artillery had found its mark. A big explosion rocked the plane. *Our howitzers must have hit an ammo pile.* More shells rained in.

Pain. *My arm. Blood. Lots of it. An artery? Fingers sticky and red.* Tommy thumped Bogan's back. Draped his bleeding arm over Bogan's shoulder. The pilot handed Tommy an oil rag. Tommy tied it around his arm above the bleeding. It stopped. Plane dropped. The plane passed over Kim's platoon. Tommy faded but heard the words "field hospital" before passing out.

∽ CHAPTER 99 ∾

Field hospital behind Sant'Angelo d'Alife– October 27, 1943

TOMMY, ATTIRED IN A GREY AND WHITE striped cotton hospital gown, craved to scratch his arm, which was firmly encased in a plaster cast. A bullet had nicked the bone—nothing broken, but a vein cut. In another era it might have been an end of life injury or at least the loss of an arm. Field docs had staunched it, then administered a blood transfusion. While not yet fit to return to combat, Tommy tried to make himself useful at the field hospital, which until a month ago was the Santa Maria grammar school. The nurses assigned him "orange juice and coffee responsibilities," which led to a shocking encounter with his commander.

"What is Turner doing here?" Tommy asked one of the WAC nurses. "Exhaustion," she said.

Carrying a breakfast tray, using his good hand to balance it on his cast, Tommy prepared to hold a neutral expression as he entered Colonel Turner's private room. *Turner looks old. Really old. Haggard. He's pushing fifty, old for an infantry combat command.*

Turner brightened at the sight of Tommy, one of his 100th boys. "I'm here for a few days to get my energy back. I lost feeling in one of my legs," he explained, and then as if to reassure Tommy, or steer the story he might tell: "Doc said my leg will be good as new in a day or two."

"We'll be glad to have you back, sir." *Does he even believe it?*

Tommy was well aware of the coconut wireless rumors. A week earlier, the story went, Turner reported an area clear of Germans, allowing a battalion of Ryder's troops to move forward. The battalion stumbled into an SS unit supported by a barrage of artillery and mortars. *I bet that Ryder's formal written complaint citing Turner for the ambush is the trigger that sent him to the hospital. Exhaustion or mental breakdown?*

Tommy discovered that Turner wasn't the only one of his commanders in the hospital. Second-in-command Major Lowell was being stitched up from Screaming Mimi shrapnel wounds. Out for at least a month.

∞ ∞

October 29, 1943

While unable to obtain clearance to rejoin his unit, Tommy received permission to accompany Colonel Turner on his farewell visit to the troops. Tommy jumped into the front passenger seat of the commander's jeep parked aside a scruffy soccer field behind the field hospital. No one noticed the small duffel bag at his feet. The driver tightened the gas cap after a top-off. A weary-faced Turner sat in the back. *A sad day. Turner's last day as our commander.*

Still in reserve, the 100th had settled in Sant'Angelo d'Alife, halfway between the hospital and the front lines.

Turner's leg was on the mend. Not so the weather. A cold drizzle matched Turner's disposition. *This can't be the exit he dreamed about when we were setting training records in Wisconsin and Shelby.*

"I don't need a blanket." Turner's frosty voice snapped at a hospital orderly as the jeep was about to pull out. Tommy grabbed two blankets and snuggled into one. At forty miles an hour, the wind was bone chilling. A few miles down the road, Turner mumbled, "Better give me that blanket." Sitting inside the cozy cab of a transport would have been better, but Turner had refused. "Clark and Ryder visit their troops in jeeps."

Three hours later, Turner, having dropped his unwanted cane on the jeep's floor, strutted, jaw clenched, into the town's crumbling, bowl-shaped amphitheater, like Cicero preparing to address the Senate. *It's tough watching him try to hide his limp.* The granite arena was a dwarf of Rome's famous Colosseum, but the circular stone bleachers had no trouble accommodating almost 400 soldiers of the 100th excused from duty. Turner's weary voice barely reached beyond the first few rows, but Tommy was sitting close enough to hear his words.

"Men, it has been a privilege to prepare you for combat and lead you in the early days. General Ryder is sending me back to Shelby for recuperation. It will be a few months before I return. God bless you." *I suspect he has more to say, but he is tearing up. Let him wave to the cheering crowd. He led us 167 miles from Salerno, 120 of them on foot, one-fourth of the way to Rome.*

After Turner's address, Tommy ambled over to the driver. "I'm not returning with you." Tommy reached into the well of the jeep and snatched his duffel bag from the floor. Wearing an impish grin, he said, "I'm going AWOL from the hospital and staying here with my combat unit. Our field medics will know when to cut the cast. I can do light duty."

The driver, from an Iowa battalion, smiled understandingly, "You 100th guys aren't given to long hospital stays." He offered Tommy his hand. "We respect that. We understand what you're fighting for."

∞ ∞

As second in command, Colonel Lowell would have been Turner's permanent successor, had he not been wounded too. *Losing both haole commanders is tough, but we are getting battle-tested replacement leaders. Probably a good trade, despite our loyalty. The Old Man loved us, but at the hospital, I heard stories of his agonizing over casualties. A medic told me, "Each one seems to tear him apart. Like it was his fault, like he should have done something. The responsibility immobilized him."*

In war, the leader has to commit to action—that means death for some.

∞ ∞

October 30, 1943

Ryder sent one of his 133rd regimental majors, James Gillespie, to take charge of the 100th battalion. He had come up through the ranks, a straight-talker with a rep for being a fast-thinking tactical officer.

Tommy was pleased with what he heard from Gillespie's address to his new troops. "I go where the generals send me. I didn't ask to be transferred. I'm sorry you lost your pop. He is a good man, someone I admire. But trust me, this isn't the last time you will have a new commander. Let's work together and make the best of it." *There's a time to be humble and Gillespie knows now is the time. He respects how we feel about Turner.*

The next day, the mule express arrived with ammo, SPAM and mail. Along with a personal letter extolling the virtues of Angelina, Kenta had sent Tommy a copy of the 442nd Shelby newsletter that featured several recent newspaper headlines.

New York Times: JAPANESE AMERICANS: THEY BATTLE THE AXIS IN ITALY

Washington News: AMERICAN-BORN JAPS FIGHT WITH 5TH ARMY

Washington Post: JAPANESE HELP ALLIES TAKE BENEVENTO

St. Paul Pioneer Press: AMERICAN-BORN JAPS ENJOY WAR ON NAZIS

"Enjoy"? Over-the-top. "Japs"? Denigrating, but a step up from "Send the traitors to camps." The press is at least teaching Americans that Japanese living in America are loyal, and those of us born on its soil are willing to die for our country. We love a country that has no place for an emperor, no possibility of a Tojo. We not only fight for our country, but do a damn good job going about it.

Tommy's *senninbari* was as vanilla white as when Okaasan had presented it to him. He had kept it wrapped around his belly, thankful for the thousand women who needled a stitch in it, symbolically protecting him from harm. *Women who pray and root for me.*

In the beginning, some of the guys crammed their senninbari in their backpacks, thanked their moms all the while thinking how silly the old tradition. Well, that was then. Now, most of the guys wore them. *We don't believe they are magic bullet-stoppers, but it's comforting to wrap that cloth around our bodies. A piece of home that boosts hope that we will return with that piece of cloth. We silently thank all those who added a stitch.*

A couple of the Christian boys carry a miniature Bible in their shirt pocket over their heart. Same reason. Comfort. A few carry the one and wear the other.

∞ CHAPTER 100 ∞

North Shore, Oahu– November 2, 1943

"SOMEBODY HAD TO BE FIRST," said Florence, teary eyes concentrating on her cup of coffee in the break room of the Waialua branch of Bank of Hawaii. "Thank you, Haru-*sensei*, for coming with the chaplain to tell me."

Earlier that morning, Haru had received a telephone call at the Fort Street Honpa Hongwanji where she was handling her caretaker duties, informing her of the first 100th soldier killed in action. She had arrived two weeks earlier from Waimea to take her place in the rotation of custodians looking after the closed temple.

"It is my duty as the army chaplain to visit Sergeant Takata's widow," the chaplain told her, "but I know Florence was a member of your Red Cross support group. I think she might need support from friends." Actually, it was Florence's mother who had helped wrap bandages, but Haru did not correct the chaplain. His intention and purpose overrode whatever mistaken army file he must have consulted.

"You are very kind to call, Chaplain," said Haru. "Would you like me to go with you to the bank?"

"Yes. I can pick you up at the Hongwanji first."

After agreeing on a time, Haru asked, "When was Joe shot?"

"September 29." His voice, low and apologetic.

Haru didn't rebuke the chaplain. She knew the month's delay wasn't his fault.

The bank manager met them at the door and then ushered the chaplain, Haru and Florence into the empty break room. They sat around a card table that held a simmering Sunbeam coffeemaker and three empty cups. As Haru poured, her hand wobbled. Florence's sad and certain voice broke the silence.

"It's Joe, isn't it? He's been killed."

Haru placed her hands over Florence's. "Such a good boy."

The chaplain opened a leather-bound folder holding what resembled a diploma. "The army has awarded your husband the Distinguished Service Cross: 'With complete disregard for his own personal safety, Sergeant Takata took a position in front of his squad and led it in the flanking movement. He exposed himself in an effort to locate the enemy machine gunner and was mortally wounded by an enemy artillery shell. Although he only lived a few minutes after being struck, Sergeant Takata called for his platoon sergeant in order to give him the situation.'"

By the end, tears were falling from the eyes of both women. The chaplain's voice broke as he told her, "Joe died a hero, Mrs. Takata."

Florence wiped away a tear. "I remember his last words before leaving: 'I will surely come back. You don't need to cry.'"

"Colonel Fielder will formally present this award later, Mrs. Takata," said the chaplain, closing the folder. Then he lifted a cardboard box from the floor.

"His personal effects?" asked Florence.

"Yes, and your letters. Joe kept them all. Judging by the frayed edges, he read them often."

"Joe and I were married in Reverend Okumura's Makiki Church, but our parents are Buddhist." Florence let the words hang in the air. Then added, "How do we have a proper memorial service with all of our priests in camps?"

This reference to the imprisoned priests told Haru that Florence had made a religious choice for Joe's funeral.

"I can ask Reverend Mitsumyo Tottori," said Haru, referring to the one Buddhist priest on Oahu not arrested. Tottori had been an outspoken advocate of Americanization. The FBI interrogated Tottori, but in recognition of his pro-American stance made him the sole priestly exception to arrest.

"But he is of the Shingon sect," protested Florence. She covered her mouth in shame at her outburst.

"We are all one Buddhist family now. Reverend Tottori and I talked about this possibility a few days after our boys sailed to the West Coast. He is ready to help. Since martial law forbids public gatherings, we can have the service at my home."

"Only the closest of family," Florence murmured.

"That would best," agreed Haru, thankful that even in her moment of shock and grief, Florence understood an American soldier of Japanese extraction would still be denied a proper funeral.

The next morning, all of Hawaii knew they had lost their first son to war when they read the headline of the *Hawaii Times:* FORMER ASAHI TEAM STAR JOE TAKATA DEAD IN BATTLE.

The front-page picture showed Joe in his Asahi uniform, holding a baseball in his glove.

⊂⊙ ⊙⊃

A week later, after the funeral, Florence and Joe's father walked into the Waialua government office. Florence took out a packet of white envelopes bordered in black and laced together with a black ribbon. She placed them reverently on the office manager's desk.

"We received four hundred dollars as condolence gifts," said Joe's father, whose weathered, wrinkled face testified to decades of plantation fieldwork. "Rather than use this money for a memorial service forty-nine days after death, as is our custom, I think Joe would prefer we give this money to the Red Cross, the Army Relief Fund, the Honolulu Community Chest and the Navy Relief Fund. We hope other families might do the same."

And they did. Hawaii's Nisei families who lost sons and husbands continued to donate bereavement money throughout the war.

∽ CHAPTER 101 ∽

Ciorlano, on the way to Cassino – November 1, 1943

BACK TO WAR.

Penetrating mountain blasts joined the wet. Chilly Hawaii winter trade winds were nothing like the frigid bluster off the Apennines. On the positive side, the winds brushed the sky clear gifting a rare cloudless sunrise showcasing snowcapped mountain peaks to the north. The Christmas objective. One could envision Hannibal's elephants lumbering down from the Alps.

Tommy's platoon had moved closer to the front line. They were camped on a hill posturing as a mountain in a village posing as a town. Ciorlano, another way station on the road to Cassino, the perfect setting for the next Bob Hope–Bing Crosby *On the Road* movie. The men sat and waited for orders. Chow trucks had joined them. Hot meals and coffee any time.

Below the platoon lay the Volturno River. A different Volturno on Tommy's third rendezvous. A muddy delta where the river met its scrawny cousin, the Sava River. Two to three feet deep and 800 feet across at the widest. It rippled around Lilliputian islands sprouting willows. Boot-stomped barley fields and armored-vehicle-mangled vineyards filled a two-mile-wide valley straddling the river.

The unit was stationed downstream from the 133rd's First and Third Battalions. There were 30,000 soldiers from the Thirty-Fourth Division and their neighbor, the Forty-Fifth, along a twenty-mile front. With the addition of de Gaulle's Free French Forces, Mark Clark's Fifth Army had blossomed to 230,000 troops.

Fifteen miles north, German engineers and their slave labor were fortifying steep cliffs, stone ridges and rugged mountains. A mile across the river, a determined Wehrmacht prepared to fight off the 100th's looming assault long enough to provide German engineers time to complete insurmountable fortifications. The 100th's job: blow the Krauts off the immediate heights facing them before those behind-the-lines engineers completed their work.

The American–British forces were capturing territory, but at their torturous pace, the stubborn Germans were winning.

∞ ∞

November 3, 1943. 8:00 p.m.

Tommy scarfed down a hot evening meal before his solo recon river crossing. He belched contentedly during the thirty-minute trek into the night from the mobile canteen to the river's edge.

Tommy had a mission: scout Hill 550. In hours, Ryder's 133rd regiment would cross the Volturno. The 100th battalion's orders were to hold the flank, and if opportunity arose, intercept a German retreat.

Tommy stepped into the frigid rapids, more worried about trench foot than about being spotted by German patrols, as water slid down inside of his boots. The leather never dried marching in rain-drenched mud, even if you didn't soak them river-walking. Since one never knew when a German would start shooting, army doctrine dictated boots on in combat conditions—including river crossings. Tommy changed his socks often, keeping a dry pair snug under his T-shirt. The problem leading to trench foot was simple: it took hours for a pair of socks to "dry"—they never really dried out—when tucked under a shirt next to skin and only minutes for wet boots to soak fresh socks.

Once over the river, Tommy crawled to the crest. *Stop, wait, look, listen.* Eyes were designed to spot motion. *No German patrol sighted. One could be waiting in ambush, but with so many miles of crossing, a speculative ambush isn't a good use of manpower. Marching patrols are more the German style.*

Tommy resisted the urge to reach Hill 550 quickly. *Haste on recon is a ticket to heaven* he thought. Hunched over, he weaved his way at an excruciatingly slow pace. He tapped the earth in front of him with his bayonet. A mine detector would be more useful, but they were heavy, and you had to stand up to use it. Not a good idea.

Nothing. How I love nothing. No mines under my feet. No Kraut patrols. But they know we're coming. So far, no movement, but I'm certain Hill 550 isn't vacant. Halfway up, Tommy made out the outlines of self-propelled guns and tanks covered with camouflage net. He had seen enough. Tommy crawled down a little to the left of his ascent path, so he could tap another piece of ground, thus giving his platoon a wider safe passage to assault the hill.

∽ ∾

A cave! The opening was narrow, but big enough to enter bent over. A rest stop. *I can use a five-minute respite.* Voices. *Shit!* Tommy froze. *Did I just walk into a concealed Kraut welcome party? If I get out alive, an important discovery. An artillery target. How can Jerry not know I am here? Yet there's no challenge, no life-ending bullet. No "Hands up!"*

Voices. As still as Michelangelo's *David*, Tommy's ears strained to listen. *Italian!* The whispering stopped. *They know someone is here. Me. I am the invader, a threat to their safety. Am I about to be killed by a hiding Italian who thinks I'm a German? If they are Italian, they are hiding.*

Tommy took a chance. "Americano."

Silence. Then a single voice in English. "Who is Joe DiMaggio?"

Tommy let out his breath. "The greatest baseball player ever. Italian. New York Yankee centerfielder." Tommy piled on. "Got a base hit in fifty-six straight games."

A shadow emerged. "I should have stayed in Boston," said a young man, maybe in his mid-twenties. Even in the gloom, Tommy saw he was skinny. "But no, two years ago my cousin wrote that my mother was dying. She asked to see her son once more. I arrived in time to help her to the next world. But before I could return to Boston, I'm drafted into Mussolini's army. After the surrender, I just walked away from my unit. With most of my unit." He laughed, bitter. "Went back to my village."

"You're not alone."

"Twenty-six of us. Parts of five families."

Tommy envisioned a platoon of civilians stumbling, walking upright despite instructions. Babies crying.

As if reading his mind, The Italian said, "We left the old women and small children behind. The Germans have no use for them. We've spent eight days walking and hiding. Except for apples and olives taken off trees, we haven't eaten for three days. If we don't escape to the Allied side soon, we face capture or starvation. This morning, I found an opening between the German lines. We arrived here at dawn just before the Germans occupied the hilltop. If not for the cave, the Germans would have spotted us. We pray every day. So far, God has listened to us."

He offered Tommy his hand. "You are the answer to our prayers. I'm Michael."

Shaking his hand, Tommy introduced himself.

"Moving between the lines isn't as hard as you might think," said Michael. "Lots of geography on a front crossing the whole middle of Italy. There's always a space between army camps. Patrols can't be everywhere. Still, I'm amazed I've been able to move so many people for so long without being spotted. "My people know how to keep a low profile. And be quiet."

That must be true How else could they have avoided capture over eight days? What choice do I have? How can I leave these starving families in the cave to be caught in an artillery barrage? Hopefully, the guy has good intel Ryder can use. "We need to move now. Artillery barrage to begin in a few hours."

The group spilled silently out of the cave. The younger women were in their teens and twenties. Fear and hope in their eyes. Bodies slumped. For protection or simply from malnutrition? *Ripe peasant girls the Germans would have used and discarded. Young men prime for slave labor. I can hardly wait to see Kim's face when I walk into our bivouac with twenty-six bedraggled Italians. If we make it.*

Make it, they did. Without incident. The group knew how to move like ghosts. After feeding the group, Kim sent Michael, a treasure trove of intel, to Ryder's HQ.

The Jerries threw a few practice shells across the river to make sure the Americans knew what awaited them. Ryder ordered his artillery to toss a couple back to let the Krauts know his artillery fury would rage at a time of his choosing. Tommy understood the "message." *We don't march troops across the Volturno until we unload an hour or two of ordnance.*

∞ ∞

November 3, 1943. 11:30 p.m.

Feeling the rumble in his groin from the division's bombardment smashing into Kraut defense positions, Tommy observed the inverted pyramids of granite and earth burst into the air from thousands of 105 mm howitzer shells. *How can anyone live through that? Us One Puka Puka boys might be new to the game, but we've learned that for all the sound and fury of our ordnance, most Krauts—as well as most of their concealed tanks and self-propelled Screaming Mimis—will survive inside their mountain caves. I know Jerry is pissed off and ready. So am I. Many mothers will lose sons tonight. Could be my turn.*

∞ CHAPTER 102 ∞

November 4, 1943. Midnight.

TIME TO BOOGIE.

Even as the artillery barrage rained down at high tempo, Kim's platoon jumped off Ciorlano's "mountain top" and marched into the valley at the muddy junction of the Volturno and Sava rivers. Just a quarter mile down from Hill 550 where Tommy had scouted earlier. *Why wasn't I assigned to scout our crossing area? That's the army for you.*

Approaching the river's edge, the Nisei advanced one mud-sucking step at a time. Their target: a junction on Highway 85. A Sunday morning's drive to Rome. Ryder's 105s went silent.

Halfway across the Volturno, Kim held a field phone and barked, "Halt." Paused, phone to ear. Kim strained his vocal cords. "Our artillery boys want to send a few more greetings."

Just great! Love standing up to my nuts in fast-moving, snow-sourced water. If my balls were made of steel, they'd be clanging like a Salvation Army Christmas bell. A short howitzer shell splashed downstream, sending a waterspout into the air like an elephant doing a belly flop off a high dive. *A dud, but even a hurtling steel dud hurts if you're in the way.* The subsequent human shriek diverted Tommy's preoccupation with his numbing testicles. *Dear God, don't let me be killed by one of our own shells.* His knees shook in the chilled ripples of the Volturno.

After the twenty slowest minutes of Tommy's life, the shelling ceased. Kim jerked his arm in the "Go, go, go!" command. At the forefront of his platoon, Tommy high-footed to the river's edge and began the climb to combat.

Before Tommy had climbed five feet, one of Ryder's gunners let loose one last shell. Aimed poorly. Short. The sixteen-pounder exploded on impact in the middle of the river. Chunks of shrapnel whirled in a five-foot killing arc. Screaming men fell into the water. Outside the arc of death, Tommy sloshed back into the river to collar an unconscious companion. He tugged him back to the kick-off point at the river's edge where waiting medics were patching up wounds and splinting broken bones. "I got him," said a medic in a voice that conveyed, "Don't dilly dally—catch up with your unit on the other side of the river."

The mid-water explosion from the stunted shell exposed the platoon's position for a second. That was enough for German forward observers. German artillery lit up the crossing with multi-colored flare shells like floodlights at a baseball game. *We're like outfielders with Germans in the bleachers—armed with tanks, artillery and mortars. We're taking on casualties. Medics overwhelmed. Who gets morphine? Who is passed over as hopeless in favor of one who might actually make it?*

The men sprinted, hunched over. German machine guns fired from concealed nests. Ahead of Tommy, Ohata, a sergeant from the earliest days who outranked him by a stripe, led his squad right into a trip-wire minefield strung among an olive orchard. Ohata made it unscathed, but his third man in the rear stepped on a mine. Body fragments from three of Ohata's men, bunched too closely, flew into the air. *The body bag men will never be able to match up all the parts.*

Kim rushed his platoon to the lead, the map image in his head as clear as it was at the HQ briefing. *Kim easy to follow—the only soldier wearing a Boston Red Sox cap.* "Can't think straight with something heavy on my head," he said often.

Tommy spotted a ribbon of rare tarmac. *Must be Highway 85.* He turned back to inform Kim. *Oh no, here comes Captain Know-It-All Suzuki.*

Suzuki stood on the edge of the tarmac and shouted to Kim, "Turn here!"

Kim snapped, "No!" a fraction of a second before a German mortar fell ten yards away. The nearby men hit the deck. No one was hurt. Kim rose as if he had just picked up a dropped bag of peanuts. "There's an olive orchard ahead, then we turn. We can find cover behind one of those stone walls." Suzuki puffed out his scrawny chest. Before he could speak, Kim challenged, "You just broke your promise after the last time you ordered us into fire!" Kim pointed to where he knew cover lay. A bullet ripped Kim's pointing arm. He dropped, landing on his back.

Tommy yelled, "Open fire!" Those in hearing distance shot covering rounds.

Like a whack-a-mole, Kim bounced up. "Flesh wound. Nothing broken." *How can he be so sure?*

But he was sure enough for Suzuki. "I'll report to HQ you're under attack." *Good riddance!*

The platoon scrambled forward into the orchard. In seconds, a stone wall appeared. Football-field length. *God lives.* The soldiers stooped behind the stout barrier for a brief reprieve. A medic sulfurized Kim's wound, threaded four stitches into the flapping flesh and taped a gauze wrap. Kim took a cursory look at the medic's handiwork. "I'm going over, taking a look." As soon as the medic scissored the tape holding the gauze, Kim slopped one leg over the short wall. A machine gun fusillade greeted his climb-over.

Kim fell into the ditch. A death-rattle yelp.

The platoon, bunched up along the low stone wall, heard the pain in Kim's voice but couldn't see him. Then silence. *Dead?* The angry men planted their rifles on the wall and triggered a salvo aimed at the Kraut gun cacophony and flashes. Wakamoto and Ikari, the platoon's Browning automatic rifle gunners, dropped down, set their BARs on squat tripods atop the wall and fired away.

Technical Sergeant Robert Ozaki bellowed, "They got Kim." A wrathful Ozaki ran hunched over along the wall, shouting, "They got Kim. Fix bayonets … They got Kim. Fix bayonets … They got Kim. Fix bayonets."

The platoon was primed, chomping at the bit like horses in the gates at the Kentucky Derby. Anger flooded Tommy's skull. His stare bored into Ozaki's eyes. Anticipating. Legs taut like steel springs ready to snap.

Ozaki rose. "Banzai!" He leaped over the wall, his roar filling the air.

The enraged men followed, all of them screaming like banshees. In seconds, disciplined fighting men had mutated into a frenzied mob, a killing mob. They ran at whirlwind speed, firing at will, feeling immortal. Stunned at the human onslaught, the Krauts ran for their lives. Slow runners were bayoneted. A stunned Jerry froze in place five feet in front of Tommy. Bayonet extended, Tommy braced for the killing charge. The frightened, wide-eyed German raised his hands. High. Tommy's bayonet stopped at the Kraut's shirt buttons. Tommy raised the razor-sharp knife to the Jerry's chin. Blood leaked. Tommy stared into eyes filled with terror, his righteous bloodlust just barely under control. *Dead Krauts don't give intel.*

Silence.

Ozaki strode over. Studied Tommy's menace. "I'll take the prisoner, Sergeant."

Tommy nodded. He couldn't speak. He lowered his rifle. His knees wobbled. His breath, short gasps.

It's over. Adrenaline still pumping, his heart still pounding, Tommy stared back at the stone fence. Kim! He was trying to hoist himself up using the fence as a prop. Tommy rushed down. Grabbed Kim's arm to help him stand. Dazed, Kim managed to say. "I was worried about you guys stepping on me as you jumped over the fence."

Tommy managed a reply, "You taught us running up a hill fast and sudden has its advantages."

So ended the first American bayonet attack in Italy.

∞ Chapter 103 ∞

November 4, 1943. 2:30 a.m.

ONLY TWO HOURS SINCE KIM'S PLATOON dropped down from Ciorlano. A lifetime. Still in an exuberant fog over their impromptu audacity, the platoon dug a slit trench parallel to the rail tracks. Only gradually did the euphoria dissipate. Combat, and the threat of imminent combat, left little time to feel good. That battle, that night, was a beginning, a foretelling. Like the edge of a glacier in summer, their platoon was shrinking. Prior to and during their banzai charge, they had fired at will without a thought of conserving ammo. Now, short of bullets, they were very much aware of their vulnerability to assault. They kept digging, expecting a German counterattack they hoped would not come.

Cold rain. Windy, cold rain on soaked clothes. Windy, cold rain on soaked summer uniforms on exhausted bodies drained of adrenaline.

Shivering, Tommy hugged himself. He had placed a few branches over him as a blanket. It didn't make any difference, *but at least I tried.*

His last thoughts before drifting off to an uncertain sleep concerned his feet. *I wish I could rip off my boots and go barefoot. Sloshing across rivers and marching through mud has puffed up my toes. Soles are cracked and leaking blood. Next step of trench foot is gangrene, and if not treated in time, bone docs start pruning toes. But until my toes start turning black, I'm not leaving the line. There's no one to replace us.*

Tommy's sleeping ears perked up: engine noises.

Peering over the slit ditch, a suddenly awake Tommy spotted an armored German troop carrier cruising for opportunity. Usually held two-dozen Krauts. Twin machine gun turrets rotated atop in tight arcs. Tommy pressed his binoculars to his roving eyes looking for a lurking tank that often trailed behind. *Doubtful we have the firepower to make it a fair fight. A rifle platoon thinks twice before opening fire on mobile armor. Big guns beat little guns, especially little guns short on bullets. Drizzle and night working in our favor at least. We hunker down in our ditch and stay quiet about it.*

∞ ∞

First lieutenant Richard Mizuta, who had taken command while Kim was at the aid station, called in coordinates of the passing troop carrier. Nothing. Mizuta's call didn't make the priority list. Tommy let out a sigh of relief as the troop carrier growls faded.

Breathing easier, Tommy reached inside his backpack to rummage for his K-ration chocolate snack. *The sweet sounds of silence. No shelling. No rat-a-tat machine gun firing. No engine noises. Maybe we are not the only exhausted troops.*

∞ ∞

A drowsy hour later, a rustle of movement behind Tommy stopped his breath again. Instantly alert, his hands grabbed his rifle. *Kraut infiltrator!* Tommy pivoted, gun in hand, finger on the trigger. Mules! One, two, three. Behind them, Roberto was flicking his switch and prodding his charges. Behind Roberto, a man wearing a Red Sox baseball cap followed. Kim!

Tommy dropped the point of his rifle to the ground and hustled over to Kim, who wore a pained grin. "A couple nicks on the leg that didn't make it over the wall in time and a helluva bruise on my elbow that took the fall. Nasty, but nothing broken," Kim explained as he eyed the mules. "Mostly ammo, but half a mule of K-rations." *Oh, yummy! More K-rations means no chow truck today.*

A new sound. Kraut mortar launched. More than one. A barrage. *Spotted the mules?* Tommy and Kim hunkered down into the trench. *Where did Jerry get all the ammo?* Seconds ticked by. Tommy and the banged-up Kim scooped the slit trench deeper, then crouched like twin fetuses in the womb. *Somebody is going to die. Hope it's not me. And please don't hit a mule loaded with ammo. What I am thinking? I need to help unload and disperse that ammo.* Many bodies, many arms appeared, and in minutes, mules were unloaded, ammo shared. The men hustled back to the trench without taking a hit.

Seconds later, the scream: "Medic!" A chilling battlefield call. Another "Medic!" plea on the other side. The only battle scream worse was "Mother!" A bleeding soldier's clarion overture lamenting his rush to eternity. Tommy counted three stretcher-bearer teams carrying guys. *Not good. No one wants to be carried out.*

After thirty minutes, the barrage turned sporadic. *Ammo depleted? Arms tired?* As Tommy welcomed the respite, a Jerry plane skimmed over, dropping anti-personnel bombs. Fetal position tighter than ever.

Then quiet again.

"Too quiet," Kim said as the first glow of gray light softened the Kraut-held mountaintops. "Not a coincidence. Time to take a peek."

That's Kim's "suggestion" for me to don my scout cap. Tommy's mouth neared Kim's ear. "If I were a Kraut, I'd be slipping down that gully looking for a gap in our lines. Lots of overgrowth for cover. We've been up all night. Jerry must think we're low on ammo."

"That's what I'm thinking," said Kim, pointing. "That vineyard is good for cover."

Not the best I've seen, but it will do. I still have thirty minutes of pre-dawn dimness.

Tommy eased out of the ditch and climbed bent-over at a steady, weaving pace. He safety-stopped every ten yards to take a peek. At the ninth stop, he stood up next to a vine growing around a roughhewn post. He lifted his binoculars … no movement. Until his fourth head pivot when he froze, allowing a steady look. Slithering shadows. *Time to hotfoot it back to Kim.* At that moment, the Germans released a smoke screen. *Works for me—I can run without being seen.* Tommy waited for the nasty smelling mist to envelop him. He tingled with excitement. *Krauts are unaware their surprise party isn't a surprise.*

Working on energy reserves the men didn't know they had, the platoon had formed up by the time Tommy returned.

"Smoke screen tells me something is up," said Kim.

"A line of Germans slinking down the gully. They have no idea they've been spotted."

We're too bunched up for my liking. One artillery shell and twenty KIAs. But the platoon needs to hear Kim's orders.

"Men, we got a line of Krauts weaving down that gully. They'll be here in ten minutes. We can't see them. We can wait here or crawl up the hill on both sides."

There's no question what Kim will do. We are not the waiting type. Kim divided his platoon into two groups. "Let's use that smokescreen while it lasts. Run up that hill for three minutes and stop. Crawl as close to the gully as you can. When you see the first German, let him and others pass. No one fires until I toss a grenade into the Kraut line." Kim paused. "I'm waiting!"

Soft "Yes, sir"s.

Kim ordered Private Shizuya Hayashi, one of the BAR men to stay put. "The front of the German line will rush forward when the shooting starts. Don't spare ammo. Fire at will with everything you got."

Since Tommy had just ascended the hill, Kim made him the point man on the right side. Sixteen to a side, less Hayashi … eight manpower short from when they landed on Salerno.

Tommy plucked out his last chocolate bar and waved it in the air. *Now is the time for a little sugar energy.*

The smokescreen lifted. The men dropped to the prone position and alligator-crawled under dispersing clouds. A blue halo peeked over the mountains. Only minutes to the first revealing rays of dawn.

The First German Tommy spotted was an officer. *Oh-so-tempting to blow his fucking head off.* Eager to pull the trigger, Tommy waited, watched the slinking Germans slip by him. *So many targets. Any second now.* He aimed his gunsight at a target, his finger light on the trigger, ready to tighten.

Kim tossed his grenade into the back of the German line.

At the sound of the detonation, Tommy pulled his trigger on the target he'd been following with his sights. One Kraut down. As drilled, Tommy and thirty other riflemen aimed and fired at one confused target at a time. Hitler's soldiers fell like bowling pins. Then the sweet sounds of Hayashi's BAR swept the hill. Befuddled Germans started throwing their rifles down, raised their hands. The gesture saved a few but not all.

Kim's voice boomed. "Cease firing!"

The few remaining fighting Germans flung their rifles to the ground and bellowed in English, "Surrender!" Loud and often. Terrifyingly loud. They had seen some of their comrades shot while raising their hands.

The platoon took twenty prisoners. Eight of them wounded. Tommy observed a medic attend a dying German. *Moments before, he was trying to kill us. Baby-faced kid. Can't save him, but he knows we Americans are not the beasts he'd been told we were. He doesn't look like an anti-Nazi propaganda-poster monster, either.*

Kim had been shot again but didn't know it until someone pointed to blood dampening his left trouser leg. "Not a big deal," Kim said. Then he collapsed like a sack of rice falling off a truck. A medic rushed to wrap a tourniquet on Kim's thigh. Lots of blood. The medic jabbed a vein to stick in a plasma drip. *Kim isn't walking back from this one in the morning.*

Tommy helped carry a gray-faced Mizuta. His arm was bloodied, his hip busted by shrapnel, his breathing shallow. *Might not make it.* As Tommy's stretcher team neared the aid station a haole soldier stepped aside, stopped, took off his helmet, stood at attention, and held a salute while the men carrying Mizuta passed him.

∞ ∞

Back with his unit at the bottom of the hill, Tommy counted the dead now in neat rows. "Forty-eight," he told Hayashi, who was also counting.

"Right."

"I know I nailed three for sure," said Tommy

"Two of us killed, and six needed to be carried off in stretchers," added Hayashi.

Tommy studied the German bodies. Not really the bodies, the clothing.

Hayashi didn't miss the eyeball statement. "Those Jerries are not going to need their winter clothing."

Tommy bent over a body and started to unbutton a German shirt. "I'm tired of freezing my ass off every night."

Hayashi picked out a corpse and followed Tommy's lead.

Tommy was working on the heavy woolen shirt's fifth button when the "dead" hand swiped at Tommy's rifle lying aside. *How stupid I am.* Tommy head-butted the struggling German and reared back to do it again when he heard a guttural "I surrender." The soldier's defeated eyes told Tommy he had lost the will to resist. But Tommy took no chances. He snatched his rifle and stuck the tip of his bayonet into the German gut. Tommy rose, all the while keeping his bayonet tip on the German's mid-section. Once up, Tommy motioned his prisoner to rise. Tommy two-stepped back. The Kraut rose slowly. Big guy, maybe two hundred pounds. With Tommy's bayonet prodding him along, the prisoner limped to the aid station while rubbing his right hip. *Feigned or real? Doesn't matter. I got the gun.*

Israel Yost, the newly arrived chaplain, greeted the prisoner in German as Tommy entered the aid station. As a medic led the German to a bed, he spoke to Tommy. Yost translated, "Only a miracle can win Germany the war. The Nazis are helping their sons avoid the draft."

Tommy answered with more than a tinge of bitterness. "You might meet my father in a POW camp."

Tommy searched his prisoner for maps and intelligence. Finding a letter, he handed it to Yost.

"It's to his father," Yost said. Tommy watched the blood drain from the chaplain's face. Yost read out loud: "We already liquidated our 1,200 Jewish slaves. We sent them to another ghetto beyond the borders of life."

∞ CHAPTER 104 ∞

November 4, 1943. 8:45 a.m.

EXHAUSTED, THE PLATOON HUNKERED DOWN in their muddy slit trench, parallel to the railroad line lying directly under a Kraut-occupied ridge. Quiet now, but German artillery was expected any moment. Casualties from the successful ambush reduced unit strength to twenty-five, including four soldiers with bloody nicks who refused to leave the line. Not enough men to withstand a full-frontal attack. Ammo was no problem, though. The platoon kept the ambushed Germans' weapons. Just not enough trigger pullers.

Tommy munched on his K-ration breakfast after adding water to the dehydrated scrambled eggs and oatmeal. Perked up with army sustenance, Tommy crawled out of the trench and duck-walked to a boulder twenty yards ahead, a bit to the left. He trained his binoculars on the ridge. Heard a loud pop on the hill followed by a firecracker flash signaling a rocket launch. Tommy shoved his face into the damp ground. The whistling sounds howled louder. He pressed his face deeper. The mud squished under his cheek. Explosion. Tommy's body bucked inches off the ground. *Am I hit? No. Don't think so.* More pops. Artillery. Mortars. *This is not the place to be!* Tommy high-tailed it back to the trench. Flung himself in. A barrage of screaming shells. Earth-jarring explosions. Debris rained down on the trench, but no direct hit. Yet.

A sudden lull. Tommy peeked over the trench. *Germans can't have enough manpower to try another counterattack. Yet, here they come spilling over the top. So many! Where are they pulling reserves from? Is our little patch of turf so strategic? Or is some senior Wehrmacht officer pissed off over our wipe-out ambush of his morning infiltration attempt?*

Krauts advanced in wavering columns. Kim's platoon held the advantage of shooting from a trench, but as military doctrine dictates, at a three-to-one manpower superiority, the Germans would overrun the Nisei. *If a bullet has my name on it, what can I do? But being prepared to die doesn't mean I don't try to avoid it.*

An explosion rocked Tommy. *So close.* "Medic!" rang down the line.

Where's our artillery support? Mortar support? Tommy looked right, left and behind. *Yes! He spotted three of their guys, crawling up a pimple of a hill to the right and not far behind.* Tommy focused his binoculars on the battalion's forward observer team. His eyes brightened watching Lieutenant Neil Ray and Corporals Bert Higashi and Katsushi Tanouye lug telephone equipment and their guns. Once on the hilltop, Higashi waved. Tommy was enthralled watching the FOs watching the Germans. *But if I can see them on that hill, so can the Germans. A small target. Hard to pinpoint a shell directly on the top of a tiny rise, but the Krauts will try.* Tommy's anxiety turned to joy as he observed Lieutenant Ray talking into the telephone. *Gotta be coordinates.*

Back to the task at hand. Incoming Germans closed enough to open fire. Tommy crouched down. Rifle over the parapet, he aimed, fired. *Damn! Germans still too far away for our M1s. So many of them; so few of us. This is not going to end well.*

∞ ∞

8:55 a.m.

The 100th Battalion's mortar unit began launching 81 mm ten-pound shells and not a moment too soon. First, scattered register shots that gauged the range. *Fellas, we don't have all day!* Tommy's balls shriveled as a Kraut shell rocked him. Mud and dirt sprayed his body.

Salvation! The mortar guys fired a concentrated volley. When called upon, each three-man mortar team could launch up to eighteen ten-pound shells a minute. Simple. Drop the shell down the thirty-inch steel tube. At the bottom of the tube, a firing pin triggered the charge that propelled the rocket up to two miles.

Tommy stared at what a minute ago was an advancing German company about to wipe out the platoon, now a macabre scene of flying Kraut body parts and scattering frightened German soldiers. With the spotter team directing the fire, the mortar shells followed the running Krauts like a hunter shooting ducks in flight. But they still ran forward. Not as many, not as fast. Two beautifully placed shells slammed into the center of the German advance. That stunned them, stopped them. Heads turned all which way. One German soldier pivoted and began sprinting back up the hill. That's all it took. Like lemmings, every Kraut turned and raced back up the hill. A confused retreat. Mortar shells put more down. A rout! *What did Churchill say about his British pilots in the Battle of Britain? "Never have so many owed so much to so few." That's how I feel about our forward observer unit right now.*

The day is ours!

Intermittent Jerry artillery continued. The dilatory pace revealed that their gunners didn't have their hearts in it. Medics took two men on stretchers, IV lines stuck in their arms with a medic holding the bags. Bleeding, but not dead. Tommy stood up and shook caked mud and dirt off his uniform. His breathing steadied. *How close were we to being overrun?*

∞ ∞

A haole lieutenant leading two platoons strolled up to Kim and barked, "Gillespie's ordered you off the line." Then, in a warm tone, he added, "What you have done today is beyond words. There's a pile of medals for your men and the heroes who made the ultimate sacrifice." Another pause. "I'm proud I can serve with such men."

Kim's coalescing platoon smiled. They know they had done something important today. An unfair test had been passed. Tommy watched the artillery spotters crowding the tiny hill. They were eyeing the scene. Tommy raised his hand. Then brought it down into a salute. The entire platoon saluted the forward observers. The three men on the hill saluted back.

A distant sound. Unmistakable in its echoing volume: a Screaming Mimi. In horror, the platoon watched the rocket explode on the hill. The three spotters shot into the air like athletes on a trampoline. In stricken silence, Tommy stared at debris and stickmen careening down the hill. *A lucky German shell. So capricious. If not for them, I'd be dead or a POW right now. No way we could have stopped the Germans from overrunning us. Math is math. And death is death. Soon Western Union boys will be cycling to their parents' homes. Every family on the street with a son serving will be praying, "Don't stop here."*

∞ ∞

Ordered into reserve status, the depleted platoon marched like zombies for three miles. Tommy munched a Mars bar. *I know that when I get to bivouac, I'll be too tired to eat. Too distraught.*

The unit was assigned a farmhouse that included a spacious barn. *Where there's a barn, there must be hay.* Tommy turned out to be wrong. *Doesn't matter. At least it's dry ground.* Tommy discovered a leather harness that he bunched up for a pillow. He didn't like what he saw when he pulled off his boots and socks. *I'm too tired to do anything about it now.* Tommy reached in his backpack and pulled out a German wool shirt he'd taken off a corpse in the aftermath of the attack. His blanket.

Tommy settled his head down on the harness. *What would have happened if Kim or I had not been suspicious, had settled for setting a guard parameter and gone to sleep happy we had carried the day with the banzai charge? Or if there hadn't even been a banzai charge? If the spotters hadn't found that hill to observe? If Lieutenant Ray had decided the hill was too exposed, too dangerous to climb? If. If. If.*

He drifted off to sleep.

∞ ∞

November 5, 1943

Coffee aroma woke Tommy up. *I've slept all day.* He glanced at his watch: 5:37. The slender sunlight making its way through the wide barn doors was emanating from the east. *Dawn! I slept all day and all night.* The urge to relieve his bladder sped him out of the barn. A few men moved about. Slowly, sluggishly. Tommy watered a bush. *Yesterday like a dream. Banzai charge. Ambushing Germans. The three spotters. Gone.*

Chow truck! A hot meal. And then Sears on wheels. The army supply truck arrived with winter overcoats, heavy underwear and the most precious item of all—fresh socks. A few enterprising soldiers had shaved damaged jeep tires into sandals so boots and various stages of trench feet might dry out.

Later, Tommy shoved grass, leaves and shrubbery into Kraut pants and shirts to fashion a mattress. Lumpy, but better than the naked barn floor.

∞ ∞

Memories of haole officers doubting the 100th's fitness and willingness to fight faded. The 100th men were warming up to Gillespie, awarded for gallantry in Tunisia, who loved to yack on about his hero, Jeb Stuart. He sported a Rhett Butler mustache but with points that he was prone to twirl. The Nisei joked about his mustache, but not his ability to lead. The ten-week seasoned men had learned the difference between good and bad leadership and the consequences of each.

∞ ∞

November 8, 1943

Tommy's body was mending after six weeks of nearly nonstop fighting. *That banzai charge and subsequent ambush sucked out every last bit of my reserve, everyone's reserve. Guess the brass figured that out too, which is why we're miles from the front line, in reserve. My energy is almost back to normal. Almost.*

Shrapnel from sporadic German artillery nicked two men, but nothing serious. Medics bandaged their wounds on-site.

∞ ∞

November 10, 1943

Medics conducted another toe check. Tommy's toes had almost returned to normal color.

Gillespie upgraded Kim's platoon to ready reserve. If there was a break in the line, they'd be sent in to fill the gap.

∞ ∞

November 12, 1943

Life Magazine dropped by with photographers and reporters. Proof the Japanese Americans were winning the war of acceptance.

∞ ∞

November 15, 1943

Payday on the first and fifteenth each month—$50 for privates, $78 for buck sergeants like Tommy. He allocated $10 to life insurance and sent $50 to Okaasan for savings. He took the remaining $18 in cash. The kotonks sent money home too, for their families who needed the cash for better food and winter clothing.

Dollars worked wonders, but cigarettes were an even better currency, especially for the nonsmokers. Everyone received a free carton monthly. A couple cigarettes were included in many K-ration packs. Soldiers were allowed to buy a carton of cigarettes for fifty cents once a week; that "currency" was worth ten times that amount on the black market. Tommy traded his cigs for food and wine. Women camp followers preferred payment in cigarettes over dollars.

∽ CHAPTER 105 ∽

November 16, 1943

DURING ALMOST FOUR MONTHS of non-stop fighting since the landing in Salerno, the Allies suffered 10,000 casualties, including 3,000 KIAs. Kesselring's Winter Line blocked all roads to Rome. Battered docks in Naples slowed supplies. Exhaustion and supply shortages compelled a reluctant Clark to pause the offensive. He ordered the 100th into reserve for two weeks rest.

The 100th sustained seventy-eight KIAs: three officers and seventy-five enlisted men. Another two hundred and thirty were wounded seriously enough to be taken out of action. Companies E and F were disbanded to fill out Companies A, B, C and D. Even so, companies were at one hundred and fifty actives instead of the regulated one hundred and eighty-seven.

A shortage of tires, batteries and spare parts kept three of the 100th Battalion's ten trucks out of commission. Tommy wondered when they would be issued fur-lined combat boots.

The 100th needed replacements. Injured or dead haole officers were replaced from Division, but only an AJA can replace an AJA. When Tommy heard that some 442 boys might arrive by Christmas, he hoped Kenta would be among the replacements.

∽ ∽

The battalion left the farm as the men were getting comfy. Twenty-seven men, including Tommy and three guys recently returned from the aid station squeezed into a single truck. No one complained. Any transport beat marching.

The entire 100th moved into Santa Maria Olivetto, another hillside village, with enough houses—such as they were, given all the signs of an ugly battle—to sleep the entire battalion. Sappers cleared the mines and booby traps left behind by retreating Krauts. Engineers bulldozed debris off the roads and smoothed over potholes.

A dozen snowcapped peaks rose in the far distance. Beautiful and deadly. After a brief respite, the 100th would be assaulting those mountains. Not far beyond lay Monte Cassino, home of a Benedictine abbey built around AD 529, now home to dug-in German troops blocking the eighty-one-mile road to Rome.

On the side of a shell-ripped post office, neat graffiti proclaimed, "*Avanti con Mussolini.*" This meant the townspeople had not trickled back into their homes. The first thing returnees did was scrape off any "Forward with Mussolini" signage. The Italians arrested Mussolini in late July, only to see him rescued by a daring German raid on September 12. Hitler made him the head of northern Italy under German occupation, a shrinking country El Duce called the Italian Social Republic.

Kim assigned Tommy and Hayashi's squad of eleven to a six-room house that was mostly intact. Tommy took a walk through. A few shell holes, but patchable, and baths, an inside toilet—even running water. Lucky. All the comforts of home in a once-idyllic Italian town. A couple empty cans of German food were in the kitchen near dirty pots and cigarette butts on the floor, but it wasn't too dirty. *Maybe these German soldiers have mothers like ours. I guess not all Germans are barbarians. Yet one of them would be happy to kill one of us, and us them.*

Tommy roomed with Ohata and Private Hayashi. Ohata and Tommy took the kids' bunk bed leaving the floor for Hayashi to spread out his sleeping bag. After Tommy unpacked his backpack, he descended the stairs just as an old man entered the front door. The man leaned on a crooked cane to negotiate the two stone steps into the house. A bronze, weathered face. Eyes radiating benevolence. He studied the men in the living room, amused, curious. His eyes settled on Tommy.

"*Benvenuto in casa mia.*"

"Welcome to my house." *I guess he accepts his "guests." Marching armies bivouac where they can without regard for home ownership. When the owners are present you can only hope there won't be trouble.* In his limited

Italian, Tommy managed a courteous "Grazie." *Inane, given that this is his home.*

He repeated, "Benvenuto in casa mia," with unmistakable warmth. "One Puka Puka OK."

So he knows who we are. Given how we treat the locals, should be good news.

Ohata came to the top of the stairs and the old man glanced at the chevron on Ohata's shirt sleeve. "Sergeant, benvenuto in casa mia."

The old man walked gingerly into the living room, tapping his cane with each step as he surveyed the soldiers lounging about. He tapped his chest. "Marco."

Tommy tapped his own chest. "Tommy."

Marco about-faced, spun his cane in a style that suggested he was former military and walked back to the front door.

He winked at Tommy and rapped his cane on the floor three times, hard. *A signal? What a Sherlock I am.* Like rabbits out of a hat, three little boys bounced into the entrance. Maybe aged two, four and six. The old man picked up the youngest. The oldest boy, more curious than afraid, looked the squad over, keeping his body close to Marco. *Their grandfather?* The middle boy yelled, "Mama!" A tall woman appeared, walked slowly, stately. Her windblown black hair was cut short. Her face thin, her complexion flawless, her nose narrow, her lips full, rosy without lipstick. She wore a dull, baggy, black dress that couldn't completely hide her figure. Her stunning beauty—its own kind of danger during war.

Ohata bowed in a gesture meant to reassure. Tommy and the others followed suit. *I think the act of courtesy might tell the family we mean no harm after what must have been weeks of brutal German occupation.* Tommy, closest to the door, reached into his shirt pocket and pulled out a Hershey bar for the kids to share. He caught the mother's worried face and handed it to her, realizing belatedly that chocolate was currency. *If I give the Hershey to the children, they'll be eating money that could be used for medicine or food.*

"Grazie," she said. Then in English, "I am Guilia." She carefully unwrapped the Hershey, snapped off one piece and broke it into three and handed a taste to each child. She dropped the remainder into a slit pocket in her dress.

Ohata strolled over. "I am Sergeant Ohata. My men respect women. We have mothers."

Tears formed on the edges of Guilia's eyes. "Grazie." She pinkied a tear away. In a subdued but toughened voice, she continued. "The Germans killed my husband." She paused to gain her composure. "An SS officer was found knifed near the town square shortly after the Italians surrendered. My husband ... he was one of ten shot by a firing squad against the church wall."

None of the hardened soldiers spoke. They waited for more.

"Of course, all the women knew what to expect when the Germans approached our village. They occupy Italy as their colony." Her face filled with loathing. "I grabbed my children and fled into the bush. On the third night, I walked through the German lines and came across Company A of the One Puka Puka. I did laundry for American soldiers." Tommy glanced at her hands, rough and red that verified her claim. "When the Americans drew close to Santa Maria, I visited our farm three kilometers south of the town. No Germans had touched it. I could hear the fighting. My father-in-law and I agreed we would meet at our farm when the Germans left our village. The next day, he found us sleeping in our tool shed."

Guilia turned to talk to the old man in Italian, then back to Ohata in English. "My father-in-law says we will stay in the storage room in the back. You will have the house. If you have food, I will cook. If you have laundry soap, I will do your laundry. If you have money or cigarettes, I can buy food and firewood."

Tommy glanced at the fireplace. The stiff breeze blowing through the front door foretold a frosty autumn night. He closed the door.

Guilia smiled. "I can find rice."

The squad's smiles lit up the room. The promise of rice confirmed she had indeed met some One Puka Puka boys.

⚮ CHAPTER 106 ⚭

THANKS TO GUILIA, on the first night in Santa Maria Olivetto Tommy and the squad ate chicken and rice.

"We will wait," Ohata ordered, eyeballing Tommy holding a chicken wing, "until Guilia can sit down with us." At that moment she was fussing over the children's plates at their small table off to the side of the living room.

"Grazie," she answered as she smiled at Ohata while sitting down next to Marco at the head of the table. Marco was fighting back tears. "My father-in-law wants to say a prayer of thanksgiving."

Tommy listened to his invocation. Guilia didn't translate. *She must assume we get the idea. Or maybe after losing her husband to a German firing squad, she doesn't see much to be thankful for.* Tonight, wearing nicer clothing, Guilia was stunning. Tommy "heard" his mother's admonishment "to treat women like you want people to treat your two sisters." He resisted the urge to stare at her blue eyes and deep natural rose lips. *Admonishment or no, I can't help but wonder what lies beneath her dress.*

"Tomorrow, I will find some carrots and onions," said Guilia, having collected two cartons of Luckys from the squad. It took a minute for the words to register as her eyes set on Tommy. "The cigarettes will last almost a week." As the unofficial food commissary clerk, Tommy nodded. "If the Germans don't counterattack, we will be here for two weeks. We'll see that you have all the cigarettes you need."

Toward the end of dinner, Marco rose without the aid of his cane and limped to the kitchen. He returned with a bottle that read "Grappa."

"My father-in-law would like you to empty your water glasses."

The squad gulped the water in their glasses. Marco poured everyone a generous measure as he talked and Guilia translated.

"Ours is an ancient town. Santa Maria was founded in the 11th century. We have suffered earthquakes. Our farmland has never been far from being a battlefield. We have empty houses. So many of our sons and daughters have left for America. I resisted my brother and two of my older sons' pleas to join them in Boston." He stopped, contemplating the wall as if he could see through it. "Maybe I was a stonehead. Yet, if I immigrated to America, who would farm my land? Land that has been in our family for generations."

Marco sat down and poured himself the last of the grappa, then hoisted his glass. "*Salud!*"

The Nisei held their glasses high—still unsure what grappa was—and as a chorus exclaimed, "Salud!" Tommy took a big swig. He immediately coughed and sprayed out the firewater he was drinking. The old man laughed. Everyone laughed. Half the men were bent over, mixing their laughter with choking and shooting spittle.

Guilia laughed so much that tears glistened in her eyes. "Welcome to grappa. Grappa is the pride of Italy. We distill the leftovers from winemaking—the skins, pulp, seeds and even some stems. We do not add water. Just let it ferment." Trying to stifle her laughter, she continued. "And as now you know, it's very high in alcohol. About fifty percent. Five times more powerful than wine."

Marco spoke up softly, Guilia translated. "Grappa is best enjoyed taking small sips."

"We got that," said Tommy, starting to laugh again. He started a chorus of "Grazie."

Marco's face turned serious. Guilia resumed her role as translator.

"Santa Maria slept through the war. We read about the battles, almost like a student reads history. Our village went about daily life as before. We grew crops, tended our vines. We cheered when Mussolini got the boot by King Emmanuel." Marco shook his head sadly and sipped his grappa. "We didn't foresee, couldn't imagine Hitler's response. Angry German troops occupied nearby towns. But not ours. We sighed in relief. We heard stories. Abuse of women. Assassinations. Then the Allies' advance toward Cassino made our sleepy town a strategic location. And the Germans came.

"When I complained to the German officer in charge that my Fiat had been taken, he answered, "Do you want to us to take your car or your son?" A tear formed in Marco's right eye. "They took both." Another pause. "Our city became a fortress. The Germans placed anti-tank weapons and machine gun nests on top of our homes." He tilted the glass to his lips, held it to catch the last of his grappa. Swallowed. His Adam's apple swelled as if he had sent a large piece of food down his throat. The color left his face. *Is he having a stroke?*

"Two girls. So young. Ten and eleven years old. The Germans shot them for disobeying the regulation not to drink from the water fountain in the town square."

He grabbed the edge of the table with both hands. All eyes were riveted on Marco even as English words poured from Guilia's lips. Her voice was losing strength. Tommy's attuned ears heard every word. "They took our mules. They threw dead sheep into our wells. They ordered all men aged fifteen to forty-five into the town square. Earlier, many had escaped into the hills, caves and small hamlets. The ones who remained regretted not trying to escape and expected to be shot. They couldn't believe in German brutality despite the reports.

"But they were not shot. They became slaves. They carried ammo and dug trenches. Fed one meal a day. Why feed men who in a week would be disposed of? And when the fighting began, the Germans didn't trust the boys. The commander let most of the men run into the hills. Everyone else left and Santa Maria became a German village."

Marco pushed his chair back, leaned on his cane, then limped towards the back door. "Benvenuto in casa mia."

"My father-in-law is thankful. As am I. Americans are dying to liberate our towns and villages. The Germans have lost the war. But many of you will die before they give up." She glanced at each of us as if wondering who would survive. Then she turned her attention to Ohata, and in a more normal voice said, "Bring me your laundry. I will do one man's laundry each day."

∽ ∾

The next day after lunch, Marco took the children for a walk into the town square. Guilia asked Ohata to come to the shed to pick up the laundry he'd dropped off at daybreak. Half an hour later, he returned, laundry in hand. Quiet.

Tommy leered at him, questioning.

"Bring out the dice," he snapped.

Wordlessly, Tommy reached into his pocket.

∞ ∞

Tommy was the last man for laundry day. Guilia had not only laundered the uniforms but also pressed them with her charcoal iron. He entered the dim room, not sure what to expect, but with high expectations. Soldiers usually bragged about their sexual experiences, yet no one had actually said anything about their laundry day.

Tommy stood just inside the door and glanced at his laundered uniform, neatly folded on a side table next to the cot. *Is what I think has been happening here is actually happening?* Then Guilia, so beautiful, a woman who blossomed as she entered her thirties, took two slow steps towards Tommy. He felt her breath. Stirred. Guilia tousled her hair as she moved beside and behind him to close the door. She laid her hands on his shoulders, turned Tommy around and hugged him tight, her lips to his right ear. She spoke softly.

"Alberto and I wanted five children." Her husband's portrait, recently rehung in the living room, flashed before Tommy's consciousness for the briefest second. "I want another child. A child from my saviors. I won't know who among you is the father, but I will know my child's father is a hero."

What can I say?

Guilia leaned back and began unbuttoning her blouse. "I want you to have a memory."

∞ ∞

Tommy left dazed. *These last moments with Guilia are the most beautiful moments of my life. Almost spiritual. To ever speak of it would diminish the memory, dishonor the woman.*

Walking slowly back to the house, laundry in hands, Tommy thought of Guilia's last words, knowing he would relive them often, never forget them. "You must never come back to Santa Maria Olivetto. Never. No letters, no visits, no speaking of what has happened here."

I promised, but I will always wonder if I have left a son in Italy.

⊗ CHAPTER 107 ⊗

Hill 1017 – November 25, 1943 (Thanksgiving)

O N THE OUTSKIRTS OF CERASUOLO, Italy, near Monte Cassino, the platoon waited for orders to move out. Anticipation, excitement lifted their spirits. Clear skies! Three sunny days in a row. And the promise of a Thanksgiving dinner. General Ryder and General John Lucas, VI Corps commander, announced they were "pleased with the 100th's fighting conduct." Tommy swelled with pride that the brass had recognized the Puka Puka's no-retreat determination, particularly during those three bloody Volturno River crossings under fire.

Yesterday, while marching away from Santa Maria, the unit ran across locals dressed all in black. A funeral procession. In moments, the keening at the gravesite resonated over the marching to the front. *An omen. None of us has spoken of laundry day.*

⊗ ⊗

Back on the line, Tommy dodged occasional incoming German artillery. The Germans were dug in on their winter Gustav Line across Italy's narrowest point, eighty-five sea-to-sea miles. A line of mountains, mud, rivers and artillery. He recalled his early optimism of reaching Rome by Christmas. *We were so naively optimistic then. The Krauts keep building fortifications and Hitler keeps giving Kesselring more troops.*

In olden days, winter meant a pause in the fighting. Not in modern warfare.

The big picture. Clark issued the order-of-battle for the resumed offensive to envelop Monte Cassino, home of Saint Augustine's fourth-century monastery and the staunchest German defense redoubt blocking all roads to Rome. British I Corps and American II Corps would attack two topographic "guards," the Camino Hill mass and Mount Sammucro dominating the Mignano Gap leading into the Liri Valley—a two-hour northwest Sunday drive to the Roman Coliseum.

The 100th, along with the rest of VI Corps were marching off their captured mountains at the head of the Volturno Valley.

A small part of the big picture. The One Puka Puka, which had moved to occupy Hill 1017 a mile outside the German-vacated town of Cerasuolo, focused only on the next hill crammed with Krauts. Ohata, Hayashi, Hasemoto and Tommy laid claim to a cave—a hollow might have been a better description—just big enough for them to stretch out.

Big Bertha, an enterprising woman who had followed the Puka Puka from Santa Maria, lugged up two pails of water. "*Lavanderia!*" she sang. You didn't have to speak Italian to get the idea. Technically, women shouldn't have been in a combat zone. The Germans were half a mile away shooting mortars and artillery sporadically. In a day or two, the attack would begin. Although the Krauts were hunkered down in a defensive position, who was to say they wouldn't engineer a surprise attack. But for the laundry ladies short on food, the risk was worth it. Big Bertha had also brought a chicken, a couple of potatoes and a young "chick" with flirtatious eyes, introduced as Nicole, to help with the laundry. *I don't think so.*

"Sarge," Tommy said to Ohata, "Big Bertha wants a chocolate bar and two packs of cigarettes for the chicken."

"One and one," countered Ohata, having learned it was bad form to accept the first offer. Taking off his shirt and trousers and handing them to Big Bertha, he added, "We're already paying too much for the washing." It cost a K-ration kit for each uniform washed. Ohata excused himself to the back of the cave and shucked his underwear, then tossed his shorts and T-shirt to the front. As he donned fresh underwear he said, "We got at least a day before we jump off, might as well get shot in a clean uniform."

The younger girl giggled at Ohata's modesty, a signal Tommy was eager to interpret. He waved a pack of Luckys at her and held up five fingers. She coyly nodded her head. Confident she knew the hollows and caves well and could find a private grotto, Tommy grabbed her hand and walked off carrying a GI-issued blanket. Big Bertha snapped the back of her hand at Tommy's genitals as he passed, giving him her seal of approval. *What war and starvation do to traditional morality.*

While Tommy listened to Big Bertha pound the dirt out of Ohata's uniform, he performed well enough to give Nicole three extra cigarettes. *Damn decent of the Krauts not to charge over the ridge right now and counterattack.* Nicole picked up his clothes and mimicked a scrubbing gesture. *Sure. Why not. The sun and wind will dry my duds in just a couple of hours.*

Wrapping his blanket around him, Tommy strolled back to his cave in time to watch Ohata snap the neck of a chicken. Some kid had lugged up two more buckets of water to Bertha. Ohata scooped his helmet in one of the buckets and set it atop a fire he built. Once the water hit the boiling point, Ohata dropped in the chicken. Pulled it out. Plucked it. Dropped it back in. Boiled chicken and K-rations. A gourmet treat.

Later that afternoon, half the platoon trekked to the supply depot. It was so steep, the men scrounged walking sticks to keep them from pitching forward. The laundry ladies led the way. Big Bertha claimed she knew the safest twists and turns. Nicole walked with them, as beatific as a nun. A demeanor for the purpose at hand.

An hour later, the men's backs were strapped with forty-five-pound boxes of C- and K-rations, ammo and five-gallon water cans brought to the depot by mules who had already been sent back to ferry more supplies to the field depot. The box strapped to Tommy's back was stenciled "Thanksgiving."

"Why walk when we have mules?" asked Tommy

"Our rocky hill is too steep, paths too narrow, with too many crevices for even mules to negotiate," said the supply officer.

"No wonder Hannibal never made it to Rome," answered Tommy.

"And maybe more important, we need those mules going back to carry more supplies. You are the last mile. The slow mile."

"OK. Got it," said Tommy adjusting his backpack. *More likely the real reason, but understandable.*

Random German artillery fell along the trail as Tommy made the ascent back. Not precise, not heavy. No casualties that night, but a reminder that war was lethal even when not in active combat.

As soon as Tommy reached his unit, he opened his box. "Shit, my box is nothing but sliced bread."

"Well, we partners then," said Ohata. "My box is all meat."

Tommy looked over. "Yuck, look at the edges. Half of them are turning green."

"SNAFU," said Ohata.

Tommy finished the thought. "Situation normal, all fucked up."

"We adapt," challenged Ohata.

"Right," said Tommy, who, along with other gathering soldiers, grabbed two slices of stale bread, a couple cuts of turkey, scraped off the green mold and ate. "Happy Thanksgiving."

Less than an hour later, Tommy bolted for the slit trench that served as the unit latrine. In minutes, there wasn't enough room for all the squatters and barfers. To no one in particular, a squatting Tommy proclaimed, "If the Krauts knew our condition, they could overrun us quicker than Big Bertha's laundry girl took me to ecstasy."

∽ ∾

November 26, 1943

Hill 1017 overlooked the double-ridged neighboring hill where the Germans waited. Tommy's stomach was still wobbly, but he knew that was no excuse to skip his nightly scout crawl. *Just need a quick snooze before my probe.*

∞ ∞

Kim poked Tommy with the tip of his rifle.

Tommy was pissed about being awakened but controlled his reaction. "I've been dreaming I'm back in Hawaii roasting a pig on the beach." He glanced at his watch. His eyes opened wider. 2:30!

"I gave you five hours. You needed it. How's the stomach?"

Tommy stood up slowly. "No cramps. I'm good to go." Tommy tilted his head upward. Observing a sliver of moon and scattered clouds, he said, "I hate rain and mud, but I'd welcome them tonight. A scout's best friend when crawling about."

"The hill's trees, mostly leafy despite the autumn chill and mostly undamaged by shelling, and the rain-drenched scrub will give you good cover," consoled Kim. He handed Tommy a scope. "Put this on your rifle."

"Lieutenant, with all due respect, I'm a scout, not a sniper."

"The army doesn't have snipers. That's a German thing. A Kraut sniper has been on the lower ridge halfway up their hill for a day. But we do have dedicated marksmen. You had three kills in the ambush. You earned a sharpshooter's badge in Wisconsin. If you spot a roving German squad, observe, don't fire, and come back. Use this only if there is opportunity. If you are about to be captured …"

Tommy cut him off. "Bury the scope. I know what happens to snipers … regardless of what we label ours."

Once Tommy attached the scope atop his rifle, he wrapped a leafy vine around his helmet. Kim strung branches around his back.

Foliage-covered, Tommy hunched into the night. Upon reaching the German-controlled neighbor hill, he crawled. Slowly. Tommy was well aware that German scouts were roaming, searching, looking. Like him, they were trained to notice movement. A fast-moving scout was soon a not-moving scout.

The first long hour, no movement ahead of Tommy. Then a sound. A motor. *Damn, a motorcycle on the lower ridge. Gutsy tactic by a Hun or stupid? Searching for a lost or dead comrade? Intimidation? A trap? Possibilities are endless. If a trap, I'm crawling right into it.* The sound receded and then increased. The engine sounds were both enticing and worrisome. *Whoever is on that bike is trolling back and forth.* Tommy pushed hard on his toes and knees, inching up to the crest.

There! A bush, but not a bush. A man-created bush. Boulders moved together behind the bush. A sniper's blind. Tommy slithered over to a rock outcrop adjacent to a small tree that gave him the concealment he needed to spot his prey. *The cat and mouse game. I hope I am the cat.*

Conscious of the twin threats, Tommy scanned ahead, right and left. No sniper. Nothing. Silence. The tree line gave the motorcycle good cover.

Tommy's night vision picked up something out of place. *There it is. A shadow outline of a two-man cycle. Soldier in the side well holding a MG42 machine gun. If I shoot, I give away my position. If I miss, I'm facing a BAR that fires a flurry of bullets against my M1. If I hit the gunner or driver, I win—unless a patrol is waiting for exactly that moment to grab a prisoner to interrogate.*

"Go for broke" sang in Tommy's mind, like a siren calling Ulysses. *The element of surprise belongs to me.* The urge seduced Tommy. He set his scoped M1 atop the lip of the boulder. His eyes roved to check the sniper's blind for movement, to check any movement on the ridge. *Still nothing. I'll get one chance.* All concentration on the motorcycle. The engine revved. *He's moving!* Tommy clicked his M1 on auto-fire. He followed the moving shadow, his left eye on the sight. *I have only seconds. Do I go for the gunner or driver? The driver. Hard for the gunner to shoot if his motorcycle is careening. He's approaching a break in coverage. There he is. So clear in my scope.* Tommy pressed the trigger on automatic. Emptied his cartridge. The driver's body convulsed. The cycle tipped over. Driver and gunner were tossed out. Tommy shoved in a fresh clip. The gunner popped up, and without looking for his machine gun, sprinted like a rabbit. Tommy emptied his second clip. Missed him.

Do I run after him or search the driver for intel and skedaddle? A dead driver or an only-stunned driver who will pull a Luger as I approach? Or do I get the hell out of here now? Is there a nearby German patrol alerted by the gunfire closing in on me? Will the running gunner have second thoughts and return, ready to duel with maybe a sidearm? All this conjecture in less than a blink of an eye.

Go for broke! Tommy scampered to the crest. *No use peeking right and left. If I missed the patrol, it's too late now. I'm a goner.* The driver was dead. *Not sure my shot killed him.* Blood oozed from the driver's chest, his neck appeared broken, his eyes were open. Tommy drew the driver's bloodied Luger from his holster and stuck it in his waistband. *Good gun.* Tommy quickened his search of the pockets. A picture of an older woman. A letter. A map!

Rifle shots came down the hill. *Time to scoot.* Tommy ran for his life. Bullets pinged dirt and trees. Tommy felt a sting on his calf like a wasp, but knew it wasn't a wasp. *Run. Run. Run.* As he approached his platoon, Tommy screamed, "Hula Girl," the password. Hasemoto yelled in return. "Hold your fire! Hold your fire!"

The instant Tommy leaped the trench line, the platoon opened fire on whoever might still be chasing Tommy. Tommy collapsed on the ground, adrenaline pumping, heart pounding. Lying on the ground, Tommy studied the crumpled picture of the older woman he had grabbed and put it in his pocket. He couldn't read the back of the photo. *I bet it's his mother hoping her son comes back alive.* Tommy pictured the dead driver's eyes staring at him. *A guy like me. Family. Brothers. Maybe a wife or girlfriend waiting for him. How do the Germans inform their parents? We send Western Union telegrams. Maybe he thinks Hitler's a shit. They can't all be Nazi believers, or the Krauts wouldn't need the SS and Gestapo.*

In that moment, with my rifle aimed at the driver, all that I've learned about "Thou shalt not kill" had to be discarded. Sure, I hate the Nazis, but not that soldier. I am conflicted, even sad. But if I don't keep killing, then I get killed. I shot him while he was hunting for a GI to kill. What makes men and nations settle their disputes with death? Demonizing the enemy as subhuman, not worthy of life, deserving of death. His buddies are hunting for the guy who killed their motorcyclist. So it goes.

"There's blood on your trouser leg," said Kim, breaking Tommy's reverie. "Get it patched and I'll put you in for a Purple Heart."

"A Purple Heart for a Band-Aid wound? I don't think so, Lieutenant," said Tommy, as he stood up.

"Listen up, Tommy. A Purple Heart tells your folks, your unit and the press you put yourself in harm's way. If that Kraut had moved his rifle a fraction of a fraction of an inch, you might be in a body bag."

"But ..." Tommy protested.

"But nothing, soldier. As our unit collects Purple Hearts like kids collect candy on Halloween, we are telling America we came to fight. We are willing to die."

Tommy focused on Kim's steely eyes.

"Yes, sir."

⚭ CHAPTER 108 ⚭

November 29, 1943. 5:00 p.m.

HILL 1017 WAS THE PROVERBIAL hill from hell. It seemed like just another hill in a series of hills until it wasn't. At 3.28 feet per meter, Hill 1017 was 3,337 feet higher than the beaches of Salerno. It offered the battle line's highest, coldest, windiest, most diverse topography. On postcards or in Monet or van Gogh paintings, hills rise gently, almost symmetrically, green-treed and flowering. Picnic-inviting. Those weren't the hills of middle Italy—for sure not Hill 1017. It was an ill-defined crest, not a smooth plateau, rather ridges and mini-crests. Not even a real bottom, but part of a series of rises or little hills. A *lot* of geography. The Nisei held what passed for a crest and part of the northern downside facing the Germans, who after skirmishes following Tommy's motorcycle kill, controlled the bottom and adjacent hills on their side, well-defended.

∞ ∞

Frost rimmed the edge of the cave occupied by Tommy high up on the German side of the hill. Out of rifle range; within mortar range. Shoes laced. Backpack stuffed with K-rations and ammo. He was ready.

Tommy exhaled puffs of fog as he boiled water in his helmet over a campfire for instant coffee and a K-ration tin of a bacon and cheese concoction which could be eaten cold but tasted better warm. Gourmet yuck. And biscuits. No matter the "main course," there were always biscuits.

Another night of crawling around. Routine? Never. In the few short weeks of nocturnal sneaking around, Tommy found he looked forward to the rush of adrenaline, the heightened sense of awareness. The tingle. The Germans sent out patrols, but by now he was aware that they were only checking if the 100th was probing rather than looking for a firefight that might wedge a break in their line.

In the few days of scouting downhill, Tommy had worked out a stealthy path of granite outcrops, scrawny bushes, narrow gullies and shell holes. His confidence was rising to the danger point as he came closer to German lines than ever before. So far downhill, he could see uphill of the little hills that made up part of Hill 1017. He settled in a fresh depression, courtesy, he assumed, of a 105 Howitzer round. His night vision was alert, the binoculars tight against his eye sockets. He studied movement below. Nothing out of place. Knew where he watched was being watched. But at five hundred yards he passed as a bush. He was certain.

Then he looked up at the surrounding hills. *Shit. Double shit.* His sphincter tightened. *I need to get back. Quickly.* Quickly was a mistake. Soldiers see quick. Tommy heard shouts. Then bullets pinging in his direction. Now he really had to move quickly. When stealth fails, speed counts. More shouts. From his left. *A German patrol.* Gunfire. Not well aimed. The patrol knew he was there, but unlike the spotters below they hadn't seen him. Tommy carried three grenades with him. Throwing them required movement, making him an easier target. On the other hand, dodging grenade shrapnel tended to make shooting a doubtful enterprise. Tommy the baseball pitcher threw the three grenades in succession towards where the gunfire had emanated. He didn't wait to see his results. But the gunfire stopped long enough for Tommy to escape unharmed.

Shortly, Tommy reported to Kim, "The Krauts solved the problem of artillery at close quarters. I saw them pulling three anti-aircraft guns on the ridge of this hill." He pointed on his map to a series of concentric circles that were part of Hill 1017's expansive contours.

"Good to know," said the unflappable Kim. "While you were trekking, Clark confirmed what we expected. The general offensive begins at six a.m. The 100th is charged with clearing the Krauts off our hill."

∞ ∞

November 30, 1943. 4:00 a.m.

A cacophony of rude noise woke Tommy. Ryder's artillery roared, lit the sky and smashed into German positions. *No more skirmishes. Today's the real thing.*

At Kim's orders, the platoon rechecked their backpacks. Six K-ration packs and ammo for what was expected continuous combat for perhaps several days. Who knew how long?

∞ ∞

4:45 a.m.

Even as the division's howitzers continued the furious barrage, Tommy's amazed eyes watched an army chow unit chugging up a field kitchen. *A hot breakfast!*

∞ ∞

5:30 a.m.

Tommy stomped his feet to keep warm. He was eager for the "move out" command even as he wondered if he would live out the day. He thought of Okaasan in her yukata, palm trees shading her vegetable patch. He daydreamed of sitting in his humanities class at the university. He envisioned how the Nisei survivors would lead the voting charge to overturn the political landscape of Hawaii. Then he came back to reality. *What better claim do I have of living through today, tomorrow, or the war than any other guy in a foxhole?*

∞ ∞

5:55 a.m.

"Form up!" commanded Kim. No "Win one for the Gipper" speech. Not Kim's style. *He knows we know what we need to do. We're not the greenies that landed in Salerno.* Kim assigned Sergeant Ohata, carrying his BAR weapon, Tommy and privates Hasemoto and Hayashi to protect the left flank.

A pop-pop sound barely heard over the artillery noise was followed by mist. The 100th's chemical mortar unit was firing smoke shells. The manmade fog, helped by the morning's quiet winds, enveloped the ground ahead of them in range of Kraut machine gun nests, which, like hidden Easter eggs, waited concealed with rolls of steel bullets ready to spit out deadly mayhem.

∞ ∞

6:00 a.m.

The artillery barrage ceased. In seconds, Kim's voice boomed, "Move out."

∞ ∞

6:15 a.m.

Tommy and his fellow flankers filed downhill. No contact with the enemy yet, but the newly deployed German anti-aircraft guns Tommy had spotted the night before were blazing at the smoke-covered mass of troops descending over the upper crest of Hill 1017. Mortar shells exploded like a popcorn machine. The thunderous noise muffled Tommy's hearing.

Some pissed-off Kraut commander targets all his ordnance into one small piece of turf. Mine! When it can't get worse, it's getting worse. Kraut machine guns at full throttle. Still I'm unscathed.

∞ ∞

6:35 a.m.

The platoon closed in on the Krauts. Like at Bunker Hill, they saw the whites of their eyes. Tommy looked for cover that wasn't there. He heard the screams of "Medic!" or "Mother!" *Will I be screaming next?*

Ohata positioned Hasemoto on his extreme left. Tommy dropped down behind one of the few boulders big enough to hunch behind for cover. He looked, couldn't spot Hayashi. Krauts straight ahead. Tommy cradled his M1 on the granite to steady his aim at four charging Jerries. One fell, rolled, tried to sit up. *No time to think about a man down, it's the ones shooting I must focus on.*

Tommy barely heard the dings of bullets bouncing off the other side of his granite protection. He slid his M1 on the rock and, without aiming, let loose a clip. Looked up. Jerries ten yards ahead. He threw a grenade and ducked. Germans spotted Tommy's throw. They scurried to avoid the explosion rather than aim and shoot.

At that instant, Hasemoto rose from behind a ditch and standing like Washington crossing the Delaware, fired his automatic rifle into a hail of bullets. While he was reloading his third magazine in a blur of motion, a German bullet slammed into his gun, making it useless. Incredibly, Hasemoto wasn't hit. He shouted, "Sarge!" at the top of his lungs.

Watching his unprotected private under assault, Ohata ignored all the safety rules and broke from his coverage to race across the fifteen yards to Hasemoto's exposed position, all while blasting away at incoming rifle-firing Germans. He mowed down ten of them bunched up like sardines.

Hasemoto sprinted backward. Under a barrage of continuing gunfire, he grabbed a rifle off the ground a dozen yards behind Ohata's covering fire. He rushed forward to join Ohata and blasted away. At least twenty Krauts lay on the ground. Still more Germans advanced. Hasemoto and Ohata fired on full automatic, reloading like they did in training when a sergeant held a timer.

More Germans fell. Hasemoto's gun jammed. Once more, he dashed back, snatched an M1 off a fallen comrade and returned to Ohata's side. Firing hip to hip, the Ohata–Hasemoto killing machine brought down ten more Germans. With only three Germans left in their field sector, the duo rushed forward, killed one, wounded another and captured the last German standing. One lucky Kraut who would wonder all his life why he lived. He was sent down with the medics.

But the Germans weren't finished. A second wave of Jerries descended. Only fourteen this time. Courage makes its own luck. Still fighting astride each other, Ohata and Hasemoto stopped that second wave and then a third.

Amazingly, Ohata and Hasemoto retreated from the carnage without a nick. When the counting was done, they had left fifty-one dead Hitler boys on the field.

☙ Chapter 109 ☙

8:50 a.m.

The Ohata–Hasemoto heroics cleared the area where Tommy had crawled about the previous evening, but the Jerries still controlled their defense line. After a brief lull, regrouped Germans charged at Kim's platoon, attempting a flanking maneuver.

From a freshly dug foxhole—*more like a shallow bowl*—Tommy lay prone, shooting at the new onslaught. *More targets for me, and more of the enemy targeting me.* Tommy's noise-damaged ears heard all sounds as low bass decibels. The anguished cries of "Medic!" seemed to emanate from a distant room. The taste and tang of dust laced with cordite particles irritated his lungs and stung his sinuses. His body hummed as the earth rumbled under the shock of ordnance. He struggled to aim his rifle while the shell-burst ground heaved angry debris in the air and then pelted down. The haze of exploding earth, shattering shells and smoking guns filtered the sun.

☙ ☙

9:35 a.m.

A blur of movement to Tommy's left. Hayashi! He bobbed up alone from what two hours earlier had been a German foxhole and charged like a comic book hero into a hail of grenades, mortar fire, snipers and a fusillade of machine gun fire. Seconds later, Tommy, along with Ohata's squad, sprung up like a string of dervishes.

Hayashi raced ahead, firing his BAR from the hip. He charged a machine gun nest from the side. Kraut gunners reached for their sidearms. Leaping into the nest, Hayashi's burst of fire ended the war for five slow-reacting Jerries. Two Germans that Hayashi missed bolted like frightened deer out the side of a dirt-and-stone parapet but weren't fast enough. Hayashi slammed a new clip into his BAR, aimed and squeezed the trigger. The two convulsed into death.

When Tommy reached the nest, the seven Germans lay like giant rag dolls, mouths open. Eyes staring, none moving.

The rest of the squad moved up. German troops on both flanks had left an unprotected path to the ridge rising midway down the multi-contoured Hill 1017. Directly up and ahead, Tommy studied the three Wehrmacht anti-aircraft guns he had spotted on last night's scouting foray. *A clear shot at our ascending men. Big shells, but hard to maneuver precisely. Not effective at close range, but we are not at close range. Yet.* Hoping to hit a gunner, Tommy started firing in the direction of anti-aircraft guns. He was soon joined by most of the squad.

Hayashi yelled, "Cover me." He sprung out of the nest he just captured. His gun roaring on automatic he charged the anti-aircraft gunners. In seconds, all was quiet. Tommy ran to the crest of the hill where only seconds ago a Kraut-killing machine blazed death. Four Germans with hands up stared at Hayashi. Nine tangled bodies were bunched around a smoking anti-aircraft gun.

Incredibly, given the limited manpower of the squad, the Germans manning the other nearby anti-aircraft guns abandoned the field.

"The day is ours," said Hayashi, grim, but smiling. The remaining Germans might have been the ones to claim the day if they had charged Hayashi, who was almost out of ammo. The Krauts blinked first. They had had enough and gave up the blood-soaked ground to Ohata's weary squad.

Tommy stood awed, admiring Hayashi. *Seventeen kills on a double one-man charge following the earlier two-man killing machine that left fifty-one Germans on the field. Sixty-eight enemy dead, the result of spontaneous courage. Who can predict or understand such men? They charged, completely disregarding personal safety to carry the day. How the Germans didn't even nick the three samurai is a curiosity I'm sure I'll never understand. The element of surprise, yes. But so many Germans, so many bullets, so many incoming mortars. I know more of us would have died that day without the inspiring spontaneity of Hayashi, Hasemoto and Ohata.*

Ohata's squad didn't have the manpower to keep the ridge longer than the time it took for the sappers to drop timed charges down the barrels of the anti-aircraft guns. Tommy didn't stand around to watch. Germans were massing for a counterattack. *Despite Hayashi's heroics, they will reoccupy the ridge, less the big guns. How long can they absorb huge losses and refill their foxholes? How long can we? The Krauts gave us their best. We held. They paid the higher price.*

∽ ∾

10:05 a.m.

Downhill, Ohata's squad stumbled upon the platoon's wounded mortar spotter, Corporal Masaru Suehiro, his pallor grey. Blood on his shirt glistened. Only fresh blood glistened. Field phone in hand, he was trying to call in coordinates.

"Let's give our prisoners some stretcher-bearer duty," said Tommy, looking at Hayashi.

Weak-voiced, Suehiro countered, "No, I'll stay here until they send a replacement."

Tommy crouched down. "I am the replacement. You know I'm the platoon scout. I might not be as good as you when you're healthy, but how long are you going to be able phone in coordinates with all that bleeding?"

A big German POW pointed to himself. He peered down at Suehiro and mimicked throwing a sack over his back. Hayashi nodded his head affirmatively. Like a fireman carrying a victim from a burning building, the Kraut eased Suehiro over his back. *If I become a POW, will I adapt to prisoner status so easily? Then again, maybe the Kraut knows many POWs on both sides never make it to HQ for interrogation. In the heat of battle, it's easier, more efficient, to simply shoot prisoners and move on.*

Tommy studied Suehiro's bloodstained maps. Having just been atop the hill, he chose two targets and called in coordinates. "We're of out shells!" rang in Tommy's ear.

Noon

Sunny. German artillery sporadic. Not exactly a truce, but neither side had the appetite to maintain the morning's level of violence and death. Medics and stretcher-bearers shuttled back and forth. Germans broke their practice of shooting at Red Cross-marked men. In turn, the 100th held their fire as the Germans picked up their dead.

1:35 p.m.

The respite was short-lived. First the Germans fired mortars, then charged.

Kim's platoon dug in. His strong voice commanded, "No one leaves their foxhole. Hunker down and fire." The Wehrmacht stormed Kim's thin line. Tommy fired one carefully aimed bullet at a time. *Keep coming, you Nazi fucks, we ain't leaving. No one, no army will outwill us!*

1:48 p.m.

With Germans within ten yards, Hasemoto raised his hand, showed Tommy his forefinger. *One more clip.* He shoved it in his BAR. It didn't matter. Hasemoto's luck ran out. Shrapnel from a mortar shell ripped his head. He collapsed in a heap.

Ignoring Kim's instructions, Tommy rolled out of his foxhole and sprinted to Hasemoto's prone body. Grabbed his gun. Tommy's eyesight had never been so clear. His concentration smothered the sounds and sights of battle. He entered another world. Just Tommy, his gun and Nazi targets. The BAR clip emptied. Tommy picked up the M1 holding his last clip. *Our guys are firing as if we have a huge supply depot next to us. How long can we last?*

Tommy's last clip took out two Germans. Dead or wounded, it didn't matter. What counted was two Germans not shooting. Tommy attached his bayonet to his rifle. He looked at the still-coming Germans and yelled, "Come and get it."

∞ ∞

1:57 p.m.

The Krauts' firing rate slowed. The Nisei were not the only soldiers running out of bullets. The Krauts retreated in good order. The last fusillade took the starch out of them. They blinked first. Kim's platoon fired whatever ordnance they had left, hoping the Krauts would think their enemy had ammo to spare. One by one the platoon's guns went silent as the Germans retreated to the crest of the hill. If they had kept advancing, who would have carried the day?

∞ ∞

2:10 p.m.

Kim ordered ten exhausted men, a third of his platoon, to the supply depot to carry back ammo. Exhausted or not, the men were motivated. Could they make the three-hour roundtrip journey before the Krauts come down the hill again?

They did.

The Germans were finished for the day. Along the entire line of the 100th, the Germans killed sixty-eight Nisei. Coincidently, Ohata, Hayashi and Hasemoto had killed the same number of Krauts.

The Germans still held the ridge.

∞ CHAPTER 110 ∞

December 1, 1943

TOMMY AWOKE TO FROST ON THE GROUND. He eased out of his sleeping bag and stepped out of the pup tent into the chill. Nickel-colored clouds floated over the mountains. Mist was morphing to sleet. Foxholes were turning to slosh.

Canteen empty. Water jugs empty. Tommy licked the chilled dew off sparse leaves to quench his thirst, shook scraggly shrubs to catch the drops in his palm. His helmet lay face up in case of rain. This lull in fighting provided a chance for the supply units to trudge up the hills. *Where are they?*

Kim picked up his newly issued TA-312 field phone receiver to call HQ. "We need food and ammo. If attacked, we'll be overrun." Tommy listened to Kim's voice straining to keep to the soft-talk rule. Tommy had spotted German acoustic mirror "listening ears" on the ridge. Kim glared at his phone. No response from the other end. Communications line was cut. An artillery shell or a Kraut sneaking behind our lines with a sharp bayonet? Kim eyeballed Tommy, even though it was the signal corpsman's job to splice and tape.

Kim beckoned Tommy. His command voice maintained the quieter, safer decibels. "I need someone credible to demand supplies. Grab the line repair kit, find the cut, patch it and then keep going down to HQ. Tell them I can't spare the manpower for a three-hour roundtrip supply run." He gritted his teeth. His eyes roamed over the platoon. "Tell 'em we're fucked if we're not resupplied. Immediately."

"Got it ... Sir."

Kaneta, the signalman, handed Tommy his repair-kit pouch. Tommy had crawled with Kaneta before as scout and rifleman protector. He had watched and learned how to splice lines. Simple. Cut the rubber off the tip of the two lines. Twist them together. Cover in tape. Tommy grabbed the wire extending from Kim's phone set, placed it in his hand between his thumb and forefinger, and began walking. Lots of slack. Signal guys laying wire always looped it at intervals.

Sleet was turning to snow. A better safety factor? Depended. Kraut visibility would be impaired, but green khaki on fresh snow was more revealing.

A string of three random mortar detonations boomed some twenty yards to Tommy's left. Dirt chunks fell with the snow. *A morning courtesy call or have I already been spotted?* Tommy dropped to the ground and began crawling. More mortar shells. *A Hitler boy working his mortar tube must've decided now is a good time to remind us they control the crest. Not a good time to be in the open. Another hundred yards and I'll be out of the target range. Unless the Germans switch to artillery.*

Whoosh! An explosion. Close. *Shit. I'm hit.* Shrapnel ripped Tommy's thigh. A shard or rock sliced his forehead above his aiming eye. More annoyance than critical. Tommy continued crawling. Blood flow from his thigh was steady. *Worse than I thought. Doesn't look like an artery cut. If I yell "Medic!" am I far enough away for the medic to hear and not the Krauts? Will anyone hear me? More blood. Not looking good.* Tommy tore open his med kit. He yanked out a tourniquet and tied it around his thigh. Bleeding reduced to a trickle. *What is lack of blood flow doing to my leg below the tourniquet? If I end up a peg leg. I won't be alone.* Since Tommy couldn't crawl one-legged, he rolled—slowly, keeping his hands in the air to hold onto the telephone wire.

The wire dropped from Tommy's hand. The end. The break. His eyes searched for the other piece. Tommy's concentration faltered. His muscles weren't obeying commands. A narrow channel of blood oozed from the head wound and dripped into his right eye. A weakened Tommy rolled and crawled painfully on his good leg and rolled again. And again. Down and sideways, back and forth. *Where is that line? Can't give up.* Tommy's vision fuzzy. Another mortar. Tommy felt the ground tremble, but the sound seemed so distant. Dirt fell on him. *Can't function. Need to crawl back or hurry forward to aid station. Legs not moving right. What direction should I be going?*

Darkness approached. Tommy lost feeling in both legs. His numbed fingers fumbled in his jacket for a Mars bar that wasn't there. *I just need five minutes of sleep.* He put his head down.

↞ CHAPTER 111 ↠

Camp Shelby – December 18, 1943

MASTER SERGEANT ADAMS walked into Colonel Pence's ciga-rette-smoke-infused office an hour after morning mess and handed him a telegram: "Send four hundred replacements for the 100th. M. Clark."

Pence read, nodding slowly. "Finally," he said, as if learning of the death of a terminally ill relative.

"A hundred less than we expected, Colonel," said Adams.

As casualty numbers accelerated in the foothills of Monte Cassino, he and Pence had privately discussed whom to send when the anticipated request came. The battalion commanders tried to make the case to Pence and Adams for sending the troublemakers in their ranks. "Better for the harmony of my battalion if I shipped out a couple of men who are more acquainted with the MPs than their own sergeants," charged one captain.

Adams, one of the few men at Shelby who had actually been in combat, said "The 100th needs battle soldiers. What's going on over there is no place for men better suited for a day in the brig." There was nothing more he could say that hadn't been said before.

"Call in all the battalion leaders and HQ staff with the rank of captain and above. At …" Pence looked at his watch. "Eleven hundred. I want the men at their sharpest."

"And close enough to lunch to cut down on the …" Adams paused, looking for a less accusatory word than procrastination. "… dilly-dallying."

"Exactly," said Pence.

"Tell each battalion leader to bring a list of six men he recommends as replacements. The remainder will be chosen on marksmanship records." Then he added, "No one from the 522nd Artillery Unit."

Adams snapped his feet together and saluted. "Yes, sir!"

∽ ∾

Kenta hobbled over to the hospital to have the nurse check the splint on his hairline-fractured big toe, for what he hoped would be the last time. He had almost removed the splint himself that morning but then changed his mind, not wanting a lecture. Each visit reminded him not to kick the base of a 105 howitzer in frustration over a missed target, especially while ignoring the "keep your boots on at all times" rule. It was a rule frequently breached. The hospital visits had one upside—an excuse to check his and Tommy's private mail service. It had been longer than usual since the last letter.

Letters from Tommy's special channel were more revealing than letters sent through regular channels. Censored channels. Tommy had suggested he could tell his brother what to expect when he got to Italy if he communicated privately. Given that the wounded coming back as Tommy's carriers could also provide the same info, Kenta assumed there was another reason. "Someday, somebody needs to write a book telling the world what we are doing," Tommy had said more than once.

Kenta thought about the letter he had received that morning through regular channels, Taka writing to tell him that he and Angelina had been accepted into the MIS and were heading for Australia. Last week, he had received a letter from Angelina telling him all about her Fort Ritchie assignment translating captured documents, but no word about Australia. How did Taka know before she did?

"Morning, Nurse Allie," Kenta greeted Allison Butler, a civilian nurse known as Angel Allie among the Nisei for her infectious smile, charming

Southern drawl and competence. "How's your application coming along?" Allie had applied to join the Army Nurse Corps.

"I'm in. Induction in two weeks. I'll be stationed in England." Her pleasant expression shifted to worry. "They'll be needing a lot of us." It was an open secret that this year or next, an Allied invasion of France would be launched. "All right. Let's have a look at that toe."

Kenta sat down on the end of a gurney to take off his sandal—the same one he had been wearing when kicking the cannon—and lifted his leg so she could remove the tape tying the injured toe with his "buddy toe" for support. She wiggled the toe forward and backward.

"Ouch!"

"Are all you Hawaii boys so brave?" she asked, bending the toe more slowly.

Kenta winced again, but kept his mouth shut.

"Well, it's been four weeks. I think it feels okay," she pronounced, tossing the tape and gauze into a trashcan filled to the brim with bandages and other hospital detritus. "You can wear boots again. You're off restricted duty." Then her smile turned conspiratorial. "Big announcement today at noon." She paused for dramatic effect. "General Marshall is going to announce all Nisei will be subject to the draft."

Wow, at last!

Kenta almost blurted out, "How do you know?" He held back, thinking he might as well be asking, *which senior officer are you fucking?* Instead, he said, "We owe a lot to the 100th guys proving we're as red-blooded as any other American."

"Also, a Corporal Koizumi came in last night. He has a mail packet for you." Kenta smiled at this unexpected good news.

"He was one of the lucky ones to be air transported," Allie explained. "When brass are flown in, they pack the seriously wounded onto return flights. He's over in Ward Six."

"Ward Six?" Kenta's face fell. "That's ... that's the amputee ward."

"Yes. He paid a high price for his valor. But he survived the war. And the army is doing wonders with prostheses these days. He'll be sent to Battle Creek, Michigan, where the army has taken over a hospital and set up an amputee recovery unit."

You don't "recover" from an amputation, thought Kenta, but he understood what she meant and the good will with which she said it. "Hey, thanks for helping with my mail," he said. "We're all going to miss you, even though we're damn proud the army recognized a good nurse."

∽ ∾

At the Ward Six nurse's station, where the astringent fumes wafted more sharply, a woman who looked like she had come out of retirement for the war effort directed Kenta. "You'll find Corporal Koizumi down the hall," she said with a schoolmarm pause to make sure Kenta was paying attention. "Third door on the right, second bed."

Despite the advance warning, Kenta fought the shock he felt upon finding Jerry Koizumi with a missing leg. Neighbors on both sides in the overheated room were missing parts of an arm. It was one thing to be told you would find a buddy in the amputee ward, but quite another seeing men short body parts.

"I hope you took out a few Krauts before this," said Kenta, forcing a smile.

Koizumi manufactured a chuckle as he read Kenta's name patch on his left pocket.

"Takayama. You must be Tommy's brother."

"Guilty as charged." Kenta glanced at a small packet of aerograms—the top letter addressed to him—atop Jerry's bed table. He fought the urge to rush his chat to ask for his brother's letters. Instead, Kenta made himself look at the reddish leg stump, sawed a good six inches above the knee, and asked what happened.

"Stepped on a Bouncing Betty. In a few days, I'll be sent to a rehab unit. Then I'll petition to stay in the army as a clerk typist. Before the war, I could do fifty words a minute. I'll have a lot of time to improve on that this year." Delighted to have a visitor, Koizumi segued into a battlefront report. "Don't know if I killed any Germans. Shot at lot of them where the dead littered the field. The Germans, they keep retreating, but not easy. We know we will win. I am not sure the Germans still believe they can. Yet, they fight like demons. We aren't better soldiers than their good soldiers. But lots of Kraut KIAs are young. The master race is running out of manpower while we're just tapping ours."

Noticing Kenta's eyes roving to the side table, Koizumi reached for the mail packet. "Tommy almost joined me."

"What? He got shot?"

"Shrapnel in the leg. He would have bled out if a supply unit hadn't climbed up the hill where he got hit and found him passed out. The tourniquet he tied around his leg saved his life, but cut off the blood flow, almost making him a fellow amputee. Touch and go. Which field doc you get often decides if you keep a leg or an arm. Tommy had one of the best. Still, your brother fought like hell to stay in Italy. He was in a wait-and-see situation when I got transported out."

"You One Puka Puka guys are taking a lot of casualties."

"Since the first crossing of the Volturno, Clark sends us where the Germans are the toughest." Jerry stopped and looked around, as if worried someone was eavesdropping. Kenta waited. "None of us really understands why we march into the rain of fire time after time, even knowing many of us are spending our last minutes alive. Haole units retreat under the attacks with no harm to their reputation. Once we Nisei start up a hill or cross a field, we just keep going until we're hit or reach the objective. We keep going because it's our nature. Go for broke, right? But if we retreated, would the army decide it's not because the battlefield situation was impossible but because we are sorry-assed Japs who don't have what it takes?"

Jerry paused and stared down at his blunted leg, then locked eyes with Kenta. "Something else we all wonder about ..."

Kenta noticed the two men on the beds flanking Koizumi's, leaning in to hear.

"Are the generals sending us Nisei on so many dangerous missions because we're the best fighters, or because, as Japanese Americans, we're expendable? Tommy will tell you we are too good for our own good. If a hill has to be taken, senior officers know we won't quit halfway up. But I'm not so sure. We're not the only brave unit. The 34th is tough. Earned bragging rights in North Africa. Yet we seem to get more than our fair share of impossible objectives."

Kenta listened, curbing his impatience to break in with questions. When Jerry had finished, he said, "What is Clark—"

"There you are." Short Pants, who had entered the room with his characteristic energy, walked over to Jerry's bed. He knew Jerry from high school, although Short Pants had been two years behind him. "Oh, man. A leg. When do you get a prosthetic?"

"Needs more healing. Maybe in a month at the amputee unit."

Short Pants plowed on. "The rumors about the 100th needing replacements are true. Pence has asked all his battalion commanders to report to his office in an hour."

Kenta was perplexed at Short Pants's demeanor. That was good news for those selected, hardly worth such agitation.

"But no one from our 522nd is going."

"So what?" said Kenta. "We're artillery. The 100th is infantry."

"And you are a forward observer. When our 442nd arrives, it would be helpful if we had our own FOs ready to spot the firing."

"We get artillery support from the 34th," said Jerry. "But getting in the queue is not the same as having your own."

"And, Kenta," said Short Pants, "you might be paired with your brother. As a trained scout, Tommy would be a natural forward observer."

"Right," said Kenta, looking down at his watch. He started to back away from the bed. "Sorry, just remembered I have to be somewhere." Ignoring the dull pain in his toe, he hustled toward the door. "Wait—Short Pants, can you take my brother's letters back to our barracks?" He took a step. *Sandals.* "And don't ask why—I'll explain later—but I need your boots."

At 10:45 a.m., Adams entered Pence's office. "Sir, there is a sergeant here from the 522nd. He's got a kind of an unusual request." Before Pence could voice an objection, Adams sped on. "Sergeant Takayama, sir. His brother was wounded December 1. Almost sent back. Takayama's making the argument that he should be sent to Italy."

Pence's face relaxed. He remembered Takayama. An early trouble-maker who later distinguished himself as a leader with the uncanny ability to direct artillery fire.

"Send him in."

Kenta, ignoring the discomfort of his toe and tight boots, strode in, more assured than rank and circumstances might suggest. He saluted smartly and stood at rigid attention.

Rather than give the "at ease" command, Pence said, "You have two minutes, Sergeant Takayama."

"Yes, sir. One is all I need," he said, wasting three seconds. "When the 522nd lands in May, will they have experienced forward observers? My brother is a scout wounded in action. I will not only be a replacement but will gain experience working with the 34th FOs. I could be ready to guide our artillery-firing when the 522nd arrives." Kenta paused, pleased with his speech. Of course, he omitted the part that he had no idea whether his brother would stay in Italy or be sent back. "Sir."

Pence allowed a hint of a smile. "A good point." He glanced at Adams. "What do you think, Master Sergeant?"

Knowing Pence was looking for confirmation, Adams offered, "A good point indeed, sir. Maybe I should recommend a couple 522nd forward observers."

"I hope your brother is recovered by the time you arrive, Sergeant."

Knowing he had won and been dismissed, Kenta gave his smartest salute ever, unable to hold back a grin. "Yes, sir!" Then he executed a perfect pivot and marched out.

Kenta fist-pumped and did a kind of an elated hopscotch back to his unit, but then slowed. His toe hurt. *What's the rush? Mission accomplished.* He savored the moment. He imagined himself and Tommy sneaking behind German lines together to gather information, calling in artillery, maybe capturing a German for interrogation. In his naïve enthusiasm, he ignored the fact that forward observers are not scouts who might be captured, but mission-critical components protected by infantry so they can call in artillery protection.

Regardless, it was a great day. And in the moment, Kenta had only one question.

When will I ship out?

❧ Author's Notes ❧

MOST AUTHORS ISSUE A STATEMENT claiming the characters in their novel are totally fictional and any similarities to living people are purely coincidental. Not so in *A Question of Loyalty*. Almost half the characters in this novel lived, did what I said they did, and said what I have them saying. Heroes and bigots are revealed for what they were. Happily, for both the writer and the reader, inspirational heroes predominate. Recreating the valor of three Medal of Honor recipients were poignant, reflective moments. What motivates such men!

Historical fiction is a mixture of truth and imagination—with imagination dramatizing the truth. Part One: Day of Infamy, featuring Sue Takayama, is a case in point. Sue Kobatake Isonaga was the real-life au pair to the FBI agent in charge of Hawaii, just as I describe. Agent Shivers really did have the habit of introducing Sue as his daughter.

The dialogue of Sue Takayama's first meeting with Agent Shivers is as Mrs. Isonaga told me at my home a couple years before she passed away. Other than her initial interview with Shivers, most of Sue's dialogue was conjured up by events.

Kenta's girlfriend, Angelina, was inspired by conversations with my mentor Kats Miho, a forward observer with the 552nd. He told me about a Nisei university student who was the bubbly cheerleader type, more western in demeanor than most of her Nisei sisters. This happy charmer became my (and Kenta's) Angelina.

A black guy, co-captain of a mostly non-black American college football team in 1941? Yep. Nolle Smith really did set all those running records on the eve of Pearl Harbor. He served as an officer in integrated units in the Pacific throughout WWII.

The Aviation Museum at Pearl Harbor displays a "Niihau Incident" exhibit that includes the airplane the Japanese pilot crash landed on Niihau. Allan Beekman's book, *The Niihau Incident*, has all the details of the only act of sabotage by a Japanese living in America.

Hiromi Takayama's anger over the treatment of Japanese in Hawaii, which led her to migrate to Japan, was inspired by good friend Mariko Miho's aunt, Fumiye Miho. Since I embellished her story more than just a tad, I did not use her historical name. I believe I was faithful to Fumiye's staunch character and her outrage over the lower caste treatment of Japanese living in America.

The "defense" of St Louis Heights, upon hearing of Japanese paratroopers landing, and the later shooting of a cow—true as written.

The 442nd/100th/MIS historian and lawyer Ted Tsukiyama told me his gripping remembrance of being disarmed along with all the other Nisei Territorial Guard soldiers in January 1942. Before he passed in 2019, he wrote *My Life's Journey: A Memoir*, detailing those humiliating moments and his patriotic response leading to the formation of the Varsity Victory Volunteers.

Hung Wai Ching did and said most of what I attributed to him, if you allow for a little imagination in the dialogue. Like Superman to the rescue, he pops up often in my novel—just as he did in reality. After the war, Hung Wai co-founded Aloha Airlines, among many other postwar business accomplishments.

In Part Three: Reprieve, you meet Eleanor Roosevelt. A champion of the Nisei, she did and said what I wrote.

General Delos Carleton Emmons, the military governor of Hawaii, installed after the attack on Pearl Harbor, tactfully ignored presidential and Secretary of the Navy orders (as reported word for word in this novel) to send all Japanese living on Oahu to Molokai. Emmons repeatedly recommended the formation of a Nisei military unit.

Yoshie Takayama represents the hundreds of Nisei who lived in Japan and didn't bother obtaining an American passport. As legal dual citizens, they were not required to do so. But once in Japan—without that American passport, they were Japanese citizens subject to the draft. The story of Yoshie guarding Chinese slave laborers in mines was triggered by the harrowing 1959 movie, *The Human Condition*. At the time of this writing, it's not available for digital streaming, but Amazon sells and Netflix rents out the DVD. Tough to watch.

Part Four: Southern Hospitality and Part Five: Jim Crow, Kotonks and Buddhaheads were fun to write. To hear it from the locals of the day in Hattiesburg, the home of Camp Shelby and the 442nd for a year, the relationships between the races were in perfect harmony and the last thing the segregationists needed was a new race "agitating their Negroes." Designating Nisei as "honorary whites" and the tossing of the driver off the bus really happened.

The drama between the Buddhaheads from Hawaii and Kotonks from the West Coast, which almost ended the "Nisei experiment," has been well documented, including in Senator Inouye's autobiography *Journey to Washington*. You might sense that I had troubled moments writing some of the conflict scenes.

I found the historical character of Mary Yuriko Nakahara fascinating. She existed as reported, an organizer of USO dances, though I moved her from Camp Jerome to Camp Rohwer to bring the characters together and keep the camp interactions to a single location. However, the scene where Mary solves a love problem between Angelina and Kenta was a product of my wine-infused imagination. The real Mary met her future husband, Bill Kochiyama, a Nisei solider, while interned, and later went on to a career in civil rights as Yuri Kochiyama.

The fight over buying toothpaste, the people of Marysville greeting the train carrying the 442nd volunteers to Shelby, the Nisei beating up each other's sergeants, and the "go home Japs" signs at the Hattiesburg train station all happened. The episodes dramatizing the breakdown of family relationships inside the Rohwer concentration camp were unhappily conceived through reading various reports.

What about the story of Cat Island? Nobody could really think you could train dogs to smell the "unique odors" of Japanese, right? Wrong! The dog scenes happened as and where Tommy reported. Go figure!

Hattiesburg waitress Mabel's marriage to a Nisei in Part Seven: The Women is based on a true story. Herbert Sasaki was entranced with a gal—Arnice Dyar—who worked in the base laundry room. He married her. The KKK showed their disapproval by burning a cross on her parents' lawn. I met Arnice in Hattiesburg after Herbert passed. He was active in the business community and had much to do with featuring the 442nd in the Camp Shelby Museum.

The Tokyo Rose scenes evolved from my research-based imagination, but the main Tokyo Rose, Iva Toguri D'Aquino, is presented factually. She didn't volunteer, if you catch the drift.

The November 29, 1943, heroics in Part Eight: First Blood honor the first three Nisei Medal of Honor recipients. There will be eighteen more brave soldiers featured in the sequel, *Proof of Loyalty*.

Part Eight took extra-long to write and not just because of its length. So many details to choose from. I am most thankful for *Ambassadors in Arms: The Story of Hawaii's 100th Battalion;* Thomas Murphy's day-by-day timeline, following the 100th in Italy, laid the spine of "First Blood."

Among my library of more than one hundred Nisei books, Lyn Crost's *Honor by Fire*, Bill Yenne's *Rising Sons* and Masayo Umezawa Duus's *Unlikely Liberators* stand out for parenting colorful snippets. My two tours of 100th Battalion battle sites in Italy provided the foundation for the descriptions of combat scenes and mountain villages.

The stories veterans and their families shared at reunions provided so many anecdotes from which to choose and weave into the novel. I hope you enjoy the ones I selected.

What about the sex scenes? All contrived. No books or personal interviews related an "experience." But, I listened to a number of "we were naughty boys" from Nisei vets in their eighties and more than one son or daughter of the Nisei vets told me how on reunion trips to Italy their fathers would joke, "I hope I don't see anyone looking like me."

WWII research on commingling of soldiers and Italian and French working ladies claims that eighty percent of American soldiers enjoyed sex, on average, once a month. Since I don't believe the Nisei would have been the first monogamous soldiers, I invented liaisons. The one true story (told by a vet at the 100th Club in Honolulu) was when the Nisei took over a German brothel and then stood their ground when white officers tried to confiscate it.

The lead-in to the brothel scene where Tommy, chased by German soldiers, is yanked into a home by an Italian partisan is true … but it didn't happen to a Nisei. It happened to the father of a friend of mine.

What about the story of Captain Suzuki ordering Kim up a road into direct fire? My military readers said this couldn't happen. They checked. It happened.

There really was an AWOL guy by the name of Thompson who bumped into the 100th and acted as their guide. The 100th really ate green moldy turkey for their 1943 Thanksgiving meal, a real kitchen supply officer by the name of George Grandstaff traded potatoes for rice and the real Doc Kometani induced the 100th to save $2 a month—savings that paid for the still-existing clubhouse in Honolulu.

Sadly, the letter from a captured German soldier referring to Jewish slaves is very true.

Lieutenant Kim receives a lot of print space. His almost career-ending conversation, in his first meeting with Lieutenant Colonel Turner, happened as reported, as did all the major events where he plays a role. An interesting character, well-portrayed in the biography *Unsung Hero: The Story of Colonel Oak Kim*.

You can decide if Colonel Turner was the right man for both jobs … one to train the men and the other to lead them in combat.

For me, the single most evocative moment was reading the story of how the family of Joe Takata, the first Nisei warrior killed in action, responded. What would you have done in similar circumstances?

So many stories. Too many to address here. I welcome correspondence asking me questions about my inspirations. (Email me at mgm@ malaghan.net.) I would love to hear more stories from the families of Nisei warriors who "Went for Broke." You might find your story in the sequel, *Proof of Loyalty*.

CHARACTERS AND
HISTORICAL REFERENCES

∞ TAKAYAMA FAMILY CHARACTERS ∞

Haru (b. 1893) – matriarch of the Takayama family; wife of Kenji; mother of four sons and two daughters

Kenji (b. 1876) – patriarch of the Takayama family; married to Haru; arrested December 7, 1941; sent to internment camps in Santa Fe and Louisiana

Takeshi "Taka" (b. 1910) – eldest son of Haru and Kenji; Harvard Law school graduate, secretary to Morale Committee

Yoshio "Yoshi" (b. 1913) – second son of Haru and Kenji; drafted into Japanese Imperial Army out of Todai University

Tomio "Tommy" (b. 1916) – third son of Haru and Kenji; drafted before Pearl Harbor and assigned to the 299th infantry regiment; later assigned to the 100th infantry battalion

Kenta (b. 1919) – raised as Haru and Kenji's fourth son, though not biologically theirs; a member of the Varsity Victory Volunteers until able to volunteer for the 442nd Regiment; later assigned to the 552nd Artillery

Hiromi (b. 1921) – second youngest child and eldest daughter of Haru and Kenji; living in Japan, forced into the propaganda section of the Japanese government

Sachiko "Sue" (b. 1922) – youngest of Haru and Kenji's children; an au pair to FBI agent Robert Shivers and his wife, Corrine; character is based on the real person Sue Isonaga

∞ 100th Battalion / 442nd Regiment ∞
fictional characters

Adams, Gunnery Sgt. – Col. Pence's key aid

Arai, "Short Fuse" – member of Tommy's unit

Carlesso, "Azore" Carlo – only non-Japanese member of Kenta's squad

Chad – member of Kenta's squad

"Chuckles" (Seiji Fukayama) – member of Kenta's squad

"Little Caesar" – member of Kenta's squad

Doi, Sgt. Johnny – in charge of Kenta's squad upon arrival at Camp Shelby

Fukuda, "Fats" Shigeko – member of Kenta's squad

Hata, Kats – member of Tommy's unit

Henry – member of Kenta's squad

Himada, Hiro – Christian chaplain for 442nd

Lester – member of Tommy's 100th unit

Karamatsu, "Hero" Hideo – member of Kenta's squad

Koizumi, Cpl. Jerry – wounded member of the 100th who carries Tommy's mail to Camp Shelby

Nakata, Harry – member of Kenta's squad

Okada, Jimmy – bazooka man in the 100th

Oda, Mathew – member of the 100th

Ogi, Tommy "No Ticket" – member of Kenta's squad

Shikiya, Tad – medic in Tommy's 100th unit

"Short Pants" – member of Kenta's squad

"Spud" – member of Kenta's squad

"Stonehead" – member of Kenta's squad; the character is an embellished creation inspired by Bishop Fujitani's memory of his father's arrest

Sugi, "Buster" – member of Kenta's squad

Tochikawa, "Tochi" – wounded soldier in Tommy's 100th unit

Ueda – ROTC squad leader

Walsh, Maj. – officer in charge of Varsity Victory Volunteers

Wilson, Lt. – wounded officer of 100th

Yasuda – 442nd soldier, friend of Kenta

Yoshihara – Nisei basketball player at Camp McCoy

HISTORICAL CHARACTERS

Harrison, Lt. Col. John – commander of the 552nd artillery at Camp Shelby

Hasemoto, Pvt. Mikio – Medal of Honor recipient for action, November 29, 1943

Hayashi, Pvt. Shizuya – Medal of Honor recipient for action, November 29, 1943

Higashi, Cpl. Bert – forward observer, killed while directing artillery

Inouye, Daniel – Medal of Honor recipient and US Senator for Hawaii (1963 – 2012)

Grandstaff, George – food supply officer for 100th

Gillespie, Maj. James – third commander of 100th, November 1943

Kim, Lt. Young Oak – legendary Korean American officer of the 100th/442nd

Lowell, Maj. James – succeeded Lt. Col. Turner as commander of 100th

Kometani, Capt. Katsumi – morale officer of 100th; collected $2 per month from each person for post-war clubhouse

Mizuta, 1st Lt. Richard – replaces Lt. Kim when Kim is wounded

Ohata, Sgt. Allan – Medal of Honor recipient for action, November 29, 1943

Ozaki, Sgt. Robert – led banzai bayonet charge of November 1943; awarded the Silver Star

Pence, Col. C.W. – commander of 442nd

Ray, Lt. Neill – forward observer, killed while directing artillery

Suehiro, Cpl. Masuru – earned Distinguished Service Cross for heroism, November 1943, Italy

Suzuki, Capt. Tara – B Company officer, appointed by Turner when 100th left for Europe

Takata, Joe – The 100th's "Mr. Baseball"; first Nisei killed in action, Sept. 29, 1943

Tanaka, Keichi – second Nisei killed in action, September 29, 1943, hours after Takata killed

Tanouye, Cpl. Katsushi –forward observer, killed while directing artillery

Thompson – AWOL soldier who bumps into the 100th

Turner, Lt. Col. Farrant – first commander of 100th Battalion

Yamanaga, Thomas – awarded Distinguished Service Cross for taking out German machine gun nest

Yost, Israel – German-speaking chaplain of the 100th Battalion

∞ OTHER CHARACTERS ∞
FICTIONAL

Adcock, Joseph – first chaplain assigned to the 442nd

Alberto – Guilia's husband, killed by partisans

Allie – nurse at Camp Shelby

Miss Beatrice – manager of the colored USO, Hattiesburg

Bernardo – Italian partisan who saves Kenta from capture

Big Bertha – Laundress in and around Santa Maria Olivetto, Italy

Bobby – Newspaper boy in Camp Shelby and Hattiesburg

Bogan, Capt. – Piper Cub pilot who flies over German lines

Carter, M.Sgt. Sunny – 69th Division

Crockett, Sgt. Davy – 34th Texas Division, enemy of Kenta

Delight, Lillian – Proprietress of the Pink Palace brothel

Ditmar, Jack – Hattiesburg Chief of Police

Doi, Fumiko – mother of Johnny Doi; internee, Camp Rohwer

Doi, Gabriel – Boy Scout brother of Johnny Doi; internee, Camp Rohwer

Doi, Jane – sister of Johnny Doi; internee, Camp Rohwer

Doi, Patrick – brother of Johnny Doi; internee, Camp Rohwer

Doi, Ruth – first-grade sister of Johnny Doi; internee, Camp Rohwer

Doi, Shigeru – father of Johnny Doi; internee, Camp Rohwer

Earl – Hattiesburg police officer

Eddie – ROTC friend of Kenta's; son of a naval officer

Fehner – postman in Waimea, Big Island

Forte – Colonel Pence's headquarters' master sergeant

Fujimori – 100th Battalion soldier in Kim's platoon; killed in action

Fumiko – Angelina's friend who married right after high school

Fumio – Japanese soldier serving with Yoshio on Siberian border

Gloria – hooker at Lucinda's brothel

Goto – Hiromi's boss at NHK Tokyo; in charge of Tokyo Rose voices

Guilia – daughter-in-law of Marco in Santa Maria Olivetto

Harwood, Mrs. – secretary to Johnny Logan at Hattiesburg newspaper

Hata, Kats – member of Kim's platoon

Henry – member of Kenta's squad

Ida, Candi – Fictional sister of historical character Horace Ida

Irie – husband of Ume; a coffee farmer in Kona

Jonesy – a lieutenant; pilot in the Tuskegee squadron

Kago – sergeant at 442nd headquarters

Koizumi – Wounded 100th soldier who carries Tommy's mail to Shelby

Logan, Johnny – editor of the Hattiesburg newspaper

Lucinda – madam of Italian brothel "captured" by Tommy

Mabel – Hattiesburg diner waitress; marries 442nd soldier Chuckles

Marco – owner of Tommy's bivouac "home" in Santa Maria Olivetto

Michael – Italian partisan leading refugee families escaping German occupation through enemy lines

Marumoto, Angelina – University of Hawaii student; Kenta's girlfriend

Murikami, Takashiro – Hitomi's bucho (section chief) at Japan Ministry of Foreign Affairs

HISTORICAL

Ching, Elsie – Hung Wai Ching's wife

Ching, Hung Wai – Morale Committee leader; real estate broker; YMCA director

Clark, Gen. Mark – commander of US forces in Italy

Cousens, Maj. Charles – Australian captured in Singapore; in charge of Tokyo Rose programming

DeWitt, Gen. John – commander of Western Defense; oversaw internment of West Coast Japanese

Emmons, Gen. Delos – commanding general of Hawaii Dept. of the Army

Eisenhower, Gen. Dwight – commander of Allied Forces, Italy/North Africa

Farrington, Joseph – Hawaii's non-voting delegate to Congress

Fielder, Col. Kendall – Emmons's Director of Intelligence; liaison with Hung Wai Ching

Fountain, Col. Ray C. – General Ryder's adjutant; commander of 133rd Regiment; worked with Nisei at Guadalcanal in 1942

Frazier, Maj. Charles Rusty – regular army commander of ROTC & Hawaiian Territorial Guard

Grew, Joseph – US Ambassador to Japan

Harada, Yuya – freed Japanese pilot who landed on Niihau on December 7, 1941

Hemenway, Charles R. – Chairman, University of Hawaii Regents; famed community leader

Hoover, J. Edgar – Director of the FBI

Hopkins, Harry – special assistant to President Roosevelt

Hull, Cordell – President Roosevelt's Secretary of State

Ida, Horace – Defendant in the Massie Trial, the "trial of the century"

Kai-shek, Chiang – President of China

Kanahele, Ben – Hawaiian Niihau field hand

Keene, Coach – Head coach, Willamette College football team; played against University of Hawaii on December 6, 1941

Kesselring, Albert – German commander of Wehrmacht forces in Italy

Kimmel, Adm. Husband – Commander-in-Chief, US Pacific Fleet

Kin-san & Gin-san – Nicknames (Gold and Silver) of California Issei yakuza in Santa Fe POW camp; the names are manufactured, but the men are real

Knox, Frank – Secretary of the Navy

Kuchiba, Bishop Gikyo – Fort Street Hongwanji bishop after Imamura; Kenji serves under him

Lodge, Cabot, Jr. – Massachusetts senator

Lucas, Gen. John – commander of the US VI corps; as such, he also commands Ryder's 34th Division and thus the 100th Battalion

McCoy, John J. – Assistant Secretary of War

Montgomery, Field Marshall Bernard "Monty" – British Commander of forces in Italy and North Africa

Nimitz, Adm. Chester – commander of all Pacific naval operations

Otani, Matsujiro – fish peddler who founded Otani fish market; arrested December 7, 1941

Nakahara, Mary – teenage internee in Camp Rohwer; a "super organizer," elements of her character have been fictionalized, though she is primarily based on the real Mary Yuriko Nakahara, who was later known as Yuri Kochiyama

Patton, Lt. Col. George – Army officer assigned to investigate Japanese loyalty; WWII hero

Poindexter, Joseph – governor of Hawaii, 1934 – 1942

Eleanor Roosevelt – wife of President Franklin D. Roosevelt

Roosevelt, Franklin D. – President of the United States

Ryder, Gen. Charles W. – commander of the 34th "Red Bull" Division

Shivers, Robert – FBI special agent; opened the Honolulu FBI office in August 1939

Shivers, Corrine – Robert Shivers's wife

Short, Gen. Walter – Army commander of Hawaii when Pearl Harbor is bombed

Smith, Capt. Nolle – black University of Hawaii football hero; a captain in ROTC

Stimson, Harry L. – Secretary of War

Takata, Florence – wife of Joe Takata

Thomas, Lowell– radio broadcaster for NBC

Toguri (D'Aquino), Iva Ikuko –first and primary voice of Tokyo Rose

Tojo, Hideki – Prime Minister of Japan (1941 – 1944), Minister of War (1940 – 1944) and Chief of the Imperial Japanese Army (1944)

Tottori, Mitsumyo – Only Buddhist priest in Hawaii not arrested; advocate of Americanism

Tully, Grace – secretary to President Roosevelt

Turner, Lt. Farrant – Leader of 100th Infantry Battalion

Yoshida, Shigeo – Statehood and Morale Committee leader

Yoshikawa, Takeo – Japanese consulate spy who monitored US fleet from Natsunoya Tea House

⸌ HISTORICAL REFERENCES ⸍

Camp Livingston, La. – POW camp that held many of Hawaii Issei leaders arrested by FBI

Camp Ritchie, Md. – MIS (Military Intelligence Services) training facility translating Japanese documents into English

Camp Rohwer – internment camp in Arkansas

Camp Savage, Minn. – MIS training center

Camp Shelby – Army training base, Hattiesburg, Miss.

Chinatown (Honolulu, Hawaii) – Chinese restaurant and retail area; nefarious night club area next to downtown Honolulu

Council of Interracial Unity – committee planning to keep Japanese out of internment camps when war starts

Fort Oglethorpe, Ga. – Army base hosting WAC (Women's Army Corps) training during WWII

Fort Street Hongwanji – main Buddhist temple in Hawaii

Hattiesburg, Miss. – town hosting Camp Shelby

Hotel Street – downtown Honolulu's bar and brothel street

Kapiolani Park – large park across from eastern end of Waikiki Beach

KGU – Honolulu radio station that guided Japanese pilots to Pearl Harbor

MIS (Military Intelligence Services) – military unit that collected, analyzed and disseminated intelligence; 6,000 Nisei served in the Pacific as interrogators and translators, listening to Japanese communications, and sometimes accompanied GIs in combat

Moiliili Hongwanji – Buddhist temple servicing Moiliili and University of Hawaii students

Otani Fish Market – River Street fish market; known today as United Fishing Agency

Washington Place – Governor of Hawaii's residence and office

Salerno, Italy – September 1943 Southern Italy landing site for the 100th Battalion

Sand Island – Honolulu port area where a tent city was established to hold interned Japanese

Sumitomo Daibutsu – Japanese trading company

VVV (Varsity Victory Volunteers) – a civilian unit considered the genesis of the 442nd Regimental Combat Team; 169 men discharged from service in the Territorial Guard after the bombing of Pearl Harbor volunteered as members of the labor battalion, serving the army in construction gangs

WRA (War Relocation Authority) – entity in charge of internment camps

Yasukuni Shrine – Shinto shrine honoring all Japanese military who died defending the empire

Yomiuri Shimbun – largest Japanese newspaper by circulation

Waimea – Haru's "hometown" on the Big Island, adjacent to Parker Ranch

∽ ABOUT THE AUTHOR ∽

A lover and reader of history, Mike Malaghan has had the good fortune to visit 203 countries and territories, beginning with Africa in 1966 during his service in the Peace Corps.

Born in Wisconsin, and raised in Florida from age twelve, he paid his way through the University of Florida by selling books door to door. Mike finished his 41-year business career as president of a Walt Disney licensee in Japan and Taiwan. His legacy business book, *Making Millions in Direct Sales*, was published in 2005 by McGraw Hill.

As part of his research for *A Question of Loyalty*, Mike and his wife, Tomoko, visited most of the places where the novel takes place, including Camp Shelby, Mississippi, and battle sites in Italy. They divide their time between homes in Atlanta and Tokyo.

Mike is currently working on *Proof of Loyalty*, the next novel in the Picture Bride trilogy, featuring the 100th Battalion/442nd Regimental Combat Unit Nisei soldiers fighting in Europe and those serving in the Military Intelligence Service in the Pacific.

Mike Malaghan welcomes your comments about the Picture Bride trilogy. Please contact him at mgm@malaghan.net.

www.mikemalaghan.com